In a Place ...

'A magnetic mix of creepy places, dark humour,
horror and violence'
Sun

'Dark and brilliantly written'
Linwood Barclay

'MacBride is a damned fine writer'
Peter James

'MacBride's thrillers just keep getting better'
Express

'Crime fiction of the highest order'
Mark Billingham

'Fast, hard, authentic – and different'
Lee Child

www.penguin.co.uk

By *Stuart MacBride*

IN A PLACE OF DARKNESS

STUART MACBRIDE

PENGUIN BOOKS

TRANSWORLD PUBLISHERS
Penguin Random House, One Embassy Gardens,
8 Viaduct Gardens, London SW11 7BW
www.penguin.co.uk

Transworld is part of the Penguin Random House group of companies
whose addresses can be found at global.penguinrandomhouse.com

First published in Great Britain in 2024 by Bantam
an imprint of Transworld Publishers
Penguin paperback edition published 2025

A CIP catalogue record for this book
is available from the British Library.

ISBN
9780552178334

Typeset in Stone Serif ITC Pro 9.25/13pt by Jouve (UK), Milton Keynes.
Printed and bound in Great Britain by Clays Ltd, Elcograf S.p.A.

The authorized representative in the EEA is Penguin Random House Ireland,
Morrison Chambers, 32 Nassau Street, Dublin D02 YH68.

Penguin Random House is committed to a sustainable future
for our business, our readers and our planet. This book is made
from Forest Stewardship Council® certified paper.

In loving memory of Gordon Ferguson Reid,
a braw wee man,
who always said 'aye' tae a pie,
knew that sausages is the boys,
and spent time in a Syrian prison on suspicion of spying for the
British Government (questions were raised in the House of
Lords to get him, and his colleagues, released).
1937–2023

—Friday 01 March—

I

God's sake, why did everything have to be such a sodding . . . *trial*?

Kevin braced himself against the weight of far too many bags-for-life and struggled the car keys from his pocket – squinting in the septic streetlight to find the right button – then plipped the locks on the little Fiat 500 Douglas *insisted* they buy because it was *so much cuter* than a Range Rover, which would've been a hell of a lot more practical, thank you very much.

But would Douglas listen?

Of course he bloody wouldn't.

It was the same with the house.

Not for them a nice cottage out in the country, with a big garden, a couple of spaniels, and a PERFECTLY PRACTICAL RANGE ROVER. Oh, they'd be *so* much happier in a two-up-two-down rabbit hutch in a cut-and-paste housing estate, in Blackwall *Sodding* Hill.

Bottles and jars clink-clanged against each other as Kevin lumbered up the short path, past the tiny rectangle of moss-infested grass.

Wasn't even a decent view: more identikit housing estates sweeping up the valley behind the house, and the nettle-strewn railway cutting to the front.

Couldn't even see the stars from here.

A booming *rattle-clank-rattle-clank-rattle-clank* grumbled beneath a diesel engine, and when he turned there was yet another sodding goods train hauling more *sodding* whisky off to be sold in sodding super-sodding-markets.

And those trains would be running all night, wouldn't they. Every two hours. WHEN HE WAS TRYING TO SLEEP.

Kevin gritted his teeth and hauled his keys up to the front-door lock, weighed down with bags stuffed full of wine and pickles and potatoes and beans and cream-of-tomato, and . . .

'Bloody, cock-wanking, shite, bastard—'

The outermost bag slipped from his aching fingers and cracked down against the front step.

'Oh, for . . . *Christ's* sake!'

He put the other bags down and stared as dark-purple liquid seeped through the dropped one, oozing out to drip down the concrete slabs.

Like blood.

'Great. Thanks. Thanks a *sodding* heap!'

Kevin unlocked the door, grabbed the stupid bags and stomped inside.

Grey fluff gathered along the hall skirting board, dust taking the shine off the laminate floor, a lone cobweb draped in the corner of the walls that Douglas insisted were 'cheerfully blue', but were actually the colour of depression and . . . drowned babies.

Socks and a gilet draped over the end of the stairs.

God, the man was a pig.

Music oozed through the kitchen door: one of those cheesy love songs Douglas adored – because, deep down, not only was the man a pig, he had the soul of a teenaged girl.

Honestly, how did anyone . . .

A drip of dark purple splotched onto the laminate.

And you *know* that crap was going to leave a stain.

'Buggering hell . . . Douglas?'

Nothing.

Just that stupid saccharine song.

'DOUGLAS!'

Still nothing.

'Fine, I'll just do everything myself, shall I? *As usual.*' Kevin dumped the other bags on the mat and hurried down the hall, one hand cupped beneath the leak, catching the drips. 'And it's like a sodding oven in here. Again!'

4

He bumped through the door into what would've been a nice big farmhouse kitchen if he'd had the sense to stand up to Douglas for once in his sodding life.

Instead, it was barely big enough for a wee fitted kitchen, a fridge-freezer that didn't even have an ice maker, a half-size dishwasher, and a dining area more suited to Sylvanian Families than actual human-sized ones. The place was only saved by sunshine-yellow walls, peppered with framed photos of the pair of them on God-knew-how-many holidays.

None of which Douglas paid for. Or helped organize. The man couldn't even pack his own frigging suitcase.

The French doors were a black mirror, hiding the equally tiny back garden, reflecting the happy walls.

Douglas was at the kitchen table, sitting in his favourite chair, with his back to the room. Chronologically: ten years younger than Kevin. Emotionally: light years away. Even if he did have a six-pack and an arse you could bounce pound coins off – a tight Fiddersmuir Brewery T-shirt showing off every lump and bump of muscle across his back.

Which didn't make him any less of a lazy prick.

Kevin glared at those broad shoulders on his hurried way across the kitchen. 'God's sake, is it too much to ask for a little help?' He dumped the whole bag in the sink – dark purple oozing out onto stainless steel. 'Sodding stuff's everywhere!'

The tap sputtered into life with an angry twist.

'And would it *kill* you to turn the bloody heating down? Electricity's through the roof again, but do you care? No, because it's muggins here who pays all the bills!' A squirt of soap, lathered up beneath warming water. Scrubbing scarlet stains from his hands. 'It's not even as if I *like* pickled beetroot.'

The schmaltzy song died a death, followed by a man's voice sharpened with insincere bonhomie. *'Hey, hey, hey! That was Hello Mr Magpie and their latest smasharoonie toonie, "Feathers"!'*

And still nothing from Douglas.

Probably sulking from this morning. Just because Kevin wouldn't buy him an electric scooter. Douglas didn't want a husband and a soulmate; he wanted a sodding sugar daddy.

5

Well, it was about time he learned that Kevin wasn't running an all-you-can-eat money buffet.

Kevin marched over to the thermostat and didn't turn it down. Oh, no: he made a big show of turning it off completely.

That would show him.

Still nothing?

This rivalled The Great Why-Can't-We-Have-A-Bulldog? Sulk of 2022.

Child.

Kevin dipped into the leaking bag, pulling the contents out one by one and running them under the tap, before thumping them down on the draining board. Shiraz, morello cherry jam, roasted peppers . . .

'You're listening to Sensational Steve's Drive-Time Goldmine!*'* An explosion of honking horns and the kind of trumpet fanfare you'd expect an egotistical dick to find amusing battered out of the radio.

Fine. Two could play that game.

Kevin let the sarcasm drip like beetroot juice: 'Good *evening*, Kevin. How was your *day*, Kevin?'

. . . Chenin Blanc, capers, harissa . . .

'Don't forget, we've got the one and only Zeb, from Four Mechanical Mice, coming on to tell us all about this year's Tartantula festival . . .'

The harissa went down with a particularly spiteful clatter. 'Well, it was *crappy*, thanks for asking. That . . . *bitch*, Jennifer Bloody Prentice, said my prose was, and I quote: "tedious and pedestrian"!'

'. . . going to be even better than last year. So, why don't we get ourselves in the festival mood with last year's headliners, Catnip Jane, and "Here Comes The Winter Sun"!'

Music surged from the radio – upbeat and drum-heavy.

Kevin picked up the harissa again, scowling at the label. 'Writes a couple of trashy true-crime books and suddenly she's Salman Fucking Rushdie? *Catching the Coffinmaker*, my arse. It's like a drunken monkey vomited up one of those poetry-fridge-magnet . . .' This time the harissa clattered down hard enough to bounce. 'Are you even *listening* to me?'

Douglas's reflection shimmered in the kitchen window.

Were his shoulders trembling? Like this was *funny*?

The words barely made it out through Kevin's pinched lips and clenched jaw. 'Thanks for your support.'

He jammed his hand into the bag again, then yanked it out as if stung by a cut-glass wasp. 'Buggering . . .' Beetroot juice stained his fingers a deep angry purple, but fresh scarlet welled up from his thumb and index finger, trickling around to drip into the sink as tears made the world ripple. Distorted and *unfair*.

'I only buy this bloody stuff for you!'

Kevin grabbed the tea towel they got on a trip to Stirling Castle – back when they loved each other, and Douglas wasn't a spoiled, ungrateful *brat* – wrapping William Wallace around his injured hand. Storming over to the table, glaring down at Douglas.

Look at him: sitting there, shoulders trembling with the effort of keeping it all in. Because this was *so* hilarious.

'Don't you *dare* laugh at me! Don't you—'

Kevin's right foot scooted forward a couple of inches, nearly dumping him on his backside. There was something wet on the laminate floor – a puddle of white wine, or apple juice, that Douglas clearly hadn't bothered to clean up. Like the rest of the house. Like the dust and the cobwebs and the washing.

'You're such a pig!'

That was it. Enough. No more.

Kevin picked his way out of the puddle, moving around to confront the useless, lazy, ungrateful . . .

Oh God.

Douglas *wasn't* sulking – the reason he'd not said anything was because he *couldn't*. Someone had stuffed a rag in his mouth, held in place by a rectangle of duct tape. And the reason he hadn't *moved* is they'd fixed both his hands to the kitchen table with half a dozen long brass screws.

Bright scarlet oozed across the polished beech. Eyes wide and spilling tears as he stared at Kevin. Moaning behind his gag, flicking his eyes towards the French doors.

Pleading.

Kevin tightened his grip on the claret-stained tea towel. 'Douglas?' Shrinking back from the table. 'Douglas, what did you do?'

The moan turned into a high-pitched wail.

'WHAT DID YOU DO?'

Kevin's back bumped into the French doors and they burst open, letting in the *rattle-clank-rattle-clank-rattle-clank* of the never-ending goods train and a gasp of cold night air.

A dark shape surged in with it – something hard smashed down on Kevin's head.

His legs stopped working.

The puddled floor swung up to meet him.

And that's when the nightmare *really* began . . .

—Wednesday 13 March—

2

The patrol car turned the corner onto Balvenie Row.

'Bloody hell.' Its driver pushed herself back in the seat, arms braced against the steering wheel. 'Feeding-frenzy time.'

A spotty PC, all elbows and Adam's apple, squirmed in the passenger seat. 'Not liking that, Colly. Not liking that one little bit.'

Sitting in the back – behind the driver, away from the dreaded 'piddle patch' – Angus leaned over to peer between the front seats and out at the windswept scene.

Row after row of identical, teeny terraced houses marched down the left-hand side of the road, facing a railway embankment covered in weeds and speckled with litter. Looking like the kind of community a kid would build if they didn't have enough Lego for something decent.

About halfway down, the road was blocked with journalists and camera crews and outside-broadcast units and rubberneckers – all people who thrived on human misery, either professionally or vicariously. There was even a wee cluster of nutters with placards: 'PROSECUTE VACCINE MURDERERS!!!!', 'THE END IS NIGH ~ MARK 13 IS COME TRUE!', and 'BEWARE THE GREAT RESET!!!!!' Doing their best to get in the background as people did pieces to camera, because *God forbid* their whack-job personal crusades didn't get rammed down the public's throat every five minutes.

Bouquets, football scarves, and teddy bears smothered the street sign, leaving only the 'ALV' and 'OW' visible.

On the other side of the mob, the top half of a grubby scene examiners' Transit van poked up into the grey sky. A similar chunk of white plastic marquee did the same – attached to the front of the house, hiding the front door. But everything else O Division had deployed was hidden behind the milling crowd.

PC Collier sniffed. She didn't look comfortable in the full Police Scotland black, an impression not helped by a stab-proof vest that was two sizes too big. Her neck poked out the top like a turtle from its shell, bobbed dishwater curls stuffed into a sagging hairnet. 'We're never getting through all that.' She pulled in behind a lumpy van with a satellite dish on the roof and the Channel 4 logo down the side. 'A'biddy oot.'

Took a bit of shuffling, but Angus unfolded himself from the back seat and wriggled out into the blustery morning. Stretching his spine from side to side to free the knots.

PC Collier looked up at him towering over her. 'Right, King Kong, you're on your own from here. Me and the boy are door-to-dooring. Try no' break anything, OK?'

'Do my best.'

They set off, back towards the junction, clutching their clipboards and high-vis jackets.

Rather them than him. No more slogging around housing estates, trying to convince members of the public to tell the truth, for Angus. Not any more. He'd moved up to the *Premier* League.

He straightened his brand-new fighting suit – dark grey, machine washable, from Asda – and marched along the pavement. Past the outermost fringes of the media encampment, where a beefy-faced posh boy clutched a BBC Scotland microphone, looking serious for the camera.

'That's right, Siobhan, but sources close to the investigation have expressed their frustration at the lack of tangible leads.'

Behind the reporter, a youngish woman with shoulder-length black hair, dyed pink at the tips, hefted her placard: 'PROSECUTE VACCINE MURDERERS!!!!' She was pretty. Smoky eyeshadow with wing tips, pouty lips and an upturned nose. Lots of earrings. Black leather biker's jacket, tight V-neck top, and combat trousers. Kinda—

Angus walked right into an old mannie in a hand-knitted duffel coat.

'Whit the hell do you think you're—'

'Sorry! Sorry. My fault.' Sidestepping around him, cheeks instantly hot. 'Sorry.'

Keeping his head down, Angus marched on – the reporter's voice fading into the background:

'. . . *showing no sign of abating, one thing's for certain: everyone expects the killer to strike again.*'

Angus waded into the crowd, making for the cordon. 'Excuse me. Sorry. Thank you. Can I just . . .? Thanks.'

A hand grabbed his sleeve. 'Hoy!'

Sod.

He pulled on his professional face and turned, ready to apologize for standing on whoever-it-was' toes, but instead of an outraged civilian, the person looking up at him beamed.

'You going to lumber past and not say "Hi"?' Ellie – bundled up in a thick, bright-orange duvet jacket, with a woolly hat, pink ears, and a red nose. She hoiked a thumb at number twenty-one, with its crime-scene marquee. 'Bit of a cock-up, isn't it? *Three* sets of victims in just six weeks. The *Daily Standard*'s going with "Fortnight Killer", which, in my humble opinion, is a load of old wank. Don't you think it's a load of old wank? You're right: it's a load of old wank. I'm going to come up with something *much* better, you watch.'

'Morning, Ellie.'

'And look at you, in a brand-new suit!' She fussed with his lapels, brushed some invisible dust from his shoulders. 'All grown up and detective-constabling. Bit of a step-up from eating worms at playtime. First-day nerves?'

His cheeks flushed hot again. 'I'm fine.'

'Course you are.' Her eyes drifted skyward as a large drone snarled by overhead, shredding the grey air like an angry, oversized wasp. 'Don't let them push you about, OK? Anyone messes with my Angus they answer to me.' She produced her phone and pointed the microphone at his face, putting on an OTT American accent: 'Ellie Nottingham, *Castle News and Post*.' Cheesy wink. 'Constable MacVicar, what do you have to tell our readers about this horrible murder?'

He pursed his lips. Raised an eyebrow. 'Can I . . . ?' Pointing over her shoulder. 'Cos I'm going to be late.'

Ellie lowered her phone, the smile slipping away. 'I worked with him on a couple of stories: Kevin Healey-Hyphen-Robinson. And, yeah, he could be a bit of a wanker, but mostly he was one of the decent ones.' Her eyes narrowed as she looked out over the crowd. 'Unlike *some* people.'

Angus followed her gaze to an older man – chunky with wide shoulders, thick sideburns, and frameless glasses. Dundas Grammar School tie at half-mast, the top two shirt buttons open, exposing one end of a thick pink scar. A photographer stood beside him, snapping pictures of the crowd with an oversized digital camera.

Angus turned to Ellie again. 'Your Mr Healey-Robinson, how come nobody from the paper reported him missing till now? Twelve days. You'd think someone would've noticed.'

'It's cos he'd just been beaten to this massive corruption exposé by Slosser the Tosser' – jerking her chin at the bloke with the bypass scar – 'and if there's one thing Kevin loves—' Ellie stopped. Licked her lip. 'Loved.' She looked away. 'He made a big thing of storming off in a huff whenever stuff didn't go his way. Honestly – like a wee kid. You wouldn't hear a thing from him for ages. Not till the next deadline. And when he missed that . . .' A big, long breath. 'So, here we are.'

'Yeah.'

She gave herself a little shake. 'Anyway, come on: make with the exclusive.'

'Got to go.'

'Hey! I shared with you.'

Angus gave her a pantomime shrug. 'First day on the case, remember?'

'Yeah, yeah.' She watched him wade into the scrum again. 'Give 'em hell, Tiger.'

'Bye, Ellie.' Making for the cordon.

Her voice cut through the general hubbub behind him. '*I can still make you eat worms, you know!*'

Yeah, probably.

At the far edge of the crowd, Angus flashed his warrant card at the PC guarding the double line of blue-and-white 'POLICE' tape, behind which lurked a couple of manky patrol cars, that SE Transit, and the Healey-Robinson crime scene.

Angus ducked beneath the cordon.

No idea why, but for some reason things always felt different on this side of the line. As if the simple act of bobbing under a ribbon of plastic was the same as stepping through a magic mirror, or an enchanted wardrobe, into a world that most people would never experience.

If they were lucky.

He nodded at someone in the full SOC kit – no idea who, could be anyone, but better safe than sorry – then slipped into the marquee.

Inside, the light was thinner. Meaner. Dampening everything down. Even Abir didn't look his usual vibrant self, despite the tartan turban and greying beard. Overseeing his miserable kingdom.

Which today consisted of two folding tables, a collection of cardboard boxes, and a pair of camping chairs.

'Hey, Abir. DCI Monroe about?'

'Inside.' Abir raised his clipboard, blocking the way. 'You gotta sign in first.' He hooked a thumb at the nearest table. 'Smurf suits is over there.'

Angus scrawled his signature in the appropriate place. 'Any news?'

'Aye – rather you than me. Take a deeeeeeep breath before you go in.'

'OK . . .' Ominous and not in the least bit helpful.

Angus wriggled his way into an XXL SOC oversuit, the white Tyvek material crinkling and rustling as it strangled his bits and armpits. 'Any chance we can get some of these big enough for normal-sized people, Abir?' Looking down at the bunched-up crotch. 'Might want to have kids someday.'

'Now there's a horrible thought.'

The suit was joined by a pair of blue plastic booties, a facemask, safety goggles, and a double set of purple nitrile gloves.

Right.

Time to go in there and show them what he was made of.

Angus huffed out a breath, pulled his shoulders back, stood up tall – winced as the suit tried to nip his balls off – hunched over again, and finally pulled the plastic sheeting to one side, exposing the front door.

Keeping his voice low. 'You can do this . . .'

He opened the door and stepped through into a small hallway, painted an electric shade of blue that emphasized the fridge-like temperature. Even with the mask on, Angus's breath steamed in the chilly air. Every inhale brought with it the stench of decay and the taste of tainted meat. Not sure which was worse.

He popped his head through the first open door.

Living room: burnt-umber walls; lots of framed photos; big TV; impressive stack of audio equipment; a whole bookcase full of LPs; and three SE techs in their crunchy SOC suits, taking photographs, lifting fingerprints, searching for fibres and DNA . . .

Next up: downstairs toilet – a tiny space painted orc-green.

He paused at the foot of the stairs as muffled voices pulsed down from above. Too low to make out any real words, but the tone was clear enough. Serious. Worried.

The last door was shut, but opening it revealed a small kitchen with a space at one end for a wee wooden table and four matching chairs. That cloying stench of meat long past its sell-by date avalanched out into the hallway.

Good job he'd not stopped for breakfast this morning.

The SE team had set up another marquee in the back garden – probably to stop the press and lookie-loos from having a good ogle through the kitchen window and patio doors. Because nothing sells newspapers like a pixelated bloodbath. The back-garden marquee wasn't white like the one out front, though: it was blue. Giving the light a mourning, underwater feel.

As if the whole house had drowned.

Over by the table, a lone SOC-suited figure womanhandled another huge digital camera, the clack and whine of the flash sending jittery shadows racing around the room as she shifted a ruler-for-scale and took another shot.

Someone had laid out a common approach path – an elevated

walkway of skateboard-sized metal rectangles, on short little legs that clanged as Angus stepped up onto the one nearest the door. Keeping him from treading in the evidence.

And there was a lot of it.

What was clearly blood had dried to a sticky Marmite brown – spattered and smeared across the collection of holiday photographs that covered the wall behind the table. More dried blood had puddled on the tabletop, caught in congealed drips around the rim. A vast loch of the stuff spread across the floor.

The taste of decay mingled with the sharp-yellow scent of a pub urinal.

Maybe best not to breathe too deeply in here.

Angus followed the path, past the butcher's table and into the kitchen area. A collection of jars and bottles sat on the draining board, a hessian bag in the sink: stained dark purple, but flecked with green mould. Fingerprint dust covered the worktops and units. Turned a fancy chromed coffee maker dull and matt. But it looked as if all the horrible stuff happened in the dining part of the room.

He picked his way back along the walkway, frowning down at the tabletop.

The SE tech lowered her camera and raised her eyebrows. 'That's where the vic was.' She snapped another pic. 'You new?'

'First day on the team.'

A little snort. 'Well, you picked a good one to start with. Wanna see what you missed?' She fiddled with the camera, then held it out, turned so the screen on the back was facing him.

Angus leaned in.

It was a wide shot of the kitchen table, taken from the corner beside the patio doors. Only now, the seat nearest the kitchen, where all the blood was, had someone in it. Male . . . probably. They'd been stripped to the waist, but the skin was so discoloured and swollen that it was difficult to be sure. Black, purple, blue, grey, the dark yawning holes of what might be knife wounds, the deformed shapes that spoke of shattered bones, all wrapped in a revolting khaki-green tinsel where the mould had spread. Both hands were fixed to the bloodstained wood with what looked like wood screws.

Whoever it was, they hadn't died an easy death.

A stained yellow Post-it had been nailed to their forehead – though the camera's screen was too small to make out the words – and their eyes were no more than thin black slits.

Angus swallowed. 'Jesus . . . They cut out his eyes?'

'What?' She turned the camera around the right way again, squinting at the picture. 'No. What kind of sick sod would do that? No, your eyeballs are one of the first bits to go. Bacteria love a tasty jelly-filled feast.' A sniff. 'Nearly two weeks, just sitting there, *decomposing*. We're lucky someone switched the central heating off, or we'd be scraping the poor sod off the kitchen floor.'

Now there was a lovely thought.

He pointed at the tabletop, where half a dozen small circular holes punctured the wood either side of where their victim sat. Three on the left, three on the right. 'What about these?'

The SE tech lowered her camera. 'Eighty-mill self-tapping wood screws.'

Another half-dozen screw holes marred the table, directly opposite. 'Same again?'

'Just like the other two crime scenes: all the way through the table and out the other side.' A blue nitrile glove hovered above one of them. 'See how there's nowhere near as much blood on this—'

A man's voice groaned across the kitchen – sounding as if all the energy had been battered out of it. *'Detective Sergeant Massie, please, for the love of all that's holy, explain why there's an unauthorized hulking-great lump wandering around my crime scene.'*

Ah . . .

That would be Detective Chief Inspector Monroe.

Angus stood up straight, ready to snap off a salute as he turned.

A thin, rustling, SOC-suited shape slumped in the doorway. What with the facemask and goggles it was impossible to see the expression on Monroe's face, but he still radiated disappointment.

Behind him, a second figure looked over Monroe's shoulder at Angus and the SE tech. DS Massie tilted her head to one side, as if that would make the answer any clearer. 'I . . . er . . .'

Time to make a good impression.

Angus stuck his hand out. 'Detective Constable Angus MacVicar, reporting for duty.'

The man frowned at the proffered hand, then at Angus. 'No offence, but you *have* heard of cross-contamination, haven't you . . . Allan, is it?'

'Oh.' Heat swarmed up his neck yet again. 'Yes. Of course. Sorry.' He lowered his hand. 'And it's Angus. Angus MacVicar. Sorry.' Cleared his throat. 'We were just—'

'Rhona, how many times do we have to go over this? Only people on the list get into crime scenes. You're *killing* me here.'

DS Massie's shoulders drooped. 'I was with you the whole time, Boss!' Before holding her hand up. 'But I'll have a word with who-ever's on the door. Refresher course, et cetera. All that stuff.'

'I need a clean crime scene, Rhona. What if someone com-promises evidence? *Then* where will we be?'

That hand went on her heart. 'I'll have a word. I swear.'

The SE tech put her camera away. 'Actually, we're all finished in here. You can call in the crime-scene cleaners, if you like.' A hope-ful lilt slid into her voice. 'Unless you'd like us to give it another once-over?'

'And double my Forensics bill?' Monroe gave a wee snort. 'I'll pass.'

'Fair enough. Pics will be on the server in an hour – if you put a rush on the DNA you could probably get it tomorrow. But it'll—'

'Cost me. I know.' He stared at the gore-soaked table. 'Do it. If this really *is* a pattern, our killer will be gunning for his next pair of victims day after tomorrow. I want that DNA on my desk today.'

The SE tech blinked at him. 'Today?'

'*Today.*' He tilted his head towards DS Massie, then looked up at a blood-free section of wall. 'What do you think of this colour for the new kitchen?'

'Bit lairy, Boss.'

'Hmmm . . .' Monroe turned to Angus. 'And as for you—'

'I got an email!' Backing away, sticking to the common approach path, cos falling off would only make things worse. 'This morning. I was meant to be joining CID, but I got an email, and it said to come here straight away, and report to you, and . . . It's—'

'Ah-ha!' DS Massie jabbed a finger in his direction. 'He's *Bonnie*'s replacement, while she's on that crime-scene-management course.'

'Oh, the irony.' Monroe looked Angus up and down. 'Angus MacVicar: any relation?'

'Well, I live with my mum, but—'

'To the writer.'

OK, today just wasn't going well at all. 'Ah, right, yes. No. No relation.'

Monroe shook his head. 'Pity.' He swivelled on his blue plastic booties. 'Well, if you're the new Bonnie, you might as well tag along.' Heading off down the corridor. 'Gather the posse, Rhona: War Room in the lounge, ten minutes.'

'Boss.' And she was off as well, leaving Angus all alone in the blood-drenched room that stank of death.

He slapped his palms against his legs.

Looked around at the torture table, and the marquee, and the drowning light, and the mouldy bag in the sink . . .

Huffed out a long breath.

'Great.'

The scene examiners had finished in the living room too, leaving every surface liberally coated with globs of white and black fingerprint powder.

There were only three people in here, but the place was already getting crowded.

Angus took up as little space as possible by standing in the corner, while DS Massie perched herself on the arm of the red leather sofa. Scooping from a tin of Irn-Bru. She'd peeled off the top half of her forensic oversuit, tying the arms around her waist. Without the facemask and safety goggles, her face was frog-belly pale, thick grey teeth with a lot of gum on show. A weird, curly, bobbed haircut, turned lank after its stint in her personal SOC-suit sauna.

DI Cohen was the shortest officer here, but bulky with it – muscle, rather than fat. Black, semi-bouffant hair, streaked with white above the ears. He'd stripped down to his real clothes, sweat staining the back of his pink shirt as he perused the

Healey-Robinsons' record collection. Hairy fingers walking along the LPs' spines. 'Told you so.'

Rhona grimaced. 'Blah, blah, blah.'

He paused, somewhere between Nirvana and Muse. 'Don't "blah, blah, blah" me: you're setting a bad example for the wee loon.' Back to the record collection. 'Always be nice to detective inspectors, Angus, cause we can be a vindictive bunch of bastards when we put our minds to it.' Then DI Cohen's finger came up to point at DS Massie. 'Besides, I *did* tell you so.'

'I never said it *wasn't* a serial killer. Three sets of victims, two weeks apart: of course it's a serial killer. Any idiot could see that.'

'And yet, there was everyone wanging on about a homicidal lovers' tryst. I – told – you – so.' He slipped an LP from the shelf. 'Isn't that right, Angus?'

Angus stood up a little bit straighter. 'Don't know, Guv: I only joined the team today.'

DI Cohen's mouth tightened. 'What did I say about "vindictive bastards", Constable?'

'Yes, Guv. You *definitely* said it was a serial killer.'

Another scoof of Irn-Bru. 'Leave the boy alone, Badger, he's in enough trouble as it is. Trampling all over the crime scene.'

What?

'But I got an email . . .'

'Aye, I know you did. I sent it.' Suppressing a little burp. 'Didn't say to come galumphing in like a pissed-up cave troll, though, did it?'

'It said to report to DCI Monroe ASAP!'

She shook her head. 'Angus, Angus, Angus, Angus . . .' Sigh. 'You turn up at the SOC-entrance tent and you *ask* to see the Boss.'

Yeah, when you put it like that.

'Sorry.'

DS Massie narrowed her eyes at him. 'Thanks to your great, clumsy meanderthalling the Boss called me "Detective Sergeant Massie". Hasn't used my Sunday name since I accidentally set fire to that patrol car . . .'

A snort from DI Cohen. ' "Accidentally".'

The living-room door swung open and in rustled DCI Monroe,

putting his phone away. 'Good news – our forensic psychologist lands at Heathrow in an hour, and he'll be on the next flight up.'

Everyone else seemed to know what that meant, so Angus didn't ask. No point making a tit of himself twice in one day.

Monroe took off his facemask and pulled back his SOC suit's hood – exposing an angular face with a sharp nose and sharper chin. No-nonsense short-back-and-sides, military moustache. He turned to Angus. 'The Chief Super's got us an FBI serial-killer specialist.' Unzipped his suit. 'I know: sounds expensive, but he was coming over for a forensic conference in London next week anyway, so we only have to fork out business class to Oldcastle and back.'

DS Massie rolled her eyes. 'About bloody time! That hairy idiot from Tulliallan was about as much use as barbed-wire toilet paper. "Murderous love triangle", my tattered arse.'

Cohen stuck the album back on the shelf. '*I* said that.'

'Of course you did.' Monroe sagged his bum against the dusted couch, making his SOC suit crackle. 'The guy's got some weird preconditions, but he's helped catch a lot of killers, so you' – pointing at Rhona – 'and you' – pointing at DI Cohen – 'will make sure no one pisses him off, OK? As of today we need all the help we can get.' He snapped off his gloves and rubbed at his face. 'Anything on the door-to-doors?'

Massie bared those grey teeth. 'Work in progress, Boss.'

'Badger?'

One shoulder rose then fell. 'Your guess is as good as mine. Trouble with Oldcastle is we've got about seventeen trillion different places to dump a corpse.'

Monroe unzipped his suit and wafted the edges. Turned to Angus again. 'Victims are always in pairs: he kills one and leaves the body at the scene. The other gets tortured and then . . . Who knows? He's got to dump the remains somewhere.'

DI Cohen plucked another LP from the shelf. 'Could spend a decade combing Moncuir Wood with cadaver dogs and still not get close.'

Silence as Monroe peeled himself like an albino banana, then bundled up the rumpled suit. 'Come on, Angus: you're new. Any insights you want to share with us? First impressions? Wild hunches? Beginner's luck?'

'Er . . .' Angus licked his lips. Nothing like being put on the spot. 'Are we sure the other victims are dead? Maybe he's keeping them alive somewhere?'

DS Massie shuddered. 'There speaks a man who's never seen the crime-scene photographs.'

'Given what he does to the ones he leaves behind? There's no way they're still alive.' Monroe wiped his hands down the front of his jacket. 'Not after that.'

Going by the photo of the most recent victim, he had a point.

Silence settled in again.

A deep breath, then: 'Right.' Monroe pushed himself off the couch. 'Rhona: clear up here, then back to the shop – I need an office for our new profiler. And get someone to pick him up from the airport; flight gets in at three forty-seven.'

'Boss.' She wrote that down. 'We got a photo?'

'Nope. Remember those "weird preconditions"? Our guy's notoriously camera shy. No pictures; no press coverage; completely incognito.' Monroe tucked the crumpled SOC suit under his arm. 'Badger: liaise with the Media Office. We need some sort of expectation management that makes everyone think we *actually* know what we're doing.'

A nod. 'Boss.'

'Just make sure they keep our American friend's name out of it, OK? Actually, far as they're concerned, he's not even here.' Monroe checked his watch. 'Meanwhile, I need to chase up Forensics.'

Angus stood to attention. 'What about me, Boss?'

'Rhona?'

She took one last swig from her Irn-Bru, then tossed the empty can to Angus. He caught it, like a pro.

If that impressed her, it didn't show. 'Go see Mags: tell her I said you could help with the door-to-doors. Just make sure you're back at the station for the four-o'clock.'

So much for the Premier League.

Angus crushed the can in one huge fist. 'Yes, Sarge.'

'And remember: no initiative! Leave that for the grown-ups.'

3

Mrs Anita Clarkson: 30 Macallan Avenue – 12:50

'OK, thanks. Bye.' Angus clutched his standard-issue clipboard, with its stack of badly photocopied witness forms, and marched down the path again. Back to the pavement. In the rain.

Well, *technically* it was drizzle, but it was cold and wet and that's all that counted.

Forty minutes of freezing his arse off . . .

A second officer stomped their way from door to door on the other side of Macallan Avenue, doing the odd numbers, but the lucky sod was in the full padded-waterproof-high-vis-and-peaked-cap outfit. Insulated from the wind that ripped along the street like an angry polar bear.

Balvenie Row was barely visible from here – just a hint of the terrace's backside, glimpsed between the cloned semis opposite – with the railway embankment looming behind as yet another freight train rumbled by, hauling a long line of rusty carriages behind it. The rattling soundtrack of diesel and metal drowning out the media circus hubbub.

Angus watched it go.

Scrunched up his face.

Come on: at least he was *doing* something.

Making progress.

Well, maybe not personally, because so far no one had seen anything, but that wasn't the point. An investigation was a team sport, and Angus was doing his bit.

Helping catch a killer.

So what if it was cold and wet?

Everyone had to be spoken to. Every avenue explored. Every lead followed up.

Still, a warmer jacket would've been nice.

Ms Louise Banks: 34 Macallan Avenue – 13:03

Ms Banks waved her cigarette about, gesticulating every word into being with a curl of pale grey. 'What, them poofs over there?'

Her smoking hand jerked towards the other side of the road, in the vague direction of the crime scene.

She had another scuba-diving pull on her cigarette, enveloping Angus in smoke with: 'Nah. Never seen nothing. Well, you don't, do you?' Pulling her dressing gown tighter at one o'clock in the afternoon. 'Just in case they're up to something *unnatural* . . .'

Mr Michael McKenna: 36 Macallan Avenue – 13:12

Mr McKenna sniffed. 'Oy, yes, I heard. I heard. Terrible. Simply terrible.' He had to be eighty if he was a day, with a walking stick, pale wobbly jowls, watery eyes, and a shirt and tie on under his jumper.

The drizzle had thickened, hiding the railway line in a blanket of drifting grey. Soaking through Angus's jacket and shirt, making his hair stick to his forehead.

'But did you *see* anything, Mr McKenna?'

An arthritis-twisted hand worried at the knot on the tie. 'One worries so much these days, doesn't one? What with all the crime and the murder and the young people in their hoodies . . .'

Miss Michelle Norris: 52 Macallan Avenue – 14:32

Miss Norris grimaced. 'Sorry.'

Cloying waves of jasmine and lavender strangled the air as she stood there with her peroxide quiff and enough eyeliner, blusher, foundation, and the rest, to record a million YouTube make-up tutorials.

Angus ticked the box on the form, shielding it from the rain with his back. 'OK, thanks anyway.'

She gave him an apologetic I'd-invite-you-in-to-dry-off-but-you-know-how-it-is smile, then shut the door in his face.

He slumped for a second, then trudged his way back to the pavement.

The drizzle had officially given way to proper actual rain about half an hour ago, driven in on that Arctic wind like galvanized nails.

Angus checked his watch – 14:33.

Another hour before he could legitimately call it quits and head back to the station for the four-o'clock briefing.

Assuming he hadn't caught his death by—

'Spring' from Vivaldi's *Four Seasons* sprung into life, deep within his inside pocket. He pulled out the small ziplock freezer bag his phone lived in. Because this stuff was expensive, and had to be looked after, and there was no way in *hell* his mum would let him spend that kind of money on another one.

Leaving it in its bag, he pressed the button.

'DC MacVicar.'

'*Angus?*' Damn. Should've checked who was calling before answering. '*You forgot your lunch! You know how important it is to eat right.*'

Still, too late now. 'Yes, Mum. Sorry, Mum.'

'*I make you a packed lunch for a reason, Angus. Do you not even care?*'

'No, I care, Mum.' He squelched his way along the pavement towards the next house on the street. 'It's just . . . and I wanted to be early for my first day in CID, and—'

'*I don't know why I bother, honestly I don't. Do you have any idea how much food costs these days, Angus? Do you think we're rich enough to just throw it away? Because we're not rich enough, Angus, those days are long gone.*'

He stopped, eyes screwed tightly shut. Keeping it out of his voice. 'I'll take it with me tomorrow, Mum. I promise. But I've got to go, the DCI's shouting for me.' Angus took the phone from his ear and put his clipboard between him and the microphone. 'Be right there, sir!'

Then back to the phone.

'Sorry, Mum: got to go. Bye. Speak to you later. Bye . . .' Hanging up before she could say anything else.

Angus huffed out a breath, put the phone and its bag back in his pocket, slumped for a moment, then squished up the path to number fifty-four.

It was going to be a *lonnnnnnnnnng* day.

Angus shifted his bum along the radiator, steam rising from his new fighting suit's trousers.

Everyone had congregated in the incident room, facing the front, where DCI Monroe was twenty minutes in and still going strong. One detective chief inspector, two detective inspectors, three detective sergeants, nine detective constables, four police constables, four support staff, and Angus.

And all of them were *considerably* drier than he was.

The room was arranged around a central well, surrounded by blue-felt-walled cubicles – each one containing a scuffed desk and a half-knackered office chair. Only most people were standing, giving the DCI their full attention as he paced in front of the twin whiteboards, adding boxes and lines and words printed in block capitals with a squeaky red marker.

A skull-and-crossbones went in the box marked 'TOMORROW TASKS!', joining 'DTD', 'MEDIA CAMPAIGN', and 'VICTIM REVIEW'.

Monroe underlined his piratical addition. '. . . post-mortem's at nine tomorrow morning. And I know the press are going to be all over us, given Kevin Healey-Robinson was one of their own, but we're sticking with strict radio silence on this case. Operation Telegram remains a closed box to these people, OK?'

Everyone nodded.

'Good.' He stuck the cap back on his marker. 'Who knows: we might actually be the first operation in O Division history that doesn't leak like a hedgehog's colostomy bag.' The pen came up to point at the exit. 'If you haven't done it already: check the roster by the door for who your investigative buddy is. We've got a dozen new team members today – make sure your buddy is up to speed by Morning Prayers tomorrow.' Pause for effect. Big smile. 'And speaking of new people: Alasdair?'

DI Tudor took the floor. He was almost as tall as Angus, but *way* older, and not as broad. He looked like the kind of middle-aged man they used to advertise pro-biotic yoghurts and expensive holidays on TV, with his *Peaky Blinders* haircut and salt-and-pepper stubble. A chiselled jaw that wasn't afraid to ask: Are you paying too much for your car insurance?

He gave everyone a smouldering look. 'As of last night, we know our unsub has a two-week kill cycle. The Healey-Robinsons disappeared off the radar twelve days ago, that means our next murder-abduction is day after tomorrow.' He wrote 'Two Days!' on the whiteboard. 'To make sure we've got every tool at our disposal, Chief Superintendent McEwan has secured the services of a forensic psychologist.' Tudor glanced up at the wall clock. 'Who was supposed to be here half an hour ago. Maybe—'

The incident room door thumped open, and in strode a very short man. Or, at least, his *arms and legs* were short; the rest of him was regular-sized. Which meant it was achondroplasia, rather than primordial dwarfism, because Angus paid attention in school. A scruffy mop of dirty-blond curls shrouded his face and broad forehead, his chin and top lip hidden by a big, greying Vandyke. White shirt, squint tie, suit jacket, army greatcoat – which must've been taken up a fair bit, but was still nearly sweeping along the carpet tiles – boot-cut jeans, and a sort of cowboy-boot-platform-shoes mashup that added at least two-and-a-bit extra inches to his height.

Even then, the top of his head probably only came up to a hand's span above Angus's belly button.

His voice was a weird mix of Scottish hard consonants and American drawl: 'Maybe he just knows how to make a dramatic entrance?'

Everyone stared. A couple of people muttered. After all the rumours and speculation about the hotshot FBI profiler about to join the team, they'd clearly been expecting someone a bit more Mulder-and-Scully and a lot less hangover-at-the-Hard-Rock-Café.

Their new forensic psychologist marched to the middle of the room, dug into a pocket, and tossed a USB stick to one of the support staff.

Pieman Bob fumbled the catch, eyes wide as he scrambled to stop the thing hitting the ground with his pork-sausage fingers.

'Be a sweetheart and pop that into whatever's hooked up to your projector. Just something I cooked up on the flight from LA.'

Finally, the Pieman got the USB stick under control, then stood there, like a damp fart, looking at DI Tudor for guidance. Who rolled his eyes, then nodded.

Off scurried Pieman Bob.

The forensic psychologist clapped his hands. 'Now then, ladies and gentlemen, on my business cards it says *"Dr Fife"*, but you can call me Jonathan. Not *"John"*, or *"Jonny"* or *"Jo"* or *"Nathan"*. *"John-a-than"*. I shall do my best to learn your names, but I can't promise anything.'

Monster Munch sidled up next to Angus, warming her bum on the radiator. She didn't take up much room, being petite but solidly built, with her long dark hair wrestled into an elaborate French plait. God knew what her mum and dad were thinking of, christening her 'Chantelle': she was clearly much more Monster Munchy. Her skin boasted of a proud Indian heritage, her voice: one of those uncompromising Scottish accents that could sandblast granite, even at a whisper. She leaned in close. 'Aye, Tudor wasnae kiddin' – yer man really is a "tool".'

The tool in question thumped a Cuban heel down like a judge's gavel. 'Next up: my presence here is gonna remain *strictly* confidential! Given how modest and shy I am, I'm more than happy for you guys to take all the credit, just as long as no one knows I'm in town, deal?' He looked around, as if actually expecting a response, but it wasn't a panto kind of a crowd.

Monroe put a hand on his heart. 'I can assure you: my team will keep you out of the public eye.'

'Cos otherwise I'm outta here and you can go back to failing on your own.'

At long last, Pieman Bob got the projector working, and a PowerPoint slide covered both whiteboards: the words 'DR JONA-THAN FIFE' all wobbly and distorted until someone pulled the screen down.

Someone else killed the lights.

Dr Fife didn't thank them. 'I understand half of you are new to the team, so think of this as your orientation.'

Silence.

Nobody moved.

'Well?' Dr Fife clicked his fingers a couple of times. 'Remote?'

Pieman Bob handed it over.

Dr Fife didn't thank him either, just pointed the remote at the projector – the opening slide disappeared, replaced by a photo of a living room that had no living left. Minimalist, with blood-spattered white walls, a couple of plain, white cabinets, and the kind of dining table you buy from a catalogue.

A man sat behind it – early forties, in a replica Oldcastle Warriors football shirt that was stained almost black, his porn-star moustache thick with congealed blood, his nose flattened hard enough for shards of bone to poke through. Parallel lines of bruising reached out from the corners of his mouth, and both hands had been fixed to the tabletop with dirty-big wood screws.

Just like Douglas Healey-Robinson.

Only much fresher: the blood still neon red, rather than Bovril brown.

The killer had nailed a small yellow square of paper to his fore-head, but the Post-it note was too far away and too smeared with scarlet to read.

Dr Fife tapped the screen. 'Second of February – Michael Fordyce, forty-one, chartered accountant.' The remote came up again and Michael Fordyce's corpse was replaced by a cheery pic of a woman in a pink sweatshirt with kittens embroidered all over it – but the sleeves had been ripped off, revealing shot-putter's arms that bulged with muscles. Shoulder-length blonde hair, big smile, and big round glasses. 'Michael's wife: Dr Sarah Fordyce; forty-nine; GP at the Blackwood Medical Centre; Oldcastle Iron-Woman finalist, three years in a row. Current whereabouts unknown.'

The slide changed, zooming in on Michael Fordyce's dead face, so the Post-it note was centre stage: 'DON'T BELIEVE THEIR LIES!!!' printed in black Sharpie capital letters, just visible between the scarlet smears.

Dr Fife's lip curled. 'The initial investigation assumed Sarah killed him and ran away. This was, of course . . .' his right hand drew small circles in the air, 'let's be polite and call it "*ridiculously ill-informed bullshit*".'

'Oh aye.' Monster Munch leaned in for another whisper. 'Tool and a fuckin' half.'

No point rising to it: would only encourage her.

'You guys might think that anyone with half a brain would take one look at this photo and know it wasn't a lovers' tiff. Look at the note: "Don't believe their lies".' He paused. 'Anyone?'

No one.

'"Their" lies. "Don't believe *their* lies". Not "Don't believe *his* lies". "*Their*" lies: plural.'

'*Actually* . . .' DS Sharp raised a finger. She'd got herself a new pixie cut, with frosted tips, and a pair of big square glasses that exaggerated her dimples and gave her the air of someone who kept a bag of emergency sweeties about her person. Like everyone's favourite aunty in a dark-brown fighting suit. 'Could be non-gender specific.'

'That's an excellent point!' Dr Fife slapped his forehead. 'I'd forgotten how people always make sure they use respectful pronouns while *torturing someone to death*.'

DS Sharp harrumphed, the tips of her ears glowing angry pink.

'Hmmm . . .' Monster Munch nudged an elbow into Angus's ribs. 'I'm gonnae go out on a limb here, and promote him from "tool" to "twat".'

The next slide was the same table, in the Fordyces' no-longer-living room, only from the other side, zoomed in on half a dozen empty screw holes. Each one crusted in congealed blood.

'Keep those in mind, OK?'

Up came the remote, and now everyone was looking at a swanky home office: wooden panelling to waist height, oil paintings on the wall, a bookcase full of leather-bound volumes. A large mahogany desk dominated the middle of the room, but the usual topping of monitor, keyboard, and papers had been swept onto the floor, leaving nothing between the camera and Victim Number Two.

Her long, greying hair was pulled back in a ponytail, exposing the necklace of bruises around her throat. She had the kind of wrinkles that implied she smiled a lot, though there was sod-all to smile about now. Someone had gone to work on her face with fists and a hammer. They'd stripped her to the waist, but there was nothing sexual about the scene – just blood and pain. She was slumped to the side in a plump leather office chair, both hands screwed to the desktop. Another Post-it nailed to her forehead.

Everyone winced.

'Sixteenth of February – fourteen days later – Jessica Mendel, also forty-nine, heir to the "Brabingdon's Sausages" fortune. Whatever the hell *that* is.'

Jessica Mendel was replaced by a grinning middle-aged man in the process of outgrowing the waistband on his best suit. Hair thinning at the front, but combed forwards in an unconvincing attempt to hide that fact. Big saggy bags under both scrunched-up eyes as he grinned for the camera.

'Husband: Councillor Thomas "Tom" Mendel, fifty-six, Labour, on the city council since 2003. Missing.'

The image jumped to a close-up of the Post-it attached to Jessica Mendel's forehead: 'DON'T BELIEVE THEIR LIES!!!'

Dr Fife leaned back against a desk. 'Now, you'd think at this point some bright spark would have put two and two together, but, alas, bright sparks seem to be in short supply round here. Which is why *I* was drafted in.'

Ooh, yeah. That wasn't good.

Everyone looked at DCI Monroe, who had a wee bit of a squirm. Probably wondering if getting a forensic psychologist in, all the way from America, had been such a good idea after all. Because Monster Munch was clearly right about Dr Jonathan Fife.

She leaned in again as the slide changed to a second set of empty, bloody screw holes on the other side of the desk. 'Told you: twat and a half.'

Kind of hard to tell if Dr Fife was oblivious to the atmosphere he'd created in the room, or if he was actively enjoying it.

'Believe it or not, at this point it was mooted that Dr Fordyce and Councillor Mendel had colluded to murder their spouses and run off together, in order to live the high life, somewhere sunny, on Jessica Mendel's inheritance. Staging the crime scenes to look like some psycho did it, so you wouldn't suspect them.' A bright smile lit up Dr Fife's face. 'And if anyone would like to put their hand up to *that* little act of genius, I'm sure we'd all love to give them a big round of applause.'

The only sound was the radiator, pinging and clicking beneath Angus and Monster Munch's bottoms as Dr Fife looked around the room. Jaws clenched, hands tightened into fists, but nobody said a word.

'No one? Ah, well . . .' He raised the remote again.

'Aye.' DI Cohen folded his arms, chin down, scowling. 'It was some *fanny*, drafted in from Tulliallan.' He turned to Monroe. 'I *told* him it had "serial killer" written all over it, but you know what fannies are like.'

'Only too well.' Monroe nodded at Dr Fife. 'That's why we sacked him and asked for you.'

A condescending smile. 'Probably the only sensible thing this police department's ever done.' Up came the remote again. 'Then the third victim pair turn up.'

This time the screen displayed an almost identical photo to the one Angus was shown this morning, back in the kitchen of horror.

'Douglas Healey-Robinson, thirty-seven. Worked from home. Author of nine homo-erotic police procedurals set in Edinburgh and Glasgow. Body wasn't discovered till eight o'clock last night, but everything points to him being attacked twelve days ago: first of March. How do we know this?' Dr Fife picked a random PC and held a hand out, inviting a response.

Didn't get one.

He was going to learn eventually, right?

'*We know*, because his husband, Kevin, was Political-and-Lifestyle Correspondent at the *Castle News and Post*, and that's the last time he was seen alive. He's also missing.'

The mouldering body was exchanged for a full-length shot of a guy in his mid-forties, grinning away in the full kilt outfit, with a white-heather spray in his buttonhole. Pointing at the shiny ring on his left hand as if it was the most amazing thing anyone had ever seen. Swept-back hair, big eyes, perfect teeth.

He beamed down at them for a couple of breaths, then a close-up of the note nailed to his husband's forehead appeared. Unreadable and buckled under all the dried blood.

Swiftly followed by a photograph of the extra screw holes.

Dr Fife fiddled with the remote, and a little red dot sparked into life on the far wall – sweeping it around the room like a man enticing a cat, till it came to rest on the projected holes. Drawing a wobbly swirl of ellipses around them in scarlet laser light. 'Now, just in case we've got a budding Columbo in the audience, who's gonna tell me what the significance of *these* is?'

Nope, he still hadn't got it: not a panto crowd.

'No? How about we downgrade to a Jessica Fletcher. Any takers?'

Monster Munch chewed on the inside of her cheek for a moment, but she kept her voice low: 'Think I'd get a cheer if I went up and punched the twat one?'

One more try from Dr Fife: 'Scooby-Doo . . . ?'

Angus put his hand up. 'He made them watch.'

4

'Bless your cotton socks, yes!' Dr Fife treated him to a big smile, as if Angus was a Labrador who'd just performed a trick. 'He makes them *watch*. Let's hear it for our oversized friend!'

Dr Fife launched into a round of applause.

Shockingly enough, no one joined in.

Heat blossomed across Angus's shoulder blades, prickled across his scalp.

Monster Munch shook her head. 'Rookie mistake. You *never* answer a twat's questions. Just encourages mair twattishness.'

'Our killer targets couples – he gets off on the power of torturing one while the other *watches*.' Dr Fife thumbed the remote and the screw holes faded to black, then up came six head-and-shoulders portraits, lined up like a graduation yearbook: Michael Fordyce, Jessica Mendel, and Douglas Healey-Robinson on the top row; Dr Sarah Fordyce, Councillor Tom Mendel, and Kevin Healey-Robinson underneath. 'Three victims left behind, and three victims removed from the scene. There's a reason he does this. Something that makes sense only to him.' Dr Fife milked a pause, one eyebrow up, deepening the creases across his brow. 'We just need to figure out what it is.'

Angus stuck his hand up again, getting a groan and a whisper from Monster Munch:

'You never soddin' learn, do you?'

'Well, well, well, aren't we *keen* today, Officer . . . ?'

'MacVicar.' Angus lowered his hand. 'Is there any chance Sarah Fordyce, Tom Mendel, and Kevin Healey-Robinson are still alive?'

Monroe winced. 'Constable MacVicar, A: we've been over this, and B: can we save the questions for the end, please? I'm sure Dr Fife doesn't want—'

'No, it's fine. At least your resident yeti's asked a half-decent question.' Dr Fife fiddled with the remote and the images wheeched back through the slides until Jessica Mendel's remains dominated the room. He stared at Angus. 'When we look at Mrs Mendel's body, what do we see?'

This time, Monster Munch put a bit of force into her elbow. 'Don't you *dare*.'

Angus shifted his bum on the radiator, and kept his big gob shut.

'No?' A disappointed sigh. 'He's a *planner*: he worms his way into his victims' homes; he establishes and manages his crime scene; he screws their hands to the table so they can't move while he gets to work. It's all controlled, measured, contained. But, soon as the torture starts, all that self-discipline evaporates like spilled petrol.' Dr Fife abandoned Angus and spoke to the whole room instead. 'Given the levels of violence on display, I'd put fifty bucks on Mr Mendel lasting a day, *maybe* two, tops. Assuming he even survived the initial encounter. You see—'

A pounding guitar rhythm ripped free as Motörhead's 'Ace Of Spades' got going. DS Massie pulled out her phone, answering it just as Lemmy asked if anyone wanted to gamble. She stuck a finger in her ear and wandered off into the corner, away from the gathering.

Dr Fife watched her go. 'No, please: don't mind me. I'm only giving you the benefit of my twenty-plus years' experience.'

Clearly, DS Sharp decided to run interference. 'So: there's going to be more victims.'

He stared at her as if that was the stupidest question he'd ever heard. '*Of course* there are. He's got away with it three times already; the police are clueless and their investigation's floundering; why would he stop now?'

DS Sharp's face darkened, her mouth pinching as she stepped forward to have a go. But one look from Monroe and she retreated to her desk. Folded her arms like DI Cohen. Glowered.

'Anyway: in two days' time, there's going to be another corpse in the morgue, and one more missing. We—'

'Mortuary.' She stuck her nose in the air. 'We don't have "morgues" in this country, we have mortuaries.'

'Isn't that interesting.' Making it sound anything but. Dr Fife clicked forward through the slides again. 'You'll have to excuse me . . . Officer Whatever-Your-Name-Is, I'm more accustomed to catching serial killers for the FBI: Seattle Strangler, KTR Killer, Nashville Ripper, Rocky Mountain Murderer, Detroit Cannibal . . .' The smile couldn't have been more patronizing if it tried. 'But I won't bore you with the full list.'

The words 'PRIORITY QUESTIONS' sat at the top of the projection screen, with a gap, then four empty bullet points below.

'Now, who wants to guess what questions we need to answer?'

Still reaching for the panto crowd.

Still getting nothing back.

'WHAT? WHY? WHO?' appeared on the slide.

'One.' Dr Fife pointed the remote again, reading out each bullet point as it popped up on the list: ' "What does our Killer do?" Two: "Why does he do it?" Three: "How does he select his victims?" And by answering these questions, we solve the big one. Four: "Who *is* he?" '

Monster Munch let out a wet, hissing tut. 'Aye, and we needed some American twat to tell us that?'

The bullet points vanished, then the words: 'REMEMBER: DR JONATHAN FIFE IS NOT HERE!' appeared in big red letters.

A sniff from Monster Munch. 'Is that it?'

One last press of the remote and they were all left in darkness.

'Like I say, this is just what I threw together on the flight over. We'll need to sift through everything if we're gonna get a proper profile.'

The lights flickered on.

Monroe didn't say anything, but he looked as if someone had kicked his puppy.

Dr Fife shrugged. 'It's not like TV, where "whoosh!" the forensic psychologist gets visions from the great beyond – this stuff takes time and brainpower. We don't even know how he transports the missing victims when he's finished butchering their other halves. Could be *weeks* before we make a proper breakthrough, so—'

'Boss?' DS Massie hurried back from her corner, phone pressed against her chest. 'Think we've got something!'

Monroe looked up from the printout, swivelling back and forth in his office chair. 'From the door-to-doors?'

The room thrummed as Operation Telegram got on with tidying up before the end of shift. Making last-minute telephone calls, printing off actions on the rattling printer, holding murmured conversations – probably about what a wanker Dr Fife turned out to be.

While they got on with that, DI Tudor, DS Massie, and a yawning Dr Fife gathered around Monroe's desk.

Angus hovered on the periphery of the little group, partly out of nosiness, but mostly because no one had given him anything *else* to do.

Monroe had decorated his cubicle with a couple of pinned-up cartoons, cut from the *Castle News & Post;* a handful of family photographs; and three pages out of some *Better Homes and Kitchens* magazine, showing unfeasibly happy middle-aged couples enjoying polished granite worktops and genuine oak cabinets.

DS Massie perched her bum on the edge of Monroe's desk. 'I was going through the daily reports, as you do, and there's this line that bugged me – a guy who lives at number seventeen, two doors down from the Healey-Robinsons, moaning about how he had to park miles away the night of the murder, because, and I quote: "Some inconsiderate bastard abandoned a dirty-big self-drive Luton van" outside his house.'

Tudor crinkled his eyes. 'Yes, but that's hardly—'

'But the thing is: *none* of the other door-to-doors mentions a Luton van. So I got 'Tash to check with everyone on Balvenie Row again: a couple of the neighbours spotted it, but no one *hired* it.'

Now that made Monroe sit up. 'Rhona: please tell me you've got a number plate.'

She produced another sheet of A4, slapping it down on the desk. 'We're not that lucky. But the van's livery *was* pretty distinctive, so I tracked down the hire company: Toucan Youcan. Based in Shortstaine. They had four Luton vans rented out when the Healey-Robinsons were killed. One on its way to Sheffield, one headed for Inverness, two local.' She tapped the sheet with a ragged fingernail. 'Hirers' names, addresses, and PNC checks. Local hires are highlighted in yellow.' She waggled her eyebrows at him. 'Notice anything?'

Angus leaned in for a squint, but Monroe wheeched the printout off the desk and had one of his own.

'Let's see . . .' Mouth pursing as he read. 'Francis McCurdy: project manager, six points for speeding, bunch of parking tickets, half a dozen complaints from the neighbours about excessive noise.' Monroe's eyes widened. 'Better yet: *Patrick Crombie*! Three years for rape, two for sexual assault, eight months for illegal imprisonment. You wee beauty!' Leaping to his feet. 'Right, I'm on the warrant. And we'll need backup.' Raising his voice, cutting across the bustling room. 'BADGER, I WANT AN OSU TEAM, ASAP!'

DI Cohen grabbed his phone. 'ON IT, BOSS.'

'LAURA, GET ME A DOG UNIT!'

DS Sharp was halfway through a Tunnock's tea cake, but she ditched it. 'ONE DOG UNIT, COMING UP . . .'

'BYRON, YOU'RE WITH GEORGE. TAKE A POOL CAR AND STAKE OUT . . .' Monroe checked the paperwork again, 'SEVEN-TEEN MUCHAN ROAD, JUST IN CASE. MONSTER MUNCH, PAUL, MAGS – YOU'RE WITH KATHERINE, COLLY, AND 'TASH. TWO TO A CAR, FULL M.O.E. GEAR. WE'LL BRIEF ON THE WAY.' Clapping his hands. 'LET'S MOVE, PEOPLE!'

The room exploded into action – everyone scrambling to their allotted tasks as Monroe marched for the door, with DS Massie hot on his heels.

Angus just stood there. Unneeded, unwanted, and un—

'Well?' Monroe threw the words over his shoulder. 'Don't just stand there, Constable, we're going hunting!'

'Yes, Boss!' Snapping to attention.

The DCI came to a halt and turned, hauling on his jacket. 'Consider this a mentoring opportunity.' He looked Angus up and down. 'Besides, you're huge: if something kicks off we can all hide behind you.'

*

The dual carriageway crawled by the pool car's windows, all four lanes stuffed with people who thought they'd make a break for it before rush hour started, but left it far too late. Now it was one minute to five, and they were stuck like everyone else. Miserable faces glooming out at the rain and a snaking ribbon of brake lights.

DS Massie sat behind the wheel, jaw clenched, fingers tightening and relaxing and tightening and relaxing, keeping a constant eight feet between them and the patrol car in front. Windscreen wipers going full pelt. Monroe: in the passenger seat, on his phone – one finger in his ear to block out the engine-and-wiper noise. Angus and Dr Fife in the back.

The forensic psychologist sagged in his seat, releasing the occasional deep sigh, the corners of his mouth turned down so far they pulled his Vandyke out of shape. As if Operation Telegram *wasn't* on its way to dunt in a serial killer's door.

He'd taken Patrick Crombie's criminal records with him, flicking through the file as they crawled along Camburn Drive with the soggy rush-hour traffic.

Angus turned in his seat, sneaking a look out the back window, where the rest of the convoy crept along behind. Two more pool cars, then a Dog Unit, an Operational Support Unit in its minibus/van hybrid, another patrol car, and a scene examiners' Transit that not even the torrential rain could wash clean.

'What? . . . No.' Monroe curled to one side, as if that would improve his mobile reception. 'Fifty-*two* Breechfield Crescent. Breech-field. Bravo, Romeo, Echo, Echo, Charlie, Hotel— . . . Yes, I know it's not normal procedure, Marjory, but this is urgent.'

'Urgh . . .' Dr Fife looked up from his file. 'Does it normally take this long?'

Angus swivelled frontwards again, glancing down at the printouts in Dr Fife's lap. Patrick Crombie's latest mugshot glowered back.

Mid-twenties, bulked up from the prison gym, shaved head, close-trimmed beard. Sticky-out ears. The kind of guy who'd glass you for looking at his pint funny.

DS Massie gave the rear-view mirror the same kind of look. 'You didn't have to come.'

'Yes.' Monroe nodded. 'That's right: we've reason to suspect Mr Crombie is responsible for six murders, possibly more . . .'

A small snort broke free, as Fife turned the page. 'Only when you're used to helicopters, and SWAT teams with machine guns, this is all a little . . . tame.'

'Well, I'm *sorry* we can't give you a bit more *razzmatazz*!'

'. . . on our way there now. You know the media's gone full-on feeding frenzy here, Marjory, imagine if we miss the chance to catch him before he kills someone else . . . Yes . . . Of course I'll hold.'

Dr Fife grimaced. 'The risk assessment was a particular high-light. I've never done one in the back of a slow-moving vehicle before.'

'Do you *want* me to pull over and let you out?'

'And miss the grand finale?' He turned the page again, voice like a bored teenager. 'How ever would I live with myself?'

Monroe twisted around to address the car, phone against his chest. 'I'm on hold.' Then faced front again, mobile clamped to one ear, finger jammed in the other.

Dr Fife leaned forward and poked DS Massie's shoulder. 'And why does it take till tomorrow to line up an autopsy? Do you guys do *everything* at half speed?'

The rear-view got another glare. 'It's not an "autopsy", it's a post-mortem. This isn't the United States of Unable to Speak the Language Properly.'

'How terribly gauche of me.'

'There's a backlog at the mortuary, OK? We're already jumping the queue.' Her knuckles whitened on the steering wheel. 'If you're just going to complain, you should've stayed back at the station.'

The windscreen wipers squealed and thunked.

Rain crackled on the car roof, like handfuls of gravel.

They crept forwards, coming to the end of Castle Hill, the dark mass of Camburn Woods looming up ahead. Ready to swallow them.

And still no one said anything.

Angus cleared his throat. 'So . . . what do you think Crombie does with the bodies? Of the partners, I mean.'

Dr Fife sat forward and poked DS Massie again. 'Besides, I *had* to come. What if there's a hostage situation and you need someone who isn't a moron to negotiate with your Patrick Crombie?'

'Have you always been this big an arsehole?' Soon as the words left her mouth, a tsunami of pink rushed up her cheeks. She bit her lips. And this time it wasn't a glare she gave the rear-view mirror.

Dr Fife raised an eyebrow, staring back.

Camburn Woods opened its maw and wolfed them down.

'I . . . When I said "this *big* an arsehole" . . . That . . . It wasn't meant to be a comment about your disability.' Her voice sharpened. 'Just the amount of arseholeishness you bring to any situation.'

'None taken.' He went back to the file. 'And for the record: disabled or not, I can still fight, drink, and fuck with the best of them.'

Because things weren't tense and uncomfortable enough.

The dark woods wrapped around the dual carriageway, the canopy cover thick enough to shut out much of the downpour and shroud the slow-moving traffic in gloom.

One by one, car headlights bloomed.

Angus shifted in his seat.

Come on, say something.

Yeah, but what?

Monroe nodded. 'Yes, I'm still holding.'

'As for "assholeishness"' – the barest hint of a smile toyed with one side of Dr Fife's mouth – 'it depends who I'm with. Some people deserve it more than others.'

DS Massie rolled her shoulders. 'Well, you better dial it back a bit or "some people" are liable to twat you one.'

God, it was getting *worse*.

OK, how about this:

Angus held up a hand. 'Do you think he took them as trophies? Patrick Crombie. Or is it more like a Dennis Nilsen situation? Or maybe Jeffrey Dahmer?' Trying not to sound too hopeful. 'Can't turn on the telly or open a book without some serial killer eating their victims.'

That hint of a smile became a definite suggestion. 'Are you usually this forthright, DS Massie?'

But Angus wasn't giving up that easily. 'Because Crombie's got to be doing something with the bodies, right? Otherwise he wouldn't go to all the trouble of hiring a van.'

Massie sniffed. '"Depends who I'm with. Some people deserve it more than others."'

And with that, Dr Fife broke into a proper smile. 'Why, Detective Sergeant, are you *flirting* with me?'

'No!'

Actually, that was a really good point, wasn't it: about Crombie hiring a full-sized removal vehicle. Angus held up a finger. 'You know, a Luton van's huge: you could get dozens of bodies in there, right? I mean, an estate car would probably—'

'Marjory?' Monroe sat up straight. 'What's the— . . . Excellent. Thank you!'

Dr Fife put a bit of honey in his voice. 'Are you sure? Because it really sounds like—'

'Oh, I'm absolutely *sodding* positive.'

'No, that's great . . . Cheers, Marjory, I owe you one.' Monroe hung up. Slumped back in his seat, completely oblivious to the atmosphere in the car. Huffed out a long breath. 'Thank God for that: we would've looked a right bunch of pricks, otherwise.' He produced his Airwave and poked at the keypad.

Right on cue, both Angus and DS Massie's handsets gave three answering bleeps as Monroe broadcast to the team.

His voice echoed out of their Airwaves, about a second out of sync.

'All right, everyone, Sheriff Barland's given us the thumbs up. We have our warrant. Let's rock!'

DS Massie hit the button on the steering column and the pool car's siren yowled into life, the lights hidden behind the radiator grille flickering blue and white against the vehicle in front.

The patrol car's light swirled on too, then the whole convoy was at it. Well, except for the grubby SE Transit van.

As the howling sirens rose, the cars in front parted, creating a temporary middle lane that the lead patrol car accelerated into.

DS Massie followed them, hands tightening on the wheel. Her grin shone in the rear-view mirror. 'God, I love this bit . . .'

*

The pool car was back to walking pace again, drifting around Breechfield Crescent – a circle of two-storey houses in grey harling with faux-stone details, brown pantiles, and rust-flecked satellite dishes. The gardens weren't *huge*, but they were still bigger than the ones on Balvenie Row. Older too; more lived in. But every bit as soulless.

The convoy had reordered itself, with the OSU taking point, followed by the Dog Unit and two patrol cars. And last, but not least, Angus, Monroe, Dr Fife, and DS Massie.

Her Airwave bleeped, then Monster Munch's delicate tones crackled out into the car.

'*That's us in the back garden, Sarge. Ready when you are.*'

Massie pressed the button. 'Any sign of Crombie?'

'*Naw. But someone's home: can hear their shite music* pounding *out through the walls.*'

DS Massie shared a look with Monroe.

He nodded. Grabbed his handset off the dashboard. 'And we're GO, GO, GO!'

Everyone floored it – vans and patrol cars leaping forward, around the last arc of Breechfield Crescent.

Right up ahead, a lurid lime-green Luton Transit was parked in the driveway outside number fifty-two. A cheesy advert covered the near-side panels: 'TOMMY THE TOUCAN SAYS YOUCAN DRIVE THIS VAN TOU!' featuring a grinning cartoon mascot with a massive multicoloured beak.

The OSU van screeched to a halt, blocking the driveway, its side clattered open and a team of absolute bruisers piled out into the rain, so big they made Angus look weedy. They were dressed for rioting – shin guards, gloves, pads, helmets, overalls, boots, stab-proof vests. Extendable batons at full mast . . .

They swarmed towards the house, parting around the hire van, and meeting up on the other side, where they flattened out into a single line along the front of number fifty-two. Keeping clear of the windows.

A particularly huge officer bustled her way to the front, carrying the big red door key.

One of her colleagues tried the door handle, shook his head, then got out of the way *fast* as the big red door key battered into the door, rattling the UPVC in its frame.

Once, twice, three times . . .

Behind them, the Dog Unit pulled up, half on the kerb.

Out came the driver, followed by the biggest, *hairiest* Alsatian the world had ever seen. Police Dog Bawheid strained at the end of his leash, dragging his handler towards the scrum.

Then it was the two patrol cars, blocking the road, disgorging their officers to set up a cordon and move into defensive positions.

DS Massie slammed on the brakes, and everyone clambered out into the rain. Everyone *except* Dr Fife.

Number fifty-two's front door exploded inwards, the whole frame tearing free of the wall in a shatter of white plastic. It crashed down, like an inverted drawbridge, and the OSU team charged inside, pursued by PD Bawheid, who seemed to be having a terrific time of it and looking forward to biting someone.

Dr Fife buzzed down his window and looked up at Angus. 'You do know that it's raining, right?'

Voices thundered out from the ruined doorway:

'POLICE!'

'NOBODY MOVE!'

Accompanied by a *lot* of barking.

Angus dragged his eyes from the dunt. 'We just caught the Fortnight Killer.'

That seemed to amuse Fife. 'Let's wait and see, shall we?'

'CLEAR!'

'CHECK THE BATHROOM!'

Monroe shifted from foot to foot, fists clenching and unclenching as he stared at the house. Talking to himself. 'Come on. Come on . . .'

Angus curled his lip. 'What do you mean, "wait and see"?'

'Well – and this is just me speaking from twenty-plus years of experience – crimes like this usually take a *bit* longer to solve.'

Eh?

'You think this isn't our guy?'

'CLEAR!'

'IF YOU'RE IN THERE, COME OUT WITH YOUR HANDS WHERE I CAN SEE THEM!'

'Look at it this way:' Dr Fife held up the file. 'Patrick Crombie starts out molesting women in his local supermarket: gets slung in jail for two years. Six months after he's released, he rapes a single mother in a city park: does another three years. He's still on parole when he lures his social worker to his house, chains her up, and locks her in the bathroom. Claimed he was "teaching her a lesson" because she "disrespected him" in front of her team.'

'*POLICE!*'

'*CLEAR!*'

'That's a classic path of escalation. You can bet he woulda raped her too, if the cops hadn't got to him first.' The file went back on the seat. '*Maybe* he spent his time in jail working out where he went wrong? He's spent nearly six years behind bars – rehearsing the fantasy over and over. Getting bolder every time they let him out.'

Well, there you go then.

Angus nodded. 'So he's *definitely* our man.'

Glad that was settled.

'*CLEAR!*'

'Hmmm . . .' Dr Fife made a see-saw gesture with one hand. 'It's a big jump from there to torturing six people to death. Plus there's the whole "sex problem". When Crombie—'

'*YOU! ON THE GROUND!*'

'*DON'T MOVE!*'

'*ON THE GROUND, NOW!*'

'Ha!' Monroe bounced on the balls of his feet. 'Here we go . . .'

The barking was interrupted by an almighty *crash*, followed by a banging echo, what sounded like shattering glass, then a familiar hard Scottish accent blared out behind the house:

'*COME BACK HERE, YA WEE SHITE!*' Definitely Monster Munch.

A look of horror smothered Monroe's face. He snatched up his Airwave. 'What the hell's going on in there?'

A wee scream from the back garden, then a howl of pain.

'*OFFICER DOWN!*'

'*AYA BASTARD!*'

DS Massie covered her face. 'Oh, for God's sake . . .'

'*HE'S HOPPED THE FENCE! GOING RIGHT, GOING RIGHT!*'

DS Sharp sprinted for the house on the right – number fifty – with Massie and Monroe hard behind her.

Nope.

Angus went left instead, towards the final house in the street: number fifty-four. Hurdling the little hedge between the properties, and hammering up the lock-block driveway. Running down the far side of the house. A seven-foot-high wooden fence blocked the way, but he leapt, put a foot on the recycling bin, and heaved himself over the top.

It was time to show DCI Monroe he was more than just something to hide behind.

5

Angus staggered to a halt in the back garden.

Rain drummed on the roof of a plastic Wendy house; a weeny shed; and a metal whirly that bore one lonely, sodden bright-pink sock. A yellow dumper truck, about the size of a breeze block, lay on its side beneath a leafless fruit tree.

The garden was enclosed by more tall wooden fencing, with a small veg plot planted along the boundary between here and number fifty-two. Green knobbly stalks of Brussels sprouts protected by a cage of bamboo canes and green netting – everything else dug over and ready for the spring to properly kick in. A rake, spade, and hoe propped against the fence.

No sign of Patrick Crombie.

Sod.

A pair of glazed patio doors showed off an open-plan kitchen/ dining area/living room. At the small table, a frazzled woman tried to get a pair of blue-and-pink twins to eat their peas by doing 'the aeroplane thing'. Going by the slick of little green pellets on the floor, it wasn't working.

She looked up to refuel the plane, and her eyes went wide, mouth falling open as she spotted Angus. More peas tipped off the spoon, bouncing off the tiles as she stared.

Grunting and thumping came from next door, then *clunk* and the scramble of feet on wood as Patrick Crombie's shaven head and neat wee beard appeared over the fence. They were followed by arms and legs, and finally the rest of him – tumbling down to crash through the green netting. Snapping bamboo canes and Brussels stalks. Flailing limbs as he struggled free.

Mud clung to his grey joggy-bots and white T-shirt; both arms thick with muscle and clarted in tattoos; shiny white trainers not so shiny any more.

Angus stepped in front of him, one hand up, barring the way. 'Patrick Crombie, I'm arresting you under Section—'

'GRAAAAAAAAAAA!' He charged, head down, arms out, slamming into Angus's chest and lifting him clear off the ground – then *thump*, flat on his back in the soggy grass with Crombie on top.

Angus jerked his knees up, rolling with it, keeping the momentum going, flipping Crombie up and over.

The tattooed lump was briefly airborne, before clattering, upside down, into the whirly, setting the metal pole ringing as water cascaded off the drooping lines.

They both scrambled to their feet.

This time when Crombie attacked, Angus dodged left, and he went stumbling by – brought up short by the fence. Sending the abandoned gardening implements clang-rattle-crashing.

'Come on, Patrick, be reasonable.'

Instead, Crombie grabbed the fallen rake, yanked it free of the netting, and took a double-handed grip on the haft. Swinging the thing like a battle-axe. Bellowing as he lunged.

The rake ripped through the damp air – metal tines flashing a hand's breadth from Angus's face.

Yeah, this wasn't good.

Angus rolled, going right this time, and the rake slammed into the grass, burying itself a good four inches.

Only now Angus was within arm's reach of the remaining gardening tools. He grasped the spade's handle and leapt up, clutching it like a muddy broadsword – pointed at Crombie's ugly mug. 'Where were we?'

Crombie swung his battle-axe again.

Angus parried it. 'Ah, right: Patrick Crombie, I am arresting you under Section one of the Criminal Justice, Scotland, Act 2016—'

Another bellow and the axe returned at speed.

Angus knocked it to the side, lunged, and the flat, back side of the spade *pannnng*ed against Crombie's skull. Not hard enough to break anything, but hard enough to make a point.

Crombie stumbled sideways.

'—for the murder of Douglas and Kevin Healey-Robinson.'

He shook his head, as if trying to get the metallic ringing noise out of it. Blinking. A wee bit unsteady on his pins.

'The reason for your arrest is that I suspect that you have committed an offence—'

And Crombie was at it again, teeth bared, spittle flying as he wheeched the rake towards Angus's cranium.

Block. Counterstrike.

Only this time Crombie was fast enough to get his faux axe up to stop the spade making contact.

Angus repeated the move: *pannnng* . . .

A woman's voice slashed through the rain. *'COME BACK HERE!'* Then another face appeared over the fence. PC Urpeth clambered up until she was perched on top, one leg dangling on either side. Her dirty-blonde hair was coming loose from its prison of hairpins, her stabproof vest and high-vis all smeared with grass stains. She'd lost her peaked cap somewhere along the way, and a fresh scrape grazed across one cheek. Her eyes were large at the best of times, but now they were positively owlish as she took in the scene.

Crombie went for an overhead strike.

Angus caught the rake halfway down with the spade, stopping it dead, then stepped forward, twisting as he went, swinging the spade to thump flat against Crombie's backside.

Well, now that he had an audience, might as well make it look good.

Crombie staggered forwards a couple of paces, then whipped the rake around, backhand.

Nope.

Swap the spade from right to left.

Block.

Step back to open up a bit of space.

'—and I believe that keeping you in custody is necessary and proportionate for the purposes of bringing you before a court—'

Double-handed swing from Crombie, slashing down left to right.

Feint left.

Twist.

Spin the spade, like Conan the Barbarian.

Pannnng . . .

This time Crombie battered into the shed.

More blinking and shaking. 'Bastard . . .'

'—or otherwise dealing with you in accordance with the law. Do you understand?'

An incoherent snarl burst free and Crombie launched himself at Angus, swirling the rake round and around, 'KILL YOU!'

Time to end with a flourish.

Angus blocked the not-axe's arc, setting the wooden haft juddering, then made a tight circle with the spade, over the haft, then under, twisting the thing out of Crombie's grasp. It sailed away to clunk against the Wendy house.

Two steps back, twirling the spade from side to side – once, twice, three, four, five, six, seven, eight – then spinning it around his back, into his left hand. And both hands together, in full Conan pose.

Crombie glared at him.

Spat.

Growled.

Here we go . . .

And charged.

Pannnnnnnnnnng . . .

Crombie spiralled sideways, feet slipping out from under him, *crump*ing face-first into the soggy grass and skidding on his front about a foot and a half, till his head boinked to a stop against that discarded dumper truck.

Angus ditched the spade-sword and pinned him there – twisting his right arm into a full lock.

'GET OFF ME! HELP! POLICE BRUTALITY!'

The cuffs ratcheted into place as PC Urpeth thumped down into the veg patch. Squashing anything that had survived Crombie's landing.

The woman with twins-and-peas was still staring, so Angus gave her a cheery thumbs up. Community policing, and all that.

Soon as the cuffs were on, Crombie wriggled and thrashed. 'HELP! POLICE BRUTALITY! CALL THE PAPERS! I WANT MY LAWYER! HELP!'

A scowl from Urpeth. 'Shut up.' She frowned at Angus's discarded weapon. 'Where'd you learn to swing a spade like that?'

'HELP! I'M INNOCENT! POLICE BRUTALITY!'

'Ill-spent youth.' Modest shrug. 'You OK?'

She prodded her scraped cheek with a fingertip. Winced. 'Little sod broke Monster Munch's nose.'

'HE ASSAULTED ME! I HAVEN'T DONE ANYTHING! POLICE BRUTALITY!'

She nudged him with her mud-and-Brussels-sprouted boot. 'If you don't shut up I'll "police brutality" you. Want a faceful of pelargonic acid vanillylamide?'

Crombie twisted his head around, glaring through the patio doors at the woman who'd pea'd all over the floor. 'THIS SLAG THREATENED ME! YOU HEARD IT! POLICE BRUTALITY!'

Angus shook his head. 'We don't PAVA people in custody.'

'Speak for yourself: I'm not built like a Sherman tank.'

'POLICE BRUTALITY!'

Between them, they hauled Crombie to his feet. Where he kicked off again, struggling hard as they frogmarched him down the side of the house. 'POLICE BRUTALITY! POLICE BRUTALITY!'

The householder, mouth like a goldfish, watched them go.

Luckily, the gate opened from the inside so they personhandled him through it.

The streetlights flickered into life, warming from a feverish orange to sickly yellow.

From here, halfway up the valley wall, you could see them blooming all over Oldcastle, stars against the gloom, twinkling through the rain. Above the rim of the valley, on the north side of the river, a sliver of sky shimmered with vibrant bloody red as the sun slowly died.

They marched Crombie towards the driveway, but before they'd cleared the house he lurched to one side, body-slamming Angus into the wall. Hard enough to strip the breath from Angus's lungs and loosen his grip. Knocking him off balance and sending him sprawling.

Crombie twisted around and slammed his forehead into Urpeth's face.

A meaty *thunk* and she went over backwards, leaving an arc of blood sparkling in the streetlights' glow.

And Crombie was off – running for it.

Lying on his side, back pressed against the house wall, Angus jabbed an arm up and out, snatching a fistful of Crombie's grass-and-mud-stained joggy-bots.

His grip on the soggy grey material was enough to pull the jogging bottoms down past Crombie's knees, tangling the nasty wee sod's ankles and sending him toppling forwards.

With both hands still cuffed behind his back.

No way to break his fall.

There was just time for a panicked scream, before the lock-block driveway rushed up to meet his face with a resounding *crack*. Followed by a stunned silence. Then a howl of pain.

PC Urpeth clambered up the recycling bin, and lurched over there on stiff legs. Fumbling out her canister of PAVA. 'SPRAY!!!'

On the TV, this kind of thing was always depicted as an exciting *whoosh* of orange gas, but in real life the special effects were a lot less impressive: like a wee squirty water pistol, sending a spoot of clear liquid into Crombie's face.

He screamed again – eyes clenched shut like angry sphincters. Tears streaming down his face.

They joined the blood pulsing out from what was left of his nose. Looked as if he'd lost a couple of front teeth as well.

Angus huffed his way to his knees. 'Was that *really* necessary?'

Urpeth wiped a dribble of fresh scarlet from her swollen lip and adopted the standard giving-evidence-in-court voice: 'The prisoner was violent and refusing to cooperate. Having assessed the situation, I deemed it appropriate to deploy my PAVA spray to protect myself and my colleague from further attack.' She put the canister away. 'Now you going to help me get him up, or what?'

They dragged Crombie to his feet again, where he stood all loose and dangly, whimpering and crying, with his joggy-bots round his ankles.

Angus pointed. 'Should we not . . . ?'

'Nah. Might stop the bugger running away again.'

They shuffled him down the driveway and out onto the road, heading for the nearest patrol car.

By the time they got there, Monroe and DS Massie were emerging from number fifty – the pair of them on their Airwaves, making urgent worried noises that trailed off as they clapped eyes on Angus, Urpeth, and their prisoner.

Then their eyes widened as they took in the bloody, *battered* state of Patrick Crombie.

Monroe came to a halt, just in front of them. 'What did . . . It's . . .'

Crombie let loose a bubble of pink frothy snot, inflated by a wee sob. 'Help . . . call the papers . . . police brutality . . . police brutality . . .'

Less than twenty feet away, Dr Fife watched them from the back seat of their pool car. Smiling as if this was all *kind of* funny, but not laugh-out-loud.

Monroe grimaced at PC Urpeth. 'Katherine?'

She dabbed at her lip again. 'He fell over.'

The only sounds were the rain, pattering on the patrol car roof, and Crombie's gurgling snivels.

'OK.' Monroe nodded. 'Excellent work, Katherine.'

'Don't look at me, Boss.' She patted Angus on the back. 'It was all Godzilla here.'

'Good lad. See? I said all that bulk would come in handy.' Monroe pulled out his Airwave. 'Gary? House is clear: let's get the team in.'

A nasal voice crackled from the handset: *'On our way.'*

'Right.' Monroe squared up to the prisoner. 'I'll give you one chance, Patrick: what did you do with Tom Mendel, Sarah Fordyce, and Kevin Healey-Robinson?' Pointing the Airwave at the house. 'We going to find them under the floorboards? Buried in the back garden? Where are their bodies?'

Crombie spattered out a frothy pink gobbet of phlegm. It fell just short of Monroe's shoes. 'Never touched them. Never even *heard* of them.' He stood up straight, bloody chin in the air. 'And I'm saying nothing else without my lawyer.'

The last scrapings of daylight had long gone, the sour-yellow street-lights robbing everything else of colour. Well, everything other than number fifty-two, where a ring of four industrial spotlights were hooked up to growling diesel generators. Bathing the house and garden in harsh white.

A row of scene examiners worked their way across the squelchy grass on their hands and knees, doing a fingertip search.

Behind them, a blue plastic marquee had been set up over the front door, hiding the investigation's comings and goings. Every curtain and blind in the property: shut.

A lone PC stood on this side of the blue-and-white 'POLICE' cordon, looking drookit and dreich in his sodden high-vis and peaked cap, keeping the crowds at bay.

The media, nutters, and lookie-loos, bustled on the other side of the tape: a swarm of people, with their cameras, brollies, micro-phones, mobile phones, and placards. That morning's trio of protestors were back, and they'd brought a new friend with them: '5G GENOCIDE! WAKE UP!!!' Jostling for position as several of the camera crews did live broadcasts for the six o'clock news.

Sheltering in the lee of Patrick Crombie's garage, Angus shifted from one soggy foot to the other – little bubbles of water squishing through the lace holes.

Still hadn't dried out from last time.

DS Sharp was on the pavement in front of the house, pacing back and forth with her head down, umbrella in one hand, mobile in the other. Her voice had that frustrated-mother tone to it: cajol-ing, annoyed, peacemaking. 'I know that . . . I know . . . Look, I said I'll get it for you, and I will!'

OK, so he could march out there and barge past her, but it seemed a little rude.

He waved, but she kept going.

'Because I always have, haven't I? Have I ever let you down? No.'

Angus cleared his throat.

No joy.

'I'll get it . . . Because I *said* I will.'

He tried again, much louder.

DS Sharp looked up from beneath her brolly. Made a face. 'OK . . . I promise . . . Got to go.' She put her phone away, then sagged. Hissed out a long breath. Gave Angus a small, sad smile. 'I love my dad to bits, but Alzheimer's can bugger right off.'

He stepped out from the garage's rain shadow. 'Sorry.'

She ran a hand across her face and sagged a little more. 'No, *I'm* sorry, Angus. I know your dad . . .' One shoulder twitched. 'At least I've still got mine. I should be grateful.' She raised her brolly, inviting him in. 'Found anything yet?'

He scurried in beside her, hunching over to stay beneath the thrumming fabric dome. 'Still searching, Sarge. Any word on the interview?'

'Crombie's in with his brief, last I heard: coordinating lies. He'll read out some bollocks prepared statement, then it'll be "no comment" this, and "no comment" that, till we have to charge him or let him go.' She glanced over at the pool car, where Dr Fife should've been, only there was no sign of him. 'Think our dwarf friend can rig the interview? Trick Crombie into confessing?'

'Actually, Sarge, people with achondroplasia don't like being called "dwarfs".'

She stared at him. 'Achrondo . . . ?'

'There was a girl with it in my year at school, so we all had to do a project. She'd clype on any kid who made fun of her condition, then wait till home time and beat the living shit out of them.' Frown. 'Think she's a barrister now.'

DS Sharp blinked at him for a bit, then shook her head. '*Anyway*, we'll need Dr Fife back at the ranch, helping with the interview. Drop him off on your way home.'

Home?

'But, Sarge—'

'On the plus side, with Crombie in custody the Fortnight Killer's reign of terror is over.' She kicked a wee stone across the driveway, sending it skittering into the overflowing gutter. 'We saved two lives today, Angus. That's not nothing. And all because *you* didn't let the bastard get away.' She patted him on the arm. 'Proud of you.'

Heat bloomed in Angus's ears and cheeks. 'Thanks, Sarge.'

'Now sod off home; shift ended an hour ago.' She pulled out a set of car keys and tossed them to him. 'Take our *friend* with you.'

Angus looked back at the house. 'You sure, Sarge?'

'We're going to be at this for hours, no point us *all* drowning . . .'

Fair enough.

She headed back inside, taking the umbrella with her.

Angus hurried towards the pool car, but he'd barely gone a couple of steps before his phone launched into its violiny ringtone.

When he dug it – and its protective ziplock – out, there was Ellie's name glowing away on the screen, beneath an icon-sized photo of her sticking her tongue out.

He pressed the button. Smiled.

'Ellie.'

She sounded as if she was trapped inside a Dalek. *'You busy tonight? Blagged two comp tickets to that new* Jumanji *musical at the King James.'*

The smile faded. 'Ellie, we've been over this.'

'Martyring yourself is more fun than a night at the theatre, eh?'

He stomped his way towards the pool car. 'It's not about "martyring" anything: it's about accepting gifts as a police officer and—'

'Truth, justice, integrity. Wank, wank, wank.'

She never got it. Or never wanted to.

'The rules are there for a reason, Ellie. If *I* don't follow them, how can we expect anyone else to?'

'You're a big, daft, damp, lump of gristle, aren't you.'

Possibly.

'Besides, Mum's making a special tea – celebrate my first day in plainclothes. Can't be late.'

'Yeah . . .' Ellie dragged the word out, seasoning it with foreboding. *'I've been on the receiving end of your mum's celebratory teas. Love her to bits, but macaroni cheese needs to have some* actual *cheese in it.'*

A whistle screeched out across the cul-de-sac, one high note, one low.

'Well? Give us a wave.'

What?

He did a slow three-sixty – the houses opposite with light glow-ing in their windows, number fifty-four at the end of the street with its slick of blood slowly washing away in the rain, number fifty-two with its spotlights and active crime scene—

'*Over here, you numpty.*'

Angus turned to scan the mob of reporters, journalists, and . . . Ellie, standing out from the crowd in her big, orange, padded water-proof jacket. Hood up. Phone pressed to her ear as she waved at him.

'*Peekaboo.*'

Damn.

Because he'd been *this* close to getting out of the rain and back to the station.

'*Come on, you love* Jumanji. *Karen Gillan running around for two hours with her bellybutton out? Thought you were going to faint with the excitement.*'

He squish-squelched towards the cordon. 'Thanks for the offer, but I can't, OK? Sorry.'

'*Honestly, I swear you wouldn't know fun if it got up and spanked your pert, fuzzy bottom.*' A sigh huffed from the speaker, slightly muffled by the plastic bag. '*I'm definitely making you eat worms next time I see you, Angus MacVicar. And it'll serve you right for being a mis-erable sod.*'

By the time he'd got there, Ellie had made her way to the far edge of the cordon – beneath the lamppost, away from the other journos.

He put his phone away. 'Do you ever get tired of being horrible to me?'

She hung up. Grinned. 'Nope.'

Behind her, one of the protestors shuffled over to the cordon, still clutching her placard: 'PROSECUTE VACCINE MURDERERS!!!' It was her, from this morning: the pretty one with the smoky eye-shadow and the pouty lips. Though the pink tips on her black hair had lost their colour in the streetlight's septic glow, hanging lank and wet from the brim of her rain-soaked bobble hat.

Angus pulled on his professional smile. 'Can I help you, miss?'

'Sorry.' Up close, her breath smelled of strawberries and roses, carried on a soft, lilting, Highlands-and-Islands accent. Her cheeks flushed, and so did the tip of her little upturned nose. 'I was just . . .' She pointed at Ellie.

Ellie dug her hands deep into the padded jacket's pockets. 'Gillian and I had a nice chat about murder investigations, and pandemics, and how some newly appointed detective constables are complete killjoys. Didn't we, Gillian.'

Those smoky eyes widened. 'I've never been interviewed for a *major newspaper* before.'

Angus didn't move.

Didn't say a single word.

Ellie thumped him anyway. 'Shut up. The *Castle News and Post* does *so* count.'

Hard not to stare at that placard.

He frowned. 'Is this *all* vaccines, or is there any one in particular? With the "Murderers".'

Gillian hugged the wooden support tighter. 'It's . . . Just it wasn't even a vaccine, it was an experimental gene therapy, and people died from it.'

Angus nodded, kept his voice nice and neutral. 'Wow.'

'Only you never hear about it, because the mainstream media always suppresses anything that contradicts the establishment's narrative. They lie to us all the time!' Waving her hand at the assembled press. 'The world's drowning in *misinformation* and *conspiracy* and *stupidity*, and instead of throwing us a lifebelt, the media's punching holes in the boat and cheering on the bloody crocodiles!' She winced. Then gave Ellie's arm a squeeze. 'Not you, of course. You're one of the few honest ones.'

'Darn tootin'.'

'See' – Gillian turned back to Angus – 'how are people supposed to give informed consent if the media won't tell the truth about all the people who died? That's why I'm here: getting the message across.'

'Right. Gotcha.' Difficult to know how to put this without sounding condescending, but: 'Is this about them putting teeny computer chips in the vaccine to track people?'

The placard drooped and she stared at him, eyebrows pinched, lips squeezed in a hurt pout. 'See what I mean? The Bill Gates

Microchip Plot's nothing more than a false-flag disinformation campaign promulgated online by the Global Elite to discredit free thinkers and make us look like delusional weirdos.' All said with one hundred percent complete conviction.

'Well . . . I'm glad it's not true, anyway.'

'My friend's dad died from the vaccine. It damaged his brain, and he got dementia, and then he died.' The placard drooped a little more. 'Only it was lockdown, so they couldn't even have a proper funeral.'

God knew far too much of that went on, back in the day.

Mrs Farooq had been forced to say goodbye to her husband, Kabir, on a borrowed iPad. She'd cried for months – sobs racking through the building's thin walls until Wee Hamish whimpered in sympathy.

'I'm sorry for your loss.'

Because what else could you say?

Gillian placed her free hand against her chest, fingers splayed, biting her bottom lip as she blinked up at him. Eyes shimmering. Though that might've been the rain. Mouthing the words 'Thank you'.

The other journalists finally seemed to notice that there was something going on over here, because a handful were working their way through the crowd towards them. Cameras and microphones at the ready.

Time to escape.

'Well, it's been lovely talking to you, but I better get back to work.' Angus turned to go, but Ellie grabbed his sleeve.

'Speaking of work . . .' She produced her phone, thumbing the 'RECORD' button. 'I hear you've got yourself a swanky American FBI profiler on the team now.'

Sod.

Angus pulled on his nonchalant voice. 'Where did you hear that?'

'Oooh . . .' Gillian's placard got a sudden shot of Viagra. 'An FBI profiler? Like in the movies?'

Yeah.

He glanced back at the pool car.

Not like in the movies *at all*.

Ellie tugged at his sleeve. 'Well? Come on, then: was he instrumental in identifying Patrick Crombie? Bet he was. Did his profile lead you straight to the Fortnight Killer's door? When are Police Scotland going to release a copy of it? The *Knap*'s readers have a right to know.' She stuck her phone in his face, the little red light winking away on its screen. 'In your own time.'

' "Knap"?'

'*Castle News and Post*. Keep up, Grandad.'

He gave her a little smile and wriggled free. 'Bye, Ellie.' Waved at Gillian. Then turned and got the hell out of there. Striding across the puddled tarmac.

Ellie's voice rang out behind him: *'Come on, Angus, at least give me the guy's name!'*

Nope.

'Angus!'

Still nope.

'IT'S DOUBLE WORMS FOR YOU NEXT TIME, MISTER!'

6

Angus opened the driver's door and thumped in behind the wheel. The seat pressed the soggy suit against his back and legs – cold and clammy and horrible.

Dr Fife was scooted down in the passenger seat, so far that even the top of his curly head didn't poke above the bottom edge of the window. He had Crombie's file open again, reading with the aid of a little LED pen light.

He looked up. 'Did you *swim* here?'

Angus wiped the rain from his face, shook the droplets into the footwell. 'Thought you weren't hanging around.'

His hooded eyes drifted up to the rear-view mirror, narrowing as he watched the assembled press reflected there. 'I've got sex on my mind, Andrew.'

Great.

'Angus.'

Those bushy eyebrows raised. 'Really? Oh.'

'And I'm flattered, but you're not my type.'

'Not me, you idiot: Patrick Crombie.' He tapped the file. 'Crombie's a sex offender; most serial killers are. Oh, maybe not on the surface – maybe they'll claim God or aliens made them do it, or they're getting their own back on their mother, but in the end it's all about the fantasy. The thing that keeps them up all night, stiff on the power of what they've done. And what they're going to do next time.'

Now there was an image.

'So . . . he's abducting the victims' partners for *sex*?'

Dr Fife's eyes drifted back to the mirror. 'That's what worries me.' Tapping the file again. 'You see, I read this and I think to myself: is Patrick Crombie the kind of guy who gets his kicks torturing men, and women, in front of their partners?' The frown deepened. 'Because he doesn't *feel* the type to me.'

Bloody Americans.

'He's got convictions for abduction, rape, and sexual—'

'Yes, I *know* that. But there's a big difference between *raping* someone, and fixing them and their partner to the kitchen table with three-inch wood screws then torturing them to death.' He held up a hand. 'Which is not to downplay the seriousness of rape, or the need to stick all rapey sons-a-bitches in prison and kick them in the nuts till their dicks fall off.' His eyes remained fixed on the reflected mass of journalists and cameras. 'It's just different.'

The rain-drenched street faded as fog spread across the car windows. Most of it rising from Angus's soggy suit.

Dr Fife sat there, immobile as a concrete bollard.

Angus: motionless as a standing stone.

Their stillness filled the car as the outside world disappeared from view.

'Let's look at the evidence.' Dr Fife smoothed a hand across the open file. 'Three sets of victims. Each time: our killer gains access with no sign of forced entry. He controls his victims, makes it so one has to watch the other get tortured to death, then abducts whoever's left.'

'Assuming they're not already dead.'

'Which they probably are, but we're gonna pretend they're not, for now.' He stared at the rear-view mirror, but the only thing reflected there was the misted back window. 'Even if you ignore everything Ressler, Burgess, and Douglas say in *Sexual Homicide Patterns and Motives*, or the *Crime Classification Manual*, the whole set-up here just feels sexual, doesn't it? Voyeuristic: one partner watching the other. Sex and death as performance art.' Pause. 'It's like some twisted peepshow, in a skeezy strip mall, in Hell.'

Silence settled in again.

Angus struggled his way out of the wringing-wet jacket – not easy with the sleeves sticking to his soaked-through shirt.

Dr Fife closed the file. 'The problem is Patrick Crombie. He's got all the hallmarks of an organized, serial, sexual killer: the escalating sex offences, the increased violence, the time in prison to work on his fantasies, and yet . . . ?' That wide forehead crinkled into deep ruts, as if he was genuinely thinking it through rather than milking the moment. 'Can I see him torturing women? Definitely. Can I see him torturing Michael Fordyce and making his wife watch, then abducting and raping her? Hundred percent.' Dr Fife pursed his lips. 'Can I see Crombie torturing Jessica Mendel to death, then killing her husband? Yes. Drunk on the power of doing that to another man's "property" . . .'

Angus slipped the key into the ignition.

'But the ultimate expression of *dominance* didn't happen.'

OK, that was just stupid.

He went to say so, but Dr Fife waved it away.

'There's nothing in the autopsy report about her being raped.' Back to pondering. 'And why abduct Jessica's *husband*? What does that get you?'

The starter whined three, four times, before the engine sputtered into life. 'Maybe it *is* a Jeffrey Dahmer thing after all?' He cranked the blowers up full, and stuck on the heated rear windscreen to shift the fog.

'And finally, we have Kevin and Douglas Healey-Robinson. Crombie's a raging misogynist, why would he find that sexually stimulating?'

It wasn't a bad point.

Angus turned in his seat. 'What if he's . . . confused? You say he's escalating, right? So, maybe he starts off killing the husband and abducting the wife, then tries it the other way around, likes it, then goes the whole hog and targets a gay couple?'

'Well, that's certainly a *theory*.' Not sounding convinced at all. 'Suppose we'll find out when we interrogate him.'

Thin black lines appeared on the rear window, spreading as the heating elements did their thing. Giving a partial view of the press and onlookers.

Dr Fife's eyes went back to the mirror again.

Angus twisted all the way around, staring out through the

spreading bands of clear glass. 'What?' Facing front again. 'What are we looking at?'

'Have your CSI team found anything yet?'

'CSI . . .? Oh. No. The scene examiners haven't found anything.'

Dr Fife tore his eyes from the mirror to examine Angus instead. 'When the officer round the back shouted "Crombie's jumped the fence and gone right", everyone else ran right, but you went left.'

'I figured, as 'Tash was behind the house, his right would be our left.' Shrug. 'Seemed obvious.'

'"'Tash".' Dr Fife snorted. 'Does everyone in this half-assed police department have stupid nicknames?'

'People in teams *like* nicknames.'

He sooked at his teeth for a bit, eyes drifting back to the rear-view. Until, finally: 'Call me a pessimistic old sex god, but – given the way Crombie makes my balls itch – I think we should go have a word with the guy who hired the other van.'

Oh, for God's sake.

'But we *caught*—'

'Then I'll look like an asshole for dragging you off on a moron's mission, won't I?' He scooted even further down in his seat, till he was well below the window level. Then pulled his greatcoat over his head. *'Just don't stop, OK?'*

Angus sat there, staring at the complete and utter weirdo in the passenger seat. 'Any chance you could tell me why you're hiding in the footwell?'

'The illusion is somewhat spoiled if they can see you talking to me.'

'Insane . . .' He wiped the side of his hand across the windscreen – clearing as much of it as he could reach. Which was quite a lot. Tears of condensation wept onto the dashboard. 'Have you ever thought about seeing a psychiatrist?'

'It's not as much fun as you'd think. Now can we get going?'

Man was an absolute Topic bar.

Angus stuck the car into reverse and performed a shuffling seven-point turn in the narrow cul-de-sac, till they were facing back the way they'd come. Crawling forward – going half up on the pavement to squeeze past the patrol car that blocked the road this side of the cordon.

Then the media frenzy kicked in. Cameras up, flashes going, TV crews repositioning to get the pool car in the back of their shot.

The poor soggy sod in the dripping high-vis nodded at Angus, then waved the crowds out of the way.

Just in case, Angus kept most of his mouth shut, barely moving his lips as he smiled at the people outside. 'This isn't normal. You know that, don't you?'

'I made the rules very clear: either I'm not here, or I'm not here.'

'Yes, but why?'

'Because that's the rules!'

The PC raised the line of 'POLICE' tape, till it was clear of the pool car's roof, and ushered them through.

Ellie and Gillian stood on the pavement, waving as they drove past.

One last barrage of flash photography, and the car was out the other side, accelerating up to twenty, following the curve of Breech-field Crescent.

Angus gave it half a dozen houses before pulling into the kerb again.

An irate voice muffled out from beneath the greatcoat: *'I told you not to stop!'*

He hauled on the handbrake. 'The press are all the way back there. And I'm not going any further till you put on your seatbelt.'

They drifted onto a curved residential road lined with decent-sized two-storey homes built about thirty years before Angus was born. About half had abandoned the concept of gardening, swapping lawns for gravel so boy-racer hatchbacks and school-run four-by-fours could park there.

The rain had called a truce for now, leaving the street shiny and dark in the streetlights.

Up here, on Blackwall Hill, they were pretty much opposite Patrick Crombie's house in Shortstaine, but the other side of the valley was little more than a spider's web of streetlights, individual details lost in the night. Castle Hill was clearer, with its swirl of old-fashioned streets and the blank black blade of granite, with the spotlit castle on top. The twin red lights, blinking atop the hospital's incinerators as they belched steam, or smoke. And the radioactive amoeba of the old glass-roofed Victorian train station in Logansferry.

'This is us.' Angus pulled in behind one of O Division's manky pool cars – easy to spot in this collection of suburban vehicles, because A: it was a Vauxhall, B: it was filthy, and C: someone had scratched the word 'BACON!!!' in big letters across the boot.

Two silhouettes lurked inside, smoking cigarettes and keeping tabs on number seventeen.

The rain resumed its attack, sweeping down the valley and up the other side, fizzing and sparking in the streetlights' glow as it clattered off the car bonnet.

Dr Fife took one look at the fresh downpour and crossed his arms. 'Go on then.'

Great.

'Monster Munch was right about you.' Undoing his seatbelt.

'*More* stupid nicknames.'

Angus rolled his eyes, clambered out, and hurried through the deluge to the other pool car, with his soggy jacket pulled up in a makeshift umbrella.

He knocked on the driver's roof.

The window buzzed down all the way, releasing a swarm of cigarette smoke to fly around Angus's head, before the rain wheeched it away.

PC Gilbert smiled up at him. He was a right farmer's loon, with his ruddy cheeks, sideburns, yellow tar-stained fingers, and receding hairline. The squint didn't help. Nor did the full-on teuchter accent. 'Aye, aye; it's the boy.'

DS Kilgour leaned over from the passenger seat to look across the car. There was more than a hint of the 'shaved bear' about him – a broad-shouldered, rounded bulk, with huge hands and little beady glittering eyes, all topped off with a pork-pie hat. As if Paddington's Uncle Pastuzo had an unfortunate run-in with a bucket of Nair. 'Angus, isn't it? We heard you handcuffed Patrick Crombie, then beat the living hell out of him. That's what we call "Very Naughty".'

'I didn't: he tripped.'

Gilbert nodded. 'That's progress for you. In my day, they used to "fall down the stairs".'

'He tripped!'

A smile spread across Kilgour's muzzle. 'What can we do for you, Angus the Terrible?'

Don't rise to it, and maybe it won't stick.

Angus pointed at number seventeen. 'Is Francis McCurdy in? Have you spoken to him?'

Kilgour turned to his driver. 'Have we spoken to him, George?'

'Nope. Not so much as a word, Sarge. On account of us secretly staking the place out and that kind of thing being frowned upon.'

He mimed a big what-ya-gonna-do shrug. 'Sorry.'

Dr Fife appeared, as if by magic. No sound, no warning, just bang – there he was, sheltering beneath a collapsible black brolly. 'Can we get on with this, please? Oldcastle is considerably colder than California. And wetter.' Taking a quick look around. 'And shittier.'

PC Gilbert scowled. 'Hey!'

'Now, now, George.' Kilgour held up a hand. 'The nice forensic psychologist might be horribly rude, but he's not wrong. Oldcastle *is* a shitehole.'

'Thank you.' Fife turned on his Cuban-heeled boots, then stopped. Turned back again. 'If you know we caught Patrick Crombie, why are you still here?'

'Because it wouldn't be the first time some tit arrested the wrong man.' The hand came up again. 'Present company excluded, of course. I've just found it's wise to keep my mind, and options, open.'

Dr Fife stared at him for a couple of breaths. Then nodded. 'Very true.'

Kilgour stared right back. 'And in the spirit of open-mindedness: if Patrick Crombie isn't our man, any idea who the Fortnight Killer's going to murder on Friday? Finding out before it happens would be what we call "Helpful".'

'I'm working on it.' This time Fife clopped away through the downpour, taking his umbrella with him. 'We're gonna give Mr McCurdy a knock. We'll scream if we need you.'

'Please, don't hesitate.' A wink for Angus. 'Try not to beat this one up, eh, Champ?'

'He *tripped*!' Angus stuck his nose in the air and marched after Dr Fife.

Number seventeen seemed nice enough, with a shiny red Porsche sitting in the driveway, blocking in a small sports-utility thing with oversized bull bars.

Angus reached the door a couple of steps before Dr Fife. Rang the bell. 'Do you have to alienate everyone?'

'I find it's quicker. They're gonna hate me anyway; the least I can do is give them a reason.'

Yeah. Who knew acting like a *colossal* dick would get people's back up? What a total shock-horror.

He pressed the bell again. 'Yes, but maybe they wouldn't—'

The door jerked open, and a woman glared out at them. She was maybe late twenties? With a toddler on her hip and fierce tear-reddened eyes. Dressed in colourful, but baggy, sweatshirt and joggies. '*What?*' Her lip curled. 'If you're here to complain about the *bloody* noise again, you can *sod* right off, because—'

Angus flashed his warrant card. 'Is Francis McCurdy in? We need to have a word.'

A smile dimpled her cheeks – cold and sharp. 'Oh, do you now? If it's "You're under arrest"' – her voice jumped up a couple of decibels as she turned to hurl it over her shoulder – '"YOU TWO-FACED, LYING, CHEATING WANKER!"' – back to Angus – 'then: yes, he is. But not for long!'

Perched there on her hip, the toddler gurned and whined. Pudgy little hands grasping for her hair. 'Shh, Baby, shhhh . . .'

Dr Fife peered past them, into the house. 'Trouble in paradise?'

Angus gave him a good hard stare, because how the hell was that helpful? Then back to the householder. 'Can we come in?'

She reversed out of the way, leaving the door wide open. Waved her hand at the stairs. 'He's up there. Don't be afraid to taser the bastard.'

A whole load of crummy kid's drawings were framed on the wall; a pair of bright-red wellies lined up with the adult shoes. The open living-room door showing off a mess of Duplo and stuffed animals.

The woman stood at the foot of the stairs, scowling after them as they climbed up to the landing. Where more horrible kid's pictures were interspersed with family holiday snaps. For a toddler, he'd been a lot of places. None of the pictures featured Daddy, but there were gaps where frames had been – leaving nothing but the hooks and a line of dust behind.

Four doors off the landing, but only one was open.

Angus poked his head in.

It was a single-bedroom-cum-study, with a wall of bookshelves, a desk, and an office chair. No sign of a computer, though.

A middle-aged man, with slicked-back hair and a weeny pony-tail, was stuffing clothes into a bin bag. He'd clearly been away somewhere, because his nose and forehead were the classic Scottish shade of been-in-the-sun beetroot, the skin peeling around the edges. Dressed far too young for his age, in Levi's, a black leather jacket, Four Mechanical Mice T-shirt, and green Vans. And, up close, it was obvious that slick-backed hairdo was doing its best to hide a spreading bald spot. A scarlet handprint marred one cheek, tears sparkling in his eyes as he rammed a cashmere sweater in with the rest.

Dr Fife wheezed his way onto the landing. Rubbing at his knees.

The man hadn't seen them yet, or if he had, he didn't care.

Angus cleared his throat. 'Francis McCurdy?'

There was a high-pitched *screek* and he spun around, nearly leaping out of his trendy-young-person shoes. Soon as he saw Angus standing there he flinched back, one arm up to protect his face. Whimpering.

Dr Fife pushed past, into the room. 'Looks like your reputation precedes you, *Detective Constable*.'

'You're *police*?' McCurdy lowered his arm and puffed out his chest: the big man once again. He jabbed an indignant finger at the carpet. 'Whatever she told you, it's a lie! I never laid a hand on that . . .' His mouth clamped shut, as if thinking better of what was about to plop out of it. 'I came home today and she'd been through my wardrobe with a carving knife!' Snatching a suit jacket from the nearest bin bag. The sleeves and back hung in clean-edged tatters. 'Ruined!' He rammed it back in the bag. 'I *tried* to be reasonable. I did everything they tell you to in the books. I even said she could keep the house! And what did *she* do?'

Dr Fife tilted his head on one side. 'Let me guess – you've been screwing around, haven't you, Francis?'

He stuck his nose in the air. 'We've grown apart, that's all.'

OK, as usual, none of this was helping.

Angus pulled out his notebook and put on his official police voice. 'Mr McCurdy, did you hire a Luton Transit van from Toucan Youcan?'

'Lemme guess: you hit the big five-oh, and you thought – "there must be more to life than this". Found yourself a young wife, knocked her up, but that didn't satisfy the itch, did it?'

McCurdy stuffed a pair of *extremely* ripped jeans in the bag. 'It wasn't like that.'

Angus had another go. 'Can we focus, please? Mr McCurdy—'

'So you got a Viagra-substitute sports car, and a ponytail, and an even younger bit on the side.'

He wouldn't look at them. 'That isn't . . . It wasn't *like* that.'

God's sake.

Angus towered over the pair of them. 'Did you, or did you not, hire a van from—'

'Only your wife, *the mother of your child*, discovered what you were up to, didn't she? And she threw you out.'

'Dr Fife, can we *please*—'

'That's why you hired the removal van. She threw you out, and now you have to move in with your side-chick.'

McCurdy bit his bottom lip, shook his head. 'You have no idea what it's like.'

'EVERYONE PLEASE *STOP* TALKING!'

There was silence, as Dr Fife and Francis McCurdy stared at Angus as if *he* was the unreasonable one.

Deep breath. 'Now, did you hire a van from—'

'And fifty bucks says I know where she lives: not far from here, in fact. Balvenie Row.'

What, was he *invisible* here?

Angus opened his mouth, then closed it again.

Hold on: Balvenie Row? Where the Healey-Robinsons died?

'How did . . . ?' McCurdy clutched the sides of his leather jacket shut, backing away till his arse bumped into the desk. 'You can't tell Denise. She's *unhinged*. She'll . . . I don't know, *torch* the place or something. Please!'

Dr Fife sucked a breath in through his teeth. 'I suppose it depends on whether you cooperate or not.'

Angus paused on the threshold, frowning out into the rain as Mrs McCurdy told Mr McCurdy exactly how much of a shit he was. Loudly and in great detail.

DS Kilgour and PC Gilbert were right where they'd left them – smoking away in blissful ignorance, but not for long.

'Suppose someone has to break the bad news.'

'Good luck.' Dr Fife popped up his collapsible brolly and scurried off towards the other, empty pool car.

'Thanks a sodding heap.'

Might as well get it over with.

Angus marched out into the downpour.

Soon as he was outside, his phone dinged and buzzed, deep in his jacket pocket. Text message.

MUM:

> You know that dinner is at seven o'clock! You should
> have been home an hour ago! I went to a lot of trouble
> to make a special meal and now it will be RUINED!

He closed his eyes, rain stabbing at his rounded shoulders. Then thumbed out a reply as he shuffled over to Kilgour's pool car.

> Sorry.
> Am busy with investigation.
> Will be home as soon as permitted by DCI.
> Sorry.

PC Gilbert lowered his window. 'Aye, aye; it's the boy again.'

A smile from DS Kilgour. 'Should I be calling an ambulance, Angus the Terrible?'

Nope: still not rising to it.

He put his phone away. 'Francis McCurdy's been cheating on his wife for the last six months, but she only found out two weeks ago. And the new woman lives at twenty-five Balvenie Row, two doors up from—'

'Oh, buggering hell.' Kilgour cringed in his seat. 'It was *his* Transit. She threw him out, he hired a van, packed his stuff, and . . .' The DS frowned. 'Wait a minute: how come they didn't cop to hiring the van when we did door-to-doors?'

'They weren't in. Pair of them only got back from Tenerife an hour ago.' Hence the sunburn. 'We're going round now to check with the young woman. Make sure his story sticks.'

'Bollocking shiteweasels. We could've been chasing down other leads!'

Hard not to sound keen about that: 'We've got other leads?'

'Course we don't. That's not the point.' Kilgour jerked a thumb at Angus's pool car. 'What about Mr FBI? Is he the golden-arsed, shiny-genius saviour Monroe thinks he is?'

Good question.

'Well, Dr Fife knew Patrick Crombie wasn't the Fortnight Killer, so . . . kinda? Hard to tell at this point.'

'Well, he better get his arrogant wee finger out. We've got . . .' Kilgour pushed back his sleeve, exposing a fat digital-watch-fitness-tracker thing. '. . . less than forty-eight hours before this bastard butchers another unlucky couple. That's what we call "Less Than Ideal", Angus.'

Yeah . . .

'There's something else, Sarge.' He shuffled his feet, making little ripples in a gritty puddle. 'The press know we've got a hot-shot FBI profiler in from the States. They don't know *who*, but they know we've got one.'

There was a groan. 'Oh, you're a little ray of sunshine in my life today, aren't you, Constable?' Frown. 'Have you told the Boss?'

'Well, no. I can't really, not with Dr Fife in the car. *He* doesn't know *they* know. And I didn't want to scare him off.' Besides, surely this was a job for more senior officers. Angus put a little wheedle into his voice. 'Don't suppose you'd—'

'I'd love to, but I'm afraid this is what we call "A Teachable Moment".'

'But—'

'While you're at it, you can tell the Boss about Patrick Crombie being innocent. He'll enjoy that.'

What?

'But . . . it's . . . Wouldn't that kind of thing be better coming from—'

'Can't hide behind detective sergeants your whole life.' If it was meant to be a reassuring smile, it didn't work. 'Besides, Monroe isn't an ogre. He even took the heat when Rhona set fire to that patrol car.'

'Oh aye.' Gilbert nodded. 'But that was totally one of them "unforeseeable accidents".' A grotesque twitch creased up half his face, as if he was having a seizure. 'Wink, wink.'

'But—'

'See? Could be worse. Give him a call – you'll be fine. Better he finds out now, before we waste a ton of time interviewing the slimy sex-offendering scumbag.'

Angus sagged. 'Yes, Sarge.' Turned. Then scuffed away towards his pool car, where Dr Fife waited, dirty-blond curls caught in the urine-tinged streetlight.

All safe and dry.

And he'd had an umbrella all this time.

Didn't bother lending the thing to Angus, though, did he.

Monster Munch had been underselling it when she'd called him a 'twat': Dr Jonathan 'Don't Call Me Jonny' Fife was an unapologetic, chrome-plated, *total* and *utter*—

Angus's phone ding-buzzed with another incoming text.

He winced, but left it unread for now.

There was work to do.

7

Twenty-five Balvenie Row was almost identical to number twenty-one, only without the Mobile Incident Unit parked outside. Or the SOC marquee covering the front door. And it wasn't cordoned off or surrounded by floral tributes.

Oh, and the homeowner was still alive.

Chloe Arbuthnot: early twenties, with an overbite and a button nose, deep-chestnut tan, long blue hair, nose ring, glaikit expression, Mr Bones T-shirt, ripped jeans, and pink Vans to go with Francis McCurdy's green ones.

Miss Arbuthnot was clearly feeling the cold – as evidenced by the protrusions in her T-shirt. One of which appeared to be pierced.

But Angus was *not* staring at it. Or them. Because he wasn't an animal.

He forced a smile. 'OK. Thanks for your time.' Then lumbered back down the short path as she closed the front door behind him.

The pool car was double-parked, flashers glittering in the rain. Angus crumpled in behind the wheel.

Dr Fife fiddled with his phone, not looking up as Angus slumped and sighed.

'I was right, wasn't I.'

The engine coughed into life, like an asthmatic smoker. 'Ms Arbuthnot says Francis McCurdy moved most of his stuff in twelve days ago. It was a Friday night, so they had "Mickey D's" for tea, went clubbing, got an Uber home at three, and "boinked porkies" till dawn.'

'At his age?' Dr Fife grimaced. 'And did she *actually* say "boinked porkies"?'

How could it all go so horribly wrong?

'DCI Monroe is going to *kill* me.'

'Maybe. But try to look on the bright side: I was right, and everyone else was wrong.' He patted Angus on the back. 'That's gotta be worth something.'

'Is this supposed to help?'

'Not really.'

Sooner today was over the better.

Angus dragged out his bagged-up phone. An unread-text icon glowed on the screen, with 'FROM MUM' next to it. Where it could stay. He called up his contacts instead and scrolled through to the 'D's, finger hovering over 'DCI MONROE'.

So much for making a good impression on his first day.

A sigh rattled out from the passenger side. 'Angus: it's a setback, yes, but imagine if we *hadn't* established this whole van-hire thing was a loada crap. The team scurry off, tracking down all of Crombie's contacts, known addresses, aliases; they wade through a thousand hours of security footage trying to figure out where he dumped Sarah Fordyce, Tom Mendel, and Kevin Healey-Robinson's bodies.' Dr Fife raised a hand, making a sweeping gesture that somehow took in all of Oldcastle. 'And Friday, maybe Saturday, we find another victim whose partner's missing, and we're right back where we started. Only two more people are dead.'

Angus stared at the phone in its ziplock bag. 'Yeah, I guess . . .' He pressed the button.

Monroe's voice barked from the speaker. *'Who's this?'*

Deep breath. 'Boss? It's Angus. DC MacVicar? From this afternoon at Patrick Crombie's—'

'Is this important, Angus? Only we're a bit busy.' The sound went all muffled, as if Monroe had put his hand over the microphone. *'Badger? Give him a long hard stare, then ask him why he hired the van again. The bastard's got to say something other than "no comment", at some point.'*

Angus grimaced at Dr Fife. 'Oh God, they're already interviewing Crombie!'

Back to full volume: *'You still there?'*

'It's . . . Dr Fife and I spoke to the other person who hired a Toucan Youcan van.'

'Uh-huh.' Not sounding as if he was paying all that much attention. *'OK, pivot back to where he was the night Michael Fordyce was killed.'*

'It wasn't Patrick Crombie's van parked on Balvenie Row, Friday before last, it was Francis McCurdy's. His mistress just confirmed it.'

An ominous silence radiated out of the phone.

'Boss?'

'He what?'

'Sorry.'

The silence returned, and brought its friends with it.

Dr Fife raised his eyebrows.

Angus wriggled in his seat.

And still the silence roared.

More wriggling.

'Boss?'

A pained groan. *'Buggering hell . . . I thought we had him. I really thought we had him.'* A hissed breath. *'Badger, it's a bust. He's not the Fortnight Killer. But he's guilty of something: find out what.'* A muffled swearword, too low to hear. Then: *'Got to go.'*

The line went dead.

Angus put his phone away.

Slouched.

'Back to square one.'

Dr Fife tapped the dashboard clock. 'With less than forty-eight hours to go.'

Urgh . . .

For some bizarre reason, they'd decided to redecorate the boardroom at Divisional Headquarters in a sort of pastel-mushroom colour. Tins and tins of 'WOODLAND WONDER' were pyramided up in the corner, by a droopy wallpaper table and about a dozen rolls of lining paper. White smears of Polyfilla dotted the stripped-back walls. Cardboard and plastic on the floor, like a serial killer's basement.

Everything smelled of dust and paint-thinner, overlain with the foul, chemical stench of floral air freshener.

Not a stick of furniture, so they all had to stand.

Monroe had the window, bum resting on the sill, arms folded. DS Massie, DIs Tudor and Cohen, and Dr Fife making a semicircle around him. With Angus steaming himself by the room's only radiator – waiting to be sent off for coffees. Because that's what *always* happened when everyone else outranked you.

DI Cohen pulled a face. 'Crombie's brief is screaming "false arrest", "incompetence", "police brutality", and "compensation".'

'Perfect.' Monroe let his head fall back to thunk against the double glazing.

'Apparently we've got a vendetta against his client, and we're engaged in a conspiracy to fit the scumbag up.'

DS Massie held her hands out, palms up, as if she was carrying a sacrificial offering. 'We've still got Crombie on three counts of resisting arrest and assault, if that helps?'

'Which we'll probably have to drop, if we're going to stand any chance of making this buggering prickfest go away.' Monroe straightened up, locking eyes with Dr Fife. '*Please* tell me you know where to look next.'

'If I had a Magic Eight Ball, I'd shake it for you, but like I said: this kinda stuff takes time. I only got the files today.' His forehead creased. 'Well, "today" for *me*. With the time difference, maybe your "last night"?'

Tudor had a go: 'What about victims? We know he's going to strike again, Friday: maybe if we can figure out who he's going to kill we can get there first and stop him?'

'Yeah . . .' DS Massie dropped the invisible baby. 'Oldcastle's got a population of nearly a hundred and fourteen thousand, so, you know, narrowing it down a bit *might* help.'

'Might it?' Dr Fife gave her an innocent smile. 'Well, that *is* good to know.' Letting the sarcasm hang there for a bit. 'Is there anything that links the victims? Anything at all?' Pacing the cardboard sheeting from here to the wallpaper table and back again. 'Did they go to the same gym? Did they go to the same school? Were they in the same book club, car pool, phone tree?

Were they Freemasons, or Elks, or whatever the hell clubs you got over here?'

Cohen shook his head. 'Not that we could find.'

'You trace their last movements? Going back two, maybe three weeks? See if they intersected somewhere?'

'Same.'

Dr Fife kept pacing, head down, as if the answer was scrawled on the cardboard somewhere. 'They all crossed paths with this bastard – that didn't just happen in a goddamn vacuum.' Face pinched, hands clenching and unclenching as he went. Getting louder. 'You don't randomly draw couples out of the hat and torture them to death!'

He kicked the pile of wallpaper, sending the plastic-wrapped rolls flying to *boing* and *poom* against the wall.

Everyone looked at Monroe.

Then at Dr Fife again as he went back to pacing, snap-snap-snapping his fingers at Angus, as if he was a sleepy waiter.

Here came the coffee order.

'OK, we got three victims. Top line: name, age, job?'

Or maybe not.

'Erm . . .' Come on, he *knew* this stuff. 'OK. Michael Fordyce: forty-one; chartered accountant. Jessica Mendel: forty-nine; heiress-slash-did charity work. Douglas Healey-Robinson: thirty-seven; wrote erotic gay crime novels.'

'Well, that's no help.'

What else . . . ? Ah, yes: 'They're all sort of middle-aged?'

'Hey!' DS Massie glared at him. 'Thirty-seven is *not* middle-aged.'

'Still not helping. There's gotta be something that links them and their partners to—' He stopped dead in the middle of the room, staring off into space, with his head on one side.

Silence.

Standing completely rigid.

Outside, a patrol car's siren split the night, wailing and then fading as the driver gunned it off to whatever tragedy had just befallen Oldcastle.

Rain pulsed against the boardroom window.

Out in the corridor, someone sneezed.

And *still* Dr Fife hadn't moved or said anything.

Maybe he'd had a stroke?

Monroe eased his bum off the windowsill. 'Dr Fife? Are you all—'

'Wait.' Snapping his fingers again. 'The partners: what did *they* do?'

'Erm . . .' At least this was an easy one. Angus rattled them off: 'Sarah Fordyce was a GP, Tom Mendel was on the city council, Kevin Healey-Robinson—'

'Lawyer!'

Nope. 'He was a *journalist*. With the *Castle*—'

'No, you . . .' Dr Fife bit down on the missing word. 'The next *victim*. It'll be a lawyer.' He stared at them all. 'You've been running round like startled geckos, thinking the ones he kills are the targets, but they're not. It's the partners. That's why he makes them watch!'

DS Massie pursed her lips. 'So he's targeting *lawyers* next?' A shrug. 'Could be worse.'

Monroe gave her a narrow-eyed glare. 'Rhona!'

'That's what the messages mean.' Dr Fife was pacing again. '"Don't believe their lies".'

Eh?

At least it wasn't just Angus – everyone else looked confused too.

Dr Fife's hand came up, fingers spread. 'You've got your four pillars of the establishment' – counting them off, one finger at a time – 'doctors, politicians, the mainstream media, and lawyers. Our guy's already symbolically killed each of the first three.'

Angus put his hand up too. 'What about bankers?'

He frowned, head tilting. 'OK: *five* pillars. Your next victim's gonna be a lawyer or a banker.'

'Or a police officer?' Going by the expression on Dr Fife's face, audience-participation time was over. Angus lowered his hand. 'Sorry.'

'Victim-choice means our guy's probably from a lower socio-economic background. These people have power over him – maybe he thinks they've abused it? They laugh at guys like him. Look down on him.' Cuban heels thunking into the cardboard, working up a little speed now. 'He's teaching them a *lesson* by torturing their partners. They're forced to watch the person they love die a horrible death and then they have to go through the same thing themselves.'

Angus's hand went up once more. 'But the sex angle—'

'It's about the power. He's not jacking off to their mutilated bodies, he's jacking off to their suffering. Because – he – has – the – power.'

Monroe settled back against the windowsill again. 'How many bankers and lawyers do we have in Oldcastle?'

'Can't be more than four or five . . .' DI Cohen drew the pause out, '. . . *thousand.*'

A snort from Tudor. 'Don't be daft, Badger, even Oldcastle's not that litigious. It'll be five hundred, tops.'

Didn't look as if Monroe liked that answer much better. 'Still too many to go through individually. Send round a patrol car and you'd still be at it come July.'

'We could put an appeal out?' DS Massie pulled in her shoulders. 'Tell everyone who works in a bank or a law firm to . . . be extra careful?' Shoogling from side to side, like a wonky metronome. 'Try and not get themselves murdered?'

'Better than doing nothing, I suppose.' Monroe pointed at Tudor. 'Alasdair: shake the Media Office out their pit. I want something drafted and ready to go on the evening news.' The finger swung around to DS Massie. 'Rhona: we'll need some sort of arse-covering retraction on the Patrick Crombie fiasco too.'

'I was only following the evidence, Boss!'

'I know, I know. But it still needs managing.' His finger picked on DI Cohen next. 'Badger: send a memo to the troops – better make it everyone in O Division, just in case. Nobody takes silly risks. If this bastard thinks he can screw with a *police officer*, let's make damn sure he fails. Hard.' And finally, the finger found Dr Fife. 'How long before you can draw up a complete profile of our killer? How do we make that happen?'

The pacing stopped, arms thrown out, as if he'd been asked to jump off a cliff. 'I need *time*, OK? I keep telling everyone: I – need – time. Even a genius like me can't just pull this stuff out my ass.'

'Anything you need.' Monroe bared his teeth. 'Other than time. Because we're looking at two more dead bodies: day after tomorrow.'

'Sonofabitch . . .' Slump. 'Fine. Unfettered access to everything. And I mean *everything*.' Dr Fife glanced in Angus's direction. 'And I'll need a minion. A henchman. An underling. Some sort of slack-jawed, knuckle-dragging yokel to do all the dirty jobs.'

'Done.' A big smile, and Monroe clapped Angus on the back.

Eh?

'Wait, what?'

'Constable MacVicar would be delighted to help, wouldn't you, Angus?'

Now wait a minute!

'Boss?'

Dr Fife sniffed. 'Well, he's certainly got the "slack-jawed yokel" bit down.'

'Angus: while Dr Fife is part of this investigation, you're not to leave his side.'

How was that fair?

'But, Boss, he's . . . Surely I can make more of a contribution by—'

'Then it's settled.' Another pat on the back. 'And you can start by accompanying Dr Fife to the post-mortem: tomorrow morning, nine o'clock sharp!'

Angus stared at him, then at Tudor and Cohen and DS Massie. And not one of the buggers leapt in to save him.

He tried not to pout, he really did.

'Yes, Boss.'

Monroe stood – shoulders back, chest out. 'If we're going to catch this bastard before he kills again, we need to do whatever it takes. Let's move it, people!'

He swept from the room, with the two DIs marching along behind him.

Angus opened his mouth. Closed it again. 'But . . .'

DS Massie gave his arm a squeeze. 'Tough luck.' Then she was gone too. Leaving him alone with Dr Fife.

The forensic psychologist ran an eye over Angus, lip curled, as if he was something to be held at arm's length with tongs. Like a dirty nappy.

His voice was cold too. 'I'll need a bunch of whiteboards for that craphole "office" you morons gave me. You can sort it out while I go for a smoke.'

He pulled out a cigar and strutted off. Slamming the door behind him.

What the hell was *that* all about?

Now it was just Angus, the tins of paint, and those dented rolls of wallpaper.

Angus's shoulders dipped even further.

'Great . . .'

He shuffled into the room, moving nice and slow to make sure not to spill or drop anything. Two hot wax-paper cups from the canteen – no lids, because apparently they forgot to order any – which had only scalded Angus's hands *twice* on the way back here; a wee stereo – about grapefruit sized – wedged under one arm; and pockets bulging with crisps, chocolate, and biscuits.

The small office lurked just down the corridor from Operation Telegram, hurriedly furnished with a squeaky filing cabinet, a scarred desk, and a trio of crappy office chairs – all the good ones having been nicked long ago. Carpet tiles that curled up at the edges. A suspended ceiling, splodged with suspicious brown stains.

Other than that, it was clean enough. But a strange . . . *meaty* smell emanated from pretty much every surface. As if someone had rubbed everything with a half-eaten doner kebab.

Oh, and the three, newish whiteboards: hunter-gathered from other offices whose occupants hadn't thought to lock the doors before heading home for the night, and wheeled in here by Angus not twenty minutes ago. Which wasn't even vaguely 'stealing', as they all belonged to Police Scotland anyway.

Dr Fife sat at the desk, accompanied by a heap of paperwork and reference books, feet propped up on a couple of file boxes. Which was probably comfier than letting them dangle over the edge of the chair. Taking notes in one of those yellow legal pads you saw in the movies.

He didn't look up as Angus eased the door closed with an elbow.

Because why acknowledge the man who could've spat in your

coffee? Not that Angus would ever do that. Because: urgh . . . But he *could* if he wanted to. That was the point.

Angus nudged a couple of crime-scene photos out of the way and put the cups down. Forced a bit of breeziness into his voice. 'They don't do "almond milk", so I got you semi-skimmed.' With both hands free, he removed the speaker from his armpit and popped it on top of the filing cabinet. 'Borrowed it from Sergeant Peters.'

That earned him a quick glance, then Dr Fife went back to his files. 'Bit small, isn't it?'

'Was lucky to get that.'

Dr Fife turned the page, every word an ice cube: 'So go raid the Lost and Found. Bound to be loads of speakers in there with more oomph.' He took a sip of coffee. Shuddered. 'Who made this, sadists?'

'I am *not* stealing things from Lost Property. They're people's possessions, not free resources.' Angus dug into his pockets for a packet of cheese-and-onion, salt-and-vinegar, two Mars Bars, a Crunchie, and four wee 'individual serving' packets of shortbread. Followed by a handful of whiteboard markers in various colours. 'Canteen aren't doing any proper food till breakfast.'

Still no eye contact. 'This really is a shithole backwater.' He produced a scratched iPod and held the thing out. 'Plug it in. "Profiling playlist number four".'

Didn't matter if Angus rolled his eyes or not – Dr Fife wasn't looking – so he gave them a good theatrical swivel, then took the iPod. Fiddled with cables and sockets and buttons till the small round stereo made buzzing noises as he scrolled through to the playlists and poked the one marked 'PP#4'.

The opening bars of something classical swelled from the tinny speakers – or as much as they could, given its diminutive stature.

Angus helped himself to the salt-and-vinegar, picked up his coffee, and settled into one of the manky chairs. 'What do you want me to do?'

'Sit there *quietly*, and try not to mess everything up. Actually: just don't touch anything.' Dr Fife finally looked at him, grimaced. 'And try not to make too much noise. I'm *working*.' He stayed there, staring at Angus for what felt like an hour, before going back to his papers.

Thank you for the coffee, Angus, you've been a great help; I don't know what I would do without you.

Angus puffed out his cheeks.

Sagged.

Sighed.

Then ate his crisps.

Quietly.

8

God, this was *boring*.

Three-quarters of an hour, stuck here, not allowed to do anything, watching Dr Wanking Fife frown at bits of paper, scribble things on other bits of paper, stare off into space, scribble things on the whiteboards . . . Now one was completely covered in drunken-Einstein squiggles, connected with boxes and lines, while Fife stood on a wobbly office chair to scrawl more nonsense on Whiteboard Number Two, pen in one hand, legal pad in the other.

With any luck he'd fall off and break his neck.

Pfff . . .

Angus slumped back, watching the ceiling tiles sweep back and forth, back and forth, as he swivelled in his chair. Making shapes out of the coffee-coloured stains up there: this one looked like Norway; that one like Marilyn Monroe; the one over there: a cat with a chainsaw.

The tinny rendition of classical music turned out to be an opera – squeezing its way out of the weeny round speaker. Like angry Smurfs, fighting over something and shouting 'Hi-Ho!' a lot.

And. Off. To. Work. We. Don't. Go.

Angus blinked at Norway. 'Can I not just—'

'I'm working!'

Pfff . . .

Whiteboard Number Two was now completely clarted in marker-pen scrawl, but instead of embarking on Whiteboard Number Three, Dr Fife was sticking sheets from his legal pad to the walls with wee strips of Sellotape. Which Building Services were *not* going to like. He'd interspersed them with photos from the crime scenes and post-mortems – adding an unwelcome splash of colour to the pale-yellow pages.

So, basically a half-arsed version of the murder board in the Operation Telegram office.

Angus sat in his office chair, with his top half slumped onto the desk, head on his folded arms, as Dr Fife taped a photograph of Douglas Healey-Robinson's bloated remains above the radiator.

Then stepped back to squint at the horrible montage. 'Will you stop *sighing*?'

For God's sake.

Enough was enough.

Angus pushed himself off the desk, sat upright, and scowled. 'Why do you always have to be such a dick?'

Dr Fife turned. 'I *beg* your pardon?'

'Ever since we got back, all you've done is treat me like a lump of . . . dog turd!'

'I'm *working*!'

'And I'm sitting here like a spare fart in a brothel.'

A hand jabbed at the door. 'Then go do something useful!'

'What? You won't let me *do* anything!'

'Oh, don't be so—'

Angus put on a lazy American drawl. ' "Just sit there and *shut up*, Angus", "Don't make any *noise*, Angus", "Don't *touch* anything, Angus", "Stop *breathing so loudly*, Angus!" '

Fife hurled his legal pad onto the desk. 'Well, what did you expect? I could've had anyone for a sidekick, but I picked you. And what did you do?'

'Sat here like a pickled prick, while—'

'You didn't *want* to be my sidekick. When Monroe offered you the job, you looked like he'd just bust a nut all over your Pop-Tart!'

Angus scowled back. 'That's not—'

'I'm a forensic psychologist – a damn good one – and I know when someone *clearly* doesn't want to work with me!'

They glared at each other for a bit.

OK, so he maybe had a point.

Even if he was a horrible, arrogant tosser.

'It's . . .' Angus squeezed one shoulder up to his ear. 'DCI Monroe doesn't . . . *I* wasn't . . .'

'Sonofabitch.' The hand jabbed out again. 'After I flew halfway round the world, to this rain-drenched *craphole* in the ass-end of nowhere, to help pull your useless police department out the goddamn hole it dug itself into!' His clenched fist banged into the table, setting the paperwork dancing. 'And this is the thanks I get?'

'Well, who'd want to be your bloody sidekick anyway? All I do is ferry you about like a glorified taxi driver, stand there while you piss everyone off, and watch you act all . . .' waving both index and middle fingers about like a rabbit having a fit, '. . . Whatever weird squirrelly thing comes over you every time the press turn up!'

'I didn't have to come here. And I can just as easily go right back down south!'

Angus stared at him. 'This *matters*, OK? People – are – *dying*.'

'I know that, for God's—'

'This is my first day in plainclothes. My first chance to make a *real* difference, and I'm stuck in this shitty little room, trying not to BREATHE TOO LOUD!'

This time the silence stretched, and stretched, and stretched.

Angus looked away. 'I've waited years for this.'

Dr Fife sighed, because apparently the rules on that didn't go both ways. 'OK. Well, now we've got that out in the open . . .' He picked at the tabletop, widening one of the scratches. 'So what *do* you want?'

'Not being called a "slack-jawed, knuckle-dragging yokel" would be a start.'

'Yeah. Sorry about that.'

Outside, in the corridor, something trundled past on a squeaky trolley.

The radiator sang the song of its people.

Angus glanced over, and there was Dr Fife, regarding him with those sad droopy eyes.

Fair enough.

He bobbed his chin in Dr Fife's direction.

Fife nodded in return. Then picked one of the reference books from the small pile and tossed it across the table to him. About an inch thick, with a black cover: the title picked out in bright yellow: 'BEHAVIORAL ANALYSIS FOR LAW-ENFORCEMENT PERSONNEL (CRIME-SCENE INDICATORS, FORENSIC RED FLAGS, & INTERVIEW GUIDANCE)'.

Sounded like a great cure for insomnia.

The pages were flared at the edges, bookmarked with dozens and dozens of little sticky notes, the spine a mass of creases and wrinkles.

'If you *really* want to help, read that. Be nice if there was someone here had half a clue what they're doing.'

Angus left it sitting where it landed.

Another big sigh from Dr Fife. 'As for the "squirrelly" thing . . . I don't like the press.'

'But you hide it so *well*.'

'OK, one time, and one time only: for the hard of thinking.' He settled back against the empty whiteboard, arms folded. 'I've spent over twenty years putting murdering assholes behind bars. Not just serial killers – mobsters, made men, cartel enforcers, zealots, terrorists, and corpse-screwing cannibals. You think I want *any* of them finding out where I am?'

'Yeah, but—'

'Don't matter if we're on the other side of the Atlantic, Angus, some of these guys got long, long arms. And I ain't risking it. So I keep my name out the papers, and my face off the news.'

Well, yeah, but that still didn't make sense though, did it.

'You're literally *surrounded* by police officers, and—'

'I got a family, Angus. I got kids. I ain't putting a target on their backs either.'

Suppose that was fair enough.

And they'd sort of called a truce.

In an unspoken, stilted, manly kind of way.

So Angus got up from the table, stretched the kinks out of his back. 'You want some more coffee?' Digging out the legendary Special VIP Card only spoken of in awed whispers. 'The Boss gave me the canteen pass. All expenses paid.'

Dr Fife smiled. 'Yeah . . . No offence, but the coffee here's like diarrhoea spiked with Drano.' A low rumbling grumble gurgled out into the room. He rubbed at his stomach. 'Could murder a nice big platter of sushi, or a quinoa-and-avocado salad. They do decent ramen around here?'

In Oldcastle?

Ha.

Good luck with that.

Angus nodded. 'I'll see what I can do.'

The incident room didn't so much bustle as shuffle. Most of the team had been on since seven that morning, and now that it was quarter to ten, they were all half dead. Lots of yawning and sagging going on.

Monroe sat at his desk, phone pressed to his ear, massaging his forehead with his free hand. 'Yeah . . . OK . . . Well, put it this way, if it's not ready for the ten o'clocks, we're all screwed . . . Oh, not just a little bit screwed, *comprehensively* screwed.' He must've sensed Angus hovering there, because he looked up and raised a finger in the universal signal to haud-yer-wheesht-a-minute. 'Exactly. ASAP . . . Thanks.' He put the phone down and creaked back in his office chair. Released a big deflating exhale. Then cricked his neck from side to side. Screwed his eyes shut. 'Fifteen minutes till nearly every broadcaster out there goes live to the nation and there's *still* no approved statement.' He opened one up to peek at Angus. 'Please tell me you've got good news?'

'We're working on it.' Might as well have a go: 'Boss, I was wondering—'

Monroe's phone jangled out a jaunty rendition of a Gilbert and Sullivan number. He raised the wheeshting finger again. 'Hold that thought.' Grabbed his phone, swiped the button. 'Irene? . . . I know, but I'm rather in the middle of . . . Uh-huh . . . Well, which tiles do *you* like? . . . OK . . . OK, look, can you hold on a sec? Someone needs me.' He put his hand over the phone. 'You were wondering?'

'Erm, Dr Fife wants something to eat that *doesn't* come from the canteen vending machine, and I thought, *maybe*, it *might* come under operational expenses? Cos I'm a bit . . .' Angus grimaced, miming empty pockets.

A tired sigh wheezed out of Monroe as he pointed towards the back of the room, where the kettle and cheap biscuits lived. 'Take twenty from petty cash, and get a receipt.'

'Thanks, Boss.'

Over in the corner, someone got into an argument with the printer.

Someone else sneezed.

'And yet: here you still are, Angus.'

'Yeah . . .' Quick look to make sure no one was lugging in. 'Boss? I was wondering if you were going to have a word with Dr Fife, about the press knowing he's here?'

Monroe bared his teeth. 'Ah. No. Not as such.'

Oh dear.

'But, Boss, he's—'

'I'm worried if I tell him, he'll sod off, and Friday we're carting another poor tortured sod back to the mortuary while Christ-knows-what happens to their other half.' Monroe frowned at his desk. 'Don't want to throw away our only tactical advantage by telling Dr Fife that the one thing we *promised* him wouldn't happen . . . has.'

Made sense, but still . . .

'He won't be happy when he finds out we knew and kept it secret.'

'Long as he helps us catch the Fortnight Killer first? I can live with the guilt.'

'Yes, Boss.'

An unholy rumbling growl burst free, as if some hideous beast was lurking deep within him, ready to devour them all.

Monroe pursed his lips. 'Angus, did you get anything for *your* tea?'

Heat sizzled in Angus's cheeks. 'I'm not really hungry, Boss, it's—'

'Take another twenty from petty cash. But no beer-and-strippers: wholesome, deep-fried food only.' Pointing at the tea-and-coffee-making facilities again. 'And I want a receipt!' Then back to the phone. 'Irene? Sorry about that. Where were— ... Well, are they going to go with the new worktops? ... Uh-huh ...'

Angus left him to it.

The WWI memorial offered a bit of shelter as rain lashed down from a dirty-orange sky: three bronze soldiers, with tin helmets and fixed bayonets, charging at some unseen enemy. Kilts flying out behind them, like Batman's cape, as the angry clouds reflected back the streetlights' sulphurous glow.

Like something out of Dante's Inferno. Only colder.

Mind you, a borrowed, padded high-vis definitely helped.

Angus's breath fogged around his head, fading away as he watched the crowd of reporters and nutjobs gathered outside Divisional Headquarters, getting ready for the ten o'clock news bulletins.

The ones who *didn't* have to be live, on camera, in eleven minutes, sat in their vans and cars, eating fish and chips, while others huddled in wheezy knots wherever they could find refuge, smoking fags and bitching about the weather.

Even the protestors were taking some time off. That Gillian woman, the pretty one, was nowhere to be seen, but a hairy man had taken her place: 'GLOBAL ELITE = SATANIC PAEDOS!' He and his fellow weirdos skulked in the lee of the Sky Outside Broadcast Unit, devouring kebabs, with their placards resting against Marge Simpson's face.

Got to wonder what would have to go wrong with your life to make you actually *believe* this stuff, never mind printing it out in big letters on a sheet of cardboard, and parading about on the news.

Maybe—

'*Are you OK?*'

Angus gave a wee squeak, whirling around, ready to defend himself ...

Gillian looked up at him. 'Hello.'

'Frightened the life out of me!'

She'd swapped her placard for a tatty umbrella with a broken rib, holding it in one hand while the other cupped a bundle of chippy paper. The delicious golden smells of deep-fried potato and sharp vinegar wafted out of it. 'Sorry.' Pink rushed up her neck and into her cheeks. 'Only I saw you coming out of the station, and you looked . . . you know.' She licked her lips with a wee pink tongue. 'Erm . . . Chip?' Holding out the bundle.

Mealie pudding supper, with salt and sauce.

Angus's stomach growled again, like something off *Jurassic Park*.

'Oh, it's Gillian, by the way. Gillian Kilbride? We met at Breechfield Crescent, when—'

'Gillian. Yes. I almost didn't recognize you without your placard.'

'Even warriors for truth have to eat sometimes.' She offered up the chips again. 'You know – because you were nice to me, back there. Most people treat us like we've got leprosy, Ebola, and gonorrhoea all rolled into one.' She gave the paper a shoogle. 'I haven't licked them or anything weird. Promise.'

Which wasn't exactly reassuring.

'Thanks, but I can't. It's a police thing. Sorry. Thanks for the offer, though.'

'Ah, OK.' She pinned the umbrella between her shoulder and neck, freeing her hand up to take a bite of pudding. Crunching through fresh batter. Making happy noises as she chewed.

'So . . .' Angus pointed at the media congregation. 'Ready to get the message out again?'

'Calm before the storm.' A chip got dunked in sauce and slipped between those pouty lips. 'OBUs won't be on live feed till a couple of minutes after ten – got to do the headlines first – then it'll be lights! Camera! Action! And I'll be in the back of every shot I can.' Another mouthful of mealie pudding disappeared. 'Soon as I've finished this.'

'Right. Right.' He nodded at the other protestors, still guzzling down their kebabs. 'And your friends? Is there competition for who gets the best spot?'

'Oh, it's a very supportive community.'

He tried to keep his face neutral; he really did.

She rolled her eyes. 'Look, I know people think we're nutters – turning up every time there's even the faintest whiff of a news crew – but if we don't stand up for the truth, who will?'

'The world's run by a global paedophile ring?' Keeping his voice kind, not threatening or mocking. 'Sounds a bit . . . ?'

'I was sceptical too.' Munching and crunching. 'But if you think about it, is it *really* that farfetched? We know you can get away with anything if you're part of the establishment. Look at Jimmy Savile: they even gave him a knighthood!' She plucked a chip from the paper and gestured across the road with it. 'Cameron says it's all about adrenochroming children. They kidnap kids, then torture them, and just before they die, someone harvests the adrenaline from their spines, with great-big needles, and sells it to the highest bidder. He says millions of kids get sex trafficked for the trade every year and no one will investigate, because the Imperial Paedophile bloodlines control the media and the police.'

'Right. I thought it was the Scottish Government who controlled us?'

Her eyes widened. '*Exactly!*'

'OK.' Nodding. 'I see.'

She polished off a few more chips. 'So . . . you had to let the guy go. From earlier?'

'Yeah, I'm not really allowed to talk about an ongoing investigation.'

'The reporters have been banging on about it, and how the police can't catch the Fortnight Killer, and there's going to be lots more deaths.' The mealie pudding was almost gone now, a single drip of brown sauce making a beauty spot on her chin. 'I thought a hotshot FBI profiler would've helped with that.'

'We're pursuing various lines of inquiry.'

'I still think it's super exciting.' She popped the last nugget of pudding in her mouth and froze, mid-chew. The words came out all mumbled, flecked with batter and oatmeal. 'Not the murders! No, but, you know, working with someone from the FBI.' Chew, chew, chew, chew. 'Is it like Mulder and Scully? Is he all sort of cerebral like Sherlock Holmes, or is he more . . . I don't know, kicking down doors and shouting, "Freeze, motherfucker!"' Her eyebrows shot up, fingertips covering her mouth. 'Oh God, I'm so sorry!'

Hard not to laugh at that. 'It's OK, I'm a police officer: I've heard much worse. Trust me.'

'I'm *such* an idiot.'

'Honestly, it's fine.' He glanced across the road, not so much at the journalists, but at the small crowd of lookie-loos, drifting down Peel Place in time for the festivities. Gathering to enjoy the vicarious thrill of someone else's misery. 'Can I ask you a question? When you've been at these things, with the media – you know, about the Fortnight Killer – have you noticed anyone *strange* hanging about? Anyone giving off creepy vibes?'

She paused a chip on the way to its doom. 'Creepy *vibes*?'

'Someone who's maybe not interacting with anyone, just watching things. Like all this is a spectator sport?'

'Oooh . . .' The chip got chomped. 'Do you think they've got something to do with the *murders*?'

Shrug. 'Never know.'

'Gosh.' Gillian frowned as she chewed. 'Can't think of anybody, sorry.'

'But if you *do* see someone creepy . . . ?'

'You want me to rat on them?' She plucked an escaped curl of batter from the paper and crunched on it. More frowning. 'See, I wouldn't normally help the cops, cos of all the corruption and being tools of the establishment, et cetera, but . . .' A nod. 'OK. You know, cos you're one of the good guys.'

'Thanks.' He dug out an official Police Scotland business card – scribbling his mobile number on the back, just in case – and handed it over. 'If you think of anything.'

'Cool.'

They stood there as she shovelled in the last of her chips, masticating through the awkward silence. Then both spoke at the same time:

'Well, suppose I should really get on with—'

'Sod: they're setting up for the ten o'clocks, I have to—'

Cue blushing and clearing of throats.

Angus's ears were on the verge of spontaneously combusting. 'Sorry, you first.'

She pointed at the nearest Outside Broadcast Unit, where the journalist was already posing with his microphone for the camera. 'I'd better . . .'

'Me too. Take care of yourself, OK?'

'Do my best. And *you*, of course.'

They shuffled their feet. Nodded. Huffed out breaths.

Then finally went their separate ways.

Oh, yeah: Angus MacVicar, slick-talking chick magnet, strikes again . . .

Hangtree Road sulked in the shadow of that thick blade of granite – with the castle's remains perched on top. Couldn't actually *see* them from down here, but their multicoloured illuminations bounced off the low cloud, giving that part of the downpour a rainbows-and-unicorns edge. The curling street must've had a blocked drain somewhere, because it was growing its own loch, the surface churned up by the never-ending rain.

Angus trudged past a row of darkened shops: a newsagent's with classified cards in the window; a place selling knick-knacks, featuring a 'FOR SALE, MAY LET' sign; and a bookies with the grilles rattled down and padlocked.

Next up, a trio of takeaways.

The first one, 'COMRADE BORSCHT'S BEETS & BURGERS!', didn't look as if it'd be serving up Slavic delights anytime soon. The windows were all boarded up – the signage and stonework blackened by whatever fire had ripped through the place. Graffiti clarted the plywood sheets: 'GENOCIDAL BASTARDS!' and 'REMEMBER BAKHMUT!' and 'PUTIN BURN IN HELL!!!', all in different handwriting. Or was it handspraying? Either way, the crowning glory was a pretty decent stencil rendition of a huge zombie bear with exposed ribs, a Nazi-style 'Z' armband, and blood dripping from its teeth and claws.

Next door had escaped Molotov-cocktail hour, but 'IT'S RAMEN MEN (HALLELUJAH)' lay in darkness. Closed, according to the note sellotaped inside the glass door, because of a family funeral.

'Bugger.'

So much for the best ramen in Oldcastle.

Could try that new place in Castleview, Tsuki Usagi, but that was miles away, and the food would probably be cold by the time he got it back to the station. So Dr Fife would just have to settle for Take-away Number Three, AKA: 'THE JADE DRAGON'S GARDEN'.

Angus pushed the door open and stepped inside.

Angus shifted his bum on the hard wooden bench seat that ran along the windowsill, leaning forward to keep his back away from the condensation misting the glass. Feet making puddles on the scuffed-lino floor.

They hadn't exactly gone out of their way to give the small, soulless room a taste of the Orient. Two cheap paper lanterns and a waving plastic cat were the only attempts at decoration, but the walls *did* feature huge, blown-up pages from the menu, complete with pictures of several dishes. They'd mounted an old TV on an arm behind the counter, up near the roof, topped with a thick grey furring of dust. A serious-faced presenter was doing a piece to camera outside a bungalow somewhere in England, while crime-scene tape fluttered in the background.

The sound was off, but auto-generated subtitles blinked up on the screen:

'DENIES ALL INVOLVEMENT IN MISS STRIKES' DEATH'.

Over in the corner, by the door through to the kitchen, a fly-zapper glowed Cherenkov blue – buzzing as another bluebottle met its fate.

Which meant Angus was now the only living thing in here.

Up on the screen, the presenter was replaced by a senior UK politician looking very stern, nose in the air, finger jabbing at a row of microphones.

'DONE NOTHING ILLEGAL, AND ANYONE WHO SAYS OTHERWISE WILL BE HEARING FROM MY LAWYERS. THIS IS NOTHING BUT A PART ASIAN WITCH HUNT'.

Part Asian?

Partisan.

You'd think computers would be better at this by now.

Angus went back to his phone, poking out a text to Mum.

Am still at work.

Sorry.

Will be home when possible.

Do not wait up.

SEND.

Onscreen, the politician was replaced by a woman in the studio, mouthing away silently, as the automated subtitles struggled to catch up – leaving her with some of his dialogue.

'OPPOSITION SHOULD BE ASHAMED OF ITSELF. THE HUNT FOR THE FORTNIGHT KILLER, IN OLD CASTLE, SUFFERED A SETBACK TODAY AS POLICE ARRESTED THE WRONG MAN'.

Which in no way could be considered Angus's fault.

'EARLY EVENING RAID ON A BUN GALLOW IN THE CITY'S SHORT STRAIN AREA'.

Breechfield Crescent appeared, with Patrick Crombie's house visible in the background and a wee gang of scene examiners on their hands and knees, searching the garden. Angus's pool car was on the left of the screen, middle distance, no sign of Dr Fife on account of him being all scooted down in the passenger seat.

'GO LIVE NOW, TO HEW BRIMMED, WHO'S AT OLD CASTLE DIVISIONAL HEADQUARTERS. HEW?'

Or 'Hugh Brimmond' as the chyron had him – the beefy-faced posh boy from Balvenie Row, this morning.

'THAT'S RIGHT, SHIFFON, IT'S BEEN A DIFFICULT DAY FOR OPER-ATION TELEGRAM WITH GLOWING CALLS FOR SENIOR OFFICERS TO BE SUSPENDED AS'.

The door behind the counter thumped open and out stomped a boot-faced man in a white T-shirt and unbuttoned, shiny, red-and-gold shirt that was covered with dragons and Chinese characters.

'SUSPECT RELEASED WITHOUT CHARGE. THOUGH I HAVE HEARD FROM SOURCES CLOSE TO THE INFESTATION THAT THE MAN IN QUES-TION IS SUING FOR WRONGFUL ARREST AND POLICE BRUTALITY'.

A carrier bag bearing the Jade Dragon's Garden logo was dumped on the counter – a nice *big* carrier bag, full of delicious food.

Hopefully.

'Number seventeen!'

There was no one else there, but Angus still checked his receipt before heading for the counter.

The man in the shiny shirt barked out the order: 'Sesame prawn toast, spring rolls, salt-and-pepper ribs, Kung Po chicken, Szechuan pork, boiled rice, plain fried noodles, prawn crackers.'

Angus's stomach snarled.

'In A Brief, But Fraught, Press Conference'.

DCI Monroe appeared, looking a lot calmer and more confident than he had half an hour ago, and a lot less depressed. He was flanked by DI Tudor, and the new Media Liaison Officer – slicked-back red hair and glasses, prim and schoolmarmish. The camera zoomed in on Monroe's face, caught in the flicker-flash glare of many, *many* cameras. Mouth moving in complete silence.

'I Can Assure You That A Pretending This Individual Remains Our Top Priority. Which Is Why We're Issuing The Following Warning To Anyone Working In The Legal Or Barking Industries'.

With an expression that was far more sour than sweet, the take-away guy dipped beneath the counter, emerging moments later with a two-litre bottle of off-brand diet cola. He bashed it down next to the carrier bag.

Angus watched it fizzzzzz . . . 'But I didn't—'

'Complimentary for spending more than thirty quid, innit.' His voice darkened, till it was almost a threat: *'Enjoy.'*

OK.

'Vigilant At This Time And Report Anything Suspicious To Our Desiccated Helpline'. The automatic transcript gave up for a moment as the photo-flashes increased to seizure-inducing levels.

Someone in the scrum must've been shouting a question, because Monroe scanned the room for them, mouth pursed.

'[Inaudible] That This Raises Serious Questions About Go Division's Competence And Ability To Carry Out This Infestation? My Team And I Remain Committed To Stopping This Man.'

Angus forced a smile, then picked up the carry-out and the bonus counterfeit Coke. 'Thanks.'

Takeaway Guy narrowed his eyes, sniffed, then turned and stomped back through the door, leaving Angus all alone in the shop again.

'MICHAEL SAUCER, CASTLE NEWS AND POST. ISN'T IT TIME TO ADMIT DEFEAT AND FIND SOMEONE MORE CAPABLE TO CATCH THE FORTNIGHT KILLER?'

Monroe's face darkened.

'WE'RE PURSUING ALL AVAILABLE AVENUES AND CONTINUE TO CONSULT WITH OUR COLLEAGUES AND SPECIALISTS IN THE AFRO PIRATE DISCIPLINES. THANK YOU FOR COMING.'

Monroe stood and the camera zoomed out to watch him stalking offstage, followed by Tudor. The pink-faced Media Liaison Officer made a big show of getting her papers into order—

And the picture jumped back to Hugh Brimmond, doing his 'concerned' face.

'DETECTIVE CHIEF INSPECTOR MOSCOW THERE, CLEARLY NOT PREPARED TO ANSWER ANY FURTHER QUESTIONS AFTER ISSUING THAT A STONE WISHING WARNING TO EVERY LAWYER AND BANKER IN OLD CASTLE. IT'S NO WONDER PEOPLE HERE ARE HOLDING THEIR BREADS, WAITING FOR THE NEXT MURDER TO OCCUR. SHIFFON?'

Angus turned his back on the telly, pulled up his hood, and marched out into the rain.

9

The wet road shimmered in the headlights of passing cars and taxis, streetlights making glowing orbs of gold as the rain clattered down. Hissing as it bounced off St Jasper's Lane, gurgling around the drains.

Angus danced back out of the way, just in time, as the number eighteen bus lurched through a huge puddle – spraying the pavement with a wall of dirt-grey water.

He paused outside the King James Theatre with its billboards screaming about how *Jumanji, The Musical!* was the best thing to *ever* happen in the *entire* history of mankind: FIVE STARS!!! Music oozed out through the closed doors – couldn't really make out the tune, but there was enough bass in it to make the glass buzz.

Bet Ellie and whoever she'd taken with her were having a great time. Singing along. Ice cream at the interval . . .

Bastards.

He kept going, past closed shops and the Sharny Dug – where the bouncer took one look at Angus in his police high-vis, and tipped a non-existent hat. Angus returned the gesture – professional courtesy between those who dealt with drunken morons on a daily basis.

Then it was a boutique lingerie emporium that didn't make it through the pandemic, an off-licence with a display of Buckfast and ultra-strength lager in the window, a boarded-up Post Office, two charity shops, and a bookie's.

Angus ducked around the corner, back onto Peel Place.

Now that their evening bulletins were over, the journalists had disappeared, taking their Outside Broadcasting Units with them. And without any cameras to wave their placards in front of, the protestors had gone home as well, leaving the street to drown in peace.

Angus slowed down as he approached the WWI memorial.

A mealie pudding supper, with salt and sauce, disappearing between soft pink lips . . .

Blinking.

Deep breath.

He gave himself a wee shake.

Important job to do, remember?

This Chinese carry-out wasn't going to deliver itself.

Dr Fife lay slouched over the desk, head on his arms – just like Angus had been earlier, only unlike Angus, he was snoring. Not chainsaw-in-a-bathtub snoring, more like Wee Hamish after a long walk. Or Mum after her Christmas sherry.

Of course, the *kind* thing would be to let him sleep: poor sod must be knackered. Surprised he'd stayed awake as long as he had, really.

On the other hand, Angus had just squelched all the way to Hangtree Road and back, so a bit of sodding recognition would be nice.

He slammed the office door shut, and raised his voice to *just* below a shout. 'Dr Fife?'

The forensic psychologist flinched, then struggled upright. 'Awake! I'm awake . . .' Staring around with swivelling eyes, a line of drool glistening in his Vandyke. 'Hello?'

Angus placed the soggy carrier bag on the spare chair. 'Ramen place was shut, so I got Chinese.'

He rubbed at his eyes, yawned, showing off a mouth without a single filling. 'Time is it?' Wiping that damp patch from his hairy chin.

'Nearly half ten.'

'No. Not *here* time. *Proper* time.'

'Oh.' Angus looked it up on his phone. Seven-hour time difference, so: 'Half three in the afternoon.'

Another yawn, followed by a bit of a scratch. 'Is that today or tomorrow, though?'

No idea what that was supposed to mean.

So, instead of answering, Angus cleared a space on the cluttered desk and laid out the takeaway's plastic containers.

Dr Fife drooped in his chair. 'Was having a lovely dream, where I never agreed to come to this ass-flavoured shithole city and stayed in LA instead.'

Next up: the grease-spotted paper bags. 'They've put out that statement about lawyers and bankers. Think it'll help?'

'Nope.' He opened a bag and helped himself to a spring roll. 'Not unless it scares our guy off for a bit. Makes him think it's too risky. In which case he just lies low and waits till the heat dies down.' Dr Fife took a bite, crunching away. It wasn't nearly as attractive as Gillian with her battered mealie pudding. 'But given how careful the Fortnight Killer's been so far? He's already got his next victims picked and lined up, all ready for the dinner party from hell.' Crunch, crunch, crunch. 'Maybe Monroe warning all the bankers and lawyers just adds an extra layer of spiciness?' A pause while he ran a tongue around his teeth. 'Speaking of which, we got any hot sauce?'

'In the wee polystyrene tub.' Angus opened the prawn toasts and polished one off in three bites. Nutty and savoury and delicious. 'How you getting on with the profile?'

'Difficult to tell.' Dip. More crunching. 'We need someone to troll through the target victims' lives and see if there's a connection.'

'We've already *done* that.'

'Yes, but you were looking for a connection between the *victims*. What you *should've* been looking for is their connection to the Fortnight Killer.' He reached across and tried a prawn toast. Talking with his mouth full: 'Go through Dr Fordyce's appointments – did she have a bad experience with one of her patients? Let them down with a missed diagnosis, or something? Then you hit Councillor Mendel's records – you're looking for people who've complained to the council and feel hard done by. Finally, it's Kevin Healey-Robinson's turn – who did he write damning articles about? Who's he libelled in print?' Dr Fife opened the noodles. 'And once you've done all *that*, you hope one name appears on all three lists.'

'So it's about revenge, not sex?' Creaking the lid off the salt-and-pepper ribs.

'If there's one thing men *can* multitask on, it's revenge and sex.' Dr Fife opened the Kung Po chicken, and the deep dark scent filled the small room. 'Chopsticks?'

'Hold on.' Back into the bag, where a couple of napkins lurked at the bottom along with their free disposable wooden eating implements. 'Sporks.'

'Bloody heathens . . .' He took one anyway. 'You're gonna have to get people working on those lists.' Staring at Angus as he plucked free a burning-hot rib. 'I'm not kidding. Like, *right now*. ASAP. While we can still make a difference.'

A groan whinged free, and the rib went back in the container.

One last, longing look at the collection of cartons and bags, and Angus was on his feet, sooking his fingers on the way out the door. Because the sooner he was done, the sooner he could eat.

Dr Fife's voice followed him, like an ungrateful crow: *'And see if you can rustle up some decent hot sauce, not this sweet chilli shit!'*

The energy levels in the incident room had picked up a bit. Now that most of the day shift had gone home, it was the back shift's time to shine. And while there was only about half a dozen of them, at least they were awake.

Monroe stood centre stage, clapping his hands as he finished issuing the orders. 'Quick as possible, people: find me those names!'

And off they scurried to fetch file boxes and search through HOLMES, leaving a moment of stillness behind.

Soon as they'd gone, Monroe leaned in towards Angus, keeping his voice down. 'How confident are we with this?'

'Dr Fife seems to think it'll work. Probably.'

Monroe crossed fingers, eyes to the ceiling tiles. 'Please, God, let *something* go right for a change . . .' Then back to Angus. 'When am I getting my profile?'

'Work in progress, Boss.' Took a bit of doing, but Angus stifled a massive yawn without dislocating his own jaw. 'Sorry.' Shake. 'Not sure how long he's going to last tonight. Was asleep when I got back from the takeaway.'

'Which reminds me.' Monroe raised his eyebrows, then stuck his hand out.

Angus nodded, then shook it.

'No, you great, daft . . . *Receipt*.'

'Ah. Yes, Boss, sorry.' He dug it out, along with the change – a whole two pounds and fifteen pence – and tipped it into the offered palm. 'Only he's still awake from whenever he got on the plane from LA.'

Monroe chewed on his cheek for a moment, then huffed out a long, low breath. 'Push him as far as you can, then make sure he gets back to his digs.' He gave Angus a quick once-over. 'After *that*, you'd better head home, too. Going to be a big day tomorrow.' He closed his fist around the cash. 'One way or another.'

Dr Fife wasn't slumped over the desk this time. Instead, he was sparked out, sitting upright in his wonky office chair, feet up on his improvised footstool, hands loose in his lap, head down. Those snuffly Wee Hamish snores had escalated to something more like an elephant with a head cold.

Smelled lovely in here, though – all spicy and savoury.

The takeaway containers were exactly where Angus had left them. He hadn't even made a dent in the Kung Po, before falling asleep again.

Angus thumped the door shut, but he didn't stir.

'DR FIFE?' Raising his voice over the trumpeting din.

Still nothing.

He gave Dr Fife's shoulder a wee shoogle. 'Dr Fife?'

That jerked him into life, blinking and snorking. 'Awake! I'm awake . . .' Looking around as if he'd never seen this room before in his life. 'Time is it?'

'Twenty to four, your time – P.M.'

'Urgh . . .' He ground the palms of his hands into his eyes. 'We need someone to dig into the target victims' lives and see if there's some sort of connection.'

'We've already had this conversation. When I came back with the carry-out, remember?'

That broad forehead creased for a bit, followed by a grunt and a sigh. 'OK. Yeah.' He scrubbed at his face. 'Come on, Jonathan, you can do this.'

'You're no use to anyone knackered.'

'I'm awake. Everything is dandy. All I need's some coffee. Even your canteen swill will do.' Dr Fife opened his right hand wide and slapped himself on the cheek. Then reached for the yellow legal pad and a pen. 'Just make sure it's plenty hot and plenty caffeinated.'

He wrote the words 'VICTIMOLOGY MATRIX' at the top of a fresh sheet and blinked at it, as if trying to get the letters to stop wriggling. 'Right.'

Angus made for the door again.

'And maybe grab a couple energy drinks while you're at it.'

Angus bumped back into the little office – big wax-paper cup of the canteen's finest blend in each hand, pockets bulging.

And stopped dead.

'Oh, for . . .'

Dr Fife had made a gap in the containers, and was slumped onto the table again. Eyes shut. Snores ringing out like a drunken monkey taking a hacksaw to a length of metal pipe.

Well, that was that, then.

The cups went on the table, and Angus sank into the least creaky of the two remaining chairs. Helped himself to another prawn toast.

Instead of being crisp and delicious and warm, the thing was soft, greasy, and stone cold.

He swallowed, put the remains back in the bag, then picked up the other containers, one after the other.

Everything was the same: oily and congealed.

'Great.'

Perfect end to a perfect day.

Angus pulled the tins of Rampant Gorilla – 'SO MUCH CAFFEINE IT'S OB-SCENE' – from his suit pockets, slipped them into the filing cabinet's middle drawer, and buried them under the post-mortem files. Where, if they were lucky, none of his sticky-fingered fellow officers would find them. You could leave cash, electronics, even jewellery lying around the station, and no one would touch them. But biscuits? Crisps? Fizzy drinks?

Even the most prolific of housebreakers had nothing on the officers of O Division.

Angus sipped at his horrible coffee.

Crunched on a prawn cracker.

Then cricked all the lids back onto the containers again.

Monroe had sprung for a pretty decent hotel: the Bishop's View, on Jessop Street. Five storeys of seventeenth-century sandstone, with small windows and thick walls, sitting directly opposite St Jasper's Cathedral.

The place could probably pass for 'quaint' in the daylight, but in the steetlights' sickly glow they might as well have carved 'ABANDON HOPE ALL YE WHO ENTER HERE' above the door.

High above, the sky was the angry, burnt-orange colour of an indicted ex-president, adding to the whole Gates-of-Hell atmosphere.

Still, at least it'd stopped raining on the short drive here from the station, leaving the road puddled and the gutters gurgling.

While Dr Fife scuffed his way up the steps to the hotel's front door, Angus hefted the luggage from the patrol car's boot.

A big wheelie suitcase and a much bigger, stainless-steel trunk thing. Awkward to shift, especially if you were trying not to drop a bulging carrier bag from the Jade Dragon's Garden.

And yeah, the trunk was heavy, but nothing he couldn't handle.

He parked it on the pavement and looked in through the open passenger window. 'Thanks for the lift, guys.'

Tim grinned up at him with a mouthful of squint teeth – they went with his crooked nose and wonky ears. 'Nae probs. Put Captain Sleepy-Pants to bed and we'll give you a hurl home, if you like? Nothing else on, have we, Ronny?'

His partner in crime still looked fresh out of school, with a ratty-pube moustache and two big plukes on both cheeks. He turned in his seat and draped one arm across the steering wheel. 'Sod, and indeed, all.'

Angus smiled back. 'That would be great; save me a massive-long bus journey!' He pointed at the stairs and the slowly climbing forensic psychologist. 'I'll just—'

The car radio bleeped, and a sharp woman's voice crackled out of the dashboard. *'Oscar Charlie Six from Control, safe to talk?'*

Ronny grabbed the Airwave clipped to the chest of his stabproof vest. 'Oscar Charlie Six. What's up?'

'Break-in in progress: Unwin and McNulty undertaker's, one thirty-seven Hodgson Drive. Can you attend?'

Tim bared his teeth at Angus. 'Sorry, mate.'

The patrol car's roof lights flickered blue-and-white, strobing against the ancient buildings as Ronny hit the switch. 'Roger that, on our way.' He let go of his Airwave. 'Aye, aye: someone's nicking deid folk!'

Angus backed up as the engine revved.

The rear wheels spun on the damp setts, then off they roared – siren kicking in halfway down Jessop Street, wailing and chirruping like a huge electronic kid's toy.

So much for a lift home.

He drooped for a moment, gathered up the luggage and cold carry-out, then followed Dr Fife inside.

They'd given him one of the swankier suites, on the third floor. Old-fashioned, in a dark-wood-and-wainscoting kind of way. And the view wasn't bad.

OK, the windows were small and mullioned, but they looked out over the cathedral – lit up in all its spiky-granite Gothic glory.

In here: a huge TV hung on the wall, facing a leather sofa and matching armchairs. Tartan rugs on polished floorboards; a drinks cabinet, hi-fi, and sideboard bearing tastefully curated curios; a coffee table with an array of expensive magazines. There was even a nice big pot plant by the window – some sort of fern with lush green fronds – lurking beneath a brass standard lamp.

This one room was almost bigger than Angus's entire flat. Well, Mum's flat. And it was certainly nicer.

Three doors led off the lounge: two closed, one open – revealing an even swankier bedroom, in tasteful, muted colours with a *massive* bed.

Dr Fife slouched in that direction, dumping his greatcoat on the carpet as he went.

Angus placed the cases by the coffee table. 'Don't forget: post-mortem's at nine tomorrow. They get really pissed off if you're late.'

That got him a dismissive wave, over the shoulder, as Dr Fife bumped into the bedroom.

OK . . .

He held up the carrier bag that had promised so much but hadn't been allowed to deliver any of it. 'Where do you want me to put the takeaway?'

'Bin it. Burn it. Eat it. I don't care. I – just – want – to – sleep!'

Then the bedroom door clunked shut, leaving Angus standing there like a damp sock.

Right.

He licked his lips. Smiled. Gazed at the lovely bag full of Oriental delight. 'Sweet.'

Angus hurried for the door, before Dr Fife could change his mind. Pausing on the threshold to switch off the lights. 'Nine o'clock, on the dot!'

And he was free.

Why did people have to be so shitty?

Angus shuffled sideways, putting as much distance between himself and the truly gargantuan puddle of vomit that covered a large swathe of the bus-shelter floor. Whoever did it had managed to get the entire row of narrow bum-rest-shelf seats, too. And some-how, with half the world underwater, the rain had failed to wash *any* of it away.

Its sharp, parmesan stink filled the plastic rabbit hutch, tainting the air with a bitter metallic taste.

He checked the information banner, little orange dots glowing away up by the curved roof: '157 KINGSMEATH – LAST SERVICE – EXPECTED 23:41'.

Nine minutes to go.

Still, on the plus side, he had a virtually untouched Chinese carry-out to look forward to. And enough left over for Mum to have a treat tomorrow, as well.

She'd like that.

Been a *long* time since they'd had takeaway.

He checked his watch, then the display again: '157 KINGSMEATH – LAST SERVICE – EXPECTED 23:42'.

OK: call it forty minutes to the front door, takeaway in the microwave – so dinner at twenty-five past midnight? Half an hour to eat and clear up. Teeth. Bed by . . . one-ish? Alarm at half five.

Could be worse.

A sniff.

Then a wince as that rancid, cheesy, bitter smell filled his nose, throat, and lungs.

Jesus . . .

Maybe it was worth the risk, standing outside?

Out of the smell?

Yeah, but these modern bus shelters had sensors in them, didn't they, and the number 157 might not stop if it wasn't registering someone standing inside. Not unless a passenger was getting off here. And, given this was the last bus home, it wasn't worth the risk.

Still, wouldn't hurt to get a breath of fresh air, would it? Bus wasn't expected for another . . . ten minutes now. Could take a five-minute break out of the pukey pong and—

The whole street lit up in a flash of bright white, followed by a deep rumble of thunder, and the heavens opened – flinging it down hard enough to bounce off the uneven paving stones.

So much for that.

It clattered against the plastic roof, ran in thick ribbons down the clear sides, and went nowhere near that vast puddle of sick.

A Volvo and a pickup truck drove by.

Then a taxi – sending up a splooosh of spray to shower against the shelter wall.

Someone hurried by on the other side of the road.

'157 KINGSMEATH – LAST SERVICE – EXPECTED 23:45'.

An auld mannie scurried into the shelter: short and grubby and dripping wet. It was hard to see where his ancient parka jacket ended and he began, what with the long tatty beard blending in with the matted fur collar. Filthy backpack, dirty clothes, and ancient leather boots held together with duct tape.

Newspaper stuck out of his collar and cuffs. A sad, filthy set of tabloid thermals. Towing a whippety dog on a string.

He nodded at Angus in his cosy, fluorescent-yellow 'POLICE' high-vis.

The brown-toothed smile hid a surprisingly posh Scottish accent. 'Don't mind me, Officer, just looking for a little shelter on this cold and stormy night. No pun intended.'

The dog took one look at Angus, and whimpered around behind its master, sniffing at the puddle of vomit.

Please don't eat it. *Please* don't eat it.

Angus glanced out at the frigid monsoon. 'You're not sleeping rough in this, are you?'

'Alas, the hostel on Gallows Alley is full to capacity, and owing to an *unfortunate* misunderstanding I find myself temporarily excluded from my gentlemen's club.' He dug a grimy hand into his sodden parka and produced a small metal tin, winkling a roll-up from the contents.

He paused for a moment, then offered the tin to Angus. 'Worry not, dear Officer, they contain nothing more illicit than a smidgeon of Golden Virginia. Which I almost certainly did *not* shoplift.'

'Don't smoke. But thanks.'

'Do you mind if I . . . ?' He waited for Angus to shake his head before lighting up – drawing on his weeny homemade cigarette as if it was the very breath of life itself. 'We all have our vices to bear.' He stuck out a grimy hand, not palm-up for a donation, but sideways for shaking. 'Dr Vincent Rayner, at your service.'

Angus shook it – the skin rough like sandpaper against his palm. 'Pleased to meet you. I'm Angus. MacVicar.'

'Angus! A *fine* Scottish name.' Dr Rayner struck a pose, free hand pressed against his chest, eyes narrowed against the smoke curling out of his roll-up.

> 'Now does he feel
> His secret murders *sticking* on his hands;
> Now minutely revolts upbraid his *faith*-breach;
> Those he commands move only *in* command,
> Nothing in love: *now* does he feel his title

Hang *loose* about him, like a giant's robe
Upon a *dwarfish* thief.'

OK, that was . . . weird.

The recitation ended with a theatrical hand gesture, '*Macbeth*, Act Five, Scene Two,' and the guttural growl of an empty stomach. 'Please do excuse me. How *rude* to sully the Bard with such base corporeal gurgles!'

'When did you last eat?'

He plucked the roll-up from his mouth and considered the glowing tip. 'What, food?' A small laugh. 'Sadly, like the unnamed protagonist in Knut Hamsun's *Hunger*, I must wander these streets unsatiated – trapped in my own personal Christiania. Though I dare say the Norwegian weather would probably be an improvement.'

Sod.

Angus frowned at the carrier bag from the Jade Dragon's Garden, all weighed down with Kung Po chicken and noodles and ribs and Szechuan pork and rice and spring rolls and prawn crackers and those delicious prawn toasts . . .

Sodding, sodding sod.

He'd been *so* close.

'Do you like Chinese?' He held the bag out. 'I was going to have it for my tea, but . . . well, you know.'

'How lovely and unexpected!' Dr Rayner beamed up at him. 'Kind sir, I shall not insult you by refusing this *magnificent* gift.' Taking the offered bag and peering inside, then sniffing the rank air in the vomity bus shelter. 'Though I think I shall seek out slightly more salubrious surroundings to enjoy your largesse.' Performing a small bow. 'A *thousand* thank-yous.' He patted his dog's head. 'Come, Dogstoyevsky!' Hurrying out into the downpour. 'A veritable feast for us both, old girl. A succulent Chinese meal!'

Angus watched his dinner scurry off down the street, then disappear around the corner onto Doyle Lane, never to be seen again.

Why did 'doing the right thing' always have to be such a kick in the nads?

His phone vibrated, announcing an incoming text message, its accompanying *ding* lost in the clatter of rain pounding on the shelter's roof.

ELLIE:
> That was BRILLIANT!
> JUMANJI! JUMANJI! JUMANJI!
> And you missed it, you silly, silly sod!

There was nothing like having your nose rubbed in it.

His shoulders dipped a little further as he put his phone away – message unanswered.

The information banner flashed a couple of times, then changed from: '157 KINGSMEATH – LAST SERVICE – EXPECTED 23:50' to: 'SERVICE CANCELLED'.

Of course it was.

He closed his eyes and let his head droop.

No takeaway.

No bus.

No money for a taxi.

Which meant he'd have to walk, all the way home, in *this*.

Angus pulled the hood up on his high-vis.

What a great end to a *spectacular* day.

—Thursday 14 March—

10

Wasn't easy, keeping the yawn in, but Angus did his best.

Everyone had congregated in the incident room, watching DCI Monroe wrapping up Morning Prayers.

Twenty past seven and the sun was barely clawing its way above the valley's rim, painting the sky a dark, ominous scarlet that glowed in through Operation Telegram's windows as if the whole world was burning.

Angus stood at the back, in his still-damp suit, clutching one of those tins of Rampant Gorilla from the filing cabinet – which, wonder of wonders, the thieving gits on night shift hadn't found. He took a scoof and stifled the resultant burp, waiting for the 'obscene' caffeine to kick in.

'. . . OK?' Monroe pointed the remote, switching off the projector. 'That means, if we don't catch this bastard *today*, two more people die. Get yourselves out there and dig till you find something.'

The team creaked into life, people heading to phones and computers, or grabbing their coats.

Monroe raised his voice. 'Anyone who doesn't know their assignment: Rhona has the list.' Clapping his hands. 'Let's do this!'

Angus pulled out his phone and switched off flight mode, connecting to the station Wi-Fi as he slouched towards the door. Then brought up a web browser and thumbed 'DR JONATHAN FIFE, FORENSIC PSYCHOLOGIST' into the search bar.

There weren't a lot of results. Surprisingly few, to be honest: less than two pages. And most of those seemed to be for things like *The*

Journal of American Psychological Science. A lot of the links dead-ended at paywalls, but the couple that did let him through were bone-dry research papers about serial killers.

Nothing on YouTube or TikTok, and no image results.

He followed a clump of PCs out into the corridor – 'Tash and Colly arguing about whose football club was crapper, while Monster Munch complained loudly about the packed lunch her girlfriend had made that morning.

Might be worth having a look on Facebook: see if Dr Fife was kicking about on there. He wasn't.

Angus scuffed his way down the corridor, ignoring the notice-boards and motivational posters, as he had a bash on Twitter, then Bindle, Threads, and Instagram.

Getting sod-all for his trouble.

He'd almost reached the sanctuary of their wee borrowed office, when the clatter-clack of heels closed in from behind. But when he turned, it wasn't Dr Fife following him, it was DS Massie, in a dark-blue fighting suit, with a clipboard tucked under her arm.

'Sarge.' Nodding a greeting. 'Don't suppose there's any news on—'

'If you're asking about the appeal for people not to get murdered – far as we know, it's working. Till it doesn't.' She looked around. 'Where's your Dr Fife?'

'He's not mine, *really*, Sarge, I just—'

'Oh no.' She held up a silencing finger. 'No, no, no. Until we catch the Fortnight Killer, he is *very much* yours.'

Bugger.

Angus opened the office door, holding it as she marched inside.

It looked much as he'd left it last night, except for the wee decorative touch added by whichever member of night shift hadn't managed to find the energy drinks Angus had planked in the filing cabinet: a framed portrait of Hannibal Lecter, perched on top of the reference books.

DS Massie did a slow three-sixty, taking in the squiggle-clarted whiteboards, the taped-up sheets of yellow legal pad, the crime-scene photographs. Given the curl of her lip, she wasn't that impressed. 'So where is he?'

Angus draped his jacket over the back of the nearest chair. 'Still at the hotel, I guess. He was really knackered, so—'

'Does this look like the face of someone who cares about forensic-psychologist-sleepy-times? He's got a profile to finish, a PM to attend, and a killer to catch.'

'But—'

Her finger poked into Angus's chest. 'The Boss put a lot of faith in you when he made you Dr Fife's liaison-slash-minion-slash-minder. *Don't* let him down.'

Angus drooped. 'No, Sarge.'

'Cos if you do, you might just find yourself on my Naughty List.' She stepped in close, face like a lump of carved granite. 'And believe me when I say you do *not* want that.'

'Yes, Sarge.'

'Glad we had this chat.' She patted him on the shoulder. 'Now go find Dr Pain-In-The-Arse. Last thing we need is this bastard getting away with murder because Fife's snoozed through the bloody post-mortem.'

Angus hunched over in his squeaky office chair, phone liberated from its plastic bag and pressed to his ear – unable to prevent the wheedling tone that had infected his voice. 'I know I did, but he's not answering his phone, so if you could just try again, *please*?'

The hotel manager sighed, sounding posh and bored and won-dering what on earth had gone wrong with his life that he had to deal with idiots like Angus. *'It's not even eight o'clock yet. Maybe your friend wants a long lie?'*

'Please: I wouldn't ask if it wasn't important.'

'I've got other guests to look after here, you know.' Getting sniffy now. *'Mary's off sick, and breakfast for six Romanian businessmen doesn't cook itself. And none of them will even* look *at a vegetarian sausage!'*

A voice echoed out in the little office, right behind Angus. *'DC MacVicar? Er . . . Angus, isn't it?'*

Oh, bugger.

Angus swivelled around in his chair. Forced a smile.

DS Sharp stood by the door, clutching this season's fashion accessory: yet another clipboard. Grimacing as she sniffed the air. 'Why does it smell of wet dog in here?' And then she saw the make-shift murder board. 'Wow. Isn't that . . . interesting.'

'Sarge?' He scrambled from his seat, one hand covering the phone. 'Just trying to get hold of Dr Fife. He didn't show for the briefing.'

'So I saw.' She checked her clipboard. 'You're on my list for the PM today. Ever attended a post-mortem before?'

'Suicide, when I was a probationer: mother of three OD'd on sleeping pills, antidepressants, and tequila.'

'In for a shock today, then. Don't worry though, I'll be there to keep you right. Come find me in twenty minutes and we'll get you kitted out, go through the procedures, then head over there.'

'Yes, Sarge.' He cleared his throat. 'How's your dad?'

'Pfff . . .' Rolling her eyes. 'And make sure you've got warm socks on. Bloody mortuary's like a fridge since the refit.'

The word *'Eric?'* rattled around the corridor, outside.

Oh sod, it was DCI Monroe.

Angus searched the little office for hiding places, but there weren't any.

Maybe he'd get lucky and Monroe would go the other way?

'Eric?' Definitely getting closer.

'Sorry, got to go.' Angus hung up and scrambled in behind the open door – just in time, because Monroe knocked on the door-frame and stuck his head into the room.

'Laura? You seen Eric?'

Angus squeezed himself back against the wall.

'Think he's doing a bacon-roll run, Boss.'

'Better be.' A worried edge slid into Monroe's voice. *'Any sign of our forensic psychologist, yet?'* Sniff. *'And what's that horrible smell?'*

'DC McVicar will know.' She turned. 'Angus . . .' Stared at him hiding behind the door. Blinked a couple of times. 'Oh. I . . . sent him off to review all the post-mortem policies and procedures. Want to make sure he's all up to speed and—'

'See if you can find him. We're on the clock here.'

'Yes, Boss.'

'*Thanks, Laura.*' Oh God, he was coming into the room. '*Well, at least we know they've been doing something.*' Most of him was still obscured by the door, but his arm and hand appeared, pointing at the whiteboards. '*Any of this make sense to you?*'

She followed his finger. 'Not really, Boss.'

'*Me neither.*' He turned, voice fading as he walked away, heading down the corridor. '*Now, where's Eric with my sausage butty . . .*'

As soon as he'd gone, DS Sharp closed the door, exposing Angus in all his hiding shame. 'Having fun?'

Come on: quick convincing lie.

'I . . . thought maybe I'd . . . be in the way?'

Well, that was crap.

She puffed out her cheeks, tilted her head on one side as she stared at him. Then smiled. 'You're a very, *very* strange man, you know that, don't you, Constable?'

Heat flooded Angus's face. 'Sorry, Sarge. It's just . . . Sergeant Massie made it clear I was responsible for Dr Fife, and stressed the importance of not letting the Boss down.'

'Let me guess: threatened you with the Naughty List?'

He nodded.

DS Sharp sooked air through her teeth. 'Yeah, you *really* don't want that. Sounds like you'd better go find your forensic psychologist, then.'

'Yes, Sarge.'

She checked her watch. 'So why are you still standing there? PM starts at nine.'

'Yes, Sarge!'

He grabbed his jacket and scurried off.

Not exactly dignified.

Angus jogged up Jessop Street, the beginnings of a stitch burning its way into his ribs.

The blood-red sky had faded to an anaemic glow, trapped between the valley's rim and the thick lid of clay-coloured clouds. Wasn't raining *yet*, but that was bound to change.

Without the illumination, St Jasper's Cathedral was a dismal lump of spiky granite, weighing the city down for its sins. What little daylight there was hadn't done a lot for the Bishop's View Hotel, either. Eighteen shades of grey, and all of them miserable.

He hurried up the stairs, taking them two at a time, and shoved through the hotel door into an old-fashioned reception bedecked with tartan and tweed, where dusty stags' heads glared down at him from the walls. A carpeted staircase led off to the upper floors.

A TV burbled away in the dining room: breakfast news to go with your full Scottish.

'. . . *localized flooding, causing travel disruption to the Aberdeen–Inverness line. And there's* more *rain and wind on the way . . .'*

Of *course* there was.

Half a dozen youngish men in sharp suits bustled down the stairs. All slicked-back hair, sunglasses, and neatly trimmed beards.

The one in the lead pulled out a silver cigarette case. '*Doamne, cred că ăştia au fost cei mai infecţi cârnaţi pe care i-am mâncat în viaţa mea.*'

One of his friends grimaced. '*Parcă ar fi fost făcuţi din rumeguş combinat cu păr de câine.*'

A third shook his head. '*Rahat de câine, mai degrabă.*' The others laughed. '*Putem, te rog, să ieşim mâine în oraş pentru micul dejun?*'

Angus held the door for them. Just because he was in a hurry, and they looked like an Eastern European Yakuza tribute act, that was no reason to forget his manners.

They hustled past.

A nod from Mr Cigarette Case. '*Mulţumesc.*'

Angus nodded back.

At the rear of the pack, someone had gone for the full Tony Stark. He gave Angus a cheery wave. '*Băi ce mare-i ăsta!*'

The guy next to him patted Angus on the arm on the way past. '*Vezi să nu-ţi manânce căpcăunul toţi copiii!*'

More laughter, and they were gone, heading out into the blustery morning.

No sign of a receptionist, or the grumpy, posh hotel manager, so Angus wheeched himself upstairs, making almost no sound at all on the carpeted steps – past landings and closed doors and more tartan than could possibly be healthy – to the third floor.

Only three rooms, each with a brass plaque screwed to the heavy wooden door.

He knocked on one marked 'BISHOP ISBISTER'. Not hard, just a polite *rap-a-tap-tap*. Then stuck his ear to the door. 'Dr Fife? Hello? It's Angus.' Didn't sound as if anyone was alive in there, so he had another go: *rap-a-tap-tap*. 'We've got the post-mortem at nine, Dr Fife.'

Angus peeked at his watch: twenty past eight, *already*.

DS Massie was going to kill him.

He knocked again, louder this time. 'Dr Fife! Are you awake?'

You know what? To hell with it.

Angus broke out his official Police knock. Three blows, hard and loud. 'DR JONATHAN FIFE, OPEN UP: THIS IS THE POLICE!'

What sounded like a strangled scream howled out somewhere inside, followed by a thump.

What if someone had got in there?

What if the press weren't the only ones who knew Dr Fife was in town?

What if the Fortnight Killer had decided to kill two birds with one hammer?

He backed away from the door, making enough space to kick the thing off its hinges, in five, four – raising his boot to slam it into the wood, just beside the handle – three, two—

The door opened a crack and a sliver of crumpled face peered up at him.

ABORT. ABORT.

Angus staggered sideways, pulled himself back upright again.

If Dr Fife noticed he'd *just* missed a boot in the gob, it didn't show. Instead, he blinked, smacking his lips as he ran a hand through his scruffy curls. Eyes bloodshot and baggy. He was wearing a long-sleeved T-shirt with a dragon on it – and going by the bare chunk of hairy knee and shin on show between the door and the doorframe, very little else. Something weird made a bulge in the dragon's forehead, about the size of a milk-bottle top. As if Dr Fife had a weird piercing in the middle of his chest, though it could've been a lumpy pendant necklace. Which would make more sense. 'Where'm I?'

Angus stared.

He wasn't even *dressed*.

'The post-mortem starts in thirty-eight minutes!'

Dr Fife had a scratch. 'This isn't California . . . ?' Then a huge yawn cracked his mouth wide open, showing off that American dentistry, leaving him even more droopy than before. 'Who are . . . Why are *you* here?'

'Because the post-mortem *starts* in *thirty-eight minutes*! You already missed Morning Prayers.'

'Like all sensible deities, I don't answer prayers till after lunch.' He closed the door in Angus's face. *'Come back later.'*

Oh no you don't.

The Official Police Knock rattled the wood. 'I WILL KICK THIS SODDING DOOR IN!'

It opened again, revealing a lopsided glare. 'It's twenty past one in the morning!'

'Get dressed. We've only got *today* to catch this guy, before someone else dies!'

Dr Fife crumpled sideways, groaned, then gave the door a wee dunt with his forehead. 'Have you Neanderthal assholes never heard of jet lag?' He squinted up at Angus. 'Get me some coffee and I'll think about—'

'I . . . just . . .' Jaw clenched. Blood fizzing. 'If you're not . . . in like, *two* minutes!'

'All right, all right.' He shut the door again. *'God, I hate morning people.'*

II

Come on, come on . . .

Angus checked his watch, waiting for a gap in the traffic so he could charge across the roundabout and onto Castle Hill Infirmary grounds. Quarter to. Fifteen minutes till they opened Douglas Healey-Robinson up on the cutting table. He could do this. He could.

If only the bastard traffic would stop for *five seconds* and let—

A woman in a cherry-red MX-5 flashed her lights at him.

He ran for it, waving a thank-you on the way.

Oldcastle's main hospital was a sprawling mass of ugly buildings. Some red-brick Victorian, with mean little windows and cheerless façades, others in concrete-and-steel with all the personality and visual appeal of a haemorrhoid. And both types needed a bloody good wash.

The twin chimneys of the hospital incinerators loomed over everything, spewing clouds of thick porridge-grey out into the awful morning as whatever the hell they were getting rid of burned. Red lights winking away at the top, warning aircraft to steer well clear.

He jogged between the maternity hospital and the kids' unit, towards the main building – a rambling jigsaw of a place with various bits and wings sticking out – getting slower, the pain in his side jabbing and stabbing with every breath. Thighs chafing against his damp trousers. Shoes slapping against the wet pavement as he stumbled on.

A gap between two wings led to a gloomy canyon that descended a good twenty feet below street level, lined with scuffed concrete, pipes, wires, and ducting.

He ducked under the black-and-yellow barrier blocking the road, and hurpled into the shadows.

A loading bay lurked at the bottom – easily big enough to take an articulated lorry – but the roller door was down, exposing the words 'MORTUARY SERVICE ENTRANCE ~ AUTHORIZED VEHICLES ONLY'.

Angus limped to a halt at the security door, set off to one side. Clutching his aching ribs with one hand as he mashed the intercom button.

Buzz, buzz, buzz, buzz, buzzzzzz . . .

Come on, come on, come—

A distorted voice crackled from the speaker, bearing the squished vowels of a heavy Polish accent. '*Yellow?*'

Took three goes to get his voice to work, through all the wheezing and coughing. 'It's DC . . . MacVicar . . . Here for the Healey-Robinson . . . post-mortem?'

'*You are cutting it a bit fine, are you not, Detective Constable?*'

As if he didn't already know that.

'Please, I'm going to be late!'

'*Probably, yes.*'

But the intercom buzzed again, and the door clicked open.

Angus barged through into a bare concrete space that echoed his footsteps as he hurried past a small, clean, silver-grey van with 'MCCRAE & MCCRAE ~ FUNERAL SERVICES' picked out in discreet gold lettering.

Its rear doors were open, but there was no sign of anybody. Or any *body*.

A black line ran across the floor, disappearing under a pair of battered double doors.

Right.

He limp-jogged over there, shoving his way into a short, manky corridor. The walls were scuffed, the waist-high trolley plates all dented and scratched, because this was the one bit of the hospital where it didn't matter how rough or careless you were – the patients weren't going to complain.

The black line ended at a double-wide lift in battered stainless steel.

He jabbed the 'Down' button three, four, half-a-dozen times.

'Please, please, please, please, please . . .'

His phone jingled into life.

Probably DS Sharp, or DCI Monroe, wanting to know where the hell he was.

But when he pulled it out, in its ziplock freezer bag, it was Ellie's name that glowed in the middle of the screen. Along with the time – 08:51.

Which meant he really didn't have time to talk to her.

Especially if she was just going to rub his nose in it about missing the show last night.

What in God's name was taking this *rotten* lift so long?

He stabbed the button a few more times.

Then answered Ellie's call.

'I can't really talk right now.'

'And here's me trying to do you a favour, you ungrateful sod. But if you don't want my help . . . ?'

Finally: the lift dinged at him, the doors juddering open slow as treacle. Soon as there was enough of a gap, Angus squeezed inside and jabbed 'Close Doors'. Over and over and over again.

Shockingly enough, it was every bit as miserable in here. Sagging ceiling tiles, and a faint whiff of mildew and mouldy sausages. Dents in the walls, the terrazzo floor patched with duct tape. A smattering of stickers ran around the inside, just above the handrail: lots of them wheeched off Fyffes bananas; a good few marked 'Easy Peel Satsumas'; several 'Are You YES Yet?' saltires; half a dozen explicit ads for escort services; and, for some strange reason, a whole litter of bright-pink Peppa Pigs.

And the doors *still* hadn't closed.

He gave up on the button and battered the one with 'Mortuary' on it instead.

'Look, Ellie, I'm sorry, but now's not a good—'

'How was your super-special celebration dinner, Mr I'm-Too-Moral-and-Bum-Faced-to-Go-to-the-Theatre-with-My-Oldest-Friend?'

The doors finished their painful crawl into the walls and started in again. Creaking and groaning like Methuselah's knees.

'I'm on my way to a post-mortem, so—'

'*Macaroni cheese again?*'

'Liver stroganoff.' Which would've been sad enough at the best of times, but when you were looking forward to a massive Chinese blowout feast? 'And I was late home, so it'd been sitting out since—'

'*That's great.*'

The doors clunked shut at long last and the lift shuddered its way down into the building's depths, while Angus stared at the illuminated letters. Which changed so slowly it *hurt*: LB, B1 . . .

Ellie's voice fizzed and *burrrrr*ed from the phone's speaker, getting more distorted the further down he went. '*Your top-secret FBI Profiler woulddddn't happen to . . . a Dr Jonathan Ffffife, wouuuld he?*'

Oh, bugger.

Angus went very still. 'Ellie? Please don't.'

'*. . . get him to talllk . . . me, we couldddd . . .*'

'*Please*: you can't publish anything about him, or he'll stop helping and people will die!'

'*. . . fnnnn . . . in . . . tomorrrrrrow's pappper . . . itttttt . . .*'

'Ellie?'

Nothing but the grinding moans coming from the lift's mechanisms.

'Ellie!' He pulled the phone from his ear and gawped at it.

'No Signal'.

Oh, this was *not* good.

This was not good *at all*.

The lift convulsed to a halt, with a *ding*, and the doors started their interminable crawl open again.

Angus didn't wait. He stuffed the phone back in his pocket and shoved himself sideways through the gap, soon as they were far enough apart.

Down here, in the guts of the building, far below the bits patients ever got to see, it was a warren of grubby corridors and hidden rooms – the ceiling obscured by a thick layer of yet more ducts and cables and wires and pipes.

He picked up a bit of speed, hurtling into the labyrinth, following the black line past storage cupboards and caged-off recesses full of abandoned equipment.

Around the corner, elbows and knees pumping – straight past yet another pair of bashed double doors.

Wait, wait, wait . . .

The black line had disappeared from beneath his feet. Angus skittered to a halt. Turned and backtracked to the doors. A wee plastic plaque sat beside them: 'MORTUARY SERVICES'.

OK.

Angus barged through into an antiseptic corridor, bathed in the dark-brown scent of death and disinfectant – wheeching his jacket off on the way.

He grabbed a white Tyvek oversuit in the changing room, ripping it from its plastic cover and scrambling into the thing's groin-and-armpit-constricting embrace in record time. Swapping his shoes for a pair of white wellies, before snatching purple nitrile gloves, a facemask, and safety goggles from the dispensers. Yanking them on as he waded through the ankle-deep antiseptic bath on his way to the cutting room.

Stainless-steel workbenches and cupboards gleamed in the LED spotlights. Slate-grey tiles on the floor. A couple of big flatscreen tellies, hooked up to a laptop.

Three of the walls were that wipe-clean plastic finish you could use as a whiteboard, but the fourth was completely made up of refrigerated drawers, a winch running on rails along the ceiling in front of it.

Two cutting tables dominated the room, beneath matching CCTV globes – like the glittering black eyes of some vast morbid insect.

Luckily, the extractor fan was going full pelt, because Douglas Healey-Robinson's bloated remains were laid out on the nearest table. Before, he'd been covered in dried blood and mould, but someone had washed him, meaning the bruises stood out in harsh contrast to his pale waxy skin. Every puncture wound a black slash.

And even with the extractor running, you could still taste him in every breath. Sour and rank and sickly sweet, all at the same time.

Three people, in the full SOC protective gear, had gathered in front of the table, and they all turned to stare as Angus staggered to a halt – wellies squeaking on the floor. The PPE would've made it impossible to tell who was who if they hadn't written their names on them in black Sharpie: 'PROFESSOR MERVIN TWINING', 'LAURA SHARP', and 'BLAIR MONROE'. No sign of Dr Fife.

DS Sharp checked the clock mounted above the eye-wash station. Nine o'clock, on the dot. 'Talk about skin of your teeth.'

Monroe stiffened. '*Constable*. You should've been here half an hour ago!'

'Sorry . . . sorry, Boss.' Propping himself up against the nearest worktop, breathing like a leaky bicycle pump, sweat running down the small of his back and soaking into his pants. 'I had . . . had to wake . . . Dr Fife up . . . and . . . and he's—'

'*Surprised it took you this long.*' Fife emerged from behind the table – the rotten sod had been hidden by DCI Monroe.

'How . . .' Angus *stared*. 'How did you . . . ? But . . . ? I waited . . . waited outside . . . for ages!'

'Did you? Wondered where you'd got to.'

'But . . . It . . .' He blinked at DS Sharp. 'Sarge?'

She breathed out, inflating her mask like a wee fabric airbag. 'Well, the important thing is everyone's here now.' Her gloved finger came up, purple and pointing. 'But don't *touch* anything, break anything, or get in the way.'

He sagged. 'Sarge.'

Then glared at Dr Fife.

This was all *his* bloody fault.

Fife hadn't bothered to write his name on his chest, presumably because it would be hard to mistake him for anyone else, but his SOC suit fitted perfectly. Which was kind of *weird*, because wouldn't he need to roll up the legs and sleeves? And if not: how come *his* was impeccably tailored when Angus's suit was doing its best to crush both testicles and Heimlich his oxters.

Unfortunately, Angus's glower failed to wither Dr Fife to dust, or cause him to spontaneously combust. Instead, the cheeky bastard launched into a jaunty whistled rendition of *Entry of the Gladiators*.

A side door opened, and in lumbered someone else in the full SOC kit, carrying a lumpy wooden stool thing. 'PAVEL WIŚNIEWSKI', according to the Sharpie words printed across his chest. So probably the guy who'd buzzed Angus through the security door. The accent confirmed it: 'Here we go. I knew he was back there, somewhere. The refit, she has been good, much easier for cleaning, but everything so difficult to find now!'

He unfolded the stool into a tiny set of steps and put them down in front of Dr Fife, who climbed up, till he was much the same height as everyone else. Well, everyone except Angus.

'That's better.' Fife rubbed his gloved hands, as if he was *actually* looking forward to this. 'Shall we begin?'

Professor Twining nodded. 'Pavel, start the recording, will you?'

His own personal Igor limped over to a bank of switches and poked at them until red lights winked on in the nearest CCTV unit.

A solid *bleeeeeeep* came from a speaker somewhere.

'Thank you.' Twining cleared his throat. 'Post-mortem beginning on IC-One male: mid-to-late thirties, one metre eighty-one – or five foot eleven and a quarter in old money – eighty-two point five-six kilos; preliminarily identified as one "Douglas Matthew Healey-Robinson". Present are Professor Mervin Twining, APT Pavel Wiśniewski, DCI Blair Monroe . . .'

Angus sidled over to Dr Fife as the pathologist went through the preliminaries. Keeping his voice low and sharp. 'How? *How* did you get here before me?'

He matched Angus's whisper: 'I drove. You were the one said we were in a hurry.'

'Why didn't you tell me you had a car? I *ran* here!'

Professor Twining moved on to lifting the victim's limbs, peering at them and dictating away, while Pavel snapped photographs with a big digital camera – its flash turning everything into a strobe-light freeze-frame, bouncing back from all that stainless steel.

'You weren't in the corridor when I locked up, so I *naturally* deduced that you'd be waiting for me in the car park, round the back.'

'I was out front!'

'Well, how was I supposed to know?' A lopsided shrug. 'You didn't show, so I drove myself over here – on the wrong side of the road, I might add, in a strange city, without caffeine, after only a couple hours' sleep.'

'Oh, for God's sake.'

'Ahem!' DS Sharp turned and gave them both the evil eye.

Dr Fife nodded, back to full volume again. 'Quite right.' He turned and placed a gloved finger against Angus's facemask. 'Shhh . . . Constable. You're spoiling the autopsy.' Then faced front again.

Leaving Angus standing there, making frustrated little penguin gestures.

Because what the hell else could he do?

External examination over, Professor Twining placed the blade of his scalpel into the little dip between Douglas Healey-Robinson's clavicles, slicing through the skin from there, down the midline, up and over the bloated stomach, and down through the tangled mat of belly hair to just above the poor sod's willy. 'Abdomen is distended, probably as a result of decomposition, but we'd better check if there's been a puncture of the gastrointestinal tract.'

His assistant fetched a squeezy bottle as Twining made delicate slices and worked his left hand into the body.

'We start by making a small pocket in the extraperitoneal soft tissue of the anterior abdominal wall . . . there we go. Pavel?'

Pavel stepped in and squirted water into the freshly made pocket, then backed away from the table.

'OK.' Twining readied the knife. 'I'm going to nick the peritoneum, so you *might* want to hold your breaths for this bit.' Whatever he did, the water bubbled and frothed in the cavity, while the stench of death got much, much worse.

Angus's throat contracted, stomach clenching as if someone was trying to turn it over with a shovel.

DS Sharp flinched.

Monroe coughed, shifting from foot to foot.

Everyone else seemed completely unaffected.

Dr Fife leaned in towards Angus, dropping into a whisper again. 'Steady . . .'

Wasn't easy, but he swallowed down the rising tide, forehead prickling, the sweat turning chill on his back.

As the gas escaped, the body slowly deflated, leaving Douglas Healey-Robinson's once swollen stomach slack and baggy – a miserable balloon, two weeks after the party's over.

Twining nodded. 'And that answers that.' He swapped the scalpel for a much bigger, curved knife. 'Right, let's open him up!'

Pavel hefted the bulky, purple-black slab of liver out of Douglas's abdomen. There can't have been much left in there, because a sizeable array of innards was already spread across two stainless-steel trolleys. All of it dark and slimy and *stinking*.

After two weeks, the liver had decomposed to the point that it oozed between Pavel's gloved fingers like some sort of beetroot jelly.

Angus wobbled. 'Oh God . . .' It was barely more than a breath, but Dr Fife squeezed his arm, leaned in close for another whisper:

'Are you gonna barf?'

'I'm fine . . .'

Deep breaths.

The liver splatched down on the scales and Angus gagged as the whole world shrank – till there was nothing in it but that seeping, foul, glistening mass. A whistling noise grew louder as warmth pushed its way through from the back of his skull, tinting everything yellow. Some sort of weird, furry, *floating* thing was happening to his knees. And a bead of sweat trickled down the side of his face.

Dr Fife squeezed again. 'You *owe* me.' Then cranked his voice up to full volume, patting at his SOC suit as if it had hidden pockets. 'Goddamnit – I've left my notepad in the car. I *can't work* without my notepad.' Laying it on a bit thick.

'Are you . . . ?' Monroe stared at him. 'We're in the middle of a *post-mortem*!'

Pavel wiped his gloves on some tissues, turning the blue paper black. 'We have notebooks in office. I get you one.'

'No, I need to keep observations and insights in a *very* particular fashion, otherwise my system doesn't work. I simply *must* have my notepad.'

'Sorry.' Professor Twining looked up from the remains, both

arms elbow-deep in Douglas Healey-Robinson. 'Much though I'd love to, I can't just put everything on hold. I've got three more bodies to get through before lunch.'

Dr Fife snapped his fingers. 'DC MacVicar: my keys are in locker six. Be a good little detective constable and fetch my notepad. Back seat of the green hire car' – pointing vaguely towards the multistorey outside – 'in that big parking garage. Might be a Ford?'

Angus blinked at him.

'You heard the man.' Monroe clapped his gloved hands a couple of times. 'But for goodness' sake: get a move on. We need all the help we can get!'

Stiff as a board, Angus marched from the room, back into the changing area. Where he struggled out of his wellies and sprinted for the toilets. Barging into the nearest cubicle, throwing the seat up – followed by everything he'd ever eaten in his whole life.

12

Angus made his way along the parking bays, past row after row after row of wobbly-looking hatchbacks, rusty estate cars, and the odd four-by-four that might have managed three-by-three at a pinch.

Why did no one visiting hospital have a *nice* car?

Not that he could talk.

Even a manky old Fiesta, held together with cable-ties and hope, would've been better than Shanks's pony.

This floor of the multistorey was wrapped in metal cladding that hid the outside world from view, but clearly wasn't waterproof, because the puddles stretched across the concrete, joining up to form lochans and lakes. Shimmering with oil in the gloom.

Maybe he should get another bicycle?

Trouble was: the flat wasn't big enough to store it inside, so the little gits would probably steal it. Again.

He stopped and held Dr Fife's keys out. Pressing the button. Doing a quick spin around to see if anything flashed its lights at him, because '*It* might *be a Ford*' wasn't exactly a lot of help.

Nothing flashed, or beeped.

Time to try Ellie again.

He wandered towards the ramp up to the next level – five down, one to go – and selected her name from his contacts. Held the phone to his ear, while he tried plipping a few more locks.

'*You've reached Ellie Nottingham. I can't talk right now, but if you've got a breaking story for me: leave a message.*' Followed by a harsh electronic '*Bleeeeeeep*'.

'It's me. Again. I need you to call me back, Ellie – it's *important*. OK? Soon as you get this. Bye.'

He hung up and tried one last plip.

No joy.

Angus slogged his way up the down ramp, ignoring the big red 'NO PEDESTRIAN ACCESS!' sign, and out onto the top layer.

They hadn't bothered putting a roof on this level, leaving it open to the elements instead, but wrapped around in more of that waffle-metal screening. There should've been a view down the valley and across the river from here, maybe a nice vista of the castle, or Kings Park; instead, he was treated to a cluster of miserable concrete buildings, poking up above the screens – full of miserable people, with their miserable ailments, lying in their miserable hospital beds.

OK, so Ellie wasn't answering her phone. Time to try a bit of lateral thinking.

He dialled the main office number.

'Castle News and Post, *Regional Newspaper of the Year, three years running. How can I direct your call, thank you?*'

'Hi, can I get Peter Ackerman, please?'

Hold music offended its way out of the phone's speaker: a pan-pipes rendition of Status Quo's 'Rockin' All Over The World', as Angus tried the plipper again.

There can't have been more than two dozen vehicles up here, but the first go produced nothing.

Creepy Pete's voice scrunched out of the phone, sounding as if he had a bag of crisps on the go. *'Fa's this?'* Munching away.

'Pete, it's Angus MacVicar. Ellie about?'

'Oh aye, sniffin' around, are you?' Crunch, munch, munch, crunch. *'Well, you can put it back in your pants: she's no' at her desk.'*

'Any idea where she's got to?'

'Nah. Women, eh? She's a bugger to pin down.' Swear to God, you could hear him licking his lips. *'But see when you do? Goes like a shonky washing machine on spin cycle, eh? Eh?'*

Angus tightened his grip on the car keys.

As if Ellie would *ever* have *anything* to do with a greasy wee shite like Creepy Pete . . .

She wouldn't. Would she?

'Look just get her to call me, OK? Soon as she's free. It's important.'

He plipped the key again and a bottle-green three-door Mini flashed its lights in reply. It had 'CAMBURN CAR HIRE' decals down the side and a big smiley emoji on the roof.

'Tell you: she's got an arse you could chew for weeks, *know what I—'*

'Got to go!' Angus hung up. Looked at his phone as if it had just peed in his hand. Shuddered. Then jammed it back in his pocket. Good job the thing was in a plastic bag, because there was something . . . slug-sticky-slimy about it now.

Angus marched over to the Mini and opened the driver's door.

The seat was pushed all the way forward, and a pair of Heath Robinsonesque pedal extenders filled the footwell – one attached to the accelerator, the other to the brake. No clutch, so an automatic.

But all that paraphernalia made it difficult to access the back seat from this side. He tried the passenger door, but there was nothing on the rear seat, or in the footwell, or the door pockets. Official bumf from the hire company in the glove compartment, but no notepad. Or in any of the vehicle's little cubbyholes. Or under the seats.

He popped the boot.

One cardboard box: marked '法夫醫生的特別訂單', containing dozens of rolled-up SOC suits in individual plastic wrappers. One small stepladder. And a holdall with various bits and bobs, none of which were a notepad.

Shitting hell.

He locked the car again and stood there as wind raked its claws across the parking level, head back, eyes closed.

Had to be here *somewhere*.

Try again.

He went back for another, more methodical rummage – splitting the car into quadrants and working his way through each of them, as if this was a crime scene.

Angus's phone rang when he was halfway through the back seat again.

About bloody time!

He yanked the thing from his pocket, but it wasn't Ellie's name glowing in the middle of the screen, it was 'Mum'.

Ah . . .

His thumb hovered over the button as his shoulders drooped.

Come on, he had a *job* to do. They were holding up the post-mortem, waiting for this stupid notepad.

Deep breath, and he let the call go through to voicemail. Then stuck his phone back in his pocket.

After all, if it was important, she'd ring back.

That didn't make him a terrible son, did it?

Probably.

But he resumed the search anyway.

Angus clumped down the stairs and out into the blustery morning – heading back to the mortuary.

Empty.

Sodding.

Handed.

Monroe was going to kill him. So was DS Sharp. And Dr Fife too. Doubt Professor Twining would be very happy either. Nearly an hour wasted.

He drooped his way past a clump of old brick buildings with a massive concrete extension out back. Stepped onto the grass to let a cluster of nurses hurry past in their scrubs and trainers. Watched an ambulance tear out of the A&E car park with its lights and sirens blaring.

There was no point in dragging it out: if he was in for a bollocking, might as well get it over with.

Shoulders back.

Chin up.

March . . .

Angus scuffed to a halt.

On the other side of the crossroads, at the heart of the Castle Hill Infirmary complex, was Dr Fife. All bundled up in his greatcoat, curly hair bouncing around in the wind.

Looked as if Angus wouldn't have to go all the way to the mortuary after all: the bollocking was coming to him.

Dr Fife scuttled across the road, Cuban heels clattering on the damp tarmac. 'Constable.'

'I couldn't find your notepad.'

But Dr Fife didn't stop to call him useless or incompetent, or a slack-jawed yokel – he kept on scuttling, straight past. 'Is your stupid bloody city always this cold?'

Eh?

Angus turned and strode after him. 'I said, "I couldn't find—"'

'That's because it's in my coat pocket, you idiot. Do you *really* think I'm unprofessional enough to attend an autopsy without my notebook?'

'But ...' Angus pointed towards the mortuary. 'Aren't we going—'

'Told them I'd seen enough to form my conclusions. No point hanging around for the whole squelchy performance.'

'But—'

'You seen one guy's skull sawn open and his brain scooped out, you seen them all.' Dr Fife dug his hands deep into his pockets. 'Actually, I knew this medical examiner in New Jersey who'd show off by removing the brain with the spinal cord still attached. Strangest thing you ever saw: like Satan designed a birthday balloon.' He glanced up at Angus. 'Point is, we showed willing, and no one saw you blowing chunks all over the body. You're welcome, by the way.'

Oh, for ...

'You could've *told me* it was a wild goose chase!'

A frown. 'You know what gets me about your Fortnight Killer? He's not very good at it.'

'I searched that *bloody* car, top to bottom. Twice.'

'Believe me, I've *seen* torture victims. The cartel people in Florida will keep you alive for days, sometimes weeks, while they go to work. Make an example of you that'll frighten children for generations.'

'I must've looked like a right twat.'

'But our guy? He's letting them bleed out in half an hour – forty-five minutes, tops.'

The car park loomed up ahead, in all its crappy-concrete glory.

'Maybe he gets overexcited?'

Dr Fife cut across the corner, heels squelching in the soggy grass. 'You read that book I gave you?'

'Give us a chance!'

'Read the book.' He hauled open the door to the multistorey, pausing on the threshold. 'Much though I hate to call your pathologist a useless sack of bullshit, someone needs to go back and review the autopsies on the first two victims. Figure out how our killer's MO is developing.'

'Want me to get you the PM reports?'

'Yeah, because I *love* paperwork.' He stepped inside. 'Ah, why not? I read the summaries on the plane over . . . yesterday? What day is it?'

Angus followed him into the echoing stairwell. 'Thursday.'

'Urgh. OK: get me the full autopsy reports. And the CSI – whatever-you-call-them-here – I want those too.' Straight past the stairs, to the door labelled 'Lifts To All Floors →', and into a cramped, grey, windowless room with a drift of empty crisp packets, Cornish pasty wrappers, and Pot Noodle containers in one corner. Because why *not* have your lunch in the most depressing spot possible?

Dr Fife hit the button. 'And I want access to all your crime scenes. Let's walk the ground, see the sights, smell the smells.' A sly look and a raised eyebrow. 'You'll like that.'

Oh ha, ha.

'It was the *liver stroganoff*, thank you very much. Which would've been a miserable enough dinner, but I was looking after *you* till half eleven, and it'd been sitting out all night.' The lift dinged its arrival. 'Not surprising I was unwell.' The doors slid open, smooth and silent. 'You'd've boaked too.'

Dr Fife clattered in. 'But first, it's time for an X-rated amount of caffeine. And breakfast! You got somewhere good does huevos rancheros?'

'Huevos . . . ?'

He reached up and poked the button for the top floor. 'You'll love it, settle that queasy stomach of yours right down.'

Angus grimaced at the closing doors. 'Can't wait . . .'

*

The stomach-rumbling scent of frying onions and sizzling batter frittered out from the hatch of Bad Bill's Burger Bar: a converted Transit van, parked between the pillars that supported the southern end of Dundas Bridge. Its dented side panels were painted matt black, and Bad Bill had chalked up the day's specials on them, in a multicoloured rendition of artery-hardening delights.

Bangs and clangs rang out across Queen's Quay, as the docks got on with their work – neon-blue flashes of arc welding strobing from the last industrial unit in the row.

Dr Fife sat behind the Mini's wheel, all bundled up, with the engine running. Frowning at the wodge of files Angus had liberated from Divisional Headquarters.

Douglas Healey-Robinson's post-mortem photographs lay spread across the dashboard, so it was probably just as well they'd got here before the lunchtime rush. They were a sight to put you off your Double Bastard Bacon Murder Burger and chips . . .

Angus hurried back towards the car, carrying a hot cardboard container, a large wax-paper cup – with a lid this time – and a wodge of napkins, which meant he'd had to pin the phone between his ear and his shoulder. Giving him a distinct list to the left.

'Can we not, Ellie? I didn't call to talk about—'

'No, I know that. It's . . . I was going to say something yesterday, but with the murders and everything – you seemed all excited and happy, and I didn't want to spoil it.'

'Then don't.' Sidestepping a venomous seagull. 'We need to—'

'All I'm saying is: if you want to do something next week – you know: mark the day – I'll help.'

No, he really didn't.

'He was your dad, Angus.'

That seagull was following him, eyeing the cardboard carton with avaricious yellow eyes.

'Angus?'

He popped the container and the cup on the Mini's roof and freed his phone. Kept hold of the napkins though, because they'd just disappear in this wind. 'I don't want to talk about it, OK? I want to talk about . . . what you said this morning.' He ducked down for a quick peek into the car.

Dr Fife had the lid of a highlighter pen sticking out the side of his mouth like a cigar stub. The rest of the pen made fluorescent-pink streaks through the text of what looked like Councillor Mendel's post-mortem report.

The important thing being: Dr Fife wasn't paying any attention to what was going on *outside* the car.

But Angus lowered his voice, just in case. 'You know? When we got cut off.'

Faux innocence radiated from the phone. *'This morning?'*

'You wanted to "do me a favour"?'

'Did I?' Like low-fat spread wouldn't melt.

'God's sake, Ellie, *please*!'

The seagull hopped up onto the Mini's bonnet, head cocked to one side as it worked out how to steal the lot.

'Urgh. You're no fun.'

Angus put an arm around the container and glared back. Which made no impact on the evil feathery sod whatsoever. 'Ellie!'

'Fine. There's going to be a big splash in tomorrow's paper: "FBI Specialist Helps Hopeless Cops". Front page; spread on four and five; comment – seven; a half-page vox pop; and a half-arsed opinion piece by some local D-list "celeb" wannabe I've never heard of.'

Well, that was just . . .

Yeah.

The seagull edged closer.

'I'm giving you a chance to present the investigation's side of the story. Cos I can tell you right now, you guys do not *come out well.'*

He held the phone against his chest and waved his napkins at the huge bird. 'Go on: bugger off!'

Didn't pay the slightest bit of attention.

Back to the phone.

'Don't tell me *to bugger off, Angus MacVicar! I'm doing you a solid here, you ungrateful—'*

'Not you: seagull.'

'Oh.' The anger drained from her voice. *'So what's he like, then – the mysterious Dr Fife?'*

'We need you not to, OK, Ellie? We . . . *I* need you to not publish anything about this guy.'

'*Really.*' And there it was, back again. '*You're censoring the press, now?*'

'Look, he's only here on condition we don't *tell* anyone he's here. If you publish: he's gone and we've got two more dead bodies tomorrow.'

'*What makes you think I can—*'

'Tomorrow, Ellie! Two people.' A shudder jiggered its way down Angus's spine. 'I've seen what this bastard does to his victims. You don't want that happening to *anyone* else.'

'*Not even Slosser the Tosser?*'

Two webbed feet landed on the Mini's roof and there was Captain Greedy-Feathers, only a couple of inches away, beak gaping open.

'WILL YOU *BUGGER* OFF!'

It scrambled into the air in a flurry of clattering feathers. *Scraw-wwwk*ing and *kyeee-kyeee-kyeeeee*ing as it wheeled away.

'Sorry. Seagull again.' He ducked down and looked into the car.

Dr Fife stared back.

Angus held up a hand and mouthed another 'Sorry'. Then back to the phone. 'Come on, Ellie, I'm begging you here.'

Captain Greedy-Feathers settled on top of Bad Bill's Burger Bar, lurking in the bridge's shadow, glowering avian hatred in Angus's direction.

A guy in grubby overalls scuffed past on his way to the food van; earbuds in, bum wiggling in time to the *tss-tss-tsss* that escaped from his ears.

Out on the river, a tiny, half-knackered fishing boat chugged past, dragging a pall of blue diesel smoke behind it.

'Ellie?'

A huge sigh. '*If – and this is a big if – but if I can get them to spike the story, they're going to need something juicier than a pat on the back for doing their civic duty.*' She let the pause hang there. '*I want an exclusive.*'

Of course she did.

'I can't promise, but I can ask.'

'*Better get your finger out then, hadn't you.*' The line went dead. She'd hung up.

Angus sagged against the car, head back, staring up at the grey blanket of clouds.

DCI Monroe was going to *love*—

The Mini let out a sharp *breeeeeep!* and this time, when he checked, there was Dr Fife doing a pantomime 'Well?'

Right.

He opened the car door, grabbed the container and cup, and squeezed himself into the passenger seat. Wouldn't have thought someone his size could fit, and yeah it was a bit tight, but it was nice enough inside – still had that new-car smell too.

Angus held out the wax-paper cup. 'French-roast arabica cappuccino, double shot, with almond milk.'

'Hmmph.' Dr Fife turned back to his file, taking the coffee without looking. Or saying thank you. 'Bet it tastes like dishwater and battery acid.'

Ungrateful sod.

Cardboard container, next. 'And they don't do wavy ranchers, so I got you a Kitchen Sinker.'

The coffee's lid was cricked back and Dr Fife took an experimental sip. Grunted. 'Could be worse. At least it's drinkable.'

'You taking this or not?'

There was a big theatrical sigh. Then Fife closed the PM file and accepted the carton, opening it to peer inside: one oversized Glasgow roll stuffed with a fried egg, a tattie scone, smoked bacon, slab of Lorne sausage, slice of black pudding, and a good dollop of own-brand ketchup – all topped with a slice of processed cheese. To complete the three-Michelin-star experience, Bad Bill had piled in a good handful of chips around the bun.

Angus stuck Dr Fife's change on the horror-covered dashboard, followed by the receipt and that wodge of napkins. 'You're welcome.'

The forensic psychologist grimaced at his breakfast. 'Can't imagine why people think coronary disease is a competitive sport in Scotland.' Hunching over the thing to risk a bite.

Manila files covered the back seat – a mixture of crime-scene reports and post-mortem results – each one marked 'OPERATION TELEGRAM' and 'NOT FOR DISTRIBUTION!' Angus gathered them up, sorting through the pile as he faced front again. 'Find anything?'

'Bet when you lot were cavemen, you deep-fried rocks.' Chewing away. 'Battered mammoth, anyone?'

'Must be *something* that can help.'

Another bite. 'What's wrong with a nice avocado and goat's cheese . . .' Horror broke across his face. 'God, there's yolk going everywhere!' Scrambling a couple of napkins off the post-mortem photos and scrubbing at his sleeve and chin. Then scowling at the eggy result. 'Of course there's something. There's *always* something. You just gotta know where to look.' Dr Fife twisted the Kitchen Sinker from side to side, as if working out the best angle of attack. Then went at it like a great white shark, talking with his mouth full. 'And I was right about your pathologist being a useless nutsack: any medical examiner worth her salt would've raised red flags all over the place.'

There was no point rising to it, so Angus flipped through the PM file on Michael Fordyce instead. 'There's that winning personality of yours again.'

'It's a simple matter of observation.' He pointed at Angus's file as the page turned, exposing a photo of the remains, laid out on the cutting table – stab wounds dark as night against the pale-moon skin. 'This guy probably thought the half-dozen three-inch screws stuck through the back of his hands was the worst thing that'd ever happened to him, but it was *nothing* compared to what our guy did next.' The shark went in for another mouthful. 'We begin with the percussive trauma – hammer blows to the elbows, forearms, collar bones, shoulder blades. None of it fatal, but by Christ that would've *hurt*. And you can scream all you like behind the gag, but no one's coming to save you.' A couple of chips succumbed to the feeding frenzy. 'Then the cutting starts: short, triangular blade; narrow profile; so probably a utility knife. And that seems to trigger something. No more than two-dozen shallow slashes and boom – suddenly we're stabbing and carving, veins and arteries, blood everywhere, only you can't escape, you're *stuck* there, screwed to the tabletop, *screaming*. And this whole time, the person you love most in the whole world sits right across the table watching it all. Unable to help . . .'

Jesus.

Angus swallowed.

The seagull glared.

And Dr Fife ripped into another egg-dribbling bite.

There couldn't have been much left in Angus's stomach, but what there was *lurched*. 'How can you eat and—'

'Because I do this for a *living*. And if you can't detach yourself, you'll end up in a padded cell or drinking yourself to death.' A slurp of coffee washed down the half-chewed mouthful. 'Then we turn to Jessica Mendel.' He raised his eyebrows at Angus. 'Go on, then.'

OK . . .

Angus closed the file on Michael Fordyce, and shuffled through the others till he got to the right one. Took a breath. Then turned to the post-mortem photos.

'We start exactly the same way: hands screwed to the desktop, hammer, utility knife. Then *boom!* Carotid artery, twenty-seven stabs to the back of the head as blood fountains . . .' He took a big greasy bite, the words barely making it out through chunks of sausage and black pudding. 'Douglas Healey-Robinson.'

Angus grimaced, turned the file face down, and scooped the photographs off the dashboard.

Little flecks of food tumbled onto Dr Fife's tie. 'Same damn thing, all over again.' He sooked the fingers clean on one hand, then plucked his wax-paper cup from the car's built-in holder. 'See, people don't set out to be serial killers. They don't wake up one morning and decide today's the day to go full-on John Wayne Gacy. They just have this *need* that's been festering away, back of their skulls, like an itch for years. Till finally, they just gotta scratch it.' A sip of coffee, frowning off into the middle distance. 'That first murder's the culmination of months, maybe *years* of fantasizing. Then he goes home and relives everything, over and over: what worked, what didn't; what made him scared, what made him hard. And he refines the fantasy to make it even better next time. To make it last.'

Angus shuffled the Healey-Robinson photos into a pile and turned them face down in his lap.

'Only with our guy, it doesn't: Jessica Mendel dies just as quickly as Michael Fordyce, and so does Douglas Healey-Robinson. He wants their partners to suffer, right? He shoulda learned *something* by now.'

'Maybe he's not very bright?'

Dr Fife sank his teeth in again. 'Bright enough to outsmart *you* guys for six weeks.' Catching a dribble of yolk. 'The longer you can keep Victim A alive, the more you can torture them, the worse it is for Victim B. So why's he so shit at it?'

The last chunks of Kitchen Sinker vanished, chased down by more coffee.

Angus returned the folders to the back seat. Not wanting to even *touch* them any more.

The chips went, one by one, dipped into spilled yolk and tomato sauce. Which was enough to make any sane man puke.

Chew, chew, chomp, chomp. 'See if it was me? I would've googled "how to use a tourniquet" at the very least.'

He tried not to shudder as Dr Fife cleaned the cardboard container with a finger – scooping up melted cheese and sauce and greasy bits of deep-fried detritus.

'Maybe . . . ' Angus frowned as that huge evil seagull dive-bombed the guy with the earbuds. 'Maybe the rage is part of the fun? He hammers and he cuts, and it gets him excited, and the rage is . . . I don't know. Like him climaxing or something.'

'It's a thought, anyway.' Dr Fife shut the carton and scrubbed his hands on napkin after napkin, till they were *slightly* less greasy-sticky, then stuck his phone into the little plastic mount thing slotted into one of the air vents. Leaving slick fingerprints on the screen as he brought up the satnav and poked in an address. 'First, we go check out Dr Fordyce's place. See if we can't get a feel for our guy.'

'Sure you don't want to go back to the station for a pool car?' Clicking the seatbelt into place.

'And give up my independence?' Dr Fife started the car, revving the Mini's engine a couple of times, like a boy racer. 'Besides, you drive like an asshole and I'd like to get back to the States in one piece.'

13

It was weird.

Back when he was a kid, Fiddersmuir always made him home-sick. Not for the crummy wee flat in Kingsmeath – for the place they had to leave behind in Aberdeen. OK, Fiddersmuir was far more out-in-the-country than Cults ever was, but it had the same feel of well-heeled wealth with its big houses and large gardens. Or it did if you stayed away from the more modern bits, which were all bungalows and turning circles. Plus it was right on the edge of Brae-cairn Forest: lair of monsters and elves and dragons and wee boys who'd lost everything and been moved down to a horrible flat in a horrible part of a horrible city.

And it was so much *brighter*, up here, beyond the lip of the valley. Free of the oppressive gloom that coated Oldcastle like black slime in a stagnant pond.

Mind you, going by all the Plot-For-Sale signs that sprouted in the yellow-grey fields, it looked as if Fiddersmuir was in for a crop of yet more bland, tiny, overpriced houses.

The developers had already laid a Harvest Road – a lopsided curl of tarmac that ended in a roundabout to nowhere.

Dr Fife took a right, onto Burnett Crescent, and Angus went back to the post-mortem file on Michael Fordyce. Avoiding the photos, because he wasn't an idiot.

Why did pathologists have to talk in medical doublespeak? Didn't help that they couched everything in 'conceivably's and 'possibly's, not wanting to be pulled up in court for saying something useful.

The car came to a halt and Dr Fife killed the engine. 'Well, this is . . . lovely.' He removed his phone from the dash-mounted holder and climbed out, letting in a jostle of cold air as the wind shoved at the car. 'You coming, or what?'

Angus shut the file and rubbed his eyes. 'Sorry.' Undid his seatbelt. 'Did you see anything in the PM results about needle marks?'

'Our guy didn't inject them with anything; it would've shown up on the tox report.'

Angus extracted himself from the passenger seat then reached in to grab a second file from the back: 'FORDYCE CRIME SCENE'. Clutching them tight as the wind tried to rip both from his grasp. 'It's not him putting stuff *in* I'm worried about.'

Instead of the usual cloned wee houses, someone had put up a line of apartment buildings – not tall enough to be blocks of flats – in a semi-Scottish-Baronial style, with crenellations and corbie steps.

There was a strange randomness to the blocks, with square and rectangular bits sticking out. Like a game of Tetris gone horribly wrong.

The development sat opposite a scabby expanse of grass and reeds masquerading as an 'EXCITING DEVELOPMENT OPPORTUNITY WITH OUTLINE PERMISSION FOR 120 HOMES!' The hoarding was falling to bits, though, so it'd been there for a while.

Angus checked the crime-scene file, then pointed. 'Eight C.'

According to a sign, there was a car park at the back of the building, but it clearly wasn't big enough, because several small cars were abandoned out here, parked with two wheels on the pavement.

Dr Fife bundled himself into his greatcoat, holding the collar shut with one hand as he clomped along. 'What, you think he's some sort of vampire, drawing blood? Didn't you have one of those already? Couple years ago?'

'No, I—'

'You did.' Lumbering up the stairs towards a door with a large cast-iron '8' beside it. 'There was a true crime podcast: *Kingdom of the Bloodsmith*. I listened to it on a stakeout. Half-assed sensationalist crap.' He ducked into the shelter of a tiny portico, stomping his feet and blowing into cupped hands.

Angus would've joined him, but it was too small to take both of them. 'That's not what I—'

'Any chance we can get a move on? I'm freezing my nuts off here.'

Angus pulled the bundle of keys from his pocket – all signed for, and labelled with little cardboard tags that fluttered in the wind like tethered moths. He slipped the one marked 'FORDYCE ~ MAIN DOOR' into the lock and pushed it open.

The stairwell was a lot plainer than the outside: magnolia walls, concrete steps, and a metal balustrade. Cobwebs blurring the upper corners, with a smattering of dead flies in them. A drift of takeaway leaflets on a small ledge. Two bland, flat doors leading off to Apartments A and B – one of which boasted a *serious* number of locks. The sound of a kid's TV show, turned up too loud, vibrating out from somewhere in the building.

But at least it didn't smell of wee.

Not that Dr Fife was impressed. 'Is *all* of Oldcastle this miserable?'

Angus stepped past him and headed up the stairs. 'If you hate it here so much, why did you come?'

'This is where the first victims lived.'

'Not *here*. Here: Oldcastle.'

The stairs doglegged around to the left, and when Angus looked over the banister, there was Dr Fife – struggling to keep up, pink-faced and already breathing hard.

'Call it . . . a moment . . . of weakness.'

Because of the wonky-lump architecture, the landing had three doors – one for each apartment and a glazed one that led to a small patio with stairs down to the car park. Which explained why people had parked out front. The rains had turned three-quarters of it into a lake.

Apartment C was still sealed off behind a cross of blue-and-white 'POLICE' tape. Angus tore it down then went hunting through the tags for the right key. 'No, look – the Fortnight Killer tortures them, but only for an hour or so, right? Before killing them? What if he's . . .' There it was. Angus slipped the key into the lock. 'Ever heard of something called andreenacoxing?'

Dr Fife staggered onto the landing and slumped sideways against the balustrade, wheezing and coughing. 'Why . . . do people . . . always have . . . to die . . . upstairs?'

'I heard, if you torture someone you raise their adrenalin levels, then you can harvest that from their spines and sell it.'

'Oh, you mean *adrenochroming* . . . and it's the kinda . . . conspiracy theory . . . bullshit . . . QAnon dickweeds . . . lap up . . . like spilt lube.'

'But I heard it was—'

'Think it through.' Dr Fife waved a hand, taking in the stairwell and the world beyond. 'There's a global conspiracy . . . to torture kids and . . . sell their body fluids? . . . And the only people . . . who can see the truth . . . are social-media halfwits . . . who all wear tinfoil underwear . . . in case the CIA are monitoring their balls?'

A sniff. 'Just a *suggestion*.'

He unlocked the door and stepped inside.

Wow.

The hall was completely bare: no coats, no coat hooks. No boots, no shoes, just a sisal mat, an ankle-high beech rack thing, and laminate floor.

The first door opened on a minimalist bathroom, the second: a minimalist bedroom. Then a minimalist study, a minimalist kitchen, and finally a lounge/dining room – which was the minimalistest of them all. It gave the whole place a . . . sterile feel, which was kind of ironic, given what had happened here.

A small white leather sofa divided the room in two. In front of it was a flatscreen TV, a white TV unit, and a glass-topped coffee table. The other half was home to a row of Ikea cabinets and the small dining table from the crime-scene photos, all of it grubby with a patina of fingerprint powder. The oatmeal carpet still had dimples in it from the common-approach walkway, but even though the scene examiners had taken it with them, they'd left the bloodstains and grubby grey footprints behind.

Angus put his hands in his pockets, not touching anything. 'Speaking of social media – I tried to find you on Facebook. Thought I'd send a friend request, as we're working together.'

Dr Fife limped into the lounge. 'My closet's bigger than this.'

'Only there was no sign of you, so I tried Twitter and Bindle and—'

'I got better things to do with my time than post pictures of my breakfast and beg randos for likes.' He ran a finger along the couch, clearing a white stripe through the grey. 'Don't think the neat freaks who lived here would approve.' Stepping into the middle of the room and turning slowly, frowning at everything. 'Tell me what you see, Angus.'

OK . . .

'Loads of blood?' Angus did a three-sixty of his own. 'How can you *not* be on social media?'

'Try harder. Look at the scene like it's a puzzle' – making a circle with his index finger – 'what's present' – he twisted the circle so it pointed at the floor – 'and what's *missing*?'

Angus went around again.

OK: blood on the wall behind the table, blood on the ceiling, blood on one half of the Ikea units. Which was understandable: you torture someone to death, that crap gets everywhere . . .

He stopped turning. 'Where's all the footprints? Not the dirty ones – that'll be the first responder and whoever declared death. Where's the *bloody* footprints?'

A raised eyebrow from Dr Fife. 'Because?'

'You do something like this, it gets on your clothes, it gets on your shoes. You'd tramp it all over the place.'

'Now look under the table.'

It was mostly clean on the side facing the couch, but the other side? Like someone had tangoed through an abattoir.

'The footprints just stop.' Angus straightened up. 'And unless the Fortnight Killer levitated out of here—'

'There we go!' Grinning like a parent whose kid went potty for the first time. 'And what can we hypothesize from that?'

There had to be a reason, right? Footprints don't just stop, unless . . .

Angus nodded. 'He's set up some sort of changing area in here. Somewhere you can strip off your bloody clothes and shoes without getting anything on the carpet.'

'And *that's* what we mean when we say "organized serial killer". Our guy's been planning this for a long time.'

Maybe Angus was quite good at this after all?

He paced in front of the table. 'You're leaving one body behind, but you're taking the other away. So you've brought a body-bag or something with you. Plastic sheeting?' Made sense. Ohh, and if you did that: 'Maybe you could repurpose the changing area? After all, it's got to be water-slash-blood-proof anyway.'

'And how do you get Dr Fordyce's body out of here? She wasn't exactly petite – not with all those muscles.'

Simple: 'Chuck her over your shoulder.'

'Yes, thank you, Paul Bunyan; most of us aren't built like a fork-lift truck.' Dr Fife rested his bum against the back of the sofa. '*We* would have to drag the body out, and what *don't* we see in this nice oatmeal carpet, where everyone who enters has to take off their shoes and put them in that silly, prissy little rack by the front door?'

Warmth seeped through Angus's cheeks and ears. Bit close to home, that. 'Drag marks.'

'So either our killer's a gorilla troll like you, or there's two of them.'

Angus opened his mouth, then closed it again.

That was genius.

'It's how he controls his victims! You need one hand to hold the screwdriver, one to hold the screw, and a friend to hold the victim's hands in place.'

'Knew you'd get there eventually.' Dr Fife beamed again. 'Actually, it's more likely to be a cordless drill-driver, but other than that you're bang on the nail. Well done. The Fortnight Killer has an accomplice.'

Bloody hell.

Angus puffed his cheeks out. 'Does the Boss know?'

'Gimme a chance: I've only been here five minutes.' He wandered from the room, fingertips tracing along the wall. 'I take it your fellow idiots were bright enough to check for CCTV?'

'Bound to.' Angus followed, in time to see him stroll into the study.

'Question is: where's he taking them, and why? Dr Fordyce, Councillor Mendel, Kevin Healey-Robinson. Could just leave their bodies at the scene and be done with it. Why go to all the extra effort, and risk?'

Angus stopped in the doorway.

It was the least austere room in the place, but that might have had more to do with necessity than aesthetics. The clean lines of three white Ikea bookshelves were spoiled by medical and accounting books. A pair of framed degree certificates blemished the walls. An uncluttered desk, dusty with fingerprint powder.

Dr Fife tilted his head on one side. 'No computer?'

'Erm . . .' Into the file again, flipping through the productions inventory. 'Looks like it was one of those all-in-one monitor-and-processor Apple jobs. Says here it's with the Forensic IT Unit.' Urgh . . . Hard not to grimace at that. 'Which means we can expect a result sometime next year. Or the year after. Half the IT team's got long Covid, and the other half's bloody useless.'

'Normally, you see a multi-victim crime scene, the perp leaves the bodies behind. Maybe stages a revolting little tableau before he goes.' Fife pulled out the office chair on its silent castors and clambered into it. 'There was one guy I caught: Bradley McCarthy, killed a family of six. Sat Mom, Pop, and the three kids round the dining table like they were eating Granny. She's laying there, on her back, all opened up like a blood-soaked Christmas turkey. Everyone with their own portion of breast and thigh.' He swivelled the chair from side to side, head cocked, eyes narrowed on the middle distance. '*This*, though: killing one, making the other watch. Then spiriting them away . . . That's kinda special.' Swivel, swivel, swivel – still squinting off into space. 'What would *you* do with Dr Fordyce, Angus? If you were a first-time serial killer, what would you do with your victim's wife?'

Easy: 'Kill her.'

The swivelling stopped. 'She's a *pillar of the establishment*, for God's sake. Her kind think you're scum. You're beneath her. The whole *point* here is to *punish* her!'

Ah, right.

So, what would be the worst thing you could possibly do to someone who'd been through all that?

'I'd . . . make her relive it, before I killed her. I can remember every single wound I've inflicted, but I want to hear *her* tell it. I want to hear what it's like to watch the person you love die. Means I get an extra wee frisson of excitement before I do the same to her.'

'Well, aren't you a sick little puppy.' The swivelling started again. 'And "frisson"? Better watch out, Detective Constable, people might think you've got some brains to go with all that brawn.' He huffed out a long breath, then hopped down from the chair. 'Think we're done here. Wouldn't mind a rummage through that computer, though – if your IT morons ain't gonna touch it. Any chance?'

'And screw with the chain of evidence? PF would throw a fit.' He followed Dr Fife out into the hall, where the forensic psychologist opened the front door and had a good peer at the lock. Then the handle. Then the frame. Then closed the thing and opened it three, four, five times.

Angus waited till he'd finished. 'We already know the locks weren't picked and the door wasn't forced.'

'Never trust someone else to do a thorough job. You'd be shocked how many morons wear a badge.' Smile. 'No offence.' Dr Fife stepped out into the hall, turned around and knocked. Stood there, as if he was expecting something to happen.

'Erm . . .' Angus shuffled his feet. 'Come in?'

'*Exactly!* They let him in. They opened this door wide and said, "Please: come inside and murder us!"' Dr Fife's heels clopped on the concrete landing, all the way to the glazed door, pulling what looked like a thick silver pen from an inside pocket. 'What's a PF?'

Angus joined him on the landing, locking the door to Apartment C with the borrowed keys. 'Procurator Fiscal. Are we telling the Boss there's two of them or not?'

Silence.

He was standing there, staring out through the door at the windswept patio with its swirl of leaves and puddled stairs down to the flooded car park.

'Dr Fife?'

'Be a good sidekick and check upstairs. See if you can spot a security camera anywhere. Maybe have a quick word with the neighbours.' He poomed the end off the pen and tipped a fat cigar into his palm. 'I'm away for a think.' But when he tried the door handle nothing happened – either jammed solid, or locked. 'Does *nothing* in this goddamned city work?' Then Dr Fife stuck the cigar in his gob and stomped off down the stairs.

Leaving Angus behind to do the grunt work.

'Lovely.'

Deep breath.

Sigh.

Who'd be a sidekick?

And up the stairs he went.

Angus thumped down the last flight of stairs and out onto the ground floor, into the lung-scraping fug of Dr Fife's cigar.

It *couldn't* still be the same one, not after over half an hour.

But there he was, leaning against the stairwell handrail, one foot up on the bottom step, puffing away. Looking disgustingly pleased with himself.

Well, that would stop right now.

'Hoy!' Angus folded his arms and loomed. 'You can't do that inside.'

A grin. 'Can't I?' Puff, puff, puff – thickening the fogbank. 'I'll have to remember that.'

Glowering at him didn't make any difference, so Angus knocked on the door to Apartment B instead. 'No one upstairs saw anything. Not even the auld mannie who smells of bin juice and hates foreigners.'

The grin widened, engorging the cigar's angle where it poked out of Dr Fife's mouth. 'Oh no. What*ever* will we do?'

No reply from Apartment B, so it got another go – the official *police* knock this time. *Boom, boom, boom . . .*

And when that didn't work, Angus wrote a quick note on one of his Police Scotland business cards and slipped it through the letter-box. 'Where now, Councillor Mendel's?'

'Oh, let's not be so *hasty*, Constable.' Pointing across the hall. 'Still got one apartment left, remember?'

Typical.

Would it have killed him to talk to the householder while Angus was upstairs visiting everyone else? Instead of lazing about, stinking the place up with that stupid cigar?

Bet Watson got this all the time.

Bet Holmes never lifted a finger to actually help out.

Angus grunted, turned, and raised his fist to knock on Apartment A's door. No messing about this time, straight to the police officer's hard three—

'Aren't you going to ring the bell?'

God's sake.

Fine.

He poked a finger into the glowing circle, and cheery, chirping birdsong warbled out from somewhere inside. Because why have a . . .

Wait a minute.

Angus edged closer to the door, staring at the doorbell.

Oh, you wee *beauty*.

He flicked through the Fordyce crime-scene file – going back and forward through the paperwork, but there was no mention of it at all.

Bloody hell.

Dr Fife pulled on a faux-English accent. 'By *Jove*, I think he's got it!'

They'd probably just cracked the case . . .

14

Angus pressed the bell again, kicking off another dawn chorus inside the apartment.

Still no response.

One more go, holding his thumb down till the birdsong got to the end of its recording and looped back to the beginning: tweeting and chirruping and trilling and answer the buggering door for *Christ*'s sake . . .

The birds were on their third encore when a muffled voice came trembling through the wood. *'Who is it? I've got a big dog in here! I'll call the police!'*

'Hello? Mrs . . .' Angus checked the list of residents. 'McManus? My name's Detective Constable MacVicar.' Producing his warrant card and holding it up to the spy hole. Then the doorbell. 'You can call the station and make sure I'm real, if you like?'

The only sound was Dr Fife, puffing away on his cigar – the end fizzing as he inhaled.

Finally a *click* rang out, followed by a *clack*, *rattle*, *clack*, and *clunk*, before the door eased open a couple of inches. Held in place by a pair of much-thicker-than-normal chains. Exposing the business end of three mortice locks in addition to the five-point security mechanism built into the door itself.

Looked as if Mrs McManus was keen on her security.

She peered out at them through the gap. A little old lady, with thinning grey hair, in a 'GARDENERS DO IT IN FLOWERBEDS!' sweatshirt, baggy denim skirt, tan tights and Clarks sandals. Wobbly fingers grasped the glasses hanging on a string around her neck, and pulled them on so she could blink at Angus's warrant card.

Then the door clunked shut, followed by more rattling, before opening all the way this time. 'It's about poor Sarah and Michael, isn't it? I heard on the radio you caught a man last night! How could he do something so *horrible*?' Every time she moved a tiny pale puff of animal hair floated out into the hallway.

'Mrs McManus, you . . . All the extra security' – pointing at the locks – 'is this new? Did you put it in after what happened upstairs?'

She nodded, setting free yet more hairy wisps. 'My Clint did it for me. He's a good boy: a solutions architect for a global IT company!' The proud little smile soured. 'But his taste in men is terrible.'

'I'm sorry to hear that. But did he install the lock and doorbell after . . .' Angus looked towards the ceiling, then back again. 'Or before?'

Please, please, please, please . . .

'Oh, he came round and put my new locks in the *very day* after we heard.' Pressing a palm against her chest. 'He's always worried about me, living here on my own! What if the Fortnight Killer comes back?'

Bugger.

And they'd been so close.

Wasn't easy, hiding the disappointment. 'No, no. It's . . . Clint sounds like a good son.' One last lingering gaze at the doorbell. 'I suppose it was too much to hope for.'

The smile returned, creasing dimples into her cheeks. 'If you like I can give you his phone number? You could meet up for a drink? Or a nice romantic dinner?' Looking Angus over like a freshly plucked chicken. 'I think he'd like you.'

What?

Yeah . . .

Angus puffed out his cheeks. 'That's very . . . *kind* of you, Mrs McManus, but—'

Dr Fife slapped him on the arse.

'Hey!'

'He'd be delighted to get Clint's number. He's just been telling me how *terribly* lonely it is, being a policeman.'

Angus stared at him. 'Now wait a—'

'Shut up.' Dr Fife shouldered his way forward, pushing Angus out of the way. 'Mrs McManus, you said Clint installed the *locks* after it happened; but the doorbell's been there a lot longer, hasn't it.'

She clearly wasn't expecting to see someone like Dr Fife standing on her doorstep, because she blinked down at him for what felt like a long, long time.

Then shook herself out of it. 'Oh, ages and ages. There were *burglaries*, and Clint said you couldn't be too careful.'

'There we go!' Dr Fife rubbed his hands together, cigar standing to attention. 'Now, we just need to come in and take a look at the footage.'

She pursed her lips, eyes fixed on the thing smouldering away between his teeth.

He took it out, holding the cigar closer so she could get a good look. 'Does this bother you?'

A wee sigh brought with it the sweet, buttery scent of Werther's Original. 'Reminds me of my Albert. He used to smoke one every Sunday after dinner, as a special treat.'

'Excellent.' Dr Fife stepped forward, but Mrs McManus didn't budge.

Instead, she folded her arms, hoiking up her bosoms as she scowled down her nose at him. 'I made the miserable sod stand out in the garden. Stinking, horrible things.' She jerked her head towards the main door, releasing a swirling miasma of fine hairs. 'You can come back when you've finished. And not before.'

Mrs McManus's apartment was a lot nicer than the bleak uncluttered crime scene upstairs. Her living room was filled with dark furniture, every surface covered with knick-knacks and porcelain figurines and glass fish and wee wooden things that looked a bit like mice from a distance. The walls were festooned with framed family photos, but pride of place – above the fake mantelpiece and fake fire – was a fake oil painting of a corgi dressed as Henry VIII.

An identical, though naked, corgi wheezed away on a rainbow hearthrug, licking its bits. Surprisingly difficult to ignore as it schlurped away.

Angus shifted on the floral-patterned couch, focusing on the TV instead – burbling away to itself in the corner of the room.

It was tuned to one of the rolling news channels, where a cheery-looking spud in a suit and tie waved at his weather map. '. . . *which means it's likely Storm Findlay will hit slightly further* south *than expected tomorrow, so watch out for travel disruption in those high winds.*'

Dr Fife sulked in one of the armchairs, feet up on a little footstool, hair even curlier than usual after being made to finish his cigar outside in the rain. He narrowed his eyes at Angus and made a wee snorting noise. ' "Adrenochroming." '

'In fact, there's an amber warning *in place across the Central Belt and we're likely to see some local flooding as the day moves on.'*

'At least I'm trying, OK?'

'So do take care if you're out and about.'

'Think it through, Constable – what sort of idiot's shooting up tortured-kid adrenaline? How many diseases are you gonna get? A billionaire's risking hepatitis, syphilis, and HIV for something like that?'

'. . . *best of the weather will be in the northeast, where it's going to be unseasonably warm and dry. Temperatures in Aberdeen and Oldcastle could even get as high as* thirteen *degrees . . .'*

Angus poked the couch. 'If it's a global trade worth millions, how come a lab can't purify it? Or maybe they test the kids for blood-borne diseases *before* they torture them?'

'. . . *perhaps catch a scattered shower or two, but only if you're very unlucky.'*

'Don't be an asshole.' Brushing a soggy ringlet from his forehead. 'See, *that's* how conspiracy theories get you. Soon as you start trying to justify this snake-oil bullshit, you're halfway there.'

'Into Saturday, and those winds are going to fall away, but there's still this area of low pressure . . .'

The dog stopped cleaning its undercarriage and sagged there, panting at them. Grinning, as if their bickering was the best entertainment it'd had all week. Then went back to schlurping.

Angus cleared his throat. 'How did you know?'

'Not the first time I've dealt with conspiracy-spouting—'

'No: the doorbell. You *knew* it wasn't new. That's why you were being so unbearably smug out there.'

'*. . . unsettled weather from lunchtime across most of the country, but the good news is that by about eight o'clock . . .*'

'Elementary, my dear MacVicar. There's at least two layers of paint visible on the thing's plastic casing – where it's not been masked off properly last time they redecorated. You just have to know *how* to look at—'

'Here we go.' Mrs McManus shuffled in, carrying a tea tray laden down with three china cups, a teapot, sugar bowl, milk jug, a plate of fruit scones, and a battered iPad. She paused, frowning at the ancient corgi still polishing its bits. 'Missy! The nice policemen don't want to see you doing that.'

Schlurp, schlurp, schlurp.

Mrs McManus placed the tea tray on the coffee table, then hunted out the remote from beneath a pile of *Gardeners' World* magazines and pointed it at the telly.

'*. . . but keep an eye on this new weather system, moving in off the Atlantic. That's likely to—*'

'You'll have to excuse Miss Garland, she's got absolutely *no* decorum.' Pouring the tea, through a strainer, into a delicate cup. Eyebrows raised at Angus. 'Milk? Sugar?'

Those scones looked good. Nice and plump and full of raisins.

'Thank you, Mrs McManus.'

She was clearly a bit psychic, because she put a buttered scone on a wee side plate and handed it over with the tea.

And he was right about the scone. 'Mmmm, lovely.'

She poured another one. 'And for you?'

Dr Fife nodded. 'Black. Lemon if you've got it.'

'We have *milk* and *sugar*.'

He shrank in his armchair. 'Black's perfect. Thank you, Mrs McManus.'

'And no shoes on the furniture.'

He snatched his boots off the footstool, leaving his lower legs dangling over the edge of the seat. Which didn't look all that comfortable. 'Sorry.'

Didn't think it was actually possible, but Dr Fife genuinely seemed chastened. Humbled even. Which had to be a first.

Mrs McManus sniffed, then handed him his tea and scone.

Soon as he was eating, and making appreciative noises, she nodded. Opened the iPad. And poked at the screen. Before handing it to Angus, because clearly *he* was her favourite. Putting on a saucy-old-lady voice and batting her eyelashes. 'Maybe I should've deleted my browser history.'

'I won't look. Swear.'

An old-fashioned, black-and-white webpage filled the screen: 'WHOISATMUMSDOOR.CMCMANUS.DUNDASITWEBSPHERE.COM/ ?SV=22&P=DASHBOARD'. No fancy graphics or buttons, just a list of dates – in reverse chronological order, with today at the top – each one an underlined link.

Mrs McManus sighed. 'Not that there's anything dodgy in there. Unless Alan Titchmarsh in a cardigan gets your knickers fizzing.'

Angus scrolled, working his way back through time. 'Erm, Mrs McManus? There's nothing in the police files about your doorbell. Did no one ask about it?'

She settled into the other armchair and poured for herself. 'Oh yes. I spoke to a *nice* detective constable about it. Big lass. Needed her roots done. Not fat-big: *big*-big, like you' – Mrs McManus held her hands a good three feet apart – 'with the shoulders.' She stood, taking her tea over to the cluttered mantelpiece, where she popped her glasses on again and dipped into a Toby jug shaped like Charlie Dimmock. 'But there was a problem with the server, and Clint was in Belgium, and I promised to get in touch soon as it was fixed, and . . .' Her mouth drooped at the edges. 'And I forgot.'

She pulled a Police Scotland business card from the jug and held it out, the other hand covering her lips as her forehead pinched.

Angus took the card. 'DC BONNIE LINTON.'

Name seemed familiar. Not entirely sure why, though.

Mrs McManus turned her back on the room. 'I'm such a silly old *fool*.'

'It's OK.' Dr Fife hopped down from the armchair and patted her on the arm, voice soft and kind. 'We all make mistakes.' Then shuffled over beside Angus, leaning on the sofa and frowning at the iPad's screen. 'Soon as you're ready.'

Angus's finger slid up the smooth glass, setting the list birling away until the beginning of February appeared. And there it was: 'FRIDAY, 2ND FEB →'. The day Dr and Mr Fordyce met the Fortnight Killer.

He tapped the screen and the list of days disappeared, replaced by another one, made up of fifty or sixty filenames, each one linking to a timestamped video.

Dr Fife pointed. 'Start with the last one.'

>> {#Link.VideoObject} 23:24:19_HALLWAY. MP4 →

The hall outside Mrs McManus's front door appeared, slightly distorted through a fisheye lens. Then the main door swung open and in shambled Mrs McManus and Miss Garland, returning from what must've been a late-night walk. There *was* sound, but it was all tinny and pretty much inaudible. Even whacking the iPad's volume up full didn't help.

The real Mrs McManus peered over Angus's other shoulder. 'We like to have our constitutional last thing before bed, don't we, Missy?' Lowering her voice to a whisper, presumably so Miss Garland wouldn't hear. 'Don't want any night-time accidents.'

He closed the video, and tapped the next file:

>> {#Link.VideoObject} 23:09:48_HALLWAY. MP4 →

A man and woman staggered in, laden down with shopping bags. Both dressed in jeans and heavy coats. He couldn't have been more than thirty, but most of his hair had already abandoned its post. She sported a bobble hat and a disappointed pout.

'Bob and Dianne. His mum's in a home with dementia. Dianne's got a funny womb, but they're trying IVF.'

Soon as the door closed the bickering started – all jerky chins and bared teeth as they disappeared into the apartment opposite.

Mrs McManus tapped Angus on the shoulder. 'Ooh, I know: would you like to see my Clint?'

Her *what*?

Dr Fife stared at her, both eyebrows up.

Oh, her *Clint*. Her son. The systems architect.

But before Angus could decline the offer, she was off.

>> {#Link.VideoObject} 22:51:26_HALLWAY. MP4 →

A big grey blob filled the screen, then faded into the middle distance where it transformed into the back of Mrs McManus's head. The rest of her appeared as she hurpled away from the camera, with Miss Garland trotting along at the end of her lead. Heading out for their no-night-time-accidents walk.

>> {#Link.VideoObject} 22:02:49_HALLWAY. MP4 →

A weary woman in a faux-fur coat trudged past the camera and lumbered her way upstairs. Yawning.

Angus pointed. 'Apartment D: Miss Jensen; does the money-slash-business show on Castlewave FM. Took two Valium and zonked out for the night.'

Mrs McManus reappeared in the living room, holding out a framed photo of a middle-aged man with a neatly trimmed beard, in a shirt and tie, at some sort of presentation dinner – holding up a pointy award in Perspex and stainless steel.

'Well, that is a coincidence!' Dr Fife nudged Angus with an elbow. 'He looks *just* your type, doesn't he?'

Oh, ha sodding ha.

'My Clint came top of his class at Dundas University, you know. He likes horse riding and sea fishing and he's a *huge* Oldcastle Warriors fan.'

Took some doing, but Angus forced a smile, and clicked on the next link.

>> {#Link.VideoObject} 19:38:02_HALLWAY. MP4 →

A woman, dressed in a soggy blue tracksuit, staggered through the main door, puffing and panting, face shiny and puce. She stood there, hunched over and steaming – a headtorch making a puddle of light around her mud-spattered trainers.

'Poor Molly's been struggling to lose the baby weight, especially since her John ran off with a traffic warden. Apartment E.'

>> {#Link.VideoObject} 19:08:27_HALLWAY. MP4 →

A much-fresher-looking Molly-From-Apartment-E jogged down the stairs, pausing to run on the spot while she checked her sportswatch-fitness-tracker thing, before clicking on her headtorch, hauling the door open, and boldly setting forth into the evening gloom.

Mrs McManus hugged her son's photo – his face pressed against her sweatshirted bosom. 'It's just a shame Clint's always drawn to these *broken* people. His last boyfriend, Mark, was nice enough, but oh my Lord, the things he came out with!'

>> {#Link.VideoObject} 18:42:49_HALLWAY. MP4 →

The latest star on *What Happens in the Stairwell* was a woman, wearing what Mum's catalogues liked to call 'active leisurewear' – early thirties, medium-height, straight nose, glasses, with a messenger bag slung diagonally across her chest. Her brown hair was stuffed under a red baseball cap with something written on it. No idea what, though, because she didn't look left or right as she marched over to the main door and out of the building.

'Oh, according to Mark the Earth's *flat*, but we're all too brainwashed by the mainstream media to realize it. I said: "Well, if that's true, why didn't I fall off when I won that round-the-world cruise?"' She lowered her voice as if about to impart some flat-world-shaking secret. 'You had to say why Branston Beans are best, in twenty words or less.' Then back to normal again. 'But Mark swore blind that ships and aeroplanes just go round and round the edges.'

Wow. Clint really *did* have crap taste in men.

>> {#Link.VideoObject} 18:20:58_HALLWAY. MP4 →

The same woman entered the building and went straight to Apartment B, dipped into her messenger bag, and came out with a handful of fliers. Popped one through the letterbox.

'And don't get me started on his silly "Why NASA faked the moon landings" nonsense.'

The flier woman crossed the hall, giving the doorbell's camera a distorted close-up, making her nose look even longer than it was. It also revealed what was written on her baseball cap: 'MAKE PIZZA GREAT AGAIN!'

Then she was bounding upstairs, taking the steps two at a time. Off to dole out more junk mail.

Mrs McManus put down her cup and examined the pot. 'Would you boys like some more tea?'

'That would be lovely, Mrs McManus.' Anything to distract her from playing matchmaker.

She poured Angus's tea first, throwing in a wink for good measure.

>> {#Link.VideoObject} 18:01:22_HALLWAY. MP4 →

This time, the people stumbling in from the cold February evening didn't need an introduction from Mrs McManus – they were familiar faces to anyone who'd been paying any attention to the news over the last month and a half. Dr Sarah Fordyce and her husband, Michael. Coming home for the last time.

They looked happy, all swaddled up in matching parkas, noses and ears pink from the cold. He was cradling a big plastic bag in his arms, with the Punjabi Castle logo on it.

'Sarah and Michael.' Mrs McManus blinked, eyes glistening in the iPad's glow as she welled up. 'Oh, I can't look.' She grabbed the empty scone plate and bustled off.

Onscreen, the Fordyces kissed.

Then raced upstairs, laughing.

Angus's shoulders dipped.

They seemed nice, even if their flat was horribly bleak.

And a few hours later, they were dead.

>> {#Link.VideoObject} 17:27:30_HALLWAY. MP4 →

Next up was a pizza-delivery guy, complete with one of those big padded backpacks in the shape of a cube – the Pizzageddon logo was plastered all over it, another one on his cap. It was on his jacket too. *And* the two pizza boxes in his hands, carried like a sacrificial offering to the gods of Can't Be Arsed Cooking Tonight. Even his trousers were striped with red, white, and green.

He was maybe late twenties? Just shy of six feet, wide face, prominent ears, shoulder-length hair, and a stubble/beard combo. The kind of guy who wouldn't have looked out of place fronting a rock band. Not a very successful one though, or he wouldn't be dressed like a bell-end and doing this for a living.

Straight past the camera and up the stairs he went.

>> {#Link.VideoObject} 17:03:19_HALLWAY. MP4 →

Mrs McManus and Miss Garland made their third appearance, hobbling inside after another constitutional. The woman and her dog both looking their age: tired and cold and lonely.

Maybe her system-analyst son wasn't the catch she thought he was.

Angus shook his head. 'Beginning to think we got our hopes up for nothing.'

No response from Dr Fife, though. He just stood there, squinting at the screen, forehead all wrinkled and creased. Chewing on his bottom lip.

>> {#Link.VideoObject} 16:40:51_HALLWAY. MP4 →

Mrs McManus and Miss Garland headed out for their walk, the wee corgi straining at the leash, dancing about, excited to be off on a new adventure. More like a puppy than an OAP.

Which was sweet.

>> {#Link.VideoObject} 14:09:11_HALLWAY. MP4 →

A postie trotted down the stairs, Royal Mail pouch bouncing against his leg as he made for the door.

Angus sat back on the couch. 'And that's us all the way back to lunchtime.' He gave the room a half-arsed shrug. 'Worth a try, though, wasn't it?' His finger drifted up to close the browser, but Dr Fife's hand snapped out and slapped his wrist. 'Hey!'

'Go back.' Swiping a thumb on the screen. 'There.'

>> {#Link.VideoObject} 17:27:30_HALLWAY. MP4 →

The delivery guy shoved in through the main door, carried his pizzas past the camera and off up the stairs.

Dr Fife minimized the video, then clicked on the one immediately before it in the list:

>> {#Link.VideoObject} 18:01:22_HALLWAY. MP4 →

Dr and Mr Fordyce bundled in from the cold, with their Indian carry-out. A kiss, then, laughing, they climbed the stairs to be tortured to death.

'Thirty-four minutes later.' The toast-rack creases smoothed across Dr Fife's brow. His mouth twitched into a smile that bloomed into a grin. 'He doesn't go out again.' Poking the screen.

>> {#Link.VideoObject} 17:27:30_HALLWAY. MP4 →

The pizza-delivery man entered the building, carrying two boxes in his hands, crossed the hall, and disappeared upstairs.

Dr Fife thumped Angus on the arm. 'The guy comes in, but he never goes out!' Then Fife was off, bustling from the room.

Great.

Angus grimaced at Miss Garland. 'The man's a total nightmare.' But he wrestled free from the sofa's chintzy embrace and followed him, down the hall and into a cosy kitchen full of travel-the-world tea towels and biscuit tins in the shape of corgis.

Mrs McManus was standing over the sink, propped up by the worktop, shoulders quivering. Barely making a sound.

'It's OK.' Dr Fife took her hand. 'It wasn't your fault.'

She gave a little hiccupy breath. Sniffed. 'I forgot to call . . . the policewoman. If . . . If I wasn't such a . . . *stupid* old bat, maybe those other . . . those other people wouldn't have died!'

'It's not your *fault*.' Voice gentle as he stroked her arm. 'Sometimes this is just how life works.'

'I'm so . . . I'm so sorry.'

'Hey, you're helping now, right? Course you are.' He glanced back at Angus. 'Mrs McManus, can my friend here borrow your iPad for a minute? I need him to check something with the upstairs neighbours.'

Soon as he stepped outside, bitter air clamped around Angus like a fist – squeezing the last gasp of warmth from his lungs. It plumed in the chilly afternoon for a second, before the wind ripped it apart. Above, the sky was tarmac grey, low and threatening.

Angus hurried down the steps and across the road to Dr Fife's Mini.

He was conked-out in the driver's seat, reclined all the way back, gob hanging open. A wee trickle of drool seeping into the hairy bit at the side of his mouth.

Suppose it was a shame to wake him.

Still . . .

Angus rapped on the window, good and hard.

Oops.

Dr Fife jerked awake, staring about at his surroundings like a startled mongoose. Then the door opened, and he scrambled out. 'Jesus.' Instantly clenching, then pulling the greatcoat tighter around himself as wind screeched in across the unfulfilled Exciting Development Opportunity. He rubbed his eyes. 'Awake. Definitely awake.'

'I checked with the upstairs neighbours – none of them ordered a pizza that night.'

'Is it always this *cold*?' Dr Fife wrapped his arms around himself. 'I got a big fridge freezer: goes down to minus twenny-five and it's *still* warmer than goddamn Oldcastle.'

'And we know the Fordyces got a curry.'

'Hell, my *first wife's* warmer than this.'

'But . . . what if it was just the wrong address? Maybe he went out the other door? The one onto the patio?'

Dr Fife stomped his feet. 'Yeah, but *why*? Where's he going with these pizzas nobody ordered? Mrs McManus says the car park's been flooded since before Christmas. What: this guy's *wading* back to his car, for funzies?' A shiver. 'Nah, you do that if you're shifting a body and don't want some asshole seeing you. Plus there's the takeaway rucksack. Guy's got it on his back, but he's *still* carrying two pies by hand?'

Eh?

'*Pies*?'

'Pizza pies: keep up. Why take them out before you get to the customer's door? Lot more hassle to carry them up the stairs in your hands, right? *But* it means your nice big takeaway rucksack's got loads of space for a couple tarpaulins, a body bag, change of clothing, and a cordless drill.'

So Angus had been right the first time: they really *had* cracked the case.

A huge grin pulled his face wide. 'Wait till the Boss hears we've—'

'Oh no you don't.' Dr Fife hugged himself tighter, nose and ears turning cranberry red. 'We're gonna check it out first. Just because it quacks and waddles, don't mean it's a duck.'

'But—'

'It's OK for *you* – you're just a detective constable – I got a reputation to protect. I'm not going to Monroe with some half-assed theory without doing some due diligence.'

Noooo . . .

If Monroe found out they'd kept something this big from him, he'd make Stalin and Pol Pot look like Teletubbies. Not to mention what DS Massie would do. And Angus was *not* going on her Naughty List.

'But—'

'Unless you *want* a repeat of Patrick Crombie? If that's the case: be my guest.'

Ah.

Yes.

Well.

When you put it like that . . .

15

The stomach-rumbling scents of hot cheese and garlic wafted through the pizzeria like a siren's call, and Angus's stomach sang a wistful lament in reply. Gurgling and growling away.

Pizzageddon sat halfway down Clay Road, in Castle Hill, wedged in amongst a handful of other restaurants. The place was bigger inside than it'd looked from the street – kitted out with bare wooden boards on the walls, red-leatherette booths, industrial lighting, with soft rock dribbling out of the speakers. Kind of faux-Italian-trattoria-meets-Manhattan-diner style.

A big wood-fired oven radiated heat from the open kitchen area, supplying those delicious smells for the handful of people who'd braved the wind and rain on a crappy Thursday lunchtime in March.

Dr Fife looked up from his eight-inch Pepperoni Apocalypse, a long string of mozzarella looping from the slice in his hand to the plate below. 'Will you sit still and eat your pizza? Look like you've got rats in your pants.'

Angus glanced at the untouched *twelve-inch* disc of ham and mushrooms and cheese sitting in front of him, then away again as his stomach yodelled. 'I . . . I'm not hungry.'

They'd taken a booth at the rear of the restaurant, because apparently it was *deeply* important that Dr Fife sit with his back to the room, just in case any paparazzi happened by.

Not sure if that was paranoia, rampant egotistical delusion, or both.

'You're the size of a school bus, of course you're hungry.' Another bite, chewing as he talked. 'So how come *you* don't have a nickname? "Teams like 'em", right?'

Angus kept his eyes on the door. 'Some people are more nicknamey than others.'

'We could call you "Frisson"?'

'When we first moved down here, a bunch of kids at the new school called me "Silent G", till I pointed out how not funny it was and asked them *nicely* to stop.' He held out both hands, flexing them into fists. 'I got a two-week suspension. No one bothered me after that.'

Over by the counter, a small child wailed that it wanted McDonald's instead.

Someone in the kitchen dropped a metal tray, setting it ringing against the tiled floor.

The insipid music blanded on.

Dr Fife shrugged and wolfed down a chunk of crust. 'Eat your pie.' He picked up the next slice and used it to point at Angus's plate. 'Ain't nothing wrong with this. And I spent seven years in New York, so I *know* pizza.'

Might as well get it over with.

Angus sat up straight. 'Look, I've no idea how much they pay detective constables where you come from, but over here it's not a lot. OK? That's why *I didn't order anything.*'

Bite. Munch, munch, munch. 'You ever thought about marrying into money?' Wiping cheese off his hairy chin with a napkin. 'I tried it once: the second Mrs Fife, *very* successful psychiatrist with a Manhattan firm. Her father owned half a dozen canning factories and meat-processing plants, upstate. Absolutely loaded.'

Well, that explained a lot. 'So you're rich.'

'She got the house, the cash, the stocks, the shares, the wolfhound, the inheritance, and custody of Megan. *I*, on the other hand . . .' drawing it out for effect, '. . . got screwed.'

Oh.

Dr Fife went in for another bite. 'Never get romantically involved with a psychiatrist, Angus, they're far too devious by half. Plus, they know what you're up to long before *you* do. And that's—'

'Here we go.' The manager was back, carrying a plate of garlic bread in one hand, a mixed salad in the other, and a laptop jammed into his oxter. His wasn't a *big* man, but he had the kind of sagging wattle neck that suggested he used to be much larger, then lost a lot of weight too quickly. He wasn't fooling anyone with the wispy dyed-black combover, or the fake orange tan, though. Like the rest of the staff, he was dressed in the restaurant's signature uniform of jeans, black T-shirt, and a red-white-and-green-striped waistcoat clarted with USA-type badges. 'Sorry that took so long, we're having problems with the chip-and-pin machine.'

The bowl and plate went on the table, followed by the laptop, then he scootched into the booth, beside Angus. Frowned at Angus's plate. 'Something wrong with the Mushroom Hamageddon?'

'I'm sure it's lovely, Mr Wilson, it's just—'

'DC MacVicar's skint.' If there was any justice in the world, the forensic psychologist's head would've exploded under the force of Angus's glare, but he helped himself to a forkful of salad instead.

Mr Wilson waved that away. 'Don't, please. Your lot caught the wanker painting swastikas and "Jews go home!" on every window in the street. Least I can do.'

A deep rumbling howl sounded deep within Angus's stomach. But he stuck to his principles and left the pizza alone.

'God's sake . . .' Dr Fife rolled his eyes. 'If you're worried someone's gonna accuse you of taking bribes—'

'It's a question of *propriety*.'

'It's a question of being an idiot.'

Mr Wilson opened the laptop. 'If it helps: your Chief Superintendent is in here every fortnight with his wife and I've never let him pay once.' Poking at the keyboard, waking the thing up. 'Now, I checked all the takeaway delivery logs and there's nothing down for Fiddersmuir on the second of February. It's outside our free-delivery zone, so there would've been a five-pound surcharge too.'

Hello . . .

Dr Fife polished off another curl of crust. Voice all calm and neutral, as if that hadn't confirmed their theory. 'What about delivery drivers? Anyone quit round about then? Or got fired?'

'No. We're one big, happy, Pizzageddon family. Lots of our staff have worked here since we opened.' Mr Wilson reached for a bit of garlic bread, but halfway there seemed to realize what he was up to and slapped his own wrist.

'Do you sell merchandise? Baseball caps, jackets, that kind of thing?'

Angus dug out his phone and brought up a screengrab of the pizza-delivery man from Mrs McManus's doorbell camera.

The picture wasn't great – bit blurry and grainy – and only in profile as the guy marched past Apartment A, but it was all they had.

Mr Wilson frowned at it. 'We sell *hats*, but not the . . .' His eyebrows shot up. 'Bobby!'

Yes.

Angus held the phone closer. 'You recognize him?'

'What? No. Bobby, one of our delivery team – someone broke into his car and cleared out three Tattie Tornados, a Pepperoni Apocalypse, two Chicken Cataclysms, and an Anchovy Earthquake. Took the uniform, hot-bag, everything. It was just before Christmas and the poor sod thought we were going to take it out of his pay.'

Urgh . . .

So close. *Again.*

Mr Wilson shrugged. 'Sorry.'

Dr Fife crunched his way through a forkful of salad, frowning in silence as the manager fidgeted – eyes drifting back towards that plate of garlic bread.

Then: 'Can you get your security cameras up on that thing?' Dr Fife pointed his fork at Angus. 'He's carrying two pizza boxes, right? Might make a more convincing disguise if they were hot, so you get the smell.'

'Ah, yes.' Mr Wilson closed the delivery log and called up a much more professional-looking system than Mrs McManus's Clint had cobbled together. 'You're in luck – we upgraded everything, including the computers we keep our footage on, when that swastika-spraying Nazi wanker appeared. We've got weeks and weeks and weeks on disk.' He clicked and scrolled, tongue poking from the side of his mouth. 'Second of February, second of February . . . Here we go.'

Click, and the laptop screen split into eight separate views of the restaurant's interior, each with a timestamp in the corner, reading '08:30'. Mr Wilson selected the camera overlooking the counter and till. 'Assuming he didn't get it delivered to another address, he'd have to come *here* to collect his order.'

The video whizzed, fast-forwarding through the day, but although plenty of people came and went, there was no sign of their man.

When the timestamp flickered through 17:27 Angus groaned. And not just because his stomach was tying itself in knots at the prospect of that Mushroom Hamageddon sitting right under his nose. That was the time the pizza-delivery man was marching into number eight Burnett Crescent. 'Anything after this is too late.'

Dr Fife scowled at his slice. 'Sonofabitch.'

'Sorry.'

'Run it again; slower this time.'

Mr Wilson clicked the footage back to the start and set it running while he helped himself to a slab of garlic bread. Not bothering to slap his own wrist as he took a big buttery bite.

Onscreen, families marched in and out of the restaurant, people paid, servers added up bills.

Then, not long after ten to five, a woman wandered up to the counter – early thirties, active leisurewear, messenger bag, red baseball cap.

'Why do I . . . ?' Dr Fife frowned as she spoke in silence to the man behind the till.

Angus pointed. 'Must've been in to collect her fliers.'

'Sorry, fliers?' Mr Wilson pulled his chin in, concertinaing his wattles.

'For the restaurant.'

'Oh, no. We don't do one-shot marketing: nobody wants them through their letterbox anyway, so it's basically spam. Not to mention the potential littering problem.'

Dr Fife shuffled closer. 'Play that bit again – normal speed.' He glanced at Angus. 'It's *her*, isn't it?'

'Hold on . . .' Angus logged onto the restaurant's Wi-Fi and brought up the web page Clint had built – username: 'MUM', password: 'MISSGARLAND' – and wheeched through to the appropriate footage. Watched the clip, then held it out. 'She's the one handing out fliers.'

'On the very same night two people died.' Dr Fife plucked the last slice from his plate and ripped out a triumphant mouthful. 'Nature and criminal investigations *hate* a coincidence.'

On the laptop's screen, the woman stayed at the counter as the guy she'd been talking to headed off – returning a couple of minutes later with a pair of pizza boxes. She paid with contactless, then disappeared out of shot.

'Where'd she go?'

'One sec.' Mr Wilson minimized that video and brought up another one showing the front of the restaurant: three tables, the entrance and the big plate-glass window overlooking Clay Road.

The woman took her pizzas across the screen, and out through the door. She turned right, which meant she was still visible through the window as she handed both boxes to a man. The picture wasn't great, but he definitely had shoulder-length hair and a beard.

The pair of them headed off down the street, leaving the shot.

'Where's the outside cameras?'

There was a bit of *erm*-ing, then Mr Wilson brought up a camera mounted above the front door. Not that it was any use – there was a reason people up to no good wore hoodies and/or baseball caps. 'Maybe we need another camera? Sorry.'

Everybody frowned at the table.

Mr Wilson helped himself to the last slice of garlic bread.

Angus's stomach howled.

And then a slow smile dawned across Dr Fife's face. 'She paid for her pizzas with a card. That means *we know who she is*. Right?'

The laptop's keyboard rattled as Mr Wilson brought up what looked like accounting software, clicking through it until a popup appeared. 'Six minutes to five, one medium Veggie Volcano and a large Meaty Maelstrom. The card issuer doesn't give us names or addresses. We don't even get the full card number, just what kind of card it was, the last four digits, a bunch of asterisks, and an authorization code.'

'Goddamnit.' The smile faded.

Time for Angus to save the day: 'Yeah, but if we can get a *warrant*, the bank will give us everything else.'

Dr Fife's smile was back. '*Now* it's time to call Monroe.'

Every day in Oldcastle brought another blow to your faith in humanity. Like the pair of tossers walking their dogs in the wee toe-nail curl of parkland on McDonald Crescent, a two-minute walk from Pizzageddon. One greyhound, one bulldog, both landmining the grass with turds.

And did either of their owners stop to pick up the steaming munitions?

Did they hell.

Angus shifted in the passenger seat of Dr Fife's Mini, phone clamped to his ear as the silence grew.

Should march right over there and arrest the pair of them for contravening the Dog Fouling (Scotland) Act 2003. Well, maybe not *arrest*, because enforcing the Act was *technically* down to the local authority, but that wasn't the point. It was the principle of the—

'*Hold on, wait.*' It'd taken a while, but DCI Monroe had finally found his voice again. '*There's* doorbell *footage? Why is there doorbell footage? Why don't we already have that?*' The sound went all muffled as he did something to the phone. '*Rhona! Burnett Crescent: Angus says there's film of the Fortnight Killer on someone's video doorbell! What the pricking prick is going on? Why haven't we seen it?*'

Her voice was barely audible in the background. '*Give us a minute . . .*'

Angus scowled as the greyhound's owner sodded off down Buchan Road, poopless. 'We haven't got a name, but we're one hundred percent it's the same man on the Pizzageddon security cameras.'

Monroe was back to full volume, suspicion oozing from his voice. 'Definitely, *definitely*?'

'Well, eighty percent definitely. Maybe seventy-five? But we're certain it's the same woman.'

More silence.

The bulldog owner watched her dog scraik its back paws through the wet grass, then hauled it off towards Dunstan Drive. She'd almost reached the edge of the park when she came to a sudden halt – both arms out for balance as she peered at the underside of her shoe.

Hmph . . .

Served her right.

She limped away, scraping her foot along the grass like Quasimodo in a pencil skirt.

'Boss?'

No reply from Monroe, but DS Massie had clearly returned from her task, sounding more than a little sheepish. *'It was buried in the actions. Bonnie was supposed to chase it up, but then she had to go on that course, and . . .'* Cough. *'And it kinda got lost in the shuffle?'*

'Oh, for God's sake, Rhona, this stuff's important!'

'I know, I know, but she went on that crime-scene-management course, and she was meant to hand everything over, and then we found Douglas Healey-Robinson's body, and . . . Sorry?'

The driver's door popped open and in climbed Dr Fife, bringing a takeaway pizza box with him. Flaunting his leftovers.

Angus covered the phone's microphone. 'DCI Monroe. There's been a bit of a cock-up.'

'What a shock.' He held out the pizza box. 'Here: take.'

They'd been *over* this.

'I'm not accepting—'

'And give me the phone.'

Oh. Right.

Angus did what he was told. 'Don't use all my minutes.'

A frown. 'Why's this thing in a goddamn baggie?' He ripped the plastic off. 'Monroe? . . . Fife. If it *is* our guy he fits the profile we've got so far. There's pre-planning: stealing the uniform; means of entry: "Hi there, pizza for Dr Fordyce? Oh, you didn't order it? Must be a thank-you from a grateful patient, it's paid for anyway, so you might as well have it"; and most importantly: an accomplice.' Dr Fife listened for a bit, rolling his eyes. 'Yeah, well, how do *you* think he gets the missing victims' bodies out of there? . . . Yeah, *exactly*. And that's why we need the warrant . . . Cool . . . OK . . . Uh-huh: soon as you like . . . Thanks.' Dr Fife hung up and tossed the phone back to Angus. 'He's gonna get us a court order for Flier Girl's credit-card details.'

Angus gave the phone a quick look over for greasy fingerprints, then hid it away in a pocket before anything else happened. Passed the pizza box back across the car.

Only Dr Fife wouldn't take it. 'Don't worry – I explained about the stick up your ass, and Mr Wilson decided to give the free pizza to *me*. It's mine now. And I'm loaning it to you.'

'But—'

'You can pay me back later.'

. . .

Fair enough.

And it did smell delicious.

16

Technically, this end of Sadler Road was in the posher bit of Kingsmeath, north of the railway line – where the council houses looked a bit more prosperous, fewer bone-thin Alsatians roamed the streets, and almost no one had a clapped-out washing machine or saggy old sofa in their front garden. Yeah, there was the occasional rusty, wheelless car up on bricks, and you could buy hash, snork, coke, E, jeelies, and meth from any number of local entrepreneurs, but it was *still* nicer than the bit Angus lived in.

Sadler Road connected the two halves – bridging the gap between the have-nots and the have-even-lesses.

Angus checked his watch: 16:30.

Pfff . . .

They'd parked four doors down from number one-thirty-two: a semi-detached, post-war two-storey in a big, long row of identical houses. All grey-and-beige-stained harling, corrugated tile roofs, the paintwork peeling on their door-and-window-frames. Tiny gardens with rampant box hedges that encroached on the pavement.

All except for number one-thirty-two.

Its other half, one-thirty-one, looked as if it'd been left to rot for at least a couple of decades, but one-thirty-two boasted new uPVC windows, a bright-blue door, a fresh paint job, and a tiled portico. Very swish. A driveway ran up the side of the neatly trimmed garden, ending in a new-ish garage, whereas next-door's ended in a knackered Transit van and a Jenga pile of pallets.

Dr Fife gave a little snore and shifted in the driver's seat – reclined all the way back, greatcoat draped over him like a blanket, eyes closed, gob open.

Angus looked past him, through the window, and out across the playing fields that bordered the other side of the street. Separated from Sadler Road by an eight-foot-high cage of saggy chain-link. A bunch of wee kids were out playing a game of after-school rugby, slogging their way through the muddy grass while a miserable clump of parents looked on and a masochistic PE teacher blew his whistle.

Today was turning into a proper trip down memory lane.

Meathmill Academy must've shrunk since Angus escaped its academic clutches, because it seemed absolutely massive at the time. The buildings lurked on the far side of the playing fields, about as welcoming as a bus shelter full of sick. The primary school next door was a bit better, with its colourful play equipment, but both backed onto the railway embankment – a towering, thirty-foot mound of grass and weeds, sealed off behind yet another line of chain-link fence.

All a massive culture shock for a wee boy who'd arrived from private school in Aberdeen not long after his dad died . . .

Angus opened the empty pizza box again, searching for any crumbs of crust or flecks of cheese he'd missed the last three times.

Nothing but greasy stains remained.

Dr Fife cracked an eye. 'You'll wear the pattern off the cardboard.' He closed the box again. 'So why *aren't* you on social media?'

'Cos it's a complete waste of everyone's time.' He shifted in his seat, pulling the greatcoat up to his nose. 'Besides, you gimme someone's username, and fifty bucks says I'll have them geolocated in twenty minutes, tops. And I do *not* want people geolocating *me*.' He closed his eyes again. 'Now shut up. Trying to sleep here.'

Pfff . . .

The wind played a mournful tune on the chain-link fence.

High up above, clouds whipped across the dirty sky.

A walker-less dog ambled by, pausing only to tag the nearest lamppost.

'Don't know how you can sleep when we're *this* close to catching the Fortnight Killer.'

Dr Fife scrunched his face up. 'I *can't* sleep, because you keep yammering on!'

'You know what I mean.'

A pained growl, then a sigh hissed free. 'OK, look: stakeouts are five percent running about, kicking in doors, and shooting people; the other ninety-five percent is this. Sitting on your ass, waiting for something to happen, even though you know it probably ain't gonna. Like they say in the military, "You sleep whenever you can, wherever you can."' He wriggled beneath his greatcoat. 'Guy on a SWAT team in Nebraska taught me the method they taught *him* when he was a Navy SEAL. I can sleep on a rollercoaster if I need to.'

Cool.

Angus sat up. 'Can you teach *me*?'

'No. You're on lookout.' Dr Fife settled beneath his makeshift blanket again. 'Now shut your yap.'

Charming.

The overgrown hedges cowered and shivered in the wind.

A feral shopping bag billowed down the street.

Those poor kids lurched and staggered around the rugby pitch, slowly turning blue with cold.

Angus checked his watch again –16:32.

Urgh . . .

'Should've been here with that search warrant by now. Do you think I should chase them up? I don't want to come off all high and mighty.'

Dr Fife forced his reply out through gritted teeth. 'Then don't chase them up.'

Angus pulled out his phone – now ensconced in a fresh ziplock bag, because it never hurt to be prepared. No new voicemails. No new messages. 'But they should've *been* here by now.'

'Then chase them up.'

'Yes, but—'

'For God's sake! Chase them up, *don't* chase them up. I don't care, just pick one!'

Bloody hell. Bit unnecessary.

'I was only—'

'Graaaaaaagh!' Dr Fife cracked open one baleful eye. 'I got ninety minutes' sleep last night, my back's killing me, my body thinks it's seven in the morning, and I'm stuck in a stupid tiny car in a stupid freezing, windy, *shithole* city with a lumbering great halfwit WHO WON'T SHUT UP!' Glaring.

Angus folded his arms and thumped back in his seat, staring out the window.

Wind buffeted the Mini on its springs.

An eightsome-reel tornado of empty crisp packets danced by.

Dr Fife groaned. 'Sorry. I'm . . . tired. I don't think you're a halfwit.'

'Hmph.' He pulled one shoulder up in a non-committal shrug. 'Right.'

'But Oldcastle's definitely a shithole.'

Looking out at the crappy houses, it was hard to disagree.

Angus poked the contacts icon and scrolled through. 'I'm going to call them.' Listening to it ring and ring and ring, then:

'*DS Massie.*' Her voice was distorted, almost drowned out by the wail of a patrol car's siren and engine roar. '*Hello?*'

'Sarge? It's Angus. DC MacVicar? Erm . . . when the Boss got the search warrant approved, he said we should wait here for backup, and I was just wondering when it's going to—'

'*Did no one tell you? We got a DNA hit off the Healey-Robinsons' house.*'

He put a hand over the phone. 'They've got an ID!'

Dr Fife sat up at that, eyebrows raised.

'*Ask your arsehole doctor friend if the Fortnight Killer's got form for violence.*'

'They want to know if the Fortnight Killer's got a criminal record.'

Wrinkles concertinaed the forensic psychologist's forehead. 'If he *does*, it's more likely to be for minor stuff. He's been saving up his savage desires for this. Experimenting in secret.'

Back to the phone. 'Only wee stuff. Nothing violent.'

Dr Fife poked him. '*Probably!*'

'Probably.'

The siren changed pitch, yelping as the driver ponked the horn. '*Sounds like our boy: Sean McGilvary, got a list of shoplifting and vandalism behind him long as a snake. We're on our way to Calman Road now, mob-handed. There's—'*

Someone muffled something in the background.

'It's DC MacVicar, Boss . . . Erm, OK.'

She must've handed over the phone, because DCI Monroe boomed out of the handset. *'Look, I know we said we'd be there, but we need to pick up this Sean McGilvary ASAP. Soon as we've done that, we'll wheech right over to Sadler Road, OK?'*

Angus sat to attention. 'Calman Road's in Cowskillin, right, Boss? We can be there in—'

'You're not going anywhere. If this Kate Paisley woman really is the Fortnight Killer's accomplice, we need her behind bars too! You and Dr Fife keep an eye on the property: make sure she doesn't do a runner when we dunt her boyfriend's door in.'

'But it's—'

'I'm sending you backup.' Monroe's voice faded a bit. *'Rhona, get Colly and 'Tash round to Sadler Road. Hotfoot.'* Then back to full strength: *'You're to observe only! Safety first, understand?'*

All the excitement sagged out of him. 'Yes, Boss.'

'I'm counting on you, Angus. We put an end to this today and no one else has to die.' And with that, the line went silent. He'd hung up.

Angus deflated even further, protruding bottom lip reflecting in the phone's blank screen.

A snort from Dr Fife. 'Let me guess: no backup?'

'Patrol car's on its way. We're to keep watch till the Boss's got his suspect in custody.'

Dr Fife cranked his seat into the upright and locked position. 'With couples who kill, there's always one dominant and one submissive. Pizza Guy is *clearly* dominant, so we can safely assume that Kate Paisley won't put up much of a struggle.' He looked Angus up and down – stuffed into the Mini's passenger seat like a bear in a kitchen cabinet. 'And I think you can *probably* handle her without backup.' He hopped out of the car, swirling the greatcoat around himself.

What?

No!

No, no, no, no, no . . .

'Hold on, you can't just . . .' Angus scrambled out after him.

A gust grabbed the car door and tried to wrench it from Angus's grasp. He wrestled it closed. 'Hoy! We have to wait for 'Tash and Colly!' Hurrying across the road, wind shoving at his shoulders with icy hands.

'Keep telling you knuckle-draggers: I've been catching killers since you were sucking on your momma's titties. Think I know *something* about how to do this properly.' He strutted past the intervening houses, hands deep in his pockets, head bent, shoulders up.

'The Boss *specifically* said to stay out of it till they get here!'

Which made sod-all difference whatsoever.

The rotten sod slipped through the neat little garden gate to number one-thirty-two.

Angus hurried after him. 'Dr Fife!'

But he kept going, up the short path to the new blue door. Reaching up to ring the bell.

'Hoy!' Angus staggered to a halt beside him. 'Have you got neeps between your ears?'

'Too late, we're here now.' He pointed. 'Put your thumb over the spyhole.'

'What?'

'You couldn't look more like a plainclothes police officer if you tried, and we *don't* wanna spook her. Finger: spyhole.' He rang the bell again.

This was all going to come back and bite them on the balls, wasn't it.

Angus blocked the spyhole with a fingertip. 'Maybe she's not in?' Which meant they could get out of here before Monroe or anyone else found out. 'You know, it's not too late to sod off back to the car. No one has to—'

The door opened and Angus staggered forward a step, catching his balance after leaning on his spyhole finger a bit too heavily.

Which might have come across more like an aggressive lunge than a trying-not-to-fall-flat-on-his-face, because the woman opening the door flinched back, eyes wide as he and his finger swooped towards her.

Long nose, glasses, early thirties, active leisurewear.

Flier Girl.

'Kate Paisley?' Dr Fife grinned up at her. 'Delivered any good pizzas lately?'

Angus went for his warrant card, but she wasn't hanging around.

'Shite . . .' Deep breath. 'RYAN, IT'S THE PIGS!' She tried to slam the door, but Angus was too far forward, after his stumble, and it bounced off his head with a hollow-plastic *thwannnnng*.

He staggered back a couple of paces and she legged it – tearing away down the hall. Leaving him standing there with the noise ringing through his skull.

Dr Fife grabbed his arm, steadying him. 'That's assaulting a police officer, right? Go get her, Tiger!' Slapping Angus's arse, like something off a Hollywood sports movie.

Angus shook his head, blinked, and barged inside.

The hall was every bit as tidy and well maintained as the outside: all the woodwork painted, nice laminate floor, a couple of framed posters on the wall. A set of boxed-in steps led upstairs, but you had to go to the end of the corridor to get to the foot of them, presumably to accommodate the tiny understairs loo.

Three other doors, leading off.

'RYAN: PERIMETER BREACH!' Kate Paisley was already at the end of the hall, skidding on the laminate as she made a hard left turn and vanished through one of them. *'CODE BLACK!'*

He lumbered after her, leaving Dr Fife hovering on the doorstep.

Three steps in and Angus was building speed, shaking off that door in the face. By the time he hammered past the end of the stairs he was going full pelt – having to scramble around the corner to avoid slamming into the door at the end of the corridor, so he could make it through the one she'd taken instead.

Following Kate Paisley into a nice fitted kitchen with black granite worktops and oak units. Must've cost a fortune.

She was jiggering about from foot to foot at the back door, fumbling with the key. 'Come on, you *fucker* . . .'

This time, Angus really did lunge for her.

The lock clicked, the handle swung downwards, but before she could haul the door open more than an inch, he was on her. They both thumped into the door, slamming it shut again. Which seemed to set off an *enormous* dog in the back garden. It launched itself at the other side of the uPVC, barking like a howitzer going off.

Kate Paisley struggled, throwing elbows and knees about, trying to hit something delicate. 'CODE BLACK! CODE BLACK!'

He tightened his grip, bracing one foot against the kitchen wall to force her face down onto the floor. Gritting his teeth as needles jabbed their way through his forearm. 'No biting!'

'GET OFF ME! RYAN! CODE BLOODY BLACK! RYAN!'

Angus struggled his right hand down her arm, grabbed hold of her wrist and bent it back on itself. Putting a bit of weight on the joint till she screamed into the tasteful tiles.

Stopped her struggling, though.

'Kate Paisley, I am arresting you under Section one of the Criminal Justice, Scotland, Act 2016 for assault. The reason for your arrest is that—'

'*ANGUS!*' That was Dr Fife, yelling from the front of the house, sounding as if something horrible was just about to happen. '*I REALLY NEED YOU HERE RIGHT NOW!*'

Oh, in the *name* of . . .

As if he didn't have enough on his—

'*NOW, ANGUS!*'

Fine.

He yanked out his cuffs and slapped one end on Kate Paisley's twisted wrist, then struggled it around so he could get the other one clicked into place too.

Scrambled to his feet. 'Don't go anywhere.'

The back door rattled and boomed as the dog hurled itself against it. Barking and barking and barking.

Yeah . . .

Angus locked the door and pocketed the key. Just in case.

'*RYAN, ISN'T IT? COME ON, RYAN, I KNOW YOU DON'T WANNA HURT ANYONE.*'

Bugger.

For once, Dr Fife wasn't just being a pain in the arse.

Angus rushed back out into the hall again.

'*ANGUS, FOR CHRIST'S SAKE!*'

Feet slipping on the laminate, he made the turn, *just* missed tripping over the end of the stairs and charged towards the panicked shouting.

'HELP ME!'

No idea what was going on – whoever 'Ryan' was, he must've been in the understairs loo, having a wee, because the door lay wide open, obscuring that end of the corridor.

'NO! DON'T BE . . .'

Then yelling and some muffled thuds.

Come on, *move* it.

Angus lowered his shoulder and barged into the open WC door, slamming it shut as he barrelled past and out the front door.

Skidded to a halt on the path.

Dr Fife was curled up in a ball, spine pressed against the neatly trimmed hedge, hands and arms covering his head as a man rained down punches like artillery fire.

Tracksuit bottoms, a black hoodie – hood up, baseball cap obscuring his face – a grey gilet, bright-white trainers.

'STOP! POLICE!'

The guy didn't say anything, just stopped pummelling Dr Fife and leapt the gate instead. Bolting for the playing grounds, hoodie and gilet flapping in the wind behind him.

And he was *fast*.

Across the road and up the chain-link fence – scaling it as if it was barely there.

Angus scuttled over and checked on Dr Fife, pulling his hands away from his face. 'Are you OK?'

Which was kind of a stupid question, because blood pulsed out of the forensic psychologist's nose and red welts blossomed on his forehead and cheek. More blood oozing from a split lip.

He peered up at Angus, wrenched his arms free. 'Go!' Voice all bunged up and nasal. 'Ged himb!'

Right.

'Kate Paisley's in the kitchen: don't let her leave!' Angus hurdled the gate, charging after the disappearing Ryan.

Because this bastard was *not* getting away.

17

The chain-link rattled and wobbled as Angus scrambled up the fence. Which wasn't anywhere near as easy as Ryan made it look.

Puffing and panting, fingers digging into the gaps between the wire, shoes scrabbling for purchase . . . And he was up! One leg over the top, then the next and—

A horrible ripping sound, like fabric parting.

Sodding . . .

Angus plummeted down the other side, landing in a heap on the grass. Forcing himself upright and lumbering into a run again.

Ryan's lead had grown – cutting across the rugby pitch, elbows up, knees pumping, still going strong.

No you don't.

Angus sped up, leaning into it, breath whooping in and out.

Near the middle of the pitch, a wee knot of seven or eight kids were arguing with the referee. Ryan ploughed straight through them, shoulder checking the ref and sending the kids flying like skittles.

Slowed him up a bit, meaning Angus was finally closing the gap.

Something must've taken a good thump in the impact, because Ryan had developed a bit of a limp. But he'd already cleared the last player, hurpled past the goal, and was heading for the far side of the playing field – making a beeline for the primary school.

'STOP! POLICE!' Well, it was worth a go.

And for the first time, in the history of ever, it actually worked.

Ryan slowed to a jog, then stopped completely – barely a dozen feet from the wooden fence that encircled the playground's rust-flecked roundabouts, swings, and climbing frames.

Can't believe that *actually* worked.

No one ever stopped when you shouted at them.

Yelling 'STOP! POLICE!' only made the buggers run faster.

But there was a first time for—

Ryan dug into his hoodie's pocket and pulled out a black revolver.

It was a replica.

Right?

It had to be, because—

A hard *CRACK* rang out across the playing field.

Angus skidded to a halt on the churned-up grass, right beneath the goalpost. 'GUN! EVERYBODY DOWN!'

The gun barked again, immediately followed by the metallic screech of a bullet ricocheting off the metal upright.

The snap of another bullet, whizzing past.

Sod this.

Angus dived for the ground, splatching into the mud as the gun fired again and again.

Another shot set the goal above his head ringing, showering him in flecks of white paint.

Someone screamed.

Someone sobbed.

Someone swore.

But there were no more shots.

He raised his head.

Ryan was nowhere to be—

No, wait – over there. On the other side of the playground, hoofing it across the car park.

Angus struggled to his feet.

Please don't let anyone be dead, please don't let anyone be dead . . .

Every single grown-up was hugging the ground, and a few of the kids too. But most of them just stood about, watching Ryan leg it. They grew them tough in Kingsmeath. And thick.

'IS ANYONE HIT?'

People sat up, shaking their heads.

No sign of anyone bleeding or lying dead with a hole in their head.

When Angus turned back again, Ryan was Spider-Manning his

way over the final line of chain-link fence – between the primary school and the railway embankment.

'SOMEONE CALL NINE-NINE-NINE – ACTIVE SHOOTER, OFFI-CER IN PURSUIT!'

A bloody stupid officer.

Angus set off at a run again, getting faster, leaping the fence into the playground.

Bloody Ryan was already at the crest of the steep bank, pausing for a moment to look back down at the chaos he'd wrought, before disappearing.

Angus hauled himself up the chain-link, wrestled his way over the top and more or less collapsed down the other side. Blood whoomping in his ears; breath rattling in his throat. Sweat trickling its way down his back. Face burning. Peching and heeching as he scrabbled up the bank.

When he finally reached the summit, there was no sign of Ryan at all. Without the embankment getting in the way, the wind ripped across the valley, shoving against Angus's chest. The first strike of rain stabbing him in the face.

He staggered towards the railway lines, stopping on the concrete sleepers and bending over to grab a knee. Holding himself upright as his chest heaved cold gritty air into his hot peppery lungs.

Where the hell had Ryan gone?

From up here most of Oldcastle was laid out like a windswept blanket – all the way down Kingsmeath, across Kings River, then up the valley to Moncuir Wood in all its malevolent darkness; and the bland sprawling mass of Shortstaine beyond.

And still no sign of the guy he'd been chasing.

Angus straightened up, still breathing like a punctured Space Hopper as he staggered across the railway tracks to the embankment's other side, standing at the edge of the drop down to the arse-end of Forbes Drive, a good fifty feet below.

He wiped a hand across his face, blinking away the sting of sweat in both eyes as he scanned the overgrown back gardens and crummy council houses – because why bother building somewhere nice, when you could just jam all the poor people into cheap-and-nasty shiteholes and forget about them?

How could Ryan just vanish?

The bastard had to be *somewhere* . . .

There: off to the right.

A screech of tyres whined out as an engine revved, and a manky green VW Polo accelerated off in a plume of blue-grey smoke. The exhaust sounded as if it was more holes than metal.

Then an angry voice wafted up from the street below: *'HOY!'* A figure ran out into the road, shaking their fist at the departing car. 'COME BACK HERE, YOU THIEVING WANKER!'

Angus pulled out his Airwave, wiping away another faceful of sweat as he thumbed the button. 'DC MacVicar . . . to . . . Control?'

He got a cheery *'Oh, aye?'* in reply. *'And what can we do for you, DC—'*

'I need a . . . lookout request . . . on a . . . on a green Volkswagen Polo . . . heading west . . . on Forbes . . . Forbes Drive.' He stepped back, up onto the rails for a better view of the car as it shrank into the distance. 'Driver is . . . armed . . . handgun. Shots fired.'

The jolly edge was replaced by something much more professional: *'Vehicle registration?'*

'Don't . . . I don't know.' Then an invisible gremlin rammed a knife into his ribs. 'Argh . . . Stitch . . .'

'OK: I can't trigger the ANPR without a number plate, but we'll sort something.' A computer keyboard rattled in the background. *'Injuries?'*

A weird noise vibrated through the air – the atonal *ping-twang-pwooom* of metal singing somewhere beneath his feet.

Angus hauled in great coughing lungfuls of air. Spluttered himself to a wheeze, drooping as sweat dribbled down his back. 'What?'

'You said "shots fired": any casualties?'

'Don't think . . . think so.' Dear God, was he ever going to breathe properly again? 'I need backup to . . . to one-thirty-two Sadler Road . . . One prisoner in custody . . . Dr Fife may need . . . medical attention. Better scramble . . . ambulance . . . just in case.'

'Stand by.'

An ear-splitting *HONK!* blared out behind him and Angus cleared the ground by a good foot, spinning around to see a massive goods train rumbling down the tracks towards him. The thing was barely moving at a walking pace, but he limped off the tracks anyway.

'*Do we have an ID?*'

'IC-One male . . . five-eleven, fourteen stone . . . dark hair. First name . . . Ryan . . . No idea what his surname—'

HONNNNNNNK!

'He's . . . our Pizza Man . . . The Fortnight Killer.'

'*How can he be? DCI Monroe just arrested the scumbag in Cowskillin.*'

'It's just . . . I don't know, OK?' Another coughing fit shuddered his ribs. Soon as he could haul in a serrated breath, Angus howked a gobbet of froth onto the singing rails. 'Urgh . . .'

HONNNNNNNNNNNNK!

'I'll try . . . get a number plate for that . . . Volkswagen.'

HONNNK! HONK-HONNNNNNK! HONNNNNNNNNNNNNNNK!

The train couldn't have been more than a five-a-side football pitch away, bearing down on him with all the speed of an auld wifie and her tartan shopping trolley.

'Got to go.' Angus stuck the Airwave back in his pocket, waving at the train as he hobbled back to the embankment's far edge, overlooking the heady delight of Forbes Drive. 'Right.'

Deep breath, then he slithered down the steep slope on his rip-arsed trousers – doing his best to avoid the clumps of nettles and thistles.

And failing.

Could today *get* any worse?

18

Trapped between the lowering clouds and the valley rim, the sun painted Oldcastle with blood as Angus limped along Sadler Road.

He followed the line of chain-link fencing, skirting the playing fields, making for number one-thirty-two where a wee police circus was setting up. Two patrol cars blocked the street, along with an ambulance, their lights spinning slowly in the falling gloom.

Almost there.

Be nice to get a sit-down out of the howling wind. And a cup of tea. And a lovely warm bath . . .

Angus's phone ding-buzzed with an incoming text.

Maybe it'd be good news for a change?

He fumbled his mobile out with cold-stiffened fingers and checked.

It wasn't.

ELLIE:

> I'm hearing rumours about a shooting in Kingsmeath.
> That got anything to do with the Fortnight Killer?
> You promised me an exclusive, remember?
> WE CAN STILL PUBLISH!

Lovely.

Right.

Angus thumbed out a reply:

> Unable to confirm or deny.
> Awaiting approval from superior officer.
> Request

... was as far as he got before the thing rang in his hands – launching into Vivaldi's 'Spring' as Ellie's name appeared in the middle of the screen.

An unwashed patrol car wheeched by, blues-and-twos going full pelt. Momentarily deafening, then Dopplering away, before falling silent as it pulled up in front of number-one-thirty-two.

Yeah . . .

Angus gritted his teeth and let Ellie's call ring through to voicemail.

Deleted the word 'REQUEST' then finished his text.

> Unable to talk: working.
> Please remain patient.
> Sorry.

SEND.

Not sure that would hold her for long, but it was all he had.

The new arrivals dug a roll of blue-and-white 'POLICE' tape from the boot of their patrol car – securing one end to the chain-link and the other to the scruffy box hedge that bordered number one-thirty-one. Then headed off to do the same on the other side. Isolating one-thirty-two from its neighbours.

Their cordon *brrrrrrrr*ed and thrummed in the wind.

Which seemed to amuse the audience no end.

About fifteen kids in muddy rugby strips – none of them older than eight – had clustered on the playing-field side of the fence, crunching down bags of crisps and scoofing tins of high-caffeine energy drinks while they watched.

One of them spotted Angus hobbling along the pavement and pointed. Their high-pitched Kingsmeath accent cut the cold air like a bandsaw: 'Hoy! It's yer man!'

Another kid turned to look. Breaking into a huge, gap-toothed grin. 'Heeeeerrrrrrro! Heeeeerrrrrrro!'

A little girl skipped closer, fingertips running along the chain-link, auburn curls bouncing around her angelic wee face. 'Hey, mannie! D'ye get him? The fuckin' radge wie the shooter?'

Angus gave them a wave and a pained smile.

'Heeeeerrrrrrro! Heeeeerrrrrrro!'

PC Collier kicked her heels beside Patrol Car Number Two, keeping one eye on the occupant in the back seat: Kate Paisley. Glowering away at everyone and everything.

Colly looked up when the cheering started. Staring at Angus as he ducked under the new cordon. 'What the hell do you think you were doing? Getting shot at!'

'Afternoon.' He stumbled to a halt and she thumped him on the arm.

'Hulking great idiot.' Her voice softened. 'Are you OK?'

'Missed me by miles.' He took a peek through the passenger window. 'She give you any trouble?'

Kate Paisley bared her teeth at him, baleful as a gargoyle.

One of the kids kicked off a sort of football-chant thing, waving his hands over his head. 'There's only one Giant Bastard . . .'

His mates joined in:

'One Giant Baaaa-stard,
There's only one Giant Baaaa-stard . . .'

Colly shrugged. 'Naw. Well, not *me* anyway. Tried to boot 'Tash's nuts into orbit, though.' She nodded towards the ambulance. 'Your twat mate always this much of a pain?'

The back doors were open and there was Dr Fife, sitting on the trolley – slouched forwards, clutching a big wodge of gauze over his nose. It probably started out nice and white, but now most of the fabric was stained a rich beetroot red.

A paramedic wrestled a blood-pressure cuff into place, even though his patient clearly was *not* cooperating.

'Oh yeah.' Angus rested his bum against the patrol car's bonnet. 'Anyway: nothing to do with me. Only known him a day.'

'There's only one Giant Bastard,
One Giant Baaaa-stard,
There's only one Giant Baaaa-stard . . .'

'Aye?' Colly smiled. 'I heard you were besties and you *love* him.' She stuck two fingers in her mouth and let rip a shrieking whistle. 'You know the arse is hanging out your breeks, right?'

He stood, twisting around a few times, trying to catch sight of his own bum. Which was exactly the kind of thing they laughed at Wee Hamish for doing – birling round and round on the living-room mat, chasing his tail. Angus stopped spinning and grabbed the seat of his trousers instead, feeling his way along a huge rip that was jaggy with the occasional thistle spike. 'Oh, in the name of . . .' How did it get to be so big?

'*Well done.*' 'Tash appeared through the gate to number one-thirty-two. A stabproof vest kept his middle-aged spread under control, but he seemed to have developed a knock-kneed mincing walk since that morning – presumably in reaction to Kate Paisley's boot. It gave him a semi-piratical air to go with his big droopy moustache, big droopy nose, and sad droopy eyes. 'Now see if you can tell which one's your elbow.' 'Tash wrung his hands together, as if he'd just washed them. Probably been examining the testicular damage in Kate Paisley's understairs bog. He grimaced at Colly. 'Boss is on his way.' A sniff. 'Which is typical. Top brass only ever turn up after all the hard work's been done and there's no chance of being kicked in the nads.' Adjusting his groin brought on a shoulder-curling wince. He waited for it to fade before limping past Colly to the patrol car. 'Orders are: sod off back to the ranch. Get Paisley charged and processed.'

'There's only one Giant Bastard,
One Giant Baaaa-stard,
There's only one Giant Baaaa-stard . . .'

Angus tilted his head towards the ambulance. 'Thanks. For looking after him.'

Colly grimaced. 'I'd say "my pleasure" but it wasn't.' She opened the driver's door. 'Just make sure you get that arse of yours covered. Don't want to start a sexy riot.' A wink and she slipped in behind the wheel.

'Tash winced his way into the passenger seat, and they were off.

Angus raised the cordon for them, holding the tape high so the patrol car could slip underneath. And all the way, Kate Paisley glared at him.

Definitely made a friend there.

Pfff . . .

Sirens howled in the distance, getting closer. That would be the Boss and his entourage.

Dr Fife struggled free from the paramedic's grip and clambered down from the ambulance, still holding that wodge of bloodied gauze to his face. The welts and scrapes from Ryan's attack stood out in angry shades of red against his pale skin; by tomorrow he'd have an impressive array of bruises. But for now, he stomped across the road towards Angus.

The football chant came to an abrupt halt as all the kids *stared*.

'Hoy, Dobby! You seen Harry Fuckin' Potter anywhere?'

'That's no' Dobby, ya prawn, that's a genuine Oompa Loompa!'

The little girl with the curls bounced in place. 'Aye: sees a Twix, ya chocolaty wee bastard!'

Little shites.

'Goddamnit . . .' Dr Fife's face clenched, shoulders curling up.

Right.

Angus stepped towards the fence. 'HOY! That's enough: you don't talk to people like that!'

'Oh, no! Shrek's mad at us.'

'Aye, leave us alone, ya great-big paedo!'

'Peeeee-dowww! Peeeee-dowww!'

Every single one of them produced a smartphone, swiping away and holding them up, ready to record him reading the riot act. No doubt destined to become memes and reaction gifs all over the internet.

Well, tough, because Angus wasn't playing.

He turned his back on the lot of them, and . . .

Where . . . ?

Dr Fife had disappeared.

'Hello? Dr Fife?'

He was crouched behind the nearest patrol car, clearly hiding from the impromptu film crew. Glaring up at Angus. 'I don't need you to fight my battles!'

'I was only trying to—'

'I'm not a child!' The glare became a snarl. 'If they didn't have cameras, I'd march over there and *kick* their asses.'

Angus leaned back against the car roof. 'They're just stupid kids.'

'They're assholes!' Jabbing a finger at the ground. 'Like I haven't had enough crap to deal with today! Whatshername' – his finger stopped threatening the ground and stabbed after Colly's car instead – 'the one with the ugly haircut. She said you *lost* him. Ryan.'

Oh no you don't.

'He tried to *kill* me. With a gun!'

'Don't be so melodramatic: everyone tries to kill everyone else with a gun all the time!'

The paramedic ambled over, hooking a thumb at the ambulance. 'Are you getting back in this thing or what?'

Dr Fife scowled at him. 'I'm *busy*.' Then the jabbing finger poked Angus. 'You wouldn't last a day back home.'

'Fine.' The paramedic folded his arms, nose in the air. 'Die of a delayed concussion, see if I care.'

'Go away! Leave me alone!' Jerking his head in Angus's direction. 'Or I'll set Sasquatch on you.'

Lovely.

Angus waved at the guy. 'Sorry.'

'Hmmmph . . .' The paramedic turned on his heel and strolled back to the ambulance, hands in his pockets. 'But if your man drops dead, can't say I didn't try!'

Soon as he'd gone, Angus pulled himself up to his full height. 'He was only doing his job.' Towering over Dr Fife. 'And we don't *have* guns in Scotland, because we're a civilized country, not a bunch of yee-haw, bible-thumping, ammosexual, redneck . . . wankers.' Banging his palm down on the patrol-car roof and making it *boom*. 'This shite is *not* normal!'

They glowered at each other as the approaching sirens fell silent and two unmarked pool cars stopped in front of the cordon – blue-and-white lights flickering through their radiator grilles. An OSU van and a Dog Unit pulled up behind them.

DCI Monroe got out of the lead vehicle, looking around as DS Sharp and DC Stephen 'Ernie' Wyse scrambled out after him.

Wyse struck a pose: nose up, fists on his hips, broad shoulders pulled back. His suit was just a bit too flash to be a proper fighting one – didn't even look machine washable. That and his short-back-and-sides-plus-quiff combo screamed 'wide boy' rather than 'police officer'. On the plus side, the mole on his top lip had a permanent-cold-sore feel to it. He pulled on a pair of shades, as if he wasn't enough of a tit already.

Last to emerge was Monster Munch, sporting a brand-new bright-white plaster across the bridge of her nose. Courtesy of Patrick Crombie.

DI Cohen appeared from the second pool car, and joined Monroe, the pair of them talking in low voices and pointing at the far end of the playing field. Then Cohen got back in his car. It jerked into a three-point turn, the siren wailing into life again as it roared off down Sadler Road. Lights blazing.

The Operational Support Unit stayed where they were – in the warm, out of the wind – but the driver got out of the dog van, went around the back, and returned with PD Bawheid, huge and slathery and barking as he strained his lead taut. Looking keen as mince to inflict a bit of law-and-order on anyone who might be tasty.

Angus pressed his bum against the patrol car, just in case it exuded 'bite me' vibes in its rip-trousered state.

One of the wee kids boggled. 'Fuck me; it's Cujo!'

'Cooooooooojoh-oh! Cooooooooojoh-oh!'

Monroe pointed, and off scurried DC Wyse and Monster Munch – pulling out their notebooks as they headed for the chainlink and that crowd of muddy kids.

Wyse struck another pose. 'All right, all right, let's have names and addresses for the lot of you.'

Soon as the words left his mouth, the children scattered in a flurry of V-signs, middle fingers, raspberries, and foul language.

Monroe marched over to Angus and Dr Fife, his face pink and pinched, eyes bulging. 'I told you to *wait*! "Wait, watch, stay safe," I said. What I didn't say was "Charge into the *violent* suspect's property without proper authorization and backup!"'

'Yes' – Angus held up a hand – 'but—'

'SOMEONE COULD'VE BEEN KILLED!'

'*Really?*' Dr Fife pulled the bloodied gauze from his nose and held it out for inspection. 'I'm fine, by the way. Thanks.'

'And now I've got a gunman on the loose in Oldcastle!' Monroe marched away a couple of paces, dragged in a deep breath or two, then marched back again. Voice a lot calmer than it had been ten seconds ago. 'Right. OK. This complicates things.' Looking up at the house. 'We've got Sean McGilvary's DNA at the crime scene. But he's in *custody*, so who's Ryan?'

Dr Fife reapplied the wadding. 'He's the Pizza Man. He and Kate Paisley were at Dr Fordyce's apartment. Fifty bucks says he's the Fortnight Killer.'

'He's not just . . .' Monroe opened and closed his mouth a couple of times. 'I don't know, some random thug weirdo?'

'Fifty bucks.'

'Then *why's* Sean McGilvary's DNA all over the Healey-Robinsons' house?'

Angus had a go: 'Maybe the Fortnight Killer's got more than one accomplice?'

The wind moaned through the chain-link as they both stared at him in silence.

'Well, it's possible, right?'

Monroe didn't look convinced. 'Dr Fife?'

'Of course it's *possible*. But so are lots of things.' He dabbed at his scarlet-crusted nostrils. 'I'll want to speak to him.'

A nod. 'Family solicitor's on her way.' Then Monroe rolled his eyes at Angus. 'More than one accomplice. Like things aren't difficult enough.'

'Sorry, Boss.'

Monroe raised a finger and pointed at the pair of them. 'I want one thing clear: in future, if I tell you to sit on your thumbs, you lube them up and you *sit*. Understand? Might not be so lucky next time.'

'*Lucky?*' Dr Fife scowled at him over the top of the blood-drenched gauze. 'Hello?'

'OK. OK.' DS Sharp had been lurking in the background, but she stepped in. 'Let's not get all heated again. The *important* thing is no one got hurt.'

Dr Fife glared at her. 'You can see this, right?'

'So to speak.' Giving him a pained smile. 'We'll send Forensics in, search the place, find out who our gunman is, and he'll be banged-up before you know it.'

Monroe huffed out a breath. Then nodded. 'Angus: hotfoot it back to the bunker and get Byron to take your statement. Then I want an eFit ready to go to the press. We'll see if anyone recognizes . . .' He narrowed his eyes as Angus grimaced. 'What?'

'Didn't really get a good look at him, Boss. He had his back to me most of the time – running away. Well, till he started shooting, and I sort of hit the ground at that point. Then he was too far away.' Angus shuffled his feet on the damp tarmac. 'Sorry.'

'Wonderful.' Monroe closed his eyes, scrunching them tight to keep down whatever was bubbling away inside. 'Dr Fife?'

'I was a bit busy getting my ass kicked.' Pointing at his battered face and the big wodge of padding. 'You *can* see this, right?'

Everyone sagged.

Come on, things weren't that bad, surely.

Angus stood up straight. 'Yes, but we've got two suspects in custody. That's a *huge* improvement, isn't it?'

Nobody said a word.

Turned out his fake enthusiasm wasn't as infectious as genuine disappointment.

Monroe chewed on the inside of his cheek for a moment, then marched away towards the house, pointing as he went. 'MONSTER MUNCH: I WANT THIS PROPERTY SECURED! NO ONE IN OR OUT TILL I SAY OTHERWISE! LAURA: DOOR-TO-DOORS!'

Monster Munch flashed a thumbs-up. 'Aye, Boss.'

DS Sharp nodded. 'Got it.' Stepping away from the car and clapping her hands together. 'COME ON, YOU LOT, YOU HEARD THE MAN: ERNIE, MAGS, WEE HAIRY, KATHERINE. LET'S GO!'

And off they went.

19

Observation Room A had the same cabbage-and-stale-feet smell that haunted nearly every police station in O Division. It also had three monitors, a single bench-style desk along one wall, a couple of teeny microphones on bendy metal sticks, and two seats.

Dr Fife had got into the filing-cabinet stash of Rampant Gorilla, and now he was on his second oversized can, vibrating gently in his plastic chair, feet twitching in mid-air.

DCI Monroe had the other seat, leaving Angus to prop himself against the back wall as they all watched the monitors.

On the plus side, it meant neither Monroe nor Fife could see him yawning. And the wall hid the rip in his trousers. So there was that.

Each of the three monitors showed a different view of Interview Room Two: a plain space with white walls bisected by a grey panic strip. Four people had gathered around the table. Kate Paisley had pride of place in the Naughty Chair – the only one bolted to the floor, for 'safety' reasons. She'd changed into a white Tyvek suit, because someone had taken her clothes into evidence, and she slouched there with the hood thrown back, casting narrow-eyed glares at the cameras. As if she could see the three of them watching her from the safety of the observation room.

Mr Coulter sat next to her, with his puffy eyes and cheeks, side parting, glasses, and the general air of a dishevelled hamster. His face glowed an unhealthy shade of puce, as if he probably wasn't going to see his sixties. Apparently being a duty solicitor really took it out of you.

DI Cohen and DS Massie had the other side of the table, an array of notebooks and files laid out before them.

Kate Paisley stopped glaring at Camera One to glare at Cohen instead. Her voice crackled out from the observation room speakers: *'I didn't say that.'*

'Then what are *you saying?'*

Her jaw tightened. *'You know fine.'* Bringing up an angry finger to point at them both. *'All you bastards do. Cos you're all in on it. I know you are, so don't try lying to me, cos you can't.'*

And she'd seemed so *nice* when Angus had wrestled her into handcuffs . . .

Dr Fife scoofed his energy drink. Cowboy boots juddering away. Monroe sighed.

Kate Paisley glared.

Onscreen, DS Massie reached into a folder and emerged with a screenshot from Mrs McManus's doorbell footage: the Pizza Man, Ryan, caught halfway to the stairs, carrying his decoy takeaways.

It went on the table. *'OK. Why don't we try* this *one again?'* DS Massie tapped the picture. *'What's your friend's name?'*

Paisley didn't even look. *'I've never seen that man before in my life.'*

'You shouted, "Ryan, watch out, the police are—"'

'No I never! That's just lies. You bastards always lie, because you're the jackboot on our neck, keeping the Elites in power. Bunch of fascists: with your lockdowns and your poison jabs and your deep-state lies!'

Monroe sat back in his chair. 'The woman's an idiot. How on earth did she qualify as an electrician? I wouldn't trust her to rewire a sieve.' He drummed his fingers on the worktop-bench. Looked over at Dr Fife. 'Can't you do something?'

'OK. How about this *man?'* DS Massie put another photo on the table. A mugshot this time, of a spud-faced bloke whose features were too small to make out clearly on the monitors.

'Told you: I – don't – know. Never seen him.'

Mr Coulter sounded as if he'd just run a marathon with a fridge-freezer strapped to his back. *'DS Massie, please. We've been over this four times now. My client doesn't recognize this person. Move on.'*

Dr Fife pushed the red button mounted beside the nearest microphone, leaning into it. Still sounding a bit bunged up, but better than before. 'Ask her if she knows Ryan's been on social media telling everyone *she's* the one who betrayed him. She's the one called the cops.'

Onscreen, DI Cohen gave a little nod, then pulled on a puzzled voice. *'Kate, if you don't want to cooperate, why did you tip us off about Ryan?'* Pausing as she shied back, then leaning in to follow her. *'The anonymous tip line: there must've been a reason you phoned it. To say he'd be there?'*

Dr Fife threw his free hand in the air. 'Oh, *now* he can improvise.'

Paisley squirmed. *'I don't know what you're talking about. If you bastards gave a toss about law and order, you wouldn't be hassling innocent people like me, you'd be arresting the paedophiles running this country.'*

'You did contact us, didn't you?' Cohen pulled out his phone, scrolling away at it as he frowned. *'That's what Ryan's telling everyone on Twitter.'*

A shuddery yawn rattled through Angus, ending in a wee burp. 'Sorry.'

Monroe turned in his chair, wrinkles bunched between his eyebrows.

Angus stared at his feet for a bit.

'They're stealing kids off the streets, and not just migrant kids: white *kids. Butchering them at these satanic rituals, cos the blood's more pure.'* Her voice sharpened. *'Drinking it gives them* power!'

Because why be a halfwit conspiracy nutjob, when you could be a *racist* halfwit conspiracy nutjob?

There was a knock on the door, and DS Sharp poked her head into the observation room. 'Boss? Sean McGilvary's solicitor says they're ready to talk.'

'Oh, does he now?' Monroe curled his top lip. 'Better late than never, I suppose.'

'Look what he posted half an hour ago.' DI Cohen peered down his nose at his phone. ' "Betrayed! Bastard pigs raided the place, cos that stupid cow, Kate, grassed me up." Hashtag "traitor", hashtag "enemy of the people", hashtag "lying bitch".'

Dr Fife poked the intercom button. 'Don't lay it on so thick!'

Kate Paisley's mouth pinched, eyebrows lowering as her bottom lip crept out, blinking and wriggling in her chair. Jaw clenching and unclenching. She stared down at her clawed hands.

'Come on' – Monroe inched closer to the monitor – 'take the bait . . .'

Her head curled to one side, left shoulder creeping up.

Another yawn ripped through Angus – a proper jaw-breaker, that even infected DS Sharp. But she covered her mouth.

Monroe turned on him again. 'For *God's* sake, will you go home and get some sleep?'

On the screen, Kate Paisley's face set into a hard line. *'Told you: you can't lie to me. I know all your tricks.'*

Dr Fife slumped in his seat. 'What an utter Nimrod . . .' Staring at the ceiling tiles. 'Amateurs. I'm working with frigging amateurs here!'

She turned to her solicitor. *'I got nothing more to say to these bastards.'*

Mr Coulter let free a big wet sigh, then put the cap back on his biro. *'Maybe now would be a good time to take a break?'*

'Pricking hell.' Monroe scowled at the screen, chewing on something bitter. Then pulled in a deep breath. 'All right. We'll go see what Sean McGilvary has to say for himself.' He pressed the button. 'Badger: take her back to her cell.' Flicking a switch killed the audio feed, so DI Cohen and DS Massie wrapped the interview up in complete silence.

One last scoof of Rampant Gorilla, draining the can. 'Well, that was a complete disaster.'

'Urgh . . .' Monroe covered his face. 'We've got, what, twenty-three hours?'

'Tops.' The empty tin got crushed and lobbed at the bin. Bounced off the wall with a clang, and went skittering across the floor tiles. 'More like twenty. If we're lucky.'

'Then let's hope Sean McGilvary's more talkative.' He stood. 'Laura: soon as Paisley's back in her cell, stick McGilvary in Interview Four. I do *not* want them bumping into each other on the stairs, or the custody suite.'

'Boss.' A frown. 'Who do you want on interview duty? Byron's done the training, or—'

'No.' Dr Fife hopped down from his seat. 'No more puppeteering halfwits through a headset: I'll do it.' Snapping his fingers. 'Angus, in case anything kicks off, I need you to intervene *before* the bastard jumps me. Unlike last time.'

'I didn't even want to ring the doorbell!'

'Meantime, I'm off for a wizz. If you could all avoid doing anything stupid till I get back, that'd be *great*.'

The door thumped shut behind him.

A grimace from Monroe. DS Sharp bit her top lip. Then they both turned and eyed Angus.

'Don't look at me. I'm just a slack-jawed, knuckle-dragging yokel.'

'Yes. Well.' Monroe plucked the crumpled can from the floor and dropped it in the bin. 'Let's hope he knows what he's doing . . .'

Interview Room Four was pretty much the same as Interview Room One, only with more disturbing brown stains on the carpet. And up one of the walls.

This time, the Naughty Chair was occupied by the potato-faced bloke from DS Massie's photo. Sean McGilvary was thin as a standard lamp, with bitten fingernails, a shaved head – not that there was much hair to shave up there, going by the thin tonsure of blue stubble – and a pronounced lean to the right.

Luckily for Mr Coulter, Sean hadn't requested a duty solicitor, so he could slink off somewhere to sleep. Or die. Instead, Sean had called in the family lawyer: Mrs Hannay.

She looked like something from an ancient BBC sitcom now repeating on an obscure digital channel: a maternal sort in an off-pink cardigan and sage-green top. Tweed skirt, heavy boots. Big hair. Nails like talons.

She ran them across the ring binder in front of her, then straightened her pen. All neat and tidy.

Dr Fife and DCI Monroe sat opposite – Monroe still as a garden gnome, Fife flicking through Sean's file. Taking his time. No rush. Whistling a jaunty American tune as he went.

Which left Angus: standing two or three feet behind Sean McGilvary, doing his best to exude an air of authoritative menace. Which wasn't easy, given he'd had to shuffle his way in here, keeping his back to the wall, so no one could see the rip in his trousers.

And the jaunty whistling warbled on.

'The Star-Spangled Banner' was on its third time around when Mrs Hannay checked her watch. 'If we *can* get started, please; I've got people over for dinner and salmon mousse will only hold for so long.'

Dr Fife held up a finger and continued whistling his way through the file.

Sean McGilvary fidgeted.

The audio-visual recording equipment buzzed.

Monroe remained perfectly still.

Angus did some more menacingly authoritative exuding.

A huge sigh from Mrs Hannay. 'Can we at least read our statement?' She unclipped it from her binder. 'Sean may have done a few *slightly* questionable things in his youth, but he comes from a good, traditional, *God-fearing* family. I assure you we can clear this up easily and get back to our guests. And investigation.' She handed the sheet of paper to her client. 'Sean?'

He fidgeted with it for a bit. Licked his lips. Then had a go, his voice all high-pitched and stilted – as if he'd never read anything out loud in a police interview room while facing a murder charge before: '"First, I wish to express my condolences to Mr and . . . Mr Healey-Robinson's friends and family for the tragic circumstances of their deaths. To lose a loved one in those circumstances must be—"'

'This is all a bit out of your league, isn't it, Sean?' Dr Fife tapped the file in his hands.

'Eh?' Sean McGilvary glanced at his lawyer for approval, then went back to the statement. 'I'm . . . Er . . . "To lose a loved one—"'

'Shoplifting's a world away from torturing people to death.' Dr Fife pursed his lips. 'What did it feel like, the first time you killed somebody?'

The talons clacked against the tabletop. 'Sean didn't kill anyone. Now can we *please* let the boy read his statement?'

A smile. 'Twenty-eight's hardly a "boy", is it? I'm just trying to make this easier for him in the long run. You don't want to do this the *hard way*, do you, Sean?'

She nudged her client. 'Keep going.'

'"To lose a loved one in those circumstances must be horrible, and my thoughts and prayers are with them. But I must stress, in no uncertain terms, that I had nothing to do with these two gentlemen's deaths."'

Back to the file. 'All this vandalism . . . petty stuff, really.' Dr Fife pulled a trio of photos from amongst the printouts and forms, and laid them on the table. Graffiti scrawled across a bookie's shopfront, a bus shelter with its windows smashed, a melted wheelie bin round the back of a convenience store.

'"I am not now, nor have I ever been, homophobic. I have great respect for the gay community and some of my best friends are LGBTQ-plus. I understand from the arresting officer—"'

'You come from a "good, traditional, God-fearing family" and you don't have a problem with *gay* people? Really? Doesn't St Thingummy say they're an abhorrence?'

Sean stiffened. 'Leviticus. Eighteen: twenty-two. "Thou shalt not lie with mankind, as with womankind: it is *abomination*." Twenty: thirteen. "If a man also lie with mankind, as he lieth with a woman, both of them have committed an abomination: they shall surely be put to death; their blood shall be upon them."'

A slow clap as Dr Fife grinned. 'Scripture: chapter and verse. You gotta love that old King James thee-and-thouing, right?' The clapping stopped. 'And here we have two gay men who've been "put to death".'

'Please let my client *finish*, Dr Fife. This is *not* helping.'

'"I . . ."' Sean licked his lips. '"I understand from the arresting officer that my DNA has been found at number twenty-one Balvenie Row. This may be due to cross-contamination as I had spoken to Mr Healey-Robinson about an article he was writing for the *Castle News and Post* earlier that week."'

'Oh. OK then.' Dr Fife closed the file. 'That clears everything up.' He hopped down from his chair. 'Sorry to have spoiled your evening.'

Sean blinked a couple of times, then turned to his lawyer. 'Is that it? Can I go now?'

Dr Fife slammed the file down on the table. 'Of course you can't, you idiot. They've got your DNA in the kitchen, the living room, both bedrooms, and the bathroom. For that to be "cross-contamination" you'd have to lick Kevin Healey-Robinson all over and rub him on every surface in the place.' He shook his head at Mrs Hannay. 'Shall we leave you two alone to cook up some *slightly* more convincing lies?'

She sat up straight, talons gripping the Holy Ring Binder, colour flushing in her cheeks. 'You being rude and sarcastic doesn't rule out cross-contamination!'

'No, but this does.' He pulled a sheet from the file and held it up. 'They found a thumb print on the banister, near the top of the stairs, Sean. Clean as a kitten's conscience. And *who* do you think's a perfect match? Hmm? Wanna guess?'

Mrs Hannay cast a sharp look at her client.

Sean blushed and took a sudden, all-consuming interest in what was left of his gnawed-off fingernails.

'You haven't been entirely honest with your lawyer, have you, Sean.'

'I . . . But . . .'

Dr Fife pulled on a pouty frown. 'And after she wrote that nice statement for you. How ungrateful.'

'I need to have a word with my *client*.' The words came out like frozen bullets, fired right into Sean McGilvary's beetroot face. 'This instant.'

'But . . .'

'Good idea.' Dr Fife gathered up the file again. 'A clip round the ear might not hurt, too.' Hauling the door open and swaggering from the room. *'I'll give you ten minutes.'*

The door swung shut behind him.

A tut from DCI Monroe. He stood, looking down at Sean McGilvary with sad eyes. 'It's only a matter of time, Sean. The longer you lie to us, the worse it'll be when it comes to sentencing.' He jerked his chin at Angus. 'Constable.' Then headed out to join Dr Fife.

Keeping his back firmly to the wall, Angus shuffled after him.

20

Just for a change, this was one of the few corridors in DHQ not plastered in motivational posters and memos. Instead, the suspects and inmates were treated to loads of adverts recommending they 'CALL CRIMESTOPPERS' and to 'SEE IT, SAY IT, SORT IT'.

Monroe paced the grey terrazzo floor from here to Interview Four and back again, curled in around his phone. 'How much? . . . For a *dishwasher*? Is it magic? Does it make the plates come alive and dance around the room? . . . OK, OK . . .' Massaging his forehead with his free hand. 'Yes . . . If that's the one you want . . . Uh-huh.'

Angus shuffled his feet. 'You don't think he did it, do you?'

'Keeping an open mind.' Dr Fife closed his eyes and let his head *ponk* back against the wall.

'No, I'm *not* being sarcastic, Irene: if it's important to you . . . Uh-huh . . . OK . . .'

DS Massie wandered up to them, bearing one of those wee cardboard carrier things with three large wax-paper cups in it. Levered one free and handed it to Monroe.

He mouthed a 'thank you' and went back to his call. 'Yes, I'm sure it is . . . Uh-huh . . . Huh. Really?'

'Angus.' Massie held out a second cup.

Which was pretty much unheard of.

A detective sergeant getting the coffees in for a lowly detective constable?

Must be because of the almost-getting-shot thing.

'Thanks, Sarge.' Ooh, it was lovely and warm in his hands.

She pulled the third one from the holder and toasted them with it. 'Cheers.' Slurping through the little hole in the spill-proof lid. 'Any joy?'

'Hold on a minute, Irene.' Monroe pressed the phone against his chest. 'McGilvary's working on a fresh set of lies with his solicitor.'

'Ahem!' Dr Fife pointed. 'Where's mine?'

Her face didn't move. 'Didn't know you wanted one.' Another sip, followed by a humming *mmmmmmm* . . . of deliciousness. 'Anyway, thought you said our coffee was like "shite boiled in battery acid".'

Monroe winced. 'Rhona.'

DS Massie rolled her eyes. 'OK, OK. He can have DC MacVicar's.' She plucked the coffee from Angus's hands and gave it to Dr Fife.

Bloody hell.

Knew it was too good to be true.

'Don't pout.' DS Massie took a good long slurp, rubbing it in. 'They've found your green Volkswagen Polo in that big patch of woods off Robertson Road.' Everyone stared at her, the expectation and hope thick enough to make the air sticky. But she shook her head. 'Nah: Ryan torched it. Nothing left but blistered metal and melted tyres. No prints, no DNA, no conveniently dropped driver's licence . . .'

Dr Fife cracked the lid off *Angus's* coffee. 'You need to put out an APB: appeal for witnesses.'

'Oh yeah, great idea. Why didn't *we* think of that?' The look she gave him could've withered granite. 'Only we don't know if it's his *actual* name, and no one from the door-to-doors had a clue who was living in the house. Only that they were "nice, but a bit weird" – which is saying something for Kingsmeath. A *description* would help, but apparently you and the Boy Wonder can't remember what "Ryan" looks like.' A sniff. 'Maybe *that's* why?'

He wiggled his eyebrows. 'You're pretty sexy when you're sarcastic.'

'But . . .' DS Massie stared at him. Blinked. Her mouth hanging open. 'Wait . . . *what*?' Her jaw clamped shut, eyes narrowing. 'Are you looking for a punch in the face?'

Monroe stopped pacing. 'Irene, I've got to go.' Sticking his phone away as he marched over. 'Will the pair of you *try* to act like professionals?'

DS Massie glared at Dr Fife; Dr Fife smiled back.

'Rhona.'

She looked away. Rolled one shoulder. Had some more coffee.

Angus stretched.

Dr Fife had an evil wee grin to himself.

Monroe sagged against the wall, gazing back along the corridor, towards Interview Four. 'I miss the good old days, when CID would dangle people off the roof by their ankles till they confessed.'

What?

He raised a hand before Angus could say anything. 'Metaphorically, of course.' The sag turned into a slump. 'We've got six dead, a gun-toting maniac on the loose, and . . .' He turned to Dr Fife. 'Any chance the Fortnight Killer *doesn't* strike tomorrow?'

'Depends.' Back to his stolen coffee. 'On lots of things.'

Helpful, as always.

A sudden burring in his pocket made Angus flinch, as if a wasp was trapped in there. But it was followed by a *ding*. Incoming text message.

He stepped away to see what it was, leaving DS Massie to have another go at Dr Fife for being about as much use as 'a chocolate butt plug'.

ELLIE:

> You missed a MASSIVE night last night, by the way. It was so good I bought the cast CD.
> But bloody Plastic Colin didn't get half of it! Never seen the film!?!

Ding.

ELLIE:

> How could any grown man not see the movie? It's Jumanji, for God's sake!
> All our schoolmates are philistines!!!!!

To be honest, calling Plastic Colin a philistine was an insult to philistines. The man had a Jar Jar Binks duvet cover.

Ding.

ELLIE:

> Now that's out of the way: WHAT'S HAPPENING WITH
> THIS EXCLUSIVE?!?
> Time's running out, we're going to press if I don't
> hear back.

Oh, in the name of the buggering shite . . .
Ding.

ELLIE:

> Oh, and your mum says to pick up some milk.

Angus curled up like a snail, face scrunched tight.

It's OK, you can do this.

Somehow . . .

He dragged in a deep breath and straightened up.

Everyone was looking at him, as if he'd just pooped – right there in the middle of the corridor.

He cleared his throat. 'Boss, can I have a quick word? In private? It's important.'

'Oh, today just gets better and better.' DCI Monroe covered his face with his hands and thumped back against the filing cabinet, setting the remaining tins of Rampant Gorilla rattle-clanking together.

The heating was cranked up full pelt, turning Dr Fife's office into a depressing magnolia sauna that still held a faint whiff of Chinese spices and takeaway grease.

Monroe peeked through his fingers at Angus. 'They *can't* print! They print a big article about Dr Fife, and Dr Fife fucks off, and this time tomorrow we've got no forensic psychologist and two more victims!'

'That's what *I* said. But the *Castle News and Post* want something in exchange.'

'Why me . . .' He dropped his hands and stared up at the stained ceiling tiles for a bit.

Angus folded his arms. Then unfolded them again.

At least it wasn't just *his* problem any more.

That was some progress.

Finally, Monroe straightened up again, decision made. 'So we give them something. Something that's not going to scupper the investigation, but juicy enough to keep them from buggering everything up.' He took a good long look at Angus. 'You.'

'Boss?' Hands up. 'I didn't tell them about Dr Fife, I *swear*!'

'No. Not that. You're now, officially, the hero of Sadler Road. Your journalist friend wants a human-interest story? Give her one.'

Heat sizzled up Angus's cheeks, what with the double entendre and everything. 'But I'm not—'

'You *want* two more people to die?'

'No, but—'

'Only don't tell her anything about *why* you went to number one-thirty-two, or who we really think you were chasing. Can't risk some smartarse defence lawyer whining that we've prejudiced the jury.'

A quick *rat-a-tat-tat*, then DS Massie's head popped around the door. Not bothering to wait for an invitation. 'Boss? It's . . .' She frowned at Angus. 'Constable MacVicar, I'm as keen on a nice arse in sexy pants as the next girl, but maybe don't show yours off at work, eh? It's not professional.'

Heat flushed up Angus's face again. He snatched a post-mortem file from the desk, using it to cover his ripped trousers. 'I haven't been home to change!'

She hooked a thumb over her shoulder. 'That's McGilvary and his solicitor ready to go, Boss.'

Monroe hissed out a long breath. 'Ding-ding, round two.'

Dr Fife and DCI Monroe settled back into their seats as Angus assumed the looming position again.

Something had changed in Interview Four, though – Mrs Hannay's face was a mask of disapproval, nostrils flaring every time she so much as glanced at her client. Sean McGilvary, on the other hand, looked as if someone had run over him with a belt sander.

Mrs Hannay made a big show of thumping open her ring binder, unsnapping the clip, and pulling a sheet of paper free. 'This time, if we could please refrain from interrupting the statement before it's been read?' She slapped it down in front of Sean. 'That would be *lovely*.'

Monroe adopted the same stoical silence, but Dr Fife raised an eyebrow. As if something had just occurred to him. But he kept whatever it was to himself – just made a little twirly after-you gesture.

Mrs Hannay sniffed. 'Go ahead, *Sean*.'

'OK . . . Right.' Deep breath. ' "I would like to begin by apologizing for my previous statement. It was wrong of me to mislead my solicitor after she has been so kind to me and my family for all these years." ' He cast her a worried look, but she kept her eyes fixed front. ' "The reason my DNA and fingerprint appeared at Douglas Healey-Robinson's house is because . . ." ' Sean's mouth worked on the words for a soundless moment, then he coughed.

Cricked his neck to one side.

Put the statement down.

Flexed his hands.

Picked it up again. ' ". . . is because I broke in on the twenty-seventh of February – which is three days *before* they were attacked – and stole a number of electronic items, jewellery, and a small amount of cash. These . . ." ' A pale-yellow tongue poked between his teeth, pulling his top lip in to be bitten. Followed by a trembling exhale. ' "These I sold to private individuals in pubs around the Blackwall Hill area. I do not know those individuals' names. Nor did I wish to know." '

He placed the statement down on the tabletop in front of him, and stared at it. ' "It was the first time I burgled a house, and I have not done so since. Having dabbled in theft from shops before, this felt like a logical progression, but I am deeply ashamed by my actions and apologize and accept any punishment the legal system deems appropriate." ' With that said he shoved the statement across the table towards Dr Fife, then drooped. Shrugged. Not making eye contact with anyone. 'That's it.'

A childish signature was scrawled at the bottom, along with today's date.

Sitting next to him, Mrs Hannay radiated righteous disapproval.

One of Monroe's eyes twitched.

Dr Fife tilted his head to the side, like Wee Hamish did when he heard a packet of crisps opening. Only instead of piteous whining noises, Dr Fife went 'Hmmmmmmm . . .'

'So you see' – Mrs Hannay straightened her ring binder – 'there was a perfectly *reasonable* explanation and Sean should be cautioned, then released awaiting a trial date if you choose to prosecute for burglary.' A grim smile flirted with her thin lips, but didn't even get to first base. 'Though I think it's fair to assume that Mr and Mr Healey-Robinson won't be pressing charges?'

Flipping heck. Talk about *heartless*.

Dr Fife's palms smacked together, then again, and again, building in speed till it was a one-man round of applause. 'Bravo! Bravissimo!'

OK . . . Not what anyone was expecting, going by the looks they were giving him.

'I *beg* your pardon?' Mrs Hannay slammed her ring binder shut. 'Is this supposed to be some sort of—'

'Have to admire the commitment there, Sean. "I broke in three days *before* they died", "I stole jewellery and cash".' Dr Fife lowered his voice and sat forward, closing the gap. 'You had these idiots going, but I'm the kinda guy who *knows* when people are lying to me.'

'I . . . I don't . . .'

'You see, when someone lies, they give off little micro-expressions without even knowing it. The way your eyes move, the muscles either side of your lips, the way your fingers curl, eyebrows twitch . . . Your body's screaming "IT'S ALL LIES!"' Bellowing that last bit out.

Sean jerked back in his seat, unable to escape because it was bolted to the floor.

Mrs Hannay glared down her nose at Dr Fife. 'I don't think this is appropriate—'

'"I am deeply ashamed by my actions." That's the only thing you've said that's true, isn't it?'

Pink flushed into Sean's face, turning the tips of his ears an angry shade of beetroot. 'It . . . I . . . I didn't . . . It . . .'

'*Isn't* it?'

He licked his lips. Stared at Dr Fife, blinking as his eyes shimmered. Then a nod, mouth clamped tight. A single tear splatched on the tabletop.

Mrs Hannay turned to look at him for the first time, her voice low and warning. 'Sean.'

'Why do you feel ashamed, Sean?'

A second tear joined the first. 'Because . . . Because of what I did.'

'I need to talk to my client again.'

'Is it because they were an "abomination", Sean?' Dr Fife poked the tabletop, emphasizing each word: 'What – did – you – do?'

Sean took a huge breath and sat up straight, fists clenched in front of him. Knuckles white with the pressure.

Mrs Hannay grabbed his arm. 'Sean!' She glared at Monroe. 'I *insist* you suspend this interview so I can—'

'I did it!' Tears rolled down Sean McGilvary's cheeks, glittering in the interview room's lights as a shiny skein of snot spread across his top lip. 'I *killed* them!'

He lowered his head, dripping tears onto his trembling fists.

Dr Fife raised an eyebrow and sat back, mouth puckered as if he was trying not to grin.

DCI Monroe, on the other hand, gave in to temptation.

'Enough!' Mrs Hannay slammed her hand down on her binder. 'I *demand* a break to talk to my client!'

The SOC suit rustled as Sean wiped his nose on its sleeve. 'They . . . They were *dirty sodomites* . . . and I killed them! I—'

'I SAID *ENOUGH*!' Mrs Hannay lurched to her feet. 'If you continue to interrogate my client, I *will* file a complaint.' Standing there, trembling and bug-eyed, finger pointing right at Monroe's face.

He looked back at her, gave a wee smiling shrug. 'Why not.' Then reached for the audio-visual controls. 'Interview suspended at nineteen fifty-eight.'

21

Angus stuck two fingers between the dusty slats and levered himself a wee gap in the venetian blinds. Peering out at the Front Podium, four floors below.

The press had gathered outside Divisional Headquarters again, braving the rain for yet another episode of *Things Aren't Going Well for Operation Telegram*. They glittered in the darkness, with their lights and camera flashes, even though there was still an hour and three-quarters to go before the ten o'clock bulletins.

Those protestors had turned up too, their number swollen to five now that 'STOP NATO WARMONGERS!' had joined the crusade for 'truth', 'justice', and the right to look like a proper tit on national television.

Ooh, there was Gillian.

She couldn't possibly see him from down there, but he gave her a little wave anyway.

Back in the real world, DCI Monroe's voice had taken on a whiny edge. *'But why?'*

Angus dropped the blinds and turned back to the incident room. Covering his mouth as a colossal yawn tried to take the top of his head off.

Not that anyone saw – Monroe, DS Massie, and DS Sharp were all too busy watching Dr Fife wearing a groove in the carpet tiles. Pacing back and forth, face scrunched up in a frown, hands twitching like unhappy spiders.

'Because if we release a statement saying we've caught the

Fortnight Killer and two more people die, we'll look like a bunch of clueless assholes.'

DS Massie glowered, arms folded, legs crossed, bum perched on Monster Munch's vacant desk. 'He confessed, for God's sake!'

'Oh, I'm *sorry*, do you *want* a repeat of Patrick Crombie?'

'It's not the same thing at—'

'Yes it is!' Dr Fife stopped pacing and waved a hand at the windows instead. 'Ryan is still out there!'

'Boss: *tell* him!'

Monroe had his arms folded too. 'Sean McGilvary confessed, Dr Fife. He's the Fortnight Killer.'

'Then what the hell was Ryan doing in Dr Fordyce's apartment block, disguised as a pizza-delivery guy when no one in the building ordered pizza? Why was Kate Paisley there *helping* him?'

'Well' – DS Sharp raised a finger – 'maybe they were casing the joint for a burglary? A real one this time.'

'He tried to shoot my sidekick!'

Angus joined the Folded Arms Club. 'Who has a name, thank you.'

Dr Fife waved the complaint away. 'Does that sound like the kinda guy who breaks in and steals your stereo?' And back to pacing again. 'No. There's more to it than that.'

She shrugged. 'We've got to tell the press *something*.'

'Maybe Sidekick Boy was right? Maybe the Fortnight Killer *does* have more than one accomplice?' He snapped his fingers, snap, snap, snap. 'Sean McGilvary: you find his DNA or prints at any of the other crime scenes?'

A snort from DS Massie. '*Course* not. They would've pinged up a hit in the database. Thieving wee git's been processed for nicking things often enough.'

'But we're supposed to believe a guy who's planned his killing spree like a military campaign suddenly can't be assed wearing gloves for a murder?' Fife got as far as the filing cabinets and started back again. 'I don't buy it. And if you do, I've got a social media website to sell you.'

Maybe it was time for Angus to save the day again?

He put his hand up. 'What if . . . they're in different cells? You know, like a terrorist organization? Ryan kills the Fordyces, Sean kills the Healey-Robinsons. Maybe someone else killed the Councillor and his wife?' Made sense, didn't it? 'Maybe *that's* why the MO hasn't developed?' This time the yawn was on him too quickly to stifle or hide, ending with a full-body tremble. 'Sorry.'

Monroe scowled. '*Three* sets of killers? That's all we need.'

The yawn got its claws into Dr Fife and he let rip one of his own. 'The boy's got a point.' Scrubbing at his face. 'It's *wrong*, but at least he's trying.'

Always nice to be appreciated.

DS Kilgour slumped into the room. Standing semi-upright he looked even more like a bear than he'd done sitting down. 'There you are.' He collapsed into a vacant office chair and slouched it around till it faced in Monroe's direction. Held up a folder. 'Preliminary search results on Sadler Road.'

'Gimme.' DS Massie snatched them.

'Loads of fingerprints, but so far . . .' The yawn claimed another victim, showing off all of Kilgour's molars. Which set Angus off again. *And* Dr Fife. Kilgour threw in a stretch for good luck. 'The only match we've got is Kate Paisley, which is what we call "Sod-All Use".'

Massie flipped through the folder. 'DNA, DNA, DNA . . . Oh, for buggering hell.' She held out a sheet to Monroe. 'Going to be tomorrow morning before they've processed and cross-checked the samples.'

'Shock horror.' Kilgour pointed at the file. 'Neighbours can't agree if there were two, three, or five-point-four million people living there. Other than that, it's just a bog-standard three-bedroom semi.' He swivelled his chair, taking in the whole group. 'I miss anything?'

'Oh yeah.'

Monroe threw his arms up, letting them slap back down against his sides. 'So what are we going to tell the press?'

'You're gonna tell them nothing.' Dr Fife made a U-turn at the whiteboards. 'Until we got corroboration on Sean McGilvary's story, it's "Someone's assisting with our inquiries", but that's all. Anything else's gonna bite us on the ass. Long as Ryan's still out there, it's too risky.'

DS Massie tossed the file back to Kilgour. 'Could have another crack at Kate Paisley?'

'Nah.' Fife shook his head. 'She won't turn on Ryan. Our dark satanic messenger is more than a friend or lover to her. More than family. She's . . .' His finger-spiders searched for the word. '. . . a *disciple*.'

'Erm . . .' Angus put his hand up again. ' "Dark satanic" . . . ?'

'The Post-its.' Tapping his forehead as he paced. ' "Don't believe their lies".'

Ah, OK.

Angus opened his mouth to point out that Ryan must be pretty pissed off that they were keeping his messages secret, but all that came out was another mammoth, wobbly yawn.

'For God's sake.' Monroe jabbed a finger at the door. 'I'm not telling you again: go home! That's an order.'

'But—'

'And make sure you take care of that . . . friend of yours.' The Boss cast a sneaky glance at Dr Fife, who was too busy with a yawn of his own to notice. ' "The Hero of Sadler Road", et cetera. Before anything horrible happens. Go.'

The finger was resolute, and so was the frown.

Fair enough.

Angus picked up his crumpled, grass-and-nettle-stained jacket and pulled it on as he slouched towards the door. Taking his time, just in case DCI Monroe changed his mind and realized what a vital cog he was in the—

'Hoy!' DS Massie threw a scrunched-up biscuit wrapper at him. 'And get something to cover your backside on the way, before some poor auld wifie has a stroke!'

Oh, for . . .

Grabbing the coat-tails of his jacket with one hand, he pulled them down as far as they would go, reaching for the door with the other.

But just as his fingertips brushed the handle, it jerked down, the door flew open, and thumped right into his chest – twice in one day – swiftly followed by the uniformed officer trying to stride in after it.

PC Pirie jerked to a halt: shortish and small-nosed, with long brown hair wrapped up in a cottage-loaf bun. *Big* bags under her eyes, as if she had a hyperactive seven-year-old to look after at home. 'Gah!' She extracted herself from the door and walloped Angus on the arm. 'Don't *do* that!' Then peered around Angus into the room. 'Boss? Sean McGilvary's brief says they're ready.'

'Thanks.' He frowned a moment. 'How's Peanut?'

'A massive pain in my arse, Boss.'

'Yeah, kids will do that.' He picked up his interview notes. 'Dr Fife, shall we?'

They made for the corridor, meaning Angus had to back out of the way to let them through – PC Pirie giving him a blast of evil eye on the way past.

She marched away towards the stairwell, with Dr Fife and DCI Monroe in tow.

Angus fell in behind them.

Monroe stopped. Turned. 'Where do you think *you're* going?'

Weird question.

'I'm . . . you know: looming?'

A quick check over his shoulder to make sure Dr Fife was out of earshot, then Monroe lowered his voice to a sharp-edged whisper. 'No you flipping aren't: you've got a journalist to distract so You Know Who doesn't end up on the front page, remember?'

Oh, sod.

'Yes, but if Sean McGilvary—'

Monroe's hand landed on Angus's arm and gave it a squeeze. 'I *genuinely* think we can cope without you, Constable. We *can't* cope without Dr Fife.' Letting go to point again. 'Go!'

Suppose he had no choice.

Angus deflated a bit. 'Yes, Boss.'

'Good.' Then Monroe turned on his heel and marched off a couple of paces, before stopping and scuttling back. 'And try to push the whole "Do you recognize this man?" angle. Be nice if the *Castle News and Post* actually *helped* for a change.' A nod, and he was off, hurrying to catch up with Dr Fife and PC Pirie.

Great . . .

Angus pulled out his phone and messaged Ellie:

Have approval from DCI.

Exclusive is on.

Will call when home.

At least *someone* would be happy.

Drizzle misted down from the scorched-terracotta clouds.

Angus tugged the hem of his borrowed XXL high-vis jacket down again, even though it was more than long enough to cover the hole in his trousers. The outfit wasn't exactly subtle – crumpled dirty suit, filthy shoes, a fluorescent-yellow waterproof with 'POLICE' across the back in reflective letters – so he slunk along the other side of the road, steering clear of the mob.

With an hour and a quarter to go till showtime, the assembled TV people were mingling with the online and print journalists, eating deep-fried foods and smoking fags before the work of setting-up began.

The other protestors had disappeared off somewhere, leaving Gillian to guard their placards, bundled up in that biker jacket of hers, knackered umbrella pinned between neck and shoulder as she poured something hot from a thermos into its plastic-cup-lid thing. She looked up, lips puckered for a sip, and must've seen Angus slinking past, because she gave him a cheery wave.

Then scurried across the road to intercept him.

Well, it would be rude not to say hello, wouldn't it?

But only hello, because Mum was *already* going to kill him for missing dinnertime two days in a row.

'Hi, Angus.'

He tugged his high-vis down again and ducked behind the WW1 monument, putting it between them and the takeaway-munching press. 'Gillian, hi. Can't stop, sorry. On a mission.'

She gazed up at him with her smoky eyes wide, a wee bounce to her stance. 'Did you hear they caught someone? I heard they caught someone. Well, *you* caught someone, I suppose, as you kind of *are* the police. How weird is that: I know someone on the investigation! Which is pretty cool.' She bit her soft peach lips. 'Ooh, sorry: want some coffee?' Holding out the plastic cup. 'It's salted-caramel latte, but with a triple shot of espresso and heaps of brandy. Great for keeping the cold out!'

He winced. 'Can't: on duty.' Which was only a little white lie to spare her feelings.

'Are you OK? You look knackered. I've got sherbet fruits, if that's allowed?' She pinned the brolly in place again and dug out a crumpled packet of sweets. 'I ate all the blackcurrant ones. Sorry.'

Couldn't refuse two things in a row, that really *would* be rude. He plucked a sherbet lime from the bag. 'Thanks.'

Didn't eat it, though.

Instead, he waited for her to look the other way and slipped it into his pocket, because good boys didn't eat sweeties from strange ladies. And neither did police officers.

Gillian lowered her voice, as if worried the monument's bronze soldiers might be eavesdropping. 'I've been keeping an eye out for anyone sketchy hanging about the press packs, like you asked. Had a good look round at Sadler Road – that's where we were before this.' A note of pride raised her chin. 'I got in the back of Sky News's coverage, flying the flag for truth, but couldn't see anyone *particularly* sketchy.' She sipped from the thermos lid. 'Well, you know what journalists are like. But then I got talking to a nice lady from one thirty-eight, and she said there was a bloke getting chased across the playing fields by some police officer who tried to shoot him! Even though there were, like, sixty wee kids right there playing football! Miracle no one died.'

'It was *rugby*; there were *twenty-four* kids; and the bloke *running away* was doing the shooting!'

She scrunched her button nose up. 'That's what they *want* you to think. Police Scotland's lying through its . . . bumhole to protect whoever this gun-happy, reckless, violent officer is.'

'Me!' Throwing his hands out. 'It was me: *I* was the officer, and it was bloody *Ryan* who had the gun!'

Her eyes were owl-wide, mouth open showing off a wee pink tongue. 'You?'

'Could've killed me, and people are saying it's *my* fault?'

'Wow.' She stared up at him as if he'd grown three feet taller, pink blooming across her cheeks. Then held out the bag of sweets again. 'Want another?'

'No, I'm . . .' Bloody hell. 'What's *wrong* with people?'

'Sorry.' Shuffling her feet.

A patrol car growled past, windscreen wipers going.

On the other side of the road, someone burst into a coughing fit.

The drizzle drizzled.

'Honest, Angus: I'm *really* sorry.' She stroked his arm with the back of her umbrella hand. 'He's the one you've arrested, isn't he. Well . . . at least this Ryan person can't hurt anyone else.'

An unhappy laugh rattled free. 'Yeah. Long story.'

'You *haven't* arrested him?'

'Don't even know his last name! Honestly, it's . . .' Angus clamped his mouth shut before anything else could fall out. Squinted at the rain fogging around that patrol car's tail-lights. 'Forget it. I shouldn't have said anything. *Please* don't tell anyone.'

'Promise I won't say a word.'

When he turned back, Gillian was gazing up at him again. She bit her bottom lip for a moment, then wobbled up onto her tiptoes and placed a soft warm kiss on his cheek.

Then she was back on the ground again, blushing like it was an Olympic sport and she was a shoo-in for gold. 'It's . . . Yes.' She cleared her throat. Pulled the sherbet fruits from her pocket and pressed the bag into his hand. 'Keep them.'

She hurried off without another word, the pink in her cheeks darkening to a rich strawberry.

After about a dozen paces, Gillian looked back at Angus, and collided with a cameraman. Stumbled. Almost hit the deck. Dropped her lopsided umbrella. 'Sorry!' Helping the cameraman up. 'Sorry. I'm sorry.' Grabbed her fallen umbrella and scurried away.

Wow.

OK.

Angus blinked, fingertips straying up to touch the spot where she'd kissed him. Still warm and tingling.

A wee smile pulled at the side of his mouth.

He huffed out a breath.

Stuffed the sherbet fruits into one of his borrowed jacket's pockets.

Right . . .

Milk.

22

A radio burbled away in the corner of Mr Mendoza's Ye Olde Corner Store ~ Est. 2014: *'. . . can't tell me they're not cocking this up on purpose!'*

The host had one of those fake radio-DJ voices, trying to bring a bit of smarmy calm to proceedings. *'That's a bit strong, Margaret, I'm sure they wouldn't—'*

'Course they are. Could've caught this guy weeks ago, but they know no one gives a toss about these wankers. Doctors, journalists, politicians? And now they're saying it's bankers and lawyers next?'

The place was a jumble of crisps and sweets and washing powder, tins and jars and bottles of off-brand fizzy juice, with a sort of Lidl-wannabe middle aisle full of unfamiliar South American things. Most of which were in very colourful packaging that had Spanish names and ingredients. All bathed in the cold, soulless light of fluorescent bulbs that hummed like blowflies.

Angus dripped his way across the grey linoleum to the fridge, rummaging through the four-pint cartons of milk in search of whichever one had the longest to go before its use-by date.

Then took it to the counter and paid for it in small change – counting out every penny. Which Mr Mendoza received with all the delight of a house brick. Or maybe it was just the big droopy moustache that made him look borderline depressed?

'Why would they want *to catch this guy? He's doing the Lord's work, you idiot!'*

Mr Mendoza looked out at the damp trail Angus had left across the shop floor and his moustache drooped even more.

'Now let's calm down a bit, Margaret, and—'

'You *calm down*. I'd line the bastards up against the wall, if it was me in charge. Them and all the paedos!'

Angus nodded. 'Thanks.' And headed for the door.

The 157 bus to Kingsmeath grumbled its way over the Calderwell Bridge. OK, so the seats were worn, and a bit dirty, and it'd been in operation long enough to still stink of ancient cigarettes, but at least it was dry, reasonably warm, and Angus had a window seat.

Condensation misted the glass, but he'd cleared a little porthole in the fog, watching the traffic go by. City lights twinkling on the other side of the river, fading as the rain swallowed them.

Someone at the back of the bus sang a sad song to themselves, slurring the words through a haze of booze and kebab fat. The joys of Ladies' Night in an Oldcastle pub.

A glowing reindeer drifted by, followed by a bow, two bells, and a parcel.

Middle of March and the Christmas illuminations were still up, but the council didn't have enough money to keep the libraries open.

Angus pulled the sherbet lime from his borrowed-high-vis pocket, turning it in his fingers, making the cellophane wrapping *crinkle*.

Should really chuck the lot in the nearest bin.

You never knew what people were trying to slip you: could be poison inside that little green lozenge. Could be drugs. Someone could've wiped their bogies on it, or something worse. And just because Gillian *seemed* nice, that didn't mean she wasn't dangerous.

There was a sergeant once, back when Angus did his probation – two years pounding the streets of Shortstaine and Cowskillin, learning the ropes from a more experienced officer – Irvine, his name was. And one day Sergeant Irvine accepted a Tupperware box of homemade fig rolls from a grateful pensioner, only to find out they'd been made with a mixture of mouldy dates, sperm, and the cremated remains of the old boy's wife. Managed to make it through half the container before the vomiting started.

Good job he'd been a greedy bugger and hadn't offered them around the muster room . . .

Yeah, but Gillian was lovely.

And she'd kissed him.

And he hadn't had a sherbet fruit for ages.

Still, remember Sergeant Irvine.

Angus returned the sweet to his pocket and went back to staring out the window instead.

The 157 pulled up at the Milbank Park stop with an angry-snake *hisssss* of air brakes. Then the doors hinged open, letting in a blast of cold air and the sound of rain hammering the bus shelter.

'Thanks.' Angus pulled his high-vis hood up and stepped out into it.

Not that the shelter provided any respite from the downpour – the plastic panels were *long* gone, leaving only a buckled metal frame behind.

Behind him, the doors clunked shut again, the diesel engine growled, and the number 157 continued on its way.

A sign welcomed visitors to 'MILLBANK PARK ~ KINGSMEATH'S FRIENDLIEST COMMUNITY', or it had done for about three weeks, before the local kids got to it – burying the message beneath so many layers of graffiti that it was caked with the stuff. And could you really call a trio of eighteen-storey tower blocks a 'community'?

Millbank East, North, and West loomed against the angry sky, in all their rain-and-dirt-streaked glory. Tombstones for a thousand murdered dreams.

Angus headed out into the rain, cutting across the car park – currently home to a Fiat Punto that was up on bricks and a handful of manky hatchbacks that wouldn't survive another MOT. A couple of stray dogs regarded him from the safety of an overturned brown sofa, eyes glittering in the gloom.

He hurried in under the large, cantilevered entrance to Millbank North, with its double doors that someone had finally scraped the posters and fliers off. Leaving ghosts of paper behind.

Off to one side, a wee play park drooped in the rain. Surrounded

IN A PLACE OF DARKNESS

by sickly trees and bollards. Where a group of five teenagers had gathered in tracksuits and baseball caps, as if it was sometime last century, swigging from two-litre bottles of extra-strong cider. They didn't seem to mind the rain, just sat there, perched on the remains of the swings and roundabout, watching as Angus reached for the door.

Their hooded eyes followed him. Wary and aggressive. Completely silent. Like hyenas disturbed at a fresh kill.

And not one of them over the age of fifteen.

Should really go have a word, but 'community policing' down here tended to get your windows panned in and jobbies shoved through your letterbox. Mum couldn't cope with that again.

Which is why you never policed the area you came from. Too many opportunities for corruption and/or revenge.

Angus pushed into the lobby, throwing the hood back on his borrowed high-vis.

It wasn't exactly the Ritz: an abandoned shopping trolley, full of empty tins, stood cock-ended on three wheels – even though the nearest supermarket was ages away; while a ginger tom with matted fur sprayed the lift doors – right below the message 'CURRENTLY OUT OF ORDER, SORRY FOR THE INCONVENIENCE AND THANK YOU FOR YOUR PATIENCE', onto which someone had scrawled 'IT'S BEEN THREE YEARS!!!'

So the cat had the right idea.

Angus shoved through the door marked 'STAIRS' into the throat-scouring stench of disinfectant. Which was better than the alternative.

Some community-spirited individual had given the stairwell a rough coat of magnolia, covering up the worst graffiti, though someone had been in after them to spray a massive cock-and-balls on the newly blanked canvas.

Angus squared his shoulders and began the long climb home . . .

Fourteen storeys later, he lumbered out of the stairwell and onto the balcony/walkway that linked the four flats on this side of the tower block. Each with its own little 'garden' of planters and concrete, and a front door onto the great, soggy outdoors. Bulkhead lights cast their wan yellow glow out into the darkness, flickering as one of the bulbs struggled to fire up properly.

A howling wind wrapped itself around the building, but the overhang of the balcony above kept most of the rain off. Even if it was brass monkeys up here.

Angus dug out his keys and slogged his way over to Mum's front door – painted a deep indigo blue, like the one back home had been – with four brass numerals, polished and shiny in the sputtering overhead light: '1408'. A wee plaque sat above the letterbox: 'MacVicar'.

At least he'd managed to persuade her not to *name* the flat.

Cos that would just be asking for trouble.

He unlocked the door and . . .

Nope. He'd only get yelled at, marching in there all soaking wet.

Instead, he stripped off his nice, warm, padded high-vis and gave it a vigorous shake. That done, he unlaced his shoes – completely sodden now – then hauled off his soggy socks and stuffed them into their empty carcases. Hissing as the cold concrete balcony jabbed his bare soles with a bazillion icy needles.

Angus high-stepped onto the front mat and hurried inside.

The hall was clean and tidy, swept and dusted, as if Mum was permanently expecting a visit from some minor royal.

And speaking of royalty . . .

A shin-high whirlwind of fur was waiting for him on the worn carpet, trembling with excitement, yapping with delight, tail going like a windscreen wiper in a monsoon. Wee Hamish launched into a bouncy twirly dance at Angus's naked feet, gazing up with pure hairy adoration and unconditional delight.

Angus bent down and ruffled the fuzzy little lad's head with his free hand. 'Hey, Hamish.'

Cue terrier-type raptures.

Must be nice to be so unbothered by bills and responsibilities and murderers and wars and climate change and all the associated horrors.

'Mum?' He hung up his borrowed jacket.

The sound of a game show dinged out through the closed living-room door, sticky with forced jollity. Upstairs, Mr and Mrs

Ratcliffe were shouting at each other again. Downstairs, someone was practising 'Smoke On The Water' on the electric guitar. Badly.

Angus slipped his damp feet into his bauchly old slippers – urgh . . . – and headed for the bathroom. Only the little red triangle on the lock was showing.

She was in residence.

He made for the kitchen instead, with Wee Hamish wheeling around his ankles.

The disappointing scent of stewed vegetables filled the small space, crowding a fitted kitchen that had probably already been out of fashion when it was installed sometime in the 1970s.

He wrung his socks out in the sink, careful not to splosh grey-brown water everywhere. Then popped them back in his wet shoes. Washed his hands.

The fridge wasn't technically an antique, it just sounded like one. Opening the door revealed the usual expanse of empty shelves, but a clingfilm-covered plate had pride of place next to a block of mousetrap cheese. Looked like some sort of casserole with a side of shrivelled peas and boiled tatties.

Sigh.

He put it on the worktop and stuck the milk into the door pocket, next to an open thing of white-wine-in-a-box. Which definitely *wasn't* usual. Not in this house anyway. A bottle of supermarket sherry at Christmas, maybe a four-pack of beer on his birthday, and that was it.

Wine in a box? Very fancy.

He clunked the door shut and took down the old Quality Street tin. Shoogling off the lid to reveal a pile of bone-shaped biscuits – one of which went into Wee Hamish, while the plate went into the microwave.

Bzzzzzzzzzzzzzzzzzzzzz . . .

Crunch, munch, crunch, wag-wag-wag-wag-wag-wag-wag.

A familiar voice squeezed into the crowded kitchen: '*You look like shite. You know that, right?*'

Angus froze. Then opened the cupboard by the kettle and pulled out the off-brand brown sauce. 'Ellie.' He didn't turn to look at her, just went about his business: salt, pepper, cutlery, glass of water. 'Was just about to call you.'

Which was true. Ish.

She pushed past him, opening the fridge and pulling out the box-o'-wine. 'Your mum's been frantic. Thought a wee Chardonnay or three might ease things a bit.' Ellie held a glass under the spigot and filled it – making widdling noises to join the microwave's buzz. She took a sip. 'Did you know the arse is hanging out your trousers?'

He turned his back to the units. 'Ellie, I really don't—'

'Hang on.' Grabbing the side of his suit jacket, she pulled it up and out, like a basset hound's ear. 'You've got moths.'

She twisted it, so he could see: a perfectly round hole poked straight through the back panel, about halfway between where his nipple and his belly button would've been.

Ellie stuck her finger through the bullet hole and wiggled it.

'Oh, for . . . I just *bought* this suit!'

Ping.

Angus snatched up a tea towel and rescued his dinner from the microwave. Thumped it on a tray with his condiments, cruet, cutlery and drink. Cursed the melty-hot clingfilm from the plate with stinging fingertips. Then picked the lot up and scowled his way through to the living room.

Like the hall, it awaited a royal visitor who would never call.

OK, so the furniture was all mismatched and second-hand – the holes in its upholstery hidden beneath layers of tartan blankets and paisley-pattern throws – and the rug by the fireplace was only there to hide a bit in the carpet that was worn down to the underlay, but no one could say it wasn't *clean*.

Mum always maintained that a lovely big fifty-inch TV would be common and obscene, which was probably easier than admitting they couldn't afford one, so a much more *modest* television sat in the corner, broadcasting a fake blonde and some fat beardy bloke as they shrieked their shopping trolley around an obstacle course, while other D-list celebrities threw oversized foam models of junk food at them. Bet the BAFTAs were watching with prizes at the ready.

'. . . *Ooh, Darren almost got them with a cheeseburger there! You could say they nearly* meat *their maker, if you'll pardon the* bun—'

Angus plonked his tray on the coffee table and hit mute.

Sod off.

He collapsed into the creaky armchair by the fire.

Wee Hamish claimed the couch.

Ellie leaned against the doorframe, toasting them both with her wine. 'Hello, Ellie. It's lovely to see you, Ellie.' Sip. 'It's lovely to see *you too*, Angus, and *thank you* for the warm welcome. *Especially* after I put my tits on the line convincing the *Knap* to spike that Dr Fife story!'

Groan . . .

He picked up his fork. 'Sorry. Been a long day.'

'So I heard.' She wandered in and thumped him on the arm. 'Any more thoughts about what I said this morning? About your dad?'

'No.' Difficult to know where to start with dinner, so he mashed his tatties into the watery gravy. 'Mum doesn't want a fuss. She doesn't like it when people fuss—'

'ANGUS! Oh, Angus!' Speak of the devil . . . She rushed into the living room, wringing her hands. Thirteen years they'd lived here, and she still looked as out of place as the day they arrived. Short and roundish was pretty standard for Kingsmeath, but not the floral skirt and layered tops: blouse, teal V-neck, and terracotta cardigan. Glasses on a chain around her neck. Neat grey hair and a lined forehead. You'd never think she was only in her fifties. She'd kept the posh Aberdeen accent too. 'My brave little boy!'

She rushed over and enveloped him in a choking hug, tears sparking in her eyes.

OK, that was . . .

He tried not to cringe.

Angus grimaced over her shoulder at Ellie – who shrugged.

Probably the wine.

Mum wasn't used to wine.

He patted her on the back. 'Are you—'

'Ellie showed me the videos, on her phone! Oh, how could *anyone* be so wicked?'

'Videos . . . ?'

237

'Oh yeah.' Ellie settled on the arm of the sofa. 'The kids playing rugby: they filmed the whole thing and posted it on YouTube. You'll be all over the papers tomorrow: "Lumbering great twit gets shot at on playing field!"'

'He could've *killed* you!' Mum let go and backed up a bit, the weepy look replaced by something much harder as she clipped him on the back of the head. 'What were you thinking?'

'Ow!' Rubbing the impact spot. 'I was . . .'

Wait a minute.

He scowled at Ellie. 'Is that why you're here: winding Mum up for a bit of extra colour? I *said* you'd get your sodding exclusive.'

Mum hit him again. 'Don't be so rude!'

Soon as she moved towards the couch, Wee Hamish obediently jumped down and waited for Mum to sit, before leaping into her lap and staring up at her as if she were a god.

Ellie shrugged. 'Wanted to make sure you were OK, that's all. Didn't want your mum to be alone at this difficult time.'

'She didn't even know it *was* a "difficult time" till you turned up and showed her!'

'Angus! Ellie has been nothing but a good friend, and you're being horrible.'

He rolled his eyes and went back to his sad dinner. Scooping up some casserole, which seemed to be ninety percent veg with only a couple of chunks of what might be generously described as 'sausage'. It tasted every bit as exciting as it looked. But there was only so much brown sauce you could add before it appeared impolite.

Ellie picked the other glass off the coffee table and handed it to Mum. 'It'll probably be on the ten o'clock news anyway, so she'd find out soon enough.' Ellie clinked their glasses together. 'At least this way everyone's forewarned and anaesthetized.'

She sipped her wine, watching him eat. 'But if you want to make it up to me – for all your rudeness – *and* keep up your end of the bargain, a nice big chunk of human interest and colour *might* help . . . ?'

Rain misted down, blurring the streetlights. Couldn't even tell where the valley ended and the sky began. Everything out of focus, like a malignant X-ray.

Angus turned his back on the lack-of-view, rested his borrowed high-vis against the handrail, and took a sip of tea. Phone in his other hand, poking out a one-thumbed message to Dr Fife:

Any progress on Sean McGilvary?
Has confession been corroborated?

SEND.

The front door eased open and Ellie slipped out – all bundled up in her big duvet coat, making a big show of hunching her shoulders and shivering. 'God almighty, it's like *Siberia* out here.' She winkled a bright-pink vape from her pocket and took a hefty sook on the thing. Blowing a cloying lungful of salted caramel in his direction. Thankfully, the wind took care of that.

She sniffed. 'You still stealing Wi-Fi off Mr Rosomakha?' Leaning on the railing, frowning out into the night. 'Bit dishonest for an overgrown boy scout.'

'That was years ago. And I *wasn't* a boy scout.'

A smile curled the side of her mouth. 'Oh no, nothing so *uncool* as "Dib-dib-dib, dub-dub-dub, where's Akela? On the sex-offenders' register." No, *you* could recite the whole pledge of allegiance to Gondor. In Elvish.'

She tried again with the sweet vapey cloud – close enough this time for it to envelop him.

He waved it away, spluttering till the wind ripped it apart. 'Do you have to?'

'Don't have any worms on me.'

'And there's nothing wrong with LARPing. At least it got me out in the *fresh* air.'

'Running round swinging wooden swords and pretending to cast spells, like a bunch of idiots. No wonder you never got laid.'

'I was fourteen!'

'Blah, blah.' She sent another cloud his way. 'This guy you've got in custody: you don't think it's really *him*, do you?'

Yeah, he wasn't answering that. Especially after she'd been so rude about Live Action Role Playing.

Ellie put her vape away. 'Off the record.'

'It's complicated.' A yawn skittered up his spine and made his jaw pop. Leaving him sagging. 'Right now I'm more worried about Ryan.'

'Cos if it's *not* him, by this time tomorrow you're looking at two dead lawyers, or bankers.'

'Yes, thank you, Admiral Absolutely Bloody Obvious.' Angus turned so he was facing the same way she was – trying to pick out the vague outline of Meathmill Academy in the dark. He huffed out a breath.

Might as well ask, right?

Angus cleared his throat and warmth bloomed in his cheeks. 'You know Gillian? From the demos. The one you interviewed?' Nonchalant pause. 'What's she like?'

'Oh aye?' The smile was back. 'Got a wee touch of the hotties, have we?'

'No. Just . . . She gave me a bag of sweets and kissed my cheek.' He pulled the sherbet fruits from his high-vis pocket and showed Ellie the packet.

She raised an eyebrow, then helped herself to a strawberry one. 'The brazen hussy.' Unwrapping the thing and popping it into her mouth. 'Mmmm . . .' Smacking her lips. 'Surprised you didn't wolf all these. Thought you *loved* sherbet fruits.'

'Yeah, but you never know, do you? If members of the public give you things. Maybe they've *interfered* with them.'

'*What?*' Eyes wide, she spat the sweetie out as if it were radio-active, sending the little red lozenge spiralling away into the rain. 'You could've warned me!' Wiping her tongue. 'Gah . . .'

Now that was definitely worth a grin. 'She *probably* didn't, though.'

'That wasn't funny!'

'Serves you right.' He curled one shoulder up to his ear. 'It's just, you know, she's kinda . . . ?'

Ellie's top lip curled. 'Urgh: I was right, you *are* nursing a stiffy for her! Forgot you like them pretty and weird.' Shuffling away a couple of feet, in case it was catching. 'Remember Mary in art class? With the long red hair and that ridiculous little rabbit nose? *Two years* you followed her around like a horny, hormonal, spotty shadow, and never *once* worked up the balls to talk to her.'

Bit unfair.

He put the sherbet fruits away. 'Yeah, Gillian's a little strange – what with all the Covid conspiracy stuff – but maybe I should ask if she fancies getting a drink when the case is over?'

Ellie hit him. 'She's a *civilian*, not a suspect, you muppet. And what if you never catch this guy? Going to stay a virgin forever?'

Helpful as ever.

'Yes, but what should I *do*?'

'Whatever you like; none of my business. Shag her, don't shag her, makes no odds to me. Couldn't care less.' Ellie pushed herself off the handrail and jammed her hands deep in her pockets. 'Now are you going to give me something juicy for this exclusive or not?'

'Pursuing multiple lines of inquiry, asking everyone to remain vigilant, we *will* catch the Fortnight Killer, et cetera.' Angus puffed out his cheeks. Sagged. 'But off the record? I've got a nasty feeling about tomorrow, Ellie.' He frowned out at the storm. 'A very nasty feeling indeed . . .'

—Friday 15 March—

23

DI Tudor underlined Sean McGilvary's name on the whiteboard three times. 'And now he's clammed up tighter than a welder's rivet, so we're going to have to crack him the old-fashioned way.'

Operation Telegram's incident room was even more crowded than it'd been yesterday – extra officers drafted in from other gigs after the 'incident' involving Ryan. And the whole team had been summoned with a three-line whip: attend Morning Prayers, or *else*.

Only Dr Fife seemed to have missed the memo.

But everyone here was on their best behaviour – no fidgeting, no jokes, no talking back, no asking questions. Just watching and nodding and taking notes. The tension almost chewy in the muggy air.

Waiting for something horrible to happen.

Angus stood at the back again, where no one could make fun of the only spare fighting suit he had. An unfashionably baggy black double-breasted affair, with slightly weird lapels and a bright-red lining. Its elbows, knees, and bum beginning to go a bit shiny with wear. The kind of suit that looked as if it'd been bought cheap from a charity shop and saved for funerals and court appearances.

Ahem . . .

Tudor checked his clipboard, then swept a hand through his greying hair. 'Team Microscope?'

Four people put their hand up.

'You hit Calman Road first, then spread out through the area. Interview everyone who's ever worked with, known, met, or *sat next to* Sean McGilvary.' Another clipboard check. 'Team Tweezers?'

Five people this time.

'You're going through his life with a nit comb: I want his *car* forensicked, I want his *house* searched again, I want to know what *other vehicles* he's got access to, what *properties* he's got access to. He's hiding the bodies somewhere.' Clipboard. 'Team Spyglass . . . ?'

Another three.

'Work the phones: chase up every police station, train station, bus station, airport, and ferry terminal. Ryan is out there, somewhere – let's find the bastard. Team Postman?'

Four hands.

'You're on door-to-doors; we'll do the whole of Kingsmeath if we have to. Someone knows this guy. Team Spanner?'

More hands.

'Kate Paisley is officially your specialist subject: same as Sean McGilvary: dig, dig, dig till you *find* something.' Tudor dumped his clipboard on the desk behind him. 'Everyone else: keep working through the actions. Microscope, Tweezers, Spyglass, Postman, and Spanner are going to be throwing leads at us: it's vital we stay on top of them.' He gave the assembled officers and support staff the benefit of a motivational stare. 'I know it's unusual to have two suspects in custody and a killer still on the loose, but that's where we are. This is our *last* chance to catch the Fortnight Killer before he tortures another two people to death. We're depending on *every single one* of you.' A nod, then he turned to DCI Monroe. 'Boss?'

The whole room's worth of sphincters tightened as the 'Something Horrible' took centre stage.

Monroe glowered out at them. 'Do you remember when I said we might *actually* be the first operation in O Division history that doesn't leak?'

No one moved.

'Well, perhaps I spoke too soon?' He produced a copy of that morning's *Castle News & Post*, holding it out so they could all see the front page. Most of it was given over to a photo of Angus: half-crouched, arms out, facing away from the camera – with only a hint of ripped trousers on show. In the foreground, a scattering of wee boys and girls lay on the muddy grass, with their hands over their heads, while in the *background* a murky figure pointed a revolver at Angus. A big banner headline: 'HERO COP SAVES KIDS FROM GUNMAN'.

But that wasn't what Monroe was pointing at – instead his finger jabbed a sidebar titled 'GRUESOME NOTES LEFT BY CRAZED KILLER'.

Monroe's jaw clenched as he crushed the morning edition in one outraged fist. 'Would someone care to explain to me how the *Castle Pricking News and Pricking Post* got hold of the one thing we HADN'T BLOODY RELEASED?'

Nobody said a word.

Some looked at their feet. Others at the whiteboards.

'DO YOU HAVE ANY IDEA HOW MUCH HARDER THIS MAKES OUR JOB? HOW MUCH *FUCKING* . . . !' He hurled the paper down, where it burst like an eighteen-storey suicide. 'HOW are we supposed to weed out the whackjobs, time-wasters, and wannabes now?'

The silence stretched and stretched and stretched as he glared at every single person in the room.

'When I find out who did this you won't be allowed within a mile of a police station WITHOUT MY BOOT UP YOUR ARSE!' He turned his back on them all. 'Now get out there and do your *pricking* jobs.'

There was a stampede for the door, as those lucky enough to be on a non-office-based team got the hell out of there before the shouting started again.

Angus almost made it to the door before Monroe's voice boomed out again:

'*Not you.*'

Sod.

He turned, and there was Monroe, beckoning him with a finger. 'Here.'

Deep breath.

Then Angus scurried over, both hands up as if he was warding off a knife attack. 'Boss. I *swear* I didn't tell Ellie *anything* about the notes. It wasn't me! She didn't even write it, see?' He scrabbled up the burst newspaper, fumbling his way to the front page. 'See?' Pointing at the byline. 'It was Michael Slosser!'

'I know.' Monroe sagged against the desk. 'Someone's stabbing us in the back, Angus, and I don't like it. I don't like it one bit.' He took the paper from Angus's hands and stuffed it in the nearest bin. 'At least you managed to keep Dr Fife's name out the papers. That's something. Would've been nice if they'd put the appeal for an ID on the front page, but at least they ran it.' Frowning away at the crumpled newsprint.

'Did Sean McGilvary really not say anything else?'

A grunt. 'Bloody solicitor got him to read a statement walking back the confession. *Apparently* we "harassed it out of him", he was "too tired to think straight", was "only saying what he thought we wanted to hear" because he's such a shrinking, timid wee wallflower. And that was it: not another word till we gave up at three in the morning.'

Sounded as if Mrs Hannay had finally got her client under control.

'Nothing about how he connects to Kate Paisley and Ryan?'

Monroe looked at him, voice flat and grey as a paving slab. 'That would be part of the nothing he didn't say.' A grimace. 'Dr Fife got a plan for today?'

'No idea, Boss. Hasn't answered any of my calls or texts.'

'Then you better haul him out of his pit and find out.' Monroe stood. Clamped a hand down on Angus's shoulder, even if he had to reach up to do it. 'This is it, Angus: last chance to catch the Fortnight Killer before he murders another two poor sods.'

The sun finally scraped its way above the valley's rim, gilding St Jasper's granite façade. Looked quite pretty through the third-floor window. A big fat pigeon settled on the sill, peering in at Angus as if he was the weirdest thing it'd ever seen.

Angus stuck two fingers up at it, then rapped his knuckles against Dr Fife's hotel door a second time.

Gave it a count of ten.

Then tried again.

God's sake . . .

He pulled out his phone and tried calling as well, knocking as it rang and rang and—

'*You've failed to reach Dr Jonathan Fife. A message: leave one. Who knows, I might call back if it's interesting enough.*'

Every inch the charmer.

Angus thumbed the red icon to end the call and dialled again. Still knocking.

Ringing, ringing, ringing:

'*You've failed to reach Dr Jonathan Fife—*'

He hung up and tried again, knuckles rapping against the ancient wood.

The phone rang.

A mushy voice muffled out from inside the suite. '*What? Goway! Sleeping . . .*'

'*You've failed to reach—*'

Red icon.

Green icon.

Still knocking.

'Dr Fife? It's Angus. Come on: we've got a killer to catch!'

Ringing. Ringing. Ringing.

'*God's sake . . .*'

A *thunk*, a *click*, and the door opened an inch.

There was a flash of sleep-rumpled features. 'Pain in the ass.' Then Dr Fife turned and shambled away into the gloom, leaving the door open.

Angus stepped inside.

OK, that was . . .

Yeah.

It was dark in here with the curtains drawn and all the lights off, but Dr Fife was *absolutely* bare-arsed naked. Well, except for maybe a bit of jewellery, scratching his backside and yawning as he slouched back towards the bedroom.

Angus made for the curtains. 'DCI Monroe wants to know where we're starting today.' Throwing them open flooded the room in golden light. He kept his eyes on the cathedral opposite, in case there was anything . . . unwholesome on show. 'You want to go visit the other victims' houses? Councillor Mendel's place is next on the list.'

The bedroom door thumped shut.

Well, at least he was up.

OK, so, if the door at the far end was the bedroom, that meant . . .

Angus tried one of the other two, discovering a swanky bathroom, all tiled in dark marble: a free-standing bath, heated towel rail, wet-room shower thing, double sink, toilet *and* bidet, gleaming in the glow of recessed ceiling spotlights.

Nope.

Door Number Three opened on a kitchenette with all the mod cons and, more importantly, a *very* fancy-looking coffee maker.

Bingo.

He rummaged through the units and cupboards – coming out with two big mugs, a thing of milk, and a selection of coloured pods for the machine.

Angus raised his voice, so it would carry out into the rest of the suite: 'I've been thinking about the "terrorist cell" theory: there'd still have to be points of contact, right? They didn't all just come up with the idea on their own. And they'd need some way to coordinate the notes too.'

The coffee maker *burrrrrrrrrrrrrrr*ed and *click*ed and *whirrrrrrr*ed.

'So maybe they've got a *concierge*. Someone on the outside who directs them? Or maybe it's Ryan. Maybe *that's* why he's got the gun.' The machine ejected the pod, so he replaced it with another one.

Burrrrrrrrrrrrrrr. Click. Whirrrrrrr.

'Unless he's *not* connected to the Fortnight Killer at all, and him being there when the Fordyces were attacked was some massive coincidence. Which isn't likely, is it?'

No reply. As usual.

'Dr Fife?'

He topped the dark-brown frothy liquid off with a dollop of milk.

'Dr Fi-ife?'

Angus gathered up the coffee, two packs of wee individually wrapped shortbread biscuits, and went through to knock on the bedroom door.

Still nothing.

'Come on, today's the day, right? We need to get moving.'

He eased the door open and poked his head in.

A weird electronic-whirring-gurgling noise filled the stale air.

The curtains in here must've been heavy-duty blackout ones,

because the only light was the alarm clock's muted red blush – just enough to make out a rounded lump in the Olympic-sized bed.

Brilliant.

The rotten sod was doing his Navy SEAL impersonation again: snoozing it up.

'DR FIFE!' Angus thumped the coffees down on the bedside cabinet, then hurled the curtains wide. An anaemic blade of daylight slashed across the bed. 'WAKE UP!'

Dr Fife thrashed his way free from the duvet's embrace, surfacing with his hair all askew and his eyes like pickled eggs. 'Wake! 'M'wake . . .' Sitting up, blinking, mouth working on the sour taste of morning breath. But the weirdest thing was the mini ventilator mask covering his nose, held in place with four straps, while a length of tubing connected it to a small machine on the bedside table. Making him look like a half-arsed cosplay version of the Space Jockey from *Alien*. He struggled his head out of the harness. 'Where am . . .? Oh God, it *is* you! It wasn't a horrible dream . . .'

Jesus.

Before, when he'd let Angus into the hotel suite, it'd been too dark to see anything, but now, in the cold sharp light of day, Dr Fife's naked torso was a map of scar tissue. Not tight and shiny, as if he'd been in a fire – though, to be fair, some of them did look like small, circular burns – but as if he'd been *heavily* into self-harm as a kid.

A fist-sized, circular tattoo sat over his heart, the ink pale grey and faded, the lines blurring: an outer ring with some sort of knot in the middle – made up of four interconnected capital letter 'P's.

The same symbol was carved into a wee stone necklace that had bits of antler and tatty feathers strung onto its leather cord. Very hippy-dip.

Then there were the bruises. Including a blossoming pair of black eyes, from when Ryan punched him in the face.

Dr Fife must've realized Angus was staring, because he grabbed the duvet and pulled it right up to his chin, hiding that scar-scrimshawed chest. Then slumped back into the pillows. Snatched one up and covered his face with it, as if trying to suffocate himself.

More scar tissue wrapped around his bare arm. 'Leave me alone!'

Angus looked away. 'Whoever dies today can't afford you having a long lie.'

Another pillow was added to the pile. 'Urgh . . . I *hate* Oldcastle.'

'Up.' Angus headed for the door. Paused on the threshold. 'And if it's any consolation: it hates you too.'

'*. . . as Storm Findlay tracks* northwards *again, meaning it's all change for the next forty-eight hours!*' On the hotel TV – big enough that Mum would consider it monumentally vulgar – Valerie the weatherperson pressed the button on her wand thing and the big yellow and red rhomboids appeared across the map of Scotland behind her. '*That weather warning's been expanded to cover most of the country for today* and *tomorrow, with only the Borders and Highlands escaping the worst of the high winds.*'

Angus sipped at his fancy coffee-machine latte, munching away on his third complimentary pastry from the basket by the not-so-minibar. Which didn't count, ethically, because they were tiny, came with the room, and Dr Fife probably wasn't going to eat them anyway.

'*Which means severe disruption to trains and ferries, I'm afraid, with the vast majority of services cancelled . . .*'

He stuffed the last nugget of maple-pecan plait in his mouth and finished his text to Ellie:

Thank you for keeping Dr Fife out of papers.

Will take your advice re: Gillian.

Angus frowned at the little glowing words, then added five more.

Mary Dunwoody had lovely nose.

SEND.

'*So, let's look at today in more detail . . .*'

The bathroom door swung open with a billow of steam, and out slouched Dr Fife with a lime-green towel wrapped around him. Another kept his curly locks held fast in a turban – like Marge Simpson. He'd pulled on a white, long-sleeved T-shirt, the fabric damp and clingy. Hiding most of the scars. But see-through enough to make out the hippy necklace and the tattoo on his chest.

You'd think the shower would've woken him up, but he was just as creased and rumpled as he'd been when he'd hauled himself out of bed.

Angus slipped the phone back into his pocket. 'Heavy night?'

'Didn't stop interviewing that pair of idiots till . . . What time is it?' A jaw-splintering yawn ripped through him, followed by a loose-boned sag. 'Go on, ask me if Kate Paisley answered any of our questions.'

'Did—'

'*Of course* she didn't. And neither did Sean McGilvary.' Dr Fife made for the bedroom . . . then stopped, turned, and squinted at Angus. 'What in *fuck's name* are you wearing?'

Cheeky sod.

'More than you. Get dressed; the Boss wants us out there solving this thing.'

'You look like something from an eighties pop video.'

Angus lurched to his feet, arms wide, one foot stamping into the deep-pile carpet. 'For the love of God, can we *please* get to work before someone else dies?'

'Hmph.' Dr Fife shuffled off into the bedroom, banging the door shut behind him. *'Make more coffee and I'll think about it!'*

Were all forensic psychologists this bloody needy?

Angus glowered at the closed door for a bit.

Then headed into the kitchenette and did what he was told.

24

The TV in the dining room burbled away to itself, turned down just far enough to make none of it understandable out here in reception.

Angus checked his watch: coming up to half eight and they *still* weren't out there hunting Ryan down.

The hotel manager bobbed up from behind the desk with a worried expression on his pinched and pointy face, twitching the waxed handlebars on his military moustache. A tartan waistcoat and unconvincing combover completed the ensemble. He held up a plastic fob – about the size of a Caramac bar, with the hotel's logo on it, and 'IF FOUND PLEASE RETURN TO THE BISHOP'S VIEW HOTEL!' – a pair of keys dangling from the end. 'Are you sure this is *strictly* above board?'

'I can show you my warrant card again, if you like?'

He chewed on the inside of his cheek for a bit. 'Well, if you're sure . . .' Then held the fob out. 'But *normally* we only give duplicate keys to couples.'

Angus took it. 'You've been a great help. Thank you.' The fob had 'BISHOP ISBISTER' in fancy gold script on the other side, along with the hotel's address. Which wasn't very security conscious, but it meant no more knocking and calling and waiting. Tomorrow morning he could let himself in and drag Dr Fife out of bed if he had to.

That would show DS Massie: Angus *could* use his initiative, like a 'grown-up'.

He pocketed the key as Dr Fife stomped down the stairs, wearing an oversized pair of sunglasses, like some sort of rockstar after a three-week bender.

'Finally!'

Dr Fife flipped him the middle finger, then went rifling through the small pile of newspapers reserved for hotel guests. '*The Guardian, Glasgow Tribune, Daily Mail, Daily Express, Daily Standard, Daily Telegraph* . . . God, you people like to stick to a theme, don't you?'

'Can we go now?'

'The local rag?' He held up that morning's *Castle News & Post*, with its front page dominated by Angus's photo. 'Well, well, well. If it isn't our *favourite* oversized lump! Look at you, being all manly with your bare ass on show.'

Nope. Not rising to it.

'I'm thinking we visit Councillor Mendel's place first, see if we can turn up anything.'

He flipped the paper round to face himself again, eyes scanning the page. '"Unnamed gunman" blah-blah; "lives at risk" doodle-de-doo; "firing indiscriminately", et cetera, et cetera; here we go: "Heroic police officer, Angus MacVicar" – brackets, twenty-four – "bravely put himself between the gunman's bullets and the terrified children, risking his own life" blah-blah-blaah-blah-blah . . . Who wrote this swooning puppy-eyed bullshit?'

Heat prickled around Angus's collar. 'Then, maybe we can hit the Healey-Robinsons' house?'

Dr Fife raised his sunglasses to squint at the byline. '"Crime and Local Issues Reporter, Ellie Nottingham."' A grin. 'I think she wants in your tighty-whities, Angus.'

The heat crept northwards. 'Don't be stupid.'

He finished scanning the front page. 'On the plus side: I don't get mentioned once. *That's* what happens when you keep a low profile.' He folded the paper and tucked it under his arm. 'Well? Don't just stand there: we've got a killer to catch, remember?'

The Mini's windscreen wipers squeal-thunked across the glass, clearing twin arcs through the drizzle. Giving them an unhindered view of the back end of the number fifteen bus, before the spittering rain blurred it away again.

Angus shifted in the passenger seat, so he was facing Dr Fife. 'The thing is, the handwriting's the same, isn't it? On all three notes. So it *has* to be the same person writing them. But if it's *different people* doing the killing, that explains your problem with the MO not developing, *and* why Sean McGilvary's DNA doesn't appear at—'

Vivaldi twiddled away in Angus's pocket. But when he dug his phone out, nestled within its protective ziplock bag, the words 'UNKNOWN NUMBER' glowed in the middle of the screen. 'Sorry.'

Dr Fife rolled his eyes. 'If it shuts you up, go for it.'

'*Thanks*.' Putting as much sarcasm into that one word as possible. He hit the green icon. 'DC MacVicar.'

A woman's voice: '*Is . . . Is it OK if I call you "Angus"? Sorry. Erm . . . Oh, it's Gillian. Gillian Kilbride? You gave me your card when—*'

'Gillian.' Angus sat up straight, a smile pulling his face wide. '*Hi. How are you?*'

On the other side of the car, Dr Fife raised an eyebrow.

'*Oh, fine. You know. Not enjoying the weather much.*' She took a breath. '*Erm . . . You?*'

'Yeah. Rain, eh?'

Well, that was smooth.

There was silence from the other end of the phone.

And on this side too.

Come on – you can do this.

He took a deep breath and jumped in, at exactly the same time she did.

'Listen, Gillian, when all this is over, I wondered if you'd like to get a drink or something?'

'*You asked me to call if I saw anyone suspicious hanging around at the press packs, and I thought . . .*'

Oh no.

Sodding. Buggering. *No*.

She cleared her throat. 'Sorry.'

Should've kept his big fat *stupid* mouth shut.

Surprised his hair didn't burst into flame, given the sudden rush of nuclear heat exploding across his cheeks. 'No, *I'm* sorry. That was . . . inappropriate, I shouldn't have—'

'*No! It's OK. I just didn't think you were . . . I mean, I know I am, but . . . It's not . . .*'

Angus scrunched his face up, eyes screwed tight, and clunked his forehead off the passenger window. 'Sorry.'

The lights must've changed, because the Mini edged forward, following the grumbling bus.

You could hear the embarrassment fizzing through her voice. '*It's just I think there might've been a weird bloke outside your headquarters for last night's ten o'clock broadcasts. I stayed in the back of shot for the whole Channel Four News piece, flying the flag for truth.*'

Way to make a tit of yourself, Angus.

Good job.

He huffed out a breath then produced his notebook. Pinned the phone between his ear and shoulder. Pen poised. 'Weird bloke?'

The Mini turned left, parting ways with the number fifteen.

'*About five-ten, five-eleven? Really pale and hairy: you know, a beard that spreads right down his neck into the chest whiskers? Big furry hands. Going bald at the back. Kinda thin. Jeans, hiking boots, and one of those outdoorsy jackets people wear when they kid-on they're mountain climbers?*'

Angus scribbled all of that down. 'And you've not seen him before? At the press things?'

'*I don't know. Sorry. I wasn't really looking till you asked.*'

'No, that's OK. And when you say "weird", what do . . .'

Wait a minute: the number fifteen went across the Dundas Bridge, into Castleview. The way *they* should be going.

He stuck his hand over the microphone, and winced at Dr Fife. 'You've missed the turning. The Mendels lived in the Wynd: other side of the river.' Peering down the dual carriageway in front of them. Looking for a gap. 'We need to do a U-turn.'

'We're not going to Councillor Mendel's house.'

'But—'

Dr Fife pointed at the phone-cum-satnav in its dashboard mount. The blue arrow pointed deeper into Cowskillin. 'Anyway, thought *you* were speaking to your girlfriend?'

'She's not my . . .' What was the point? He went back to Gillian's call. 'You still there? Sorry.'

'*He was weird, because he was filming O Division Headquarters on his phone. Everyone else was filming the TV crews, or the crowd, but he seemed more interested in what you guys in the police were doing.*'

Now that *was* weird.

Angus frowned through the rain-speckled windscreen.

'*I tried talking to him, but he wasn't having any of it. Wouldn't even tell me his name.*'

Yeah . . .

'Thanks for letting me know, but *please*: if you see him again, don't approach, OK? We don't know if he's just some random guy or—'

'*Bloody hell!*' A breathy, awed tone hit her voice. '*The Fortnight Killer.*'

'Just be careful, OK?'

'*Promise.*' Silence radiated down the phone. Then: '*And, Angus? I'd love to get a drink or something. Doesn't even have to be when all this is over. If you like?*'

All the hairs stood up on the back of his neck. 'Great. Yeah. Definitely. Thanks.'

'*Right. Super. Erm . . . Sorry, got to go: traffic warden. Bye! Bye.*' And she was gone.

The smile returned.

They were getting a drink.

Which would take some pretty complicated financial juggling, but it was doable. Kind of.

Anyway, that was a worry for later. Right *now* her number was going into his contacts. 'MISS GILLIAN KILBRIDE'. Nah, that was far too formal. 'GILLIAN'.

Dr Fife shook his head. 'Oh, to be young and stupid again . . .'

Angus scrolled up the list to 'DS MASSIE' and hit the button. Listened to it ring a few times, before:

'*Detective Sergeant Massie.*'

'Sarge? Got a possible suspect for you. IC-One male: thin, bearded, really hairy, but balding. Was hanging around the station last night, watching the building.'

'*Oh aye? Thought you and Dr Arsehole were convinced it was this Ryan bloke.*'

'Yeah, but if they are operating as separate cells, there's going to be multiple killers and accomplices. It's worth a punt, isn't it?'

'Hmmmm . . .' A hush settled on the line.

The Mini drifted along Jutemill Terrace, past the Post Office depot and the conjoined tower blocks of Dalrymple Park.

'All right, I'll bite. Give me that description again and I'll get someone on it.'

'Thanks, Sarge.'

Two bits of initiative in one day. Who was the grown-up now?

Calman Road probably didn't feature on many postcards. A grey, drab slab of tenement flats, it lurked in Cowskillin, south of the dual carriageway, thrown up – in both senses of the word – back in the days when getting something built was more important than making it pretty. Six flats per entrance, arranged over three miserable storeys.

The only decoration they'd given the bland brick frontage was a smattering of wall vents and the block numbers: carved into a single stone mounted above each archway, leading into an open stairwell. Like a cave. Or the mouth of a hungry beast without teeth.

Didn't help that they overlooked a swanky new development, where the flats all had balconies and planters and actually looked like a nice place to live.

Angus unfolded himself from the Mini's passenger seat and levered his limbs out into the rain. Which had graduated from spitting to gobbing it down. Pulling his collar up as wind ripped down the street.

Should never have given back that high-vis.

Dr Fife hurried past, holding onto his umbrella like an anchor in a storm. Jogging up the path and into the toothless maw of number fifteen.

Angus followed him, footsteps echoing off the damp brickwork and puddled concrete floor. Enveloped by the smell of drab-green mildew and sharp-yellow urine.

Somewhere in the middle distance, a child's voice rose and fell – singing a filthy song about two nuns and an unfeasibly well-hung bus conductor.

Dr Fife collapsed the little brolly. 'So which one's Sean McGilvary's . . .' Trailing off as Angus pointed above their heads. 'Sonofabitch. It's *always* upstairs.'

Angus followed him up. 'Should we not be focusing on the *Mendels*, though? I mean, look what we turned up when we—'

'*HOY!*' An angry voice battered around the stairwell, reverberating off the bland walls. '*You can't come up here.*'

Turning the corner revealed the first-floor landing, where a line of 'POLICE' tape sealed off Flat Fifteen D. PC Mahmud stood blocking the way, arms crossed, glowering down at them. Today's tartan turban was all muted yellows and oranges. The scowl faded as he clapped eyes on Dr Fife. 'Oh, it's you.'

'Well, who the hell *else* would it be?'

Crisis averted, Abir sank back into his folding camp chair – complete with a breeze-block-sized Stephen King paperback and a thermos of something.

Angus nodded. 'Didn't see you at Morning Prayers.'

'Nah, been here since seven, haven't I? Keeping the great unwashed at bay.'

All three of them turned to look at the empty stairwell.

'Where's the press?'

Abir shrugged. 'Do I look like Mystic Meg?' Then pulled a face when Angus clearly had *no idea* what he was talking about. 'I don't *know* where they are. Thought someone on the investigation would've leaked McGilvary's name by now, but nope.' He dug a clipboard out from behind his chair. 'Sign in, and you too can explore "uncharted territory"!'

They both filled in their details, and Abir unlocked the door to Fifteen D with a little brass key and a flourish. 'Gentlemen.' Pushing it open.

That mildewy smell intensified, scratching at the back of Angus's throat, bringing with it the taste of mouldy bread and dust. He wrinkled his nose. 'Fusty.'

'You'll make detective superintendent in no time with deductive brilliance like that.' Abir settled back into his seat and cracked the spine on his novel. 'Try not to make a mess in there, eh? Search team's not long finished tidying up.'

Dr Fife pulled on a pair of gloves, then stepped inside.

Angus did the same, shutting the door behind them.

You could tell from the hallway that this flat was a fair bit bigger than the one Dr and Mr Fordyce lived in. Kind of outdated, though: old-fashioned wallpaper, old-fashioned carpet, old-fashioned slab doors, old-fashioned prints on the wall. Old-fashioned mould spreading out from the corners in tendrils of dark, dark grey . . .

Dr Fife disappeared through the door to the nearest room.

Angus scuffed in after him. And stopped dead. Let out a low whistle. 'So much for "uncharted territory".'

The double bedroom was an absolute tip.

If this was the search team's idea of tidy, Christ knew what *messy* would be like. The wardrobe's contents lay strewn about, like an explosion in a little-old-lady supply shop. The mattress was tipped up on its end, in the corner of the room – the divan bed it belonged to lay upside down, with its fabric slashed to expose the wooden skeleton within.

Every single bit of furniture had been pulled away from the wall, drawers yanked out, the contents scattered.

Looked as if the search team were a lot less worried about wrecking a suspect's house than they were a victim's.

Dr Fife picked a couple of drab floral dresses from the floor, stared at them for a moment, then chucked them over his shoulder. He did the same with a faded pastel-pink jacket with a smattering of mould on the sleeves. Then turned on his Cuban heels and stomped out into the hall again.

OK . . .

Next stop: the living room.

It'd been gutted as well – the couch upended, armchairs too, their fabric bases disembowelled. An old sideboard lay on its back, the contents heaped up on a small dining table.

A drift of paperbacks lay crumpled beneath the window: Aga sagas mixed in with the dirtier end of Mills & Boon's output, going by the titles.

The search team had even taken up the rug, leaving it draped over the inverted couch like the flayed skin of some strange dusty animal.

On the wall, above the fireplace, hung a framed print of the Virgin Mary, with a chubby wee Baby Jesus cradled in her arms. The pair of them hanging at a drunken angle.

Dr Fife made his way into the middle of the room and did a slow three-sixty. Frowning out at everything.

Angus nudged a broken china dog with his foot. 'Are the FBI search teams this messy?'

No comment.

Dr Fife just marched from the room.

It was never like this on the TV detective shows. Couldn't shut the main characters up on those. Forever explaining everything to the well-meaning sidekick. What was wrong with a bit of that?

Angus strode out into the hall again, catching up to Dr Fife in a damp kitchen that looked even older than Mum's – the fridge more like a museum piece than something to keep your mousetrap cheddar and cold dinner in. Every single one of the cabinets, drawers, and cupboards hung open, their contents spattered across the worktops.

Dr Fife opened the fridge door, scowled at the contents, slammed the door shut again, then marched out. All without a word.

A single bedroom sat at the back of the property, overlooking a scrubby patch of grass passing as a drying green. Complete with drooping washing lines and rusty poles.

Shockingly enough, it was a tip in here too. Mattress and divan on their side, wardrobe pulled out from the wall and eviscerated – its entrails tossed about all over the place. A large shadow marked the curling wallpaper above where the bed would've been if the search team hadn't got their paws on it. Going by the shape, a cross or crucifix must have hung there for years. And years. And years.

About twenty or thirty books were mingled in with the wardrobe's viscera, nearly all of them science-fiction paperbacks, curled and battered, their spines creased and crackling. Some still bearing the charity-shop or 'REMOVED FROM LIBRARY STOCK' stickers.

So, a man after Angus's own heart.

Well, except for the murder bit.

He picked up a copy of Larry Niven's *Ringworld*, turning it over in his gloved hands before placing it carefully on the windowsill.

Following it up with *The Martian Chronicles*, *Dune*, and *The Three-Body Problem*. 'You going to tell me what we're doing here?'

Dr Fife evicted a pair of jeans and a black, paisley-patterned shirt from a toppled wooden dining chair, and set the thing back on its feet, plonking it in the middle of the room. Then sat, feet dangling about eight inches off the manky carpet. 'You've read the book, you tell me.'

Eh?

Angus frowned down at the copy of *Neuromancer* he'd just picked up. Well, yeah, he'd *read* it, but it was hard to see how that helped in the current . . .

Ah, OK.

Bet Dr Fife meant that massive tome he'd chucked on the table, Wednesday evening: *Behavioral Analysis for Law-Enforcement Personnel*, brackets, *Crime-Scene Indicators, Forensic Red Flags, & Interview Guidance*. 'When did I get the chance to read a great-big textbook? I'm with you the whole time!'

That got him a shake of the head and a tut. 'OK, back to basics: what do you *see*?'

Neuromancer went on the windowsill with the others. 'Search team's a law unto itself.'

'Sean McGilvary was brought up in a strict, *religious* household. Trust me: that's not easy.' Gazing up at the shadow on the wall. 'See if you can find the missing crucifix.'

Sounded like a waste of time, but Angus went rummaging anyway.

'You hafta figure: if Ryan the Pizza Guy has any sense, he'll be halfway to Belgium by now. But, of course, if he had any *sense* he wouldn't be torturing people to death.'

'Uh-huh.' Angus scooped up the clothes and stuffed them back in the wardrobe – as if he was down the laundrette, filling a washing machine.

'Thing is, he's *not* an idiot. He's deluded, certainly, but the level of planning involved in stealing a delivery guy's uniform *months* in advance, and arranging a changing station so he doesn't get blood everywhere, and moving the bodies, *and* getting away with it.' Dr Fife flexed his gloved fingers. '*That* takes smarts.'

'Hmmm . . .' The divan clumped back into place, the right way up this time, followed by the *thunk-boinnnnng* of Sean McGilvary's saggy mattress.

'And he doesn't have his accomplice to help him. Cos we've got her in the jailhouse.'

'Them. We've got *them* in the cells.'

'But Ryan must've ID'd his next victims by now. Worked out the best way in, best way out.' A frown. 'Is he really gonna abandon all that? And his two-week schedule? And his *mission*?'

'Uh-huh . . .' Duvet, sheets, and pillows onto the mattress. Place was beginning to look like a bedroom again.

'Maybe yes, maybe no.'

Angus scooped up an armful of socks and pants, then stuffed them in the wardrobe too, before clicking the doors shut and shoving the whole thing back against the wall.

Which left the chest of drawers.

He tipped it back on its hind feet and peered underneath.

Nope.

It got hefted into the corner – slotted into a matching outline on the wallpaper.

Dr Fife nodded. 'It's not here, is it.'

'No crucifix. Maybe the search team took it?'

'Sean's mom's dead. He keeps the Virgin Mary in the living room, cos he can't bear to touch it, but he ditches the crucifix from his bedroom wall. No way she lets him do that if she's still alive.'

'Hold on . . .' Angus checked the file. 'Here we go: she's in Castle Hill Infirmary, hospice wing. Pancreatic cancer.'

'Same thing.' Glancing up at the shadow again. 'He can't have Jesus hanging on the wall over his bed, can he? Not when Sean does such disgusting *dirty* things there. On his own, or with friends.' A gloved finger came up to point in Angus's direction. 'You live at home with your mom, right? If she was carted off to hospital, would you take loose women back to your place?'

'What? No.' He cleared his throat. 'I mean, I *could* have people back *now* if I wanted to. Course I could. I just . . . don't.'

A smile. 'Can't get a girlfriend, eh? That why you were making goo-goo eyes when – what was it: Gillian? – was on the phone? Think she might pop your cherry?'

The room became very small and far too hot.

'That's not . . . It's . . . Shut up.'

Dr Fife sighed. 'There's worse things than being a virgin, Angus. Maybe one day I'll tell you the tale of how I lost mine to a woman twice my age.' He shook his head. 'But not today.' Then hopped down from the chair. 'One thing you see with these old apartments: they're prone to damp. And that shit's expensive to fix, so they do stuff when they're built to make sure a bit of air can get in.' He reached into his greatcoat, coming out with a handheld multitool – like a Swiss army knife, only more industrial-looking. Dr Fife fiddled a flat-head screwdriver attachment from the selection of blades and bits. Then swaggered over to the corner of the room, where a curl of wallpaper was coming away, just above the skirting board.

Lifting it revealed a small metal vent, about the size of a house brick. It was crusted with layers of old paint, to the point of being almost solid, which defeated the purpose of installing the thing in the first place. And probably explained the ever-present taint of mould in the flat. But while the metal grille was caked with paint, the screws holding it in place were shiny and new-looking.

A few twists of the screwdriver and the cover clunked down against the ancient carpet.

'There we go.' Dr Fife straightened up, put the multitool away, and made for the door. Didn't even bother to check the vent hole. 'Bag that lot up, and sign it into evidence, there's a good sidekick.'

Eh?

Angus inched over and knelt in front of the vent, tipping forward onto his elbows to peer into the tiny cavity.

Even if the thing hadn't been painted solid, it wouldn't have let any air into the room – some idiot had stuffed it full of newspaper.

Or, rather, they'd stuffed something inside that was *wrapped* in newspaper.

He placed it on the carpet and peeled back the layers of *Daily Standard*. 'Bloody hell . . .'

Contents: two insertable sex toys; one tube of lube; one

well-thumbed paperback copy of *DI Davidson and the Musclehead Murders* by D. H. Robinson; and a collection of old-fashioned gay porn magazines with titles like *Beefy Lumberjack Bonanza*, *Big Cocks for Derek*, and *Sneaky Bumhole Ninjas 3!*

Dr Fife's voice floated in from the hall. *'Think we need to have another chat with Mr McGilvary, don't you?'*

Definitely.

25

Vivaldi's 'Spring' violined into life as Angus clomped down the stairs from Sean McGilvary's flat, arms full of slithery evidence bags – all sealed and marked up with the contents of Sean's secret hidey-hole. Angus struggled the phone from his pocket, trying not to drop anything.

'DS MASSIE' glowed in the middle of the screen.

He nearly lost a hardcore porn mag answering the call. 'Sarge?'

'You got Dr Pain-In-The-Arse with you?'

Did he ever. The arrogant sod had done nothing but radiate smugness ever since finding that air vent. 'Yes, Sarge.'

'Tell him we've got DNA back from Sadler Road, at long last. Blood at the scene is a match for Councillor Mendel and Dr Fordyce.'

Around the landing, heading for the brick archway and the rain beyond. 'What about Kevin Healey-Robinson?'

'Don't you think I might've mentioned that?' She sniffed down the phone at him. Then: *'Nah. Only other matches are you and Kate Paisley.'*

'Not even Sean McGilvary?'

'Again: don't you think I would've said!' Another sniff. *'And before you ask, no one's reported a hairy balding bloke at any of the crime scenes.'*

Angus sagged. 'Sorry.'

Up ahead, Dr Fife's heels rang out against the concrete floor as he made for the exit, unfurling his umbrella on the way.

'What's he doing, Dr Tosser? Anything that might actually help?'

Good question. Suppose it depended on your attitude to secrets hidden in the walls of a mildewy flat. 'We're working on it.'

'*Better be.*'

'At least we were right about Kate Paisley and Ryan, right? Otherwise the victims' DNA wouldn't . . . Sarge?' Silence. 'Sarge?' He checked the screen – she'd hung up.

Always nice to be appreciated.

He stuck the phone back in his pocket, almost dropping the evidence bag with lube in it, and hurried out after Dr Fife.

The wind had picked up again, tugging at the sawn-off greatcoat and setting it flapping. Clattering an empty tin down the pavement.

'That was DS Massie: they've got DNA from our first two victims at Ryan's house.' Angus curled his head into his shoulder as a battering of rain hurled sideways into his face.

Dr Fife unlocked the Mini. 'Shock horror.' Climbing in behind the wheel.

'Yeah, but *think* about it.' Angus got the passenger door open, and the evidence bags performed a slippery avalanche into the footwell. 'Oh, for . . .' Arse sticking out into the rain, he gathered them up again. 'How come there's no DNA from the third victim? Because there's *another* murder cell. That'll be the one Sean McGilvary kills for.' The evidence bags got stuffed onto the back seat and Angus scrambled into the car. Thunked the door shut.

'You *still* harping on about that?'

'Well, it makes sense, doesn't it? Given the evidence?'

The reply was flat as an unbuttered oatcake. 'Oh yeah, definitely. Can't be *any other* explanation at all. Sean McGilvary's a Fortnight Killer, *for sure*.' Dr Fife cranked the engine into life. 'Seatbelt.'

Angus clicked his into place. 'Sarcasm doesn't help anyone.'

'Helps me. Now, hush your mouth: I got some strategizing to do.'

Someone had turned the heating up full in Interview Two, which should've been a welcome relief after all the wind and rain. Instead, steam rose from the shoulders of Angus's jacket, damp trousers chafing his thighs as he wrestled a tiny square desk into the room. Maybe two foot by two foot; just big enough for one person and a laptop.

He hefted it over the interview table and plonked it down in the corner, under the window – closing the blinds to shut out the rainy morning. 'You sure about this?'

Dr Fife arranged the evidence bags on the room's new desk, placing each so its contents were clearly visible as you entered the room. 'Sometimes, a bad man murders his wife, only he doesn't want to go to jail so he makes it look like some asshole broke into the family home to steal stuff, and' – pulling on an Appalachian-Cletus accent – '"Oh no! Things got outta hand and he musta *bashed* her head in with a *hammer!*"' The porn mags got swapped with the sex toys and Dr Fife frowned at both with his head on one side. 'Other killers like to arrange the bodies in new and exciting ways. Like that guy I told you about: Bradley McCarthy and his Cannibal Thanksgiving.' Dr Fife swapped the bags back again. Nodded. 'It's called "staging the crime scene".'

'Yes, but—'

'What people don't know is we can stage the *interrogation* too.' A knock rang out from the closed interview-room door. 'Right on cue.' Grin. 'Enter!'

A wee man with a crooked moustache and a baldy bit at the back poked his head into the room. Detective Constable Harry 'Wee Hairy' Black raised his eyebrows. 'You ready?'

Dr Fife gave him a thumbs-up. 'Count to ten, then wheel 'em in.' He hurried around to the police side of the table, hopped up into his seat, then made that thumb-and-forefinger-rectangle thing that film directors always did. Peering through it at the scene he'd staged. Then waved a hand sideways at Angus. 'Move left a bit. Want you looming, but not blocking the evidence.'

This was all going to go horribly wrong, wasn't it . . .

But Angus shuffled over a couple of feet anyway. 'We call them "productions" over here. You know: of the investigation.'

That must've been ten, because the door opened again and in stalked DCI Monroe, face flushed, a folder clamped to his chest, mouth puckered. He made eye contact with Angus, shook his head. Then took the seat next to Dr Fife without saying a word.

Yeah, horribly wrong and *then* some.

Next through the door was Sean McGilvary's solicitor, Mrs Hannay, in another tweed-skirt-and-questionable-cardigan combo, with matching ring binder accessory. Nose in the air, she took her seat as the man of the hour shambled in.

Someone must've brought in a change of clothes for him, because Sean's SOC suit had been replaced by a baggy Oldcastle Warriors replica shirt and a pair of tracksuit bottoms. Grubby trainers squeaking on the grey terrazzo floor.

He took two steps into the room and froze, eyes locked on the little desk with its display of once-hidden things.

Sean's mouth fell open.

'Mr McGilvary! How lovely to see you again.' Dr Fife beamed across the table at him. 'Or can I call you "Sean"?' Pointing. 'Please: take a seat. Sit, sit.'

He didn't move, little beads of sweat prickling out across his top lip and forehead.

'Perhaps you'd like a coffee? Tastes like crap, but it's hot and wet.' Throwing in a wink to go with the suggestive tone: '*If* ya know what I mean . . . ?'

Mrs Hannay rapped her long scarlet nails on the chipped interview table. '*Sit down*, Sean.'

With that, he finally creaked into motion again. Doing what he was told. But instead of facing front, he kept glancing over his shoulder at the evidence bags.

Monroe fiddled with the audio-visual controls, setting everything recording. 'Interview of Sean Colin McGilvary, on Friday fifteenth of March, nine forty-six a.m. Present are—'

Mrs Hannay hissed at her client: 'Will you *sit still*?'

He did. For a moment anyway. Growing more fidgety as DCI Monroe went through the script that kicked off every formal interview.

It was as if that little table was magnetic, and Sean's eyes were lumps of iron. Drawn to it, over and over and over again.

Intro done, Monroe sat back. 'Mrs Hannay, have you got another statement for us? Or can we proceed?'

She raised her nose an inch or two. 'I expect my client to be released once this interview is over. He's explained his presence at Balvenie Row and it's time you either charge him with burglary or let him go.'

'Noted.'

Dr Fife pulled on a sympathetic face. 'How you doing, Champ? You have a good night in the cells?'

Sean bit his lip, as if he was trying to stop any words from accidentally slipping out.

A scowl from Mrs Hannay. 'I don't see how this is relevant, Detective Chief Inspector.'

Monroe didn't answer. Instead, he slid his folder in front of Dr Fife.

'Why *thank you*, Detective Chief Inspector.' Making a big show of lining it up with Mrs Hannay's ring binder. 'Gotta tell ya: I'm just trying to build a little rapport here, Lorna. But I can see you're not a girl for foreplay.' Dr Fife sleazed it up again. 'Is she, Sean?'

'I *beg* your pardon?' Mrs Hannay's face soured. 'I don't like your tone, *Doctor* Fife.'

'"I killed them", "They were dirty sodomites and I killed them".' He raised his eyebrows. '*Did you*, Sean?'

'We've been over this! My client was over-tired and confused, and—'

'Oh, he's confused all right. Aren't you, Sean? Confused and *conflicted*.'

She clutched her client's arm. 'You don't have to answer that.'

'Now, we told you about the DNA we found at Douglas and Kevin Healey-Robinson's house, but we didn't tell you *where* we found it. Or what *kind* of DNA it was.'

'My client has already explained that.'

Dr Fife opened the folder. 'See, every time you go into a room, you leave a bit of DNA behind. Each breath carries little droplets full of it, your skin cells are constantly falling off and being renewed – same with hair. If you spit, that's loads of DNA, right there. If you bleed, that's DNA-tastic too.' A smile bloomed as he pulled out a sheet of paper. 'But there's another *big* source of DNA that *guys* have but *girls* don't. Ain't that right, Sean?'

Mrs Hannay's eyes narrowed. 'You don't have to answer *that* either.'

'So if I was to say to you: "We found a big spurt of your spunk in the bedroom", what do you think would happen?'

Colour flushed into Sean McGilvary's cheeks, darkening as it spread. Eyes shimmering as he trembled. But still not a word.

'You killed Douglas and Kevin, then went upstairs to jack off? What is it they call it here . . . ah: wanking! Did you torture them to death then go for a *wank*?'

'All right, that's enough.' Mrs Hannay stood. 'You might think you're clever, Dr Fife, with your crude language, but my client—'

'Oh God . . .' Sean clamped a hand across his mouth.

'What would your dear old mom think, Sean? Two dead bodies downstairs and you're up there jerking on your cock like a demented—'

'THAT IS ENOUGH!' Mrs Hannay stabbed a finger at the table-top. 'I'm making a formal complaint!'

Monroe's jaw clenched, but he kept his mouth shut.

'We'll have to talk to her, of course. Your mom.' Dr Fife made a big show of looking over Sean's shoulder at the display of evidence bags. 'Tell her what a *naughty boy* you've been.'

Mrs Hannay turned to Monroe. 'Terminate this interview, right now!'

'She's gonna find out sooner or later, Sean.'

A muffled wail rose behind Sean McGilvary's hand, bursting free as tears spilled from his eyes, running down his cheeks. Silent for a moment as he dragged in a gurgling breath, then howled it out again.

And that was it for Monroe. He reached for the audio-visual kit. 'Interview suspended at nine fifty-one.' Clicked the buttons and scowled at Dr Fife. 'I need a word. *Outside.*'

'. . . yet another complaint, and we're getting nothing out of it!' DCI Monroe paced the stairwell, face flushed. Voice not far off being a full-on shout as it echoed up and down the steps. Which is probably why he hadn't just led them down the corridor a little bit like last time. There was a lot more scope for bollocking people here without the suspects hearing anything. 'Are we not in enough of a *pricking* hole as it is?' Throwing his arms out. 'Have you got *any* idea how unprofessional this is?' Monroe got to the far end and started back again. 'And you can't lie to suspects!'

'I didn't.' Dr Fife leaned against the wall. 'Did *you* hear me lie, Angus?'

Angus opened his mouth, but Monroe was on a roll.

'You told McGilvary we'd recovered his semen from the bedroom!'

'No, I posited a *hypothetical*. "What would happen *if* . . ." It's right there on tape. Not one single word of a lie.' He stuck his nose in the air. 'I'm insulted you'd even suggest such a thing.'

At that, the air seemed to leak out of Monroe, sagging his shoulders and rounding his back. He slumped into a frown – probably running the interview back through his mind – then he scrubbed at his face. 'Will it work?'

'It's *already* working. Soon as he saw that pile of gay porn, Sean knew the hook was buried deep. He'll feel the need to thrash and struggle a bit more, but he's dead in the bottom of the boat and he knows it.'

Angus half raised a hand. 'Think he'll give us Ryan?'

'Nope. Because he doesn't *know* Ryan.'

Monroe thumped against the stairwell wall and groaned. 'But he *has* to!'

'And again: nope.' Dr Fife reached into his jacket, coming out with another little metal cylinder. 'You getting anywhere with Kate Paisley's phone?'

'Forensic IT strikes again. They had a couple of goes unlocking it and say if they try again, it'll erase all the data.'

He tapped a fat cigar into his palm. 'No offence, but your geeks are seriously shit. We had time, I'd ship it to this guy I know in Philly; Jamal would crack it like a pistachio in two minutes.'

'But we *don't* have time.'

'And three times, nope.' Cigar between his teeth, Dr Fife produced a Zippo with a skull-and-crossbones embossed on it. 'We got about ten hours, tops.'

'Also nope.' Angus plucked the lighter from his hand.

'Hey!'

'You can't *smoke* in here. It's against the law.'

Fife turned to Monroe for backup, but the DCI just shrugged. 'Since 2006.'

273

'*Course* it is.' The cigar went back in its tube as he muttered away to himself. 'Goddamn backwater, hick town, shithole . . .'

Angus held out the Zippo. 'This is all assuming Ryan hasn't done a runner.'

A harrumph, then Fife reclaimed his lighter. 'Gotta be kidding me. Can't *smoke*.' He put it away. 'And our boy's got too much invested to abandon it all. Sunk-cost fallacy trumps common sense every time.'

Wee Hairy came trotting around the corner. 'Boss? Ready when you are.'

'Ten bucks says I'm right about this too.' Dr Fife clacked off down the corridor. 'Dead in the bottom of the boat.'

Sean McGilvary squirmed in his seat, fidgeting with the sleeves of his replica top. Tugging on a single thread, making it longer and longer and longer . . .

His solicitor was the colour of watered-down Vimto, not looking at her client, sitting bolt upright. Mouth pinched as she opened her ring binder and produced an A4 sheet. Then slapped it down on the table in front of Sean. 'Statement.'

He picked the thing up and stared at it. Not making eye contact with anyone else. The paper trembled in his hands. ' "I did not kill Douglas or Kevin Healey-Robinson." '

On the other side of the table, Monroe sighed and rolled his eyes.

'I *didn't*! I just said that, because . . .' Sean licked his lips. Returned to his statement. ' "My DNA was at number twenty-one Balvenie Row because . . ." ' He cleared his throat. Tugged on that thread again, unravelling himself. ' "Because I was having sexual relations with Douglas." ' As soon as the words were out, his whole body drooped, as if some massive plug had just been pulled out of him. He blew a long breath at the ceiling. Swallowed. 'Wow. I've never said it *out loud* before. Not even with Dougie. We . . .' A laugh. 'I mean, I'd, you know, fumbled about in the corner of a nightclub, but Dougie was the . . .' Sean bit his lips together. 'He was my first. You know: all the way.'

Mrs Hannay was clearly trying not to squirm, and making a bad job of it.

'I couldn't say anything, cos of Mum. It'd kill her if she knew I was . . . that I was gay. And I'm gay. I'm *gay*!' His eyes widened. 'Please don't tell her!'

Dr Fife gave him a lopsided smile. 'If it's any consolation, I know what it's like growing up with religious nutjobs judging everything you do.'

Sean stared at him. 'So you're . . . ?'

'Nope. But I empathize all the same.'

'Oh.' Clearly disappointed. Sean picked up the statement and put it down again. 'We'd been seeing each other for about six months. Kevin was just so controlling, you know? Wouldn't let Dougie *breathe* sometimes. Didn't support his writing. It was just a stupid little hobby, not like the *genius* prose *Kevin* cranked out for that horrible rag.'

Monroe leaned forward. 'Is that why you killed Kevin Healey-Robinson: get him out of the way so you and Douglas could be together?'

'I never killed anybody.' He glowered at his fists. 'Oh, I'd love to have done it. Serve the bastard right.' Then let his hands uncurl again. 'But I didn't *need* to. Dougie was going to leave Kevin, soon as Netflix picked up the rights to the books. And I'd never do *anything* to hurt Dougie!' Wiping a tear away. 'I loved him . . .'

Mrs Hannay *still* couldn't look at her client – leaning away from him, as if he was infectious. 'I assume we can agree that Sean had neither the motive nor the . . . temperament to—'

Someone pounded on the interview-room door, then threw it open without waiting for an answer.

DS Massie lurched inside, breathing hard. 'Boss? Need a word. Urgent. Now.'

Monroe grimaced. 'Fine. Interview suspended at ten twenty-nine.' He levered himself out of his chair and turned to DS Massie, the pair of them putting their heads together so no one could hear what they were whispering about.

Whatever it was, Monroe snapped ramrod straight. He turned to the room. 'Correction: interview *terminated*.' Snatching up his files. 'DC MacVicar, escort Mr McGilvary back to his cell. Dr Fife, you're with me. Mrs Hannay . . . no idea. Angus can see you out too.'

She blinked at them. 'But we're—'

'Got to go. Doctor?' Monroe hurried from the room, following DS Massie.

OK . . .

Dr Fife looked at Angus, one eyebrow climbing his forehead, bunching up the wrinkles. 'Was that . . . ?'

'How would I know?'

And then Dr Fife was off too, leaving him alone with Sean McGilvary and Mrs Hannay.

'Right. Well, suppose we'd better . . .' Angus pointed at the door. 'Yeah.'

Angus strode back along the corridor and into the organized chaos of Operation Telegram's incident room.

Officers and support staff bustled about, others were on the phones, grim faces everywhere. Whatever had spooked DCI Monroe, it was clearly big.

No sign of the DCI in here, though. Or DS Massie. Or even Dr Fife.

DS Sharp stood in the middle of the room checking a clipboard and pointing at people. 'Leo! I need you on the phone to Voodoo's team every ten minutes. Nag them about that ANPR data till they're sick of the sound of you.'

A voice called out from somewhere in the grid of cubicles. 'Dialling now, Sarge!'

Angus hurried over. 'Sarge? What happened?'

She glanced at her clipboard again. 'Eric, 'Tash: grab a car and get your arses over to Fettes, McCutchen, and MacBain; solicitors; one-twenty-six Robin Thomson Square. I want every single person interviewed – don't care if they're the senior partner or the boy who delivers the sandwiches!'

'Tash grabbed his stabproof vest from the rack in the corner. 'Sarge!'

Eric ran a hand across his hairless pate and lumbered after him with all the grace of a three-legged polar bear as Vivaldi got his violins out in Angus's pocket.

'DR FIFE' glowed above the icons to decline or accept the call.

ACCEPT.

'Hello? Dr—'

'Where the hell are you? I'm in the car park: get your ass in gear!'

Eh?

Angus scanned the whiteboard, searching for some sort of clue as to why everyone was rushing about. 'But what's—'

'We got a dead lawyer: wife's missing. And according to Monroe, Ryan's gone full-on meat-grinder this time.'

Buggering hell . . .

26

Barbazza Crescent couldn't have been more different to the depressing street where Sean McGilvary lived if it tried. Instead of mildewed tenement flats built of featureless brick, it was a long sweep of dirty-big villas, in tan stone, tan harling and scalloped slate roofs. Each one slightly different from its neighbour.

Behind them rose the dark-green mass of the Swinney – branches shivering in the howling wind. Drizzle blowing sideways down the street drenching the poor sods out guarding the police cordon, making their high-vis jackets shine in the morning gloom.

Or maybe that should be *mourning* gloom.

A grubby SE Transit sat on the driveway of number eighteen, AKA: 'Lothrathven', according to the golden letters carved into a coffin-sized lump of granite in the front garden. A dog unit van was half up on the pavement outside, with two patrol cars acting as roadblocks, just outside the twin lines of blue-and-white tape. A pair of pool cars crowding the space inside.

The scene examiners had battled the weather to erect a small white marquee over the front door, making a wee airlock, and a ghostly figure in SOC white emerged from time to time, humping an evidence crate from the house to the Transit.

Then there was the press.

They'd been turning up for the last half-hour – just a couple of cars to start with, then more and more, followed by the Outside Broadcast Units. But the vile weather kept them in their vehicles. A poor PC staggered from one car to the next – struggling to keep his feet as the wind tore into him – water dripping off his fluorescent-yellow jacket, peaked cap pulled down so far that it bent the top of his ears over as he checked the occupants.

Silly sod.

Angus went back to his text messages.

MUM:

> Remember to eat your lunch Angus I made it specially
> After everything that happened yesterday its important
> to keep your strength up

Dr Fife groaned and sighed in the passenger seat, head buried in the copy of the *Castle News & Post* he'd liberated from reception earlier. Making a big production of turning the pages. Then sighing again. 'I'm just saying: what was the point of rushing over here if we're only gonna sit about like a couple of spare dicks?'

Angus went back to his text. 'It's barely been an hour.' Cough. 'And a bit.' Thumbs clicking across the onscreen keyboard:

> Promise will eat lunch.

SEND.

'And look at this crap!' Dr Fife slapped the newspaper with the back of his hand, then turned the offending article to show Angus. It was a centre-page spread on Operation Telegram. A blurry picture of Ryan took up a quarter of one page, the photo all pixelated from being blown up much further than the image's resolution could support. Must've got it from one of the kids on the rugby field. 'How's anyone supposed to recognize that? Looks like a goddamn Mr Potato Head with a beard drawn on.'

Grumble, whinge; rant, rave.

Angus looked up from his phone. 'What happened to the first one?'

He lowered the paper. 'First what?'

'Wife. You said the second Mrs Fife was a psychiatrist. What happened to the *first* one?'

A snort. 'Oh no, we're not opening *that* can of snakes, thank you very much.' Back to the paper. 'What about you – is there a Mrs MacVicar? Or a Mr? I'm open-minded.'

Ding, buzzzzz.

Incoming text.

MUM:

> Did you see the nice article Ellie wrote about you in the
> paper? Mrs Farooq showed me when I took Hamish
> out for his business
> She was very impressed

Urgh . . .

Not that there was anything wrong with Mrs Farooq. It was Ellie writing about him that gave Angus the heebs.

'Well?' Dr Fife stared across the car, both eyebrows up.

'None of your business.' *Click, click, clickity, click, click, click, click*:

> Have seen article.
> Am glad Mrs Farooq happy.

SEND.

'Hang on a minute. So *you* can ask *me* about *my* love life, but yours is off-limits?'

'I was only trying to change the subject. Stop you moaning.' He squirmed a bit in his seat. 'And it's complicated.'

'Always is: that's how people work. Spill.'

Outside, a delivery van wove its way through the crowd of media vehicles, only to be turned back at the cordon by a soggy PC.

A squall of wind thrashed at the Swinney's branches, hammering the front gardens' trees and bushes, rocking the Mini on its springs.

Rain crackled against the windscreen.

'Don't be a dick, Angus.'

He pulled one shoulder up. 'There's . . . someone I've known for ages, but I don't think she's interested. We went to school together. You know what it's like.'

'So ask her out. Turn on that awkward, lumbering-yeti, half-assed charm of yours.'

'Nah.' Angus watched the poor PC check the occupants of an ancient Volvo – grabbing the roof to keep upright as wind ripped the peaked cap from his head and sent it spinning off down the street like a flying saucer. 'Maybe if I'd done it years ago, but the moment passes, doesn't it. Someone sees you as a brother, you're never recovering from that.'

Dr Fife sighed and shook his head. 'You really are a *desperately* silly—'

Three hard raps clattered against the car roof. A police officer's knock. A wall of crumpled white had appeared at the driver's side.

Dr Fife opened his window a couple of inches and DS Massie hunched down to squint in at them, her SOC suit rustling and crackling in the wind.

'The Boss wants you both inside.'

'Sarge.' Angus clambered out – keeping a firm grip on the door handle so the storm wouldn't yank it from his hand – but Dr Fife stayed where he was.

Bit odd.

Angus ducked his head back into the Mini. 'You coming?'

Dr Fife buttoned up his greatcoat. 'Do me a favour and nip round this side first.'

'Is your door stuck? Do you need me to hold your hand?'

'Funny. You're a funny guy.' He jerked a thumb over his shoulder. 'Grab one'a them CSI suits from the boot on your way past.'

'Because clearly you're *far* too important to get your own—'

'No one knows I'm here, remember? And we're gonna keep it that way.'

God save us from forensic psychologists and their paranoid histrionics.

Angus thumped his door shut.

DS Massie stared across the Mini's roof. 'Good job we didn't issue that statement last night. "Everything's fine, we've caught the Fortnight Killer!"' A grimace. 'Looks like your arsehole friend's good for something after all.' She staggered a couple of steps as a gust of wind barged past. Then pointed at that poor soggy PC – currently chasing his peaked cap across someone's front garden, three houses down. 'And you owe Dusty a pint, *possibly* a handjob. He's looking for your mystery man: Beardy McBaldhead, every twenty minutes.'

Ah . . .

Hard not to feel a bit guilty about that.

DS Massie didn't wait for a response, just stomped back towards Lothrathven.

Four houses down, Dusty finally caught up with his cap as it tumbled into a thrashing clump of pampas grass.

Good for him.

Could whistle for that handjob, though.

Angus snatched one of Dr Fife's pre-wrapped SOC suits from the box in the Mini's boot, then stomped around to the driver's side and stood there – acting as a windbreak and privacy screen between the car door and the assembled press.

Dr Fife popped the door and hopped down onto the puddled tarmac. 'And make sure the vultures can't see me!' Plipping the locks and hurrying up the driveway towards the marquee with Angus following close behind.

The SE Transit provided a bit of cover too.

And then he was yanking open the marquee's front flaps and slipping inside before the first telephoto lens could turn their way. With any luck. Probably . . .

Inside was the usual collection of boxes – SOC suits, gloves, masks, safety goggles, plastic booties, wet wipes – a bin already half full of empty takeaway-coffee cups, two plastic chairs, and a PC with a clipboard. Only it wasn't Abir this time, it was Shirley Westbrook: a hard-edged, tattoo-clarted, dark-haired wee hard-woman. The kind of officer who looked as if she'd be committing all sorts of crimes if she hadn't joined the police by mistake. She was drawing lines on her clipboard, tongue poking out the side of her mouth.

Dr Fife wrestled his custom SOC suit from its plastic bag.

Angus helped himself to the largest one from the box in here. 'Your second wife: she didn't work on that paranoia of yours?'

'You have any idea how many death threats someone like me gets in a year? And where I'm from, assholes with a grudge can buy AR-Fifteens and sniper rifles. Fewer people know I'm here the better.'

Angus sank into one of the chairs, working his shoes through the leg holes. 'Hey, Shirley: where's the Boss?'

She didn't look up from her lines. 'Where do you *think* he is, you utter biscuit. Inside.'

'Yeah, but DS Massie says, "You always go to the entrance tent and ask to see the senior officer, cos if you just walk into the crime scene you get a bollocking."' Hauling the suit up and sticking his arms into the sleeves.

'*Or* you could hang around out here, like a numpty, and get a bollocking anyway?'

Oh, joy.

Angus donned a pair of booties, then a mask, goggles, and finally a double pair of gloves – one over the other, just in case.

By which time, Dr Fife was ready to go: all done-up in head-to-toe PPE. He tipped a wink in Shirley's direction. 'Later, Toots.' Then pushed through the inner flap and into the house.

She stared after him, jaw clenched. 'Who the *hell* is he calling "Toots"?'

'Ignore him. He thinks "being a dick" is the same as having a personality.' Angus paused on the threshold. Looked back at Shirley. 'You're *positive* the Boss wants us inside?'

An evil grin spread across her face. ''Bout to find out, aren't you?'

Lovely.

Deep breath. Then Angus plunged between the layers of plastic and out the other side, emerging in a . . .

Jesus.

It had been a nice hallway at one point: wide, with pictures on the walls, a cupboard for coats, and that interlocked parquet flooring that Mum always mooned over in the magazines. Now, bloody handprints smeared the walls with scarlet; bloody footprints tracked all over the wooden floor.

The scene examiners had laid their common approach path down one side of the hall to avoid the heaviest staining – the little metal trays clanging beneath Dr Fife's bootied heels.

A camera's flash flickered out from an open doorway.

Angus swallowed.

Even through the mask, the air tasted of hot copper and AAA batteries.

Dr Fife stared at the nearest wall, with its crimson spatter-patterns sprayed up the museum-white walls. 'Looks like Ryan's tidy phase is over.' He clanked along the pathway, three inches off the gore-soaked carpet, looking into the other rooms.

Angus sloped along behind.

First up was a drawing room/library, full of expensive-looking furniture; a deep oatmeal carpet; and a row of swanky bookshelves, stocked with lots and lots of books. The curtains were shut, but someone had clicked the spotlights on, bathing the place in a welcoming golden glow. A sweet-musky scent of sandalwood fought against the raw butcher's-shop tang – even though there wasn't a drop of blood visible in the room.

The lounge, across the hallway, hadn't fared so well. Yes, it boasted a mammoth TV and fancy entertainment system, a sleek hyper-modern phone in a sculptural base unit, and oversized china leopards sat upright on either side of the ash-filled fireplace, but a wide smear of dark scarlet reached about eight feet into the room. As if someone had been attacked inside, then dragged out of there.

Dr Fife paused in the doorway to the dining room. Standing still as a gravestone as that flickering camera flash strobed out into the hall. Voice low and breathy. 'Son of a bitch . . .'

Angus stepped up behind him.

Wow.

It was a bright, modern room, with a long table and chairs – easily big enough to seat a dozen people in comfort. A sideboard with fancy silver bowls and two decanters on it. More paintings on the wall. A display cabinet full of awards and cups.

And someone had turned it into an abattoir.

27

The body sat on the other side of the table, facing the door. There was almost nothing left of the victim's head – it'd been battered into a shapeless bag of bloody flesh and slivers of bone. Both hands were screwed to the dining table, like the other crime scenes, but the fingers were split and flattened, the hands lumpy and misshapen, as if someone had shattered each and every bone in them with a hammer. Then moved on to the poor bastard's forearms.

Blood.

Was.

Everywhere.

Painting the walls.

Saturating the carpet.

When Angus looked up, little stalactites of congealed scarlet hung from the ceiling. 'Jesus . . .'

This time, the Post-it note was nailed to the victim's naked chest – probably because there wasn't enough left of his head – but the message was illegible. Lost in all that gore.

The traditional second set of screw holes marred the nearside of the table, but they were surrounded by hemispherical dents *battered* into the wood. As if the killer hadn't been calm enough to aim his blows, just rained them down amidst the screaming.

Four SOC-suited figures had joined the victim in here – one taking photos, one collecting swabs from the surfaces and slipping them into test tubes, one muttering into a Dictaphone, while the unmistakably thin figure of DCI Monroe stood with his back to the door.

'Dr Fife.' He didn't turn around. Kept his eyes on the remains. 'Looks like our killer has escalated.'

The forensic psychologist's foot hovered over the first segment of elevated pathway that led into the room. 'Is it safe to enter?'

'No. But this time I'm making an exception.'

Dr Fife stepped inside, heels ringing on the metal.

Angus made to follow, but Monroe raised a finger.

'*Just* Dr Fife.'

Ah.

Angus retreated to the doorway. 'Yes, Boss.'

The path split in two, circling the dining table, and Dr Fife went widdershins, looking at everything along the way, until he was standing at the victim's left shoulder. Or what was left of it. 'Who am I looking at?'

'Leonard Lundy, fifty-one, worked for a wee firm in Castleview. Did the occasional bit of duty-solicitor work.' Monroe cricked his head to one side, as if the view was physically painful. 'Good bloke. Didn't screw you around or play games.'

Dr Fife's voice lost its hard professional edge, swapped out for what sounded like genuine compassion. 'It's . . . always difficult when the victim's someone you know.'

'Wife's Olivia: corporate-law specialist at Fettes, McCutchen, and MacBain. Didn't show up for work this morning, so her assistant came round to see if everything was OK.' Shaking his head. 'It wasn't.'

The person with the Dictaphone pointed it at Leonard Lundy's ruined corpse. 'The level of violence displayed is really *quite* remarkable.' Professor Twining – the forensic pathologist who'd carved up Douglas Healey-Robinson's remains. 'Mr Lundy's skull's been reduced to little more than a soft, leaky bag.'

Dr Fife stared at it for a couple of breaths. 'This kind of ferocity is . . . Either he *knew* the victim – held some deep, dark anger towards them – or this is his frustration at nearly being caught. He knows we're looking for him.'

A sniff from Monroe. 'We've *always* been looking for him.'

'No: we've been looking for "the Fortnight Killer", now we're looking for "Ryan". We came to his house. His *picture*'s in the paper. That's a very different thing.'

Hold on a minute.

Angus raised his hand. 'But it could be anyone! A "Mr Potato Head", you said.'

'To *us*. You think he doesn't recognize his own face?' Dr Fife turned to Professor Twining. 'Gonna venture a time of death, Doc?'

'Hmmm . . .' Twining rocked a glove from side to side. 'I'd say . . . *somewhere* between when they were last seen alive, and when Mrs Lundy's assistant discovered the husband's remains this morning.'

'Thanks. Very helpful.'

'I'll know more when we get him back to the mortuary. Meanwhile, maybe have a think about catching this chap soon? We're running out of refrigerated drawers.' He marched from the room, followed by whoever it was who'd been taking the samples.

Now the only sound was mask-muffled breathing and the crack-whine of the camera flash. Strobe-lighting the room.

Finally, the crime-scene photographer lowered her lens. 'That's me done too. I'll get everything uploaded soon as I'm back at the farm.' She took one last look at the corpse and shuddered. 'I've seen some horrible shite in my time, but . . . *Christ.*'

She patted Angus on the arm as she went past. 'Hey, big guy.'

No idea who she was, though.

Back in the dining room, Monroe stared at Dr Fife. Not saying a word.

The forensic psychologist sagged. 'I know, I know. I shoulda seen this coming.' A sigh. '*He* knows *we* know he's on a two-week schedule – it's in all the damn papers – so Ryan doesn't wait till today: he goes last night. Course he doesn't have his little helper any more, cos we've got her locked up, which means he can't control the scene. And *this*' – sweeping a hand around, taking in the battered remains and the blood-drenched house – 'is the result.'

Difficult to tell what was going on with Dr Fife's face, what with all the PPE, but he lowered his head for a bit. Pulled in a deep breath. Then nodded and clanged his way back around the table and out into the hall.

Angus fell in behind him.

Monroe brought up the rear. 'Are you saying *we're* responsible?'

'Kinda.' Dr Fife wandered along the hallway, peering into every room they passed. Pausing every now and then to examine a smear of blood, or spatter-pattern of dark sticky red. 'But what you gonna do, just let him run around killing folks? No one likes it when the cops come after them.'

They stopped outside the main bedroom.

Double bed; wrought-iron frame; the pillows dented, sheets rumpled where someone had been sleeping. Duvet half on the floor.

Drips of scarlet on the carpet.

Dr Fife stared, tilted his head to one side, then walked over to the bedside cabinet and pressed a button on the alarm-clock radio. The display switched from '12:03' to '06:45'.

He let free a little grunt, then tried the room next door: a study, tidy and neat, complete with desk, computer, law books, and a smart wooden filing cabinet with bloody fingerprints on one of its drawers.

Another grunt, and he was on the move again.

Monroe tapped Angus on the shoulder, then raised his hand, as if cupping something invisible.

Yeah, like Angus had the slightest idea what Fife was up to.

They followed him into a single bedroom.

Ruby-coloured footprints scuffed in from the hallway to the bed and back again, bringing a plethora of drips with them. The bed bore the same tell-tale traces of sleep, but this time the crumpled duvet was clarted with deep crimson. More red spattered up the wallpaper in two fang-shaped arcs.

No alarm clock – just a mobile phone sitting on the bedside cabinet.

Monroe leaned on the doorframe. 'Would you *please* tell us what we're . . .'

But Dr Fife marched right past them without a word, heading back down the hallway towards the front door.

He didn't step outside, though, he took a right instead – through the open doorway, disappearing into that drawing-room-cum-library.

By the time they'd caught up, he was squatting in front of a buttoned leather couch. Staring at its legs for some weird reason. Before running a gloved fingertip along the top of the skirting board. Then sat back on his heels. 'They were in bed when Ryan let himself in. So it must've happened before the morning alarm went off at quarter to seven.'

Monroe raised a finger. 'Hold on: "let himself in"?'

'No sign of forced entry?'

'Not that we can find. SE team think—'

'Then he let himself in.' Dr Fife pointed towards the hall. 'From the look of the master bedroom, the Lundys start off sleeping together. Maybe one of them snores, so they have to move to the spare room. Enter Ryan.' Fife stared at the wall, turning to watch the imaginary action. 'He goes to the master bedroom first – probably a couple of blows to the head – renders whoever's there unconscious. Cable-ties hands and feet. Next up: single bedroom.' Miming the weight of a blunt object in his hand. 'Got blood dripping off his . . . hammer? Probably a hammer. Tracks more blood through on his shoes. This time, when he swings the *hammer* there's already enough blood on there to fly off, making lines up the walls. Two blows this time. Blood on his hands as he pulls off the duvet. Throws the victim over his shoulder and carries them through to the dining room. That's why there's no drag marks.'

Fife tilted his head, and dropped the make-believe hammer. 'Only he's not hit them as hard as he thought, and they regain consciousness halfway down the hall. Wriggle free. Try to crawl away from him, into the living room – maybe they're making for the phone, call for help.' Dr Fife stood, hands clenching around something only he could see. 'But Ryan grabs them – drags them back into the hall. Hits them a couple more times. Takes them into the dining room and screws their hands to the table. Goes back for the other one.'

'But . . .' Monroe waved a hand at the front door. '. . . "let himself in" *how*?'

'He's got a key.' Dr Fife pointed. 'See the little circular marks in the carpet? That's where the furniture's been taken out and replaced in not *quite* the same place. Probably to fit the brand-new bookshelves.' The gloved finger swung towards a set of three dents in the deep pile, arranged in an L shape. They looked about the same distance apart as the couch legs he'd been staring at, only the fourth one – back right – would be hidden underneath the bookshelves. And finally the finger stopped six inches from Monroe's face.

The DCI retreated a step, but Angus edged closer.

Fife's black nitrile fingertip bore a thin smudge of pale cream.

'Sawdust. That's why it smells of fresh wood and beeswax in here.' Dr Fife dropped his hand. 'Kate Paisley's an electrician; why *wouldn't* Ryan be a carpenter?'

Monroe *blinked*. 'Pricking hell.'

Ooh!

Angus put his hand up again. 'Maybe *that's* why there's blood on the filing cabinet! He was getting his invoice back, so there wouldn't be a trail.'

'Right.' DCI Monroe yanked out his phone, dialling as he marched off. 'Badger? . . . Yeah, it's me. I need you to get a warrant for whatever bank the Lundys used.' Voice getting fainter as he disappeared off down the corridor. *'I want full account details for the last year: money in, money out, and who it was paid to . . . Yeah: ASAP.'*

Angus nodded at Dr Fife. 'Look at you, all Sherlock Holmes.'

'Hmph.' He scrubbed the make-believe murder from his hands, scowling behind his safety goggles. 'I *was* gonna get to the bit about the filing cabinet. You stole my thunder.'

'No "I" in team, remember?' Angus stuck his head out into the hall. 'Want to check it out, just in case?'

'Might as well.'

Dr Fife clambered up onto the office chair, wobbling away till he grabbed the top of the filing cabinet for support, then hauled out the top drawer – the one with the bloody fingerprints all over it – and went rummaging inside.

Angus, meanwhile, sniffed his way along the rows of legal books, flipping through the occasional volume in case there was something incriminating hidden inside. Which there wasn't. But at least it was more interesting than standing about like a massive twonk, watching Dr Fife do the interesting bit. 'Anything?'

'Course not. You think he's going to leave a handwritten receipt behind for the police to find?' Dr Fife slammed the drawer shut. 'We need to talk to the acolyte: Kate Paisley.'

'She was up before the Sheriff, first thing. She'll be in HMP Oldcastle by now.' Locked away, awaiting trial. 'We could probably arrange a visit, though. Not that she'll tell us anything.'

'Hmmm . . .' Black nitrile fingertips drummed against the wooden filing cabinet. 'Maybe not on *purpose* . . .' An evil smile slithered into his voice. 'But we need to pick something up from evidence, first.'

Yeah.

Why did that sound borderline illegal?

28

Gloom reigned in the Records-and-Productions Store.

Angus sat in the lit part – a small area separated from the rest of the huge warehouse space by a twelve-foot-high chain-link fence. Topped with barbed wire. Rows and rows and *rows* of shelving racks lurked on the other side – about half were jammed full of dusty files, the rest were cluttered with evidence boxes. A second, top-secret zone lay at the heart of the store, secured behind an electrified cordon of steel mesh, garnished with razor wire and 'DANGER OF DEATH' notices.

It would've been completely invisible, if PC Mason didn't keep wandering through some sort of motion sensor's path, setting off the security lights as he went a-rummaging.

Back here, though, a pair of small desks sat either side of the outer fence, bolted to the floor, with a large hatch set into the chain-link at tabletop height. Awaiting the fruits of PC Mason's labours.

Dr Fife paced the boundary between the two realms, checking his watch every couple of laps. Man had the patience of a starving crocodile.

Angus shifted in his seat, all hunched up, elbow on one knee – holding his forehead up with his free hand. The other clutched his phone in its ziplock armour. 'I know, Mum. I'll do my best.'

'*What are you not telling me, Angus? You know we don't have secrets in this house.*' Then the suspicious tone disappeared, replaced by a horrified gasp. '*Did that horrid man try to kill you again? Oh Angus! Is it any wonder I'm worried sick!*'

'No, he . . .' Hard to know what to say to that. Maybe someone else could break the news to her? Angus glanced at the phone's screen. Bang on one o'clock. Well, that helped. 'Turn on the radio, Mum. Pretty much any station.'

The sound of a door opening and closing came through the phone's speaker, followed by some scrunching, a weird *squarrrrk*-tinged buzz, then another door. *'I always said you shouldn't join the police. It's* far *too dangerous, but you never listen to your mother, do you?'*

A sharp click rang out, followed by a serious newsreader's voice, distorted through the kitchen radio. *'. . . denies all allegations and insists his dealings with the Saudi government were above board . . .'*

Mum sniffed, no doubt with her nose in the air. *'You could've got a nice little job at Mr Nwachukwu's pest-control business. I said, didn't I?'*

'You're the one who wanted me to be a police officer! Said it might make up for all the . . . for Dad.'

'. . . demanding the Home Secretary be suspended pending criminal proceedings.'

'Oh Angus!' Mum let loose another gasp. *'How* could *you? Mentioning that . . . man.'*

Great.

Here we go.

He slumped back in his seat, drooping like a discarded teddy bear.

'. . . crash investigators say the eight thirty-nine to Aberdeen was intentionally derailed just north of Kennethmont . . .'

Angus pinched the bridge of his nose with his free hand. 'Mum, it's not—'

'I don't know why I bother, I really don't.'

'Mum, *please* . . .'

The sniffy tone was back. *'And Hamish needs more doggie bickies. Don't forget to pick some up on your way home.'*

Dr Fife came to a halt, right in front of him, voice loud and cutting. 'For God's sake, DC MacVicar, get off that bloody phone and DO SOME WORK!'

'. . . to contact the police with any information.' The newsreader left

a little pause, then: *'The Fortnight Killer has struck again in Oldcastle, bringing the total number of victims to eight—'*

'I've got to go.' Angus hung up before Mum could say anything else. Put his phone away and glowered at Dr Fife. Bristling.

Where the hell did he get off, yelling at him like that? When there was nothing they *could* do till PC Manson got back. What was he supposed to—

'Sorry.' Dr Fife shrugged. 'Sounded like you needed rescuing.' He turned, interlacing his fingers through the chain-link. 'What's taking this asshole so long?'

Deep inside the store, those security lights snapped on again, revealing Manson's silhouette as he shambled past.

Angus put his phone away and drooped some more. 'Not like there's any rush, is there.'

'Are you kidding me? *Ryan's* out there, and—'

'Yes, but the clock's reset. We screwed up and didn't catch him.' Going from discarded teddy bear to shipwrecked jellyfish – his tentacles brushing concrete floor. 'So there's fourteen days till the next victims get tortured to death.'

Dr Fife opened his mouth, then closed it again. Pulled his shoulders in. 'Not the point.' Then paced the fence again. 'And as of this morning, we know Ryan is flexible with his timings. Just because it was two weeks last time, doesn't mean we get a fortnight now.'

'Do you think that's even his real name? "Ryan".'

'Be a pretty crap nickname if it isn't.'

'Suppose.'

Angus's phone ding-buzzed in his pocket. And when he dug it out, there was 'ELLIE' glowing away in the middle of the screen at him. Probably heard the news on the radio and wanted to horrible some information out of him.

'What about you?' Angus glanced up as Dr Fife reached the far end of the 'public' cage and started back again. 'Bet you had a crap nickname growing up – that's why you kicked off the briefing with the whole "don't call me "John" or "Jonny" bit. How bad was it?'

Frowning, Dr Fife scuffed to a halt, as if it was a question no one had ever asked before. 'It . . . kinda depends on your perspective . . .'

ELLIE:

> Mary Dunwoody's a plus-size porn star now: here's a
> link to her stuff on PornOnTheCob. You can wank off to
> her screwing a whole rugby team till your dick wears
> down to a tiny(ier) nub.

Well, that was . . . unnecessarily nasty, even for Ellie.

Wonder what'd flown up *her* bum and laid eggs.

'Here we go!' A figure emerged from the shelved depths, carrying a cardboard box about the size of a small microwave. PC Manson had a sort of unwell-Gollum thing going on, with his threadbare scalp, wonky teeth, and gammony skin. The big square glasses didn't help – magnifying his jaundiced eyes as he shambled up to the desk on his side of the fence and thumped the box down. 'Forensic IT Unit signed a job-lot back into evidence this morning. But did they fill in the correct paperwork?' Tutting as he opened the box and rummaged inside.

Dr Fife glared. 'About goddamn time.'

There was that winning charm again.

Manson paused for a moment, as if processing that, then took a much smaller cardboard box from the bigger one – a phone-specific evidence container, with a form printed on the beige surface. He checked it against a clipboard, then placed it on the desk. 'One mobile phone.'

'Give.' Sticking his hand out, then clicking his fingers.

'You *do* understand this is highly irregular? And I'm only doing it because DCI Monroe says so?'

'For the love of *Christ*, just gimme the goddamn phone!'

'Hmmph.' Manson opened the hatch and slid the clipboard through to their side. '*Sign* for it.'

'Yeah, yeah . . .' Fife scrawled his signature on the dotted line then shoved the clipboard back. 'Happy?'

'Delighted. And there's no need to be an arse about it.' He reached through the opening and plonked the phone box down. 'You can see yourselves out.' He flared his nostrils for a bit, picked up the bigger box, and slithered away into the gloom.

Angus cringed. 'Do you have any idea how *embarrassing* it is to sit here and watch you do that?'

'Yeah.' A sneer. 'Maybe, if your police department didn't hire useless half-wound-clockwork assholes, I wouldn't have to.' He ripped open the cardboard carton and tipped Kate Paisley's mobile into his hand.

It had a purple case with a bunch of kittens tooled into the leather, and a sort of scruffy-rosary-bead-dangly-bit hanging from the bottom corner. Very twee for a serial-killer's assistant.

Dr Fife flipped the cover open and poked at the side buttons till the phone powered up. Frowned at the lock screen when it finally appeared. 'What kinda cell you got?'

Cell?

Ah, right. *Americans.* 'Samsung.'

'Shit. Need a Google Pixel.'

PC Manson's voice drifted out of the gloom. 'I've *got a Google Pixel.*'

'Cool.' Dr Fife held out his hand again. 'I need to borrow it for a couple of hours.'

'*Then you shouldn't've been such a dick, should you.*' A *clunk* echoed through the warehouse and about a third of the lights on this side of the fence died. '*Like I said: see yourselves out.*'

Clunk. Another third.

Angus scowled at Dr Fife. 'Because that pre-emptive pissing-people-off thing you do is working *so* well.'

Clunk.

And they were in darkness.

Great.

'Cos I say so, *that's* why.' Dr Fife shoved the incident-room door open and barged inside.

Angus paused in the corridor for a moment, voice barely more than a whisper. 'Manson was right about you. You *are* a dick.' But he followed him in anyway.

Operation Telegram was three-quarters empty – probably because Teams Microscope, Tweezers, Spyglass, Postman, and Spanner were off doing their thing, and every other available officer was either going door-to-door in Castleview or trying to trace Leonard and Olivia Lundy's last movements. Which left a handful of support staff to answer every single phone in the place as they rang and rang and rang . . .

No sign of DCI Monroe, but DI Cohen was here, squinting at a spreadsheet. Clicking numbers into it with two-fingered typing, the tip of his tongue poking out between his scrunched lips.

DS Sharp wrote names and dates on a whiteboard. Monster Munch fought with the printer.

'Hoy: *Wind in the Willows*!' Dr Fife strode to the middle of the room and did that annoying finger-snapping thing at DI Cohen. 'Where's Monroe?'

There was a very long and pointed pause as Cohen sat back from the laptop and ran a tiny hand through the grey streak above his left ear. 'Do I *look* like a waiter? Or more like someone who rips people's clicky fingers off?'

Dr Fife stuck his hands in his pockets. 'I need a Google Pixel phone and *this one*' – nodding at Angus – 'won't let me raid the Lost and Found.'

'*Why?*'

Angus stood up straight. 'It's not communal property, Guv, it's—'

'Not that, you vast twit.' He swivelled his chair in Dr Fife's direction. 'Why do you want a phone?'

'I wouldn't *need* a phone if your Forensic IT team wasn't dumber than a bag of hammers. Speaking of which: who's looking into Kate Paisley's social media accounts?'

'Forensic IT deals with all electronic communications and—'

'Oh, for Christ's sake! They couldn't find their assholes with a map and a tour guide!'

Cohen glowered. 'It's *procedure*. That's how these things work.'

'Screw that.' Dr Fife clambered up onto the nearest chair and from there to an unoccupied desk. Stamped his Cuban heel like a flamenco dancer, stuck two fingers in his mouth and let loose a shrieking whistle. 'LISTEN UP, MOTHERFUCKERS!'

The whole room stopped what it was doing to stare at him, open-mouthed.

'Everybody: get on the internet and search for "Kate Paisley". Twitter, Facebook, LinkedIn, Bindle, Truth Social, Clarion Digital . . .

Any time-wasting sack of social media shit you can think of.' Then, when no one moved: 'Go! Go! Go!'

They still didn't.

Instead, the team all looked to DI Cohen. Who sighed. Rolled his eyes. And finally nodded. 'Do it.'

Cue an explosion of activity – poking at phone screens, clicking computer keyboards, and hunching over laptops.

Cohen shook his head. 'You certainly know how to make friends, don't you?'

'I don't *need* friends, I need results.' Dr Fife clambered down from the desk. 'This is what happens when police departments put everything into goddamned silos, and nobody talks to anyone else.'

Monster Munch waved. 'Guv? I've got a Kate Paisley on Bindle. Photo matches.'

Two seconds later, DS Sharp was at it too: 'I've got her on Instagram.'

A smug smile. 'See?' Dr Fife bustled over to Monster Munch's desk, with Angus and DI Cohen hot on his Cuban heels.

She held out her smartphone, so they could see the scratched screen. 'That's her Bindle profile.' A photo of Kate Paisley sat next to a brief bio – which didn't include being apprentice to a mass murderer.

'How do you find out who she follows?'

'Who's in her bundle? Hud oan . . .' Monster Munch poked at the screen. 'She's bundled three-hunner and thirty-nine people, and twenty-two have bundled her.'

Cohen curled his lip. 'That make sense to anyone in long trousers?'

'Can you order who she follows by date? Look at who's been there the longest.' Dr Fife turned to Angus. 'The first people we follow are the people we know.'

Made sense. 'Like Ryan.'

'Exactly.'

Monster Munch scrolled through the list. 'Nope. No one called Ryan, just a bunch of made-up handles like "Chunky Love Three-Four-Nine-Two-Six" and "Bongo Dog Mummy".' She went back and poked the other list. 'Let's try people who've bundled *her* . . .' Wheeching through all twenty-two of them. 'No "Ryans".'

'OK.' Dr Fife leaned closer. 'Let's see the profile pics.' Squinting at the screen as she worked through them one at a time. 'Angus?'

'Difficult to tell. No one's got long hair and a beard.' Shrug. 'Might be an old photo, though.'

'Goddamnit . . .'

DI Cohen straightened up, voice raised so everyone in the room could hear him, nice and clear: 'Now, if we've quite finished with the *Everyone Look at Me Because I'm So Special and the Expert at Everything* show, perhaps the rest of us can get back to work?'

29

If there was one thing worse than an arrogant Dr Fife, it was a miserable one. Sulking away behind the wheel, face clenched like a toddler's when a seagull's just nicked their ice cream.

Angus did his best not to sigh. Forced a bit of faux positivity into his voice instead. 'Maybe Ryan's not his real name? Or they're using pseudonyms? Call signs. Something like that?'

Outside, Camburn Woods drifted by the passenger window. Dark as a raven's back, branches scrabbling at the sky as gust after gust howled down the valley and rain bounced off the road.

No reply from Dr Fife.

One hand let go of the wheel and poked the dashboard-mounted phone, scrolling the map around on the screen.

'You're not supposed to adjust your satnav while driving.'

Still no reply.

They followed the road around onto McLaren Avenue.

More poking and scrolling.

'Look, I know Badger can be a bit of a dick, but he's not wrong about policies and procedures. They do things a certain way here and there's probably a perfectly good reason to . . .'

Dr Fife took a left at the lights, onto Pudding Lane, even though the arrow on his phone's screen pointed straight ahead.

Angus turned in his seat, watching the junction receding through the rear window. 'It's faster if you keep on McLaren Avenue till the dual carriageway.' But it was OK. Still fixable. He faced front again, pointing. 'Take a right, just past the big Asda. We can cut through to Jutemill Terrace.'

But Dr Fife took a left instead, into the big supermarket car park.

'You're really not good at directions, are you.'

Dr Fife grunted. 'Need to pick up a couple of things.'

My God, it speaks!

He parked diagonally across two 'FAMILY FRIENDLY' spaces, right in front of the main doors, killed the engine, and hopped out into the rain. 'Won't be a minute.'

'But . . .'

The driver's door clunked shut and off he went – disappearing inside. Leaving Angus sitting there like a boiled fart.

Without the windscreen wipers and the blowers, the outside world had turned into a ribboned, wobbly special effect, rapidly disappearing into the fog.

Angus frowned down at that last text from Ellie:

> Mary Dunwoody's a plus-size porn star now: here's a link to her stuff on PornOnTheCob. You can wank off to her screwing a whole rugby team till your dick wears down to a tiny(ier) nub.

He poked out a reply:

> Text V unkind.
> Why so nasty?

Nah, that made him sound like a becardiganed schoolteacher. Angus deleted the whole message and tried again:

> Who rattled your bumhole?

Much better.

> Mary always nice to you.
> Unable to watch pornography at home.
> Parental lock on Mr Rosomakha's router.

Yeah, that struck the right tone. It was still missing something, though . . .

Ah. Of course:

> ;)P

SEND.

Then he sat there, grimacing out at the fog.

'A whole rugby team . . .'

Angus rubbed the side of his hand against the passenger window, unblocking the porthole he'd made. Again.

Outside, a woman in a dripping fleece struggled past, pushing an overloaded trolley through the storm, with a screaming toddler in the seat. She scowled at the badly parked Mini.

For which Angus took no responsibility.

He gave her an apologetic little wave, by way of explanation. Then huffed out a long breath. Which had the bonus of remisting the porthole again, so she couldn't hurl daggers at him any more.

His phone ding-buzzed.

Probably Ellie with some suitably cutting remark about his text. But it wasn't.

GILLIAN:

> I was wondering if you fancied getting that drink tonight after work?
>
> Or a coffee.
>
> We could meet somewhere local after the evening bulletins if you like?

Didn't have to think about *that* twice:

> Would like very much.
>
> 18:00 at the Shoogly Peg?
>
> Investigation permitting.

SEND.

The reply was almost immediate.

GILLIAN:

> Can't do six, sorry. Reporting Scotland's live at half past.
> Seven fifteen's good, though. Is that OK for you?
>
> Yup: Perfect.
>
> See you there.

SEND.

A huge grin spread across his face.

It had grown even bigger by the time the driver's door opened and Dr Fife clambered in out of the downpour. Shuddering the rain off his even- curlier hair like a soggy spaniel.

A frown spread across his face, deepening the wrinkles as he stared at Angus grinning bigly. 'What've you been up to?'

Which just made Angus grin biglier. 'Nothing.'

'Yeah . . . Never take up poker, you'll get reamed. And not in a good way.' Dr Fife started the engine, turned the blowers up full, and the windscreen wipers too. 'Let's go see if we can't break Kate Paisley.'

Not exactly politically correct, but right now Angus was too happy to care.

Angus smiled, leaning back against a hot-pink wall punctuated with heavy blue security doors.

The opposite wall was floor-to-ceiling toughened safety glass, overlooking the exercise yard and one of the prison blocks. Normally it'd be full of bustling prisoners: taking the air, playing five-a-side, running laps . . . but today only a single sodden prisoner braved the storm – battling the wind and rain as he tried to sweep up a clump of leaves that swirled and spun away from him every time he got near them with his bin bag.

Be nice to read Gillian's texts again, but they'd confiscated his phone when he'd signed in at reception. Securing it in a locker, by the metal detectors, till it was time to leave.

Going out for a drink with an actual, real-life, attractive, genuine woman-type person . . .

How cool was that?

And the Shoogly Peg was—

The sound of trainers-on-prison-flooring squealed around the corner as a prison officer appeared. A big one – almost as tall as Angus – with tattoos wrapped around both muscular arms, covering every inch of skin from her shirt's short sleeves all the way down to her scarred knuckles. 'FAITH' on one set, 'HOPE' on the other. Short grey hair with frosted blonde tips. White shirt, black tie, black jumper with 'HMP' epaulettes, black trousers, black trainers. And a wee white clip-on badge: 'SPS ~ HMP OLDCASTLE ~ BARBARA CRAWFORD'.

Behind her came Kate Paisley – all done up in prison blues – with a second huge prison officer bringing up the rear.

Officer Crawford jerked her head at the door. 'He ready yet?'

'Hold on, I'll find out.' Angus opened the door to Family Room Number Three and slipped inside.

It was the sort of space that got billed as an 'intimate welcoming environment' in the prison literature, but in reality was a wee room with yellow hessian wallpaper and a plastic pot plant that looked in need of a bloody good watering. The decor was rounded out by three mediocre landscape paintings – all screwed to the wall – a semi-manky coffee table, and four plastic chairs.

The room's only window looked out on a blank, twenty-foot-high concrete wall topped with razor wire.

'Intimate' and 'welcoming'.

Dr Fife sat with his platform cowboy boots up on the coffee table, fiddling with Kate Paisley's phone.

Angus hooked a thumb at the door. 'That's them, now.'

'Yeah. Gonna be *two* minutes . . .' He produced his copy of that morning's *Castle News & Post* and spread it out on the coffee table, opening it to the centre-page special about Operation Telegram. Then aimed the phone's camera at the blurry, pixelated 'HAVE YOU SEEN THIS MAN?' photo of Ryan, and poked the screen. The fake-shutter click rang out. More poking and fiddling.

Angus *stared*. 'You got it to work!'

'Told you.' Dr Fife didn't look up, fingers still tapping away. 'I got me some nerds *way* brighter than your Forensic IT morons.' A nod. 'OK. We're good to go.' Slipping the phone into his pocket. 'Show 'em in.'

How the hell did he do that?

Amazing.

Angus popped his head back out into the corridor and gave Officer Crawford a thumbs-up, then held the door open for the three of them as they marched inside.

Dr Fife had cleared away the newspaper and now he slouched in his seat, hands behind his head, feet up, legs crossed at the ankles. Wearing a great-big smugtastic grin.

Kate Paisley scowled.

'Right.' Officer Crawford stuck her chin out. 'You know the rules?'

'Yup.' Dr Fife pointed at a sign, mounted on the back of the door. 'All laminated and everything.'

'One hour. No drama.' Narrowing her eyes at him. 'From *anyone*.' Then she motioned for Kate to sit.

Which she did, bolt upright in her plastic chair, arms crossed, defiant as she glared at Dr Fife.

The grin widened, and he produced that morning's *Castle News & Post* with a flourish – making a big show of turning to the centre-page spread again, placing it on the table so it was the right way up for her. Paused for a count of about ten. Then plonked his feet on Ryan's face.

Kate Paisley sniffed. 'This supposed to impress me?'

'Have you ever noticed how scared right-wingers are about everything? Migrants, refugees, foreigners, kids, the "woke", "leftie" lawyers, sports commentators, celebrities, vaccines—'

'That's not fear, that's anger!' Pulling her arms tighter. 'You bastards stick your needles in kids – pumping them full of experimental, DNA-altering, *untested* chemicals that cause heart attacks and strokes – but if we stand up for what's right, *we're* the monsters?'

'What about Ryan? He's into all that "Great Replacement Theory", isn't he?'

'We're *not* racists.'

Angus scribbled that down in his notebook. 'Thought you said you'd never seen him before in your life?'

'All right, DC MacVicar, I think Kate and me can manage fine here.' Dr Fife reached into his greatcoat again, coming out with Kate's phone in its purple cover. 'Forensic IT guys can do wonders these days. Most folks, they think their phone's nice and secure, but our nerds can crack them in, like, thirty seconds flat.' He flipped the cover and held the phone out, showing off the unlocked home screen. 'Changed your backdrop to Ryan's photo in the paper.

Knew you wouldn't mind. Had to tidy up the apps and icons, though. What is it with you women and organizing stuff?' Smiling up at Officer Crawford and her colleague. 'No offence.'

Clearly some was taken. 'You're supposed to hand *all* mobile phones over when you sign in!'

'Am I? How naughty of me. Tell you what: don't think of it as a *phone*, more as a . . . conversation starter.' He turned the screen to face himself again, and poked at it. 'I like your Bindle quote, Kate: "Live life like it's a nail and you're the hammer." Exclamation mark, smiley face, cake emoji. Very inspirational.'

Kate shrank back in her seat, eyes fixed on her phone.

'It's amazing the secrets people keep on these things, isn't it? All the little things *hidden* away in their diaries, texts, and messages.' Wink. 'End-to-end encryption's great . . . till someone gets hold of your password.'

She licked her lips. 'That's not legal. You've no right to invade my privacy!'

'And the *photos*! Let's not forget those.' He raised the phone so the camera pointed at her, and pressed something on the screen. That fake-shutter *click* sounded once more. 'Did you know, ninety-three-point-seven percent of people convicted of bestiality get banged up because they've taken photos of themselves balls-deep in the family dog? Or goat, sheep, llama: whatever.'

Her face pinched, tiny dots of sweat swelling out of her forehead to gleam in the strip lighting.

'Isn't that *weird*? I mean, why would you take photos *incriminating yourself*?'

Kate's left leg developed a tremble, the heel going *dunk-dunk-dunk-dunk-dunk-dunk* against the lino.

'Still, good job they don't have the death penalty over here, am I right, Kate?'

It was as if her eyes were welded to the phone now.

'Only question now is: do you want to cooperate and maybe cut a few decades off your sentence, or don't ya?' He lowered the phone. 'Ryan got the lawyer and her husband, by the way. Mr and Mrs Lundy. You probably saw that on the news.'

The faintest smile slid across her lips. 'Don't know what you're talking about.'

'OK, so you were *in here* when they actually died, but you're still on the hook for conspiracy to commit. Which makes it eight counts of first-degree murder!' Dr Fife gave her a wee round of applause. 'Even *without* the death penalty, you're gonna die in here. Alone and unloved.' He raised an eyebrow. 'Unless . . . ?'

She kept her eyes on the phone. Bit her top lip as a single bead of sweat trickled down the side of her forehead. 'I . . .'

'Let's make it something easy, shall we? To start with. How about: what did you do with the bodies? No one can complain about that, can they?'

She shifted in her seat, hands turning to claws – gripping her sides.

'And you *want* people to know, right? Want it in all the papers, so they can be afraid?'

'You *know* what happened; you've seen the photos.'

'Yeah, but I need to hear you say it. Part of the process.'

And Kate Paisley finally tore her eyes away from her phone, voice barely more than a whisper: 'I buried her. The doctor woman.'

'Good. Where did you bury her, Kate?'

'The Gallowburn, out by Braecairn Forest.'

Angus's old childhood haunt.

Looked as if orcs and trolls weren't the only monsters out there.

Dr Fife clapped his hands together, making her jump. 'There we go! Isn't it *nice* to be helpful?'

And she was on her feet, glaring down at him. Claws out. 'I'M NOT *HELPING*!'

Officer Crawford stepped in, putting a hand on Kate's shoulder. 'All right, settle down.' She pointed at Dr Fife. 'This situation de-escalates *now*, or I pull the plug. Understand?'

Kate sank into her seat and glowered across the coffee table at him. 'Must be strange, sitting there with your wee legs not reaching the floor. A kid in a high chair.'

'Ryan doesn't need you any more: he's got himself a new disciple. Someone bright enough to not get caught.'

'What must your dad have thought when you slithered out of your poor mum? Like something off a horror film.'

There was a pause. 'My father thought all his prayers had been answered.' Then Dr Fife shuffled forwards. 'Ryan's going to let you rot in here. He thinks you're too stupid to rat him out, even to save yourself.'

'The Great Reset is coming, whether we like it or not. Some people will get trampled; some will do what they're told, like good little sheep; and some will stand up and *fight*.'

He raised the phone again, flipping the cover shut. 'But I will say this for Ryan: at least he sent you a lovely text, thanking you for your service.' Then tossed the phone onto the table – right in front of her.

Officer Crawford jabbed a finger at it. 'No phones!' Glaring at Angus. 'Thought you knew the rules.'

Eh?

'It wasn't me! I—'

'It's OK, Officer' – Dr Fife smiled like a cowboy-booted Buddha – 'she's gonna give it *right* back. Aren't you, Kate?'

Sod that.

Angus reached for the phone, but Kate snatched it off the table-top before he could get there. Flipped it open.

Well, he'd just have to take it off her, wouldn't—

'Don't!' Dr Fife raised a hand. 'Leave her alone. I'm gonna take full responsibility, OK? This is all fine.'

Officer Crawford loomed. 'It *better* be.'

He hopped down from his seat and strutted his way around the coffee table, coming to rest at Kate's side.

Yeah, given what happened last time, that probably wasn't a good idea. If she decided to kick off, she'd get a good few blows in before they hauled her off him.

Angus moved over, till he was right next to Dr Fife and just behind Kate Paisley. Ready to intervene.

Looked as if Dr Fife had changed her lock screen to the same blurry pic of Ryan.

'Oh, I disabled the fingerprint and facial recognition' – wink – 'for obvious reasons.'

Her shoulders tightened. But curiosity got the better of her, and she poked in her passcode instead. 'What?'

She tried again.

'Stupid thing . . .'

One last go.

A growl swelled in her throat, turning into a snarl as she slammed her phone down on the tabletop.

Dr Fife pulled on a pantomime pout. 'Well, that's just *rude*.'

OK: no more wanking about.

Angus wheeched the thing off the coffee table.

Dr Fife nudged Officer Crawford with his elbow. 'See? No harm done.' Then sauntered back round to his side of the coffee table, producing a different Google Pixel phone from his pocket on the way. Prodding the screen with a finger. 'Three, six, nine, one, four.'

'*What?*' Kate Paisley stared at him, mouth hanging open.

He held the new phone up to show them the home screen – so cluttered with app icons that the backdrop was barely visible. 'That wasn't so difficult, was it?'

This whole thing had been a con to get her passcode.

Devious sod.

'Bastard . . .' Kate's eye bulged, teeth bared. 'You think you're so *clever*, don't you.'

'I have my moments. And now: I have your phone. And *all* those little secrets we talked about.'

'Yeah? Well, *we* know *your* secrets!' Scraping her chair back and jabbing a finger at him. 'With your underground paedophile ring, and drinking the blood of murdered kids. We *know* about your satanic rituals!' Taking a step closer, spittle flying: 'WE KNOW!'

Officer Crawford grabbed her shoulder. 'All right, that's enough.' Scowling at Dr Fife. 'I *said*: de-escalate!'

Tears sparked in Kate's eyes. 'They murder kids and *I'm* the one in prison!'

Dr Fife settled back in his chair again, feet up on Ryan's face. Grinning. 'Kate, the whole Pizzagate thing was a *lie*. You really think the Evil Global Elite are abusing kids under a pizza place called "Comet *Ping Pong*"? It doesn't even have a basement.'

'THAT'S WHAT THEY WANT YOU TO THINK!'

Officer Crawford nodded at her colleague – they both took one of Kate Paisley's arms. 'Come on, Kate. This visit's over.' They 'escorted' her to the door.

'HE'S COMING FOR YOU, FREAK! YOU'RE DEAD!'

'Think it through: if they're drinking murdered kids' blood, wouldn't they do it at some swanky private club in the Hamptons? Who goes to a pizza place, on a busy intersection, in downtown DC, where everyone can *see* them?' Dr Fife barked out a mocking laugh. 'What *happened* to you, Kate? When did bullshit like this start to make sense?'

She wriggled free of the prison officers' grip and surged towards the table, fists at the ready.

Angus blocked her way, hands out. 'Don't.'

'I CHOOSE THE GREAT AWAKENING!'

Officer Crawford grabbed her again. 'That's enough!'

The other officer took hold. 'Behave yourself.'

But Kate struggled and thrashed, teeth bared in a vicious smile as they wrestled her towards the door. 'We *will* rise up. And you – and *all* your bloodsucking, liberal-elite, paedo friends – will *burn*!' Her right foot lashed out, connecting with one of the plastic chairs and sending it wanging off to batter against the wall.

Dr Fife gave her a wee wave. 'Ryan's going to forget all about you, Kate, but you won't forget about *him*, will you. No, you'll build a little shrine in your heart and your cell, where you can worship him till they cart you out of here in a pine box. A faithful, stupid little disciple who's already been replaced.'

The vicious smile sharpened. 'You don't know *anything*.' Her eyes widened. 'Ryan doesn't *need* to replace me. WE ARE LEGION!' Laughing and laughing and laughing as they dragged her from the room.

30

Angus stuck a finger in his ear and had yet another go: 'No: *Brae-cairn* Forest. Bravo, Romeo, Alpha, Echo, Charlie—'

'*Oh,* Brae-*cairn.*' DS Massie finally twigged. '*Why didn't you say so?*'

'I was trying, Sarge.'

On the other side of the corridor's great-big windows, that poor sod was still at it: doing battle with the leaves. And losing.

Dr Fife leaned back against the wall, fiddling with Kate Paisley's real phone – now returned to its purple-leather kitten case – pulling faces as he scrolled through her photographs.

Angus, on the other hand, was on the *fake* Google Pixel, using up the ten quid's worth of free credit it'd come with. Which was cool, given his was still stuck in a locker downstairs.

'Hey.' Fife clicked his fingers a couple of times, eyes still focused on Kate's camera roll. 'Tell her they buried Dr Fordyce near a sort of twisted tree thing. Maybe a pine? Possibly?' He held out the phone. 'This nature shit all looks the same to me.'

No wonder Kate Paisley had squirmed when Dr Fife mentioned idiots taking self-incriminating photos. There she was, pouting for the camera, flashing victory Vs with Dr Fordyce's tattered remains in the background. The body lay broken like a shotgun, at the bottom of a shallow grave, about a dozen paces from an ancient, twisted oak. Going by the gashes and the blood and the bruises, she'd suffered a death every bit as horrible as her husband's.

Somehow, Kate's posturing selfie made it all seem even worse.

How could anyone be *proud* of that?

He looked away, phone to his ear again. 'Sarge? They buried Dr

Fordyce out by the Gallowburn. You know the tree they used to hang sheep thieves from, back in the day? Near there.'

A scrunching noise drowned out some muffled shouting on the other end of the phone. Then DS Massie was back: *'Did he really trick Kate Paisley into unlocking her phone for him?'* Sucking a breath in through those tombstone teeth. *'He's a sneaky wee shite, I'll give him that.'*

'Yes, Sarge.' Angus risked another glance – Fife was logging into her WhatsApp messages now.

'I want it back at the ranch A-sap. See if we can't get these useless IT dicks to actually forensic something.'

Another bout of finger-snapping. 'And tell her everyone needs to be on their guard. Chances are fifty-fifty Ryan's going after a cop next.' Frown. 'Probably more like eighty-twenty.'

'Dr Fife says—'

'I heard.' DS Massie sighed down the phone. *'Fuck.'* Pause. *'What happened to targeting bankers?'*

Good question.

Angus poked Dr Fife, making him look up from Kate's no-longer-private messages. 'Why not bankers next?'

'Because he's seen the morning papers. Not only are you guys jackbooted pillars of the establishment, you're actively hunting *him*. Ryan might think it's rude not to return the compliment.'

A groan from DS Massie, who'd clearly heard that too. *'I'll put out a call. Anything else while you're depressing the hell out of me?'*

'Think that's us for now, Sarge. I'll let you know if something turns up.'

Her voice went Sahara dry. *'You do that.'* And then she hung up.

The faux Google Pixel didn't have a case, so Angus powered down the screen and held it out to Dr Fife. 'Can't believe you just *bought* a new phone.'

'Don't worry: I'm claiming it back on expenses.'

Expenses?

'It must've cost hundreds of pounds!'

'Oh, yeah.' He slipped it into an inside pocket, then set off down the hot-pink corridor, towards an internal balcony that overlooked the admin wing's four-storey atrium – each level picked out in a different primary colour. 'You want it when we're finished?' A set of stairs jutted out into the space, looping around a fifty-foot, dangling, art-installation-cum-chandelier thing, but Dr Fife clomped straight past, making for the lifts. 'Seriously – I'll tell Monroe that Kate Paisley smashed the thing to bits, and we had to bin it. He'll never know.'

'I'd know! I can't accept a stolen phone!' Angus pressed the down button. Changing the subject before the forensic psychologist worked his manipulative mojo on him. 'How come you didn't ask her where Ryan was, or what his last name is?'

'Cos she's hardly gonna believe I've got access to *everything* on her phone if I start asking stupid questions like that.' He poked away at the screen some more. 'Besides: answer's on here, somewhere.'

'You tried her contacts?'

An electronic voice clattered out of nowhere: '*THIRD FLOOR. DOORS OPENING.*'

And, as if by magic, the lift *ding*ed, and the doors slid open.

Dr Fife stepped inside. 'Course I tried her bloody contacts.'

It was surprisingly clean in here, certainly a huge improvement on the one back at Divisional Headquarters. But then maybe prison officers weren't as manky as police ones?

Angus pressed the green button marked 'G'. 'What about texts?'

'*DOORS CLOSING.*' And so they did.

'All deleted. Same with WhatsApp, her call history, and every one of her social-media DMs.'

'*GOING DOWN.*'

Dr Fife frowned at his reflection in the shiny stainless-steel doors. 'They're on a war footing, Angus. You don't leave anything lying around the enemy can use.'

'Except for all those photos.'

A smile. 'Gotta love stupid people.'

The lift slid down through the floors as Dr Fife went back to frowning.

'So, what now?'

'Lunch.'

Just the word was enough to set Angus's stomach rumbling. Which felt a bit . . . *off*, given eight people had died and there was a killer roaming the streets of Oldcastle. 'But we've—'

'We've got *fourteen days*, give or take. And I don't know about *you*, but I didn't stop being human when I got into law enforcement. I still need to eat, drink, and take a shit from time to time.'

Suppose he had a point.

Plus it was a *long* time since those complimentary mini pastries.

Dr Fife tapped Kate Paisley's phone against his palm. 'You know what worries me?'

Ding.

'*GROUND FLOOR. DOORS OPENING.*'

The atrium appeared, complete with indoor shrubs and bushes and a trapped sparrow flittering about from one planter to the next.

'We've got blood from Dr Fordyce and Councillor Mendel at Sadler Road, but . . .' His frown deepened. '. . . what if it's *not* just trace evidence trailed in from the crime scene? What if both victims were actually *physically* there?'

'How?' Angus joined in with the frowning. 'Why would they be there?'

'*DOORS CLOSING.*'

The atrium disappeared again.

'Exactly. And where would you put them?'

Angus pressed the '←I→' button. '*Why* would you put them, more like.'

'*DOORS OPENING.*'

The atrium appeared again.

'Doesn't make sense.' Angus pulled his shoulders up. 'Far better to leave their remains in the car-slash-van-slash-whatever till you bury them. Shifting bodies about is just asking for trouble.'

'And yet . . .' Dr Fife sucked his top lip in, making the hair on his chin jut out like a greying hedgehog. 'Hit the button: first floor. I wanna do a bit of snooping. *Then* lunch.'

Typical.

Angus's shoulders drooped again. But he pressed the button anyway.

'*DOORS CLOSING . . .*'

*

Officer Orton was a small, slight woman who looked as if she wouldn't say 'mint sauce' to a lamb. Well, except for the ring of barbed wire tattooed around her neck, like a choker. She clunked a plastic tray onto the custody suite's twelve-foot-long reception desk – scowling down at them because A: it was raised a couple of feet above ground level on *her* side, and B: word had clearly travelled about what had happened in Family Room Number Three.

The processing centre for HMP Oldcastle's new arrivals had a loading bay at the far end, hidden behind a pair of security doors; a mini-barcode of red, green, and blue lines set into the floor, leading off to various bits of the prison estate; cubicles down one wall, for people to change out of their civvies and into their state-issued blues; with shower facilities opposite.

Welcome to jail.

Officer Orton shoved the tray towards Angus. Contents: one large brown paper bag, with a preprinted form on one side – all filled out in red biro. She narrowed her eyes. 'We don't appreciate people winding up the inmates.'

Even on his tiptoes, Dr Fife's eyes barely cleared the desktop. He stared up at her. 'And *I* don't appreciate assholes who torture eight people to death.' Then did that annoying clicky-finger thing again. 'Angus?'

Ah.

There was no way he could see what was in the tray from down there.

Angus bent over and reached out to—

'I'm not asking you to pick me up, you idiot! Take the tray somewhere I can look at it.'

'Oh, right . . . Sorry.'

Officer Orton didn't bother to hide her schadenfreude smile. She plonked a box of nitrile gloves beside the tray. 'It's all inventoried, and I'll be checking everything's still there when you're done. Understand?'

Charming.

Angus helped himself to a quartet of blue gloves, then took the tray over to a small table set beneath a sign with 'SHOES HERE!' on it.

He unlaced the trio of treasury tags holding the brown paper bag shut, and tipped its contents out into the plastic tray. 'This is daft: they'll have been through all this when they processed her at the station yesterday.'

'Yeah, because I *totally* trust your colleagues not to screw things up.' He snatched one of the gloves from Angus, then grimaced at it, before pulling the thing on. Officer Orton must've given them the extra-large ones, because the blue nitrile fingers were about twice the length of Dr Fife's, leaving the rubbery tips dangling like drunken-octopus tentacles. He worked them into place with a vaguely . . . *obscene* motion, then did the same with his other hand, before poking through everything Kate Paisley had on her when she was arrested: a wee drift of small change, a couple of hair ties, two pens, a takeaway menu from Pizzageddon, a wallet, and a bunch of keys.

Angus looked up, in the general direction of Family Room Number Three. 'What do you think she meant by that "We are legion" thing?' Nodding to himself. 'I was right, wasn't I? There's different cells of them, all over the city, killing people.'

'Or maybe she was talking about all the online conspiracy douchebags out there, just like her. Now, shut up, and let me work.'

Emptying the wallet produced twenty quid in creased plastic fives, a photo of two old people holding a little girl's hands, a Tesco Clubcard, the debit card Kate Paisley used to pay for those decoy pizzas, and a tiny bunch of pressed forget-me-nots that'd been laminated.

Dr Fife got to the end of his rummage and frowned, forearms resting on the tray's lip, hands dangling. 'Hmmm . . .'

'Told you.'

He flexed his right hand, setting one of the tentacles flopping free again, before lunging to pluck the keys from Kate Paisley's possessions. Holding them up to the light, as if they were precious jewellery.

A raised eyebrow paired with a smug wee head wobble. 'Notice anything?'

Not really.

It was a perfectly ordinary bunch of keys: two Yales, what looked like one for a padlock, and one for a Honda Civic. All held together by a *very* old-fashioned, grubby key-chain-and-fob: a small pink baby, with oversized eyes and a great long shock of lime-green hair sticking straight up from its head.

'Is that a troll? Haven't seen one of them for years.'

'Call yourself a *detective*.' Dr Fife gave the troll a shoogle and something rattled about inside its little plastic body. He held it up to the light again. 'I think the head comes off.'

Oh no.

Angus reached for the keys. 'You can't just go about damaging prisoners'—'

Too late: he'd popped the thing's noggin right off. Dr Fife peered in through the open neckhole, smiled, then tipped whatever was inside onto his palm. A dark-grey, round-ended cylinder with a red band across the middle. Slightly smaller than a pen top. The smugness was palpable: 'Know what this is?'

It took a moment to recognize the shape, but eventually Angus got it. 'Some sort of USB stick.'

'*No.* It's a proximity key fob: radio-frequency ID. The kind of thing you use to open electronic locks.' Tossing it in the air and catching it again. 'Now *why* would Kate Paisley need one of these? And why hide it in a troll?'

'Well, she's an electrician, right? So, probably something for work.'

'Yeah. Probably.' He frowned at the fob nestled in his palm.

'We should check back at the station: Team Spanner've been looking into her all day. Bet they'll know.' Plus, Angus could hand over Kate Paisley's phone, and avoid DS Massie's Naughty List.

Dr Fife shoved the troll's head back on again – the wrong way around – and dumped it in the tray. Pointed at the former contents of Kate Paisley's brown paper bag. 'You can give that lot back to Smiler there. I'm off for a piss, a smoke, and a think. In that order.'

Shaky Dave's Tattie Shack was a cheery-wee-wooden-house-shaped trailer – hooked up to the back end of a Range Rover and a portable generator – plying its potato-based wares in Gallipoli Park. It had a fake-shingle roof, a fake-brick chimney, and even a couple of fake seagulls, screwed down to stop them taking off in the howling wind.

On a sunny day, you'd have an excellent view of the big war memorial that sat in the middle of the park, pan left, across acres of municipal grass and trees, then out over Kings River to the pristine granite spires of St Bartholomew's Episcopal Cathedral. But *today*, what you got was a vague tumorous shape lurking in the twisted shrouds of rain, a big expanse of grey, a slug-grey smear of water, and the ghostly shadow of some vast spiky monster.

The car park was virtually empty – just Dr Fife's Mini; a fogged-up Nissan Qashqai, rocking rhythmically on its springs; and Shaky Dave's Tattie Shack.

The man himself was reassuringly round, with a baldy head, Hawaiian shirt, and once-white apron. Oriental tattoos covered both arms and he whistled along to some sort of opera as he bustled from deep-fat frier to plancha to stove to prep area and back again.

All that catering equipment didn't just exude delicious smells, it radiated a reasonable amount of heat too. Which was why Angus stuck as close to the serving hatch as possible. Plus, the side flap was up, forming a welcome shelter from the hammering rain.

'Yeah.' Angus grimaced out at the downpour, phone pressed to his ear. His *own* phone this time. In its safety-first ziplock bag. 'But did you have to lay it on so *thick*?'

Ellie snorted. *'Course I did. You want everyone to think you're a hero, don't you?'*

'No! . . . Well, maybe. It's just a bit—'

'My editor wants a follow-up for tomorrow's paper. "Get to know the man behind the heroics" sort of thing. Maybe a couple of photos. Nothing sordid – very artistic. You could probably keep your socks on.'

A gust lifted an Oldcastle-Council-branded recycling bin and sent it spinning across the car park, spraying crisp packets and empty drink bottles and tins out into the gale.

Rain sheeted off the tattie shack's faux-shingle roof.

Shaky Dave whistled away.

'I'm joking! I'm joking. Well, about the naked pictures, anyway.'

'Definitely not.'

A sleekit tone wormed its way into her voice. *'Or you could give me the skinny on this morning's murders? On account of me doing you a massive favour keeping your forensic psychologist out of the papers? Rumour is the Fortnight Killer hacked off the husband's head with an axe!'*

'He didn't. And *a thousand percent* not.'

'Hmmmm . . . I'll take that as a "maybe".' Strange clonking noises rattled down the phone, as if something had come loose at her end. *'You getting shot at's been a godsend, by the way: they're bumping me up to* senior *crime reporter. OK, there's already two other* senior *crime reporters, but that's Oldcastle for you. Always plenty murders to go around.'*

As if that was something for a city to be proud of.

Angus looked out across the car park to where Dr Fife sat behind the Mini's wheel, fiddling away on Kate Paisley's phone – with its camera roll full of blood and horror.

He forced a bit of cheer into his voice. 'Congratulations.'

'We should celebrate. You, me, Plastic Colin, Burps, and the Captain. We'll have a Cocktail Calamity at Wobbly Bob's and—'

'No!'

Sod. That'd come out far harsher than necessary. Heat burst across his cheeks, warm enough to put Shaky Dave's deep-fat fryers to shame. Angus cleared his throat. 'I mean . . . I can't be late for dinner three nights in a row. Mum'll change the locks. Sorry.'

A sigh. *'Honestly, Angus, I love your mum to bits, but she's got you tied to her apron strings like a—'*

No idea how that simile ended, because everything else was drowned out as Shaky Dave slammed his palm down on a wee reception-style bell. *Ding.* 'GREEN: FOUR-SIX-TWO!' Bellowing it out as if Angus wasn't the only one there. 'ONE PICKLE-FRENZY DIRTY DUCK-FAT FRIES WITH FETA AND AVOCADO; AND A SPECIAL POUTINE, EXTRA LOADED, WITH ONION RINGS AND SPICY SLAW; JUMBO LATTE!'

Angus held out his raffle ticket. 'That's me.'

Shaky Dave exchanged it for a pair of eco-friendly cardboard containers, two bamboo sporks, a small wodge of napkins, and a big wax-paper cup with a plastic lid. Meaning Angus quickly ran out of hands and had to pin the phone between his shoulder and his ear. He turned, holding everything tight to keep the storm from stealing it. 'Yeah, so I can't make it tonight. Sorry.' Hurrying across the car park.

'They'll carve that on your gravestone, you know that, don't you? "Here lies Angus MacVicar, he's 'sorry'."'

Angus sidestepped a puddle. 'You've had a right hedgehog up your bum ever since I asked about Gillian.'

A sniff. *'Why would I care about Gillian? No business of mine who you're shagging. I'm sure Mary Dunwoody would do a sixteensome for you, if you bung her a couple of quid.'*

Bloody hell. Talk about *bitchy*.

Never mind a hedgehog, that was a full-on porcupine.

His bottom lip poked out.

And how come she was taking whatever-this-was out on him?

Well, if she was going to be like that:

'Got to go. Sorry.'

She groaned down the phone at him. *'Of course you are.'*

Angus stuck Dr Fife's coffee on the Mini's roof and hung up. Yanked open the passenger door, rescued the wax-paper cup, and lurched inside. Thumped it closed again, shutting out the storm. 'Bloody hell . . . Could you not've parked closer?'

Dr Fife didn't look up from Kate Paisley's phone. 'Fresh air's good for you. Builds character.'

Get, and indeed, stuffed.

'Here.' Angus held out the containers and cup. 'Take.'

Dr Fife tossed Kate's phone onto the dashboard, selected the top box – opened it, sniffed, closed it again – then did the same with the other one. Weighed each one in a separate hand. Then plumped for the poutine. 'Let me guess: sporks?'

'Cos we're all "bloody heathens".' Angus plonked the receipt and a clattering of pound coins next to Kate's phone.

He sat there, stomach growling, as Dr Fife chewed his way through a few sporkfuls, and the car filled with the mouthwatering scents of chips-and-cheese-and-gravy . . .

Which was more than a little cruel, given that all Angus had to look forward to was a mousetrap-lettuce-and-brown-sauce sandwich, an apple, and a wee square of rock-solid traybake that tasted like bird-seed and carpet fluff. And even *that* was back at DHQ. Hidden away in the bottom of the filing cabinet in Dr Fife's temporary office.

Assuming some sticky-fingered food-hoover hadn't already found it.

Swear to God, some of his fellow officers were like bloody sniffer dogs when it came to other people's food.

Angus's stomach snarled again.

Dr Fife sporked up an onion ring and dipped it in the gravy. 'Kate Paisley: who checked out the company she works at?'

'Don't know. Can find out easy enough. Why?'

'We should go there.' Munch, munch, munch. 'Have a word. See what we can find.'

'But someone's already—'

'If you learn *one* thing from our time together, Angus, it's that the vast majority of people are assholes and idiots. Never trust them to do anything important. That's *your* job.' One last sporkful, then he closed the box and tried the Pickle-Frenzy chips instead. Nodding as he chewed.

Then handed Box Number One back to Angus.

'What?' Creaking the lid open an inch to peer inside. 'Something wrong with it?'

'Nope, I just like *this* better. You have it.'

Scraps from the master's table.

As if he were a stray dog.

Or a weird little man quoting Shakespeare in a vomity bus shelter . . .

But Angus had his *pride*.

'Told you: I've got sandwiches back at the station.'

'No skin off my ass; I'm claiming everything back on expenses anyway. I'll call you a consultant for accounting purposes.'

Angus stiffened. 'You might be happy, gaming the system, *cheating*, but I'm not.'

'Oh, for Christ's sake, what is *wrong* with you?'

His jaw clenched, the familiar heat crackling up his neck and ears. 'I . . . I'm skint, OK? I'm always skint.'

'So do some overtime!'

'It's not *like* that.' He puffed out a breath. 'We pay the bills, and everything else goes to charity: the Molly Ormond Foundation.'

'*Everything* else?' Spearing up a couple of perfectly golden chips, loaded down with all manner of tasty things. 'No little treats? Soccer matches, burgers, night at the movies with some hot chick?'

Angus stared at his hands. 'Mum and me get a fish supper once a month.'

'Jesus. And Courtney thought *I* was screwed up. So, you're living like a monk for this Molly Ormond woman? That doesn't sound like a cult at all!' Another mouthful disappeared. 'How many yachts she got?'

'She doesn't have . . . Her mum and dad started the charity in her memory. Wanted to help kids who've got megalencephalic leukoencephalopathy with subcortical cysts, like she did.'

Dr Fife put the spork down and sat there, with his head on one side, studying Angus like an injured puppy. 'Let me guess: your dad died from the same condition.'

If only.

He frowned out through the passenger window, watching the rain bouncing off the waterlogged tarmac.

Deep breath.

'He took his own life. You're not allowed to say "committed suicide" any more, cos "committed" makes it sound like he did a crime.' Hard not to laugh at that – short and bitter. 'I mean, he *did* do a crime, but that wasn't it.'

Dr Fife's voice lost its mocking sharpness. 'Which is why you became a cop.'

'We're all atoning for something . . .'

'And now you're stuck giving every penny you've got to this charity for a condition that most people couldn't even pronounce. Aren't families *great*?'

Silence settled across the Mini as Dr Fife contemplated his Pickle-Frenzy. 'Hey.' He held them out in one hand, taking the poutine back with the other. 'You need a slab of fancy fries *way* more than me.'

Angus glared. 'I'm not a charity case.' Then cleared his throat. 'You know what I mean.'

'Have them, don't have them – doesn't matter. Either way they're paid for. At least this way they won't end up in the trash.' A smile. 'And cos I've *tried* them, that makes them technically leftovers. Ethically: no biggie, right?'

Unburdened by the shackles of pride, his stomach howled.

After all, it would only go to waste otherwise.

Which wasn't exactly environmentally friendly. Or sustainable. Yeah . . .

Angus accepted the Pickle-Frenzy carton. 'Thanks. Sorry.'

He took the other spork and stabbed an unpeeled chip – all crisp and golden and loaded with bacon and capers and battered pickles and avocado and salty feta.

God, it was *delicious*.

'That's more like it.' Dr Fife scooped up some poutine. 'Soon as we're done here, we hit Kate Paisley's work. Find the missing clue. Solve the case.' He grimaced through the windscreen at the battering wind and howling rain. 'Then get out of this goddamn city before we all evolve gills.'

31

Dr Sparky was a cartoon man in blue overalls, with a big smile and pointy nose, screwdriver in one hand, lightbulb in the other, posing above the company name and the words 'EMERGENCY ELECTRICAL REPAIR & MAINTENANCE SPECIALISTS!' The logo dominated one wall of the small reception area – more like a minicab office than an electrician's – hidden away in an anonymous business unit, in an anonymous industrial estate, on the anonymous outskirts of Logansferry.

A saggy grey rubber plant spidered its way up the corner of the room. The poor thing looked in need of either water or euthanasia. And so did the saggy grey receptionist.

He drooped behind the desk, cheek propped up on one fist as he perused the *Daily Standard*, lips moving as he read along, strip lights gleaming off his shiny head.

Dr Fife poked away at Kate Paisley's phone again, forehead creased up like a sideways rollercoaster, sitting in a creaky plastic seat, feet dangling off the cracked lino floor.

Which can't have been comfortable. But at least he *had* a seat – all the other chairs were heaped with electrical bits and bobs, leaving Angus to lean against the wall. Counting the spiders and cobwebs. And trying not to check his watch every two minutes.

Finally, the door through to the warehouse opened, and in marched a sturdy woman. Greying hair pulled back in a ponytail. Wearing a smile that would've fallen off her face if it was any squinter. She posed: one hand on her hip, the other making a gun that she aimed at the pair of them. 'Dr Fife, Constable MacVicar? Jean Barber. You want to come through?'

She didn't wait for an answer, just turned on her heel and headed back out the door again. 'Bob, hold my calls, OK?'

Shiny-headed Bob didn't even grunt.

Angus followed Dr Fife into a smallish warehouse just about big enough to fit a couple of double-decker buses side by side. Most of the space was taken up with modular shelving racks, but they'd left a space at the front, just inside the roller doors, for a grey Vauxhall Vivaro with the Dr Sparky's logo and 'IT'S NOT A PARTY WITHOUT DR SPARKY!' on both sides.

Ms Barber headed for the van. 'So . . . I had your colleagues in here for an hour this morning. One smug git with a quiff and a cold sore; and a wee nyaff with sideburns and eyes that point . . .' Her twin index fingers wiggled off in random directions. 'Wanting to know about Kate.'

That sounded like Ernie and PC Gilbert.

She picked a big drum of cable from a pallet and hefted it up onto her shoulder, the weight pulling her sideways as she shuffled between the shelving racks. 'Kate's a good worker, excellent sparky, doesn't embarrass herself at the Christmas bash, and as long as you steer clear of vaccines, the royal family, Hollywood, and international politics: you're fine.'

The drum thumped down on a shelf with three or four others, and Ms Barber lumbered back to the pallet for another one. 'Did her apprenticeship with the council, started working here two years ago, and other than a parking ticket on the van, she's never given us a bit of worry.' Hoisting up a second drum of cable.

Angus pointed. 'Shall I . . . ?'

'Be my guest.'

He stacked four of them in his arms and trailed after her, back into the rows of shelving.

Dr Fife didn't offer to carry anything, though. 'Did Kate Paisley *really* never mention anyone called Ryan?'

'Nope.'

'What about her home life? Girlfriend? Boyfriend?'

'She lives with a guy. Only met him once, 'bout six months ago.

Kate wanted to borrow the van. Said she had to move some wood and tools and shit. I said OK.' The new drum banged onto the shelf with its mate. 'We like to be flexible, you know? Keeps the team happy and loyal. One big family' – Ms Barber winked at Angus – 'right, Slugger?'

He lowered the four reels of cable into place, without so much as a thud.

Dr Fife leaned back against a stack of plastic ducting. 'This man got a name?'

'Probably. No idea what, though. Kinda Dave Grohl wannabe – you know, with the hair and beard? Buncha tattoos. Not bad-looking, if you like that sorta thing.' A frown. 'Think his van failed its MOT, and they had a homer in Auchterowan that weekend.'

A puzzled look curdled onto Dr Fife's face, so Angus translated:

'"Homer". It's when you do a job for someone who isn't your employer, off the books, usually for cash.'

He nodded. 'So, you're OK with that?'

'Long as I know about it, and it's not a client who would've come to the company?' Ms Barber shrugged. 'No problem. You've got to use your own supplies and tools, though. And you *never* turn up here too knackered to work cos you've been rewiring your mate's house all night. I didn't build this company up from nothing just so some . . .' She trailed off as Vivaldi *Four Seasoned* his way out from Angus's pocket.

'Sorry.' He checked his phone: 'DS MASSIE' glowed on the screen. 'Sorry.' Hurrying off to a quiet corner by the workboard. 'Sarge?'

'*Where the* hell *are you? Told you I wanted that phone back here, ASAFP!*'

'Dr Fife wanted to see where Kate Paisley worked.'

'*Did he now? Well, you can tell that pisshole egomaniac tosspot there's procedures and a chain of command in place for a reason!*'

He did his best not to sigh. 'Sarge.'

'*Back here. Now.*'

'Right.' As if he had any bloody say in the matter. Time to change the subject: 'How's the dig coming?'

'*It's only been an hour. Give the poor sods time to set up the tent.*'

'Sorry.' He picked at the nearest shelf. 'Don't suppose anything's come of that search on the Lundys' finances? You know, whether there's a payment to Ryan for the—'

'Oh, Angus, *am I not keeping you up to date with all the teeny minutiae of the investigation?*' A sarcastic tut stabbed its way out of his phone's speaker. '*How* terribly *remiss of me!*'

He had a quick look around, then lowered his voice, just in case. 'Not my fault Dr Fife can be a bit abrasive, Sarge.'

'*He's not abrasive, he's a* dick. *But no, there's no sign of a bank transfer, card payment, or cheque. We've got a grand withdrawn in cash a month ago, another grand two weeks after that, and one more last Friday.*'

'Final payment on completion.'

'*Yup. Poor bastards paid him a fortune; gave him a key; and he came back, in the middle of the night, and . . .*' DS Massie sighed. Couldn't blame her. '*I've got Mags and Pauly going through the other victims' financials, see if we can't find a better hit.*' Then she put a bit of steel back in her voice. '*Anyway: Forensic IT's all lined up and ready to get cracking on Kate Paisley's phone. The only thing missing is . . . ?*'

'Yes, Sarge.'

'*Should think so, too.*' And that was it – she'd hung up.

He hurried back to the pallet, but Ms Barber was nowhere to be seen. Instead, Dr Fife was all on his own, fiddling away with the phone in question.

'You shouldn't . . .' Angus pointed. 'You're interfering with the chain of evidence.'

'How ever *will* I cope?' Fiddle, scroll, fiddle. 'Kate Paisley might've deleted her texts and messages, but she's kept photos of the jobs she's done.'

Maybe they'd *finally* got lucky?

'Ryan?'

Something higher-res than the crappy effort the *Castle News & Post* had published would be nice.

'Not yet, but I live in hope.' Scroll, fiddle, scroll. 'It's—'

'Here we go.' Ms Barber appeared from behind a stretch of shelving, carrying a sheet of A4. 'Told you I was organized.' She held it out. 'Kate's homers. Or at least the ones she told me about.'

Dr Fife accepted the printout, giving the list a quick skim. 'And the other officers: they got the same list?'

Her mouth scrunched down, her shoulders up. 'They would've if they'd *asked* about homers.'

Typical.

Ernie and Gilbert – a pair of utter numpties with warrant cards.

'Thanks.' Fife folded the list and slipped it into his greatcoat. Turned. Clacked away a couple of paces. Turned back again. 'If you're one big happy family, how come you don't know Kate's boyfriend's name?'

'She was *kinda* private about her love life.' Ms Barber gave them a squint wince. 'And with Kate, you *don't* want to dig too deep, in case you set her off on another . . .' Ms Barber's finger came up to describe a little circle, right beside her ear. 'Now, you guys want anything else, or can I get back to running a business here?'

The Mini crept forward another car length, still waiting for its turn on the roundabout with Kings Drive.

Sitting in the passenger seat, Angus read through the list of Kate Paisley's homers again – fifteen sets of names and addresses, from Cowskillin to Fiddersmuir. 'Don't see the Lundys on here.' He lowered the printout and sighed at the sheer extravagance of it: 'Custom-built bookshelves . . .' You didn't stick charity-shop paperbacks and removed-from-library-stock hardbacks on something like that. No, you went into an actual bookshop and bought them brand new.

He looked across the car. 'Was it nice being rich? When you were married to that psychiatrist?'

Dr Fife moved up into the space just vacated by a prolapse-pink Bedford Rascal with copulating sausages painted down both sides. Meaning they were next for the roundabout. 'Way better than being poor. Right up to the point I found out Special Agent Morrison was boning my wife.' Leaning forward in his seat, searching for a gap in the oncoming traffic with a huge smile. 'I laughed for a *week* when someone shot him, right in the dick.' A ScotiaBrand Chickens lorry rattled past, engulfing the Mini in a deluge of filthy spray. 'Where am I going?'

Probably Hell.

Angus pointed. 'Straight across. DS Massie needs Kate Paisley's phone, soon as.'

The smile blossomed into a full-on laugh. 'Took one of his balls clean off, too. *Pow!*'

Yeah, definitely Hell.

A gap opened up and Dr Fife put his foot down – the Mini surged forward, but instead of going straight across, onto Castle Drive, he swung them nearly all the way around the roundabout, provoking an outraged blare of horns.

'Where are . . . No: that way!'

But Dr Fife accelerated up Kings Drive South instead. Making for the Calderwell Bridge. 'We're gonna pay a visit to one of Kate Paisley's side hustles. Have a sniff about. See what we can turn up.'

Nooooo . . .

'But DS Massie—'

'Chicks dig a bad boy, Angus.' Wink. 'You give them what they want all the time: that's how you end up in the Friend Zone.' He let go of the steering wheel for long enough to punch Angus lightly in the arm. 'But you know all about that, right?'

And all Angus could do was glower.

It took over half an hour of strained silence before they reached the genteel streets of Auchterowan. Well, Angus did his best to make it strained, but Dr Fife didn't seem to notice.

Completely oblivious.

Yet again.

Trebuchet Row was a fancy residential street on the outskirts of the village – fine Georgian sandstone buildings, facing each other across a wide tree-lined street and nice big gardens. Four-by-fours, sports cars, and SUVs parked outside three-storey detached homes with names rather than numbers.

'BALMORAL' even had a turret on one corner. Like a mini castle . . .

A howl of wind shuddered the naked branches as rain flickered against the Mini's bonnet. Even rich posh people got crap weather sometimes.

Angus turned his collar up and struggled free of the passenger seat. Clunking the door shut before the wind could get at it. Turned his face away from the icy needles being driven into his cheeks. 'Could you not've picked one of the nearby jobs?'

Dr Fife scurried around from the driver's side, straight past him and through the gate. Hurrying up the path, and not stopping till he reached the relative shelter of Balmoral's columned portico.

'All the way out to sodding Auchterowan.' Angus stomped up the path, shoulders up, hands deep in his pockets. 'DS Massie's going to kill me!'

'Stop whining. Besides, we know Kate and Ryan were both here, right? She borrowed the work van. Now shut up and ring the god-damn bell.'

Angus stomped his feet beneath the portico, gave Dr Fife the benefit of a scowl, then did what he was told. Holding his finger down till a deep *bing-bong* resonated out through the wood-and-stained-glass door. It was *immediately* followed by the scrabbling sound of claws on tile and an artillery salvo of barks from howitzer-sized dogs.

Yeah . . .

Angus backed away from the door a bit. Just in case. 'They've got a team going through the other victims' bank accounts. See if they took out money for Ryan too.'

'Morons.' Dr Fife held up a hand before Angus could object. 'If they only preyed on people they'd done work for, why would Ryan need to steal a pizza-man disguise? The Lundys were a lucky acci-dent for him. Call them self-selecting victims.' Pointing at the bell. 'Again.'

Ringing it hyped the massive dogs to even more enraged heights.

'Maybe they were assholes while he was doing the work? Wouldn't make him a cuppa coffee or something? Or maybe he had the key, and *we* were after him, so he needs to let off some steam?' Dr Fife curled his lip. 'Only an idiot craps in his own bath.'

A posh voice joined the baying ruckus. *'Benedict! Dominic! Down, you naughty muffins!'*

'And Ryan *ain't* that stupid.'

There was a clunk and the door popped open about a hand's

breadth, then a woman's thigh wedged into the gap before the dogs could get their teeth into biting range.

She smiled up at Angus, making little wrinkles line up either side of her mouth. Her greying hair was immaculately styled, as was the rest of her, in a slate-coloured pashmina shawl, layered floaty top, and a pair of ripped-knee jeans that looked way more expensive than Angus's suit. 'Hello, hello!' She grabbed hold of the hellhounds' collars, only without the door in the way they'd transformed into a pair of Labradors – one black, one yellow – tails going full-pelt. 'Don't mind them. All mouth and no trousers, as my dear old dad used to say. How can I help?'

The living room was much nicer than the Lundys' – not only was it blood-free, it had a cosy lived-in feel to it, with stained glass set into the windows, lots of polished wood, a set of comfy-looking armchairs, a crackling fire, and a whole wall of bookshelves. Busts of Shakespeare, Byron, and Emily Brontë gazed out blindly from the mantelpiece.

Dr Fife stood, still as the three dead writers, hands curled up against his chest as Benedict padded around him.

Dominic had abandoned all pretence of decorum and wiggled about on his back so Angus could rub his tummy.

Mrs Baldwin-Cooper emerged from the hallway, bringing with her three mugs. 'Only instant, I'm afraid. Bloody machine's on the blink again.' She handed them out. Then toasted the bookshelves. 'So, what do you think? Lovely, aren't they.' Her brow crinkled. 'Benedict, leave the nice man alone!'

Tail between his legs, Benedict slunk off to his mistress's side.

'OK.' Dr Fife wiped his hands down his greatcoat. 'Mrs Baldwin-Cooper: where'd you find the guy who built them?'

'Please, call me Patricia. Mrs Baldwin-Cooper sounds so horribly *formal*, don't you think?'

'Cool. Now, the bookcases?'

'Oh, someone at Rupert's club recommended him. *Lovely* chap. *Frightfully* good with the old woodwork. Been saying for years we really *must* get those mouldy old bookshelves replaced, and here we are.' She took a sip of coffee. 'One doesn't like to blow one's own *trumpet*, but it's nice to have one's books *properly* looked after.'

'Was his name "Ryan"?'

'And when I say "one's books" I do actually mean "*one's* books".' She pulled a volume from the shelves – a hardback, featuring a generic historical-romance cover, with 'P.B. COOPER' in gold embossing along the top and '*L'AMANTE DEL VIAGGIATORE NEL TEMPO*' at the bottom, bracketing a painting of a man in full Elizabethan gear reaching for a bosom-balconied redhead who was armed with a cutlass and musket.

Dr Fife's eyes were on Benedict's gaping muzzle, though. All those scary Labrador teeth. Tongue lolling out the side. 'Right.'

'Italian edition. Though *why* they had to change the title to *The Time Traveller's Mistress* is beyond me.' Sigh. 'Still, they invite me to the most *darling* little festivals in Napoli and Bologna, so I forgive them.'

'The man who built your bookshelves, was his name—'

'Oh, he didn't just build the *bookcases*! He did something much more special than that.' Mrs Baldwin-Cooper lowered her voice to a whisper. 'I've wanted one of these ever since I read *The Famous Five*, by torchlight, as a little girl.'

She flipped Shakespeare's head back, exposing a hollow neck, reached in and pulled out a little round-ended cylinder: black with a green band around it, instead of the red-banded one in Kate Paisley's troll.

Mrs Baldwin-Cooper carried her RFID token over to the wall of bookshelves, removed a copy of *Diamond Hearts on the Spanish Main*, and inserted the fob in its place.

Click.

She placed both palms on the bookcase and pushed – causing a whole three-foot-wide chunk of books and wood to slide into the wall. Then, after it'd sunk in a good four feet, it hinged away to the left, revealing a hidden room on the other side.

'Isn't it simply *divine*?' She wafted through the secret door with Benedict and Dominic in tow.

Angus stared. 'Wow.'

Dr Fife raised an eyebrow. 'Interesting.' He stepped inside.

Come on, it was more than 'interesting'. When the thing was shut there hadn't been so much as a crack on show. The workmanship was phenomenal.

Angus followed them both into what had to be the base of the turret they'd seen from outside.

The walls were free of any distraction, painted a bright white; the floor carpeted in dark-blue deep-pile; an upholstered window nook; a fancy office chair, a roll-top desk, and a wafer-thin laptop. The only books in evidence were a pair of thick reference tomes about seafaring and geopolitics in the late sixteenth century. A journal sat next to the laptop, the page filled in a curling fountain-pen script with today's date at the top. All very, *very* swanky.

Mrs Baldwin-Cooper stuck her arms out and gave them a wee twirl. 'My study.'

'What was his name? The man.'

'Oh, it was double-barrelled something. Nothing wrong with that, of course, all the best rogues are.' Flirty wink. 'And he was *magnificently* piratical, with a lilting west-coast accent.' Her head tilted to one side, eyes misty. Then she gave herself a little shake. 'Let me see . . .'

Putting the coffee on her desk, she crossed to the window nook and pressed a knothole on the polished wooden sill. A hidden compartment popped open, showing off a collection of identical leather-bound notebooks, just like the journal. 'Now, where are we . . .' Mrs Baldwin-Cooper walked her fingers along the spines, then plucked one from the collection and flipped it open. 'As the great Charles Dickens once said, "One keeps a journal not for oneself, but for *posterity*." '

She slipped on a pair of reading glasses and leafed through the pages. 'October, October . . . Ah, here we go.' Shoulders back, deep breath. ' "*Outside* the leaves are like lips of fire, *kissing* the branches as the evening sky *burns* in gold and amber. Oh, *October*! Your pale, autumnal embrace—" '

'If we could just skip forward to the name, Patricia.' Dr Fife checked his watch. 'We're kinda on a clock here. With all the murders . . .'

Pink bloomed in her cheeks. 'Of course. How silly of me.'

Running a finger down the page. 'Here we go: Lachlan. Lachlan Ballantine-Reynolds.'

'Jesus.' Dr Fife winced. 'No wonder he goes by "Ryan".'

Angus held up a hand. 'You didn't lend him a *key*, or anything, did you, Mrs Baldwin-Cooper?'

'You keep saying "Ryan". Not the man from the papers: the one with the gun, who *killed* all those people?' The colour drained from her face. 'I . . . I mean, we *had* to so he could do the work.' She blinked up at Angus. 'But we got the key back, I'm *sure* we did.' Clutching her shawl closed around her neck. 'Didn't we?'

'Yeah . . .' Angus patted her on the arm. 'Might be a good idea to change the locks. Just in case.'

32

'*What?*' DS Massie didn't sound convinced at all. '*You're kidding, right?*'

'Lachlan!' Dr Fife kept pulling faces and shaking his head as he piloted the Mini through Auchterowan's rain-battered streets, heading for the main road back to Oldcastle. 'What kinda monster calls their kid "Lachlan"?' A snort. 'No wonder he turned into a serial killer.'

Angus swapped the phone over to his left ear, popping a finger in the other one to mute the non-stop muttering. 'No, I'm serious, Sarge, we've got a name!' Checking his notebook, because accuracy was important when you were kicking off a manhunt. 'Lachlan Ballantine-Reynolds. Lima, Alpha, Charlie, Hotel—'

'*Yes, I know how to spell "Lachlan", thank you very much. And your writer woman:* please *tell me she paid him with a cheque or bank transfer?*'

'Sorry, Sarge. Cash only.'

'*Typical.*' The volume dropped on Massie's end, probably muffled by a hand. '*Hoy, Dusty! I need a PNC check on a Lachlan Ballantine-Reynolds . . . Yes: now!*'

They followed the road, past a couple of truly palatial sandstone houses.

'How's it going with the shallow grave, Sarge?'

'*Slowly and carefully. What do you think: they're going to howk the remains out with a JCB? It's a depositions site, Constable, not a fairground claw machine.*'

Fair enough.

'*Now: get that phone back here!*'

'Sarge.'

The line went silent. She'd hung up. Because when you were a detective sergeant, you didn't have to bother with niceties like saying goodbye. Or thank you.

Angus put his phone down. 'Still, at least now we know what that lozenge thing was in Kate Paisley's troll. Spare key to Mrs Baldwin-Cooper's secret room.'

'Nope.' Dr Fife reached into his greatcoat and pulled out a familiar liquorice-torpedo shape with a red band around the middle. 'Tried it while *darling* Patricia was calling the locksmith. Doesn't work.'

'How have you got . . . You're not supposed to steal suspects' property!'

'Besides, this one has a *red* band; Patricia's was green. This . . .' waggling it from side to side, '. . . fits somewhere else.'

Unbelievable.

And *illegal*.

'Have you never heard of "chain of custody"?'

He popped it back in his pocket. 'The question is: where?'

The Mini slipped out through the village limits, swapping genteel sandstone buildings for waterlogged fields and drooping woodland. Dr Fife put his foot down and poked at his phone/satnav. 'What's the fastest way to Kingsmeath from here?'

'We have to go back to the station!'

A smile beamed across the little car. '*Of course* we do. How silly of me. Divisional Headquarters, here we come.'

Thank God for that.

The Mini pulled up to the kerb on Sadler Road, opposite number one-thirty-two with its fluttering banners of blue-and-white 'POLICE' tape. The cordon had shrunk since they were last here, and now only sealed off Kate Paisley's front garden from its neighbours.

For some reason, floral tributes and teddy bears had appeared on the chain-link fence, like sacrificial offerings to a murder that never happened. The stuffed animals sagged under the weight of all the water they'd absorbed as yet more rain scatter-gunned down from an ink-dark sky, wind battering through the wire – ripping leaves and petals from those petrol-station bouquets.

By rights, there should've been a Mobile Incident Unit parked outside, but it'd been moved on somewhere else.

Always plenty murders to go around.

Dr Fife killed the engine. 'Will you stop going on about it?'

'We have to call this in!'

'We're taking a punt, Angus, nothing more.' A shrug. 'Be shocked if this isn't a complete bust, to be honest.'

For God's sake. 'Then *why* are we doing it?'

He opened the driver's door – nearly losing his grip as the wind grabbed hold – and scrambled out. Curled his face away from the rain. 'DON'T BE SUCH A DWEEB!' Then wrestled the door shut again.

Angus sagged in his seat.

No prizes for guessing who DS Massie would blame for all this.

Outside, Dr Fife hurried across the road, bent almost double, greatcoat flapping and snapping in front of him. He ducked under the thrumming cordon, let himself in through the gate, and legged it for the front door.

Where he'd have to stay, because Angus had the keys.

Could just leave him out there.

Maybe the wind would batter a bit of sense into him?

Standing on the front step, Dr Fife turned to face the car, making jabby pointing gestures at Angus and the house.

Angus groaned.

They were going to be in *so* much trouble . . .

Dr Fife pretty much collapsed over the threshold soon as Angus turned the key. Stumbling forward into that nice, neat hallway.

Angus bustled in after him and thumped the door closed. He slumped back against the wood and dripped on the laminate floor-ing. Catching his breath. Then clicked on the lights. 'If this is such a long shot, why are we here?'

'Because that's how you crack cases.' Standing in the middle of the hall, Dr Fife did a slow three-sixty, staring at everything. 'You *take* the long shots. Dream the impossible dream. Poke your nose in where it doesn't belong.' A lopsided shrug. 'Be an asshole: rile folks up.' Three-sixty complete, he wandered down to the end of the hall. 'If you were putting in a secret room, where would you hide it?'

'Dunno.' Unlike Mrs Baldwin-Cooper, Kate Paisley didn't have a swanky library full of her own books. 'Upstairs?'

'Urgh . . . It's always goddamn stairs, isn't it.' He puffed out his cheeks. 'Good a place as any.' Then headed back to the foot of those backwards, boxed-in stairs and lumbered up them, holding onto the balusters for support.

Angus gave him a decent head start then wandered up after him, emerging on a small, doglegged landing with three doors leading off it. All of which hung open, exposing the search team's legendary bull-in-a-china-shop finesse.

Dr Fife nudged a small mound of frilly pants out of the way with his cowboy boot, and stepped into the front bedroom.

Click, and light spilled out onto the landing.

It was nicely kitted out, with fitted wardrobes on the far wall, a window overlooking the playing fields, and a double bed with a tasteful headboard. Nice light fitting. Decorated in neutral estate-agent-friendly tones.

Just a shame that every drawer and cupboard door in the place had been thrown wide and ransacked – the contents strewn everywhere.

Angus gave those pants a wide berth. 'What are we looking for?'

'Walls in the wrong place, I suppose. Hidden cubbyholes.' He paced the room like a high-wire walker – heel to toe – as if measuring it. Knocking on all the walls with his ear pressed to the wallpaper. Then clambered into the open wardrobe to do a bit more knocking. Poking and prodding. Waving Kate Paisley's RFID fob about.

He emerged in a clatter of wire coat hangers. Held the fob out to Angus. 'Here: try the upper shelves.'

OK . . .

So Angus did – working his way from one shelf to the next, slow and methodical. But nothing clicked or swung open. 'Maybe it *doesn't* operate a secret catch? Maybe Kate Paisley really did have it for work?'

'Not according to Dr Sparky; they don't use this brand.'

Angus stepped down from the wardrobe. 'When did you—'

'While you were on the phone. I *can* actually investigate stuff without you supervising.' He stuck his hands in his pockets and headed out into the hall again. *'You coming or not?'*

Might as well.

Bedroom Number Two was a lot like the first one, only without the blizzard of searched-through clothing.

Angus ran the fob over everything, while Dr Fife paced the room and knocked on the walls. 'Anything?'

'Nope.' And Dr Fife was off again.

In Bedroom Number Three, angry red light oozed in through the rain-rattled window as the sun sank behind the valley rim.

Once again: Dr Fife paced; Angus fobbed.

Nothing.

The forensic psychologist hopped up onto the edge of the bed, then flopped over onto his back. 'Telling you: I'm not feeling it.'

'If it's not for *her* work, doesn't mean it's not for someone else's, right? Or maybe it opens a gym locker, or a bicycle shed?'

'Hmmm . . .' He stared up at the ceiling. 'This place got an attic, don't it?'

Angus stuck his head through the loft hatch, holding his phone out and sweeping its torch beam across a skeleton's ribcage of rafters and insulation. Dust motes hung thick in the air, wind howling in the guttering and growling across the pantiles, searching for a way in.

No boxes, no crates, no bits of old furniture. Just an empty attic.

Dr Fife's voice filtered up from below. *'Anything?'*

'What do you call that thing when they paint fake perspective on walls?'

'Trompe-l'œil.' In an almost perfect French accent.

'Unless Ryan's shit-hot at that: no.'

Just in case, Angus grabbed a little nugget of plaster sitting by the hatch and hurled it at the far wall. It sailed through the dusty air and bounced off the brickwork, exactly as expected.

He dropped back down onto the landing, leaving the hatch open, and brushed the fibreglass wool off his hands. 'Not upstairs, then.'

They trooped back down to the ground floor and tried the lounge instead. It was OK. Not flashy. Couch, matching armchairs, a TV just small enough not to fall foul of Mum's 'vulgar' rule, and a double-width rack for DVDs – though the *actual* DVDs were scattered across the carpet.

Outside, rain punished the city, hiding the other side of the valley in dark, swirling sheets. Angus closed the curtains, shutting it all away.

Which is what the search team should've done in the first place, hiding the room from the vulgar gaze of both press and public.

Dr Fife launched into his low-wire act again, wobbling across the room, knocking on the wallpaper, while Angus took the fob for a walk.

Nothing.

'Same size as the bedroom.' Fife knocked the toe of his cowboy boot against the skirting board. 'Which is pretty much what it should be.' Then frowned at the bland colour scheme. 'Who owns the place?'

'Technically: Kate Paisley's aunt on her dad's side, but she's in a care home. Parkinson's.'

'Hmmm . . .' He wandered out into the hall.

Rolling his eyes, Angus followed him. 'Neighbours can't agree how many people lived here, but we've got three bedrooms, so could be maybe six people? Think they're all in on it?'

'Don't be dense.' Stepping into the kitchen.

Cheeky sod.

'Who are you calling "dense"?'

The kitchen was a lot messier than the last time Angus was here: all the drawers and units and cupboards lay wide open and empty, their contents unceremoniously dumped all over the work surfaces and floor.

Dr Fife kicked a path through the debris. 'Three bedrooms, but only *one* looks like an explosion in a Goodwill store. So, either your mates in the search team have sticky fingers, or . . . ?'

Bugger. He was right.

'There was only two of them.'

'Only two of them *here*.' Dr Fife paced his way across the floor. 'Kate Paisley said Ryan-slash-Lachlan was never alone. "We are legion", remember? Could be houses like this all over Oldcastle.'

Ha.

Angus poked him. 'See! I *said* it was lots of different murder cells, didn't I?'

A withering glance. 'Don't push it.' Dr Fife turned, frowning at the devastation. 'Besides, having a whole bunch of serial-killing bastards running around the city is *not* a good thing.'

33

The bathroom was *just* big enough for Angus and Dr Fife, a toilet, and a jacuzzi bath. Sparkly tiles in shades of slate and petrol blue.

Dr Fife paced the room, then had a go with the RFID fob.

No joy.

He perched his bum on the closed toilet seat. 'Let's pretend that our Murderous Messiah has disciples *other* than Kate Paisley—'

'And Sean McGilvary.'

Dr Fife snorted. 'If Sean McGilvary's the Fortnight Killer, I'm Buffy the Vampire Slayer. He's been so screwed up by his religious-Fruit-Loop mom, it was easier to pretend he's a serial killer than come out of the closet.'

'But we've got him banged up for murder!'

'Yeah, you should probably let him out again.' Dr Fife kicked his heels, letting them swing back to *doink* against the porcelain. 'Where was I? Yeah – other disciples. Could be four, six, or maybe he's gone for the full Jesus dozen? Depends how many whacka-doodles you got running round Oldcastle, looking for an excuse to kill people.'

Bit of a sore point, in the Serial-Killer Capital of Europe.

'Thousands.'

A groan.

Angus shrugged. 'Apparently it's got something to do with all the mercury in the environment, cos we made heaps of mustard gas in the First World War. It can cause "developmental issues".'

'Yeah, that explains a lot.' He looked Angus up and down. Shook

his head. 'OK: where did they find the DNA? The blood CSI found –
Dr Fordyce and Jessica Mendel?'

'Understairs bog.'

Going by the look on Dr Fife's face, he had no idea what that was.

'Bog. Loo. Or as my mum likes to say: water closet. First door on
the right as you come in?'

'Oh, the *restroom*.' He hopped down from the seat. 'Why didn't
you say?' Pushing past and out into the hall.

'Because we don't *have* "restrooms" in Scotland.' Following him
to the panel door at the front of the house, squeezed into the space
beneath the stairs. 'Who "rests" in the toilet anyway? What kind of
house do you live in if *that's* the best place to put your feet up?'

Dr Fife pulled the door open, blocking most of the hallway.

Angus peered around it.

If the bathroom was a tight squeeze for two people, the understairs loo was barely big enough for one. A small WC and sink were
wedged in there, with a heated towel rail and nothing else. Soon as
the light clicked on, an Xpelair whirred and jittered into life.

They'd gone for less of a glittery-disco feel in here: slate tiles
on the floor and halfway up the wall, petrol-blue paint from
there to the sloping roof. With a line of thumb-sized pebbles sep-
arating the two.

Dr Fife stepped into the teeny space and turned. Mouth pursed.

Angus closed the door far enough to slip past, then opened it
wide again. 'Forensics think they were probably washing blood
residue off their hands.'

A finger appeared, pointing at all four sides of the understairs
loo: 'Outside wall, outside wall, hall, which leaves *this* one.' Because
of the sloping ceiling, it wasn't much more than waist height. Dr
Fife reached out and knocked on the tiles.

The sound came back flat and dead. No echo from a nice hollow
space concealed on the other side. 'Damn . . .' He sagged against
the sink. 'Really thought this was it.' Head falling back to pout at
the Xpelair. 'Maybe I'm losing my touch?'

Vivaldi broke the disappointed silence with those jaunty violins, making Angus flinch.

When he pulled his phone out, there was 'DS MASSIE' glowing away on the middle of the screen like an ominous warning.

Yeah . . .

He bared his teeth, hissed in a breath. Then held the phone out. 'Maybe *you* should answer it? It's you she wants to speak to anyway?'

And Vivaldi fiddled on.

'Move it.' Dr Fife wriggled past, fighting his way around Angus and the door, into the hall, to knock on the ever-decreasing section of wall that ran along the side of the stairs. Getting a hollow echo for his trouble.

Well, *someone* had to take responsibility.

Angus took a deep breath and answered the call. 'Sarge. Hi. I was just about to—'

'If the next words out of your gob aren't "walk into the office" you're in trouble.'

Bugger.

Dr Fife tried again, a little further on: still hollow.

'Funny you should say that, Sarge.'

'Oh, is it now?'

Another knock. Another hollow noise.

'Tell me, Constable MacVicar, when I told you I wanted a major *piece of evidence in an ongoing multiple-murder investigation brought in, did you think I was having a laugh?'*

Fife had reached the bit where the stairs were only a couple of feet off the ground and the plasterboard tapered to a triangular point. Gave it a wee kick with his platform cowboy boots.

'It's just the Boss said I had to stick with Dr Fife, and—'

'Put him on.'

Ah.

Angus held the phone out again. 'DS Massie would like a—'

'Outta my way.' Pushing past again and into the understairs loo. He frowned at the short section of wall – where it blocked off the underside of the stairs – for a moment, then gave it a hefty kick.

Thunk.

Definitely *not* hollow.

Angus stuck his head into the teeny room, one hand over the phone's microphone. 'Are you going to talk to her or not?'

'This wall's *solid*, but it *should* be hollow – cos it's just the space under the stairs. That ain't right.'

'Maybe they bricked it up?' Angus held out the phone again. '*Speak* to her.'

But instead of taking the thing and sweet-talking DS Massie, Dr Fife stared at the slate-grey floor tiles. 'No scratch marks, so if it *is* here, the door has to open inwards.' He produced the RFID fob again and ran it along the wall – doing one row of tiles at a time, from the ground up to where it joined the sloping roof. Then up past that as well, till he was standing on his tiptoes.

Angus went back to the phone. 'Sarge? He's in the middle of something, can he maybe call you—'

'*You remember that talk Badger gave you about detective inspectors being a vindictive bunch of bastards if you cross them? Well, detective sergeants are a thousand times worse.*'

Dr Fife leaned back against the sink, forehead a rugged valley of peaks and troughs. 'Come on, Jonathan: you can do this. *Think.*'

'I'm doing my best, Sarge.'

'*Really? Cos as of now you're right at the top of my bloody list!*'

A step closer, and Dr Fife rapped on the tiles with his knuckles. 'Or *maybe* we're just looking at it the wrong way? What if it's *here*, but it's a bit more old-school?'

'*Put me on speakerphone. Now.*'

Running his fingers over the tiles. 'What if they built this before they got their hands on the fancy RFID kit?'

Angus pressed the button. 'You're on.'

DS Massie's voice boomed out of the phone's speaker. '*Dr Fife!*' You'd think the ziplock bag would've acted as a muffler, but instead it seemed more like an amplifier.

Fife didn't look around, just kept prodding at the tiles. 'DS Thingy. Stop bothering my sidekick: he's working.' Giving up on the tiles, he tried the line of pebbles that marked the boundary between grey slate and blue paint. Press, poke, press, poke . . .

'*I'm guessing the FBI used to mollycoddle and indulge you, "Jonathan", but Police Scotland expects you to be part of the bloody team!*'

He'd prodded all the way to the cistern before a sharp *click* sounded and a sliver of black appeared at the base of that suspiciously-not-hollow wall. The whole thing had hinged up, exposing an inch of gloom where the wall no longer met the floor. Like some sort of weird, tiled cat flap.

'When I say we need that mobile phone back at the station, I mean: We – need – it – back – at – the – station!'

The gap remained visible for a count of three, then it narrowed and narrowed and narrowed . . . until *click*: it disappeared again.

Dr Fife beamed. 'Sonofabitch. You see that?'

'See what? What are you talking about?'

He pressed the pebble again.

Click.

This time, he put his hands against the wall and pushed, before it could seal itself shut again. The whole thing hinged upwards – not stopping until it came to rest against what had to be the underside of the stairs.

'Bloody hell.' Angus squeezed into the room, head bent sideways to avoid the sloped ceiling.

'What's going on?'

Dr Fife stepped forwards, till the toes of his pointy boots disappeared over the edge. 'HELLO?'

His voice echoed back at him from the darkness below.

He raised his eyebrows at Angus, grinned, then dug out his phone and switched on the torch.

'DC MacVicar, I'm not kidding about here! Either you—'

'Sarge? We've found something.'

The secret door started its slow-motion descent again. Dr Fife pushed it back up, the glow from his phone's torch glinting off a little catch you could use to keep the thing open. 'And *that* is why they pay me the big bucks.'

The torch traced around the opening – chipboard walls on either side, more chipboard on the underside of the stairs, and a set of wooden steps, leading down into complete darkness.

An uncomfortable scent of bleach and copper oozed up from down below.

'If someone doesn't tell me what's going on, this instant, I'm going to make you wish the Spanish Inquisition was in town!'

'So, Angus, you thinking what I'm thinking?'

'Don't you dare!'

A wink, and Dr Fife stepped into the secret passage.

'No! We need to call it in!'

'Call what in? AAAAAAAAAAAAARGH!'

Angus lunged for a handful of greatcoat, but there wasn't enough room to turn and grab at the same time, and Dr Fife disappeared down into the torchlit gloom.

Oh, for God's sake . . .

What if Dr Fife was walking into a trap?

Yeah, but one person stomping all over the crime scene was bad enough. Two would give DS Massie *and* DCI Monroe conniptions.

Protocol said he *had* to wait here for a search team.

But what if something happened . . . ?

At least there was no one here to see him doing the Dance of Uncertainty, as if needing a pee.

Come on: man up.

Back to the phone. 'Sarge? We've found a secret passage under the stairs at Sadler Road.'

A voice echoed up from the depths: *'Are you coming or not?'*

'Stay there. Do not *touch anything – I'm sending backup and Forensics.'* Her voice went all muffled. *'Monster Munch: get a car sorted!'*

Angus did the dance a little longer.

That was a direct order from DS Massie.

He had no choice, now.

None at all.

He wedged the phone between his ear and his shoulder, freeing up both hands to snap on a pair of nitrile gloves. Voice low, talking to himself. 'Everyone's right: you *are* a hulking great idiot.' Then back to full volume again. 'Don't touch anything!'

'Correct. And don't let Dr Arsehole screw around with the crime scene!'

No way he was fitting through that tiny little gap face-first, so Angus turned, hunching his back as he reversed into the low, slope-ceilinged space, climbing down the stairs like a ladder.

After all, what could go wrong?

34

Walls pressed in on both sides of Angus's shoulders – the stairs narrow, steep, and dark. And he had to navigate the sodding things backwards. Every step a mystery, with no idea what he was descending into.

But it probably wasn't good.

DS Massie's voice hissed and crackled from his phone: *'We'll be there in ten min—* . . . *for God's sake, don't—* . . . *sss* . . .*'

Then silence.

Hope this was worth getting fired for . . .

The last step thudded beneath his searching foot. Concrete, from the sound of it. He'd arrived.

The basement was little more than a short corridor, with the stairs forming the upright of a 'T' shape. LED strips glowed in the ceiling, but they were turned down so low they barely made any difference. And there was no obvious way of turning them up, leaving the room cramped, gloomy, and creepy. With an eye-stinging stench of bleach.

Dr Fife stood at one end of the corridor, tracing his torch beam over the bare chipboard walls.

There was *just* enough room for Angus to stand up straight in here, but his hair brushed the ceiling.

He held his phone up: no signal.

Great.

'She's going to kill us.'

Light swept across him as Dr Fife turned on the spot.

'This *ain't* right. No one goes to all this trouble to hide an empty . . . cupboard.'

Angus switched on his phone's torch and held out a pair of nitriles. 'Gloves.' Watching to make sure he put them on. 'Maybe it's a bolthole? The door self-closes, so you could hide in here if someone comes to the house.'

'What, *someone* like the police? Like *we* did?' A sarcastic sniff. 'Ryan-slash-Lachlan ran when he saw us, remember? Leading you *away* from the house.'

True.

Angus stared at the stairs. 'And he came out of the understairs bog! The door was open.'

Fife turned to look too, bringing his torchlight with him.

A weird little shadow flashed in and out of existence.

'Hold on. Swing the light back this way a bit.'

Dr Fife did – and there it was again. A strange crescent-moon shape set into the chipboard. It'd probably be invisible from the forensic psychologist's eyeline, but it was right there for Angus.

He stepped closer, running his own phone's beam around it. 'Little . . . finger hole, or something.' Plucking a pen from his pocket gave him something to poke into it, wiggling the biro about, rattling it off the edges.

That got him a raised eyebrow.

'Well, I don't know if it's booby-trapped, do I.' First rule of dungeon-crawling: do not stick *any* part of your anatomy into something that might conceal hidden blades. But nothing nipped the top off his pen, so Angus risked slipping his index finger in the hole.

There was a small space on the other side of the wood. Enough to hook the first two joints of his finger into. 'Hold on . . .' He pulled. Gently to start with, then a bit harder. Harder still . . . and *clunk*.

A section of chipboard came free – three-foot-wide, five and a bit feet tall. It didn't come on its own, though: it was attached to a wodge of thick white insulation, then a layer of spiky grey acoustic foam, then a final layer of chipboard. All glued together into an eighteen-inch-thick sandwich, like the lid of a chest-freezer. Only upright.

The stench of disinfectant got much, much stronger.

Dr Fife grimaced. 'OK, all that soundproofing is *not* a good sign.'

Angus shifted the 'lid' to the other side of the corridor, leaning it back against the wall. 'We need to go back outside, *right now*, and wait for Forensics.'

'Yup.'

Neither of them moved.

Dr Fife looked at him. Shrugged.

This was such a terrible idea . . .

Angus took a deep breath of bleach-tainted air and leaned into the opening.

His phone's light bobbed across the walls of what could only be a cell – maybe six feet square. Going by the sides of the doorway, the whole place was wrapped in the same acoustic insulation.

Reddish-brown stains made abstract shapes on the pale concrete. Not dark enough to be *fresh* blood, but maybe if you heavily doused it with Domestos . . .?

The torch picked out more bare chipboard on the ceiling, and finally came to rest on some sort of *cocoon* of clear plastic sheeting, bundled into the far end of the cell. Big enough to take a body.

A blurred face stared out from inside it. Eyes wide. Mouth open. Lips purple. Bald on top, with a tonsure of hair around the sides. A pale belly pressing against the plastic. The cocoon distorted most of the fine detail, but it was obvious from the waxy colour and dark smears that the body was naked and covered in bruises.

Jesus . . .

Angus jerked his head back out into the secret basement and released a shuddering breath. Then wrestled the cell door back into place.

Dr Fife looked up at him. 'What?'

Bloody hell.

'Angus, for *Christ's* sake: what's in there?'

He cleared his throat. Backed towards the stairs. 'I think we just found Councillor Mendel.'

35

Streetlights cast their wan light through the downpour, shivering like limbless trees in the wind. Doing their best to hold back the darkness.

Angus shifted in his seat, gazing out through the Mini's passenger window as the SE team battled to get their blue plastic marquee up in number one-thirty-two's front garden. Looked as if it'd come adrift from its moorings, though, because the thing was making a bid for freedom, walls snapping and furling in the storm.

Rather them than him.

The circus had arrived – with its filthy Transit vans and patrol cars – and now a pair of high-vis officers tied another cordon of 'POLICE' tape into place, sealing them all in.

God, it was all such a bloody disaster.

He shoogled around in his seat again as a new set of headlights appeared outside the blue-and-white tape. BBC News had arrived. Which meant the rest of the press pack wouldn't be far behind.

A groan rattled out from the other side of the Mini, where Dr Fife had his seat fully reclined, lying there with his eyes closed, greatcoat draped over himself like a blanket. 'Will you sit *still*?'

'We just found a dead body!'

'Meh. When you've seen as many as I have, it's difficult to get that excited.'

Unbelievable.

Ding-buzzzzz.

Angus pulled out his phone.

GILLIAN:
Angus? Are you OK?

That was nice of her to . . .

'Shite!' He sat up so quickly the whole car rocked. Eyes wide, followed by full-face clampdown. 'Shiteing, shitty, shite . . . shite!'

Another groan. 'Just a *half-hour's* sleep, is that too much to ask?'

'I'm supposed to be meeting Gillian for a drink!' Seventeen minutes ago, according to the clock on his phone. '*Shite* . . .'

Well, he'd royally screwed *that* up, hadn't he.

Deep breath.

Huge sigh.

Then he thumbed out a reply:

> Sorry.
> Meant to call.
> Has been development in investigation.
> Still at scene.
> Sorry.

SEND.

Dr Fife raised an eyebrow, but didn't bother opening his eyes. 'Oh yeah? And who's Gillian? She that school friend you been too scared to shag all these years?'

'What? No!' He squirmed a little. 'Gillian's just a . . . someone I met the other day.'

Thumbs clicking away at his phone screen:

> Sorry.
> Really wanted to meet for drink.
> Will you be free later?
> Again: sorry.

SEND.

'Word of advice from an old man who's been there, Angus: this job screws with your sex life. You gotta move fast if you wanna get laid.'

'It's not about "getting laid", you sexist dinosaur, it's about—'

A policeman's knock hammered on the car roof. Then DS Massie loomed at the passenger window, all done up in a rain-crackled SOC suit. She did *not* look happy.

Angus opened his door. 'Sarge?'

Her face hardened. 'Inside. The Boss wants a word.'

Not happy at all.

Angus scrambled out and hurried after her. Wind battering at his back. 'Sarge? Is there—'

'If you're going to ask about the burial site: yes. They found a body.' She turned and poked a finger into his chest. 'Now guess what *I'm* going to ask about.'

A quick check over his shoulder – Dr Fife was getting one of his custom SOC suits from the Mini's boot, so out of earshot. But Angus lowered his voice, just in case. 'He kept coming up with other places he wanted to be! I did my best, but you don't know what it's like – he's—'

'Oh, I *am* sorry, Constable. I didn't realize.' Placing a hand against her chest, a wee pout to her lips. 'There was *me* thinking that you were a *police officer*, and might have some *authority* in these cases!'

'Doing my best, Sarge.'

She poked him again. 'Just because the Boss made you Fife's minion that doesn't mean you get a holiday from doing what I tell you! And if you're thinking' – she put on a thick yokel accent – ' "But Sarge, a man can't have two masters." ' Back to normal. 'I'm not your *master*, I'm your *god*.' Poking him in time with every word: 'And – I – *will* – smite – you!'

Eek . . .

'Yes, Sarge.'

Another poke, harder this time. 'I don't care what Dr Arsehole wants, when God says "jump" you bloody well ribbit! Understand?'

'Yes, Sarge!'

Dr Fife plipped the Mini's locks as he marched over to them. 'Hey, Sweet Cheeks. If you're giving the lump a hard time, don't bother. He's *my* sidekick, he does what *I* tell him.'

'You . . .' Her eyes bugged. 'I am *not* your bloody "Sweet Cheeks"!'

'Course you are! And I'm the man who gets results.' He gave her a wee theatrical bow. 'You're welcome.'

DS Massie *stared* at him, fists clenching and unclenching, trembling with what had to be a volcanic, mammoth-sized heap of rage.

But Dr Fife didn't hang around for the eruption, he swaggered past, and ducked inside the scene examiners' marquee.

Angus grimaced. 'You see?'

Her whole face tightened, muscles rippling along her jaw, then DS Massie stormed after him.

Oh joy . . .

The marquee walls billowed in and out as the wind buffeted them, as if Angus had just stepped into some vast artificial lung. The SE had set up an inner airlock over the house's front door, a sort of mini-gazebo made of semi-translucent plastic. Presumably because the entrance to their subterranean crime scene was just inside.

No Abir today, instead it was DC McClarty who wielded the clipboard, all bundled up in a houndstooth fighting suit with a padded high-vis over the top. Breath misting in the chilly air. She held the sign-in sheet out, but DS Massie pushed straight past.

'Who the *hell* are you calling "Sweet Cheeks"?'

Dr Fife paused, halfway through unwrapping his SOC suit, to bend and peer at her backside. Because clearly he had a death wish. 'Yeah, it's flat and square, but I'd still tap that.'

She stepped up, fist raised – but Angus lunged in front of her. Blocking the way.

'Sarge: the phone! I've got it right here.' Pulling Kate Paisley's mobile from his pocket, now secured in his spare ziplock bag. 'To sign into evidence?'

She snatched it from his hand, glaring at Dr Fife. 'This isn't over!'

The front door opened with a *phooom*, sucking the marquee walls in, as if taking a deep breath, and an SOC-suited figure appeared. Indistinct and blurred behind the semi-translucent airlock. Coming into focus as he pushed through into the marquee proper.

DCI Monroe pulled his shoulders back. 'What's all the ruckus out here?'

'Just turning over some evidence.' Dr Fife pointed at the phone with a smile. 'I stuck the passcode on the screen, by the way. Cos I'm a team player.'

'Hmmph.' DS Massie wriggled the cover open – not easy, because of the bag – and scowled down at the Post-it with '36914' printed on it. 'You should've been back with this *hours* ago.'

'Instead of which, we found *two* of your missing victims.' A faux-modest shrug. 'Like I said: team player.' He finished by tipping a wink in DS Massie's direction. Throwing rocket fuel on the fire.

She stiffened, ready to swing, but Angus stayed where he was, a dirty-great-big human shield.

'Sarge . . .'

Monroe sighed. Frowned at the pair of silly buggers. Then shook his head. 'In case anyone's keeping score: I've got a serial killer on the loose, the media breathing down my neck, the Chief Superintendent looking over my shoulder, and a kitchen refit that's turned into a never-ending money-bonfire – I *don't* need you pair getting into a dick-measuring contest every time my back's turned!' The frown turned into a scowl. 'Understand?'

The only sound was the wind scrabbling against the marquee walls.

Dr Fife looked at the ground. Kicked a paving slab. 'Yes.'

DS Massie glared at him for a couple of breaths, then nodded. '*Fine.*'

'But for the record, mine is much bigger.'

Her jaw clenched again. 'Why do you have to be such a—'

'Like a toddler's leg.'

'Just . . .' Monroe massaged his temples with a purple-nitrile hand. 'Rhona: go rattle the Media Office. Tell them we'll need a *lot* of press management on this one. I want a statement prepped and ready to go.'

No reply.

A warning tone crept into his voice: 'Rhona?'

She huffed out a breath and cricked her neck. 'Boss.' Clacked the phone's cover shut, turned, and stomped out again.

Angus sagged. 'Thanks, Boss.'

He snapped off his gloves and dumped them in a black bin by the airlock. 'Three bodies in one day. I'd like to say that's a record for Oldcastle, but it's more like a Wednesday . . .' He patted DC McClarty on her high-vis shoulder. 'Clarty, why don't you go get yourself a cuppa.'

Big grin. 'Boss.'

Soon as she'd gone, Monroe slumped into one of the plastic chairs, covering his face with his hands. '*Three* bodies.' Shoulders drooping. 'Thank God we didn't tell everyone Sean McGilvary was the Fortnight Killer.'

Dr Fife unfurled his custom SOC suit. 'Look on the bright side: at least now we gotta name, right? Can't be too many Lachlan Ballantine-Reynolds in Oldcastle.'

'There aren't *any*. The PNC came up blank, so I got Monster Munch to do a wider search. Turns out "Lachlan Ballantine-Reynolds" is a character from some obscure American comic book. Hunts vampires, zombies, and werewolves in ye olde Wild West.'

Sod.

Monroe made circling gestures with one hand. 'Byron and Mags are off to visit your writer woman, see if we can't get a decent eFit of this guy. Got to be better than the out-of-focus blur in the papers this morning.' He grimaced. 'You two: call it a night. We've got more than enough dead bodies for one day. Don't need you finding any others.'

'But—'

'It's *half seven*, Angus; shift officially ended at five. Go. Have a drink or something. Blow off steam. Come back tomorrow morning, ready to catch this bastard.'

'But—'

'Good idea.' Dr Fife grinned. 'Besides: Godzilla here's gotta hot date with a sexy chick.' Slapping him on the back. 'Ain't ya, Champ?'

'I don't have a—'

'Mind you, given how skint he is, doubt Loverboy could paint the town pale peach, never mind red.'

Heat rushed to the tip of Angus's ears. 'Will you *please*—'

'Here.' Monroe dug into his rustling SOC suit and produced a wallet, liberating three twenties. He held them out. 'I hereby officially declare this to be petty cash. We'll call it "team building".' With that he groaned himself upright and lumbered back through the airlock again. '*Just make sure you get a receipt!*'

The house door clunked shut, leaving Angus and Dr Fife alone in the marquee.

Dr Fife fingered the cash. 'That went pretty well.'

In what world?

Angus scowled at him. 'Why do you *always* have to do that?' Jabbing a finger in the general direction DS Massie had gone. 'And "Sweet Cheeks"? Have you *any* idea how misogynistic and patronizing that—'

'*Of course* I do! That was the whole point.' He rolled his eyes as Angus blinked. 'Means she's too busy being pissed at *me* to be pissed at *you*.' He scrumpled his unworn SOC suit up and pitched it at the bin. Missed. 'Besides, me and DS Massie: unresolved sexual tension is kinda our thing.' Leaving the crumpled Tyvek where it fell, he turned for the marquee's exit. 'Now where are we meeting this Gillian woman?'

Angus backed away, both hands up. 'Oh no – you're not meeting anyone! I've seen what you're like with *police officers*, I'm not letting you anywhere near someone I actually like!'

36

The Mini weaved a path between the waterlogged potholes on Mortsafe Road, past dirty sandstone buildings and gurgling gutters. Not the swankiest bit of Castle Hill by any means – the kind of street where a kebab shop rubbed shoulders with a bookie's and 'HONEST TONY'S VAPE EMPORIUM'.

'Son of a *bitch*.' Dr Fife scowled out through the windscreen as the wipers thud-squealed their way back and forth. 'This ain't how a wild night out starts!'

Tough.

'I have responsibilities, OK?' Angus pointed. 'That's us, over there.'

They pulled up outside a glum red-brick building with big windows. It looked like a small recycled supermarket from the seventies or eighties – probably part of a chain that went bust long before Angus was even born. The current owners had done a half-arsed job of painting over the old signage, replacing it with a tattered banner: 'PETOPIA! DISCOUNT PET WAREHOUSE ~ EST. 2019'. So they'd timed that well.

'You said we were going to a bar!'

'Brief stop.' Angus climbed out into the rain. 'And now you know what it's like.' He turned up his collar and ran for the entrance.

According to a sign sellotaped to the glass, opening hours were '08:00 – 20:00', meaning they'd made it with a whole four minutes to spare.

Angus yanked the door open and charged inside.

The owners had put the same care and attention into renovating the interior as they had the façade. The stained chess-board linoleum still bore the marks of old supermarket shelves, but now everything was piled up on wooden pallets – pet food in huge bags; cardboard trays of tins; stacks and stacks of boxed pouches . . .

A section at the back was made up of racked cages, each featuring a miserable gerbil or a depressed rabbit, while Simply Red's greatest hits played over the tannoy.

Angus hurried to the canine section and grabbed a pale-grey sack with 'SCOTIABRAND TASTY CHICKENS LTD. BUDGET-FRIENDLY MECHANICALLY-RECOVERED-MEAT DRIED DOGFOOD ~ 15KG' printed on it. Swung it up onto his shoulder and sprinted for the checkout.

It *banged* down on the motionless conveyer belt, and a boot-faced man rang it up. His expression darkening further as Angus paid with seven pound coins and a big clattering fistful of small change.

Angus hefted the dogfood back onto his shoulder and legged it out to the car again – placing the sack in the back and fastening its seatbelt, like a chubby, limbless passenger. 'See?' Fastening his *own* seatbelt this time. 'Didn't take a minute.'

Dr Fife pulled out onto the road. 'I could be *at home*, having *dinner* on the deck, with *friends*. 'Stead of picking up dogfood, in a rainy shithole, with an idiot.' He slowed for the junction with McLaren Avenue. 'Where are we meeting this sexpot of yours?'

'She'll be long gone by now.' And who could blame her? 'Maybe you should just drop me home.'

'No way. We're hitting whatever bar you were taking her. He raised a finger. 'One: it won't be some dive, cos you're trying to impress her. Two: you're not exactly a pickup artist, so it won't be anywhere too swanky. Three: you ain't the sort to hump on a first date – assuming you've ever humped at all, and the jury is *way* out on that one – so it's gonna be a place where you can actually talk. And four: you're a cheap bastard, so the booze ain't gonna cost a fortune.' He narrowed his eyes and stared at Angus. 'Fifty bucks says it's old-fashioned and quaint, with a cute folksy name.'

Warmth fizzled across the back of Angus's neck.

'Shows what you know.'

*

STUART MACBRIDE

The Shoogly Peg was a proper, old-fashioned Scottish pub, with booths and tables arranged around a central bar that looked a *bit* like an unpainted fairground carousel. Only without the horses. And a lot more bottles of Bell's, Grouse, and Grant's.

A place free from the taint of theme nights and karaoke competitions and darts leagues and live music.

They'd even rejected the sinful allure of *recorded* music, preferring instead the gentle hum and susurrus of auld mannies hunched over their pints, and the occasional click of a domino.

Angus sat next to the bag of dogfood, a pint and a nip on the table in front of him as he slipped his clip-on tie into a jacket pocket.

Dr Fife filled the other side of the booth, sprawled out, taking up as much space as possible, contemplating a pint and a nip of his own. He raised the small glass. 'In just three days we've come *this close* to catching a serial killer, duped his disciple, located a hidden grave, got the aforementioned serial killer seriously pissed at us, then sat through an autopsy, discovered a secret hidden basement *and* a dead body, and been given the night off.' A lopsided smile. 'Even for me, that's a record.'

They clinked glasses and Angus took a sip: sweet and smoky and corrosive, and not too dissimilar to drinking burnt varnish. Shuddering as it went down, eyes closed, tongue poking out. 'Dear God . . .'

Turned out bourbon was nowhere near as nice as a proper Scottish whisky. Or creosote. Or Toilet Duck.

Dr Fife just sniffed his. 'When I got away from the Brethren, I went on a bit of a bender. After all those years of strict fundamentalist Christian horror, I was *all* about the tits and beer . . . You know what a decade of hedonistic excess gets you, Angus?'

'Who's "the Brethren"?'

He waved that away. 'A liver the size of Tibet and a lot of very happy memories. The ones you can remember, anyway.' Sigh. 'Thirty years on the wagon . . .'

Angus shifted in his seat. 'Sure you want to fall off now?'

'Not like I gave up for religious reasons. 'Sides: kinda interested to find out if I've lost the taste for it.' He knocked back the whole

360

glass of bourbon in one. Closed his eyes as he rolled it around his mouth, savouring the horrible taste, before swallowing. 'Ahhhh . . . Like riding a specially adapted bicycle.' He nodded at Angus's glass. 'Drink up. Got a lot of catching up to do, and *a whole sixty pounds* to do it with.'

The pub's patrons had swelled with the addition of a professional drinker – in a tweed bunnet, sports coat, jogging bottoms, and dress shoes – and a trio of after-work types in sharp suits, drinking imported beer and talking in some kind of Eastern European language.

The second round lay empty on the table, and a warmth had inhabited Angus's chest. A nice one, not an embarrassed flush this time. Bourbon wasn't so bad once you got used to it.

Dr Fife leaned forward, poking the table. 'See, Ryan's just swapped one cult for another. That's what conspiracy theories are – online cults. You don't have to travel to Waco or Jonestown, you can join up from the safety of your laptop or iPhone. Feel superior cos you're part of the select few who *understand* secrets no one else does.' The finger traced an invisible circle between the empty glasses. 'You draw a Venn diagram of people with paranoid tendencies, people who believe in conspiracy theories, and people who're into cults, the three circles would *so* overlap.' Then Fife's finger came up to point. 'Want another one?'

'Can't, my bus is in . . .' He checked his watch: half eight, *already*. 'Oh buggering hell. Missed it.'

'Then one more ain't gonna hurt.'

The barman put a nice sharp head on the second pint of Stella and placed it on Angus's tray. Then turned and chugged a couple more bourbons from the optics behind the bar.

Angus nodded. Smiled. And made sure not to get any of the words wrong, because his tongue was going a bit floppy. 'Thank you. And can I have a receipt, please?'

That got him a grimace, but the barman printed one out on the till anyway.

The Shoogly Peg was beginning to feel *almost* busy as two

gentlemen laid claim to one of the empty booths. One looked like Wayne Rooney's uglier cousin: close-cropped hair on a scarred Easter Island head, while his companion had a definite extra-from-*Braveheart* vibe: curly red pigtail, big moustache, and John Lennon sunglasses. Bit of a dick thing to wear indoors, but what the hell.

The barman plonked the receipt on the tray, along with a smattering of change. Raising his voice weirdly loud: 'There you go, *Officer.*'

At which, the two newcomers gave Angus matching grins.

Which was really friendly of them.

He gave them a cheery nod on his way past, carrying the tray back to the booth. Putting it down nice and slow in case anything spilled. 'That's the last of the float.' Scooping the change from the bottom of the tray. 'Got enough for a packet of crisps?' A couple of five-pence pieces slipped from his hand and skittered across the tabletop. He lunged – slamming a hand down to stop them escaping. 'Oops.'

Dr Fife helped himself to a pint and a nip. 'You know, for a big lad, you ain't so good at holding your liquor.'

'I'm perfectly sober, thank you very much.' Only slightly spoiled by nearly missing the bench as he sat down. 'Where was I?' Ah, right. 'OK, so people think LARPing is just for spotty kids, but it's so much more than that. You get to *be* someone else for a bit, you know? Step out of yourself and suddenly you're like . . . a *wizard*, or a mighty warrior.' He took a sip of cold fizzy beer. 'It's basically all the fun of role-playing, but you're out in the fresh air battering each other with padded swords and things. Win, win.'

'Sounds like an idyllic childhood.' Dr Fife's eyebrows drooped a bit. 'Must've been nice.'

'And we had a lovely big house in Cults – that's on the outskirts of Aberdeen. Only after Dad's death there were all these debts Mum didn't know about and she had to sell up. Everything. House, furniture, car, computer, all her fancy clothes . . .' Another sip. 'Course her friends abandoned her, cos of what Dad did, so we packed up what was left and moved to Oldcastle. "Fresh start," she said.'

Which was a joke. 'Only place we could afford was a tiny crappy flat, in a crappy tower block, in crappy Kingsmeath. *Kingsmeath!* I had a huge garden and a golden retriever.'

'In a tiny flat?'

'*No.* When we moved, Westminster had to go away: live on a farm.'

A nod. Then Dr Fife reached across the table and patted Angus's arm. 'If it's any consolation, I wasn't allowed pets, because keeping an animal for fun was a sin.' He opened his mouth to say something else, then clicked it shut again. 'Back up a bit. Think we missed something important there. What *did* your father do?'

'Not supposed to talk about it.' Angus took a good long scoof of lager, chasing down a slurp of bourbon. 'Anyway, I still had my LARPing gear, so I joined a club in Blackwall Hill and we had all these epic adventures in Camburn Woods, and out by Braecairn . . . Best thing was, other than a few rolls of duct tape and some foam rubber, it didn't cost a penny.' He wagged a finger at the big bad world outside. 'See, what's wrong with kids having a bit of imagination? These days it's all served up on tablets and laptops and smartphones! How's that progress?'

There was a *ding* on the other side of the table. Dr Fife pulled his phone out and checked the screen. 'That identikit image's come through.' He pursed his lips, eyes narrowed as he stared at it, moving the phone closer then further away. Before flipping it around. 'He look familiar to you?'

A black-and-white, computer-generated face filled the screen: male; long, straight, dark hair and a trimmed beard; large ears; sharp cheekbones; dark eyes. As if Dave Grohl from Foo Fighters and Captain Jack Sparrow had popped out a love child.

'Tell ya, Angus: that woman spends *way* too much time fantasizing about pirates.'

He unfocused his eyes a bit, tried to conjure up a muddy rugby pitch in Kingsmeath . . . 'Sort of? Like I said, I didn't *really* get that good a look at—'

'*Angus?*' A woman's voice. Soft, with a west-coast lilt.

Dr Fife covered the eFit with his palm and slipped his phone back in his pocket.

When Angus looked up, there was Gillian in her combat trousers and leather jacket, holding a stripy beanie hat like a little Victorian orphan. Lots of smoky eye make-up. Hair plastered to her head. Dripping rainwater onto the pub's wooden floor.

'Gillian!' He tried to stand, but the booth's bench seat and table got in the way, restricting him to an awkward half-bow. Very slick. 'Sorry I wasn't here when . . . but the investigation . . .' He cleared his throat. 'Sorry. Thought you'd gone home.'

'Did. Lost my hat.' She held up the stripy beanie. 'Someone handed it in at the bar.'

Dr Fife looked her over. 'So *you're* the legendary Gillian? Angus never told me you were *beautiful*.'

Her pink cheeks went bright as a strawberry. 'Oh, I . . . It's . . .'

He stuck out his hand. 'Jonathan. Or Dr Fife, if you want to step behind the screen and show me where it hurts?' Wink.

Gillian shook his hand, but the sleazy sod kept hold of it. 'Sorry. Er . . . Are you . . . ?'

'Angus's mentor? Well, you *could* call me that, but I like to think of myself more as a wise friend, helping to guide him and his colleagues.' Another sodding wink. 'Please, join us.' He turned to Angus. 'Why don't you get Gillian a drink?'

How?

They'd burned through the float already; all they had left was crisp-money.

Dr Fife held up a finger. 'It's OK, it's on me.' Then whipped out a twenty and passed it across the table. Just so everyone could see that *Angus* couldn't afford to buy a round. Because Angus had planned to visit the Cashline machine on the High Street, back when Gillian was still going to be here, and didn't because it was just meant to be him and Dr Fife and if he'd *known* she was going to come back for a missing hat he would've raided thirty quid from his savings as planned instead of standing here like Scrooge's ghost begging for charity and how was this bloody fair?

Gillian brushed a strand of wet hair behind her ear. 'Thanks. Er . . . a pint of Camburn Beasties, please? Thanks.' She gave Angus a pained smile. 'Sorry. Thanks.'

'Camburn?' Dr Fife stretched out in the booth, marking his territory. 'Like the woods?'

She nodded.

'You know: Angus was just telling me how he likes to run around down there, dressed as an elf. Hitting people with sticks.'

Oh, for God's sake . . .

If the pub's floorboards could just open up, right now, and swallow him whole, that would be *great*.

Things had got worse by the time Angus returned with the drinks, because Gillian had shuffled in on his side of the booth.

To *start* with, that seemed like a great thing, because when he got back from the bar with two lagers, two bourbons, and a pint of Camburn Beasties, that meant she was sitting right next to him. Sitting together. Side by side.

But after twenty minutes the reality sank in – she wasn't sitting *next to him*, she was sitting opposite Dr Fife, gazing at the bastard with awe as he told his *completely unfunny* stories about how he'd caught loads of American serial killers. Like the current rambling, uninteresting, humble-brag, buggering-awful one:

'. . . and I swear to God, he's standing there, with his trousers round his ankles, dick in one hand, and a partially skinned human skull in the other – and he takes one look at the SWAT team and says, "What? Never seen a man getting head before?"'

There was a sharp intake of breath from Gillian, then she burst out laughing. Clapping both hands over her mouth, stifling the giggles that followed. 'Oh God, that's so *horrible*!'

Dr Fife settled back in his seat, arms along the top, dominating the space. 'Worst thing is: wasn't *his* dick. Hacked it off a security guard in Baltimore.'

'No way!' She shook her head, then turned to Angus. 'Sorry. Gotta go to the bathroom.'

He got up and she shoogled herself out of the booth. Straightened her top. Gathered up all their empty glasses like someone who'd done regular bar work. 'Same again?'

Dr Fife grinned. 'Excellent idea.'

And off she shimmied.

Angus waited until she was out of earshot before squeezing back in and poking the table. '*What* are you doing?'

'Being charming?'

'Well, stop it! No more being charming.'

He tilted his head on one side. 'Are you *jealous*, Constable MacVicar? I'm old enough to be—'

'A dirty old man!' He poked the table again. 'How am I supposed to compete when you've got money and two decades' worth of "funny" FBI serial-killer stories?'

'It's not a competition, Angus. Women aren't prizes; they're not goldfish at the county fair.'

Typical.

'I liked her first! You're such a *wanking*—'

Oh bollocks – Dr Fife was staring over Angus's shoulder, mouth pulled out and down, one eyebrow raised.

She was behind him, wasn't she?

She'd been there the whole time, listening to him ranting away like a jealous tosser.

Angus closed his eyes. Groaned. Turned. 'Gillian, it's not what you . . .'

Only it wasn't Gillian, it was Ellie.

'Think?'

She was wearing her thick duvet jacket and a serious expression.

Not sure if this was better or worse.

But knowing *his* luck . . .

She backhanded Angus's arm. 'Budge up.'

He did what he was told and she slid in next to him, opening her coat and pulling out her phone.

She placed it on the table, with the microphone facing Dr Fife and pressed the glowing red icon marked 'Record'. 'Ellie Nottingham, *Castle News and Post*.'

Dr Fife eyed the phone as if it were venomous. 'Angus?'

'He's not the one you've got to worry about, *Doctor* Fife. If that is your real name?'

OK, wasn't expecting that.

Angus tapped her on the shoulder. 'Ellie, why are—'

'See, I've been doing some digging, and I don't think you exist. Not till 1992, anyway, when you graduated from Stanford. Before that there's no sign of a Jonathan Higgins Fife being born or educated anywhere in the United States.'

'Sonofabitch.' His eyes narrowed. 'How did you know my middle . . . Never mind.' He folded his arms. 'That's because I was born in *Scotland*. What, you think I put this accent on for fun?'

'There's no mention of a Jonathan Higgins Fife being born here either. And I went way back to the fifties.'

Dr Fife licked his top lip. Shifted in his seat. 'My dad was an abusive asshole. Mom changed our name after the divorce.'

'Oh.' Ellie raised her eyebrows. 'You know what? That makes *perfect* sense. Sorry to trouble you.'

The exact same trick he'd played on Sean McGilvary.

She stayed where she was, staring at him.

He stared back.

And the air in the booth sizzled like a live toaster dropped into a bubble bath.

'Ellie! How cool to see you again.' Gillian was back, carrying a tray with another round on it. 'Sorry: didn't get you one. What would you like?'

No one said anything.

Ellie and Dr Fife glared at each other.

Gillian lowered the tray. 'Jonathan, what's going on?'

Dr Fife kept his eyes on Ellie. 'Just a little misunderstanding.'

'He's not who he says he is.'

'Jonathan?'

Ellie leaned forward. 'There's not a single photo of "Dr Jonathan Fife" on the internet. No social media accounts. Nothing.'

'And yet: here I am.'

She glanced at Angus. 'How do you know he's who he says he is? You guys got no idea what he looks like, so you, what: went to the airport, held up a crappy sign with "his" name on it, and believed the first person to say "Yeah, that's me"?'

Dr Fife dug out his wallet. 'You wanna see my driver's licence?'

'And now he's embedded deep in the investigation. Leading it around by the nose with that half-arsed American accent of his.'

He shuffled sideways, out of the booth. 'I'm not gonna indulge this . . . idiotic speculation for a—'

'And *somehow*, Satan's Messenger always manages to be one step ahead!'

'Satan's . . . ?' Angus blinked a couple of times, turning from Ellie to Dr Fife and back again. 'Are you saying *he's* the Fortnight Killer?'

Her smile was as triumphant as it was cold. 'And his first victim was Malachi Ezekiel McNabb.'

It was as if Dr Fife's entire world had just tumbled out of his backside. He stood there, mouth hanging open for a moment, then covered his face with both hands. Knees curling. 'Oh, for . . .' Dragging in a huge breath. 'I HATE THIS *FUCKING* CITY!'

37

The Shoogly Peg wasn't exactly jumping to begin with, but it went *completely silent* as everyone in the place turned to scowl in their direction. It was one thing for *natives* to badmouth Oldcastle, but strangers?

Dr Fife flipped them all the middle finger. 'Screw you, I'm outta here.' And away he clomped.

Angus pushed his way out of the booth – forcing Ellie to scramble clear – hurrying after him. Clamping a hand down on Dr Fife's shoulder. 'No: you're not.'

'Get off me!' He tried to wriggle free, but Angus tightened his grip.

'Sit your arse back down, *right* now.'

A fist clenched, and for a moment it almost looked as if he was going to start swinging. Then Dr Fife huffed out his cheeks. Cricked one shoulder up. And unclenched his hand. Which was just as well, because that would *not* have ended well for him. He looked away. 'Fine.'

Angus let go and Dr Fife stomped back to the table. Slid into his seat again:

'Let's get this over with.'

'OK.' Angus pointed at Ellie. 'You better not be fishing.'

'Don't worry – I've got receipts.' She shuffled in, opposite Dr Fife. 'Malachi Ezekiel McNabb, fourteen years old, disappeared from hospital in Wick, thirteenth of September 1983. His remains were discovered by a pair of hillwalkers, near Achavanich Standing Stones, two weeks later.'

Dr Fife shook his head. 'No, they *weren't*.'

'Malachi's father identified the remains. Said the only thing missing was his son's necklace. A family heirloom, passed down for generations. A small chunk of granite, carved with a Celtic shield knot, held in place by silver wire and decorated with wee bits of stag's antler.'

Hold on.

Angus frowned – this morning in the Isbister suite bedroom. Fife's hippy necklace. '"Celtic shield knot" . . . is that like a little roundy thing?'

'Lots of serial killers keep trophies, don't they, *Doctor* Fife?' She prodded her phone, waking it up and unlocking the screen. Scrolling through to the photo gallery. 'You might be notoriously camera shy, but not every member of your family is so careful.'

Ellie spun her phone around so they could all see the picture of a pretty little girl, with golden ringlets and a gap-toothed smile, clutching her headless Barbie in one hand while she took a selfie. Dr Fife was clearly visible over her right shoulder, in shorts and flip-flops, holding a Coke and a hotdog. Smiling as he talked to someone off camera.

His scarred chest was covered in a white long-sleeve T-shirt, but the necklace had somehow managed to escape its confines to lie over the fabric. No sign of the tatty feathers it had this morning, but the bits of antler were there.

Ellie pinch-zoomed in on the necklace. 'Got it?'

Yup – it was *definitely* the same one.

She swiped, bringing up the next image: an article from some old newspaper – the text was far too small to read, but the headline was clear enough: 'FAMILY OF MISSING TEEN APPEAL FOR HELP'. A chunk of the page was given over to a black-and-white line drawing of the same necklace.

She zoomed in on that too. 'Malachi was sexually abused, strangled, and his skull battered in with a rock. Isn't that right, *Doctor* Fife?'

Angus pointed at the phone. 'How did you . . . ?'

'Senior crime reporter, remember?' Ellie threw that cold smile in Dr Fife's direction again. 'You killed him.'

'Hmmph.' Sitting back with a sneer. 'You're not buying this bull-shit, are you?'

Time to do a bit of professional looming. 'Just answer the question.'

Over in the corner, the auld-mannie contingent finished their game of dominoes, marked by unhappy muttering, the words 'Jammy sod . . .' and the mouse-bone rattle-click of tiles being shuffled for a new game.

One of the Eastern European businessmen took a call on his mobile.

The bartender polished glasses.

And still Ellie and Dr Fife glared at each other.

He gave in first, though. 'Yeah, OK. *Great!*' Throwing his hands in the air. 'I killed him. I put an end to his *miserable* little life then buggered off to America in the sincere hope I'd never have to hear that bloody name ever again!'

Wow.

Gillian covered her mouth with both hands, but there was no giggling this time, just a look of pain.

'Happy now?' Dr Fife thumped back in his seat. 'Knew coming to this shithole city was a mistake.'

Angus pulled out his cuffs. 'Jonathan Fife, I am arresting you under Section one of the Criminal Justice, Scotland, Act 2016 for murder. The reason for your arrest—'

'Seriously?' He curled his lip. 'I was right when I called you a "slack-jawed yokel".'

'The *reason* for your arrest is that I suspect that you have committed an offence and I believe that keeping you in custody—'

'Oh God.' Gillian uncovered her face. 'It's *you* . . .' She leaned into the booth, wrapped her arms around Dr Fife and hugged him.

How was *that* fair?

Or appropriate, given the confession.

'And I believe that keeping you in custody is necessary and proportionate for the purposes of—'

'You don't *understand.*' Gillian gave Dr Fife another squeeze. 'He didn't *kill* that boy: he *is* that boy. He's Malachi Ezekiel McNabb.'

Ellie rolled her eyes. 'Don't be daft, Gillian. Malachi's father identified the remains. Think he couldn't tell the difference between his fourteen-year-old kid and a dwarf?'

'Why did I bother?' Dr Fife's head fell back to scowl at the pub's smoker-varnished ceiling. ' "You should go to Scotland, Jonathan"; "It's time you faced your demons, Jonathan"; "You'll never get past this if you don't confront it, *Jonathan*!" '

Angus poked Ellie. 'You're not supposed to call people "dwarfs", it's demeaning.'

'Don't *you* start: he raped and killed a fourteen-year-old boy.' She picked up her phone and held the thing across the table. 'Any comment, before Angus drags your murdering arse off to prison?'

Gillian still hadn't let go. 'Leave him alone!'

Got to admit, that hurt a bit.

Angus poked Ellie again. 'How did you figure all this out?'

'Because this' – tapping her forehead – 'works just fine. And before you say anything else: a journalist never reveals their sources.' Giving the phone a jiggle under Dr Fife's nose. 'Well?'

A deep breath. 'My loving pop ID'd some poor dead schmuck's body? I mean, I always knew he was an asshole, but still . . .' Dr Fife downed his bourbon in one. 'The son of a bitch wouldn't want the authorities looking for me, cos if they *found* me, what's gonna happen to him and the rest of the Brethren? Think Jedediah Gideon McNabb's gonna spend the rest of his days in a jail cell?' A cold hard laugh. 'Not when there's the End of Days to bring on.'

Gillian slid into the booth next to him, one hand stroking his arm. 'You poor thing.'

'Oh, you got no *idea*.' He downed Angus's bourbon as well. 'Hark: gather round me, sinners, for cometh now the time of darkness, where only *one* can summon holy light . . .'

Dr Fife finished his pint with a frothy sigh.

Gillian hadn't let go of his arm, the whole way through, while Angus had to sit next to Ellie, watching the pair of them. As if he didn't even exist . . .

Ellie sniffed. 'So, basically, it was a cult?'

'Not basically – *completely*. Church three times a day, hellfire and brimstone, hard manual labour, everything's a sin.' A shrug.

'Turns out there's only so much purging and shriving and *goddamn* prayer a teenaged boy can take. So I'd run away. And they'd catch me, every single time. Drag me back. Beat the ever-lovin' crap outta me. And I'd be a good little boy till next time.' He fiddled with his empty glass. 'Then one day, my dear old pop gets a bit carried away and the Brethren panic – rush me off to hospital, before I croak right there on the church floor. Needed about a dozen blood transfusions.'

'I'm sorry.' Gillian curled in, bumping her forehead against his shoulder. 'My dad used to beat me, too.'

'Sounds like he and my old man would get on like an orphanage on fire.' Dr Fife sniffed, as if he could smell the smoke. 'Soon as I could *walk* again, I went on the lam – and far as I know, they're still looking for me. Nobody leaves the Brethren of the Sacred Thorn, not even in a coffin. Yea, unto the third generation.'

Suppose it was hard not to feel sorry for the poor sod.

Even if Gillian was all over him.

Angus cleared his throat. 'Then why did you come back?'

'Cos it's been years. Cos my therapist's been banging on about it for nearly a decade. Cos even after all this time it's still screwing with my life. The nightmares; flashbacks; waking, middle of the night, soaked in sweat, screaming – oh yeah, better believe my ex-wives *loved* that.' He glowered into his empty glass. 'And it was just gonna be baby steps. "Go to the forensic conference in London, Jonathan, won't even be in Scotland. What's the worst that can happen?" Only I hafta get cocky, don't I? Cos the old bastard's probably dead by now, right? Might not even *be* a Brethren of the Sacred Thorn any more. Maybe they . . .' He waved a hand. '. . . I don't know – swallowed a shitload of Vicodin, washed it down with Drano, and finally got the Rapture they always prayed for?' The hand thumped down again. 'So when the call comes in: "Hey, we need your help!" I think yeah, why not? I am un-fucking-touchable. *That's* why.' He pushed the empty glasses away. 'But if it's gonna be plastered across the papers, I'm outta here.'

Oh no. 'But the Fortnight Killer—'

'Ain't my problem.' He pointed in the vague direction of the fire exit. 'If my *loving* family find out I'm here, swanning round

Oldcastle: bet your ass they'll come looking. And these fuckers don't take no for an answer.'

Angus sat back, chewing on the inside of his lip. Then looked at Ellie. 'You don't *actually* have to publish anything, though, do you?'

'Not me you've got to worry about, it's Slosser the Tosser. Got jealous I "stole" the front page from him; thinks he can do a character piece just as good as the one I did on you.'

Dr Fife sagged. 'Tomorrow.'

'Tomorrow.' She raised an eyebrow. 'But he *doesn't* know about "Malachi".'

Good. That was something, anyway. 'And he won't have a photograph, so there's that.'

Ellie winced. 'Actually, yeah. He does.'

'Oh, for . . .' A groan rattled out of Dr Fife; he covered his face again. '*How?*'

No reply, but Ellie had one hell of a shifty look on her face as she shrugged.

'OK. Well, then.' Gillian wriggled out of the booth. 'I think, maybe, we could all do with another drink?'

Three crisp packets lay on the sticky wooden tabletop, their bags ripped open and innards exposed. Like a tasty post-mortem – attended by police officers dressed as pints of Stella and shots of Jim Beam.

Angus swallowed down a burp, because there were ladies present and Mum was always very strict about that kind of thing. 'That's . . . *terrible!*' Swaying slightly in his seat.

'I *know*, right?' Dr Fife wasn't as wobbly, but his face had gone all pink and ruddy-cheeked.

'Everything's a sin?'

'That or a punishment from God. Rains blight the harvest? Punishment from God. Calf's delivered stillborn? Punishment from God. Your brother, Elijah, falls out of a tree and breaks his leg?'

Gillian fidgeted with her tin of Diet Coke. 'Punishment from God.'

'Nah. I pushed him.' Big grin. 'He always was an asshole.'

'Punishment from God . . .' Angus reached across the table and squeezed Dr Fife's shoulder. 'Must've been hard, growing up like that.'

He raised an eyebrow, then frowned, clearly trying to work out the subtle *and insightful* message Angus had just laid on them. But finally he got it:

'What? No, no, no, no. That little shithead, Kate Paisley, was talking out her ass. Was my father "upset" when I "slithered out" like "something off a horror film"? Course he wasn't! I wasn't a *punishment*, I was what that bunch of mirthless dicks had been waiting for. Generations of them: praying and praying and praying.' He threw his arms out in a wide *ta-daaaa!*, then winked at Gillian. 'I'm quite the big deal.'

Which was fair enough, so Angus gave him a wee round of applause.

Dr Fife raised his chin and put one hand against his chest – the other hand held out and up, as if he was about to tell everyone to be most excellent to each other. 'For *I* am the Chalice!' He dropped the pose and leaned towards Angus. '*That* was my nickname.' Then leaned back again. 'And lo: the Chalice shall sire the Dawn Child, and the Dawn Child shall bring forth the End of Days, when fire shall rain from the skies and the dead shalt consume the earth, and the Rapture shall raise the True Believers to God's right hand, and all others shall be cast into the pit, yea to burn for all eternity.' A sour burp slithered free, because he hadn't had the same kind of upbringing as Angus. 'Only when they say "the True Believers" they mean the Brethren of the Sacred Thorn. Everyone else is screwed.'

'Bloody hell.'

Dr Fife toasted him. 'Quite literally.'

Which was when Ellie returned from the ladies', wiping her wet hands on her jeans. 'What? I miss something important?'

'Yes!' Fife dug out his wallet and slapped it on the table. 'It is *time* . . . for tequila!'

The pavement outside the Shoogly Peg was all uneven: going up and down beneath Angus's feet, as if someone was sailing it into the wind . . .

Only it wasn't a sail that reared up at the end of the narrow dead-end street, it was the vast granite shark's fin with the Old Castle perched on top. All lit up like an oversized Christmas decoration.

A sparkle-shark.

Sparkle-sharkle.

Someone had tried to gentrify this end of Doocot Lane, by swapping out the concrete-and-steel lampposts for ye-olde-worlde cast-iron ones, and sticking in a row of planters. But drunken morons had ripped out the flowers and shrubs quicker than the council could replant them, and now the only things that grew in the rectangular wooden boxes were cigarette butts; empty bottles, tins, and glasses; and vomit.

Keeping it classy, Oldcastle.

The good thing, though, was with the castle on one side, and the great-big tall buildings on two others, it blocked the storm, cutting the shrieking wind and hammering rain down to gentle breeze and a misty drizzle.

Sparkle-Shark would be a great name for a band, wouldn't it?

Should write that down.

But if he went rummaging for his pen, he might drop Wee Hamish's dinner. And that wouldn't be good. Not on an uppy-downy pavement like this one. So Angus hugged the fifteen-kilo sack of ScotiaBrand Tasty Chickens Ltd. Budget-Friendly Mechanically-Recovered-Meat Dried Dogfood tighter. Like a deformed teddy bear.

Dr Fife had propped himself up against one of the quaint lampposts, cos he was suffering the effects of the wobbly pavement too.

The only ones who *didn't* seem bothered by its lurching about were Gillian and Ellie.

Ellie hooked a thumb over her shoulder. 'Are you sure? My car's just around the corner.'

'Honestly, I'm good, thanks.' Gillian pointed. 'I'm only five minutes that way.' She walked to the lamppost and slipped a hand in under Dr Fife's armpit. Gave the greatcoat's sleeve a squeeze. 'I'll drop him off on my way past the hotel.'

Fife blinked up at her. 'I don't . . . don't need a babysitter. I'm not' – a belch barked out – 'oh, 'scuse me. Not . . . a *child*.'

'I know.' She beamed down at him. 'But I'm going that way anyway, and you can keep me safe, in case any perverts are on the prowl.'

'Oh.' He gave Gillian a wobbly salute. 'In that case, it would be . . . my pleasure.'

'Thank you.' Then she paused for a moment. Let go of the forensic psychologist. Stood on her tiptoes. And kissed Angus on the cheek again.

Twice in two days.

She gazed up at him with those smoky eyes. 'As first dates go, this certainly beat curry and a cheesy movie.' Then off she went, taking Dr Fife with her. Leaving Angus with the lingering scent of strawberries and Coke, and a warm-fuzzy glow.

Dr Fife's cowboy boots clacked against the wavering paving slabs. 'I ever . . . ever tell you 'bout the time I caught this guy . . . who liked to skin his victims?' Another foghorn burp. 'Damnedest thing . . .'

Fading away as they were swallowed by the drizzle.

Angus beamed. 'I really like her.'

'I'll bet you do.' Ellie rolled her eyes. 'Come on, Casanova, let's get you home.'

Ellie's ancient Ford Fiesta scunnered its way across the Calderwell Bridge – exhaust sounding as if an elephant was gargling treacle – buffeted by squalling rain. The windscreen wipers went full pelt *clunk-clunk-clunk-clunk-clunk-clunk*, back and forth across the glass while the radio played a sad love song at them both.

Ellie hunched forward over the wheel, squinting out through the streaked windscreen, making for the lights glittering on the other side of the river. 'You know what worries me?'

'Hmm? No. Maybe.' He hugged the dogfood tighter. 'Is it dying alone?'

'Is it *what*?'

'It worries me. I mean, I'm . . . you know? Totally.' Which was true.

Ellie pulled a face at him. 'Why are you such a sodding lightweight?'

'I mean, how sad . . . how sad would that be?'

'Two shandies and you're falling over, talking shite, and belting out "Scotland the Brave".'

He gave the sack another squeeze. 'Gillian's *nice*, isn't she?'

'Will you listen? What *worries* me is this story about his dad being some weird cult leader. I mean, we've only got so-called "Jonathan"'s word for that.'

'I think she's nice.'

Ellie hung a right at the roundabout, along Montrose Road, following the river. The old train station glowed on the other side of the water, like a vast demonic slug. Behind it, the lights of Logansferry and Shortstaine reared up the valley wall – broken only by the dark ribbon of Moncuir Wood – until they disappeared into the low cloud.

'Hoy!' She reached across the car and bashed him one, on the arm. 'Divert some blood away from your nadgers to your brain for a minute: how do we know he's telling the truth?'

That was easy: 'Call the hopsital.' Hold on. Angus had another bash: 'Hobspital. Hops-sittle. Why'd they make that word so difficult to say?'

'*Total* lightweight.'

'Call 'em and *ask*. It'll be on his notes, right? From nineteen thingummy, if the real . . . real Malachi Ezekiel McNabb's got achondroplasia.'

'Oh, so you can say "achondro . . . whatsit", but "hospital"'s too tough?'

Ha!

He snapped his fingers. 'That's the one: hopsital!' No, wait, still wasn't right.

Ellie puffed out her cheeks. 'Don't know if they'll divulge medical records to *me*, but luckily I know a police officer who owes me lots of favours.'

'Who's that?'

'You! You complete and utter tit.' She hit him again.

'Oh.' He blinked at all the blurry lights. 'Do *you* think Gillian likes me?' A burp burst free, and he slapped a hand across his mouth, but it was too late to catch the thing. 'Sorry. Very rude.' Angus stuck his elbow out and nudged her. 'Come on. 'Mon. All together.'

Deep breath, then he belted it out:
'Land of the heart diseases,
Eating pies and deep-fried pizzas,
Smokers making bagpipe wheezes,
Scotland the brave!'

'And there it is.' Ellie rolled her eyes. 'I should've made you *walk* home . . .'

Wind whipped through the gap between the three tower blocks, snatching at discarded rubbish and making it dance like a pagan rite. The buildings didn't offer much shelter from the rain either – it *clattered* down, sparking off the playground outside Millbank North, because not even stoned teenagers were daft enough to be out drinking super-strength cider in this.

Angus cradled the fifteen-kilo sack of dogfood against his chest, tucked safely inside his jacket so it wouldn't get wet, as he leaned on the Fiesta's roof and peered in through the driver's window. 'Thanks . . . Ellie. You're a . . . a good friend.'

'Yeah, well, just remember it when I call asking for that favour tomorrow.'

He beamed at her, then threw in a nice sharp salute, and lurched off towards the main entrance. Because, somehow, that wonky-pavement thing outside the Shoogly Peg was spreading throughout the city.

Ellie's voice pounded through the storm: *'AND DON'T FORGET TO FEED WEE HAMISH!'*

As if he'd *ever* forget to feed the little man. But Angus waved a polite thank-you over his shoulder anyway.

Took three goes to get through the doors at the tower block's entrance, but he managed in the end, then turned and waved again.

Ellie flashed her lights at him, then off she jolly well drove, leaving Angus all on his alonesome.

Right.

Fourteenth floor here we come.

Just a shame the lifts never worked . . .

*

Angus wobbled in place, one leg ponking up and down to keep him upright, cos wouldn't you know: it wasn't just the pavements that'd gone all funny.

But the key finally decided to cooperate and he let himself into the flat.

Being vewy quiet.

Because he was hunting wabbits.

He removed his shoes and tiptoed through into the kitchen. Lowered the dogfood onto the worktop with care.

A plate sat beside the microwave – something grey-brown and congealed. Stovies. Allegedly. He closed one eye to get the clingfilm-wrapped horror into focus. Bet there wasn't so much as a scrap of meat in there, just potatoes, onions, and a stock cube. *If you were lucky*.

But Mum was doing her best.

Meat cost money.

You ungrateful bastard.

True.

She'd left a note for him on the fridge:

'HAVE GONE TO BED WITH MY HEAD.

I EXPECT YOU NOT TO MAKE ANY NOISE, OR WATCH TV.'

He blinked at it for a bit while the letters swam in and out of focus. Then made a shooing gesture, and opened his sackbaby, pouring a generous measure into a wee tartan dog bowl. Because why should the little man be on meagre rations too?

Soon as the biscuity nuggets rattled into the dish, Wee Hamish appeared – summoned to dinnertime. Doing his happy whirly dance, tail wagging like a mad thing, claws skittering on the kitchen floor.

Angus placed Wee Hamish's dinner beside the matching tartan water bowl. Then ruffled the fur between the little man's ears, keeping his voice low, so as not to wake Mum: 'Your favourite: ScotiaBrand Tasty Chickens Ltd. Budget-Friendly Mechanically-Recovered-Meat Dried Dogfood! Mmmm . . . Yum, yum, yum!'

Wee Hamish fell on it like a loveable, weeny terrier with big sparkling eyes and a happy, waggy tail.

Munch, munch, munch.

'You, my teeny man, are a most excellent dog.'

Angus ruffled the hair on his tiny fuzzy head once more, then lurched from the room. 'Shhhh . . .'

He picked his way down the hall – *like a ninja* – and into his bedroom. Clicked on the bedside light.

The single bed was barely big enough, but he still fit. More or less.

Shame about the faded dinosaur wallpaper, though. And the old school desk, rescued from a tip, with a trio of jury-rigged bookshelves above it. Each one of them stuffed with fantasy paperbacks, collected over the years from charity shops, discount bins, and library sales.

Just like Sean McGilvary's SF collection.

The curtains were open. Not that he had a great view: the top half of Kingsmeath, followed by a short stretch of the valley wall, then sky. But tonight there was nothing but a scattering of streetlights and a big swathe of darkness.

Yeah, Dr Fife was right. No way he could bring a beautiful woman back here.

Still wearing his soggy fighting suit, Angus half sat, half collapsed onto the edge of the bed.

Just needed to rest for a minute while the world whooshed around his room. Maybe it'd be a good idea to close his eyes for a bit, so he couldn't see it rush by?

That was an idea.

Smart thinking.

He slumped backwards, arms akimbo, gob open, feet still flat on the floor.

Yeah, that was better.

Comfy.

Just rest here for a minute, then get up, do his teeth, get changed, hang his damp suit up in the bathroom to drip dry.

Piece of cake.

The clickity-clackity of little claws approached down the hall, then in trotted Wee Hamish.

Angus peeled one eye open, watching the teeny man bimble

over to the bed and hop up onto the duvet. Then climb onto his chest, turning around twice before curling up and settling down to sleep, all soft and warm and cosy . . .

A big smile spread across Angus's face as his eye drifted shut again. 'Sparkle-Shark.'

And that was that.

—Saturday 16 March—

38

'We're bang on five thirty; please contain your enthusiasm. It's dark and wet out there, but good news! It's going to get darker and wetter today. So, let's celebrate with a slice of the Mighty Beetroot.'

A slow piano melody burbled out of the clock radio.

Urgh . . .

'If you're still here at eight, it's Holly Janowski – till then you're stuck with me, Jane Forbes. It's the Very Early in the Morning Show, and this is "Hearts In Darkness"!'

Something was wrong.

Something was very, *very* wrong.

A miserable voice burst into song:

'I wasn't meant to die today,
But you killed me all the same . . .'

Angus's eyes snapped open, and there was the ceiling of his bedroom. Looming like a hammer, and his bed was the anvil.

'I tried to give it all away,
And hate what I became . . .'

His mouth made a sticky *sssscklack* noise as he prised it open, releasing the bitter taste of last night's beer and too many bourbons.

'Cos you always breathe my final breath,
I suffocate as we undress . . .'

He blinked at the ceiling-hammer. 'Awake! I'm awake . . .'

'Our hearts live in darkness,
Our hearts live in darkness,
Our hearts live forever in the—'

His hand thumped down on the old clock radio and blessed silence settled into the room. Followed by the *whump-whump-whump* of blood in his throat. Working its way up into his swollen cranium. Getting louder with every beat.

A long shuddery breath rattled out, smelling even worse than it tasted.

Angus blinked again, looking down at the wee hairy face staring back at him from his chest as if he were the most wonderful thing in the whole wide world. Oh, to be a little fuzzy dog.

Why was . . . ? He was still wearing his jacket. And his shirt. And his trousers. And his damp socks. And everything else.

How much did he *drink* last—

There was a subterranean gurgle, followed by a burp.

Nope.

Wee Hamish had a stretch and hopped down from Angus's chest.

Which was probably wise.

Another gurgle, another burp.

Angus swallowed. Hissed out a long, sour breath.

Yellow and green burst across the back of his brain, sweeping forward in a tsunami of burning gravel, making cold sweat fizzle across his skin.

Definitely nope.

He jerked bolt upright, both hands clamped over his mouth, and scrambled from the room.

Angus lurched back into the bedroom, towel wrapped around his middle, yesterday's fighting suit draped over one arm, little nuggets of toilet paper stuck to his cheeks like mini Japanese flags. Head pounding – because there was no paracetamol in the whole house. Unless Mum had some squirrelled away in her room. And there was no way he was waking her up to find out.

Instead, he gave the suit a sniff.

Bit beery.

More than a bit wrinkled.

But what choice did he have?

Erm . . .

OK.

He hurried out into the hall, opened the cleaning-cupboard door, and gave his suit a quick once-over with Mr Sheen's furniture polish. Then took it back to his bedroom for a quick squirt of Lynx Africa, just in case.

He scrambled into fresh socks, pants, and a clean shirt, then the suit.

Tie.

Where the hell was his tie?

He was definitely wearing it in the pub last night, wasn't he?

The clock radio clicked over to 06:01.

No time to worry about that now.

Through to the kitchen, where Wee Hamish greeted a break-fast of budget-friendly dried dogfood with the usual twirly dance of delight, crunching merrily away as Angus investigated the untouched stovies.

The coagulated lump of mushy potato had leached a thin grey liquid onto the plate, like bin-juice, and . . .

Nope.

He closed his eyes, gripped the edge of the work surface, breath-ing in little shallow puffs. Not that there was anything left to bring up.

Couldn't leave last night's dinner just sitting there, though. Mum would be hurt. Worse, she might make him eat it *tonight*.

He dug an old bread bag from the recycling and scraped the stovies into it. Tied a knot in the top and rammed it into the bin. Covering it with whatever else was in there so she wouldn't see.

Then gave the plate a quick wash – abandoning it on the drain-ing board as his phone launched into the crappy-marimba tune that meant it was time to get the hell out of the flat or miss the bus.

Quick, quick, quick, quick, quick.

Angus struggled into his damp shoes and out onto the balcony.

Bloody hell . . .

If anything, the weather was even worse than yesterday. Wind snarled and whirled between the three tower blocks, rain hurling itself against the concrete, puddling across the walkway. And the sky was coal-black, with only the faintest smear of fire around the valley's lip to show the day even existed.

Even the streetlights could barely puncture the darkness.

Angus locked up and staggered towards the stairwell.

What a *great* day to have a massive hangover.

The radiator's ping-clang-gurgle filled the air with warmth, raising steam from Angus's jacket – laid along the top of it, arms hanging over the sides. His shoes were tucked underneath – stuffed with newspaper pilfered from the Media Office's recycling pile.

One huge benefit of them giving Dr Fife his own private office was no one else was here to break the calm. Not even Dr Fife, because at ten past seven, he'd still be lying in his pit, all scarred and snoring it up. Dreaming of cults and beatings and a dead boy wearing *his* real name . . .

Angus puffed out a long breath and took a scoof of Rampant Gorilla – the last one in the filing cabinet – pairing it with yesterday's stale cheese sandwich and two paracetamol borrowed from Monster Munch. Then went back to wrestling with *Behavioral Analysis for Law-Enforcement Personnel (Crime-Scene Indicators, Forensic Red Flags, & Interview Guidance)*.

Who the hell wrote this stuff? Online terms and conditions were clearer than this.

So far, the yellow legal pad he'd borrowed to take notes in only had the book's title printed at the top in nice, neat biro letters, today's date, and a big 'WTAF????!??' Underlined three times.

This must be what it was like for old people trying to work Netflix . . .

The office door opened and in slouched PC Derek McConachie, AKA: Dusty. Droopy of eye and red of nose. Sniffing.

There was more than a hint of football hooligan about him, with tattoos poking from the sleeves of his black Police Scotland T-shirt and a couple of nicks taken out of his left ear. That's what you got for getting into pub brawls wearing earrings.

He scuffed right up to Angus and flicked him on the shoulder.
'Ow!'

'Rotten sod.' Dusty hauled in a snochery sniff. 'Hours and hours and hours I was: going round those buggering cars. In the cold. And the rain.'

'Sorry.' He forced a smile. 'Find anything?'

'Nah. Almost caught my death, but . . .' One of his basset-hound eyes scrunched up, top lip twitching as he made a *gnnnnnnnnngnnnn . . .* kind of noise. He shuddered, then slumped. 'Hate it when that happens.' Dusty wiped his nose with a scabby hanky. 'If you see Noodles coming: *run.* Says she spent three hours last night watching all the CCTV footage from outside the station. Aye, *and* all the stuff they put out on the news too. Looking for your Mr Four-B.'

No idea.

Dusty dabbed a dreep from the end of his nose. ' "Bloody Beardy Baldy Bloke". She's got eyes like pickled beetroot the day.'

'Don't blame me! I just passed on a tip.'

'Yeah, well, like I said: run. Cos if there's one thing Noodles knows it's how to hold a . . . a . . . a . . .' His eye scrunched up again, but this time the *gnnnnnnnnnnnnnnnnnnnnnnnn*-ing ended in a thundering sneeze. He scrubbed at his nose and top lip. Then blinked and shook his head. 'Grudge.'

A knock rang out at the door, then it opened and in marched DCI Monroe with DS Sharp in tow. Both of them grim-faced. As if they were about to tell some poor victim's family about a car crash or murder.

Dusty nodded at them. 'Boss. Sarge.'

DS Sharp checked her clipboard. 'Thought you were on door-to-doors today.'

'Sarge.' And off he scurried, closing the door behind him.

A DEFCON 3 sneeze boomed out in the corridor.

Monroe thumped into the spare seat. 'Where's Dr Fife?' His nostrils twitched. 'And why does it smell like my nan's front room in here?'

'Boss.' Angus stood to attention, *not* looking at the steaming Mr Sheened jacket draped over the radiator. 'He's probably still a bit . . . *jet-lagged.* Doesn't like to start till nine. Ish.'

DS Sharp ran an appraising eye up and down Angus. 'You seem a bit "jet-lagged" too. Rough night?'

He kept his eyes on DCI Monroe. 'You instructed us to blow off steam, Boss.' Digging out the scrunched-up receipts from the Shoogly Peg and placing them on the desk. 'For the petty cash?'

Monroe swept them up and pocketed the lot. 'You've seen the *Castle News and Post* this morning?'

'Sorry, Boss: Dr Fife wanted me to bone-up on this.' Pointing at the impenetrable textbook. 'Did they print it?'

'Oh, yeah.' DS Sharp grimaced, eyes wide. '*Big* time.'

'Any chance we can minimize the damage, Angus? Make him see this isn't so big a deal?'

Ah . . .

Angus bit his top lip. Then pulled in a deep breath. 'We *might* have a problem there.'

Monroe sat back in his chair, mouth hanging open as Angus finished his story. 'And it's a *cult*?'

'He's convinced that if they find out he's here they'll come after him.'

'An actual religious . . .' Monroe waved his hands. '. . . woo-woo, here-comes-the-Rapture, let's-all-drink-the-Kool-Aid cult?'

DS Sharp folded her arms. 'Assuming your mate on the *Knap* is wrong, about Dr Fife not being who he *says* he is.'

'True.' More frowning from the Boss. 'Then we'd better go with Angus's plan. Laura: get on to every hospital north of Inverness – if they've treated this . . . Mordecai—'

'Malachi, Boss.' Angus gave a wee deferential bow of the head, because senior officers really didn't like being corrected. 'Malachi Ezekiel McNabb.'

'Should be a distinctive enough name. Find out if he's got dwarfism or not. And see if you can't get the original investigation notes on the murdered kid from N Division. *Might* still have them?'

She checked her watch. 'Boss.' Then bustled out.

As the door closed behind her, Monroe plucked a legal pad from the piled-up paperwork that littered the desk – it was covered with Dr Fife's drunken-chicken scrawl, punctuated by hand-drawn diagrams and footnotes. He flipped through the pages, as if they might somehow make sense. 'What's your opinion of the man, Angus?'

Good question.

After last night, with Gillian fawning all over him, that was very much up for debate. Which was petty and probably unfair. But then so was life . . .

'Are you asking if he raped and killed a fourteen-year-old boy forty-plus years ago?'

Monroe dumped the pad back on the pile. 'You're the one who's worked with him more than anyone else.'

'Yeah, but . . . That's, like, only two-and-a-bit days.'

A nod. 'Where was he Thursday night, Friday morning, when the Lundys were killed?'

Angus licked his top lip. 'Wasn't he with you, Boss? Interviewing Kate Paisley and Sean McGilvary?'

'Till half two, maybe three o'clock, tops. After that . . . ?'

'I was at the hotel, trying to wake him up: about ten to eight?'

'So nearly five hours unaccounted for.'

The radiator gurgled like an upset stomach.

A muffled conversation moved past in the corridor outside.

But in here, they just frowned at each other.

Angus leaned forward. 'We're not seriously—'

'I mean, *how* would he move the bodies?'

'Yeah, but maybe that's why the Fortnight Killer has disciples? "We are legion", according to Kate Paisley.'

'Yes, but . . .' Monroe looked up at all the notes covering the three whiteboards. 'I mean, he *can't* be.'

'No. Can't be.'

'It's just . . .' A grimace. 'If there's one thing I've learned in all my years as a police officer, Angus, it's: never trust a clever bastard, they're always up to something.'

'Yes, Boss.'

'And if it turns out he's dodgy, the press will tear us apart.' Monroe tapped a finger against the tabletop, eyes focused on somewhere just outside the room. Then nodded and got to his feet. 'Till we know he's telling the truth about the whole growing-up-in-a-cult thing, stick to him like seagull shite on a suede jacket.'

'Boss.'

'Well?' Monroe stood there, brow furrowed, staring at Angus. 'What are you waiting for? Shift.'

'Yes, Boss.' Angus grabbed his newspapered shoes and his furniture-polished jacket, and made himself scarce.

Wind whipped down Jessop Street, as if it hated the very setts beneath Angus's feet – howling rain into his face as he lumbered towards the Bishop's View Hotel in another borrowed XXL high-vis.

The downpour battered against the cathedral opposite, gurgling in the rones and downpipes, rivering its way along the gutters – making white-water rafts of empty Coke tins. Sparkling as it slashed through the streetlights' glow to bounce off the pavements and cars and hungover detective constables.

Angus hurried up the stairs and into the shelter of reception. Shaking himself like Wee Hamish after a soggy walk, sending droplets spattering onto the welcome mat and tartan carpet beyond.

The TV was playing to a completely empty dining room again as he hurried past and up the stairs:

'. . . significant damage to power lines over the last twenty-four hours, and it looks as if that trend's going to continue till Storm Findlay finally moves out into the North Sea tomorrow . . .'

Taking the steps two at a time, all the way up to the third floor.

Striding across the landing to the Isbister suite, pulling out his duplicate key on the way.

Slipping it into the lock as he knocked, then counted to ten. Nine. Eight. Seven. Six. Five. Four. Three. Two. One.

Angus turned the key and stepped inside. After all, no one else ever waited to be asked, did they.

With the curtains closed, the living room lurked in treacle-thick gloom, but what little light seeped in from the hall made it look as if an O Division search team had been through it. Discarded socks lay in the middle of the carpet, along with one platform cowboy boot. The other had been abandoned on top of the couch. A pair of trousers slumped over the back of an armchair, a shirt and leather jacket draped across the coffee table's swanky books and magazines. But it wasn't just clothes – three open wine bottles sat on the mantelpiece, next to a row of dirty glasses.

Pfff . . .

Looked as if Dr Fife had celebrated falling off the wagon after thirty years by going on a *serious* bender.

'Hello?'

Angus threw open the curtains, letting in a thin smear of early-morning light – painting last night's detritus in shades of depressing grey. *Technically* the sun had been up for an hour, but it was almost impossible to tell.

Oldcastle: got to love it.

He stripped off his high-vis, folding it so the dry side faced outwards before dumping it on the couch.

'Hello?'

Still nothing.

Angus was halfway across the lounge when the bedroom door opened. Good. At least he wouldn't have to drag Dr Fife from his bed this . . .

Shite.

He juddered to a halt and stood there. Mouth full of cottonwool, stomach full of magpies, veins full of battery acid.

'Morning, Angus.' Gillian yawned her way across to the kitchenette door, dressed in nothing but a man's shirt – Dr Fife's going by the length of the sleeves. It was long enough in the body to cover anything explicit, but stopped halfway down her forearms, showing off a forest of scar tissue. 'Can't *believe* I missed the morning broadcasts.' Without all that make-up, she was like a different person. Someone younger and a lot less . . . well, *pretty*. Which was maybe a bit sexist, but it was true.

She paused in the doorway for a yawn and a scratch.

Dr Fife was just visible through the open bedroom door – a silhouette, sitting on the edge of the mattress, head in his hands.

Scratch over, Gillian slouched into the kitchenette. 'I'm making coffee: you want some?'

Angus *stared* as the sound of cupboards opening and closing clacked and thumped out of the little cooking area. Jaw clenched so tightly his teeth squeaked.

Bastard.

Utter, bloody, complete *bastard*.

He stormed across the lounge and barged through the bedroom door.

The blackout curtains were doing their job, but a bedside light cast its soft golden gaze across one side of the crumpled duvet and the room's occupant. All very serene and romantic.

Angus clicked on the overhead lights, making Dr Fife's scarridden skin glow milk-bottle white.

He flinched away from the sudden brightness, one hand coming up to shield bloodshot, blackened eyes as he wobbled away on the edge of the bed. Wearing nothing more than a pair of boxer shorts and that stupid shield-knot necklace of his. 'Jesus!'

And yes, his body looked like a road atlas of pain, and he'd suffered a horrible abusive childhood, but tough shit, because he had this coming.

Angus hauled in a great-big breath and bellowed it into Dr Fife's face. 'WHAT THE *BLOODY HELL* IS WRONG WITH YOU?'

He winced, both hands over his ears. 'Sonofabitch . . . Can we not—'

'No!' Angus dropped into a hard whisper, every syllable sharp as an axe. 'You *knew* I liked her!'

Dr Fife grabbed the duvet and hauled it over his half-naked body. 'Get the hell out of my bedroom!'

'Here's me sticking up for you and all the time you're sticking . . . *it* in Gillian!'

He scrambled off the bed, squaring up to Angus, chin out, glaring, those battered eyes ripened into terrible fruit. 'That's enough!'

'All my life, I've had to play by the rules – work hard, do the right thing – and in you waltz like a fucking wrecking ball who can't keep it in his pants!'

Dr Fife raised a fist, as if that could do anything. 'I'm *warning* you.'

'You're a selfish *wanker*!' Angus loomed, teeth bared. 'Well? What have you got to say for yourself, you two-faced, immoral—'

The fist snapped forward, right into Angus's groin.

Fire *ripped* through his body, exploding out from the impact point like a nuclear detonation – buckling his knees, jab-stabbing through his stomach, stealing all the breath from his lungs as he clutched his aching balls and sank to the floor.

Fuck . . .

Ow . . .

Bloody . . .

Turned out, that fist was a *lot* more dangerous than it looked.

Dr Fife sniffed. 'What have I got to say for myself?' Flexing his treasonous hand. 'NYPD don't call me "The Vasectomist" for nothing.'

39

Angus perched sideways on the chaise longue, tilted over to one side so he could cup his throbbing testicles.

Dr Fife pulled a baggy, grey, long-sleeved T-shirt on over his scarred torso. A stylized skull-and-crossbones grinned out from the fabric as he scowled and muttered away. '. . . barging in here like an asshole, shouting the odds . . .' He jabbed a finger in Angus's direction. 'You pleased with yourself?'

Did he sodding look pleased?

Angus glowered back.

'Well, what did you *expect*?' Dr Fife hauled his trousers on. 'And for your information, not that it's any of your goddamned business, nothing happened. OK?'

'You punched me in the nuts!'

'Yeah, and you *deserved* it. She's a human being, not your property.'

. . .

Urgh.

He had a point.

That's what wounded pride and knackered bollocks got you.

Angus shrugged one shoulder, turned his head away, and huffed out a barely audible 'Sorry.'

Dr Fife produced a clean pair of socks from the wardrobe. 'Angus, I'm getting as far away from this horrible city as I can, before the Brethren come looking for me, but . . .' He paused, one sock on, one sock off. 'But it would be nice to know I'd made at least one friend before I go.' A sigh. 'Don't have a lot of those.'

The sound of a sad spiritual lilted in from the kitchenette, muffled by the bedroom door. Gillian had a good voice: almost haunting as she sang of the dark woods calling, and the dark things lurking there.

Dr Fife pulled on his other sock, then stood still as a gravestone, listening to her sing.

Angus let loose a big, long breath, then winced himself upright. Towering over Dr Fife, who frowned up at him. Probably wondering if this was going to devolve into another punch-in-the-balls scenario. Angus stuck his hand out.

There was a pause.

Then Dr Fife shook it.

Which meant they had *officially* reached an accord.

Truce.

Friends.

Though neither of them said anything about it. Because, you know, they were *men* and that's not the kind of thing men did.

Dr Fife cleared his throat. 'Wonder what's happened with that coffee?'

Rain attacked the living-room window, streetlights shuddering as the storm ravaged the city.

Clearly, Gillian hadn't just been busy in the kitchenette, because all the scattered clothes now sat in a neat pile on the couch, all folded and tidy. She'd cleared the bottles and empty glasses away too. Even the cushions looked plumped.

Her voice wafted out through the open kitchenette door as she bustled about with extra-large mugs and the machine:

'In darkness lead me, O my Lord,
My spirit cries to see the stars,
But in the deep woods, I did stray,
I need your light to be my sword,
In darkness lead me . . .'

Gillian turned, mouth clicking shut as she saw them both standing there, watching her. Pink exploded across her pale cheeks.

'Sorry.' She looked down at the mugs in her hands. Pulling her shoulders in, making herself smaller. 'I didn't mean to . . .'

Dr Fife smiled. 'It's OK. You've got a beautiful voice.'

She bit her bottom lip, then forced a painful smile. 'Coffee! Yes. Everyone loves coffee . . .' She crept into the room and handed one mug to him and the other to Angus. 'I hope it's OK, I've never used a machine like that before, but don't drink it if it's horrible, it's probably horrible. Sorry.' She reached out to take Dr Fife's mug back. 'I should just throw it away, better give it back and I'll try harder, and—'

'I'm sure it'll be lovely.'

'Thanks.' Angus raised his mug. 'You not having any?'

She stared at him. 'The *men* are *always* served first.' Then averted her eyes again. 'Sorry.'

OK, that was . . . weird.

Dr Fife reached out and stroked her arm, voice calm and soft. 'Hey, hey: don't worry. I know there was a bit of shouting, but it's nothing: a misunderstanding. We're all friends again. Right, Angus?'

And the weird kept on coming.

But he played along, anyway. 'Definitely.' Then took a sip of his freshly made fancy-coffee-machine frothy-cappuccino thing, with a sprinkling of chocolate on top and what smelled like caramel syrup. Very professional-looking, and it tasted absolutely . . .

Bloody hell.

He blinked as the bitter sourness gave way to sickly sugar, then back to bitter again. It took some doing, but he managed to force it down – doing his best not to shudder. 'Wow . . .'

Her whole face lit up. 'Really? You're not just saying that?'

How could anyone screw *that* up? You put the pod in the machine and you pressed the button. It wasn't rocket science. You didn't have to swim to Colombia and roast the beans yourself.

Dr Fife took a big swig. Froze. Raised both eyebrows as he swallowed. Then forced a smile. 'That's gotta be the *best* damn coffee I've had since I got here.'

Gillian gave a couple of little happy hops, clapping her fingertips together, then headed back into the kitchenette for her own mug.

Soon as she was gone, Dr Fife grimaced, mouth wide, tongue curling forwards, like a cat about to bring up a hairball. 'Jesus . . .'

Yup.

Angus wandered over to the window. 'So where do you want to start today? Could try the other victims' houses?'

'You're kidding, right? Soon as I'm packed, I'm on the first flight outta here. When the Brethren see that thing in the paper, they'll come running and I ain't hanging around. Sayonara, Oldcastle – konnichiwa, LA.'

'Ah . . . There might be a *tiny* problem with that. Oldcastle International Airport's cancelled all flights, because of Storm Findlay.'

'Brilliant. Just . . .' He took another swig of 'coffee', curled his head to one side and winced. 'Then I'll drive to Edinburgh.'

'Planes are grounded all over Scotland. You *could* get a train down south – try Heathrow, or Luton – but the trains aren't running either. You've got landslips, flooding, trees down on the line . . .'

'Then I'll *drive* to Heathrow.'

'Only everyone who can't get a flight out of Scotland's doing the same, so everything's overbooked.'

Dr Fife covered his face with his free hand and made a little strangled screaming noise.

Which was all the cover Angus needed to ditch his *horrible* coffee in the big pot plant by the window. He forced a bit of cheer into his voice and stood up straight – shoulders back, chest out, filling the space like a bulldozer in a damp suit. 'Come on, it's not that bad! You think these "Brethren" are going to try anything with *me* standing there? Course they won't.' He checked his watch. 'And it's only twenty-four hours; be back to normal tomorrow.'

'Urgh . . .' Dr Fife drooped. Took another mouthful of coffee. Cringed and stuck his tongue out again. 'Twenty-four hours.' Not sure if it was hunger, or a reaction to Gillian's foul coffee, but his stomach let loose a cluster of wheezy popping sounds, then a low growl.

'One more day.' Angus smiled. 'What's the worst that can happen, right?' That got him a scowl. 'It'll be great: we'll catch the Fortnight Killer, big party, and tomorrow you're off back to the

States with the happy thanks of Oldcastle's citizens ringing in your ears.'

Another shuddering mouthful. 'I *hate* this stupid city.'

The whirrs and clunks of the fancy coffee machine ground their way out of the kitchenette as Gillian committed another hate crime against hot beverages.

Time to change the subject, before Dr Fife decided to abandon the city and lay low somewhere less murdery.

Angus nodded towards the kitchenette. 'Any idea what *that* was about?'

'"The men are always served first"? Yeah.' He watched her through the open door. 'Remember what I said about Venn diagrams, cults, and conspiracy theories? Turns out you and me ain't the only ones carrying round a sackful of childhood trauma.'

Because everyone was broken in their own way.

Some just hid it better than others.

OK, this wasn't helping.

Angus had another go: 'So . . . Councillor Mendel's, or the Healey-Robinsons'? Or we could try another one of Kate Paisley's homers?' Doubt it would turn up much they hadn't already found out from their visit to Mrs Baldwin-Cooper's secret library, but it *had* to be better than Option Number Three: 'Or there's the PM on Dr Fordyce, *and* the one on Councillor Mendel.'

After all, who *didn't* love watching Professor Twining postmortem partially decomposed corpses? And the sights and smells would really complement a monster hangover.

'Hmmm . . .' Dr Fife frowned out through the lounge window as Storm Findlay hammered rain into the cathedral's stained glass. 'There's no point doing a geographical analysis – victims are targeted all over the place, so he doesn't adhere to boundary conditions. Victimology has *kinda* limited value here, cos he's not targeting a single type, he's targeting multiples.' Another round of popping and gurgling grumbled out from Dr Fife's stomach and he rubbed at it, not taking his eyes off the jagged granite wedding cake opposite.

'Thought you said he was going after a police officer next?'

'Yeah, but *motivationally* speaking it should be someone on

Operation Telegram. We know he likes targeting people in power, so you're looking at . . . detective sergeant and above? Probably detective inspector.'

'So that means: DCI Monroe; DIs Tudor and Cohen; or DSs Massie, Kilgour, and Sharp.'

'But from a *practical* point of view, you don't wanna go near *them* with a stick. Too dangerous – they're on their guard, right? More chance of getting caught. What you want is a victim who ain't on the case, so they're . . .' This time the pop and gurgle was drowned out by full-on intestinal whale song, forcing Dr Fife to curl up till it passed – teeth bared, eyes clenched shut. Finally, he straightened up, free hand pressed against his belly, mouth open until a belch rattled loose. Wincing, he smacked his lips a couple of times, then swigged down more coffee. Squirmed. 'Damn stuff's like Clorox mixed with burnt shit.' He grimaced into his mug. 'What I remember from my drinking days is: best thing for a hangover? Get yourself a whole heap of greasy carbs and processed meat. Think we should continue this discussion over one of your healthy Scottish breakfasts.' Dr Fife knocked back the last gulp of vile coffee, shuddering as he dropped his voice to a whisper. 'Before she makes any more of that fuck-flavoured ass-water.'

The smell of hot fat and deep-fried things permeated the Walie Nieve. Being just around the corner from the Shoogly Peg, it enjoyed the same microclimate, meaning Gillian was safe to pace about outside – just visible through the café's fogged-up windows – arguing with someone on her phone while she vaped. Behind her, the castle's granite blade towered above the sandstone buildings, fading away into the misty drizzle.

In here, it was all painted white, with scuffed, dark-red lino on the floor; little two-seater tables featured dented legs and scratched tops; and blue plastic chairs. The wooden counter boasted a till and a heated display case full of pies.

A handful of couples and a pair of lone breakfasters occupied most of the small café, working their way through full fry-ups and assorted butties; triangular wedges of toast lined up in wire racks like small crunchy stegosauruses . . .

Crappy hold music burbled out of Angus's phone as he reached across the table and liberated a spare mushroom from Dr Fife's plate. Well, he'd finished anyway: bolting off to the toilet as the whales sang their ominous tune, leaving behind a sausage, two rashers of bacon, half a disk of black pudding, a hash brown, most of a fried egg, a lump of clootie dumpling, and at least half a dozen mushrooms.

Gillian had given up on her breakfast too, abandoning a small ham-cheese-and-mushroom omelette for the 'breath of fresh air' she was currently enjoying.

They'd pushed two little tables together, now littered with plates and cutlery and mugs. With nobody to tidy up the debris but Angus.

Another mushroom disappeared.

Munch, munch, munch.

He'd wiped his plate clean with the last slice of toast – leaving not so much as a smear of bean juice behind – then plonked the thing on the counter, freeing up space for the list of Kate Paisley's homers. With a big red 'X' through Mrs Baldwin-Cooper's swanky home in Auchterowan.

OK, so there was no guarantee that Ryan had worked on every one of these, but if they found a *couple* more, that would be something, wouldn't it? They'd got a passable eFit out of Mrs Baldwin-Cooper; maybe Dr Fife was right and someone out there knew who Ryan was?

Question was: which address to hit next? Because—

His phone ding-buzzed in his hand, interrupting the Stylo-phone rendition of 'Greensleeves'.

ELLIE:
> Time to call in that favour: do Malachi McNabb's med-
> ical records show he had achondroplasia or not?
> And before you complain: you OWE me, remember?

Well, well, well. 'Achondroplasia'. Look who got all politically correct.

Angus poked out a reply:

> Team looking into medical history.
> Will advise on result if authorised.

He frowned at the cursor.

Never mind DS Sharp's medical search, should he tell Ellie the *important* news of the day or not?

She'd hardly been supportive of the whole thing.

Downright horrible, to be honest.

Yeah, but she *had* given him a lift last night.

And if you couldn't tell your best friend, who *could* you tell?

> Gillian chose him instead of

Monroe's tiny tinny voice scrawked out of the phone's speaker, freezing Angus's thumbs. *'Angus? You still there?'*

He deleted that last, unfinished line and hit 'SEND'. Then stuck the phone to his ear. 'Still here, Boss.'

'And Dr Fife's sure? About it being one of the senior officers next?'

'Kind of. Unless Ryan's playing it safe, in which case it'll be someone who isn't on the case.'

Monroe grunted. *'Well, if it's only DS and up, at least that means most of the team's safe. And we've got another thirteen days before he tries anything.'*

'Yeah . . . except it might be sooner, cos he knows we're closing in.'

You could almost hear Monroe's face puckering at that. *'I'm thinking of renaming you "Constable Pain In The Hoop".'*

'Sorry, Boss.'

'Positive thinking, Angus! We're in a better position than we've been since this whole thing kicked off.' There was a pause. *'Speaking of which, what's Dr Fife's plan?'*

'We're going to hit the rest of Kate Paisley's homers. See if we can't dig up something else on Ryan. They're good at covering their tracks *now*, but Dr Fife thinks it might've taken them a while to work out the kinks. Could be clues at the earlier jobs.'

DS Massie's voice muffled out in the background. *'Boss?'*

'Hold on, Angus.' Monroe must have turned away from the phone, because he got a lot quieter. *'If it's bad news, I don't want to hear.'*

'*Your missus on the phone: says it's urgent. Something about a knack-ered boiler and flooded kitchen? She sounds really upset.*'

'*They only just got that fitted! Oh, for . . .*' Monroe groaned like a rusty crypt door. Then he was back at full volume again: '*Keep me informed. If you find something,* anything, *I want to know, ASAP.*'

'Boss.'

And he was off.

Angus slipped the phone back into his pocket and rescued the last of Dr Fife's mushrooms.

'*I don't think there's anything left.*'

Oops.

Angus wiped his fingertips on a napkin as Dr Fife slump-scuffed out from the door marked 'TOILETS ARE FOR CUSTOMERS ONLY'.

He lurched back to the table. With his sunglasses hooked into the neck of his skull-and-crossbones top, the full horror of his post-vomit face was on show: pale skin, dark bags under his bloodshot blackeyes, a smear of dark-blue stubble on sallow cheeks . . .

'Sorry.' Angus pointed at the breakfast he'd just been pilfering, as the embarrassment of getting caught whooshed up his neck. 'Thought you'd finished.'

'Liver, spleen, kidneys, colon, stomach . . . All of it.' Dr Fife collapsed into his seat. 'Never been so sick in my *life*.'

Ahhh . . . So *that's* what he'd meant by 'nothing left'.

Dr Fife grimaced at the remains of his breakfast, then pushed it away towards Angus with a grunt.

Cool.

A sausage joined the ranks of the saved, anointed with a quick dip in red sauce. Munchity crunchity. 'Feeling better?'

The sunglasses were unhooked and slipped into place, hiding the bruising. 'Scratch that – there was this one time in Honduras, back when I was twenty-one. Jesus . . . Thought I was gonna *die*!'

'They're getting a load of calls about that eFit. Sounds like mostly time-wasters, though.' Angus popped over to the counter, where a well-thumbed copy of that morning's *Castle News & Post* lay on a pile of equally scuffed tabloids, with 'FOR CAFE PATRONS ONLY: DO NOT STEAL!!!' printed across the top in wonky Sharpie letters.

Dr Fife rubbed at his stomach. 'Think it was the haggis that did it. Blood sausage is bad enough, but haggis and . . . what was the fried grey stuff?'

'Clootie dumpling.'

'Gah . . .' Another shudder.

Angus held the paper out, finger pointing at the sidebar on the front page, where Mrs Baldwin-Cooper's eFit of Ryan had been squeezed in along with 'POLICE APPEAL FOR INFORMATION → SEE PAGE 4'. Of course, the main image was a photo of Dr Fife's face – a telephoto shot, with a patrol car and what might've been the Lundys' house in the background, beneath the headline 'FBI SPECIALIST HELPS HAPLESS COPS'.

Dr Fife took a swig of café coffee and swirled it around. Giving it a good squoosh between his teeth, before looking around, cheeks bulging. He grabbed Gillian's empty mug and spooted the gritty mouthful into it. Then held out a hand. 'Give.'

'You sure you want to—'

The fingers snap-snap-snapped.

Fair enough. Angus handed it over and Dr Fife glowered at his own face:

'"FBI serial-killer specialist, Dr Jonathan Fife" – brackets – "fifty-four . . ."' A sniff. 'Bastards. ". . . flew over from California three days ago to help struggling Oldcastle Police catch Satan's Messenger. The four-foot-five forensic psychologist . . ."' He slapped the paper with the back of his hand. 'How did these *fuckers* know what height I am? I'm wearing three-inch lifts, for Christ's sake! What was the point of that?' Slapping the newsprint again. '". . . born with dwarfism, but that hasn't stopped him working with US law enforcement to . . ." blah, blah, bullshit, bullshit, bull . . .'

A gurgling growl sounded, deep within his body, and Dr Fife's eyes went wide, his face pale and shiny as spoiled milk. 'Nope.'

He scrambled out of his seat and sprinted for the toilet again – one hand clamped over his mouth – narrowly beating a woman in a Winslow's Supermarket tabard with a copy of *Hey You!* magazine tucked under one arm.

The door slammed shut and the lock clicked.

Tabard Woman threw her arms up in frustration, dropped her magazine, picked it up again with a big, hammy, did-you-see-that?

sigh. Then took up position by the door, checking her watch and tutting every thirty seconds.

Angus retrieved the *Castle News & Post*, chewing on a cold rasher of bacon as he skimmed the front page, then flicked through to the centre spread, where Micky Slosser's 'exclusive' continued. Eyes widening as he took in the horror.

Oh, that wasn't good.

That wasn't good *at all*.

40

They'd given over a whole quarter-page to the photo Ellie had shown them last night in the pub: Dr Fife smiling away, holding a hotdog and a beer, unaware he was a supporting feature in his wee girl's selfie.

'CATCHING KILLERS TAKES TERRIBLE TOLL ON FAMILY LIFE' according to the headline.

The article was Slosser the Tosser's usual overblown mix of melodrama, gossip, and run-on sentences, but three bits stood out:

> . . . long hours on the road with the FBI, hunting killers like the Seattle Strangler and the Nashville Ripper, led to the breakdown of his first marriage, to aspiring country-and-western singer Molly-Jane Tate (41), now a dental hygienist in the sleepy town of Halfway, Oregon . . .

And:

> . . . trauma during the arrest of Theodore Washington, AKA the "Detroit Cannibal", meant Jonathan spent a gruelling six-month stay in the Ancora Psychiatric Hospital, New Jersey . . .

And best of all:

> . . . a world away from the idyllic life of his daughter, Megan (6), who attends Milton Academy, a private school, just around the corner from her mother's lavish Park Row apartment . . .

Oh yeah. Dr Fife was *not* going to like that one bit.

They might as well have printed a map to his daughter's school and ex-wives' homes.

Just have to hope the *Castle News & Post* wasn't popular with US cartel bosses, mob enforcers, and serial killers.

God, it would be *online* as well though, wouldn't it. Available all over the world to anyone who felt like googling Dr Fife's name.

Slosser the *bloody* Tosser.

Angus removed the whole centre-page spread, folding it up and sticking it in his pocket. No matter what the Sharpie warning said.

The Walie Nieve's door chimed, and in scuffed Gillian – cleaning her boots on the mat. She'd put on the full smoky-eyed make-up before leaving the hotel, transforming herself from a timorous, plain-Jane girl-next-door into a glamorous siren again.

Weird the way women could do that. Artfully apply a bit of colour, a squirt of hairspray, and suddenly they were a completely different person.

She smiled at him, and something in Angus's chest lurched.

Still, too late to worry about that now.

Too late for a lot of things.

Gillian gazed off towards the toilets and its impatient, one-woman queue. 'How is he?'

'Says it was the haggis.'

'It's a challenging breakfast item if you're not used to spicy sheep's lungs.'

True. 'And *nothing* to do with the bathtub-full of Stella and bourbon he put away last night.'

She pulled out her chair and sat. Fidgeted with her cutlery. Glanced at the newspaper, then did the same with the list of Kate Paisley's homers – though both were upside down from her point of view.

Anything to avoid making eye contact, eh?

Angus cleared his throat. 'Gillian, about that balding hairy bloke you—'

'I wanted to explain. To you. While he's not here.' Breath. 'About last night.'

'You don't have to.'

'No, it's . . .' She tore little strips from her napkin. Shifted in her seat. 'My mum and dad joined a commune on North Uist when I was three. I grew up there. You know those Christian sects that believe in tolerance and forgiveness and love and healing?'

He nodded.

Gillian slipped her leather jacket off and pulled up one sleeve of her top, showing off that network of scar tissue. 'The Apostles of the Shining Water weren't that kind of sect.'

So, it wasn't self-harm. It was child abuse.

'I'm sorry.'

'I *hated* it. The rules. The prayers. The . . . The beatings.' A sour laugh and she lowered her sleeve. 'Dad loved every minute, though. Said it wasn't enough to batter the sin out of *ourselves*, we had to confront the Great Sinful Outside and cleanse *their* sins too. On my ninth birthday the Elders caught him making pipe bombs out of fertilizer and rusty nails for a trip to Kyle of Lochalsh.' Gillian stared down at the tattered napkin. 'He wouldn't recant; said we were all too soft and full of sin – even though they beat him and *beat* him and *beat* him . . .' A tear welled over the edge of her bottom lid, dripping onto the back of her hand. 'That night, I saw them load Dad onto the Apostles' rusty old fishing boat. And that was that.'

Shit.

'Did they . . . ?'

She wiped at her eyes. 'Think so.'

'Jesus. And you were *nine*?'

Gillian reached for her coffee mug, but Angus plucked it from her fingers. You know, what with it being the mug Dr Fife rinsed his vomity mouth into.

'Probably best not. It's . . . cold. We'll get some fresh.'

'Yes. Of course.' She looked up for the first time since sitting down, gazing at him with glittering, pink-rimmed eyes. 'That's why I . . . You see, Jonathan: he's . . . like *me*. He knows what growing up with all that' – Gillian made a crackly gesture with both hands – '*craziness* is like. I'm sorry.'

Angus sat back in his seat.

What a bloody awful childhood. No wonder she'd grown into a

strange wee person: with her scars, and her inferiority complex, and her conspiracy theories. Doing her best to make sense of a world that must be a million miles from the violent, religious *hell-hole* she grew up in.

He reached across the table and patted her hand. 'It's OK. Honestly.'

A small smile made more tears break free and she wiped them away. 'Plus, my therapist says I have *serious* daddy issues, so: you know.'

He passed her another napkin. 'Did anyone tell the police – about the Apostles . . . ?'

'Dumping Dad's body in the Minch?' She blew her nose on the napkin, all wet and snottery. 'Who'd care? We're just "religious nutters", right?'

And speaking of nutters:

The loo door swung open and out slumped Dr Fife, pale and sweaty, shambling towards the table like a partially reanimated corpse.

Tabard Woman threw him a sharp 'About time!' then hurried inside to spend some quality time with her magazine. Locking the door behind her.

Gillian stood. 'Jonathan? Are you all right?'

'Feeling much better now, thanks.' Patting his stomach as he leaned on the tabletop as if it were the only thing keeping him upright. 'Yeah . . . constitution like a concrete buffalo.'

'Maybe you should go back to the hotel? Lie down for a bit.'

'I'm fine, I'm fine.' Sweat beaded across his top lip and forehead. 'Got a killer to catch.' He dug out his wallet, but it slipped from his fingers as he tried to open it – hitting the table next to his plate, setting the cutlery rattling. Dr Fife blinked at it. Swallowed hard. 'Any chance you could sort the check out, Angus? I'm gonna get some fresh air.' He walked to the café door on stiff legs, struggled the door open, then tottered out into the misty drizzle. Soon as he was six feet from the door, he grabbed the nearest lamppost – propping himself upright and looking as if he was either about to collapse or puke himself inside out.

Yeah . . .

Gillian scrunched up her snotty napkin and dumped it in the vomity coffee. 'You *will* look after him, won't you?'

'Course I will.' Angus waved for the bill. 'We're only going to visit a few places today, nothing strenuous.' Tucking the list back into his jacket pocket.

She frowned out through the window at the rounded figure. 'Thanks, Angus, you're a good friend.'

And, sadly, nothing more.

Dr Fife slouched back against the Mini's bonnet, face in his hands. 'Have you not finished *yet*?'

The car park round the back of the Bishop's View Hotel was a dark hole of a place, hemmed in by the buildings on either side – three storeys of rain-darkened grey with mean-spirited windows glaring down on the rectangle of potholed tarmac. The far end wasn't much better – a red-brick cliff face, pockmarked with mullioned glass and an archway out onto Wheelwright Road.

Angus shifted his grip on the spanner, undoing a locking nut that held Dr Fife's pedal extension in place – freeing it from the accelerator. Then went back in again for the one fixed to the brake.

You'd think it would be sheltered in here, with buildings on all four sides, but the wind swirled around the car park, spinning leaves and empty takeaway containers into a scabby semi-cyclone. But at least it'd stopped raining before the puddles had joined together into a full-blown loch.

'Ha!' One last twist and the metal contraption came free. He clanked it onto the driver's seat, along with its companion, and stood. 'Finished.'

Dr Fife didn't show his face, just groaned and drooped even further.

Angus carried the pedal extenders round to the boot. 'What was it you said about people not being able to "hold their liquor"?'

No reply.

He wedged them in under the box of custom SOC suits, so they wouldn't rattle around back there. 'Where do you want to go first? Start with the oldest and work forward, or with the newest and go back? Or with the nearest, and sort of spiral out?'

'I can hold my liquor just fine.'

Yeah, you just keep telling yourself that.

Angus closed the boot, then opened the passenger door and held it, till Dr Fife scuffed over and collapsed inside with a whimper.

'Oh yeah.' Smiling as he closed the door. '*Now* who's the lightweight?'

Angus stripped off his high-vis, then squeezed himself in behind the wheel. Fiddled with the seat till there was room to breathe and he wasn't sardined against the controls any more. Dumped his borrowed jacket on the back seat.

Dr Fife scowled across the car. 'Can we get on with it, please?'

'Hold on.' He dug into his pocket and held out a fistful of carrier bags. 'In case you're caught short. With the vomiting.' Cheery smile. 'Don't want you losing your deposit on the nice clean hire car.'

He started the engine, shifted the lever to 'R', and eased backwards out of their spot as the drizzle started up again. Speckling the windscreen.

The Mini jerked to a hard stop, lurching them both back into their seats.

A wee cry burst free, and Dr Fife grabbed the dashboard. 'Are you *trying* to make me hurl?'

'Sorry. Not used to driving an automatic.' He shoved the lever forward to 'D' and crept the Mini out past rows of expensive motor cars, making for the exit. 'So oldest to newest, or—'

The car slammed to a sudden halt again, throwing them forwards into their seatbelts as they emerged through the narrow archway, ready to join the road.

'Aaaargh!'

'Sorry. Keep thinking I'm pressing the clutch.'

Dr Fife scrunched his face up, eyes closed, teeth bared. 'Oldest, newest, I don't care. Just stop driving like a *dick*!'

'Oldest it is, then.' He pulled onto Wheelwright Road, with its expensive shops and twee tearooms, and the car lurched to another abrupt stop. Angus *definitely* wasn't smiling. Not even a little bit. Honest. 'Sorry.'

And they were off again, before Dr Fife could start swearing or crying.

Or possibly both . . .

Mrs Jessica Woodry: 32 Guillemot Crescent – 09:00

It was a bland beige-and-magnolia semi in a row of bland beige-and-magnolia semis in a bland beige-and-magnolia housing estate in Logansferry.

Mrs Woodry blew another cloud of cigarette smoke out the open lounge window, fiddling with the tie of her baggy hoody, a tabby cat rubbing against the hem of her bow-legged jeans. 'Yeah, well, it was cheaper than all the other cowboys quoted, and she did a good job.'

Outside, the sky was dark as a politician's heart – rain clattering down.

'Right.' Angus nodded, scribbling that into his notebook. 'And she rewired the whole place?'

'If she's not paid tax on it, that's nothing to do with me.'

'Uh-huh. And what about joinery: you get any woodwork done?'

Mrs Woodry sooked on her cigarette's filter, making the glowing tip *fizzzz*. 'Mind you, what's the point of *paying* tax? The buggers only spend it on giving their rich mates contracts and screwing us over!'

'Yes, but did you get any—'

'Don't need to. My Colin's father-in-law's a joiner.'

Fair enough.

Mr Albert Gartly: 144 York Street – 09:20

For some reason, Mr Gartly thought it was acceptable for a man in his late sixties to dye his hair boot-polish black. It was fooling no one. And neither were the bright-white trainers, turn-ups on his jeans, or My Chemical Romance T-shirt. His third-floor flat was all leather and chrome too, as if he'd hit a three-quarter-life crisis and set up as a 'groovy' bachelor.

He leaned against the kitchen's central island, overlooking the storm-tossed garden at the back of the building, flicking the switch on a big range cooker, off and on and off and on. 'You see, soon as I got it installed, it kept blowing the fuses every time I turned it on, and Kate was simply a marvel.' His eyes went all misty and wistful. 'I don't know *what* I would've done without her.'

Ms Imogen McCormack: 12 Miller Row – 09:40

'No woodwork at all?' Angus tried not to look as Ms McCormack bent all the way over to touch her toes in skintight Lycra running shorts.

It was a lovely big house in Castleview, part of a long Georgian terrace. Three storeys of sharp sandstone, overlooking a church where the funeral directors were busy carrying a coffin up the steps, ready for the performance to begin. Ignoring the lashing rain as if it were an earthly matter of no concern to them or their client.

Ms McCormack balanced on one leg, the other foot pulled up to her buttock. A bright-pink sweatband pinned down her bouncy brown curls, a towel draped over her shoulder as she limbered up. The elliptical trainer, in the corner of the living room, looked as if it'd never been used as a clothes horse in its life. 'Well, the Paisley woman said she had a mate who could refit the study, but the cost was *astronomical*. What's wrong with Ikea? That's what I want to know.'

'Yeah. Right.' As if Angus could even aspire to the giddy heights of a Billy bookcase.

His eyes drifted back to the window. The garden out back might be huge, but the one in front of the house was a more modest rectangle of grass, separated from the road by a wrought-iron fence. Dr Fife's Mini sat right outside it, with the man himself zonked out in the passenger seat. So no help there, then.

He frowned. 'Don't suppose this friend of hers gave you a written estimate?'

A snort. 'If they did, it went in the bin *months* ago. If there's one thing I can't stand it's clutter.' Which explained why, apart from the elliptical trainer and the yoga mat, the lounge was minimalist and immaculate. She stuck her elbows out, twisting her spine from one side to the other. 'Now is there anything else? Only I've got a Zoom meeting with the Italians at half ten and I really need to get my five miles in before then.'

Mrs Harriet Sneddon: The Elms, Dunross Street – 10:15

Angus grimaced out at the storm, zipped up his high-vis, then stepped out of the swish townhouse, just down the road from Moffat Park. Very nice. It even had an old oak tree out front – naked branches shuddering in the wind – with a Jaguar parked underneath it.

He turned and nodded at Mrs Sneddon. 'Thanks.'

She ran a hand through her grey hair, and smiled back. 'Are you *sure* you can't stay for tea?' All wrapped up in her chinos and bulky Icelandic jumper. 'I have chocolate cake?'

Which was *seriously* tempting.

Angus hunched his back against the weather. 'I'd love to, but I'm on duty.' And they had a killer on the loose. 'Thanks anyway. Sorry.'

She stayed at the open door, waving as he scarpered down the path.

He waved back, then scrambled in behind the Mini's wheel.

'Gah . . .' God, it was horrible out there.

It was horrible in here too – the cheesy-bitter stink of vomit-soured breath mingling with a sort of damp-dog fug.

Dr Fife was slumped in the passenger seat – reclined all the way back – mouth hanging open. Face pale and waxy, with a faint sheen of sweat. Snoring away.

Hard to imagine why any woman *wouldn't* find that devastatingly attractive.

Angus wiped the rain from his face and shook it into the

footwell. Then reached over and prodded him with a damp finger. 'You awake?'

'No . . .'

'How much did you drink when you got back to the hotel? I mean, I've seen hangovers before, but you belong in the record books. Or the mortuary.'

'Funny. Hilarious.' Dr Fife winced his way up, bringing the seatback with him. 'Just ain't used to it like I once was. Outta practice.' He squinted out through the shimmering windscreen. 'Anything?'

'Nah. So far everyone's had electrical work done and sod-all joinery.' Seatbelt. Engine. But Angus didn't drive off, he sat there, frowning across the car at the forensic psychologist's trembling corpse. 'You want to get some coffee or something? Maybe yoghurt? Put a bit of lining on your stomach? Or are you more a hair-of-the-dog person?'

That got him a grimace. 'If I die, don't let the bastards bury me here. I hate—'

' "This city". Yeah, you mentioned that.'

'And I'm not some sort of alcoholic, OK? Yeah, I was the kinda guy who liked to party, but soon as I stopped, I *stopped*. No cravings, no DTs, no nothing.' He wiped a hand across his sweaty face. 'Never been to a goddamned "meeting" in my life.'

'OK . . .' Angus pulled away from the kerb, pausing only for a farewell wave to Mrs Sneddon, who still stood in her open door.

A lonely old widow, with no kids and a bunch of dead friends.

What was the point of a swish house and chocolate cake if you had no one to share them with?

Christ, that was a cheery thought . . .

Shite. Buggery. Crap. Shite. Shite.

Angus high-stepped around the puddles, one hand holding his fold-out hood from flipping back, the other clutching the paper bag to his chest as he hurried across the parking area, making for the Mini.

In summer, this was a favourite spot for families and romantic trysts – overlooking the downhill sweep of Montgomery Park, past the trees, the leisure centre, the boating lake, the swathes of emerald grass . . . But *today* the whole area was drained of colour, and there wasn't much visible beyond the dark mass of Kings River: swallowed by undulating sheets of grey rain.

Not surprisingly, they hadn't exactly struggled to find a parking spot. The only other soul out here was a figure lumbering across the sodden grounds with a drookit spaniel and a misbehaving umbrella.

And good luck to them.

Angus leapt into the Mini, making the whole thing bounce as he landed in the driver's seat. 'It's getting *worse* out there.'

No response.

Because Dr Fife was sparked out again, lying flat in his reclined seat, snoring like a rusty bandsaw, with that greatcoat doing blanket duty. The kindest thing might be to pull it up over his face and call the pathologist.

But they still had work to do.

Angus poked him. 'Hoy, Rip Van Lightweight!'

He struggled to the surface, blackened eyes squinting in the cold grey light. ''M'wake. 'M'wake . . .' Then peered across the car. 'Oh, not *you* again . . .'

'That's what I get for doing you a favour?' Angus held out the paper bag. 'You want this or not?'

'Hmmph.' He thumped back onto his improvised bed. 'I *don't* need more sick bags.'

'Look inside.'

There was a suspicious pause, then Dr Fife dipped into the bag, coming out with a big carton of off-brand chocolate-flavoured yoghurt drink.

Angus nodded. 'And I bought that with my *own* money, so you're welcome.'

Dr Fife blinked at the container, then twisted off the lid and took a sip. Rocked his head from side to side a couple of times, then shrugged. 'Could be worse.'

It was *so* nice to be appreciated.

Angus unzipped his high-vis and gave it a shoogle, making his own private cloudburst in the footwell. 'You can score Steven McFall off the list as well. Didn't get any joinery done: new bathroom suite and set of smoke alarms. But it wasn't Ryan who did the plumbing and tiling, Kate Paisley brought a woman along for that bit.'

Dr Fife knocked back a much bigger swig. 'Another disciple?'

'Who knows? It was that long ago, Mr McFall can't remember her name or what she looked like; didn't ask questions; paid in cash.'

'I see . . .' Frowning out through the window at the storm-whipped park, drinking chocolate yoghurt, and rubbing his stomach. Then: 'How many we got left?'

'Half a dozen. Two more in Blackwall Hill, one in the Wynd, one in Castleview, one in Shortstaine, and number six is a fancy-sounding place just north of the city.'

'You know what I think? I think . . .' He lowered the carton as some sort of uptown funk rattled out from an inside pocket. He fumbled it out, one-handed, without looking, and held it as far away as his arm would reach. Flinching in the opposite direction. 'You . . . do it.'

Great.

Sidekick *and* secretary. Lucky him.

But Angus accepted it anyway and pressed the button. 'Dr Fife's phone. Can I help you?'

'*Angus?*' It was Gillian's voice, only higher and a bit strangled. '*Is everything OK? Did something happen to—*'

'He's fine. Just too lazy to answer his own phone.'

Dr Fife gave him the finger, but clearly his heart wasn't in it.

'*Thank God for that . . . I just wanted to make sure he was OK and you weren't . . . you know.*' A breath. '*Fighting.*'

Yeah . . .

Looking at the shrivelled, yoghurty lump in the passenger seat, chances were a stiff fart would've killed him. Never mind actual fighting.

Speaking of dead bodies:

Angus took a deep breath. 'Gillian, I think you should make a formal statement: about your dad. I mean, I can raise it with my boss, but it'd really help if we had names and dates and things.'

Silence.

'I know he was an abusive monster, and you deserved better, but if they really *did* kill him—'

'*So . . .*' Her voice positively *ached* with forced brightness. '*. . . how are you getting on with your list? Of places you're visiting?*'

'We've got a specialist unit dedicated to cold cases, and they've got a really good track record, so—'

'*Just, if you're in the neighbourhood we could maybe meet up for lunch? I could bring a picnic or something?*'

'Gillian—'

'*Well, I say "picnic"*' – the words getting faster and faster – '*I know it's not really the weather for a picnic, but sometimes that's fun, isn't it, in the car when it's raining, like you're a kid again, but you're warm and dry and safe, because nobody's trying to batter the sin out of you . . .*'

The only sound was the storm, clawing at the Mini's roof.

Dr Fife slugged away at his chocolate stomach-liner.

Angus sighed. 'Just think about it, OK?'

It was barely a whisper: '*Sorry. I can't . . .*' Then the forced cheeriness returned. '*Where are you?*'

'Drinking yoghurt in Montgomery Park. Even the ducks have gone home.'

The breath caught in her throat. '*I am sorry, Angus. For everything.*'

'Yeah.' His shoulders dipped. 'Me too.' Then he hung up, sat there staring down at the blank phone screen.

Dr Fife nudged him. 'Are you still moping about that?'

'What? No. Course not.' A half-shrug. 'None of my business.'

'Anyway, you've got Ellie.'

'I don't "have" anyone – we're friends, that's all.'

'Pfff . . . I've seen the way Ellie acts. The way she gets a bug up her ass every time Gillian talks to you.' He took a yoghurty swig. 'Sooner or later you'll both get shitfaced somewhere and try it on. And *yes*: it'll be clumsy and embarrassing, but maybe it'll go somewhere? *Maybe* you'll wind up with someone you love who loves you back.'

Chance would be a fine thing.

Angus forced a smile. 'You think?'

Dr Fife nodded, then toasted him with the carton. 'Maybe – in this wild, *crazy* adventure we call life – the real treasure is the friends we bang along the way.'

41

Mr Daniel Hilson: 72 Thurbury Drive – 11:45

Angus held on to his high-vis's hood, hurrying down the driveway, past a boxy old Volvo estate that had to be an antique. From here, high up on Blackwall Hill, there was little more than a handful of waterlogged fields between the row of nondescript bungalows and the lowering skies. No sweeping views across the city – everything had been swallowed by a maw of soggy grey.

He yanked open the Mini's door and hurled himself in behind the wheel.

Shuddered.

Dripped.

Sagged.

Dr Fife was fast asleep, yet again. Bone dry, wrapped up cosy in his greatcoat blanket, while Angus did all the running about in the horrible rain and the yuck.

Still, at least he didn't look like a greasy cadaver any more. In a dimly lit room, he might even pass for human.

Angus thumped him one. 'Are you going to actually do something today?'

'Arrgh! 'M'wake!' Fife wrestled his way upright. Blinking. 'Where . . . ?' Then a wince. 'Oh Christ . . . Not *this* again.' Dr Fife slumped back down, wiping the drool from his Vandyke. 'Anything?'

'Detective Constable Angus MacVicar saves the day.' Stretching the pause for effect. 'Mr Hilson got a built-in wardrobe made for his master bedroom by guess who?' Angus produced the eFit and gave it a shoogle. 'Ta-daaaa.'

Dr Fife sat up again. 'Ryan.'

'Only he didn't call himself "Ryan", he called himself "Jack MacKinnoch", and he left an actual invoice. Once again: ta-daaaa!' He held up the printout, but where the eFit was all creased from being folded and stuffed in a pocket over and over again, the invoice was safely ensconced in a clear-plastic document sleeve. 'There's even an address!'

Angus pulled out his phone and scrolled through the contacts to 'DCI MONROE'. Sitting there as it rang. And rang. And rang. And rang . . .

An electronic voice emanated from the handset: '*YOU HAVE REACHED THE TECHZEDMOBILE MESSAGING SERVICE FOR . . .*'

Then Monroe, awkward and stilted: '*Blair Monroe.*'

'*PLEASE LEAVE A MESSAGE AFTER THE TONE.*'

Bleeeeeeep.

'Boss? It's Angus. DC MacVicar? I think we've got an ID for Ryan. I'll try DS Massie. OK, bye.' He hung up and called her instead, putting a hand over the microphone as it rang. 'Wasn't answering his phone.'

A scowl. 'Thank you for this *important* update.'

'That yoghurt must be working if you've got the energy to be a sarcastic—'

'*What?*' DS Massie didn't exactly sound friendly. '*I'm busy.*'

'Sarge? Think I know Ryan's real name!'

'*So do half the nutters in Oldcastle. Got two hundred and thirty-six potential IDs to wade through as it is.*'

Time to impress: 'Yeah, but mine comes from an invoice he gave for a homer in Blackwall Hill. "Jack MacKinnoch", Flat Nine F, Blackburn Court.'

'*Pffff . . .*' Well, maybe impress was too strong a word. '*Hold on.*' Her voice went all muffled. '*Monster Munch: PNC on one Jack MacKinnoch . . . I know you are, but that's the upside of me outranking you. Hop to it . . . I heard that!*' Then Massie was back to full volume. '*Honestly, the Boss sods off for a couple of hours and they all think it's Lord of the Flies.*' A sniff. '*How many more places have you got to visit?*'

Angus pulled out the list, drawing a red line through 'D HILSON, 72 THURBURY DRIVE, BWH'. Which meant they had: 'Four left.'

'*Then you'll be finished in plenty of time to make Dr Fordyce's post mortem, won't you.*'

Oh, buggering hell.

Just what they needed . . .

Her voice went distant and fuzzy again. '*Monster Munch: where's my PNC check?*'

An even fainter Monster Munch grumbled out an answer. '*Aye, aye, keep yer knickers on, Yer Majesty. Jack MacKinnoch, twenty-seven; three parking tickets and a decree for no' paying his rent; chippy wi' the coonsil.*'

Excitement crackled out of DS Massie. '*You wee beauty!*'

And there it was.

Angus turned to Dr Fife. 'MacKinnoch's a joiner with Oldcastle City Council!' They sodding *had* him.

Then Monster Munch had to go and ruin it all: '*Died three years ago, when a scaffy's wagon took a shortcut through his van. Mind the Parkway was closed for twa days? Nightmare.*'

Angus groaned.

So close . . .

Dr Fife stared at him, one eyebrow raised.

Wind rocked the Mini.

A stampede of rain turned the windscreen opaque.

On the other end of the phone, all the excitement drained from DS Massie's voice. '*Let me guess, he lived at—*'

'Blackburn Court, Nine F. Got a family of Afghani asylum seekers staying there now.'

'*You hear that, Sherlock?*'

Angus drooped back in his seat. 'Sarge.'

'*So keep looking. PM's at two. Sharp.*' And the line went dead.

He covered his face with his hands and let loose a wee moan. 'Shite . . .' Before taking a deep breath and peering out between his fingers. 'Jack MacKinnoch died in a collision with a . . . you'd call it a "garbage truck", three years ago. Address was the deceased's flat.'

'Hmmm . . .' Dr Fife frowned as wind sang its way around the door seals. 'This *might* not be as bad as it looks. OK, so maybe Ryan just saw the notice in the papers, and thought "Yeah, I'm having that as an alias," or maybe he knew this Jack MacKinnoch *personally*. They're both joiners, right?' Dr Fife sat up, bringing the reclined seat with him. 'Maybe Ryan thinks "No way I'm paying tax on some piece-of-shit side-hustle job, but this guy wants an invoice, so I gotta get myself a fake name to put on it, and who better than my dead buddy? Not like he's gonna complain if the IRS turn up at his grave."'

He nodded to himself a couple of times, bottom lip pulled in between his teeth, as if he was tasting the idea. Then pointed. 'Call Massie back and tell her to get her flat ass round to whatever council department runs the maintenance and construction crews here. Flash that identikit picture about, knock some heads together if they gotta.'

Flat ass?

Angus curled one shoulder up. 'I am *not* going to tell her that.'

'Pussy.'

'Yeah. No more yoghurt for you.'

Dr Fife pulled out his mobile. 'Fine: *I'll* tell her.'

He was on his own with that one. Some people just had a death wish, and—

Angus's phone ding-buzzed.

DCI MONROE:
> WE NEED TO TALK. UTMOST SECRECY.
> Come to my house ASAP!
> Tell no one and bring Dr Fife with you.
> Edengrange, Farfield Road, Wardmill.
> Investigation compromised.
> TELL NO ONE.

Wow . . .

He stared at the screen. Read the text message again. Then a third time.

Holy *shit*.

On the other side of the car, Dr Fife was being an arsehole to DS Massie. 'Cos I say so, *that's* why. Why'd you think your boss got me in from the States: cos I *know* stuff, sweetheart, so get those—'

Angus hit him on the arm. 'Hang up.'

But Dr Fife just turned his back. 'Yeah, that's right, I said "sweetheart".'

Angus hit him again. 'Hang up!'

He scowled from the passenger seat, still on the phone. 'Oh yeah? Well—'

Time to go for the full dead-arm treatment.

Thwack.

'HANG UP!'

'Sonofabitch!' Dr Fife *finally* did what he was told, rubbing at the muscle Angus just punched. 'What the *hell*?'

Angus opened his mouth, ready to read him DCI Monroe's text . . .

Yes, but what if Dr Fife was part of the 'no one' he wasn't supposed to tell?

Monroe knew he'd be with the forensic psychologist – told him he had to stick to the guy like seagull poop – so when he wrote 'Tell no one and bring Dr Fife with you' maybe that's because it was *OK* for Angus to tell Dr Fife? But if that was the case, why say 'Tell no one'?

Angus's mouth clicked shut again.

Might be a good idea to play this safe. After all, Dr Fife would find out when they got to Wardmill anyway.

For better or worse.

Dr Fife glared at him. 'Well?'

'It's just . . . we should probably go there *ourselves*. To the council's Works Department.' OK, that was good. 'Like you said about not trusting idiots to do the important jobs?'

The glare turned into a frown. 'Yeah, I'm probably right.' He launched a backhander into Angus's arm. 'But no more hitting!' Giving Angus's arm another slap.

'Sorry. Got carried away. You know, in all the excitement.'

'Hmmph.' Dr Fife settled back in his seat, eyes closed. '*Of course* I was right. Always am.'

A long flat breath hissed through Angus's lips.

Seemed to have got away with it.

He looked at the text one last time:

Investigation compromised.

TELL NO ONE.

No way this would end well.

Angus started the car and headed off into the storm.

Wardmill was one of those old planned villages, set up by rich mill owners so they could play philanthropist as they controlled every aspect of their workforce's lives. It sat just outside Oldcastle proper, on the other side of the Swinney, a mix of terraced sandstone houses on the uphill side, and red-brick warehouses and repurposed factories on the down. The kind of buildings trendy IT firms and hipster breweries moved into.

Dr Fife snored gently in the passenger seat as Angus stuck to the *exact* speed limit. Because what if he got pulled over for speeding? Or dodgy driving? Word would get back to DS Massie and the rest of the team before you could say 'Investigation compromised' and God knew what would happen then.

Angus took the turning onto Farfield Road, a swanky street of big houses on the westernmost edge of the village, all sitting in great-big gardens with mature trees and sprawling rhododendrons – their colours muted in the cold, grey light.

Edengrange was halfway down, guarded by a pair of stone gate-posts topped with a carved mermaid on one side and a harpy on the other.

Quick check in the rear-view mirror to make sure he wasn't being followed, and Angus drove between the two, scrunching onto a gravel driveway that ended in a turning circle boasting a Range Rover Sport and a little red hatchback.

The house was *huge*. A three-storey mansion masquerading as a castle, complete with battlements and an iron-banded front door. Big double garage, off to one side. Eight-foot stone wall around the property. The only thing missing was a moat.

Don't know what DCI Monroe's wife did for a living, but there was *no way* he could afford this on a police officer's salary.

A big magnolia tree sat beside the drive. The poor thing was in early bloom, and Storm Findlay had battered the living hell out of the opened buds, scattering pink-and-purple petals all over the two parked cars and the driveway. The vast rhododendron on the other side of the garage had got as far as budding, but hadn't risked going any further – its thick green leaves shining like slabs of liver as the bush bucked and writhed in the wind.

Angus parked between the Range Rover and the hatchback.

Guess now they'd find out what this was all about.

He huffed out a breath.

Nodded.

Switched off the engine.

Then poked Dr Fife. 'We're here.'

'Mmmph! Wake! 'M'wake . . .' Snorking and spluttering upright. 'Where . . . ?' He peered out at the rain-battered garden. 'What?' Then undid his seatbelt. '*This* is the council building? Bit small, isn't it?'

'No.' Angus climbed out into the storm, slamming the car door and hauling up his hood.

Gusts of wind shoved and barged past him, whipping the bushes around the driveway, making the trees shudder and creak. Rain pummelling his back as he crunched his way towards the grand stone portico with its twee fake-portcullis and great wooden door. Off to one side, a leylandii hedge thrashed like a monster, ready to break free and devour all that stood in its way.

The portico, when he reached it, was like a little oasis of calm and sanity.

That is, until Dr Fife arrived. He bustled in out of the rain, hackles up. 'This ain't no council building. You wanna tell me what's going on?'

'Your guess is good as mine.'

Angus reached for the doorbell . . . then stopped.

Never mind *locked*, Edengrange's front door wasn't even shut. It swung halfway open, then clunked back again, deadbolt bouncing off the lock as wind billowed across the house's façade.

Dr Fife pulled his chin in. 'What kinda asshole doesn't close their front door in *this*?'

Angus reached for the handle.

'Careful!' He grabbed Angus's arm. 'Just in case.'

'Maybe the latch is dodgy or something?'

'Or *maybe* it ain't.'

Yeah . . . He was probably right.

It was a struggle, getting a pair of nitrile gloves on over his damp hands, but Angus wriggled his fingers more or less into place. 'Right.' He took hold of the handle and pushed the door wide, revealing a decent-sized porch with a bench seat down one side – wellies underneath. Coats hanging opposite. The floor: one big swathe of sisal matting.

It squelched beneath Angus's feet as he tiptoed inside. Soggy from all the rain that'd blown in through the swinging door.

The inner door was partially glazed, but the hall behind it was dark, making it hard to pick out any details beyond a big staircase lurking there. A couple of red teardrops marked the glass – glistening and sticky. What looked like a scarlet fingerprint was smeared across the handle. And the whole door rattled in its frame as the wind gusted.

Dr Fife inched up beside him, voice compressed to a whisper: 'Yeah, I'm getting a *real* bad feeling about this. We should call it in.'

'Course we should.'

Trouble was: who to call? If the investigation was compromised, any one of them could be . . . what, working for the Fortnight Killer? Nah, that sounded *insane*. But you didn't become a detective chief inspector by being an idiot, and DCI Monroe's text was very clear: *Tell no one . . .*

Deep breath.

Angus opened the internal door and slipped into a large hallway: wooden panelling halfway up the walls, beneath a liberal sprinkling of photos and paintings; black-blue-and-white tiles on the floor; that big staircase sweeping up to the left, curling around as it rose to a balcony that ran around three sides of the open space.

Cold enough that his breath misted in front of his face, before fading away.

Five or six panel doors led off the hallway, but a line of teeny red dots marked a path across the tiles, leading to – or *from* – only one of them. It lay slightly ajar on the right-hand side, nearest the entrance.

Dr Fife stayed in the porch, but his whisper got sharper. 'Why aren't you calling this in?'

'Stay *right* there.' Angus crept across the hall, following the trail of blood.

'What, you *suddenly* lost the fence post up your ass? Now's not the time to lose the fence-post up your ass!'

Angus raised a finger and leaned one ear towards the narrow gap between the panel door and the frame.

There was a faint ... *something*. Hard to make out. Maybe breathing?

He pulled back. Braced himself. Placed his palm against the wood, but nowhere near the handle – the other side, by the hinges, to avoid contaminating any potential fingerprints.

In three. Two. One.

He shoved the door wide and lunged into what was clearly a dining room.

The curtains were drawn, but a chandelier hung from the high ceiling, casting its glittering light over yet more wood panelling, oil paintings, a sideboard, and a Welsh dresser full of fancy china. A pair of mahogany standard lamps added their illumination from the far side of a large walnut dining table with matching chairs.

But all of that faded away as Angus stared at the star of the show: a middle-aged woman, dressed in a blue-and-white Breton top, sitting directly opposite the door, with both hands screwed palms-down to the tabletop.

Bright scarlet blossomed down the front of her stripy top, spreading out from the Post-it note screwed to the middle of her chest: 'COME AND GET ME!' A heavy gag of black material stretching her mouth wide.

Her eyes glittered from the dark sockets, mascara streaks running down both cheeks. Glaring at him as he stood there, staring like a numpty.

Holy crap ... She was *alive*.

42

The woman's eyes widened, throat clenching as she screamed behind the gag.

Angus *stared*.

What the hell was he supposed to do now?

> Investigation compromised.
> TELL NO ONE.

But he *had* to call an ambulance. *Had* to call for backup. Forensics. The whole circus. No matter what DCI Monroe said.

And he had to get *her* out of here.

Screwdriver.

He needed a screwdriver.

Where the hell did . . .

Wait: Dr Fife had one in that multitool thing of his – the one he'd used to unscrew the vent-cover in Sean McGilvary's bedroom.

Angus forced the tremble out of his voice: 'It's going to be OK. I need to get—'

A loud *bang* sounded out in the hall somewhere, like a door slamming.

He spun around, knees bent, hands raised in the defensive position just like they taught you in Officer Safety Training.

But there was no one there.

He glanced over his shoulder.

She was yelling something at him, behind the gag, but all that came out were muffled grunts and growls.

'Just . . . Shh . . . OK? Sorry. I'll only be a minute.' He tiptoed to the open door and peered out into the hall as she shouted and shouted and shouted at his back.

No sign of anyone.

'Dr Fife?'

The porch door was shut. Probably the wind. But you'd think Dr Fife would've been in the way. Or stopped it. Or *something*.

Angus stepped out onto the tiles, pulling his phone from his pocket – still safely cocooned in its ziplock bag.

OK.

Had to call someone.

Question was: *who*?

He eased the porch door open . . . but Dr Fife was nowhere to be seen. Nothing in here but wellies and coats and a drowned welcome mat.

The front door was shut too – which meant someone had unsnibbed the deadbolt.

He marched over there and yanked the door wide, letting in a spattering of ice-cold rain. 'Dr Fife?'

The three cars were exactly where they should've been. The wind battered more blossom from the magnolia, while the rhododendron snarled and writhed.

'DR FIFE!'

Still nothing.

Angus closed the door again.

Yeah, this wasn't good.

Deep breath.

Time to call Control.

He stepped back inside and listened to it ring.

A cheery female voice burst out of the speaker: *'Aye, aye? If it's no' DC MacVicar! Battered any good suspects lately?'*

Angus snibbed the deadbolt, making sure no one was sneaking into the house behind him, then strode across the hall. 'I need backup and an ambulance: right now!' He threw open the door opposite the dining room – a cosy lounge, with leather sofas, tastefully decorated in country tones.

No one there.

Control went straight into professional mode: *'Go ahead.'*

The next room was a study. Wall-to-wall bookcases and a standing desk.

Still no sign of Dr Fife.

'DCI Monroe's house: Edengrange, Farfield Road, Wardmill. Don't know the postcode.'

Door Number Three revealed a small WC.

Unoccupied.

'Got an IC-One female with severe injuries to both hands and chest. Possibly other trauma. Think it's Monroe's wife.'

Door Four: a brand-new kitchen, with nice units and worktops. None of which looked in the least bit flooded. Not so much as a puddle on the fancy, patterned tiles.

'Monroe's missing – possibly abducted.'

'*Shite . . .*' There was a pause, filled with the staccato clatter of a computer keyboard. '*DC MacVicar, can you—*'

'It was the Fortnight Killer.' He checked around the back of the central island: no Dr Fife. 'Don't know if I disturbed Ryan before he could kill her, but Mrs Monroe's screwed to the dining-room table.'

More keyboard noises.

Angus locked the back door, then stepped out into the hall again. 'Hello?'

'*Hud oan . . . Right. Ambulance is on its way. Rerouting nearest patrol cars . . .*'

'Might need roadblocks on Wardmill Road and the A9405.'

'*Working on it.*' A scrunching sound muffled her voice. '*Brucie! Get the Operation Telegram bods on the blower – code black, DCI Monroe's house!*' Then she must've let go of the headset's microphone, because everything was clear again. '*OK, the phone's going to go quiet for a wee bit: I need to make a couple of calls. Find somewhere safe to hole up and protect the victim till backup arrives.*'

'Roger.'

'*And don't do anything stupid, like getting yourself killed!*'

Then silence.

Not even hold music.

Not getting killed sounded like a good idea.

He did a quick three-sixty, scanning the upper balcony, then backed towards the dining room, keeping his eyes on the stairs and the landing above.

'DR FIFE! Where the wanking hell have you—'

A voice. Right behind him. Smug and cold: *'Should've run when you had the chance.'*

43

Angus spun around, already halfway into the defensive position when a pickaxe handle slammed into his shoulder.

Fire raced across his back and down his left arm, the nerves burning as he staggered.

'Hoooo-yeah!' A broad-shouldered wee hardman with a Freddie Mercury moustache grinned at him. Curly hair sticking out from under a blue Oldcastle Warriors woolly hat. Gold tooth at the front. About the same age as Angus, but in plaster-spattered grey overalls. Work boots. Yellow-and-orange work gloves wrapped around the pickaxe handle, holding it like a short sword. 'You big bastards is *all* the same. All mouth, but sod-all in the trouser department.' He tossed the handle into the air, caught it, and swung it – all in one fluid motion.

The end cracked against the side of Angus's head, sending him sprawling. Yellow-and-brown lights flashed through the walls and ceiling, accompanied by the sound of a thousand funeral bells.

He hit the ground hard, phone flying from his hand to spin across the tiles towards the open dining-room door.

'You're *surplus* to *requirements*, Big Guy!'

Bastard . . .

Angus shoved himself over, onto his front, and crawled after his phone. Blood trickled down the side of his face, spattering onto the blue-black-and-white tiles, smearing beneath his hands.

The man with the moustache followed, ambling along. Using his weapon as a swagger stick. 'Lucky for you, really.'

Don't stop: keep moving.

'See: I've got a cell ready and waiting, and a *whole heap of toys* to show you what we do with Elite wankers.' He grabbed the pickaxe handle in both hands, raised it over his head, then clattered it down on Angus's left forearm.

A horrible cracking noise rattled up to join his throbbing shoulder, followed by a deluge of rusty nails, driven into the skin by the handful.

The arm wouldn't take his weight any more, pitching him forward onto his face. The tiles cold and slick against Angus's cheek.

The Bastard laughed. 'Oops. Clumsy me.'

He raised the pickaxe handle again, probably hoping to shatter the right arm as well, but Angus rolled sideways, both legs kicking out.

One foot missed, but the other clipped the handle on the way down, knocking it out of the Bastard's hands. Sending it bang-thump-crashing away across the floor.

'You just won yourself a kneecapping!' He scrabbled off to retrieve his weapon.

Angus's right hand closed around the fallen phone, but he kept on going, crawling into the dining room.

He stuck one corner of the ziplock bag between his teeth and hauled himself up the dining table, one-handed. Ruined forearm clutched against his chest as it burned.

Mrs Monroe glared at him over her gag. As if this was somehow all *his* doing.

That ringing noise was getting louder, and shaking his head did nothing to help – just spattered drips of scarlet across the polished walnut and made the room spin like a carousel.

A singsong voice came from the doorway: 'Knock, knock.' The Bastard was back, pickaxe handle slung casually over one shoulder. An arrogant strut to his walk. All the time in the world.

Angus staggered around to the other side of the table, putting it between them. Dropped the phone into his hand. 'EMERGENCY! I'M UNDER ATTACK! REPEAT, UNDER—'

The pickaxe handle clipped the top of his mobile, and the Samsung went flying end over end into the Welsh dresser, where it smashed straight through a soup tureen.

Bastard.

Utter. Complete. *Fucking*. Bastard.

'I HAVEN'T EVEN FINISHED PAYING FOR THAT!'

''S OK.' Lining up another shot. 'Your Direct Debits keep going for a while after you're dead.' The handle swung in a flat arc, heading straight for Angus's face.

Angus flinched back, and it whistled by less than an inch away, but one of those standard lamps stopped him retreating any further. Banging into his throbbing shoulder, the tassels on the lightshade fluttering at his bloody cheek.

Wait a minute.

Oh yeah.

He took hold of the lamp and yanked it away from the wall – hard enough to strip the flex from the plug.

Time to see how arrogant the Bastard was when faced with a makeshift halberd. OK, the long poles usually came with an axe-blade, a spike, and a hook on the end, but a tasselled shade would have to do.

Muscle memory kicked in as Angus twirled the thing twice, then whacked it down. Pinning that pickaxe handle to the tabletop.

The Bastard's eyes went wide.

Damn right.

Angus snapped his new weapon up again, twisting and lunging, catching the Bastard right in the face with the lampshade. Bursting the bulb with a sharp *pop*.

A scream blared out and the Bastard stumbled back, blood gushing from his lacerated nose. Because that's what happens when someone jams broken glass and a metal light-fitting into it.

Press the advantage.

Angus leapt – left foot onto a dining chair, propelling himself up onto the tabletop, then from there into the air. Swinging his halberd with its battered shade. The chandelier exploded into a thousand glittering shards as the standard lamp ploughed through them. Angus tightened his grip on the wooden shaft, bringing it cracking down on the Bastard's head hard enough to break the lamp in two.

The Bastard wobbled, then pitched over backwards, through the open doorway and into the hall. Landing like a sack of tatties.

Oh, LARPing's really silly.

You all look ridiculous: dressing up in cloaks and cardboard armour, pretending to be elves and wizards, and hitting each other with sticks.

Well, who was laughing now?

Angus jumped down from the tabletop and strode after the Bastard, left arm clutched against his chest, right hand gripping the lamp's broken remains. The wire down the middle hadn't snapped, so now the two bits of wood hinged in the middle. Like an oversized, half-arsed nunchuck.

The Bastard groaned, scarlet oozing from the brim of his torn woolly hat to dribble down his face, mingling with the blood from his tattered nose. He rolled over onto his side and Angus swung the lamp at him.

It wasn't easy to control, now it was in two barely connected bits, but the end still battered into the Bastard's thigh with a satisfying *thwack* – making him howl. He curled into a ball, one hand holding his leg, the other clutching his head.

And now he was subdued, it was time to arrest the—

An ear-ringing *PANG* splintered the air, followed by a sizzling *crack*, and a thumb-sized chunk of doorframe exploded into tiny slivers of wood, right beside Angus's head.

Why would the doorframe . . . ?

Another *PANG* rang out and a lump of wall turned into plaster dust and fragments of torn lath.

Which is when the truth *finally* made it through Angus's pounding head.

'GUN!' He hit the deck, scrambling backwards on all threes, into the dining room.

He kicked the door shut, rolling out of the way as a trio of bullet holes punched their way through the wood. Struggled to his feet.

A muffled cry came from the hall outside.

It was followed by a woman's voice – hard and sour. *'What the hell are you doing?'*

The Bastard let loose another whimper. *'Oh God, I'm bleeding!'*

'You stupid wee shite: you were supposed to kill *him!'*

Two more gunshots ripped through the door.

Mrs Monroe screamed behind her gag as the bullets gouged tracks into the tabletop.

'He called the cops. I saw him call the cops!'

'Why do you have to screw everything up?'

A scream of pain rattled through the door.

'Get in the van.' A pause. *'GET IN THE FUCKING VAN!'*

Boots scrabbled on the tiled floor, followed by another three barks from the gun, punching splintered holes through the dining-room door. Carving twisted grooves across the polished walnut.

Then a *click*.

And a howl of rage.

Oh, thank God for that – the Bastard's friend was out of bullets.

She kicked the punctured door. *'THIS ISN'T OVER!'*

Then those boots clattered away into the distance.

After that, the only sounds were the blood whumping in Angus's ears, his own rasping breath, and Mrs Monroe hissing air in and out through her nose.

They'd *survived*.

Angus slumped against the dining-room table for a moment.

Come on: not over yet.

He gave himself a shake, then marched to the window and threw open one side of the curtains, letting in the pale afternoon light.

The Bastard hurpled out through the gateposts, moving like Igor's ghost, dragging his left leg, still trying to hold his bashed-up head together.

No sign of the gunwoman.

A long, shuddering breath abandoned Angus's lungs, and he folded forward – grabbing a knee with his one good hand. Holding himself up as blood dripped from his head to the oatmeal carpet.

Staying there till the urge to puke faded a little.

Then straightened up and moved over to the Welsh dresser, where his phone lay in the shattered remains of the soup tureen. The ziplock bag was still intact, but the phone's screen had turned into a spider's web of cracked glass.

Pressing the power button made the thing flicker into life, but the icons were smeared on one side and out of focus on the other.

Strange parallel lines of pixels glowing in magenta and cyan all the way down the screen – like the bars on a cage.

He held it up to his ear. 'Hello? Control?'

Nothing.

'Hello?'

Hard to tell if he was still on hold, or if his mobile was just totally knackered. 'Hello? DC MacVicar to Control, can you hear me?'

Complete and utter silence.

So much for that.

He stuck the bag back in his pocket and forced a smile.

'Mrs Monroe? It's OK: they've gone.' He lurched over there. 'Are you all right? Have you been shot?'

Didn't look like it.

As far as he could tell, other than the screws through both hands, the one in her chest, and the egg-sized lump on the back of her head, she was fine. Well, maybe not 'fine', but the bullets all seemed to have missed her, and that was the important thing.

He reached for the gag. 'Let's get this off you.'

Untying the knots wasn't easy with only one working hand, but he finally got it off her, and pulled out the rag stuffed inside her mouth.

Mrs Monroe coughed and spluttered. Retched a couple of times. Spat something yellow and viscous onto the tabletop. Then creased her eyes shut and took a long, deep breath. 'YOU NEARLY GOT US KILLED, YOU SILLY BASTARD!'

Angus backed away from the table as she launched into a full-on rant.

There was just no pleasing some people . . .

44

The ambulance lights strobed in through the living-room window, chasing shadows around the walls, making the whole place spin even faster as Angus propped himself up against the sill.

DI Tudor was out there, supervising as a pair of paramedics loaded Mrs Monroe into the back of their ambulance, faces creased up as the rain lashed down.

Was nice in here, though. Old-fashioned and comforting, with its piles of paperbacks on the coffee table and open tub of Quality Street. Well-padded sofa and armchairs. Happy family photos and an oil-painting of a springer spaniel. Cosy.

Even if the room wouldn't stop whirling.

DS Massie was head-to-toe in PPE, Tyvek suit going *zwip-zwop* as she paced the room, giving someone a hard time on her phone. 'I don't care if they're driving the Popemobile – everyone gets stopped and searched. *Everyone!*'

No one had given *him* an SOC suit.

She, DS Kilgour, and DI Tudor were all rustling about like crumpled ghosts, but Angus was stuck in his battered, double-breasted funeral outfit and blood-slicked high-vis. Shirt was probably ruined. As was the towel he'd found in the downstairs loo – held against his head to staunch the constant seeping dribbles of bright red.

Outside, one of the paramedics hopped down from the back and folded the elevator ramp thing up, closed the door, and hurried round to the driver's side. The ambulance's siren gave a single *Vwoooooip!* and off went Mrs Monroe. Pausing at the gateposts so a PC could shift the cordon of 'POLICE' tape.

As the ambulance disappeared off down Farfield Road, one of the scene examiners' manky Transit vans crunched onto the gravel drive, taking its place in front of the house.

The circus had arrived.

Ya-ta da-da-da-da ya-ta yaaaa-da . . .

All they were missing were the Procurator Fiscal, a handful of clowns, and a trapeze artist.

Angus blinked.

No idea where *that* came from.

Yeah . . .

Taking a pickaxe handle to the head probably hadn't been a *great* idea. As if the hangover wasn't bad enough.

DS Massie stopped pacing. 'Right. Good . . . Uh-huh . . . I know . . . OK. Will do.' She hung up and sagged. 'Buggering hell.' Then rounded on him, finger inches from his face, glaring behind her safety goggles. 'You've got *ten seconds* to explain why I shouldn't kick your arse from here to Fiddersmuir!'

'Sarge?' How was this *his* fault?

'What were you *thinking*? You should've called it in, right away!'

'I got a text . . .' Angus pulled out his poor battered phone. Took four goes on the power button to get it to start this time, and the ziplock bag was smeared with blood, but he cleaned it with a gob of spit and one of the less blood-soaked corners of the hand towel. He tapped the icon again and again and again till his text messages appeared.

DCI MONROE:
> WE NEED TO TALK. UTMOST SECRECY.
> Come to my house ASAP!
> Tell no one and bring Dr Fife with you.
> Edengrange, Farfield Road, Wardmill.
> Investigation compromised.
> TELL NO ONE.

He held his phone out. 'That's why.'

She curled her lip. 'And you *actually* believed that came from the Boss?'

'Well, yeah, I mean why wouldn't—'

'Monroe never sent a text in his life that didn't contain at least three emojis.'

What?

'But the investigation *is* compromised! Someone told the papers about the Post-it notes. Someone told them about Dr Fife working with us.'

DS Massie's face soured. 'Speaking of the narcissistic tosspot: where is he?'

Good question.

Outside, the SE team decamped from their Transit van and dragged a pair of large holdalls from the back. The entrance marquee had arrived. Not that they were going to have much luck erecting it in *this* weather. It'd be halfway to Dundee by lunchtime.

Fingers snapped right in front of his nose. 'Angus! Focus.'

'Sorry, Sarge.' Wonder what concussion smelled like. Cos right now, the whole room stank of old pennies and black pepper.

There was a knock on the door and in shambled DS Kilgour, dressed head-to-toe in rustling white. He nodded at them. 'Rhona. Angus the Terrible.' Then stuck his gloved hands on his hips. 'Well, this is what we call "An Unmitigated, Cocking Disaster".'

DS Massie glowered. 'It *isn't* funny.'

'Do I look like I'm laughing?' He peered at Angus and his blood-drenched towel. 'How's the head?'

A sharp, bitter laugh from DS Massie. 'Hollow. Or solid granite, depending on your perspective.' She snatched the phone from Angus's hand. 'The boy thinks Monroe sent this.'

'Really?' Kilgour frowned at the cracked screen. 'Where's the half-dozen smiley-slash-winky-slash-grumpy faces?'

'That's what I said.' She poked Angus's high-vis. 'Now *where's* Fife?'

'I . . . don't know. I found Mrs Monroe, turned round, and he'd disappeared. No sign of him.' With the ambulance lights gone, the room should've slowed down a bit, but it was battering around like a wonky merry-go-round. And closing his eyes just made it go faster. 'Any chance I could sit down, Sarge? Only it's getting kind of . . . ?' He made a wobbly hand gesture.

DS Kilgour fiddled with Angus's phone. Gave it a shoogle. Then a proper shake. Turning in circles, holding the ziplock above his head, as if he was struggling to get a signal. 'How come you're not off to the hospital, Angus the Terrible?'

DS Massie hooked a thumb at the window. 'Irene didn't want to share an ambulance with him, on account of his being a lumbering great tit.' Then pointed. 'Sit down, you idiot.'

Oh, thank God for that.

Angus half sat, half collapsed into the sofa. Which probably caused no end of bloodstains on the upholstery, but it couldn't be helped.

'Don't mind DS Massie, Angus, she's just grumpy because she's worried about you.'

A snort. 'Worried about *the Boss*, more like. Not answering his mobile, no GPS fix from his Airwave. Best guess is this Ryan arsehole attacked Irene, made her lure the Boss here with that call about the flooded kitchen, then abducted him. Same as he did with Dr Fordyce and all the other poor bastards.' She folded her arms, pulling them tight. 'So, yeah: I'm worried.'

Angus's phone let out a distorted ping – the 'sent message' alert – and straight away, an answering *ding-buzz* sounded inside DS Massie and Kilgour's SOC suits.

'Just sent you a copy of that text.' Kilgour returned Angus's mobile. 'We should get the phone company to triangulate Monroe's position.'

She stared at him. 'Yes, *thank you*, Captain Mansplaining. I've already got a warrant being fast-tracked for that.' Then moved around so she was in front of Angus. 'Laura spoke to the hospital, up in Teuchterville: they couldn't find any medical records for a Malachi Ezekiel McNabb. Mind you, it's forty years ago – nothing was digitized then.' A shrug. 'Doesn't prove anything either way, but still . . .'

'Oh.'

'Yeah.'

'OK.' DS Kilgour shrugged. 'Somebody want to fill me in?'

'We don't know if Dr Fife really *is* Dr Fife.'

'Are we talking . . . ?'

She nodded. 'There's plenty of serial killers who wangle their way into investigations. They get off on the power. Saw it on a true-crime documentary.'

'Which would complicate things.' Kilgour settled his bum on the sofa's arm. 'So, Dr Fife's either been abducted by a murderous bunch of scumbags, or he set this whole thing up, took the Boss hostage, and buggered off with his . . . what did he call them, "disciples"?'

'About the size of it.'

Kilgour whistled behind his mask. 'Perfect. Just. Bloody. Perfect.' A long breath. 'We need to . . .'

There was more, but he seemed to have developed some sort of speech impediment – his mouth kept moving, but all that came out was a whooshing booming barrage of noise. As if Angus had water in his ears.

Something was up with the lights in here too. The room kept slipping out of focus, the colours turning sharp and far too bright.

And for some reason, DS Kilgour and DS Massie didn't seem to notice any of it. You'd think detective sergeants would have better observational skills.

He should really tell them.

Yeah, but that would mean getting into an argument and Angus was far too comfy for that. Sitting here on this nice soft couch.

Warm and comfortable and sleepy.

He blinked.

Then did it again, only slower.

Think anyone would mind if he closed his eyes for a second?

Been a long day, after all.

. . .

. . .

. . .

. . .

'What the hell's going on in here?'

Angus's eyes flickered open to find DI Tudor standing over him, staring, mouth hanging open, facemask dangling under his chin. And he was *sideways*, which was a bit weird. But that might've been Angus's fault, because he seemed to have keeled over at some point and now lay slumped across the sofa.

Tudor knelt in front of him, one hand shaking his shoulder. 'Angus? Can you hear me?'

''M'wake.'

Then Tudor turned, jabbing a gloved finger at Massie and Kilgour. 'What's this man doing, *lying* here, bleeding on the Boss's couch, when he should be off getting medical attention?'

That seemed to come as a surprise to DS Kilgour. 'Oh, buggering . . . Er . . . We were just working on a timeline, Guv, piecing together DCI Monroe's—'

'It can *wait*. Things are bad enough without Detective Constable MacVicar dying from a head injury!'

The room slipped out of focus again, and darkness seeped in from the corners, swallowing the world.

'Get him to A-and-E, now!'

'OK, same again.' Dr Fotheringham flicked the pen-torch's light into Angus's left eye, then away again, holding a finger up on her other hand for him to focus on. She was nice, in a harassed, sort-of-haunted kind of way. Late thirties maybe? With a sensible haircut, green scrubs, pink Crocs, and pretty Asian features in an oval face.

Admissions Ward D was a windowless, soulless, eight-bed room on the second floor of Castle Hill Infirmary, whose cracked terrazzo floor was stitched together with ancient duct tape and, in one spot over by the communal sink, cardboard. And every bed was full.

To be honest, the scratchy sheets and itchy blanket was nowhere near as comfortable as DCI Monroe's couch.

'Right.' Dr Fotheringham sat on the edge of Angus's bed. 'Well, pupil response is normal, so you're probably not going to pop your clogs before the end of *my* shift.' She scrunched her face to one side. 'We *could* keep you in for observation. Unless you've got someone at home to keep an eye on you?'

'I'll be fine, honest.' Plus it would be nice to get out of this peek-a-boo arseless hospital gown.

She pointed at the swathe of bandages holding a paperback-sized lump of gauze in place, just above his ear. 'Twelve stitches; lucky you didn't fracture your skull. But if you're sure? Can't say we don't need the bed.' The penlight tapped against the fibreglass cast that covered his left arm from elbow to knuckles – the fingers poking out the end already purpling with bruises. 'Take care of that arm though, or we'll have to open it up and stick half a Meccano set in there. Ruin your sex life.'

'So I can go?'

'Get dressed. They'll give you your discharge papers and some painkillers at the desk on the way out.' Dr Fotheringham winked. 'Don't forget to tip your nurse if you want the good stuff.' She stood, gathering up her things.

'Any word on Mrs Monroe?'

'In Recovery now. Apparently, that screw in her sternum was this close' – holding up two fingers a hair's breadth apart – 'to puncturing her superior vena cava. If they'd used the same great-big screws they stuck through her hands, she'd be dead by now.' Dr Fotheringham patted his leg through the blanket. 'Now get the heck out of my hospital.' She got as far as the end of his bed. Stopped. Turned. 'Oh, and you've got a visitor.'

Angus scrambled out onto the cold grey floor. Wobbled a bit. Sat down hard on the crunchy mattress.

Dr Fotheringham stared at him, one perfectly plucked eyebrow raised.

'Got up too quick. Sorry.'

'Don't make me change my mind about discharging you.' And off she went.

Soon as she'd cleared the ward doors, Angus pulled the curtains around his bed, then wrestled his way out of that sexy bumless robe – because undoing the ties at the back was a *massive* challenge.

He dumped it on the boxy bedside unit thing, with its battered veneer door and scratched, square mirror.

Yeah . . .

Not a great sight, to be honest.

They'd given his face a once-over with a damp rag before putting in the stitches, but the naked bloke reflected back at him still had blood matted into his hair where it stuck out from the bandages. A dark-red stain started halfway down his neck, carried on across his chest, into his groin, and halfway down the left thigh.

A shower would've been nice, but there wasn't time.

Getting his pants on was another battle, but the trousers were worse. Socks: completely impossible.

A woman's voice came from just outside his curtained realm. *'Hello? Angus?'* Crap, it was Gillian.

'Hold on!' He dug his bloody shirt from the unit and got his right arm into the sleeve. No way in hell the cast was fitting the left one, though.

'Angus?'

'Yeah, just a minute!' He pinned his broken arm against his chest and had a bash at buttoning the shirt over the top. Which was every bit as impossible as putting on socks one-handed. 'Oh, for God's sake . . .'

The curtains parted a teeny bit, and Gillian's head popped in. 'Sorry. Are you all right? Only it sounded as if . . .' She watched him struggle. 'OK.' Then slipped inside and stood in front of him, a blush whooshing up her neck to the tips of her ears as she buttoned him up in silence.

Heat burned through Angus's cheeks.

Soon as she fastened the last button, he tucked his shirttails into his trousers. Thankfully, she didn't offer to help with that bit.

'How did you know I was—'

She looked down at his naked feet. 'Do you need help with your socks?' Kneeling before he could say anything.

Which meant he had to sit on the plastic chair beside the bed to free his feet up. 'Honestly, you don't have to.'

She did anyway, unrolling the things before pulling them over his toes. 'I couldn't get in touch with Jonathan anywhere, and then it was on the radio that something happened and you'd been hurt. Well, not *you*, you. Not on the radio anyway, but then they put your photo on the *Knap* website, and I was really worried, and I phoned the station, but they wouldn't tell me anything, so I came right over, and said I was your sister. Shoes?'

OK . . .

'In the cabinet thing.'

She pulled them out and slipped them on him. 'Jonathan speaks *so* highly of you, Angus. Says you're the only police officer here with an ounce of brains.' Doing up the laces. 'He *trusts* you.' And finishing off with a double bow. Then sat back on her heels, looking up at him as he stood.

'Thanks for doing that, it was . . . very kind of you.'

'No problems.'

A theatrical *'Ahem!'* entered the curtained-off space around the bed, and there was Ellie. Looking from Angus: standing there; to Gillian: on her knees in front of him; and back again. 'Kinda formal way to end a blowjob.'

Gillian scrambled to her feet, that nuclear blush of hers fizzing through the make-up. 'Oh, no! I was only helping Angus put on his *shoes*.' A smile. 'Ellie! It's lovely to see you again. I like your jacket.'

Ellie ignored her. 'What's this about you almost dying?'

'They're discharging me.' He retrieved his suit jacket from the unit. The thing was all stiff down one side – starched with dried blood, the fabric turned a matt shade of very dark brown against the original black. He shoved his right arm into the sleeve, then turned, and turned, trying to get his left shoulder into the jacket too. Not managing at all.

Gillian put a warm hand against his chest, stopping him spinning, then pulled the jacket into place, and then did up the four buttons. 'There we go.' She pulled his blood-smeared high-vis from the cupboard and popped it over his shoulders. Like a Mafia Don.

Ellie curled her lip. 'You look like crap.'

'Thanks.' He pulled the curtains back with his working hand as Ellie produced her phone and stuck it under his nose.

'Any comment for our loyal and discerning readers?'

Really? After everything he'd just been through?

No *concern*. No *sympathy*. No 'How are you, Angus, you must feel terrible!' No, it was straight to 'GIVE ME A STORY!'

Some friend.

His jaw tightened. 'No comment.'

Angus marched past her and out of the room.

There was a little nurses' station in the corridor, near the door to the lifts, where a glum-faced nurse with freckles and a perm was poking away at a computer keyboard. 'Name?' Sounding as bored as she looked.

'Angus MacVicar.'

Gillian hurried through from the ward. 'Are you sure you're OK?'

No sign of Ellie.

The nurse slapped an A4 printout on the desk and followed it with a prescription. 'Discharge papers. And we're all out of co-dydramol and co-codamol.' She plonked a small pack of paracetamol in front of him. 'That's what happens when bastards keep underfunding the NHS.'

Great.

Para-sodding-cetamol was going to make a *massive* difference to a broken arm and a bashed-up head. He scooped the lot off the desk and lumbered through the double doors.

Behind him, Gillian's voice creeped out a quiet *'Sorry'*. Then she scurried after him. 'Angus?'

He mashed his thumb on the down button. 'I'm fine. Never better.'

Ellie sauntered through, hands in her pockets. 'You want a hurl?'

The rattle-and-clank of machinery long past its best grumbled out from the lift shaft.

Angus scowled at the dented metal doors.

Gillian shuffled her feet. 'Err . . . It's OK, I've got the car with me. And you've got deadlines and stories to file, right? High-flying *senior* crime reporter and everything. It must be really exciting . . .' She cleared her throat. Stared down at her boots.

Ding.

The lift doors juddered open with a metallic squeal and Angus stepped into a scarred stainless-steel box. Graffiti on all four walls. The light guttered, exuding a miserly yellow glow that did little to dispel the gloom.

He pressed the button marked 'G: YELLOW ZONE + EXIT'.

Ellie folded her arms, nostrils flaring. *'What?'*

'I'd better . . .' Gillian pointed, then slipped past into the lift. 'Sorry.'

Angus *glared*. 'That's all I am to you, isn't it: a joke and a story.' He stabbed the '→I←' button. 'Bye, Ellie.'

The doors screeked and quivered shut, leaving her out in the corridor.

He kept his finger on the button, so she couldn't open them again.

The lift creaked and groaned, descending to the ground floor, and Gillian put her hand on his good arm. Nodded. Keeping her eyes on the scuffed and grimy floor. Didn't say a word.

Angus let his head fall back. 'Yeah.'

Because what else was there to say?

45

Angus pulled out his phone as they marched through the hospital's Yellow Zone, past rows of grey doors with little white plaques on them, and waiting areas full of misery and despair.

Bloody thing wouldn't power up on the first go. Or the second. Or third. He ripped the ziplock open with his teeth – after all, what was the bloody point any more?

The power button made a weird buzzing noise as he held it down until *finally* the display bloomed into life.

In addition to being all cracked and covered in glitching pixels, the touchscreen sensors were all out of whack, so getting his contacts up was an even bigger struggle than turning the phone on. Not helped by having to do it one-handed.

He jabbed his thumb down on 'DS MASSIE' about a dozen times before his phone registered the input and called her mobile. Only instead of ringing, it made electronic gurgling noises as the splintered screen flickered.

'*Angus? What are . . . Are you OK?*'

He forced his face into a smile. 'They let me out early, for good behaviour.'

The hospital exit was an airlock with automatic doors – lined with posters about mental health and cancers and staying the hell away from the Castle Hill Infirmary if you had a potentially fatal, highly infectious respiratory disease.

The first set of doors squeaked out of Angus's way, with Gillian trotting along beside him, still not saying anything.

'Just wondering, Sarge: any sign of the Boss? Or Dr Fife?'

'I'm going to forgive you confusing me for your bloody secretary again, because of that thump on the head, but don't push it.'

Soon as the outer doors opened, the wind rushed in.

Rain had darkened the concrete fascia, but there was enough of an overhang to keep the worst of it out. Making a wee shelter for the handful of people in their hospital pyjamas crammed in here to smoke cigarettes, beneath a sign saying you weren't allowed to do that within fifteen metres of the hospital buildings.

'But, Sarge—'

'The answer is no to both.' She sniffed. *'And that's it – you get sod-all else. You're officially off on the sick, understand? Three days' leave, minimum.'*

Angus stopped on the edge of the sheltered area. Grimacing out at the downpour as it scoured the road and surrounding buildings. 'You can't do that, Sarge! I'm part of the team; I'm Dr Fife's sidekick. I need to help!'

A sigh. Then DS Massie's voice softened a little. *'You already helped, Angus. We've got the eFit you did with Byron out to every newspaper and TV station in the country. We've got your statement generating actions in HOLMES. We've got Irene Monroe, still alive to tell us what happened – well, soon as she comes off the sedatives – because of you. I get that you need to help, I really do. But you also need to not die from a brain haemorrhage, you daft bastard. Tudor'll have my arse on a stick if you snuff it.'*

'But—'

'No.' The hard edges were back. *'And that's final. You're off the case till I get a note from a doctor saying you won't make a shite-load of paperwork for me by dropping dead!'* She left an ominous pause. *'Are. We. Clear?'*

Angus sagged. 'Sarge.'

'Now go home and get some rest!' She hung up.

He yanked the phone from his ear as a piercing squeal erupted from the speaker. The display fizzed with mismatched pixels . . . then died. And no amount of pressing, squeezing, or poking made it live again.

Up on level five of the infirmary car park, the flooding had spread across three-quarters of the sodden tarmac, leaving less than two dozen useable spaces, unless you had your wellies on. Only one person had decided to risk it: abandoning their vehicle to the cold and damp.

Wind moaned through the metal cladding, but at least they were out of the rain here, trapped beneath the concrete lid of the floor above. Which kind of begged the question – where had all this water come from?

Gillian led the way to a grubby wee Renault Clio, whose bonnet didn't match the rest of the car. Its wings seemed to be about fifty-fifty rust and filler. She stuck her key in the driver's door and unlocked it, then did the same on the passenger side. 'Central locking doesn't work. Sorry. It's a bit . . . manky.' Opening the door for him.

It wasn't easy, shoving a bit of brightness into his voice, but Angus had a go. 'No, it's fine. Thanks. Great.' He sank into the passenger seat.

Weirdly, even though the Clio's exterior was manky as a scabby dog, the *interior* was showroom clean and filled with the sharp-sweet scent of lemon. Which seemed to be coming from the cardboard Smurf that dangled from the rear-view mirror.

He wriggled free of the high-vis, and pulled his seatbelt on. 'Honestly, thanks for the lift. You didn't have to.'

'No, it's nothing. Just, you know, when you and Ellie . . .' She stuck the key in the ignition. Took a deep breath. And stared out through the driver's window, voice small and shaky. 'Angry voices are how the beatings always start.'

Poor sod.

'Was it hard: leaving the Apostles?'

The battery whined as the starter motor struggled and struggled till finally the engine caught. Coughing and spluttering into life. Sounding more like a big tractor than a wee car.

She pulled on a brave smile. 'Wasn't easy.' They rattled out of the parking spot towards the down-ramp. 'After Dad . . . after they threw his body in the Minch, I tried to run away. They chained me to the bedroom wall. Couldn't even *pee* without someone watching. I was only nine.'

Rainwater gurgled down the ramp from the floor above, which

explained the flooding on this level. Gillian negotiated the little rapids, and took them down to level four.

'They kept me on that chain, like I was a . . . rabid dog, or something, for *four years*, till they trusted me enough to take it off.' Her chin came up. 'Took me another three and a half to get out of there, but I did it.'

'How?'

'Ah.' She kept her eyes straight ahead. 'I *might*'ve set fire to something. Accidentally. Officer.'

Down the ramp to level three.

Angus smiled. 'You're lucky I'm officially off duty.'

Gillian smiled back. 'Oh, you have no idea . . .'

The further down the multistorey they went, the busier it got. Soon every level was crammed with cars – hopeful idiots circling like hyenas, hoping to pick off a parking spot, and then the Clio bumped down the final ramp and out into the storm-battered afternoon.

Stopping at the junction with Vyas Street to let a catering truck grumble past.

'Jonathan says you live in Kingsmeath, right? One of the tower blocks?'

Angus watched an ambulance roar away into the distance. 'Actually, would it be OK to head back over to Wardmill? Or is that too far out of your way?'

'Thought the doctor said you had to go home. Take it easy. Because of the head injury?'

A car horn blared out of the multistorey behind them, echoing against the concrete.

Gillian flinched. 'Sorry.' And pulled out onto the road. 'They could've cracked your skull. What if you get a brain haemorrhage or something? No, I'm taking you home.'

Behind them, a shiny, never-been-near-the-countryside-or-a-job-site four-by-four pickup truck growled out of the car park, the driver making wanking gestures in the Clio's rear-view mirror.

'He's missing, Gillian. Dr Fife. *Jonathan*. I don't know if they took him, or if he went voluntarily because he's one of them. But either way, I *have* to find him.'

'But he would *never*—'

'I know, but that's how it looks to some people. And if he's in danger, he needs me. Us.'

The Clio drifted to a halt at the roundabout, and Gillian turned to stare at Angus.

'The doctor said—'

'Just drop me off at Wardmill: I'll nab Dr Fife's hire car and go looking. Please.'

It took a while, but eventually Gillian's shoulders rounded. She shook her head. 'You can't drive.' Holding up her left arm. 'How you going to change gear?'

'It's an automatic.' He dug into his jacket pocket. 'And I've still got the keys.'

Deep breath. 'No. It's too dangerous.'

Sod.

Still, it'd been worth a go.

He'd just have to raid his savings for a taxi, because God knew when the next bus going that way would be.

Gillian reached across the car and squeezed Angus's knee. 'Like you say, Jonathan needs us. *I'll* drive you.' She checked the empty roundabout. 'Where we going?'

Yeah, but what if it wasn't safe?

What if something happened?

What if he said no, and she just followed him anyway?

She sat there, looking at him. Jaw clenched; eyes steely. Not for turning . . .

And, you know, it wouldn't *hurt* to have a little help.

He pulled the list of Kate Paisley's homers from his pocket – all battered and crumpled, with dark-scarlet stains soaked into the paper. 'We've got four left: the Wynd, Castleview, Shortstaine, and one north of the city.'

'OK.' She ran her eyes from the bandage on his head to the stiff and discoloured black suit jacket, across his bloodstained shirt, then down his scuffed trousers to the dull-red drips on his shoes. 'But first you need to get changed. Look like something out of *Reservoir Dogs*.'

Fair enough.

*

Gillian unlocked the door to Flat 4B and stepped into a friendly little hallway. 'Come in, come in.'

The carpet was so old that the pattern had worn off down the middle. A couple of jackets hung on one side of the door with a velveteen painting of the Dalai Lama, giving a thumbs up, on the other.

Four doors led off, not including the front one, but none of them were open.

'Sorry. It's all a bit of a mess . . .'

No, it really wasn't. OK, so everything was a little threadbare, but it was *clean*.

She closed the door behind him and snibbed the lock. Then pulled the handle to make sure. Helped him off with his stained high-vis.

Angus blinked at the happy Dalai Lama. 'Are you sure about this?'

'Probably. Robbie was about your size. I mean, he was a *complete* prick, but he was big with it.' A smile. 'Hold on.'

This was going to be a disaster, wasn't it.

She opened the second door on the right, exposing a double bedroom barely large enough for the mock four-poster bed and wardrobe that'd been squeezed in there. Then reached in, under the wooden bedframe, and pulled out one of those big plastic wheelie boxes. 'I know people would probably think it's weird, holding onto his stuff after he left, but he owes me, like, *three hundred quid*, and I thought he might come back if I kept it.' A frown. 'He didn't.'

Gillian folded the plastic lid back and produced a tweed jacket from the box. 'Not a splot of blood in sight.' Popping it onto the bed.

A weird scratching noise rasped out from behind Door Number Four.

Angus pointed. 'Is that normal?'

She placed a bright-yellow waistcoat beside the jacket. 'It's just Bartholomeow Farquharson McFuzzypants wanting his tea.' Tweed trousers next, followed by a checked shirt, tartan boxers, and white socks. She scooped it all up and stood, presenting it like a suit of armour to a medieval knight. 'Here.'

Angus accepted the lot, doing his best not to look ungrateful.

'I know, I know: he was a *total* young fogey. But I was kinda into that . . .' She stroked the tweed jacket. 'Like I said: daddy issues.' Then opened the third door. 'You can change in here. I'll go feed The Beast.'

At first glance, it was a dark little cupboard, but Gillian flicked the light switch, illuminating a small, windowless bathroom. It should've been poky, but it'd been done up like a miniature version of one from a swanky hotel. The bath was short, but it was deep, wrapped around with Welsh slate and topped by a fancy three-point shower. Elegant shower curtain. Small but stylish sink and toilet.

Everything in its place, no dust, no mould on the silicon, no water spots on the taps, no hardened toothpaste residue in the sink. Even the grout looked clean.

Turning on the light set a small extractor fan buzzing its way up to an idling *whummumumumum*.

'Thanks.' Angus ducked inside and locked the door behind him, before wriggling out of his bloodstained clothes. Which was much easier than wriggling into them.

The man reflected in the long, mirrored medicine cabinet looked like something out of a cheap horror movie. But the gore wasn't fake. In addition to all the blood down one side, a twin line of bruises peeked over his shoulder – exactly a pickaxe handle's width apart. He curled his top lip at the sight, then held his broken arm above his head and gave the armpit an experimental sniff.

Flipping heck . . .

Sour and oniony with hints of long-dead kebab.

He leaned towards the door. 'GILLIAN? GILLIAN, IS IT OK IF I TAKE A SHOWER? I'M ALL CLARTY WITH BLOOD.'

'*What?*'

'CAN I HAVE A WASH?'

'*Oh . . . OK. I suppose. Erm . . . hold on.*' About twenty seconds later, there was a knock on the door, and when Angus unlocked it – peering around the edge, keeping his naked body hidden behind the wooden panels – there was Gillian with a bath sheet and a bin bag. 'You want to give me your dirty clothes?'

Her eyes flickered past Angus as he handed them over, then her whole face went radish-red. 'It's . . . towel.' Holding it out as she stared. 'Towel for drying. Whhhh . . . Bag for your . . . you know . . . cast.' She crumpled that through the narrow gap between door and frame. 'Yes. I'd better . . . Sorry. Erm.' And she was gone.

Strange as a bag of herrings, that one.

Nice, and kind, and sweet, and pretty too, but *definitely* odd.

Angus closed the door and locked it again.

Not that there was anything wrong with being odd.

He turned to hang the towel on the rail and froze.

Naked Angus stared back at him from the big, mirrored medicine cabinet.

That's why she'd been acting all weird – she'd had a full-length ogle at his naked backside the whole time.

Well, that was humiliating.

He scrunched his face up and curled into himself.

Took a couple of deep breaths.

Sighed.

Then pulled the bin bag over his fibreglass cast and climbed into the shower.

Maybe a good hard scrub would wash the embarrassment away?

Even with the extractor running, after a fifteen-minute shower of shame the traitorous mirror had fogged up.

Angus flipped it the Vs as he towelled off.

Had to admit, that felt a lot better. Even if it *had* been a pain in the arse keeping his bandages dry.

He slipped into the borrowed boxers – having first checked that they were definitely clean – then stood there, head on one side, little finger wiggling away in his left ear. Trying to dislodge the water sloshing about in there. And making no difference whatsoever.

What he needed was a cotton bud.

He popped open the medicine cabinet and stared.

Wow.

There was an electric toothbrush and a bottle of make-up remover in there, but about ninety percent of the cabinet was stuffed with packets and packets and tubs and more packets of pills. All of which bore pharmacy stickers.

No cotton buds, though.

Angus closed the medicine cabinet.

That was a *massive* amount of medication.

He opened the cabinet again and had a careful rummage – putting everything back exactly where he found it. Thus ensuring he'd never get a job on an O Division search team.

Gillian had a sizeable collection of anti-anxiety drugs, antidepressants, sleeping tablets, pills for abnormal heartbeats, high blood pressure, low blood pressure, indigestion, a wide assortment of painkillers, and quite a few unopened boxes of pills that could've been anything. Like 'SEROQUEL'.

Suppose it wasn't that surprising, given she'd grown up in a commune of violent religious arseholes . . .

Most of the pharmacy labels were made out to 'MISS GILLIAN KILBRIDE', but there were a few boxes of antidepressants for 'MR ROBERT SNEETH', and one of diazepam too.

Angus weighed Mr Sneeth's escitalopram in his palm, then slotted it back into place and closed the medicine cabinet door.

None of his business.

Besides, she'd said 'Robbie' left some stuff here.

Just because she had a whole pharmacy of drugs, didn't mean she had a problem, did it? And even if she *did*, now wasn't the time to bring it up. Not with Dr Fife, DCI Monroe, and Olivia Lundy about to suffer a horrible death.

Everything else could wait.

He pulled on Robbie's checked shirt.

The guy must've been huge, because Angus's left arm, complete with cast, slipped easily into the sleeve, leaving plenty of room to spare. It was much easier to do up the buttons with one-and-a-half hands, but the front billowed out like a deflated bouncy castle. The trousers could easily have taken a couple of pillows before the waistband was anywhere near tight.

Angus gave his bloodstained belt a rinse in the sink, wiping it dry with toilet paper. That reined the trousers in. Tightening the strap at the back of the waistcoat made it more-or-less wearable, but the tweed jacket swamped him.

Not the sleeves – they were the right length – but the shoulders and front were far too big. As if he were a wee kid playing dress-up in an adult's clothes.

Still, it was better than the *Reservoir Dogs* cosplay outfit.

Barefoot, Angus picked up his new socks and padded out into the hall.

All the doors were closed, but the washing machine whirred and churned away in the kitchen, and muffled voices sounded from inside Door Number Four. Where The Beast had been scratching.

'Gillian?'

He knocked on the door – gently this time, not the Police Officer's Official Three – then let himself into a living room as threadbare and tidy as the hall. A bookcase in the corner groaned under the weight of self-help titles, next to a couch covered in a charity-shop quilt. A small TV sat opposite, playing *The Great British DIY Workshop*, in the shade of a big cat tree that'd been scratched raw in places.

Gillian was on the couch with a chunky grey cat in her lap. Stroking a rumbling purr from it as she poked away at her phone.

A brash Geordie accent burst out of the telly: *'Anthony and Donna have both decided to make their picnic tables out of recycled wood, but Anthony's decision to use reclaimed railway sleepers has come with some . . .* unexpected *problems . . .'*

Onscreen, a man in a Numbered Onions T-shirt thumped a sticky chunk of wood down onto a workbench, then sniffed at his fingers, before a look of utter horror dawned.

'And that's *why you're never supposed to go in the station.'*

Angus waved. 'Gillian?'

She let loose a squeal, flinching so hard that her cat had to scrabble to maintain its spot. She clamped her stroking hand over her heart and stared at him. 'Angus!' A deep breath was followed by a nervous laugh. 'It's been so long since I've had . . . friends over. Sorry.' She put her phone away.

The man in the T-shirt held his hands *far* away from his face. *'Oh my* God, *that's rank! . . . Oh, I'm going to be sick . . . How could anyone—'*

Gillian pointed the remote, shutting off Anthony's realization that railway sleepers weren't just brown because of the creosote. Then moved The Beast from her lap, getting a sharp, indignant *meow* for her trouble. 'Honestly: I thought you were, like, Robbie's *ghost* there for a moment. Only . . . thinner.' She gave herself a shake. 'I polished your shoes, and sponged off your fluorescent jacket. Ready to head?'

'Just about. Need help with socks again.'

She stood and took them from his hand with a wee smile. 'You look good.' Stroking his arm. 'Tweed suits you.'

No: he looked like Rupert Bear had shagged Toad of Toad Hall, but Angus smiled back and nodded anyway.

The Beast settled onto the couch and had a wash.

Downstairs, someone shouted at the television.

A bus rumbled by in the distance.

And she was still stroking his arm.

Angus swallowed. 'Better get going.'

'What? Oh, yes. Right. Sorry.' Gillian let go and turned to kiss her cat on the head. 'Bartholomeow Farquharson McFuzzypants – you're in charge. Watch the house while Mummy's away.' Then turned back to Angus. Blinked a couple of times as she gazed at all that oversized tweed. 'Ah: socks and shoes first. Yes. Sorry. Sorry.'

And she was on her knees again.

Angus kept his eyes focused straight ahead.

This was turning into a *very* confusing day . . .

46

Mrs Judith McKinnick: 8 Pearson Drive – 18:15

Angus limped down the driveway, wincing as rats sank their teeth into his stitched-together head, burrowed deep inside his aching shoulder, and rampaged up and down his broken arm with their sharp little claws.

But other than that? Just bloody dandy.

It was another swanky street: big modern four- or five-bedroom villas, in the plusher part of Shortstaine, overlooking Moncuir Wood. Where every home had flash cars parked on its lock-block driveway. For someone who whinged on about the Global Elite, Kate Paisley certainly liked her customers rich and extravagant.

The sun had barely put in an appearance since dawn, but now it glowed deep red around the valley's rim – as if its throat had been cut – bringing the streetlights flickering into life. Glowing gold in the hammering rain. The woods were a thick swathe of darkness, but the streetlights picked up again in Logansferry and Castle Hill, fading into the night as Storm Findlay swallowed Kingsmeath and Blackwall Hill.

Angus braced himself against the howling wind, opened the Clio's passenger door and tumbled inside, setting the whole thing rocking on its springs.

Closed his eyes, just for a moment, till the rats quietened down . . .

The *tick, tick tick-tick-tick tick, tick, tick* of thumbs on a smartphone scrabbled across the car.

Deep breath.

He huffed it out, wriggling in his seat, which seemed to have developed horrible lumps and angles since they arrived here ten minutes ago.

'*Angus?*'

He opened his eyes, and there was Gillian, holding out a wee hand towel.

'You'll catch your death in this.'

'Mrs McKinnick didn't get any joinery done.' He pulled his high-vis's hood back, and scrubbed his face dry. 'Didn't recognize either of the eFits.'

'Are you OK? Only you look—'

'I'm *fine*.' Which was a lie almost as big as the house he'd just left.

She lowered her eyes, picking at the skin around her fingernails. 'I was thinking. *Maybe* we should wait till tomorrow, when it's not blowing a gale?'

Just reaching for the seatbelt set his battered shoulder alight. Pulling it on poured petrol on the flames. He hissed and grimaced, clicking the buckle home. 'You want to find him, don't you? Jonathan?'

'*Of course* I do! I just don't want to lose *you* in the process.' She started the car, turned the blowers up full, and pulled away from the kerb. Headlights sweeping through the downpour as she let loose a little sigh. 'Where next?'

He checked the list. 'Castleview's closest, then the Wynd.'

'Wouldn't it be quicker to just phone? Or get a patrol car to do it?'

For God's sake. Why did everyone think they knew better? 'Dr Fife says, "Most people are arseholes and idiots."' Almost barking the words out. '"If something *important* needs done, do it *yourself.*"'

Sod. That had come out far harsher than necessary.

Gillian bit her bottom lip, eyes on the road, not saying anything.

She took a right at the junction, swapping the fancy homes of Pearson Drive for the modest bungalows of Monastery Road.

Her mouth quivered.

'I'm sorry; that wasn't meant to sound so . . .' Angus raised his good hand then let it fall again. 'Think the local anaesthetics must be wearing off, or something.' He tried for a smile. 'I'm just . . . a bit sore.' Would've helped if he hadn't left his NHS-issue paracetamol back at her place, in his blood-soaked suit. Like an idiot. 'It's not you, honestly.'

She nodded, but didn't say a single word.

Great.

He'd screwed *this* up too . . .

Mr Jeremy Dalgarno: 4 Strachan Lane – 18:41

'I'll be sure to let them know.' Angus hobbled out of the porch into the storm.

Mr Dalgarno stuck his nose in the air. 'You do that. We pay *more* than enough council tax to keep these hooligans from dropping their litter all over the riverbank!' His tweed suit was a much better fit than Angus's borrowed affair, and probably a *heck* of a lot more expensive too. With the white hair swept back from a high fore-head, aquiline nose, and busy hands, it gave him the air of a retired detective from an Agatha Christie book. Only with fewer social graces.

He threw Angus a crisp 'Goodbye', and thumped the door shut, exiling him to the lands of wind and rain.

Tosser.

Angus hauled his high-vis hood up and limped away down the drive, going as fast as his aching body would allow. Rain hissing through the leaves and branches of the massive garden, crackling against his fluorescent-yellow jacket.

Strachan Lane lay on the eastern edge of Castleview – big granite houses on one side, the wooded riverbank on the other. A view out across the golf course, the River Wynd, and on to Minch Kirk and its cemetery. God knew how much somewhere like this must be worth, but it was probably *millions*.

So what the hell did Mr Dalgarno have to whinge about? He should try living in a tower block with knackered lifts and teenage gangs roaming the streets.

The driveway ended at a set of eight-foot-high wrought-iron gates, with 'DALGARNO' worked into the design.

Angus gave them a shove, but they wouldn't budge.

Maybe it was a pull, instead?

Still nothing.

A buzzing noise sounded from the ivy-covered wall, and the gate swung open, all on its own.

He looked back towards the house, and there was Mr Dalgarno, standing in the drawing room's bay window with a remote in one hand and a whisky in the other.

Angus gave him a little wave, but got sod-all back.

Typical.

He slipped out through the gates onto the pavement and hobbled over to Gillian's Clio. The wind tried to rip the passenger door from his hand, but he gritted his teeth and held on, easing himself into the seat and hauling it shut again.

Then sat there, graveyard still, face all creased up, eyes screwed tightly shut, teeth bared as the rats threw a ceilidh for their arsonist friends.

Gillian kept her voice very small. 'You know, it's OK if you want to stop. You've been very brave, Angus, but you'll fall apart if you don't get some rest.'

He hissed a breath through clenched teeth. 'I just need a minute.'

'*Please* let me help you.'

Every muscle and vertebra howled as he edged himself fully back into the seat. 'Can't . . . just abandon him.'

'There's, like, a million cops out there, looking for Jonathan. You're knackered – you nearly *died* today.'

They sat there, in silence, as rain hammered on the Clio's roof.

Then Gillian cleared her throat. 'Look. I kinda thought this might happen and . . .' She reached across the car.

Angus's eyes snapped open, in case she was—

But she opened the glove compartment and pulled out a small tub of prescription drugs instead.

He shook his head. 'I don't—'

'They're only little ones.' Giving the tub a shake. 'You got a prescription for thirty-mil co-dydramol, right? This is just co-*codamol*, and it's only eight milligrams, see?' She showed him the label. 'These are like Smarties, really. Only less chocolatey?' Opening the child-safety cap and tipping two lozenge-shaped pills into the palm of her hand. 'You can't help him if you can't move.'

Angus stared at the pills, then out at the storm raging across the valley – whipping whitecaps from the river below, shuddering the trees, hurling rain to bounce from the tarmac and rattle the Clio's bodywork.

She had a point.

And, as Gillian said: they were only little.

He took them from her warm palm. 'Thanks.'

'Hold on, this'll help.' She dug into her door pocket, emerging with a bottle of flavoured water. Flipped open the sports cap. And held it out.

Angus washed his co-codamol down with a good swig of—

Jesus, that was horrible. Acrid and bitter – the fake-strawberry flavour barely took the edge off. And then the *aftertaste* hit.

'I know.' Gillian nodded as he shuddered. 'But it's got essential salts, minerals, and vitamins in it. The government want to ban sugar, because that means manufacturers have to put artificial sweeteners in everything, and research shows most of those interfere with your amygdala, cos the plan's to keep us all docile. Even though aspartame is disgusting *and* carcinogenic.' She took the bottle back. 'That's why you should *always* read the label.'

Bet she'd had Covid and it'd screwed with her tastebuds, because her coffee was awful too.

But she meant well.

Angus forced the bitter taste down. 'Thanks.'

She turned in her seat and stared at him. 'You *sure* you don't want to go home?'

'I can't just give up.'

She nodded. Sighed. 'The Wynd next?'

'The Wynd.'

She pulled the car around in a lurching three-point-turn and drove off into the storm.

Jack & Chloe Maxwell: Fenrith House, Persephone Avenue – 19:15

Angus hauled open the passenger door and thumped into the seat with a hissing wheeze. Blinking just seemed to stir up the dots floating across his vision, but he did it anyway. Gritted his teeth. Shook his head.

It didn't clear the dots. Or the angry buzzing in his shoulder, skull, and arm.

'Angus?'

He squinted across the car and there was Gillian, staring back at him, with a pensive look on her face.

She pointed. 'Door?'

Oh, right. Right.

The door.

Rain was getting in.

He clunked the door shut again. 'Sorry.'

'You OK?'

No.

Another blink sent the dots dancing once more. 'Jack and Chloe Maxwell. You should see their house: it's like something off an advert for rich, smug turdwads.' Not the kind of language he would normally use in front of a civilian, like Gillian, but *boy* were they *smug*. 'He's a political advisor to the local MSP, she's an investment banker, with a Bentley and a holiday home in the Dordogne. They paid Kate Paisley and Ryan to redo their wine cellar.'

Gillian's eyes widened. 'Didn't Jonathan say the next victims were going to be *bankers*?'

'That's what I was thinking.' He pulled out his phone – now liberated from its ziplock bag – and pressed the power button. Nothing. So he squeezed it instead. Still nothing. Tried again. And again.

What was wrong with the bloody . . .

Ah, right. It had gone to the Great Phone Shop in the Sky, remember?

He let a little groan rumble free, then stuffed the thing back in his pocket. 'Phone's dead.' Leaving a nice long pause for her to leap in and offer. But she didn't. So: 'Can I borrow yours? Promise I won't search for nudes.'

'I . . .' Gillian pulled back in her seat as bright pink whooshed up her neck and cheeks. 'That's . . .'

'Sorry. Sorry.' He scrubbed his good hand across his face. 'Don't know why I said that.'

A squall of rain jostled the Clio – windscreen wipers struggling to keep up.

'Maybe . . . because you're really tired? It's been a long day. Lots of stuff happening.'

'Sorry.' He gave himself a shake, sending water dribbling from his high-vis into the seat and footwell. 'Can I borrow your phone to call the station and tell them about the Maxwells? Please?'

She frowned at him, chewing on the inside of her cheek.

Angus kept his big mouth shut.

But eventually Gillian nodded. 'OK.' Then produced her mobile, unlocked it, and passed it to him.

Took three goes to remember the right number for Control, but he got there, setting it ringing.

She tugged at his fluorescent-yellow sleeve. '*Then* can we go home?'

'Just one more address left. We're—'

'*O Division, Control Room, who's calling please?*' The same voice as last time, but taking no chances with an unknown number.

'It's DC MacVicar – can you put me through to DS Massie? I've got some info for her.'

'*Hud oan.*'

The line went silent.

'Please, Angus: you're acting a bit . . .' Her fingers writhed like upturned beetles. 'What if it's a concussion? Maybe we should take you back to the hospital? Maybe something's gone wrong?'

'I'll be fine. Probably just low blood sugar. Been a long time since breakfast, and—'

'*Hoy!*' DS Massie did *not* sound happy. '*What did I tell you? Three days! Doctor's note! No being a pain in my—*'

'Sarge: Mr and Mrs Maxwell, Fenrith House, Persephone Avenue, the Wynd. Got a positive on the eFit of Ryan—'

'*Do you never bloody listen?*'

'This is *important*! Mrs Maxwell's an investment banker and she's had work done by Ryan, just like the Lundys. She's probably the Fortnight Killer's next target! You need to get a patrol car out here and—'

'*And you need to* go home*! Thank you for the tip; we'll follow it up. You. Will. Go. Home. Before. You. Kill. Yourself! I'm not telling you again.*' She left one of her trademark ominous pauses. '*I'm circulating a lookout request, Angus, and if back shift find you out and about, you're spending the rest of the night in custody. For your own sodding good. Am I making myself* plain, Constable?'

Just couldn't win, could he.

Angus closed his eyes and let his head boink, *gently*, against the passenger window. 'Sarge.'

'*Go home!*' And with those rousing words of thanks and encouragement, she hung up on him.

He scowled at the mobile's blank screen for a couple of breaths, then returned the thing to Gillian. 'Thanks.'

'Whoever it was, on the phone, they told you to get some rest, didn't they?'

He produced the list again – battered and creased and going floppy from being handled with damp fingers – and drew two red lines through Fenrith House. Then pulled in a sharp breath as those twelve stitches in his head snarled beneath their gauze padding. Which set his arm throbbing again. Then his shoulder. Like some sort of torture-filled game of KerPlunk, stealing the air from his lungs.

Angus sat there, jaw clenching and unclenching, till the spasm passed. He slumped back in his seat. 'One . . . address left.'

'We need to get you home, so—'

'Come on, we owe it to Dr Fife.' Shifting his weight from one hip to the other, struggling to find a position that didn't *hurt* so much. 'I'm just a bit stiff, that's all.'

She chewed on a fingernail, gnawing away till it was ragged and bleeding on one side. Then reached for the glove compartment.

'Here.' Shaking two more pills from the tub and holding them out, along with that horrible strawberry-flavoured water again.

He popped the tablets, chasing them down with a gulped mouthful. Grimaced and shuddered at all those essential salts, minerals, and vitamins.

Gah . . .

He handed the bottle back. 'Thanks.'

'Angus?' She squeezed his arm, a wheedling, pleading tone seeping into her voice: 'Are you *sure* we can't go home?'

'We're almost done.'

Gillian's head drooped. 'That's what worries me.'

She put the car in gear.

47

Something was wrong with the map he'd found in the glove compartment. The roads and gridlines kept slipping in and out of focus, and the paper wouldn't fold properly, and the whole thing was about as big as a duvet cover, and how were you supposed to work with *that* in the passenger seat of a rusty-but-spotless Renault Clio, parked in a half-flooded lay-by?

Didn't help that he was having to do it all by the meagre glow of the car's courtesy light.

This was *impossible*.

They'd made it up beyond the rim of the valley, north of Blackwall Hill, far removed from Oldcastle's streetlights and their sickly glow.

Out here there was nothing but darkness.

Well, darkness and the Glendorcha distillery. And its bonded warehouses. And the eight-foot-high, razor-wire-topped chain-link fence surrounding both. Other than *that*, the world had dissolved into vague silhouettes in the gloom.

Gillian fidgeted behind the wheel, worrying another nail down to a serrated, bloody stub as rain growled against the windscreen and those silhouettes writhed in the wind.

The wipers clunked and squeaked, clearing twin rainbows through the downpour, showing off the brown road sign mounted at the end of the lay-by for a moment – 'PARRACK WOODS 2 ~ BRAE-CAIRN FOREST 2½' – before the downpour swallowed it again.

'I don't like this, Angus. It's *horrible* out here. What if something happens? What if we get squashed by a tree, or the road's blocked, or there's flooding?' She nodded, agreeing with herself. 'We should go home.'

'We'll be fine. It's easy.' He pulled the map right up to his nose and squinted at it. 'Erm . . . I think we go that way.' Pointing in the same direction as the road sign.

She took a deep breath, then crawled the car out of the lay-by, skirting first the massive puddle and then the distillery's chain-link barricade. Sitting forward in her seat, hunched over the steering wheel and peering out through the hammering rain. 'Talk to me.'

'What?' He did his best to fold the map back up again. 'I *am* talking to you.'

'I'm nervous enough, driving in this. Just . . .' She tightened her grip on the wheel – knuckles bunching as the car forged through a spreading lake of muddy water, sending twin arcs of brown *spwooosh*ing up and over the bonnet. 'So you live at home with your mum? That's nice?'

Ha.

Nice wasn't exactly the first word Angus would've chosen.

'Well, she throws a wobbly when I'm late for dinner. Complains that I never do the washing up – even though I do it *all the time*. But . . . she *means* well. It's all been a bit hard for her, you know? Dealing with Dad's death.'

Another one of those brown signs went by, pointing left into the darkness: 'PARRACK WOODS 1½'. Behind it, a clump of trees thrashed, jagged arms reaching for the car like a hungry animal.

'Uh-huh.'

Angus frowned. 'Never really thought about it at the time, but I guess we used to be pretty well off. Dad worked for an oil company, so we'd have fancy foreign holidays and nice new cars. She was a "lady who lunches", and I went to private school. Had a lovely golden retriever called Westminster.' He puffed out his cheeks. Poor old Westminster. 'Don't know what you've got till it's gone, do you.' Or at least *he* didn't. 'After Dad died, it all evaporated. We moved down here and Mum got a job as a dinner lady to pay the bills. That was a culture shock.' He produced a sad smile for the little boy reflected in the passenger window, with a bandaged head and blood matted in his hair. 'But at least we had plenty of food in those days. She used to bring home the leftovers . . .'

And yeah, to begin with it felt dirty – living off the remnants of some state-school kids' Turkey Twizzlers, chips, jam sponge and custard, but it'd been better than going to bed hungry.

Bed.

Lovely soft cosy bed.

Warm and droopy with sleep.

Where you could close your eyes and just drift off.

Where nobody bullied you for your posh accent, or being taller than all the other kids.

Where everything didn't *hurt*, and you still had a nice big bed-room with all the latest toys and a golden retriever . . .

. . .

. . .

'*Angus?*'

. . .

'*ANGUS!*'

Something thumped into his arm.

'Mmmph?' He sat up straight, blinking at the squealing wind-screen wipers. 'Sorry. Yes. Where . . . ?'

Gillian hunched over the wheel again. 'Your mum's a dinner lady.'

'Oh. Yeah.' A stretch made something pop in his neck, as if he'd been stabbed with an icicle. 'Not is: *was*. Her knees went, so she's on disability now. Doesn't exactly pay the bills. And I think it *hurts*, you know? Being thrown away like that.'

Gillian blinked, and a little tear trickled down her cheek. 'She sounds like a lovely woman.'

Suppose that must be true, especially if your *own* mother raised you in a brutal, bible-thumping cult of pious island bastards.

'Oh, she's a proper nightmare at times, but . . . she's my mum. It's just . . . she gets *extra* squirrelly around the anniversary of Dad's death.' Shaking his head sent the dots swirling again. 'Kids-on she's fine, but everything becomes *that bit more* brittle. So, next Tuesday will be a bag of laughs.' He braced himself against the dashboard until it stopped rotating. 'Suppose I don't have to tell *you* about weird mums, right? Growing up with the Apostles?'

A nod. Then Gillian wiped her eyes, smudging the black wing-tips. 'I'm sorry.'

He reached across the car and patted her on the arm. 'Yeah, me too.'

A T-junction loomed in the headlights, with another road sign pointing off to the left: 'BRAECAIRN FOREST 1½'. Gillian slowed the Clio to a walking pace, easing around the turn.

Angus smiled. 'Will you look at that . . .' Pointing away into the dark. 'I used to LARP up here, when I was a kid.'

Hang on.

Angus sat up a little straighter. 'That's where we found Dr Lundy's body. You don't think . . . ?'

'No. That was on the other side of the woods, remember?'

'Was it?' A yawn made his jaw pop, followed by a little shiver. 'Yeah. Suppose it was. Maybe that's why they chose the spot – because they'd been working in the area?'

The car grumbled along like a busted tractor, blowers roaring, windscreen wipers thumping.

Gillian tapped her fingers against the steering wheel. 'Do you know the stories about Braecairn Forest?'

'Mmmm?' He settled deeper into his seat.

'Once, long ago, when the mountains were young and trees could still speak, there lived a family of cannibals in the deep dark woods. They built cairns from the skulls of their breakfast, filled the streams with the blood of their dinner, and patched together beasts and monsters from the skins of their supper . . .' She turned the blowers down a notch. Which was nice, because she didn't have to talk so loud, and she had a lovely soothing voice. 'Course, this was back at the end of the seventeenth century, when the "Ill Years" famine hit, and the Great Old Forest stretched all the way south to Kings River and north to Farrabroch. Now there's only a few wee patches left.'

Her phone ding-buzzed with an incoming text message, but she ignored it and kept on down the rain-lashed road. 'They didn't *start out* as cannibals. That only came after the famine hit. All over

Scotland about fifteen percent of the population starved to death, but in this bit of the world it was one in four.'

Bet that was a lot of people.

All hungry in their beds.

In the middle distance, a spine of darker black jutted out into the fields – its back hunched and rippling in the storm.

She bit her bottom lip, gazing out through the sweeping wipers at the stormy night. 'Can you *imagine* a worse time to be alive? You've got one of the coldest bits of the Little Ice Age, the Nine Years War is still raging, there's only been *one* successful harvest in the last five years, *and* there's rampant poverty.'

On the other side of the road, another slab of darkness reared out of the gloom, and Braecairn Forest swallowed the car. Tree trunks and branches shining in the Clio's headlights – making inky shadows slither as they passed. No other lights to be seen.

Gillian's voice faded to a whisper. 'No wonder they ate each other.'

Most of the trees were thick, heavy pines, but here and there the pale naked skeletons of beech and ash slunk between their well-fed brethren. Slippery in the twisting gloom.

These were *exactly* the sort of woods where a family of starving cannibals would live, making monsters.

Even the storm was too scared to enter.

The car slowed to a halt and Gillian cleared her throat. 'We can still turn around and go home, Angus.' Gazing across the car at him. 'Please?'

He blinked at her.

Poor Gillian, with her horrible childhood and her murdered father and her smudged, teary eyes.

Another yawn rippled its way through Angus, leaving him sagging against the door. Voice going all fuzzy around the edges. 'He's out there somewhere, Gillian. We can't . . . we can't give up.'

A sigh. A nod. Then the Clio moved forward again, heading deeper into the dark woods.

It wasn't long before a hand-painted sign flared in the headlights: 'MAINS OF INVERMINNOCH →', and she took the turning onto a gritty track that rolled and wallowed with water-filled potholes. Winding away between the looming trees.

Dark.

Even with the blowers turned down, warm air oozed out into the footwell, working its way up Angus's legs and chest. Cocooning him against the storm. Wrapping him in its tender arms.

Making his eyelids droop.

They'd be there soon.

Should really stay awake.

Yeah . . .

. . .

Should really . . .

Angus snorked. Opened his eyes and blinked out through the Clio's windscreen. 'Where . . . ?'

It was a clearing, deep in the woods by the look of it, surrounded by battlements of oak and Scots pine. And everything was still – no howling wind, no lashing rain, just the cold light of a gibbous moon, shining down through a gap in the clouds.

Maybe this was the eye of the storm?

At its centre reared a Scottish baronial tower: L-shaped; five-and-a-bit storeys tall, the lower two floors wrapped in scaffolding with a skin of poles and tarpaulin reaching all the way up the long end of the building to its steeply pitched slate roof. All turned monochrome in the moonlight.

The track ended at a wide turning circle, where a rusty builder's van sat next to a huge pile of broken slate and another of crumbling stone. It had probably all been in gravel at one point, but now grass and weeds crawled across it, blurring the line between the driveway and an overgrown lawn of tussocks and reeds. Whin and broom creeping in from the forest's edge.

Gillian's mouth pinched, her eyes glittering in the dashboard lights. 'We're here.' She parked next to the van. 'Angus, I . . . I want you to know I tried, I really did.' Patting him on the leg. 'But you . . . you're just so *stubborn*.' Then let go. 'I'm sorry.'

Eh?

'What's . . .' He shook his head, turning the car into a fairground waltzer. 'Wait a minute . . .'

The passenger door opened and a Freddie Mercury tribute act

grinned in at him. The bastard still wore his manky overalls, but he'd swapped the torn woolly hat for a swathe of bandages of his own – probably holding his head together after Angus lamped him one. *Literally.* An asterisk of microporous tape held a wad of gauze over whatever was left of his nose. His voice was as bunged-up and cheery as a decongestant commercial. 'Hey, big fella. Thought you'd never get here. How's the arm?'

Then his fist clattered into Angus's face.

48

Gillian grabbed at Angus's high-vis. 'Don't!'

Before the world stopped spinning, the Bastard reached in and unclipped Angus's seatbelt. There was a brief tug of war, but he was clearly stronger than Gillian – hauling Angus out of the car and onto the gravel driveway.

A boot slammed into Angus's stomach, folding him up, then another, and another. Sending something far bigger than rats scrabbling through his body, all claws and teeth.

He shielded his head with his arms, knees drawn up tight to protect his insides as the boot thumped home.

'NOT SO FUCKING BIG NOW, ARE YOU?'

Get up.

Get up!

But his arms and legs were lead-lined coffins full of rotten bones.

'WANT SOME MORE?' The boot stomped down on Angus's ribs, and probably would've again if it wasn't for the ominous *shclick-clack* of a gun being cocked.

'Tony! I said "Don't"!'

The Bastard, AKA: Tony, backed away a couple of paces, and when Angus unwrapped the arms from his head, there was Gillian, standing beside the Clio with a semi-automatic pistol pointed right at Tony's head.

'You gotta be *shitting* me.' The Bastard raised his hands. 'This prick is the *enemy*. He's the Elite we're fighting against!'

'Elite?' She jabbed her free hand at Angus. 'He lives in a crappy wee flat, in a tower block, in Kingsmeath, *with his mum*!'

It took almost everything Angus had to roll over onto his back, arms and legs reduced to floppy useless things that wouldn't take his weight.

Gillian glared at Tony.

Tony glared at Gillian.

Angus groaned.

The house's front door clicked open, and a woman stepped outside, crunching her way across the weed-strewn gravel. She had a paint-smeared puce sweatshirt and grey joggy-bottoms, long brown hair and heavy eyebrow-length fringe, stubby fingers, lots of teeth. A forty-something dowdy lump in a mid-twenties body.

She curled her lip. 'What's with all the wanking about? Get him inside already.'

Tony flexed his fists. 'Ask *her*. She's gone native.'

Gillian lowered the gun. 'This isn't *necessary*.' Then lowered her eyes. 'We're supposed to be *better* than that. Better than *them*.'

The Woman jerked a thumb at the house. 'In!' Then squatted down in front of Angus. 'Here's a joke for you, Pig. A journalist, a politician, a lawyer, a doctor, two police officers, and a *teeny* forensic psychologist walk into a meat grinder . . .' She flashed him a basilisk's grin. 'Stop me if you've heard it before.'

Nothing worked any more. He couldn't even pull away.

She patted him on the cheek. 'You're going to *love* the punchline.' Then grabbed one shoulder of Angus's borrowed high-vis.

Tony took the other, and together they dragged him across the weedy gravel towards the house, huffing and puffing with the effort.

The moonlight faded, and drizzle misted down from the low black sky. Wind mourned through the trees . . .

They hauled him past the exoskeleton of scaffolding to an arched recess, through an open door, and into a big fancy hall.

A stone staircase dominated the space, sweeping up to the next floor. The steps were old enough to have dips worn in the middle of them, but brand-new wooden bannisters shone in the pendant lighting. Two, maybe three doors led off to other parts of the house, and a passageway disappeared into its depths, behind the staircase. The place should've been festooned with paintings and tartan and stuffed animal heads, like the Bishop's View Hotel, but instead everything was slick and modern. Nothing interfering with the clean sweep of magnolia walls, or the unblemished oatmeal carpet.

The Woman jerked them to a halt on the patch of coir matting, just inside the door. Breathing hard. 'Hold on, hold on . . . put a . . . towel under his feet . . . for God's sake . . . Don't want drag marks . . . on the nice new carpet.'

Tony groaned, then let go – causing Angus's battered shoulder to thump down against the mat as he grumbled away.

Didn't hurt, though.

Nothing hurt any more.

Instead, the aches and stabbing and throbbing pains had been replaced by warm marshmallow.

Angus squinted up at the Woman, but she wouldn't stay in focus. His tongue didn't want to cooperate either: 'You'll . . . Won't get . . .'

'Let me guess: "You'll never get away with it", or "The police are on their way"? Cos we will, and they're not.' She grinned. 'No one's coming to save you.'

Gillian stepped into the hall, still clutching the gun, but not pointing it at anyone. She looked at Angus as if he was an injured puppy, tied to a breeze block, ready to be hurled into the river. 'I *tried* to get you to go home, but you wouldn't listen.' Her eyebrows pinched. 'This isn't how it was meant to be: I put plenty of sleeping pills and antidepressants in your coffee this morning . . . It would've been *painless*.'

Great.

And he'd let her give him *pills*.

Moron.

She hunched her shoulders. 'But Jonathan threw it all up, and I don't know *what* went wrong with yours. Put enough in there to down a hippo. Sorry.'

Angus forced himself up onto his elbows, pushing out each word like a kidney stone. 'I ditched it . . . in the pot plant . . . because your coffee . . . was *rank*.' Come on, he could do this. 'Gillian Kilbride . . . I'm arresting . . . arresting you under . . . Section one of . . . the Criminal Justice—'

'Shut up.' The Woman put her foot on his chest and shoved him back down again. 'Thought you said he was out for the count.'

Gillian winced. 'He's had four zopiclone and a bunch of sertraline and Seroquel dissolved in water and strawberry vodka; he's not going to be any trouble.' Smiling down at him as if they were old friends, not so much as an ounce of malice in her voice: 'Are you, Angus?'

The Woman snorted. 'Yeah. And my shite smells of Christmas trees.' She threw open Angus's jacket. 'I want his phone, his belt, and anything sharp.'

Gillian went through his pockets, cheeks bright red as she fiddled his belt off.

Then Tony reappeared from the passageway under the stairs, unfurling a tatty bath sheet. 'Happy now?'

'Yeah: ecstatic.' The Woman watched him lift Angus's feet and plonk them down on the towel. 'Cable-tie the bugger's wrists and ankles first, you idiot!'

'God's sake . . .' But he dug a handful of thick black strips from the pocket of his overalls and threaded one around Angus's ankles, fastening it with a *zwwwwiiip*. Then added a second one, just for luck. Before jamming a boot under Angus's shoulder and half kicking, half flipping him over onto his front.

Gillian's gun snapped up again. 'I *told* you!'

'Jesus, you're as bad as *her*!' He knelt and hauled Angus's hands behind his back. *Zwwwwiiip. Zwwwwiiip.* '*Better*?'

'No.'

He muttered something – too low to make out – then tucked the towel around Angus's feet, tying the ends together.

They didn't bother flipping Angus back over again. Instead, Tony and the Woman took hold of his armpits and dragged him through a door on the right, into an empty room. It had the same spotless beige carpet, same clean magnolia walls, but a line of fitted bookcases stretched down one whole side – immaculate, book-free, and floor to ceiling.

Now that Angus's belt was gone, there was nothing to keep his oversized, borrowed trousers from sliding down around his knees.

As if this wasn't undignified enough.

The Woman raised her voice as they dragged him into the middle of the room. 'Look what we got!' The words echoing around the empty room.

And in marched Ryan, dressed in a brown hoodie and blue jeans. His bright-white trainers discoloured and scuffed from the chase at Sadler Road. Faded Tartantula festival T-shirt. Trimmed beard and long black hair. For some reason, he looked as if he'd talk in a trans-atlantic drawl, to go with the wannabe-rockstar look, but when he *spoke* what came out was a Highlands and Islands accent almost identical to Gillian's. 'Give you any trouble?'

Tony sniffed: ever the hardman. 'Tried, but I put him straight. *Again.*'

'Oh dear.' Ryan tutted at Angus, dangling there between Tony and the Woman. 'Who's a *bad* house guest?' He took a three-step run-up and slammed his foot into Angus's ribs.

Gillian flinched, but the gun stayed by her side. Clearly, she was a lot braver around Tony than she was with Ryan.

The air roared back into Angus's lungs as he hung there, gasping.

Ryan stuck his hands in his hoodie's pockets. 'Take him downstairs.'

The Woman pulled out an RFID fob – black, with a red band around the middle. Just like Kate Paisley's one. She reached into one of the bookcase shelves, near the middle of the set, and pressed it against the wood until something inside went *clunk*. Then placed both hands on the nearest uprights and pushed.

A whole three-foot-wide section sank into the bookcases, only coming to a halt when it had retreated behind the rest of them. Another clunk and she shoved it sideways instead, hidden castors rumbling as it slipped out of the way, concealed by the shelves in front.

LED lights bloomed, illuminating a short passageway with a flight of stairs at the end. Heading down.

Tony didn't wait for the Woman to come back and help; instead, he hooked both hands deep into Angus's armpits and hauled him into the passageway, to the top of the stairs.

Then shoved him over the edge.

49

Angus tumbled down a narrow flight of steep stairs, bumping off the walls, battering off the steps, then coming to a sudden stop with a crunching *thump*.

It should've hurt a lot more than it did – which was one benefit of trusting bloody Gillian Two-Faced Poisoning Scumbag Kilbride. At least he was well anaesthetized.

And didn't drunk people survive more accidents because they didn't tense up? Which was lucky, because he could barely *move*.

More LED strip lights sparked into life as he lay there on his side, both arms twisted behind his back, legs pinned together, face pressed against a cool, smooth floor of polished concrete.

It was bigger than the secret dungeon under number one-thirty-two Sadler Road – about twelve feet square, lined with chipboard. But instead of one cell, there were two: facing each other across the room. Both secured with twin handles and a large, hinged locking mechanism. Each held in place with a chunky padlock.

Those weren't the only doors, though. A third – heavy-looking and wooden – sat beneath a wall-mounted sign that probably lit up when you switched it on. Red background with the word 'RECORDING' in white, above 'STUDIO IN USE'.

Which wasn't exactly reassuring.

Ryan's lilting Highland accent echoed down from upstairs. *'You bloody idiot!'*

'What?' Tony's hardman bravado transformed into a petulant whine: *'He tried to bash my brains in* with a standard lamp, *remember? Look what he did to my face!'*

'You trying to ruin everything? Is that it? What if he broke his neck?'

'Oh, come on, Ryan: we're killing him anyway, aren't we? He's a fascist jackboot for the Cabal! Who cares?'

Angus closed his eyes and rocked his right shoulder forward. Then back. Then forward. Then back. Putting a bit more energy into it each time until, at last, he toppled over onto his front. Breath hissing against the concrete.

Which should make it *a little* safer for what he was about to do.

He dragged in a deep breath and swallowed it. Opened his mouth and clenched his battered stomach. A gurgling, gagging sound bubbled out from his throat.

'And what if that broken neck isn't just a broken neck? What if it's a punctured lung, or a compound fracture, and he's down there bleeding all over the place? WHICH YOU'LL HAVE TO CLEAN UP, YOU MUPPET!'

'All right, all right. I get it. I'm sorry.'

Angus retched and squirmed, jerking his stomach muscles in and out as he rocked. Mouth open, throat stretched. The blood swelling in his face as he strained and strained and strained . . .

A wee dry boak hacked out nothing more than a string of spittle.

'Maybe you're not suited to this kinda work, Tony. Maybe you shouldn't be part of the team?'

The petulant tone turned into something more like fear. *'Jesus, Ryan, it was just a mistake. Didn't mean anything by it.'*

Another deep breath and Angus tried again, clenching and straining till tears blurred his vision and his eyes were about to pop.

'Maybe we should throw you a going-away party? Like we did for Shona.'

Come on, you dirty bastard . . .

A bitter, stinking wash of antidepressants and sleeping pills and water and strawberry vodka *hurk*ed from his mouth. Spattering across the polished concrete. He heaved again. And again. Getting as much out of his system as possible, till there was nothing left but bile and air.

Vomit spread out in a slick of clear-pinkish-foamy liquid – which, *hopefully*, was that colour because of the beans he'd had at breakfast, and not because all this crap was dissolving the lining of his stomach.

He forced himself over onto his back, and then again, onto his other side, keeping going till he'd put a bit of distance between himself and the foul-smelling puddle.

Then lay there, panting. Spitting out the sour remnants.

'Honest, Ryan: if he's broken anything I'll clean it up! Spick and span. Like new!'

'You better.'

'Yes, Ryan. Not a problem at all. Great.'

Angus blinked the tears from his eyes.

OK, so the world was still waltzing around his head, but you couldn't just puke this stuff up and be instantly better. It'd take a while to work its way out of his system. And at least now it wouldn't get any worse.

What he needed was a plan.

And a weapon.

Yes, but there was nothing in here, was there. Just him and the bloody cells. And even if there were something, he was in no position to wield it with his hands cable-tied behind his back.

Bootsteps clumped on the steps. Someone was coming.

OK: Plan B.

Angus went limp. Drooping, as if he'd passed out, or been knocked unconscious in his plummet down the stairs. Right eye shut, left one peeking out into the basement.

Which actually helped slow the room's swirling dance.

Tony appeared, face scrunched like a toddler's fist. Voice a muttering grumble, too quiet to be heard by anyone in the lounge above. Because he was nowhere near as brave as he thought. 'Yes, *Ryan*; no, *Ryan*; what did your last slave die of, *Ryan*.' He pulled a key from his pocket – small, with a round head. 'Thinks he's God's gift . . .'

He slipped the key into the padlock opposite the stairs, popped it open, and swung the locking bars out of the way. Then took hold of the handles and levered the cell's door from its frame. It had the same thick layers of polystyrene and acoustic insulation sandwiched between two slabs of chipboard as the dungeon at Sadler Road.

As soon as the door popped open, the stench of stale sweat and human waste collapsed out into the basement.

Tony didn't even flinch at the smell. What with his nose being standard-lamped and everything.

He propped the door up against the wall. 'I'll show *him*. See how *he* likes it when I bash *his* sodding head in . . .'

He stomped towards Angus, bending, arms out ready to grab him, and stepped right into that puddle of vomit. Turned out a frothy pool of liquid on top of polished concrete made for a very low-friction surface and Tony's foot skidded out from underneath him, arms pinwheeling as he crashed down on his arse.

The padlock key pinged against the floor, bouncing away as Tony sat there: eyes screwed shut, teeth bared, hissing and growling in pain. Then a look of disgust crawled across his face as he raised his wet hands from the concrete. 'What the . . . ?'

It soaked into the fabric of his overalls, turning the material dark grey all around his backside, sleeves, and legs.

He stared at his glistening, dripping fingers. 'Oh, you *dirty* bastard!'

Angus narrowed his hidden eye.

That key had come to rest not far from the door to Cell Number Three, a couple of feet from Angus's no-longer-shiny shoes. It glinted in the LED lights.

Tony was still sitting there, in the puke, trying to flick frothy pink bile off his hands.

Good.

Angus let free a pantomime groan – not hard, given the state of his poor ribs, and jammed his feet down hard into the concrete. Pinning them there as he curled up, dragging his torso and head closer to Cell Number Three.

'God, it's everywhere!' Tony struggled to his knees, hauling himself up the bars outside Cell Number One, boots slipping in the slithery mess.

One more groan-and-curl, and Angus was less than two inches from the fallen key.

Come on, you wee shite . . .

Tony Bambied out of the puddle and stood there, turning in a circle, pulling at his overalls, clearly more concerned about his covering of vomit than anything else. 'Gah . . . !' Then his boot flashed out, catching Angus on the thigh.

Which stung a bit, but the remnants of Gillian's drug cocktail smothered the worst of it.

A grunt burst free, and Angus curled up tight as an ammonite. Protecting his innards, and bringing the key right under his face.

He opened his mouth and scooped the padlock key up with his tongue. Biting down on it as Tony's boot landed again. And again.

The Bastard went for one more, but stepped in the slithery puddle during the run-up and nearly went his whole length. He skidded to a halt, holding onto the basement wall. Breathing hard. 'Not so . . . clever *now* . . . are you?'

Tony wiped his hands on his overalls, grabbed Angus's high-vis lapels, and hauled him backwards, through the puddle, and into the open cell.

Inside, it wasn't much bigger than the one at Sadler Road. There was even a body, like last time, only this one wasn't wrapped in plastic. Instead, it lay naked, bruised, and bloodied, slumped against the far wall – not thin enough to be DCI Monroe. So someone else . . .

What the cell *also* had was Dr Fife.

He was scrunched into the corner, furthest away from the corpse, hands behind his back, ankles cable-tied together. Blinking in the harsh LED light.

One eye was swollen almost shut and fresh blood caked his squint nose. He said something, but all that came out was an indecipherable series of grunts – muffled by the rag stuffed into his mouth, held in place by what looked like a pair of leggings knotted around his head. They'd taken his greatcoat, but left him his jeans, platform cowboy boots, and skull-and-crossbones top.

Tony dumped Angus on the floor, howched long and hard, then spat on him. 'You're gonna learn what happens when *the people* rise up against you Elite bastards.' Bending over to snarl in Angus's ear. Aping the Woman. 'And I'm gonna enjoy ripping the balls right off you.'

He yanked the towel from around Angus's feet, stepped out of the cell, and thunked the insulated door back into place.

The whole cell went dark.

The padlock's click was barely audible.

And then silence.

Complete, lightless, suffocating silence.

Slowly, the sound of someone else breathing hissed and whoomped through the pitch-black air. Because Dr Fife would be finding it hard, what with the broken nose and gag.

Angus shifted the key with his tongue, pinning it against the inside of his cheek, out of swallowing or choking range. 'You OK?'

Whatever Dr Fife's reply, none of it was comprehensible. Didn't sound happy, though. Shock, horror.

'Yeah, thought so.' He rested his head against the cell floor – smooth and cool, like the concrete outside. 'If it's OK with you, I'm just going to lie here till the world stops spinning . . .'

Again, the response was incomprehensible, but *definitely* rude.

Just like old times.

Surprisingly enough, with all that crap out of his stomach, things were settling down again: the walls no longer pulsed and whirled, and feeling was coming back to his arms and legs. Which was a mixed blessing, after all the beatings.

The real pain hadn't kicked in yet, though, so there was probably a limited window before he was unable to move again.

Better make the most of it.

'You awake?'

More muffled swearing.

'OK, then.' He wormed his way along the concrete, until his head bumped into Dr Fife. 'Scoot down, so you're on the floor.'

This time the angry mumbling went on for *quite* some time.

'For once, can you just do what you're told?'

A grunt. Then there was a scuffing noise, followed by a grunt.

OK, then.

Angus rolled over, shoogling about until he could feel the forensic psychologist's curly hair. Which put his head more-or-less level with the small of Angus's back. Angus's fingers walked, poked, and prodded till they hit face – producing outraged mumbles.

'Hold still!'

It took a while, working one-handed, but he wedged his fingers in between the leggings and Dr Fife's cheeks, hauling and twisting and pulling and yanking on the elasticated fabric till that lump of rag popped out of Dr Fife's mouth.

'*Ow! Ow! Ow! Watch the beard. Watch the beard!*'

Angus let go.

'*Jesus . . .*' A couple of deep breaths followed. Then a hissing noise. '*Ow.*'

'You're welcome.'

'*What now?*'

'This is all *your* fault.' Which was entirely true.

'*Shut up and let me think. Has to be a way out of here.*'

'You're only just starting an escape plan *now*? What the hell have you been doing?'

'*Before, it was only me, you idiot. Now I've got a blunt object to work with: you. That changes things.*'

Well, it was time for the 'blunt object' to dazzle with his brilliance.

'The key.' Slipping it from his lips onto the floor. 'Tony – the guy who chucked me in here – he dropped the padlock key. I've got it.' Shoogling about again, so the thing was grabbable with his fingers.

'*The lock's on the outside of the cell, you idiot! How's that supposed to help?*' A frustrated sigh rang out in the darkness. '*Son of a bitch . . .*'

'I *know* it's on the outside. But the key has sharp little metal teeth, *hasn't it*. Unless you've got some secret FBI trick to get these wanking cable-ties off?'

Silence.

'Didn't think so.' Angus twisted the key around in his hand, turning it so the flat edge of the blade was against his index finger, pressing the teeth against the first cable-tie, and sawed. Back and forth and back and forth across the smooth plastic. Which wasn't easy, given the position he had to contort his wrist into. But it was this or sit here, waiting for Tony to come back with a pair of pliers.

How would Ellie put it?

Ah, yes: 'Thank you, Angus, you're a *genius*, Angus. Oh, don't mention it, Jonathan. No, really, your brilliance and intellect are an inspiration to—'

'All right, all right. We get it!'

Saw, saw, saw, saw, saw . . .

'Who's the idiot now?'

Saw, saw, saw, saw, saw . . .

'I reserve judgement till it works.'

Saw, saw, saw, saw, saw . . .

Dr Fife spat something out into the darkness. *'If it does work, we have to be totally ruthless, OK? When these motherfuckers come back: we go for them. No holds barred. Kill or be killed.'*

Saw, saw, saw, saw, saw . . .

'I'm a police officer! We don't—'

'That's why we're here! Because they want to kill a police officer.'

'No: we're *here* because *you* decided it would be a good idea to shag someone who turned out to be part of the sodding conspiracy!'

Saw, saw, saw, saw, saw . . .

Dr Fife cleared his throat. *'That doesn't change—'*

'You're supposed to be this red-hot forensic psychologist: how could you be such a *crap* judge of character? Getting manipulated by that . . . two-faced . . . pill-poisoning . . .'

Saw, saw, saw, saw, saw . . .

For Christ's sake, was this bloody thing never going to break?

'I know, OK? But that doesn't change *anything.'* Deep breath. *'Angus, the chances of us getting out of this alive are vanishingly slim. You saw what they do to their victims. They turned Leonard Lundy's head into a sack of mush!'* His voice dropped. *'I'd rather die fighting.'*

Saw, saw, saw, saw, saw . . .

'Yeah? Well, I'd rather not die at all.'

Saw, saw, snap.

Oh, halle-frigging-lujah – the first cable-tie pinged off into the black.

'Got one!' Angus set to work on number two.

The only noise was the key's teeth sawing away at heavy-duty plastic.

'And I didn't "shag" anyone.'

'Yeah, I *totally* believe you.'

'I didn't!' Dr Fife huffed and puffed in the darkness. *'It wasn't because of the booze. I mean, that probably didn't help, but when I was younger I could down a bottle of tequila and still be up all night. Like a flagpole.'* A small laugh broke free, bitter as bile. *'The reason I'm so pissed at that journalist bastard publishing stuff about where Courtney lives isn't just because of cartel killers. Angus, what if the Brethren decide Megan's the Dawn Child?'*

'Cos she's your firstborn.'

'I wish. When I turned eleven, the Brethren made me sleep with some-one at the church. Well, not "sleep" sleep: screw. *Right on the altar. In front of everyone.'* Pause. *'That was a weird birthday.'*

Angus kept on sawing.

'It's no fun losing your virginity with your mum and dad and all the neighbours watching. Only the baby didn't bring forth the End of Days, she made it to three years old, before measles got her. Because vaccines are "the Devil's work".' A dull thunking sound came from his direc-tion, as if he'd just bounced his head off the wall. *'So you know what they did? They changed the prophecy. Decided I can't just knock-up some random woman, it needs to be a* specific *special lady to make the Dawn Child.'*

Jesus . . . Father to a dead child at only fourteen.

How could *anyone* cope with something like that?

And wasn't fourteen when Dr Fife's father beat him so badly he ended up in hospital?

'So go back to wherever your dad's stupid cult is, get someone pregnant and have done with it. They get their Dawn Child and their apocalypse; you get on with your life, not having to worry about them any more. Everyone wins.'

'I'm not condemning any kid of mine to live with those joyless, vio-lent, bible-bashing sons of bitches.'

This bastarding cable-tie was proving even tougher than the first one.

'So no: I didn't "shag" Gillian.' There was that laugh again. *'Casual sex is kinda difficult with all that hiding under the bed.'*

'Come on!'

'I couldn't get it up, OK? You happy now?'

'Not you: this stupid . . .' The cable-tie snapped. 'Ha!' And then the pain set in, grinding through his shoulders as he finally moved his hands around to the front of his body for the first time in ages. He flexed the fingers of his right hand, twisting the wrist as it burned and screamed. 'Cramp! Cramp . . .'

'It's a lot of pressure, not knowing if your next orgasm's gonna kick off Armageddon.'

Angus slumped back against the floor. 'Everything aches . . .'

'No wonder I'm in therapy.'

Soon as he'd got his breath back, he shuffled his bum into a sitting position, bracing his aching shoulders against the wall and pulling his knees up against his chest so he could reach the cable-ties around his ankles. Sawing away again. Pulling upwards this time and putting some muscle into it.

'Hoy! At least do my hands first!'

'What a great idea.' Angus kept going. 'Because that way . . . if Tony, Ryan, or any of the others come back . . . we'll be able to hop away like happy little Easter bunnies.' Upping the pressure on the makeshift blade by pushing his ankles forward. '*This* way, if it happens . . . I can carry you out of here.'

Come on, come on, come on . . .

Growling at the thing now, teeth bared, breath hissing in and out as he sawed and sawed and sawed and—

Snap.

Angus slumped back. Peching and heeching like a smoker on a treadmill. 'One more . . . to go . . .'

50

Angus held onto Dr Fife's wrists with one hand, the other sawing away with the key – which was getting a bit hot with all the friction. Not sure if that made it more efficient at cutting through industrial-grade plastic cable-ties or not . . .

One thing was certain, though: this would go a lot quicker if Dr Fife wouldn't keep shifting about. 'Will you hold still?'

'Ow! Cut the plastic, not the skin!'

'Told you to hold still.'

They sat in silence for a bit – the only sounds being the duddering rasp of little metal teeth on plastic, and Angus's laboured breathing.

Dr Fife hissed out a sigh. *'So, you gonna tell me what your dad did, or not? You know: the thing you're "not supposed to talk about"?'*

'I'm *busy*.'

'You got somewhere more important to be?'

Bastarding cable-ties were never going to give . . .

'Or we could talk about your inability to grow free of your mother's shadow and self-actualize towards a mutually fulfilling sexual relationship with Ellie Nottingham?'

Finally, the bloody thing snapped.

'Thank God for that.' Angus stuck the hot little key in Jonathan's hand. 'You can do . . . your own ankles.' He collapsed flat on his back, breathing hard; whoever invented cable-ties could stick their knob in a blender full of Scotch bonnet chillis and set it on pulse.

'Angus, we're probably gonna die here, so what've you gotta lose? Might do you good to get it off your chest?'

Nope.

'Angus?'

Still nope.

'Hey: I shared with you; don't be a dick.'

Maybe if he ignored him, Dr Fife would go away . . .

'I'll just keep bugging you till you tell me. Or they kill us.'

Wonderful.

'Anyone ever told you you're a pain in the arse?'

'My first and second wives may have mentioned it.'

Urgh . . .

He stared up into the featureless dark. 'Dad was a senior accountant at an oil company. Did the books for a bunch of charities in his
spare time, played golf, tinkered about in his shed, took Mum and
me to Paris and San Francisco and Rio and Rome . . .' Hard to
imagine it now. 'Then one morning, we got up and he just wasn't
there. They pulled him out the River Dee two days later. He'd got
drunk, filled his pockets with rocks, and jumped right in.'

'I'm sorry.'

'All Mum's friends rallied round, of course. Till one of those
charities found out he'd skimmed *thousands* from their accounts.
Soon as that came out, the casseroles and sympathy dried up. Then
the other charities started looking at *their* books. And so did the oil
company.'

Hard not to see her face, standing there, blinking back the tears,
as the police searched Dad's study, looking for evidence of secret
bank accounts.

'Mum had to sell the house, the car, furniture. Everything.' Angus
raised his arms, as if he was giving away the world. 'And that's how
we ended up in Kingsmeath.' He let his arms fall back, the fibreglass
cast clunking against the concrete floor. 'Happy now?'

'Hmmm . . .' A thoughtful pause. *'Let me guess: one of the charities
he defrauded was your megacysty one.'*

'Megalencephalic leukoencephalopathy with subcortical cysts:
the Molly Ormond Foundation. Yeah. So far we've paid back the
Royal Deeside Childhood Leukaemia Trust and the Smile Happy
Intervention Partnership. They do cleft-palate operations on poor
kids in Indonesia, Cambodia, and Vietnam.' It was hard, keeping

the anger out of his voice, so Angus didn't bother: 'He had a hundred and twenty-three *thousand*, eight hundred and ninety-seven pounds from the Molly Ormond bank account. It'll take *decades*.'

And that was his life, all laid out before him in a never-ending slog of long hours and overtime and scrimping and penny-pinching and never having anything nice to show for it.

What a time to be alive . . .

Dr Fife reached out in the darkness, found Angus's arm and gave it a squeeze. *'I know you might not wanna hear this, Angus, but your father was a massive, thieving asshat.'*

Yup.

Which was why they never spoke about it.

Angus gave himself a shake. 'Anyway, this isn't getting those cable-ties off. You'd better get sawing.'

The duddering rasp started up again.

'Just cos he's your dad doesn't mean you're responsible for his crimes or *his debts.'* Sawing away. *'But I suppose it explains why you've got a massive stick up your butt about everything.'*

Angus had another go at changing the subject. 'Who's our dead body?'

'Best guess? Monroe.'

'Can't be: not thin enough.'

'Then it's Kevin Healey-Robinson . . . Unless they've killed someone else we don't know about?'

'You haven't checked?'

The sawing stopped. *'In the* dark. *With my wrists and ankles* tied together, *and a* gag *in my mouth? Oh yeah: I've been exploring my* ass *off.'*

It was always the poor detective constable that had to do all the nasty jobs, wasn't it.

The sound of key-on-plastic snarled away as Angus hauled his trousers up, then got down on his hand and knees, shuffling along the wall – left arm held out in front of him, fingers reaching from their fibreglass cocoon to skitter across the concrete floor.

Searching, and searching, and searching, and—

Angus's fingertips brushed the unmistakeable clammy softness of bare skin.

'Got him.'

Kind of weird, though. You'd think a dead body would be colder than that. It was almost as if—

A soft, mushy voice whispered out in the darkness. *'Kill me . . .'*

'JESUS FUCK!' Angus scrabbled backwards. Sat flat on his bum. Staring into the void.

Dr Fife stopped sawing again. *'What? What's happened?'*

'Please . . . k . . . kill me.'

'He's alive!'

Tiny sobs jagged out of a gurgling throat. *'Please . . .'*

Come on, you silly bastard: take control of the situation, like they taught you.

Deep breath. 'Mr Healey-Robinson? It's the police. You're . . . ?' It was hard to know how to finish that sentence without either a massive lie, or a deeply depressing truth.

Luckily, Dr Fife didn't have anywhere near as many scruples. *'You're safe now. We got a SWAT team on the way; this is all gonna be over soon.'*

One way or the other . . .

Angus slipped off his high-vis jacket. 'Here, put this on.' Helping the poor sod get his arms into the sleeves. Trying not to wince at the sticky patches of fresh wounds and knobbly lines of scabbed tissue.

Soon as he was covered up, Angus scrambled back across the cell to Dr Fife. 'Have you got those bloody cable-ties off yet? I can't carry *two* people.'

'Sonofabitch.'

Saw, saw, saw, saw, saw . . .

Dr Fife shuffled back from visiting Kevin Healey-Robinson. He reached out, then poked Angus, keeping his voice down to barely a whisper. *'He's got a fever: poor bastard's hands are like* microwaves. *We gotta get outta here soon, or he's gonna die.'* A grunt. *'And so are we.'*

Angus matched the low volume. 'OK, how's this for a plan? We break down the door, charge up the stairs, batter our way through the bookcase, and arrest everyone.'

'*Excellent. Love it. Especially the bit where we make so much noise* the dead *can hear us – cos that way, by the time we get to the top of the stairs, every asshole in this goddamned house will be lined up ready to* shoot *us.*' The dull *thunk-thunk* of knuckles on chipboard sounded in their dungeon cell. '*Maybe, instead of making a racket, we could be a bit more sneaky?*' He gave Angus a shove. '*See if you can find the edge of the door.*'

It had to be a pretty snug fit, given that they'd not seen a chink of light since Tony shut them in here.

Angus slid his fingertips along the chipboard, slow and methodical. Feeling between the lumps and bumps of glued-together wood slivers, looking for a straight groove marking the join between door and . . .

'Got it. Now what?'

'*Here.*' Dr Fife's hands worked their way down Angus's arm, then pressed the padlock key into his hand. '*Try prising the wood off. Pick the insulation apart. Dig us out of here.*'

Seriously?

'With a *key*?' A crowbar, maybe, but a key? 'What happened to your multitool?'

'*Surprisingly enough, they* confiscated *it. And my phone. And my belt. The key's all we got.*'

Wonderful.

Angus sighed. Shrugged in the darkness. Then found the edge of the door again. It fitted tight against the wall panels all the way around, but there was the teeniest crack in the bottom corner, maybe a millimetre wide. Angus poked one of the key's teeth into it, because that was all that would fit, and wiggled it from side to side, up and down, rocking it, shoving it, twisting it . . . until something fell onto the back of his hand.

He ran his fingers over it – all that effort for a thumbnail-sized sliver of chipboard.

'This is going to take forever.'

'*It'll take three lifetimes if you don't get moving. His. Mine. And yours.*'

Yeah.

Fair enough.

Angus dug the key into the crack again: digging and digging and digging . . .

Christ knew how long it'd taken, but Angus finally managed to flake away enough slivers to make a hole *just* big enough to get all four fingertips into. The chipboard scratched and scraped as he forced them in there, squishing his way through the foam padding, then hooked his fingers up behind the wood.

He braced both feet against the wall. Took a deep breath. And pulled. Hard as possible. Stiffening his back. Shoving with his heels.

Come on, you utter . . .

A creak rang out, then a crack, then a splintering *bang* as a piece of chipboard broke free from the door – big as a ragged sheet of A4.

'Ha!'

'Did it work?'

'Catch.' He gently tossed the lump towards Dr Fife's voice. It *pock*ed onto the concrete.

Angus reached into the new hole. OK, so it would probably be easier with two hands, but he only had the one to work with.

Crack, crunch, scrunch.

This time the door gave up a slab of wood about the size of a laptop.

He heaved off chunk after chunk – dumping them all on the floor at his feet, until there was no more chipboard on this side of the door.

He sagged back on his heels, breathing hard. 'That's . . . that's it.'

'Give me the key.'

'Told you . . . I pulled . . . the chipboard—'

'To cut the insulation with, you lump.'

Oh.

Angus handed it over, leaning against the wall as Dr Fife went to work, filling the air with the crackling fizz of grey acoustic foam being ripped free of its gluey bonds. Followed by the chip, chip, squeak, and squeal of what had to be polystyrene.

Soon as he had his breath back, Angus reached out – fingertips searching for Dr Fife, then giving him a wee shove. 'Shift over.'

Going by the feel of it, Dr Fife had managed to make a dent in the polystyrene about the size of an orange. And he *still* wasn't through it. 'Is this all you've done?'

'Well, I don't see you doing any better!'

'Watch and learn.' He searched through the fallen bits of chipboard for the most jagged bit, took a good hold of the flattest side, and whacked the sharp edge into the polystyrene. Digging it in there like a shovel before wrenching it left and right till a hunk of the stuff shrieked and popped free.

He went exploring with his fingers again.

The insulation had to be at least three inches thick, but there was rockwool underneath so all Angus had to do was jam his good hand in there and rip the lot of it out – taking the polystyrene insulation with it, hurling it over his shoulder in great skreiching hunks till there was nothing left.

Angus dropped his voice to a whisper again. 'That's me through to the chipboard.'

'OK.' Dr Fife handed over the key. *'Nice and careful now – don't want them to hear us upstairs. Quiet as a squirrel fart.'*

Angus felt for the edge, where the outer door joined the outer wall, but before he could work the key into the minute gap, the whole sheet of chipboard popped outward, and the only thing holding it up was the padlock and hasp. Which worked as a one-point hinge. Meaning the whole slab of chipboard tilted downwards at speed.

He scrabbled forwards, grabbing the bottom edge *just* before it clattered against the basement floor.

Holy *shit* that was close.

A thin, grey light flooded into their cell.

He levered the door back up again, twisted it a couple of degrees, then pulled. Working the bottom corner back inside the cell. Shoogling and wriggling the thing until it was free of the doorway.

Oh yeah.

Score one for Team Angus.

The locking bars didn't really block the exit – there was enough of a gap between the mechanism's metal frame and the doorway to worm out through, but that wasn't going to do Kevin Healey-Robinson any good. Not in his state.

But luckily, Angus had a key.

OK, so it was a bit sticky after all it'd been through, but a bit of solid twisting and the mechanism popped open with a *click*.

He swung the bars out of the way and stepped into the basement proper.

Right: weapons.

Only there was nothing in here, other than the cells, the padlocks, and those bars.

And the 'Studio', of course.

Angus pulled up his baggy trousers and limped over there.

Dr Fife emerged from the cell. 'Where are you going, you idiot?' Pointing back into the dark. 'We need to get him outta here!'

'Thought you wanted to go down fighting.' Angus grabbed the studio door and pulled. The thing was heavy, coming open with an air-tight *pfwoom*ing noise, exposing a lightless, echoing space. Cold.

Not *refrigerated*, just . . . cold.

A line of eight or nine switches were just visible by the door, and he flicked the nearest one – setting the sign above the door glowing blood-red: 'RECORDING ~ STUDIO IN USE'.

The scarlet glow seeped past Angus into the dark, chilly space. Glinting off things hidden in the gloom.

The next switch flooded the room with eye-searing white light. It sparkled back from the stainless-steel sheets that covered every surface in here: walls, floor, and ceiling.

He hissed, shielding his eyes with his fibreglass cast, scrunching them into tiny slits. Waiting for shapes to come into stinging focus.

Though it might have been better if they hadn't.

Beneath his feet, the metal surface sloped down towards an open grate, about two-thirds of the way in – not far from a heavy-duty wooden chair. It was bolted to the floor, in the middle of the room, complete with pristine leather tie-down straps.

Network points were set into the wall opposite the lights, next to a line of electrical sockets with those 'for outside use' covers on them.

A tap stuck out of the stainless steel, within easy reach of the door, mounted at waist-height. Presumably so you could hose the place down from outside. Nothing else.

Angus flicked the switch again, plunging the room into darkness, leaving only the 'RECORDING' light on. Giving the whole basement an abattoir glow.

Yeah . . .

Dr Fife's voice whispered out behind him. *'What the goddamn hell was that?'*

Appropriate choice of words.

Blinking the swirling yellow dots from his eyes, Angus backed out of the studio, letting the door creep shut under its own weight. *Pfwoom.*

A nudge from Dr Fife. 'Well?'

He turned. 'You *really* don't want to know.'

'Of course I do. If anything, I want to know *more*.' Dr Fife stood on his tiptoes, as if that would help him see through the heavy studio door. 'What: they got cameras and stuff? A desk, and a green screen?'

Angus shook his head, but the room was tattooed across his retinas. 'Just . . . We *seriously* need to get out of here.' The opened padlock for their cell door was still hooked into the hasp. He pulled it free, weighing it in his good hand.

Might work.

Better than nothing, anyway.

'Grab the gag.'

But Dr Fife wasn't listening – he was struggling with the studio door.

'Leave it alone and go get the gag.'

A grunt, and Dr Fife hauled the thing open far enough to see inside. Whatever the blood-red light touched was enough to make him stare for a moment, then flinch away from the handle. The door eased itself shut again with that airtight sound, and he stood there. Staring.

'Told you. Now, will you *please* grab the gag?'

Dr Fife blinked at him.

'I need you to trust me, OK? Grab the gag.'

'Holy shit . . .' Dr Fife turned his eyes back towards the studio door for a couple of breaths, shuddered, then ducked back into the cell. Emerging moments later with the rag that had been stuffed in his mouth and the pair of leggings used to hold it there. He held them out. 'You realize what that room means, don't you?'

'Said you wouldn't want to know.' Took a bit of doing, but Angus undid the knot in the leggings as Dr Fife paced.

'Either they've named their torture chamber the "studio" as a sick joke, or they're *filming* this shit. Why would they film it . . . ?'

Angus shook out the leggings, held them up in the scarlet light. Couldn't see any holes in them. Still, better safe than sorry – he tucked the left leg into the right, shoving his arm down there till the toes lined up.

'Option one: they're idiots, filming themselves committing murder – AKA: Bestiality-Self-Incriminating-Moron Disorder. Option two: they're actually *broadcasting* this stuff . . .' Dr Fife's brow creased, lips moving as if he were tasting that idea.

Angus tied a knot in the newly made single leg, just above the heel, then wrapped the padlock in the rag and stuffed it through the leghole. Shoogling the whole thing till it rested up against the knot.

A nod. 'How else are they gonna get their message across? The police don't tell anyone about the Post-its, so who's seeing their warning message? No one, *that's* who. So how are they gonna change the world? They can't. They gotta go *global*.'

Another knot right next to the padlock trapped it in place. Followed by another couple, just in case.

'Are you listening to me?'

'Nope.' Angus tied another knot every three or four inches, till there was no leg left. With any luck the whole thing would be much stronger than the original fabric. He tossed the trussed-up leggings to Dr Fife, who curled his lip, as if he'd just been handed a used condom.

'What the hell is—'

'I was our LARPing group's resident armourer. Think of it as a chained flail without the handle, or a freehand mace. You hold on tight and swing it like a baseball bat.' He mimed taking a swing. 'Hopefully the padlock doesn't just go straight through the fabric.

Might only get one or two blows in before it rips, so make them count.' He grimaced at the closed studio door. 'Unless you want to end up "on camera".'

'Hmmm . . .' Dr Fife weighed the mace in his hands, then held it out. 'Wouldn't you be better—'

'I'm carrying Kevin Healey-Robinson.' Angus slipped off the tweed jacket and ripped the lining out of it, twisting the thin material into a makeshift belt to keep his trousers up. Not *great*, but it would do.

'Yeah . . .' Fife bared his teeth and looked back at the cell. 'I don't think Kev's gonna make it.'

'We can't just leave him here!'

'I know, I know, but it's gonna be hard enough getting outta this alive, without dragging extra . . .' Dr Fife pursed his lips as he frowned at the other cell door. 'You don't suppose *Monroe*'s in there?'

Angus followed his gaze.

Sodding hell.

Dr Fife stuck his hand out. 'Gimme the key.'

Ryan's people must've got the padlocks as a job lot, because the same key opened this one too. Dr Fife pocketed the lock, then swung the bars out of the way. Stepping back to let Angus take hold of the handles and lever the door-plug from its frame.

The smell that slumped out after it reeked of stale sweat and iron and raw sewage.

Angus risked a slightly louder whisper. 'Boss?'

No reply.

'Detective Inspector Monroe?'

Silence.

He glanced at Dr Fife, who shook his head.

OK then.

Angus took a deep breath and stepped inside.

51

The studio's 'RECORDING' light cast its horror-film glow through the open cell door – barely reaching more than a couple of feet into the rank, silent space.

Angus shuffled forwards, the fingertips on his left hand skiffing along the side wall, the right one out to stop him banging into the end of the cell. Moving slow and careful. Feeling his way.

If it was anything like the box they'd just escaped from, there couldn't be much further to go . . .

And then his foot bumped into something.

Soft.

OK.

He squatted down, running his good hand over a confusing mass of naked flesh with too many limbs and—

A bellow of rage split the darkness, and something slammed into Angus's chest, tipping him over backwards, thumping down on top of him as he hit the concrete floor. Bony hands scrabbling up his torso to wrap around his neck and *squeeze*.

Growling and snarling.

'Help!' He grabbed the wrists and pulled, but those fingers locked on tight, strangling the words in his throat. 'Help . . . me!' Heels shoving against the concrete, pushing himself back towards the door.

Brown blobs, like dried blood, bloomed in the corners of Angus's eyes, overlaying the darkness as he ground his shoes into the polished concrete. Pressure building behind his eyes. Lungs burning.

The grip tightened, trying to wring the life out of him.

Another shove and he'd made it back into the scarlet glow. One more and the strangling bastard's face loomed out of the gloom above him. Only there was something seriously wrong with it – the features all swollen and lopsided, a sharp nose crushed into a gristled stub.

Bloody hell.

It was DCI Monroe.

Dr Fife's voice worried in from the basement outside. *'What's happening?'*

Angus prised at the fingers, getting just enough air in to stop his head from popping. 'Get your . . . arse in here . . . and *help* me!'

'Goddamnit . . .'

'Boss! . . . Boss, it's me!'

Monroe hauled Angus's head up off the floor.

'It's DC MacVic—'

Then slammed it down, bouncing it off the concrete with a ringing *thunk*. Then another one. And another.

Dr Fife scrambled into the cell. 'Oh, for . . .' He knelt beside them, cupping Monroe's face in both hands.

A roar, and the Boss tried to drag his head away. Slamming Angus's skull against the floor.

'Stop it, you silly bastard!' Fife gave Monroe's ruined face a shake. 'It's *us*! We're *rescuing* you!'

The banging stopped, fingers loosening around Angus's throat – letting him haul in a deep rasping breath.

Oh, thank God for that.

Monroe's voice was soft and wet, the words barely there: 'Dogstor Ffffiff?'

'Yup. And I'd really appreciate it if you didn't strangle my sidekick.'

He let go of Angus and sat back – right arm curled around his ribs. Shoulders drooping as he leaned over to one side. Lungs making unhealthy rattling-gargle noises. Then, 'Wrrrs backuft?'

Dr Fife helped him to his feet. It took three goes to get Monroe upright, and even then he wobbled like a newborn foal, free hand trembling out to steady himself against the wall. Whatever had fuelled the attack on Angus had burned itself out, leaving him shrunken and trembling.

Monroe tried again: 'Wrrrs *backuft*?'

'Yeah . . .' Dr Fife helped him towards the cell door. 'Funny story.' Leaving Angus lying there.

They shuffled out into the basement.

'*Turns out we got . . .*' A sharp intake of breath. '*What the* fuck *did they* do *to you?*'

'Thrrrs nnugh backuft?' The words might've been mangled, but there was no mistaking the catch in them. As if tears weren't far behind.

Angus rolled over and got to his knees. Wheezing. Free hand rubbing his crushed throat.

Jesus – that man had one hell of a grip.

'*We got abducted by the same assholes that grabbed you. But we're getting outta here. I promise.*'

Angus inched his way deeper into the cell again, feeling his way back towards the far wall, where that fleshy lump with too many limbs had been. Because there was no way that'd all been DCI Monroe.

'Orrgh Godg, weer augh goeen dzo die . . .'

The body was pressed against the wall, still and silent.

'Hello?' He ran his hand along the clammy skin, searching for the head. 'Can you hear me?'

OK – that was definitely a breast, so the body was female. Which made it Olivia Lundy. Probably.

He followed the line up to her shoulder, then neck, searching for the right place to feel for a pulse.

Please, please, please, please . . .

It was barely a flutter, but it was there.

She was alive.

'Yes: *thank* you!'

Angus scooped his good hand under one armpit, wedged his fibreglass cast into the other, and dragged her out of there.

In the abattoir light, it was unmistakeably Olivia Lundy. Only something awful had happened to her. She was covered in *horrific* bruising, wrapping around her body like the world's cruellest

Rorschach-inkblot test. Scrapes and cuts were interspersed with scabbed-over wounds, but worst of all were her legs. It looked as if someone had twisted the bones all out of shape.

DCI Monroe wasn't much better. Welts and scratches covered his thin, wiry frame, the damage too fresh to have darkened into proper bruising. Out here, his face looked even worse: swollen and misshapen, both eyes puffed out so far it would be a miracle if he could actually *see* anything; jaw misshapen; the nose of a boxer who'd never made it past the first round. Three fingers on his left hand were crooked and hooked – broken or dislocated – but both hands were dark with blood. A trio of glistening black holes marked the palms where the screws went through. And he'd *still* managed to half-throttle Angus.

Olivia Lundy bore the same stigmata. And they both had thick, dark lines around their wrists, chest, throat, and ankles. Probably from those straps on the studio chair . . .

Angus lowered her to the floor, then picked up his baggy tweed jacket and arranged it over her – hiding her nakedness. 'Boss?'

Dr Fife pointed. 'Is she . . . ?'

'Only just.'

'So now we got *three* people to rescue.' He huffed out a long breath, looking down at her immobile body. 'Gonna have to leave them here.'

Monroe jabbed his tortured hands out. 'Nnnngh!'

Angus stripped off his borrowed waistcoat and shirt. 'The Boss is right: we can't just abandon—'

'We're *not* abandoning you.' Dr Fife squeezed Monroe's arm. 'We're not abandoning *anyone*: we're being sensible. They're crippled; you're blind. And OK, so I can maybe guide you outta here, but think Angus can carry two bodies *and* fight off a whole gang of murderous assholes?'

'I won't leave them.' Angus draped the shirt over Monroe's shoulders, so at least he was wearing something. Then climbed back into the waistcoat. Which probably looked ridiculous, but was better than having your nipples on show. 'We'll figure something out.'

'Nnnngh.' The Boss raised his broken jaw. 'Hsss riigh.'

Seriously?

'But we can't—'

'Yeah, we can.' Dr Fife's eyes drifted towards the staircase. 'Once we've *won*, we call in a SWAT team and a whole fleet of ambulances.' A small, sad smile. 'If we *lose*, we're all dead anyway.'

Angus led the way up the stairs, creeping like a ninja. Not making so much as a squeak. The further he climbed, the darker it got as they left the scarlet glow of the studio light behind.

He patted the pocket of the waistcoat, checking the key was still in there. Not much of a weapon, but protruding between two fingers in a well-curled fist it'd probably still do a decent bit of damage. The other padlock hung heavily in his trouser pocket. Not sure what it would be good for – too small for a knuckle duster, unless he wore it as a ring? Might work. Either way: when dungeon-crawling, a good adventurer never left equipment behind.

Dr Fife laboured up the stairs behind him, clutching his free-hand mace.

What could go wrong?

The illumination died just before the top of the stairs, blocked out by their bodies and the distance, leaving Angus in the pitch dark.

He took a deep breath and held out his good hand, skimming his fingertips along the surface. Of course, it would be quicker to use both hands, but then there was the risk of his cast banging against something in the gloom and tipping off the Cult of Bastards that they were trying to escape.

OK – that definitely felt like an L-shaped alcove at the end of the short passageway, which would be where the bookcase slid back and in behind the other ones, out of the way. A pair of handles were set into what had to be the shelves that moved, but a gentle tug on them did nothing, and neither did a full-on pull.

Angus let go, barely *breathing* the words: 'It's locked.'

Dr Fife's voice whispered up at him. *'Look for a door catch.'*

'Gee, do you *think*?'

He made another pass with his fingertips, spreading out to the sides of the stairwell too. Then inside the alcove. And finally, the floor and ceiling. 'Nothing.'

A pause.

'OK. *It's opened from the outside by an RFID fob, so maybe it's the same from the inside? Luckily, some of us keep our wits about us when flat-arsed detective sergeants demand we hand over all the evidence.*' The muted sound of rummaging filled the small space, then: '*Here.*' He patted Angus on the ribs, keeping his hand there till Angus reached for it. And pressed a small lozenge-shape into Angus's palm.

Like an extra-large liquorice comfit.

'The key fob you stole from Kate Paisley?' Typical. 'Wait, *where* have you been hiding . . . Actually, I don't want to know.'

He gripped it between his fingers and ran it over the wooden surfaces, searching for the same spot the Woman had used to unlock this secret passage in the first place. 'Come on, you dirty, hidden, sneaky little' – a *click* sounded, followed by a sliver of pale-grey light that marked one edge of the bookcase/door – 'beauty.'

Dr Fife poked him in the back. '*Remember:* totally *ruthless. No holds barred.*'

A horrible notion, but what other choice did they have?

Angus nodded. 'Kill or be killed.'

He took hold of the handles and eased the secret door towards himself, no more than an inch at a time, so slowly that the castors trundling in their tracks were barely audible at all.

When it was level with the recess, the bookcase changed direction – flooding the passageway with light as it slid sideways into the alcove with a faint *clunk*.

After the basement gloom, even a single lightbulb burning in the room outside was enough to render everything invisible: washed out in the unaccustomed glare.

They stayed where they were, not moving as the bare room slowly unfaded into view. Pale carpet. Pale walls. Pale ceiling. And a window, looking out on the storm-racked night.

No welcoming committee armed with guns, knives, pickaxe handles, or anything else.

A long shuddery breath rattled out from Angus's lungs.

Thank Christ for that.

He crept through the gap, keeping low, head tilting from side to side. Listening.

Other than the wind throwing its shoulder against the double glazing, it was silent. He lowered his voice even further, though. Just in case. 'Can't hear anyone.'

Dr Fife tiptoed after him, holding out the freehand mace. 'You take it.'

'Don't be daft: I'm not leaving you unarmed.'

'But I don't know how to—'

'Swing it like a baseball bat, remember?'

His brow darkened. 'Do I *look* like a jock to you?'

Angus stared at him. Standing there, all hunched over, seemingly unable to decide if it was better to bite his lips or lick them, shifting from one cowboy boot to the other.

No. He did *not*.

But it was too late to do anything about that now.

'If it all kicks off, I can't be worrying about you not defending yourself.'

'Great.' Dr Fife slumped. 'We're all gonna die . . .'

'That's the spirit.' Angus crept along the line of bookcases, making for the door they'd dragged him in through. The one that led off the hall. He pointed at the handle, then at Dr Fife.

Held the finger to his lips.

Then raised another two to join it.

Dr Fife slunk around to the other side of the door and reached for the handle. Nodded.

OK.

Here we go.

Angus held out his three fingers. Then two. Then one. And clenched his fist.

Dr Fife turned the handle and inched the door open about a hand's width.

Angus peered through the gap.

The hall was as empty as the living room, with a clear run to the front door and freedom.

He slipped out into the hallway, scanning the room with its grand staircase and multiple doors – all closed.

Time to move.

Angus gave Dr Fife a thumbs-up, and picked his way across the carpet, slow and silent, to that big square of sisal matting just inside the front door.

Dr Fife sneaked after him.

Here we go.

Angus reached for the handle and a lilting, Highlands and Islands accent boomed out behind them, echoing off the bare walls:

'*Very rude to sneak off without saying goodbye.*'

52

Sod.

Angus turned, slowly, both hands up as he stepped around and in front of Dr Fife, hiding him. 'All right, let's all stay calm.'

Ryan wandered down the big stone staircase – an iPad in one hand, that revolver of his in the other. Pointed right at Angus's face.

One of the other hallway doors opened and the Woman appeared, brandishing a lump hammer and a Stanley knife.

Bit redundant, given the gun, but OK.

Angus pulled his shoulders back, and took a couple of paces forward, making himself as big as possible. Increasing Dr Fife's shield. 'Doesn't have to go this way!'

'I should've killed you on the rugby pitch.'

Now it was the living-room door's turn. A young man stood on the threshold, in scuffed jeans and an Oldcastle Warriors replica shirt. Early twenties, lots of spots, big jaw, eagle's-beak nose, narrow eyes, and shoulder-length blond curls. Armed with a heavy-browed scowl and a vicious-looking slater's axe – like a heavy, rectangular metal trowel with a jagged spike welded onto one side.

Ryan gave the new boy a smile. 'Bob – these guys have let our other guests out of their rooms. You want to do something about that?'

Bob slapped the slater's axe against his palm. 'Oh aye.' He slipped back into the living room.

'OK.' Dr Fife's quietest whisper yet sounded at Angus's elbow. 'Door's open in three, two, one . . .'

A whoomph of cold air rushed into the hall, bringing with it the snap and groan of wind hammering the tarpaulin-coated scaffolding, overlaid by the downpour's angry-snake hiss.

'*Run!*'

Angus turned, free hand grabbing the door's edge as he sprinted through it and slammed the thing shut behind him.

Spotlights made Mains of Inverminnoch glow scabby grey against the stormy night, the landscape reduced to a trembling black smear against a dark sky.

Gillian's crappy Clio and the rusty builder's van were still parked right outside the house, both dancing with sparks of rain – caught in the spotlights' glare.

Dr Fife skidded to a halt on the weedy gravel.

Angus nearly collided with him. 'Don't just stand . . .'

Oh, no.

So *that* was why he'd stopped.

The van's engine roared into life, headlights snapping on. Then the driver's door popped open and Tony climbed out into the rain, with his broken nose, bandaged head, and pickaxe handle.

A second man emerged from the passenger side – late thirties, clean-shaven, side parting, sensible jumper. Like a cross between a golf-club bore and a Tory MP. He swung a baseball bat up to rest on his shoulder.

Then the back doors creaked, and the third newcomer jumped down. There was something oddly *familiar* about him . . . Not much older than Angus, but thin and angular, with hands like tarantulas. A thick beard that spread down his neck and disappeared into the collar of his hiking jacket. The van's headlights gleamed off the big bald patch at the back of his head as he moved to join his mates, carrying a crowbar and a claw-hammer.

Of course: he was the spitting image of the guy Gillian said had been hanging around at the press scrum outside Divisional Headquarters. Mr Four-B.

And last, but not least, the Clio's driver's door swung wide and out she climbed. Clutching that semi-automatic pistol. Giving Angus a pained smile.

Dr Fife beamed, stepping towards her with his arms wide. 'Gillian!' He jabbed a finger at the gun in her hand, then looked up at

Angus. 'See? *Finally*: someone in this goddamn hellhole has the sense to bring a—'

'She's on their side, you idiot!'

'She's *what*?' He frowned. 'Don't be . . .' Turned and stared. 'But . . .'

Gillian winced, biting her bottom lip. 'Sorry.'

'HOW COULD YOU BE ON THEIR SIDE?'

Ryan strolled out through the front door, with the Woman right behind him. 'Yeah, we wondered where her loyalties lay as well. Turns out being nice to you was just a bit of an aberration. Wasn't it, Gillian?'

'Yes, Ryan.'

'And you know who your *friends* are.'

'Yes. Definitely.' Gillian lowered her eyes and scrunched up a little. Making herself smaller. 'Death to the Cabal.'

A nod. Then Ryan smiled at Angus. 'I see you've already met Steve and William.' Gesturing at the guy with the baseball bat, then the one with the crowbar. 'Much better to do it out here, don't you think? Be a shame to get blood all over Christine's lovely paintwork.'

The Woman nodded. 'It's a bastard to clean up.'

He raised the revolver. 'What do you fancy: beaten to death right now . . . or come back inside and be an object lesson for millions? Your call.'

Angus backed away, hands up again. Squashing the tremble out of his voice. 'Come on, Ryan, we don't have to do this.' Nice and calm.

The Woman, Christine, grinned. 'Oh, we *so* do.'

Dr Fife glared at Gillian for a couple of breaths as the rain pummelled down, then shook his head and took a step towards Ryan. 'I thought, *maybe*, you were on some sort of righteous crusade, but you're just as bad as the rest of them, aren't you? Just as corrupt.' Looking him up and down. 'Christ, you're a disappointment.'

Oh great, that was all they needed.

Angus grabbed Dr Fife's shoulder, dropping his voice to a hissing whisper: 'Why are you *antagonizing* him?'

'Because that's what I do, remember?' He shook Angus off. 'See, when you were taking your frustrations out on poor bastards like Dr Fordyce, it *kinda* made sense. She represents the medical establishment, so she's gotta be held responsible for all your antivax nightmares, right? And OK, it was *cockeyed* and *stupid*, but there was a *logic* to it.'

The guy with the crowbar – William? – crept closer. So did Tony, Steve, and Christine.

'Don't matter that the vaccine probably saved millions and millions and *millions* of lives, you still made Dr Fordyce wear the thorny crown. Punished her for sins that never existed.'

Ryan narrowed his eyes. 'Bollocks. They filled their murder jab with experimental proteins. *That's* why so many people are still sick. It *destroyed* their immune systems. It fucked with their brains!'

The house glowed in the headlights and spotlights, casting a circle of light that extended twenty, maybe thirty feet out into the weed-and-tussocked lawn. All they had to do was make it *that* far, then they could run off into the darkness, right? That would make it harder to get a bullet in the back, right?

Possibly.

If they were really, really lucky.

Angus took another handful of Dr Fife's long-sleeved top and dragged him back a couple more steps.

At least this time the forensic psychologist didn't struggle free. 'Doesn't matter that Councillor Mendel campaigned for better hospitals and care homes and a decent working wage – you decided he was a paedo, because some random greasy douchebag on the internet told you politicians drink the blood of murdered kids in a pizza-restaurant basement.'

Tony slapped the pickaxe handle against his open palm. 'How do you think they *get* to be politicians? They have to take the Cabal's test, like all them TV stars in the seventies!'

'Yeah!' Christine raised her lump hammer. 'Blood of the *innocent*. They're drinking kids' blood!'

William shook his crowbar. 'Fuckin' *preach*!'

They crept closer.

'Doesn't matter that Kevin Healey-Robinson is a Political and

Lifestyle Correspondent – he spends most of his time writing about "fifteen ways to spend a wet weekend in Oldcastle", for God's sake!'

'He was a political hack!' Steve curled his lip, as if he'd just stepped in something. 'A lying, lefty, elitist bastard, pushing the establishment's war-mongering, military agenda. Hiding the truth!'

Any closer and they'd be within baseball-bat swinging range.

Dr Fife threw his hands out, getting louder. 'Olivia Lundy negotiated land deals for supermarkets. Where does *that* fit in?'

Angus kept going, pulling Dr Fife with him.

Another twenty feet and they'd cross from the pool of light into the gloom.

Ryan sniffed. 'Lawyers are the locusts of the woke plague, and—'

'Oh, GROW UP!' Fife jabbed a finger at the house. 'You're broadcasting torture-porn on the internet for clicks and *money*!'

Rain squalled across the gravel driveway, crackling off the tarpaulin as it writhed in the wind.

Tony, William, Steve, and Christine edged closer. Like the four bloody horsemen.

'You strap some poor bastard into that chair and you slowly murder them, while outraged, racist, right-wing, fascism-curious *motherfuckers* cheer and stick dollars in your G-string!'

The cultists stopped moving at that, glancing back at their Great Leader as he stood there, face darkening.

Eighteen feet to go . . .

'Revolutions cost money.' Ryan raised his gun to point at the building behind him. 'You think somewhere like this comes *cheap*? When the Great Reset happens, you'll be glad people like us bought the guns and ammunition and explosives to fight back!'

Tony punched the air. 'Great Awakening!'

Sixteen . . .

'Wait.' Angus stared. 'You're buying *explosives*? Who's selling you explosives?'

Christine crept nearer. 'Think you've got more pressing things to worry about, Hodor.'

Dr Fife gave her the finger for that. 'You lot are no better than the other far-right internet shock jocks: peddling snake oil and lies and fear and division and *hate*, just to line your own pocket.'

Fourteen . . .

'THEY'RE NOT LIES!' Ryan took a step out from the tarpaulin's cover and rain slashed across his face, wind whipping that long dark hair back as he bared his teeth. 'I *know* the vaccines fuck with people's brains, because my father was fine before they pumped that shite into his arm. Didn't even *recognize me* by the time he died!' Ryan jabbed his gun at the world. 'The truth's out there, plain as sliced white bread, but *you* . . . you've got your heads bent in supplication and deference, and you won't *look*!' He cocked the revolver's hammer. 'Well, we'll bloody well *make* you look.'

Twelve . . .

Tony took a practice swing with his pickaxe handle. 'Enough talk. Let's do this.'

Christine raised her lump hammer – a cut-price frumpy Thor in a paint-smudged sweatshirt. 'DEATH TO THE CABAL!'

Ten . . .

'Yeah.' Ryan's mouth pursed, and he looked away. Voice dead and flat. 'Death to the Cabal.'

William bellowed out a guttural war cry and charged, with Tony, Steve, and Christine right behind.

Angus had run out of time.

53

William's crowbar flew – swinging right for Angus's face.

Thankfully he missed – though only by a fraction of an inch – but Tony and his pickaxe handle were close behind. Using the gap to lunge in and slam the bloody thing down on Angus's shoulder, sending him crashing down onto the weed-infested gravel.

Bastard . . . The same aching, half-dead shoulder he'd battered back at DCI Monroe's house. And Gillian's drugs were definitely wearing off now, because a wave of burning ice pulsed through Angus's chest, radiating out from the impact point.

Steve circled closer, baseball bat up and ready to strike.

But Tony held out a hand as he danced closer. 'Watch and learn, boys!' Laughing like a hyena. Leaping, swinging the pickaxe handle overhead to slam it down on Angus's head.

Hell, no.

Angus rolled and it smashed into the driveway instead, flinging up chips of gravel.

'ANGUS!' Dr Fife: somewhere off to the left. 'FOR GOD'S SAKE: HELP!'

Angus scrambled to his feet and William rushed in, the crowbar flying in a sharp, flat arc. Close enough to take a button off the borrowed waistcoat.

Buggering hell, this was *not* going well . . .

'ANGUS, I'M NOT JOKING!' Then the scuff-clatter of feet on gravel.

'I'm busy!' He glanced towards the noise, but that just gave

Steve an opening to rush in – hammering his baseball bat into Angus's back.

He staggered forward into the Clio, stomach hitting the bonnet, bending him over as that bat came crashing down again, right across his shoulders. Hard enough to clatter his teeth together.

Over by the van, Dr Fife howled in pain.

Angus shoved himself off the car, spinning around as the baseball bat whistled towards his head.

But he didn't duck this time: he propelled himself forward, fibreglass cast raised, blocking the bat halfway along its length. Then grabbed the neck of Steve's sensible jumper and hauled him forward.

His eyes went wide. And Angus's forehead crashed right into his face.

There was a crack, a grunt, and a spatter of blood – glowing like rubies in the building's spotlights.

Angus shoved him away again, keeping hold of the jumper in case he needed another headbutt, and Steve staggered, eyes half shut now, nose shattered, mouth hanging open to show two missing teeth at the front. The baseball bat fell from his fingers.

Good.

A bellow of rage and Angus yanked him off his feet. Up and over Angus's battered shoulder, hurling him like a sack of dogfood, flipping him upside down and crashing him, full length, on his back, into the Clio's roof. Putting enough force into it to buckle the metal and send a lightning-burst of cracks shattering their way across the windscreen.

The ancient car's security system kicked in: horn blaring its Morse Code distress call as the hazard lights flashed in the storm.

One.

Angus snatched the baseball bat from the gravel at his feet, twirling around as William charged, crowbar sizzling through the rain, coming for his head again.

But *this time*, Angus was armed.

He parried the crowbar, twisting the bat in a classic circular disarm. The crowbar flew from William's fingers, twirling end over end, straight into the van's windscreen. Impaling it like the world's rustiest unicorn.

A backhand swing of the baseball bat smashed into William's knee and down he went: screaming, clutching the ruined joint in both hands as that claw-hammer of his went skittering off under the car.

Two.

Another cry of pain blared out of Dr Fife. *'ANGUS! FOR GOD'S SAKE!'*

'*Still* busy!' Facing Tony and his pickaxe handle.

The Bastard howched, chewed, then spat on William as he lay there howling. 'Fucking amateurs.' He snarled forward, charging, pickaxe handle raised high, bringing it down hard, aiming for Angus's skull.

Angus dropped to one knee, using the baseball bat as a shield – and the handle clattered into it. Which was Angus's cue to ram his fibreglass cast upward, as violently as possible, right into Tony's balls. Because Dr Fife wasn't the only one who could perform a Furious-Flying-Fist Vasectomy, and Angus was much bigger and a *hell* of a lot stronger.

Which meant Tony parted company with the ground, jerking about two feet into the air, before tumbling over Angus's head, carried by his own momentum. He cleared the Clio's mismatched bonnet and hit the gravel on the other side, tumbling across the driveway and crashing into that big pile of broken slates. Sending avalanches of sharp grey wreckage clattering and slithering to the ground.

Three.

Which left Christine, Ryan, Gillian, and Bob. Wherever he was.

Angus scrambled to his feet, baseball bat at the ready.

Wouldn't do much good against a pair of guns, but it was better than just giving in and being tortured to death.

Ryan stared at the carnage. 'Oh, for God's sake.'

Gillian hadn't moved, just stood there, clutching the semi-automatic to her chest.

But Christine seemed to be having fun. She circled Dr Fife, making him turn around and around to face her. Moving her

Stanley knife like the head of a snake. Bobbing and weaving the glittering triangular blade.

She'd already managed to carve four slashes across his arms, the blood dribbling down his long-sleeved top. Glowing bright scarlet in the Clio's headlights.

Dr Fife still clutched the freehand mace, but he wasn't *using* the thing. It was meant to be a weapon, not a sodding security blanket.

Right.

Angus stepped towards them, spinning the baseball bat as if it were Conan's sword. Whirling it left and right as he advanced across the driveway.

'No you don't.' Ryan pulled the trigger and his revolver barked like an angry Rottweiler.

The bullet crackled through the air, right past Angus's ear, making him flinch as it clanged into the builder's van.

Jesus . . .

Not sure if that was meant to be a warning shot, or a genuine murder attempt. Either way, Ryan didn't look too pleased about it. He lined up for another go.

Angus glanced from him to Dr-Fife-and-Christine and back again. Crouching low, baseball bat raised. As if *that* was going to help.

Christine slashed forward, ripping another gash across Dr Fife's right arm. 'Dance, midget monkey boy!'

'Sonofa*bitch*!' Dr Fife shuffled around again, left hand clasped over the new wound, blood welling up between his fingers. Mace dangling at the end of his right.

Another bullet tore through the night, and a spider's web exploded across the van's passenger window.

'Bastard . . .' Ryan changed his stance – feet shoulder-width apart, gun in both hands now. As if he was on a shooting range.

Christine lunged in with her lump hammer, but Dr Fife stumbled backwards, nearly losing his footing as the thing swung past.

Snarling, he lashed out with his freehand mace, chasing the hammer, and the padlock smashed right into her elbow with a crack of metal on bone.

The lump hammer tumbled from her fingers, and she staggered to a halt, staring at the misshapen lumpy joint. Then the shrieking started, curled up at the waist, holding onto her shattered elbow.

Ryan marched a couple of feet closer, took up his firing pose, and the revolver barked again. A gout of steam hissed from the van's radiator, pluming out into the downpour. Thank God shooting people was more difficult than it looked on TV.

And given that Ryan was such a crap shot, maybe rushing him wasn't a stupid idea after all? OK, so there was a very real risk of getting shot at short range, but just standing here, like a hulking great lemon, was even more risky. Ryan was going to get lucky eventually. Especially as he kept shuffling nearer.

As Christine wailed, Dr Fife planted his feet – swinging his freehand mace as if he was in a batting cage at the local ballpark.

The padlock connected with the left side of her face, crumpling the cheekbone and spinning her around in a spurt of fresh rubies. She crashed into the scaffolding, setting one of the poles ringing, then collapsed in a motionless heap.

'Ha!' Dr Fife punched the air. 'Who's dancing *now*, you prejudiced asshole?'

Four.

This time, when the revolver barked, what was left of the van's windscreen exploded, releasing its crowbar horn. 'Hold still!'

OK. Time to move.

But Angus only managed a couple of steps before the gun went off again. Three times in quick succession – one bullet vanished into the night, one kicked shrapnel out of the gravel, less than eight inches from Angus's foot, and the third punched a hole in the Clio's front wing.

How many shots was that?

Six? Seven?

Thought revolvers only had six chambers?

What kind of Hollywood-movie bullshit was this?

Ryan bellowed out his frustration, then jabbed the smoking gun at Gillian. 'Would you like to fucking *help* at some point?'

She still hadn't moved. But as Ryan glared, she lowered her eyes, shuffling her boots on the wet gravel, hair plastered to her head. 'Sorry . . .'

Angus took a deep breath and stepped forwards. 'It's *over*, Ryan. Put the gun down.'

'It's not over. It's *never* over!'

OK.

Angus took a couple of paces sideways, putting himself between Dr Fife and the two gun-toting nutjobs. Trying hard not to look too menacing with a broken arm and a baseball bat. 'Let's all just calm down. All right?'

'You Elite bastards think we'll just bend over and take it. Well, we *won't*!' Ryan launched into a rant about globalists and cabals and government agencies and viruses . . . but while Angus was *watching*, he wasn't really *listening*.

Instead he slipped a whisper from the corner of his mouth, keeping his lips as still as possible. 'Dr Fife: I'm going to move left, *slowly*. Stay behind me.' He inched over, keeping his front facing Gillian and Ryan. 'Soon as you have a clear line to the edge of the house, run like a bloody *cheetah*. Make for the woods and don't look back.'

Dr Fife was barely audible over the rain. 'You think I'm just gonna abandon you?' A grunt. 'Besides, what's to stop this asshole shooting me in the back?'

'Me.'

Ryan's face had gone a worrying shade of puce as he waved his gun at the big bad world. '. . . call them *conspiracies*, because that's what they *are*! The people have had your *fascist* boot on their necks for so long . . .' Blah, blah, blah.

Dr Fife hissed out a shuddery breath. 'I'll call for help. Try not to die before it gets here.' He patted Angus on the back. 'Three. Two. One.' And he was off – cowboy boots hitting the gravel at speed.

Soon as the first step sounded, Angus marched towards Ryan and Gillian, waving his arms like a drunk man learning semaphore. 'I'M *NOT* THE ELITE, YOU IDIOTS! I'M JUST A GUY TRYING TO MAKE PEOPLE'S LIVES A LITTLE BETTER BY CATCHING MURDEROUS ARSEHOLES LIKE YOU!'

That got their attention.

Now to keep it.

Back in his LARPing days, he'd had a *great* berserker yell that frightened the crap out of the other kids. Maybe now was the time to dust it off? He bellowed it out, whirling the baseball bat in a full sword-spinning display: left, right, behind his back, then round the front – held up in the best two-handed grip he could manage with one arm in a fibreglass cast.

And charged straight for Ryan.

Whose eyes went wide. 'Shit . . .'

Ryan fumbled the gun, almost dropping it as Angus rushed towards him, a one-man stampede, bellowing, weapon whirling, ready to break the evil bastard's—

The revolver barked like a big dog in a little house and something thumped into Angus's leg – sharp and stinging. The sting turned into an ache, then an acetylene torch, cutting its way through his thigh. All in the time it took for his foot to hit the ground again.

Then the whole leg collapsed, and down he went, tumbling along the gravel drive, until he lay in a tangled heap barely six feet from Ryan's trainers.

Holy, bastarding hell, that *hurt*.

Ryan leapt into the air, both hands up like Rocky at the end of the old film. 'YES!' He gave himself a double fist pump. 'Get *fucking* in!'

That really, seriously, *bloody* hurt.

Ryan pressed something on the gun and the cylinder hinged out, spilling brass casings to ping and bounce off the ground. Reloading it one bullet at a time as Angus struggled and growled and swore his way along the gravel – reaching for the fallen baseball bat.

Could still cripple the bastard from here. Take a kneecap out. Or rupture a testicle. Anything to stop him before he finished putting more bullets in that *buggering* gun.

Ryan slipped the last one home and snapped the cylinder back into place. 'Got to love good old Smith and Wesson.'

Angus's fingers curled around the baseball bat's handle.

Probably only going to get one go at this, SO MAKE IT GOOD.

He rolled over, swinging the bat around as fast as it would go, aiming for—

The gun roared and a bullet slammed into Angus's chest, punching him to the ground.

54

Fire. Roaring and crackling across his chest. Burning through his shoulder blade. Napalm in his veins.

Angus hauled in a tortured breath, stoking the flames. Then snarling it out between clenched teeth.

The baseball bat slipped from his fingers as he curled around the pain, good hand pressed against the source of the blaze – high on the left side, just below his collar bone.

Not – quite – dead – yet.

'See?' Ryan jabbed that bloody gun at him and turned to Gillian. '*That's* how it's done!' He kicked the baseball bat away. 'Want to know how we knew you were out of your cell, big guy? Thermal-imaging camera and microphones in the ceiling, keeping an eye in the dark.' He looked out across the scene of carnage, towards that big pile of slates. 'WHICH *SOMEONE* WAS SUPPOSED TO BE MONITORING.'

Tony writhed on his slithery throne, both hands wrapped around whatever was left down there.

'I'LL DEAL WITH *YOU* LATER!' The revolver's dark barrel pointed straight at Angus's face. 'Say goodbye, pig.'

Gillian slapped one hand over her ear, pressing the handle of her semi-automatic against her head with the other. 'STOP IT! STOP IT! STOP IT!'

Ryan closed his eyes for a moment, pinching the bridge of his nose, mouth clamped in a thin, hard line. 'You knew it would come to this, Gillian. What did you think we were going to do with them, bake rainbow-kitten cupcakes?'

'But I didn't want—'

'WELL, YOU SHOULD'VE POISONED THEM PROPERLY, SHOULDN'T YOU!'

She flinched back against the rusty van, and stared down at her boots.

'Jesus *Christ*.' Ryan paced towards the van and back again, waving the revolver about like a conductor's baton. 'He's *going* to die, Gillian. Out *here*, or in *there* – in the chair, live on the dark web.'

Her eyes glistened in the Clio's flashing hazard lights. 'Please, Ryan, he was . . . he was *nice* to me. And so was Jonathan. They didn't treat me like some freak.'

'What is *wrong* with you? THEY'RE THE ENEMY!'

They stood there in the driving rain as Angus bit down on the pain.

Short, sharp breaths.

Not dead yet, remember?

There had to be a way out of this.

Ryan stared up into the downpour. 'Why do I bother? Why? What possible . . . DO YOU SEE WHAT HE DID TO STEVE AND WILLIAM AND TONY? What that little munchkin bastard did to Christine?' Pointing his revolver at her crumpled body, then out across the driveway; taking in Steve, motionless on the Clio's roof; Tony vomiting on the pile of slates; William sobbing over his ruined knee; the van with its shattered windows.

No more steam gushed out of the radiator; instead the van's engine coughed and choked, a grinding noise coming from under the bonnet, until it finally sputtered into silence.

Rain shimmered through the Clio's headlights as the security system gave up the ghost. Killing the horn and the blinking orange lights.

It hissed against the gravel. Drummed against the tarpaulins. Soaked through Angus's borrowed waistcoat and tweed trousers.

Wrinkles bunched up between Ryan's eyebrows. 'Wait a minute . . .'

Gillian spun around, looking left and right and left again. 'But . . .'

'WHERE THE HELL'S THE FUCKING DWARF? Oh, for . . .' Ryan folded up, the gun and a fist clenched over his head as a growl of frustration ripped free. When he straightened up again, his whole face trembled. 'Don't just *stand* there: FIND HIM!'

She pulled her shoulders in, head ducking, shrinking into herself. Even her voice became smaller. 'Don't . . . Ryan, please. I didn't mean to upset you. *Please.* I'll find him! I swear, I'll find Jonathan and I'll . . .' Her mouth fell open as she stared towards the far corner of the building.

Great.

That was just *sodding* great.

Dr Fife was back, standing there with his hands up.

When he *should've* been miles away: flagging down a car, commandeering the driver's phone, and getting half of O Division charging over here ASAP.

Fife lowered his arms. 'It's not too late to do the right thing, Ryan.' Strolling past the scaffolding, voice calm, as if this whole situation were nothing out of the ordinary. 'I've called the cops; they'll be here soon. Time to put down the gun and walk away while you can.' He smiled a non-threatening smile. 'Come on, Ryan, this has all spiralled out of control, hasn't it. You don't really want to *hurt* anyone.'

Ryan stared at him. 'Have you not been paying attention? That's *exactly* what we want! That's the whole fucking point!' Jabbing his gun at the storm. 'It's how we get them to wake up!'

Dr Fife glanced at Angus – lying there with blood soaking through his borrowed waistcoat and trousers.

'I *told* you . . .' Angus forced an arm under himself and shoved till he was almost sitting up. 'I told you . . . to keep . . . running!'

'There has to be a better way, Ryan. Cos if you make yourself into a monster, how are you any different from the Cabal?'

'Let me think.' He aimed the revolver at Angus's face again. 'Gillian: take your wee friend downstairs and stick him in the chair. I'll take care of the Missing Link here.'

She bit her lip. 'But, Ryan, this isn't—'

'DO WHAT YOU'RE FUCKING TOLD!'

'Wait! Wait.' Dr Fife hurried forward, till he stood between Angus and the gun. Hands out. 'Look: I know how it feels to lose a father, Ryan. Someone you admire and respect and look up to.'

Ryan lowered the gun, so it pointed at Dr Fife instead, and pulled back the hammer.

Tears glittered in Gillian's eyes. 'Don't shoot him, Ryan! Please don't. *Please!*'

'All those years, doing everything you can to make your pop *proud* of you. Feeling like nothing would ever be good enough. And—'

'I told you to take the little bastard *downstairs*!'

'And now he's dead and you're trying to make sense of this screwed-up, *unfair* world – lashing out at the kinda people who sort of represent everything that's ever gone wrong.' Dr Fife's voice softened. 'But life's more complicated than that.'

Ryan blinked, gun drooping. 'It shouldn't be.'

'I know.' Dr Fife held out a hand, palm up, for the revolver. 'Angus is my friend, Ryan. Please don't kill my friend.'

'They don't care about us.' The gun's barrel drifted down to point at the ground. 'All they care about is their power and their money and their plans to turn us into good little sheep . . .'

'Come on, Ryan: give me the gun and we can talk about it. That'll be nice, yeah? Just you and me, putting the world to rights.'

'I AM NOT A SHEEP!' The revolver snapped up and barked again.

Dr Fife stumbled backwards, tripped over Angus's legs and went down, eyes wide. A red circle, like the tip of a magic marker, made a hole in the chest of his long-sleeved top, slightly left of centre, straight through the skull-and-crossbones printed on it.

It spread, blooming like a poppy, damp and scarlet in the Clio's lights.

Dr Fife stared at the growing stain, hands trembling in front of the bullet hole, then he slumped sideways and lay there, mouth open. Bleeding into the gravel.

Gillian howled in pain, staggering closer. 'YOU KILLED HIM!'

'THAT WAS THE IDEA! Jesus . . . Just cos you let him crawl between your legs, doesn't mean—'

Her gun thundered and a dot appeared, right between Ryan's eyebrows – the back of his head popping like an overripe tomato, spraying pink and red with chunks of white and grey.

It was as if someone had severed all his muscles with a single stroke, and Ryan collapsed like a sack of disconnected bones. His revolver rattled away across the gravel, disappearing under the knackered van. Well out of reach.

She fell to her knees beside Dr Fife – gun-hand squeezed against her mouth, the other pressed against his chest. Rocking back and forth. Face going pink, then puce, before a tortured sob wailed free.

It wasn't meant to end like this.

Why couldn't he just keep running, like he was *supposed* to? THAT WAS THE BUGGERING PLAN.

Angus gritted his teeth and crawled over to Dr Fife. Breathing hard. Hissing through the flames that roared through his leg and shoulder.

This wasn't the plan.

Gillian stared at him, mascara streaking down her pale cheeks, eyes bloodshot and shining. 'Fix him.'

Silly, silly bastard.

Why did he come back?

Angus fumbled for a pulse. 'Come on, Dr Fife, please don't do this . . .'

'FIX HIM!' The semi-automatic's barrel pressed against Angus's forehead – the metal still hot from blowing the back off Ryan's skull. 'If Jonathan dies, *you* die.'

Was that a pulse?

Something faint flickered beneath his fingertips again.

It was. But probably not for long.

'We need an ambulance, right now. Might already be too late.'

'I've got explosives; if he dies, EVERYONE DIES!' The gun wrenched away from Angus's head and two shots pounded out. One made Christine's body twitch, the other silenced William's crying. He pitched forward and lay there, bleeding out onto the weed-strewn gravel.

She swung the semi-automatic back around, shoving the searing metal into Angus's cheek. 'Now *fix him!*'

55

How? How the *living hell* was he supposed to do that?

Angus looked down the length of the gun, then along her arm to her tear-streaked face. Creased and swollen. Puffy eyes glaring back at him. Demanding he wave a magic wand and make a sucking chest wound disappear.

He placed a hand over the wound – leaning on it, pressing down. That was what you were meant to do, right? Apply pressure?

Blood seeped out through his fingers.

This was stupid.

Dr Fife would bleed to death in his arms, and then Gillian would kill him.

But he was *not* going out snivelling and begging. 'Call an ambulance, or – he – will – *die*.'

'FIX HIM!' Bellowing right in Angus's face. 'Or I swear to God: I will blow your *fucking—*'

A ringing metal *CLANG* burst across the rainy night, then Gillian's eyes rolled up in her head and she slowly pitched over onto the gravel.

God knew how DCI Monroe had managed to sneak up behind Gillian – probably the storm and all the shouting and threats and blood – but he stood over her now, holding that slater's axe in his deformed hand. Wearing nothing but the baggy shirt Angus had lent him, freshly smeared with blood and torn at the shoulder.

He looked simultaneously awful – with his swollen, battered face and damaged limbs – while also being the most lovely sight Angus had ever seen.

Monroe wobbled, as if staying upright was taking all the energy he had. But at least now they knew he wasn't blind. Not that he could be seeing much through those slashed-grapefruit eyelids.

Angus nodded. 'Thanks, Boss.'

The slater's axe tumbled from his hand and clanked against the ground. 'Isss thag augh ovv rem?' His left leg quivered, the muscles clenching and unclenching beneath the bloodstains and scabs. 'Wvvee neid tghhhh . . .' And the leg gave way, collapsing him onto the driveway. Curled on his side, with his arms at ten to four. Legs frozen as if he'd been running away.

'Boss?'

No reply. Monroe just lay there.

The wind changed direction, snapping the building's tarpaulin skin against its scaffolding skeleton as rain strafed the battlefield.

And it looked as if Angus was the only one still standing.

Well, sitting.

Well, vaguely upright, anyway.

So it was up to *him* to save the day.

Ryan's right leg was just within reach – Angus grabbed it, hauling the body towards him. That ruptured head left a slick of scarlet behind – flecked with shards of bone and soggy clumps of greyish pink.

'Gimme your phone.'

A quick rummage through Ryan's pockets turned up a scuffed Motorola. Password protected, of course, but there *was* a button on the lock screen marked 'EMERGENCY CALL'.

Angus pressed it, cradling Dr Fife's body as it rang and rang and rang . . .

Sirens wailed in the distance, then the flickering blue-and-whites of a patrol car, travelling at speed, glimmered between the trees. Then another one. Closely followed by an ambulance.

Backup had finally arrived.

Too little, too late.

At least the air ambulance had got here first.

It sat about sixty feet from the house, rotors slowly turning as rain howled down.

The paramedics finished strapping Dr Fife to the stretcher and picked the whole thing up. An oxygen mask obscured that ridiculous Vandyke of his, skin waxy and pale, a saline drip – hanging from a stand fixed to the stretcher – disappearing into one arm.

Angus limped after them as they hurried towards the waiting helicopter. Using the baseball bat as a walking stick. 'Will he be OK?'

'We're pushing fluids hard as we can, but . . .' The paramedic sucked her teeth. 'If he makes it as far as the trauma ward I'd be amazed.'

Her mate hauled the air ambulance's door open, peering up at the storm-thrashed night. 'Assuming we don't crash on the way back.'

They struggled the stretcher inside, then clambered in after it.

The woman stared at Angus – propped up against the side of the helicopter, covered in blood, teeth gritted. 'Are you sure you're OK?'

Angus nodded. 'Never better. Go. Save him.'

She grimaced, then trundled the door shut.

The moment it clacked into place, the engines picked up pace, the whine building in volume as the rotor blades quickened.

'JUST . . . TRY, OK?' Angus hobbled out of the way, staying low as the *whump-whump-whump* turned into a clattering roar.

The bright-yellow machine clawed its way off the ground, bobbing and weaving as the wind shoved and jostled, gaining altitude till it was up above the trees. Peeling away to hammer home for Castle Hill Infirmary at top speed.

Angus waved his only working arm at it as the yellow dot faded into the night, standing there till even the navigation lights had disappeared.

Then sagged.

Turned.

And shambled back towards the house, leaning heavily on the baseball bat, because right now it was the only thing holding him up.

William lay slumped where Gillian's bullet had found him, and so did Christine. Ryan was spreadeagled on the gravel, limbs all stretched out from being dragged close enough to search. But Steve had gone from the Clio's roof, and Tony no longer threw up on the pile of discarded slates.

Angus lurched the last three steps into the gap between the tarpaulin-wrapped scaffolding and the building, out of the wind and the rain. Grabbing the poles to keep himself upright.

Inside, the lounge was all lit up, warm and welcoming.

DCI Monroe sat on the bloodstained oatmeal carpet, slumped against the empty bookcases. He raised a shaky thumbs-up at Angus, then let his arm flop back down again.

Poor sod.

But at least he was still alive. Not to mention inside, out of the storm.

That was something.

And yes, Angus could've imprisoned Bob and Tony and Steve in there too, but somehow this felt more poetic.

The three of them were hunched against the scaffolding poles, one arm either side of an upright, wrists fastened together with far more cable-ties than was strictly necessary. Ankles too. And they were going *nowhere*.

Gillian got the special treatment, though: she was fixed in place with Angus's handcuffs.

She looked up at him, eyes and nose all puffy and flushed. Her make-up had smudged away to almost nothing, leaving her looking small and so much younger again. Vulnerable. Hard to tell if the blood smeared across her clothes was Angus's, Ryan's, or Dr Fife's. There was more than enough to go around, anyway.

Gillian blinked, voice trembling. 'Is he . . . ?'

Hard to know what to say.

The truth seemed unnecessarily cruel – so Angus nodded, pulled on a fake smile, and lied. 'Course he is. Medics say he'll be up and about in no time.'

A warm smile broke free. 'Good. That's good. I'm glad. He'll be fine.' Followed by a small, trembling laugh. 'Phew! Right?' Rolling her eyes. 'God, what a night!'

Angus frowned out at the storm, where William's hiking jacket twitched in the wind. 'Why did you tell me about . . . your friend?'

Though that seemed a weird way to describe him, given what she'd done. 'You know: hanging around the press packs, being creepy?'

'Dunno. Just trying to be helpful.' She sat forward. 'Do you think they'll let me *visit* Jonathan? In hospital?'

Not a chance in hell.

But he nodded again. 'We'll see.'

The sirens died, followed by the scrunch of tyres on gravel as the first patrol car slid to a halt, right in front of the tower. All four doors popped open and a firearms team piled out into the rain, guns up and ready, crouching over as they ran towards the house.

Sergeant Lincoln took the lead – thin, with narrow eyes and a flattened nose. Heckler & Koch MP5 pointing at the centre of Angus's chest. As if he hadn't had more than enough of that already today. 'ARMED POLICE, HANDS IN THE AIR, NOW!'

Easier said than done.

Angus's left arm wouldn't move at all, and the right one barely made it as high as his shoulder before the world throbbed in and out in waves of black and brown. 'You took your sodding time . . .'

—Wednesday 03 April—

56

Some manky sod had dumped a half-eaten doner kebab in the bin, filling Observation Room B with the sharp-sour scent of raw onions, congealed lamb, and sweaty garlic.

Which begged the question: had it been there all night, marinating away, or did someone have a really weird breaktime snack this morning? What was wrong with a doughnut, or a couple of biscuits with your cuppa? Or, in Angus's case, a Tunnock's tasty Caramel Wafer, discovered at the back of a cupboard in the Operation Telegram incident room.

Which wasn't technically stealing, because whoever hid it there hadn't included a Post-it-note-proof-of-ownership.

He shifted on his plastic seat.

Surely there had to be *one* position where his leg didn't ache the whole time.

Not that the rest of him was much better.

OK, so the bruises had faded to a wash of pale-yellow stains, but the stitches in his chest and shoulder itched like absolute bastards, the microporous tape holding the dressing in place kept ripping hairs out every time he reached for something, and his left arm was 'full of Meccano' and still in a cast.

At least the sling made a convenient hidey-hole for a bag of sherbet fruits, keeping them from the thieving fingers of his fellow officers.

Angus stretched the offending leg out, knocking his NHS-issue elbow crutch off the end of the worktop to clatter against the floor. Where it could bloody well stay this time.

The room's trio of monitors each showed a different view of Interview Two: Gillian, in prison blues and no make-up, sitting next to the crumpled Mr Coulter, who seemed to get less and less healthy every time he was called in as duty solicitor. He should probably see a doctor. Or an embalmer.

Stripped of the lipstick and eyeliner and all the rest of her armoury, Gillian looked more like a secondary schoolgirl than someone charged with three murders and conspiracy for six others.

She pulled a shoulder up to her ear, picking away at the nails on one hand as her voice crackled through the observation room's speakers – the vowels flattened and elongated by Gillian's newly acquired American accent. *'I guess? I mean, I suppose we were . . . trying to do something positive for the world. You know? Gonna shake it out of its complacency, before it's too late.'*

Sitting opposite, DI Cohen placed a photograph on the table. *'For the tape: I'm showing Miss Snyder item three-nine-four-dash-two. Is this what you call "something positive", Daisy?'*

She pulled back in her chair, scowling down at her twisting fingers, avoiding the picture of Leonard Lundy's remains. *'That* ain't *my name.'*

Mr Coulter sounded as if he hadn't slept in a year. *'Can we please just use my client's preferred name, Detective Inspector? Or we'll be here all flipping year . . .'*

'Fine.' He poked the photo. *'Is this what you call "something positive", "Gillian"?'*

Angus checked his copy of *Behavioral Analysis for Law-Enforcement Personnel (Crime-Scene Indicators, Forensic Red Flags, & Interview Guidance)* – open at the chapter titled 'DELUSIONAL CONDITIONING IN RELATION TO PATTERNS OF REPEAT OFFENDING' – and added a new box to the analysis matrix he'd drawn up on a spare yellow legal pad. Wrote 'MASKING & AVOIDANCE' inside it, then underlined it twice.

Had to admit, the book was *finally* starting to make sense.

Sort of.

There was a knock at the observation-room door, then in hurpled DCI Monroe, leaning heavily on a crutch of his own. His suit was sharper and more expensive than Angus's, but he held a pale mirror to the man who'd led the inquiry.

His hair was shorn to the scalp, where a handful of gauze pads hid his own crop of stitches. A black patch covering one eye. Plastic guard shielding his reconstructed nose. Bandages and splints encouraging his fingerbones to knit together in the right shape. The last hints of purple fading away across his face.

'Boss!' Angus hit 'MUTE' and struggled upright. 'Didn't know they'd let you out.'

'Sit down, you idiot. Before you fall down.'

Thank God for that.

Monroe pointed at the monitors. 'Any joy?'

'Kind of.' He hooked a thumb at the wall, towards Observation Room A. 'DI Tudor and the Tulliallan boys are next door, pulling the strings.'

'But . . . ?'

'Yeah.' Angus frowned at his legal pad. 'Far as I can *tell*, the whole thing was a weird mixture of conspiracy cult, revolutionary cell, exploitation broadcaster, property developer, and troll farm. But they *seriously* believed they were saving mankind from "the Great Reset" by standing up to some nebulous "Global Cabal".'

'Hmm . . .' Monroe nodded. 'So: nutters.'

'According to Gillian-slash-Daisy, she stopped taking her medication sometime before Christmas – defence claims everything she did after that was one hundred percent down to a massive psychotic episode, and she's not responsible for any of it.'

His good eye narrowed. 'Tell me we're still doing her for killing Ryan Miller, Christine Douglas, and William Baird. Plus the two counts of "attempted" on you and Dr Fife?'

'*And* joint enterprise on all the other murders and assaults.'

'Then diminished responsibility's her best bet, if she wants out before her ninetieth birthday.' He winced. 'Can't believe these bastards were fitting my *kitchen*.'

'Not your fault, Boss. They targeted you, just like they did the Lundys.'

'Yeah. Still feel like an idiot, though.' Monroe cleared his throat, then reached out and squeezed Angus's good shoulder. 'I didn't get a chance, back at Mains of Inverminnoch, but thanks for saving my life. Getting me out of that cell.'

Heat rushed up Angus's cheeks. He reached up and patted DCI Monroe on the back. 'Thanks for not letting her shoot me.'

Onscreen, Gillian burst into tears, covering her face as she sobbed.

Mr Coulter rolled his eyes.

Outside in the corridor, someone let rip with a coughing fit.

But Monroe and Angus just stayed where they were.

Then the observation-room door opened and DS Kilgour popped his head in, lips pursed as he watched them standing there. 'Not interrupting anything, am I?'

Monroe let go of Angus's shoulder, and Angus pulled his hand from Monroe's back. The pair of them shuffling apart, as if they'd been caught doing something naughty.

Kilgour waggled his eyebrows. 'Was this what we call "A Touching Moment"? Literally *and* figuratively speaking.'

No answer.

He grinned. 'The Chief Super's ready for you, Boss. Boardroom. Rumour has it they've laid on the good sandwiches.'

'Thanks.' Monroe turned to go, then stopped. Hobbled back around again. 'Meant to ask: how's Dr Fife?'

Difficult to tell, because it very much depended on which doctor you spoke to.

Angus went for the simple version. 'He's still in a coma. They tried withdrawing the sedatives yesterday, but he wasn't responsive. Going to try again today. Who knows: they *might* even get him off the ventilator.'

A nod. 'If he *does* wake up, tell him I said thanks. For everything.' Monroe's crutch thunked against the observation-room floor as DS Kilgour held the door open for him. 'The *good* sandwiches, eh?'

'So they tell me.'

Monroe hobbled off down the corridor. *'How come no one ever lays on a platter of pies, chips, and Quality Street? The occasional mug of Bovril wouldn't go amiss.'*

DS Kilgour went to follow him, but Angus got in first:

'Sarge? Is he OK?'

'Course he is.'

'Only, you know, if there was a video of *me* being tortured, doing the rounds on the dark web, I'd be a bit . . . unhappy about it.'

'The Boss is a big boy, Constable. He knows we've got a crack team of experts working round the clock to get it taken down and trace all of the cult's nasty little customers. This is what we call "Taking Care of Business".'

Angus grimaced. 'This "crack team of experts", it's not the Forensic IT Unit, is it?'

DS Kilgour threw Angus a little salute. 'Angus the Terrible.' Then stepped out, letting the door swing shut behind him.

Angus sniffed.

Sighed.

Yeah, they were all doomed.

Right: back to work.

He hit the 'MUTE' button again and Gillian's voice burst out of the speakers. *'Did you know that the Global Elite wanna farm our kids for their adrenaline? That's how come so many children go missing every year . . .'*

'Because you're a bloody idiot, that's why.'

Angus limped into the stairwell, phone pinned between his ear and good shoulder – freeing up his right arm so the elbow crutch could keep him upright. Which meant having his head bent all the way over to one side, pulling on the stitches in his left shoulder, while that horrible microporous tape yanked out chest hairs with every step.

Through here, the grey terrazzo floor was worn down to the concrete in patches, the handrail scratched and scarred, the walls dented and scraped.

'Ellie, it's not like—'

'The doctors offered to sign you off on the sick for months, and there's you hauling your scarred arse into work every day, like a total bloody numpty!'

He hobbled to a halt in front of the battered lift doors and pressed the button. Then leaned back against the wall to catch his breath. 'You know, I think you were nicer to me when we weren't going out.'

'Don't change the subject.' You could pretty much hear her scowling down the phone at him. *'Come on, Angus! I could really do with a juicy exclusive. Slosser the Tosser's doing a thing about that strangling in Logansferry last night, and I need a bit of oomph or I'll be lucky to make page twelve.'*

The button still hadn't lit up, so he pressed it again. And again. Six or seven times in quick succession. *Click-click-click-click-click-click* . . . Until, *finally*, the 'DOWN' light flickered on.

Of course, in the good old days, he'd have just walked. It was only four flights. That's what being shot in the leg got you.

'I haven't got anything oomphy to share – I'm helping build the case against the cult members. All the exciting stuff happened weeks ago, with the guns and the bloodshed.'

'But there must be something that—'

'And even if it *was* oomphular, I couldn't tell you. Bad enough my girlfriend's a journalist; if people think I'm giving you stories they'll crucify me.'

The lift mechanism clanged and rattled, like an ancient fairground ride. On its way.

'Urgh . . . You're no fun!'

'Yup. Probably all those worms I ate as a kid.'

A sneaky tone crept into Ellie's voice. *'How about we swap? I may have* accidentally *found out who's been leaking stuff to Slosser. About Operation Telegram?'*

Hold on a minute.

'Ellie? When you say "accidentally"—'

'Well, he should have a better email password. And not write it down on a pad in his desk. A desk that wasn't what anyone would seriously describe as "properly locked".'

Oh, for God's sake.

'Ellie!'

A grinding squeal rang out from the lift shaft, followed by a rumbling series of clunks, then a half-hearted *ding*, and the doors rattled open.

DS Sharp and DS Massie were in residence, the pair of them wearing heavy coats over their fighting suits. Heading out.

He nodded at both as he lumbered his way into the lift. 'Sarge, Sarge.'

DS Massie nodded back. 'Angus.'

Inside, someone had been at the graffiti with a wire brush or Brillo pad, leaving shiny patches on the stainless-steel walls. But the words 'SGT. SMITH IS A WANKER!!!' still stood out clear as day.

'Urgh . . .' DS Sharp slumped. 'I'm just saying: we *always* go out for noodles.'

'Who doesn't like noodles?'

Angus limped into the corner. Staying well out of it.

'All that stuff about Satan's Messenger, and the Post-its, and Dr Fife growing up in a cult? He paid some serious *wedge for it, and I know who to.'*

The doors juddered shut, and the lift clattered, creaked, and clanked on its way to the ground floor.

DS Sharp pointed in the vague direction of town. 'What's wrong with a *baked potato* from time to time? Or . . . sushi?'

'I am *not* eating raw fish.'

Angus propped himself up against the wall, taking the weight off his throbbing leg. 'Thought you journalists were all about protecting your sources.'

'Yes: our *sources. Not other people's.'* Ellie's voice went from sneaky to devious: *'You want to know or not?'*

'Oh, come on, Rhona.' Sharp buttoned up her coat. 'There's a nice Italian opened up on Jamesmuir Road, opposite the florist's?'

'I just want to know what you've got against noodles all of a sudden.'

Angus groaned. 'But I've got nothing I can swap!'

'Then you owe me a curry.' Ellie left a long dramatic pause, milking the moment. *'Ever worked with a detective sergeant called Laura Sharp?'*

'Because we *always* have noodles! Every Wednesday lunchtime for the last Christ knows how many years: noodles, noodles, noodles!'

DS Massie threw her hands in the air. 'Fine, we'll have Italian. You happy now?'

The lift lurched to a stop with a metallic screech.

'They're only noodles!'

'I'll call you back.' Angus hung up as the lift dinged and the doors grumbled open.

He reached past DS Massie and pressed the '→I←' button.

The doors grumbled closed again.

Both detective sergeants turned to stare at him.

'Listen up.' Massie stuck her chin out. 'If this is the start of some weird sexual fantasy you've got, trust me when I say it *won't* end well.'

But Angus kept his eyes on DS Sharp. 'I know who's been selling stories to the *Castle News and Post*.'

Sharp pursed her lips. Drew a breath in through her nose. Then closed her eyes. 'Ah . . . *shite*.'

57

When it wasn't hammering with rain, you got a pretty decent view from up here on the station roof. A gleaming sun shone down from the pale-blue sky, making the surrounding buildings glow. Bit of a nip in the air, but after Storm Findlay anything was an improvement.

The crumbling castle took centre stage, atop its granite mohawk, but the rest of the city was spread out around it, reaching up the valley walls in all directions. Even Kingsmeath didn't look too bad today.

Kind of . . .

Antennas, pipes, heat exchangers, emergency broadcast systems, wires and ducting made a tangled crown on top of Divisional Headquarters, alongside the cheese-wedge top of the stairwell, and the bulky lump of brick that housed the lift's mechanics. Complete with heaps of leaf litter; the carcasses of nearly a dozen pigeons; several mountains of cigarette butts; and some crumpled, empty tins of extra-strength lager; all enclosed within a knee-high boundary wall.

As if that was going to save anyone.

By the time Angus had limped up the stairs and out onto the roof, DS Massie and Sharp were standing over at the front of the building. Not saying anything.

He shambled to a halt on the other side of DS Sharp, penning her in. Just in case.

She had one foot up on the wall, leaning on her knee, frowning out at a black Mylar balloon caught in the guttering opposite. 'Sorry For Your Loss!'

She bit her bottom lip. 'So, what happens now?'

DS Massie sighed. 'You'll probably be suspended; then, *if you're lucky*, they'll demote you. Stick you back in uniform and give you a beat in Kingsmeath, till you either learn your lesson or quit. If not?' A sniff. 'Depends if they want to make an example.'

'Buggering hell . . .'

Angus poked at a mound of leaves with his crutch. 'But *why*?'

'You got any idea how much decent residential care costs?' She tensed, and for a moment it almost looked as if she was going to launch herself forward, off the edge of the building, on a swift one-way trip to the Front Podium, eight storeys below. Then she straightened up and stepped back instead. 'Suppose I shouldn't say anything else without my Federation rep present.' Turning to DS Massie. 'But I *am* sorry.'

A nod. 'Yeah. Me too.'

They headed back towards the stairwell.

DS Sharp tried for a smile. 'Angus: I meant to ask, how's your mum doing?'

'Yeah, better, thanks. I think it was all just a bit of a shock, you know, with the hospital and everything. They gave her some pills.'

She nodded. 'I know they can be a pain in the arse at times, families, but you don't know what you've got till they're gone.'

'Yes, Sarge.'

And *sometimes* the opposite was true, as well.

The bag-for-life clanked against Angus's crutch as he limp-hobbled into Room Four. Closing the door on the muted *hummmm* of the High-Dependency Unit.

It smelled of old cabbage and disinfectant in here, the air tasting as if it hadn't seen the outside world in years . . .

Sunlight struggled to find a chink in the lowered blinds, leaving the private room smothered in gloom, with only the glow of various bits of machinery to illuminate Dr Fife's tiny kingdom. The courtiers hissing and bleeping to prove he was still alive.

He lay flat on his back, sallow and sunken, hooked up to drips and monitors and the bulging bag full of yellow liquid dangling under the bedframe.

Angus popped his shopping on the wheelie cantilevered table, then untucked the oversized envelope from his sling. 'You awake? The nurses texted me you'd come round.'

No reply, but one of Dr Fife's feet moved beneath the blankets, as if he was trying to dig his heel through the NHS mattress.

Angus hurpled over to the bed. 'Hello?'

Dr Fife's eyes creaked open – tiny crusty slits in his pale face – then a full-body wince rippled through him. His lips moved, but all that came out was a dry rasp.

'Hold on.' Grabbing the plastic cup from the bedside cabinet, Angus added a splash of water from the jug, then slipped a hand under Dr Fife's head, easing him up far enough to take a couple of sips with a bendy straw.

That done, Dr Fife sank back into the pillows. Three words croaked out: 'I . . . hate . . . Oldcastle . . .'

'It grows on you. Like a verruca.' He slipped the get-well-soon card from its huge envelope: revealing a trio of attractive, athletic, and *very* well-endowed ladies, in Stars-and-Stripes bikinis, posing with machine guns, in the woods somewhere. 'Sorry, Monster Munch picked it.' Angus opened the card. 'Everyone on the team signed.' Holding the thing out so Dr Fife could see the whole inside was covered in signatures and extra-special personalized little messages, like 'GET WELL SOON!'

He propped it up on the bedside cabinet. 'We weren't allowed to bring stuff in when you were in the ICU. But . . .' He reached into the bag-for-life and came out with a bottle of Lucozade, followed by a large sandwich wrapped in butcher's paper. 'Avocado, grilled peppers, smoked halloumi, and rocket, on seeded rye. Cos A: the food in here is awful, and B: it's the most Californian thing I could find.'

Dr Fife blinked at the ceiling. 'Feel like . . . I've been run over . . . by a goddamned . . . ticker-tape parade.'

'For a man who's had about a million blood transfusions, and spent the last seventeen days in a medically induced coma, you look . . .' He pursed his lips, head on one side, taking in what was left of Dr Fife. 'Anyway, a lot's happened since you got yourself shot.' Pulling up a chair and creaking down into it. 'Olivia Lundy's doing better. Which is nice. She'll need a wheelchair, but at least she's alive. Kevin Healey-Robinson's still under psych evaluation across the road.' Pointing through the wall at the old Victorian wing, where the Mental Health Services Unit lived. 'If they don't medicate the hell out of him he just screams and screams and screams and screams . . .' Not surprising, really. 'They couldn't save his hands.'

'Thought you . . . were dead.'

Angus tapped his chest. 'Aches a bit, but I get my stitches out next week.'

'Thirsty . . .'

He helped Dr Fife take a couple more sips, then made sure he was settled before sitting down again. 'As it's the day for it: thanks. You know – for putting yourself between me and the gun.'

'I'm an idiot.' A grimace turned into a small smile. 'But I did . . . didn't I? . . . I *literally* took . . . a bullet for you . . . Turns out I might . . . not be such a selfish . . . egocentric . . . mercenary *dick* after all . . . That'll teach Courtney.' Those four sentences seemed to take it out of him, because Dr Fife sagged for a while, breathing hard from the effort. Then, 'What about . . . Ryan?'

Yeah . . .

'Gillian Kilbride blew his head off. Well, not all of it, just the . . . back half.' Which was an image that would stay with him for a long, long time. 'Turns out she *didn't* grow up in a cult on Uist, her dad wasn't murdered, and that's not her real accent. She's not even "Gillian Kilbride".'

A groan. 'Do I wanna know?'

'Real name's Daisy Snyder; she's from Leeds, originally. Spent most of her youth in residential care after her dad murdered the rest of the family with a sledgehammer. Been sectioned six times since her fourteenth birthday. And she got "the Apostles of the Shining Water" from a short story.' Shrug. 'Keeps asking after you every time we interview her, though.'

Dr Fife stared at the ceiling again. 'Can't believe I fell for her kindred-spirits-slash-ingénue shtick.'

Eh?

'On-jen-what-now?'

'Ingénue: an innocent, naive, wholesome young woman.'

'Oh.' Made sense. 'If it's any consolation, I think *she* fell for it too. Turns out Gillian's personality is kind of malleable, like plasticine. Only been in custody two weeks and she's already joined a prison gang.'

His eyelids drooped, voice getting fainter. 'Some people just can't cope on their own. Gillian needs to belong to something. A perennial cult member.'

The machines around the bed hissed and clicked and bleeped and pinged.

'Dr Fife?'

He lay there, eyes closed – perfectly still, except for the rise and fall of his chest.

Suppose that was a lot of excitement for someone who'd been in a coma for two-and-a-bit weeks.

Angus pulled out his 'new' phone – in a shiny leather case, no less – and checked the text that had arrived in the lift, on his way up here.

MUM:

> Are you going to be home for tea Angus? I could do
> you some nice fishfingers beans and oven chips

It was a long way from stovies with no meat in them, or macaroni cheese without cheese.

DS Sharp had been right about the 'don't know what you've got till they're gone' bit, but with Mum it was more like 'don't know what you've missed till they're back'. Amazing what a course of antidepressants could do.

He cradled the Google Pixel – that Dr Fife *definitely* said he could keep – against his fibreglass cast and poked out a reply:

> Thank you for offer of fishfingers.
> Unable to eat them as am planning to see Ellie tonight.
> Dr Fife has woken up.
> Will bring home pizza.

SEND.

The reply was almost immediate.

MUM:

A Mushroom Hamageddon would be lovely thank you

He slipped his phone back in his jacket and reached into Dr Fife's bedside cabinet, coming out with the breeze-block-sized library hardback hidden away inside: *Bloodfire.*

That was the only good thing about spending so much time in hospital – sitting here these last two weeks, waiting for Dr Fife to wake up – lots of opportunities for reading.

Suppose they'd be letting him home soon, though, and Angus would have to read the third book in the trilogy on his own time.

All good things come to an end, eventually . . .

A good thirty pages later, Dr Fife surfaced again. Squinting around at the private room as if surprised to find he really *was* in hospital. He groaned and slumped back. Voice like a rusty hinge: 'It's *unsettling* . . . waking up and finding you . . . sitting there watching me . . . Like a creepy, oversized . . . Labrador.'

Angus put his book down. 'You're welcome.' Then helped him take another drink of water. 'They came past with your tea, but you were asleep, so I helped. Mince and tatties. Bloody awful. You were better off unconscious.'

A disgusted grimace curdled Dr Fife's face at the mention of food.

Which probably meant that ludicrously expensive sandwich was in play as well.

Raised voices sounded outside in the hallway: one trying to calm things down, one angry and imperious. Then the door thumped open, and a middle-aged man strode into the room: five-eleven-ish; thin, but wiry with it. Broad shoulders and a dour moustache, old-fashioned sideburns mingling with a touch of stubble, lined face, hair greying at the temples. He was dressed in an ancient, heavy, woollen suit with a full-length duster coat on over the top, and a battered wide-brimmed fedora.

The kind of guy who'd heard about smiling, once, years ago, and decided he *did not like the sound of it one little bit*. But there was something weirdly familiar about him, like a slightly out-of-focus photograph of someone Angus knew.

His voice matched the retro outfit – half teuchter, half old-time preacher – as he looked down his nose at Angus. '*Leave* us.'

Oh, you think so, do you?

Angus stood, shoulders back. Towering. 'And you are?'

The newcomer scowled at Dr Fife. 'It's been a long time, Malachi. I've come to take you home.'

Dr Fife's left heel dug away at the mattress again. His eyes widened, mouth tight. 'Elijah . . .'

The brother. The one who 'fell' out of a tree. Which explained why he looked so familiar.

'OK.' Angus held out his hands. 'Let's all just—'

'I *said*: leave us!' Giving it the full fire-and-brimstone timbre. 'This is family business.'

'Dr Fife?'

He shrank back into his pillows. 'Don't you . . . bloody dare! . . . I'm not going anywhere . . . with—'

'Silence!' Elijah slammed his hand down on the wheelie table. 'It's bad enough you flee your responsibilities, big brother, but to accept yet more *impure* blood?'

'Impure . . . ?' Angus jabbed a finger at the bed, at the machinery. 'He would've *died* without those transfusions!'

'The Brethren have been patient far too long, Malachi. You *will* come back with me. You have a sacred duty to your family, to your community, to your *faith*, and to the world.' His nostrils flared. 'The time for this self-indulgent . . . whatever it is, has *ended*.'

And for the first time since Angus met him, a look of genuine fear spread across Dr Fife's face.

Angus grabbed Elijah's shoulder. 'All right: out!'

'UNHAND ME!' Swinging a backhanded fist that smacked Angus across the jaw, catching him off balance. 'No more discussion. Gather your belongings; Mother and Father are waiting in the—'

The rest of that sentence disappeared, because Angus slapped his good hand over Elijah's mouth, clamping it shut – fingers digging into his cheeks as Angus shoved him backwards into the wall with a rattling thump.

Oh, he put up a struggle, howling with outrage, but all that came out were mumbles and hisses.

Angus stepped in close, pinning him to the wall, then put a bit of hoomph into it: hoisting Elijah up until his feet dangled a good six inches off the floor.

Couldn't be very comfortable, being suspended by your *face*. Probably quite painful, to be honest.

Elijah grabbed onto Angus's forearm, pulling at it as his whole head turned puce. He tried to kick, to knee, to do *some* sort of damage, but Angus was far too close to get up any momentum.

Time to drive the point home.

Angus raised his fibreglass cast, index finger extended, and poked Elijah in the forehead – leaving a pale oval imprint on the flushed skin. 'You listen very carefully.' Another poke. 'Because you get *one* chance at this.' Keeping his gaze locked on those furious grey eyes. 'Dr Fife, do you want to go with this man?'

'*Hell*, no!'

A nod. 'Want to say anything before I throw him out of here?'

There was a rustle of bedclothes. 'You're an asshole, Elijah . . . Always have been . . . always will be.' Voice getting stronger with every word. 'I am *not* your goddamn Chalice . . . Find some other poor bastard . . . to make the prophecy come true . . . because I am *done*.'

Poke. 'Did you get that?'

Whatever was mumbled behind Angus's hand, it sounded far too angry to be an agreement.

This time, when Angus poked Elijah, he kept the finger there, *pressing hard*, as if trying to drill the digit through Elijah's thick skull. 'Let me put this in language you can understand: thou shalt go forth from this place and multiply.' Throwing in an ominous pause as he leaned in close, till their noses were almost touching. 'And if you *ever* come back, I will *personally* crucify you.'

One last squeeze and Angus removed his poking finger. Then let go of Elijah's face.

He dropped the six inches to the hospital floor, then sagged even further as his knees buckled. It took a couple of seconds before he straightened up, one hand working his jaw from side to side while the imprint of Angus's fingers faded away on those flushed cheeks.

Could almost see the cogs whirling behind his eyes, wondering if he could take Angus in a fight – fair or otherwise – or if Angus would paint the walls with him.

Which, let's be honest, would be a pleasure.

In the end, common sense must've prevailed, because instead of throwing the first punch, Elijah stuck his nose in the air and brushed imaginary dust from his antique suit's lapels. 'This is not over, Malachi. This is not over *at all*.' Then he turned and swept from the room, duster coat swirling out like a cape.

A crash sounded in the corridor, followed by an avalanche of metal things that clanged and rang as they hit the floor, then an angry nurse's yell: *'Hey!'*

'Stay out of my way, woman!' The preacher's voice fading as he stormed off to a ringing cry of:

'Wanker!'

Angus closed the door. 'Well, I can see where you get your winning personality.'

'He'll be back.' Dr Fife's heel dug at the mattress again. 'My little brother might . . . not be too bright . . . but he's a persistent son of a bitch.'

Yeah, he looked the type to hold a grudge.

'I'll have a word with security.'

'And he's gonna bring more assholes with him . . . Been over forty years . . . God knows how many Brethren there are now.' Dr Fife looked up at the bank of machinery surrounding his bed. 'Soon as they discharge me . . . I'm outta here.'

Couldn't blame him, really.

And they'd caught the Fortnight Killer.

Well, Fortnight *Killers*.

Most of them anyway.

If you didn't count the ones Gillian had shot.

The point was: they'd stopped Ryan's cult from claiming any more victims, so DCI Monroe couldn't possibly object to Dr Fife going home.

The forensic psychologist picked at his blankets, head turned away as if Monster Munch's bikini-clad card was the most interesting thing in the room. Voice light and nonchalant, in a gravelly sort of way. 'You could come with me, you know . . . To the States . . . If you like.'

'*America?*'

Bloody hell . . .

'Why not? . . . If there's one thing we got in spades . . . over there . . . it's guys who make dead bodies . . . There's more work than I can shake a severed limb at . . . You and me could team up . . . help the FBI catch serial killers.' He pointed at his chest. 'Brains.' Then at Angus. 'Brawn.'

Cheeky sod.

Angus gave him a glare.

'OK, OK: brawn . . . and also *some* brains.'

It was tempting, obviously: escaping Kingsmeath and Oldcastle for a life of adventure. Solving crimes and saving lives, like something off the telly.

And the portions over there were *huge*.

But still . . .

He sank into the plastic seat. 'I took your advice, about Ellie? We're . . . you know.'

A smile. 'She popped your cherry? . . . *Good* for her. Welcome to being a man, Angus.'

Heat popped and crackled across his cheeks. 'And things are going well at work: they're talking about putting a team together, doing behavioural evidence analysis. I've been reading that book you gave me, so I'm in with a shout. And Mum's doing *much* better, now she's on the pills. She had a bit of a turn, on account of nearly dying, but it's like she's . . . my mum again. The one I knew before Dad died.' A wee shrug. 'And now that we're not donating *every single spare penny* to charity, we can afford to live like normal people.' Angus picked at the fraying end of his fibreglass cast's lining. 'I know it sounds like a really weird thing to say, but I'm actually sort of *happy* for a change.'

A long breath rattled out of Dr Fife. 'Yeah.' His head drooped. 'I suppose you've gotta do . . . what's best for you.' The machines pinged and hissed. 'Shame, though . . . you made a pretty good sidekick.'

Angus picked up the get-well-soon card, with its pneumatic, gun-totin', yee-haw ladies, and grimaced at them. 'America. I mean, what would I even *do* there?'

—Tuesday 02 July—

58

Maasaw Airfield (100 miles NE of Flagstaff, Arizona) – 16:57

Even with the air-conditioning on, the tiny Cessna was like a winged oven as it banked into a turn. Barely a cloud in the sky, but the plane's shadow raced across the parched landscape below – all shades of beige and pale brown, with the occasional tuft of green.

They'd followed the road for the last fifteen minutes of the flight up from Flagstaff, and only seen three vehicles the whole time.

Number four was parked at the side of a tiny airstrip: a big, filthy, jacked-up, silver, double-cab pickup truck with a light-bar on the roof and a big green-and-gold shield on both front doors.

A figure leaned back against it, arms folded.

How the hell they weren't melting in this heat was anyone's guess.

The pilot's low drawl crackled over Angus's headset: *'All right, ladies and gentlemen, we'll shortly be landing in Buttfuck, USA, please make sure your seatbelts are securely fastened, and your tray tables are in the upright and locked position.'*

Ha bloody ha.

As if there was room for any of that back here – squeezed into the plane's two rear seats, trying not to squash Dr Fife against the bulkhead, because these things seemed to be designed for schoolchildren.

Of course, Special Agent Marshall had taken the front seat, next to the pilot, even though he was nowhere near as big as Angus – playing power games. Because let's face it: the man was an arsehole in a black suit and white shirt, short-back-and-sides, sunglasses, and shiny black shoes.

The Cessna sank lower and lower, shadow racing up to meet them as it wheeched across clumps of cactus and the occasional scruffy bush. Then the wheels touched down, kicking up a huge plume of orange dust. The engines howled and the wheels bumped along the runway, slowing to a walking pace, before stopping entirely – the motor idling, but *not* turning off.

Maasaw Airfield didn't have anything as fancy as a control tower or a hangar, just an old Portakabin that looked as if it was about to collapse from heat exhaustion.

'*Thank you for flying FBI Airways, I hope your flight's been a pleasant one, and don't forget to tip your stewardess.*'

Special Agent Marshall took off his headset, popped his door, and hopped out.

Heat barged into the four-seater plane.

The pilot flipped Marshall's seat forward, as if this was a housing-estate hatchback. '*Everybody out.*'

Angus struggled free from the tight space, stepping down onto gritty sand. Blinking as heat-haze rippled the middle distance, sparking sweat across his top lip, making his shirt sticky. And he'd only been here for fifteen seconds. 'Jesus Cake-Baking *Christ*, it's hot.'

Everything smelled of scorched dirt and burnt pepper.

'Little help?' Dr Fife crouched in the doorway, arms out, because there were no steps on this thing and a wee moment of humiliation was better than going flat on your face.

Angus lowered him to the ground. 'How can it be this *hot*?'

Dr Fife glowered. 'Something funny, Agent?'

And when Angus turned, there was Marshall smirking at them from behind his sunglasses. 'Just thinkin' 'bout this thing my wife said last night.' He snapped his fingers and aimed a finger-gun at Angus. 'Get the bags, yeah?' Then wandered off, across the dusty runway, towards the pickup truck.

Arsehole and a half.

'Hmmph.' Dr Fife lowered his voice, cranking up a faux-hillbilly accent. ' "Juss thinkin' 'bout this thing ma wife done sayed." ' A sniff. 'Bet it was about the size of his tiny dick.'

'Ignore him.' Angus popped open the little hatch on the side of the plane, and pulled out a pair of wheelie suitcases.

Halfway to the car, Marshall stopped, turned, and cupped his hands into a loudhailer. 'YOU LADIES COMING, OR WHAT?'

A sniff from Dr Fife. 'Gonna be a *long* couple of weeks.' Staying right where he was.

Because some people deserved to be antagonized.

Angus dipped back into the hold for the final wheelie case, two large holdalls, Dr Fife's photocopier-sized travelling trunk, a couple of rifle bags, and a cardboard box that clinked like a trip home from the off-licence. Stacking it all into a pile at the side of the runway.

He clunked the hatch closed again as a ding-buzz sounded deep in his pocket. It was *far* too hot for text messages, but he checked anyway.

ELLIE:
> Make sure you take heaps of photos so we can do a big thing in the paper!
> Your mum says: "Don't forget to wear sunscreen and drink lots of water."
> Bring me back something flashy and American, like a Stetson, or an illegal firearm.
> And no letting strange ladies make you eat worms! That's MY job.
> XXX ;)

Well, maybe not too hot for one little reply.
He got as far as . . .

> Have arrived on Second Mesa.
> Missing you.

. . . before 'HEY, ARNOLD SCHWARZENEGGER, DANNY DEVITO: MOVE YOUR ASSES! WE'RE ON A CLOCK HERE!' cut through the superheated air.

> FBI Agent is massive bellend.

SEND.

Dr Fife frowned. 'See, if there comes a time when we gotta choose: save his ass, or let him die? I'm gonna let him die.' Then marched off, kicking up dust with his platform cowboy boots.

Angus gathered up all the luggage he could carry in one go and shambled off towards the pickup truck.

Soon as he'd stepped off the runway, the Cessna's engines roared, sending a storm of dust and grit howling out behind the plane as it taxied away. Turning at the end of the runway and accelerating back again. Bobbing up into the air, showing off the strange collection of wires, antennas, microphones, and gimbal cameras mounted on the underside.

It did a circuit of the airstrip – no doubt to a running commentary from Captain 'Hilarious' about stowing your luggage in the overhead compartments – waggled its wings twice, then headed off into the wild blue yonder.

Angus followed Dr Fife to the pickup truck, heaving the luggage into the loading bay. Turned out those gold-and-green crests had 'RANGER' and 'HOPI POLICE ~ HOPI TRIBE' on them.

The ranger in question was nearly as big as Angus, and every bit as broad across the shoulders. Her short-sleeved uniform was either dark green or faded-after-too-many-washes black, with three golden chevrons on both well-muscled arms. A thick utility belt with a *massive* gun at her hip. Her long black hair was pulled back in a formidable bun, mirrored shades hiding her eyes. Heart-shaped face. Serious mouth.

She took off the shades, revealing a pair of brown eyes that turned up at the corners. She looked Angus up and down. 'Yup.' Then did the same thing with Dr Fife. 'You the serial-killer guy?'

'I try to be. This is my associate, Detective Constable MacVicar on loan from bonny Scotland, but you can call him "Angus".' Dr Fife stuck his chest out. 'On *my* business cards it says "Dr Fife", but—'

Angus gave him a wee kick on the ankle before he could launch into that stupid 'you can't call me "John" or "Jo"' speech of his.

Dr Fife cleared his throat and stuck a hand out instead. 'Jonathan.'

She shook it, her hand completely engulfing his, like a mountain lion's paw. 'Smith. Hakidonmuya Smith. And before you ask, it means "She Who Rips The Balls Off Sexist Assholes".'

Speaking of which . . .

The passenger window buzzed down and Special Agent Marshall popped his elbow out onto the sill – wrist extended so he could tap his watch. 'Save the chitchat for the car, Ranger. Wanna get there before the light goes.'

He didn't wait for a response, just buzzed the window up again.

Might have to promote him from 'bellend' to 'wanker', as Monster Munch would say.

Dr Fife stuck his hands into his pockets and kicked a stone off into the scrub. 'What we looking at, Ranger Smith?'

'Ever seen a man been skinned alive?'

A smile. '*Twice*.'

'Then you're gonna feel right at home.' She slipped her shades back on. 'Welcome to Second Mesa.' She marched around to the driver's side and climbed in behind the wheel.

Soon as her door clunked shut, Dr Fife's smile turned into a grin. 'We *like* her.'

Angus did a slow turn, one hand shielding his eyes, squinting out at the vast, flat desert, and the scrub, and the horizon rippling in the heat. A lone buzzard circled high above, searching for the dead.

The plane wasn't even a speck in the punishing sky.

He puffed out his cheeks. 'Long way from Oldcastle.'

'That was kinda the point.' Dr Fife swept a hand towards the dusty truck, making a big dramatic pantomime gesture. 'Come, DC MacVicar, mystery, adventure, and exciting dead bodies await!' Then he clambered into the back – which wasn't all that dignified, given how high the suspension was jacked up – leaving Angus alone. Outside. In the boiling afternoon.

High overhead that buzzard cried, sharp and lonely.

A bead of sweat trickled its way down Angus's back.

'Yeah . . . This was *definitely* a mistake.' But he collected the last few bags anyway, and heaved them into the pickup's load bay.

Because it was too late to back out now.

And maybe it wouldn't be so bad this time?

After all, it couldn't be anywhere near as dangerous as hunting down the Fortnight Killer.

. . .

Right?

And Last, But Not Least, Stuart Thanks Some People

Writing a book is a bit like trying to shove a cactus up your nose. The wrong way around. While people throw things at you. But something that makes it a *weenie* bit easier to get that cactus up there is the assistance of friends, so I want to say 'thank you' to: Inspector Bruce Crawford; Frankie Gray and Finn Cotton; Sarah Adams, Bill Scott-Kerr, Thorne Ryan, Kate Samano, Richenda Todd, Linda Joyce, Lorraine McCann, Katrina Whone, Tom Chicken, Emily Harvey, Bronwen Davies, Phoebe Llanwarne, Gary Harley, Louise Blakemore, Julia Teece, Louis Patel, Leon Dufour, Marie Goodwin, Emma Matthews, Lucy Middleton, Tom Hill, Alison Barrow, Phil Evans, Richard Ogle, Sarah Scarlett, Lucy Beresford-Knox, Larry Finlay, Kim Young, and everyone at Transworld; Phil Patterson, Guy Herbert, Leah Middleton, Catherine Pellegrino, Sandra Sawicka, and the whole Marjacq Scripts team; Alexandru Arion and Suzy Yuan; and the ever-naughty and helpful Allan Guthrie.

Another group of people who deserve a huge 'thank you!' are librarians and booksellers – AKA: Lovely Bookmongers of Delight. And then there's you! In an ever-stupiding world, where cruelty and ignorance are rampant, reading fosters empathy, imagination, thought, and compassion. Which is why so many authoritarian bumheads want to ban books. READING IS AN ACT OF RESISTANCE!

But the biggest thanks are reserved for Fiona, who gets to listen to me grumping about fictional people the whole time. And let's finish with the inestimable Onion, Beetroot, and Gherkin, who are all tremendously hairy and have the most excellent purrs.

Stuart MacBride is the *Sunday Times* No.1 bestselling author of the Logan McRae and Ash Henderson novels. He's also published standalones, novellas, and short stories, as well as a slightly twisted children's picture book for slightly twisted children.

Stuart lives in the wilds of north-east Scotland with his wife Fiona; cats Gherkin, Onion and Beetroot; lots of hens; some horses; and a truly staggering assortment of weeds.

For more information visit:

StuartMacBride.com
Facebook.com/StuartMacBrideBooks
X @StuartMacBride
substack.com/@StuartMacBride

NO LESS THE DEVIL
Stuart MacBride

It's been seventeen months since the Bloodsmith butchered his first victim and Operation Maypole is still no nearer catching him. The media is whipping up a storm, the top brass are demanding results, but the investigation is sinking fast.

Now isn't the time to get distracted with other cases, but Detective Sergeant Lucy McVeigh doesn't have much choice. When Benedict Strachan was just eleven, he hunted down and killed a homeless man. No one's ever figured out why Benedict did it, but now, after sixteen years, he's back on the streets again – battered, frightened, convinced a shadowy 'They' are out to get him, and begging Lucy for help.

It sounds like paranoia, but what if he's right? What if he really is caught up in something bigger and darker than Lucy's ever dealt with before? What if the Bloodsmith isn't the only monster out there? And what's going to happen when Lucy goes after them?

'Stuart MacBride is an automatic must-read for me'
Lee Child

'If you like your serial killers with lashings of dark humour, this is for you'
Peter Robinson

'Admirers of tough, modern crime novels will be in seventh heaven – or should that be hell?' *Express*

THE DEAD OF WINTER
Stuart MacBride

All Detective Constable Edward Reekie had to do was pick up a dying prisoner and deliver him somewhere to live out his last days in peace.

From the outside, Glenfarach looks like a quaint, snow-dusted village, nestled deep in the heart of Cairngorms National Park. But its streets are thick with security cameras and there's a strict nine o'clock curfew, because Glenfarach is the final sanctuary for ex-convicts who can't be safely released into the population.

Edward's new boss, DI Victoria Montgomery-Porter, insists they head back to Aberdeen before they get trapped by the approaching blizzard, but when an ex-cop-turned-gangster is found tortured to death in his bungalow, *someone* needs to take charge.

The weather's closing in, tensions are mounting, and time's running out – something nasty has come to Glenfarach, and Edward is standing right in its way …

'Written in MacBride's familiar tongue-in-cheek style, it fizzes from every page' *Daily Mail*

'Not your usual crime story, this is a darkly funny Fawlty Towers' *Sun*

'It's a high-wire balancing act, but MacBride never falters' *Scotland on Sunday*